# PRAISE FOR DALE BROWN

*And now, his newest, most exciting adventure . . .*

# DAY OF THE CHEETAH

*Berkley Books by Dale Brown*

**FLIGHT OF THE OLD DOG**
**SILVER TOWER**
**DAY OF THE CHEETAH**

# DAY OF THE CHEETAH

# DALE BROWN

BERKLEY BOOKS, NEW YORK

This Berkley Book contains the complete text
of the original hardcover edition. It has been
completely reset in a typeface designed
for easy reading and was printed from new film.

DAY OF THE CHEETAH

A Berkley Book / published by arrangement with
Donald I. Fine, Inc.

PRINTING HISTORY
Donald I. Fine edition published 1989
Published in Canada
by General Publishing Company Limited
Berkley edition / June 1990

ISBN: 0-425-12043-0

A BERKLEY BOOK® TM 757,375
Berkley Books are published by The Berkley Publishing Group,
200 Madison Avenue, New York, New York 10016.
The name "BERKLEY" and the "B" logo
are trademarks belonging to Berkley Publishing Corporation.

PRINTED IN THE UNITED STATES OF AMERICA

10  9  8  7  6  5  4  3  2  1

# Acknowledgments

I would like to thank the United States Air Force Aeronautical Systems Division (ASD), Wright-Patterson AFB, Ohio, for their invaluable assistance in gathering information on America's future fighter aircraft. ASD is a dream come true for an ex-Air Force nav, wistful fighter pilot, and fiction writer.

Space prohibits me from mentioning each of the fine persons of ASD that I had the pleasure of meeting, but I would like to thank Lt. General William E. Thurman, commander of ASD, for allowing me the privilege of a visit; to Lt. Col. George H. Peck, Helen Cavanaugh, Capt. Brian Hoey, Jo Ann Rumple, and Capt. Jamie Scearse of the Office of Public Affairs for arranging my visit and escorting me through the myriad of offices and labs; Captain Myers N. Drew, AFTI/F-16 Program Manager, from the Flight Dynamics Laboratories, who showed me how a fighter could really fly sideways; Mr. James Pruner, X-29 Program Director; Mr. Ron DeCamp, mission-adaptive wing (MAW) Program Director; Mr. James Kocher, Integrated Close Air Support System (ICASS) Program Director, all of the Flight Dynamics Laboratory, Wright Aeronautical Laboratories; and a special thanks to Dr. Wayne L. Martin, acting chief of the Visual Displays System Branch of the Armstrong Aerospace Medical Research Laboratory, for allowing me to try out some of the incredible "Buck Rogers" supercockpit systems that our fighter pilots will be using five to ten years from now. I hope I have done credit to the time you extended to me.

Source for many of the technical descriptions of aircraft,

weapons systems, and military forces of foreign nations was the United States Naval Institute Military Database, Arlington, Virginia. Other information sources include Western Union InfoMaster Research Database (medical articles, research papers, theses), CompuServe Information Service (encyclopedia, data storage, and computer utilities), and the Dow Jones News/ Retrieval Service (news articles, historical data, government statistics).

Thanks to Dennis T. Hall for helping arrange research trips and interviews. It's great having you on the team.

A special thanks to George Wieser, who helped me to focus in on the real story behind *Cheetah*, and to Donald I. Fine, editor as well as publisher, for sharing his experience and talent with me.

And, as ever, to Jean. I'm happy you're with me.

*Day of the Cheetah* is dedicated to two very special people who helped me over the years.

To my grandmother, Ruby Normandin, for her warmth and vitality, her charm and humor, for her patience when I was little and her pride now that I'm not so little. I'm happy to let the whole world know what kind of person you are and how much I love you.

To my uncle, Leo Brown, a very special dedication. I took a lot of your time, your talent, and your patience — I even took your name. I wish I had taken the time to say Thank You.

# Glossary

All terms in this Glossary are actual terms, weapons or systems unless designated "fictional."

**AA-11**—NATO reporting name "Archer," advanced Soviet close-range heat-seeking or radar-guided air-to-air missile. Carried by MiG-29 (can carry six), MiG-23 (carries two), and Su-27 fighters (carries four).

**AAA**—anti-aircraft artillery. Also called triple-A.

**ADIZ**—Air Defense Identification Zone. Specially marked areas around the United States where aircraft from outside the United States must receive permission from air traffic control before entering.

**AEROFLOT**—The national airline of the Soviet Union. Aeroflot has a major role in the Soviet Union's military strategy and planning—all Aeroflot aircraft can be expected to serve under military command in wartime.

**AFTERBURNER**—A throttle setting in a high-performance jet engine where extra fuel is sprayed into an engine chamber to increase thrust. The use of afterburner increases the rate of fuel consumption by 500% but can double or triple the engine's thrust.

AGL—Above Ground Level. The actual distance between the aircraft's belly and the ground. Usually measured by a radar altimeter.

AGM-88 HARM—HARM stands for High-speed Anti-Radiation Missile. The AGM-88 is an air-launched anti-radar missile built by Texas Instruments, Inc., that homes in on enemy ground or ship radars and destroys them from ranges as far as ten miles.

AGM-130—An air-launched rocket-powered glide bomb built by Rockwell International. Guided by infrared or TV camera, by manual data-link guidance or automatic target lock-on, it has a two-thousand-pound high-explosive warhead and can glide for two to five miles, even when launched from very low altitude.

AGM-132C TACIT RAINBOW—An air-launched winged drone anti-radar missile built by Boeing Aircraft. The missile can be pre-programmed for certain enemy radars and launched from long distances. The missile will cruise to and then orbit the target area until an enemy radar comes up, then home in on it and destroy it.

AIM-9R SIDEWINDER—Primary U.S. heat-seeking air-to-air missile, built by Raytheon Company and Ford Aerospace. It has a speed of over Mach two (twice the speed of sound) and a range of more than ten miles.

AIM-120C AMRAAM—Advanced Medium-Range Air-to-Air Missile, a radar-guided missile built by Hughes Aircraft and Raytheon. The AIM-120 has its own radar seeker in its nose-cone—unlike other radar-guided missiles, the AIM-120 does not need guidance signals from the launch aircraft to home in on its target. It has a top speed of over Mach four.

AIM-132B ASRAAM—Advanced Short-Range Air-to-Air Missile—The proposed European-built successor to the AIM-9 Sidewinder.

AIRWAY—Pre-planned routes to be followed by large or commercial aircraft entering, leaving or flying within the United States under positive control. Three kinds: "A" routes (from foreign or overwater points), "V" (for low altitude), or "J" (for higher-altitude aircraft).

ALPHA—Stands for "angle of attack," the angle, measured in degrees, between the wind hitting an aircraft's wing and the angle of the wing itself. A plane exceeding a certain angle of attack will stall (cease to fly). Most high-performance aircraft cannot fly at more than eighteen to twenty alpha, but advanced fighters will be designed to fly and attack at well over fifty alpha.

ANTARES (FICTIONAL)—Advanced Neural Transfer and Response System. A method for digitizing and transmitting neural impulses from the human body to a computer, and vice versa.

ATF—Advanced Tactical Fighter. A program developed to specify, design and build the next generation of fighter aircraft, beginning in the year 1992 and continue well into the twenty-first century. The ATF (X-22 or X-23) will use non-metallic materials in its construction, rely heavily on artificial intelligence and advanced computer graphics in the cockpit, fly in unconventional ways, fly at supersonic speeds without afterburner, and take off and land on a fifteen-hundred-foot-long runway.

AWACS—Airborne Warning And Control System. An aircraft-mounted radar that can scan for aircraft at any altitude out to two hundred miles and control air-to-air intercepts and engagements with enemy forces with a wide array of communications equipment.

BIG CHICKEN DINNER—BCD, or Bad Conduct Discharge.

BOGEY—Fighter pilot slang for unidentified aircraft.

BREAKAWAY—An emergency term used during air refueling when the two aircraft must separate quickly. The tanker aircraft will immediately accelerate and climb five hundred feet, and the receiver aircraft will immediately decelerate and descend five hundred feet.

BUS—In electronics, the point at which power is supplied to numerous other circuits.

C-21B—The military version of the Gates Learjet 35A, it is a ten-person fast airlift jet used by the U.S. Air Force. Can be used for up to eight passengers, three thousand pounds of cargo, or in aeromedical evacuation role.

CANARDS—Movable fins or stabilizers mounted on the front of an aircraft to provide additional lift, turning power, or supplement performance of the main wings.

CAP—Combat Air Patrol. Arranging fighters in a defensive or offensive role at various altitudes and configurations to counter an enemy threat.

CAYMAN ISLANDS—A small chain of islands southwest of Cuba in the Caribbean Sea, self-governed but administered by the British government.

CBU—Cluster Bomb Unit. A canister carried by a fighter or bomber that dispenses small bomblets over wide areas. Used against columns of troops, parked aircraft, or lightly armored vehicles.

CHAFF—small pieces of metal, like tinsel, that reflect radar energy and act as a decoy to enemy radars or radar-guided missiles.

COMPOSITE—A material made from metallic and non-metallic substances to increase the material's strength without adding weight.

CONNECTICUT ACADEMY (FICTIONAL)—KGB training facility that teaches young Russian agents how to act like Americans.

"CRANKED ARROW" F-16—A special version of the U.S. F-16 Fighting Falcon fighter built by General Dynamics, the "cranked arrow" resembles a large delta-winged fighter. The larger wing increases fuel load, weapons carriage, and stability.

CV-22 OSPREY—A special tilt-rotor aircraft built by Boeing and Bell Helicopter that uses two movable rotors to take off and land like a helicopter but flys like a regular airplane.

DIA—Defense Intelligence Agency. A special Pentagon unit that conducts investigations for personnel security clearances and co-ordinates intelligence gathering, analysis and dissemination for the Department of Defense.

DREAMLAND—Unclassified nickname for the restricted military airspace in south-central Nevada used by the Departments of Defense and Energy and the Central Intelligence Agency for special weapons research.

E-3B SENTRY—Modified Boeing 707-320B airliner with a thirty-foot diameter rotating saucer radome mounted atop the fuselage, plus extensive computer displays and communications systems. Primary U.S. and western reconnaissance, command and control system. Can track hundreds of aircraft and ships at any altitude. Can fly one thousand miles to and from a patrol area and then stay on patrol for six hours.

EEG—Electroencephalograph. Measures electrical activity in the brain and central nervous system.

EET—Eastern European Time.

F-15E—Modified McDonnell-Douglas F-15 air superiority fighter, with a weapons system officer and extensive air-to-ground attack systems added.

F-16F—FIGHTING FALCON—Lightweight single-engine, single pilot counter-air and attack fighter, built by General Dynamics. Designed for high maneuverability and flexibility and able to carry a wide variety of weapons.

F-20 TIGERSHARK—Modified Northrop F-5F fighter with single-engine and single pilot. Emphasis on simplicity and low-cost maintainability.

F/A-18 HORNET—U.S. Navy carrier-based interceptor and at-tack fighter, built by McDonnell-Douglas. Can change from air-to-air to air-to-ground attack role while in-flight.

FAST PACK—Fuel Armament Storage Tank Packs. Smoothly curved conformal tanks fitted to the upper side fuselages of

F-15 fighters to allow them to carry extra fuel and equipment without a significant drag penalty.

FLARES—Pyrotechnic magnesium or phosphorous devices ejected from tactical aircraft to decoy heat-seeking missiles.

Fox ONE—Call made by an attacking fighter to friendly forces to warn of a radar-guided missile launch.

Fox TWO—Warning call for heat-seeking missile launch.

G—Measurement of gravitational forces imposed on something. One G is normal gravity (weight); two G's is two times normal weight, etc. Zero G is weightlessness. Negative G's cause reversal of normal fluid motion in blood vessels or aircraft fuel systems. A trained human being can withstand as much as six positive G's before experiencing gray- or blackout, or as much as negative-three G's before red-out. Excessive G's (positive or negative) cause unconsciousness.

GCI—Ground Controlled Interception. Ground-based radars and controllers used to direct fighters to attack enemy aircraft.

GEOSTATIONARY ORBIT—An orbit of a satellite approximately 22,300 miles above Earth, where the time for the satellite to orbit the Earth is equal to the Earth's rotation. If the satellite is placed above the equator, the satellite will seem to hang motionless in space over the same point on Earth.

GPS—Global Positioning System. A system of satellites around Earth that provide highly precise position, speed and time information to aircraft, ships, vehicles and ground troops. Position information precise to four feet, speed information precise to one-quarter-mile per hour, time precise to one-hundredth of a second.

GRAY-OUT—Condition during high-G maneuvering where blood is forced out of the brain, causing a gradual loss, darkening, or tunneling of vision. Excessive G's cause complete gray-out (blackout) and unconsciousness.

GUARD—Internationally established and recognized emergency radio frequencies. VHF GUARD is 121.5; UHF GUARD is 243.0.

HF—High Frequency radio. Used for extreme long-distance communications (being replaced in USAF by SATCOM).

HH-3 JOLLY GREEN GIANT—Modified Sikorsky CH-3 Sea King helicopter, used for deep-penetration rescue missions into heavily defended areas.

HH-65A DOLPHIN—Aerospatiale SA-366G-1 Dauphin II utility helicopter, used for medium-range personnel and cargo transport and rescue operations.

HIGH-G YO-YO—An air combat maneuver where a less maneuverable but more powerful pursuer can attack a more maneuverable opponent by executing a dive, then a hard climb and descent to bring weapons in line for an attack instead of trying to outmaneuver the opponent.

HOTAS—Hands On Throttle And Stick. A carefully designed feature in many new high-performance fighters that logically arranges all necessary switches on the pilot's control stick and throttle for easy activation in busy combat situations.

HUD—Heads-Up Display. Usually a large piece of glass mounted atop the instrument panel in a fighter aircraft, used to reflect projected information in front of the pilot's line of sight. All necessary flight and weapons information is thereby presented to the pilot without having to look down inside the cockpit.

HYPERVELOCITY MISSILE—A simple, low-cost missile with no explosive warhead, designed to destroy targets by sheer force of impact. Speed of these missiles can exceed a mile a second. Warhead is usually a dense depleted uranium material that increases force on impact.

I.P.—Initial Point, the beginning of a bomb run. Usually the weapons officer or bombardier has control of the aircraft from the I.P. to the target.

ICU—Intensive Care Unit.

IFF—Identification Friend or Foe. A radio system that broadcasts specific bits of data "on demand" by compatible radar-radio systems that properly "interrogate" the system. The data are usually identification, altitude and airspeed data. Used by civilian and military agencies.

ILS—Instrument Landing System. Precise glide path (heading) and glideslope (altitude) radio beam system, widely used by civilian and military aircraft to line up with a runway for landing in bad weather. The bombing computers of military strike aircraft can sometimes simulate an ILS when no ground-based ILS is available.

ILYUSHIN-76—NATO reporting name MAINSTAY. Soviet version of the American E-3 Airborne Warning And Control System (AWACS) radar plane.

IMMELMANN—Air combat maneuver where an aircraft can change or reverse direction rapidly without a wide, sweeping turn. Usually made by executing a steep climb, rolling inverted into the desired direction, then rolling upright.

INS—Inertial Navigation System. Precise navigation unit that uses accelerometers (precise electronic pendulums) to detect and quantify all aircraft motion and compute exact position and speed.

IR—Infrared (heat) energy.

IRSTS—Infrared Search and Track System. Used by the Soviet Union on fighter aircraft in conjunction with GCI search radar to collect attack information to launch air-to-air missiles from long range without transmitting radar information that can be detected.

JP-4—Standard U.S. military jet fuel.

JUDY—Code word to ground or airborne controllers from fighter pilots that a designated target has been detected (either by radar or visually) and that the fighter pilot is continuing the attack alone.

KC-10 EXTENDER—McDonnell-Douglas DC-10 airliners modified for inflight refueling and heavy cargo transport. Able to carry all the men and equipment of an entire deployed fighter squadron for five thousand miles, including non-stop inflight refueling for the unit's fighters.

KC-135—Boeing 707 airliner modified for inflight refueling and light to medium cargo duties.

KGB—*Komitet Gosudarstvennoy Bezopasnosti* (Committee for Internal Security). The intelligence-gathering unit and secret police of the Soviet Union.

KOLLEGIYA—The main military council of the Ministry of Defense of the Soviet Union, responsible for military implementation of the policies of the Politburo and the Communist Party.

LLUYKA TANKS—Specialized fuel tanks carried by non-air-refuelable aircraft that are fitted with retractable refueling probes to give these aircraft the ability to refuel inflight.

M-16/M203—Standard U.S. infantry automatic rifle. The M-203 is a lightweight forty-millimeter grenade launcher fitted under the barrel of the M-16 rifle that can fire high-explosive rounds out to twelve hundred feet without impeding use of the rifle itself.

MAW—Mission-Adaptive Wings. Wings that can change the shape of their upper, leading and trailing edge surfaces to improve performance without the use of "hanging" devices such as flaps and slats.

MFD—Multi-Function Display. A series of computer monitors in an aircraft that replace or augment conventional aircraft instruments. Most MFDs can be programmed to display a wide variety of information in text or graphic form.

MIKOYAN-GUREYVICH—MiG. One of the many government aircraft design bureaus of the Soviet Union. Others are Sukhoi

(Su), Ilyushin (Il), Yakovlev (Yak), Tupolev (Tu), Beriev (Be), Antonov (An), and Mil (Mi).

MIL—Military power throttle setting. Usually one hundred percent or more of an engine's rated thrust.

MODES AND CODES—An aircraft properly displaying coded IFF data that are being received by a ground or airborne surveillance controller able to scan for these signals.

NRTS—Near-Room-Temperature Superconductors. A specially designed composite material able to demonstrate unusually high rates of electrical conductivity at normal "room" or operational temperatures. Most materials exhibit superconducting capabilities only at super-cold temperature levels. NRTS devices can transmit high amounts of energy without relying on large or bulky power generators or large environmental units.

NSC—National Security Council. A group that advises the President of the United States on a wide range of national security matters.

POLITBURO—*Politicheskoye Buro* (Political Bureau). The key policy-making body of the Central Committee of the Communist Party of the Soviet Union, directing the work of the Party between plenums (biannual meetings) of the Central Committee. Composed of not more than fifteen persons, they are chosen by the 307 voting and 107 candidate (non-voting) members of the Central Committee.

PULSE-DOPPLER—Long-range radar tracking system that detects changes in relative motion of a target.

RAMENSKOYE—Chief aircraft design and test center of the Soviet Union, located in west-central Asia near Moscow.

RAPIER—British-built surface-to-air missile air-defense system, developed by British Aerospace Dynamics. Self-contained, mobile, low- and medium-altitude capable to a range of five miles.

ROE—Rules of Engagement. Set of rules established before an air-to-air engagement that spells out exactly when and how a fighter pilot can begin and carry out an attack.

SA-7—NATO code name "Grail." Soviet shoulder-launched heat-seeking missile used mainly against helicopters and slow, low-flying jets. Range eighty- to five-thousand-foot altitude, five to six miles, speed of missile Mach one point five.

SA-8—NATO code name "Gecko." Soviet short-range surface-to-air missile. Highly mobile, all-weather capability from one hundred to twenty thousand feet, out to eight miles range. Missile speed Mach two.

SA-10—NATO code name "Grumble." Strategic (fixed-base) high-performance Soviet surface-to-air missile. All-altitude, all-weather capability. Can intercept aircraft, cruise missiles, tactical ballistic missiles and some intercontinental strategic missile warheads.

SA-15—Highly mobile improved version of the SA-8 surface-to-air missile.

SAC—Strategic Air Command. U.S. Air Force major command responsible for strategic nuclear, refueling and reconnaissance forces (aircraft and land-based intercontinental ballistic missiles).

SATCOM—Satellite Communications. A radio data-link network that sends coded information to a time-sharing relay satellite for rebroadcast to Earth stations. High-speed, secure global communications capability.

scissors—An air combat maneuver designed to prevent an unintentional overrun of a pursued aircraft. When an aircraft being pursued begins to slow or make sharp maneuvers to cause a pursuing aircraft to overshoot, the pursuer can begin several wide side-to-side turns to avoid overtaking the pursued aircraft without decreasing power.

SMG—Submachine Gun.

SMTD—STOL/Maneuverability Technology Demonstrator. A program developed to explore new technologies for advanced fighter aircraft to decrease takeoff and landing distances and increase maneuverability by the use of canards, mission-adaptive wings, vectored-thrust engines, computers and improved performance engines. The F-15 SMTD was one of the first high-tech fighter aircraft (precursor of the Cheetah). *See* STOL.

SR-71—Extremely high-altitude (hundred thousand feet), high-speed (Mach three) strategic reconnaissance aircraft, the fastest air-breathing aircraft on Earth. Can photograph one hundred thousand square miles of the Earth's surface an hour.

STALL—A condition when a wing can no longer produce lift. Usually occurs when airflow on top of an airfoil (wing) is disrupted or breaks free from the airfoil by slow speed, low power or high alpha (angle-of-attack) flight conditions.

STOL—Short Takeoff and Landing. A combination of high-lift wings and vectored-thrust engines to produce very short (less than one-thousand-foot) takeoff and landing distances, three hundred to five hundred percent shorter than normal.

SUPERCOCKPIT—A combination of computer graphics, multifunction displays, high-speed computers, voice-recognition and sight-pointing switch-activation systems that improve efficiency, integrate numerous battle management information sources and decrease pilot workload in a modern combat aircraft's cockpit.

TACAN—Tactical Air Navigation. A ground or aircraft based radio used mainly by the military to provide distance and bearing information between two aircrafts or between an aircraft and a ground station.

TOW—Tube-launched Optically tracked Wire-guided. An anti-tank missile launched from ground or airborne vehicles.

TR-1—Improved version of the U-2R high-altitude strategic reconnaissance jet. Subsonic but capable of reaching altitudes of eighty thousand feet. Mainly used for signals intelligence, electronic eavesdropping, and monitoring of data transmissions during Soviet space launches and missile tests.

VECTORED-THRUST NOZZLES—Nozzles and louvers on special fighter aircraft that can direct engine exhaust in many different directions, including side to side, downward, and forward. These nozzles improve takeoff and landing performance, enhance maneuverability, and can act as speedbrakes or drag devices.

X-29—An experimental aircraft developed by Grumman Aircraft Corp. in the early 1980s, featuring forward-swept main wings, canards, strake flaps and aeroelastic computer-controlled wing surfaces in place of conventional flaps and ailerons. Used as a technology demonstration aircraft to explore the problems and advantages of forward-swept-wing aircraft. Airflow on a forward-swept-wing aircraft is channeled along the fuselage, increasing maneuverability and performance over conventional aircraft.

XF-15F (FICTIONAL)—Modified two-seat McDonnell-Douglas F-15E fighter, designed as test-bed aircraft for the U.S. Air Force's Advanced Technology Fighter program. First fighter to combine SMTD, mission-adaptive wings and supercockpit technology in one operational aircraft. Capable of air-to-air and air-to-ground missions.

XF-34A (FICTIONAL)—The first fighter aircraft to combine forward-swept-wing technology, vectored-thrust engine systems, mission-adaptive wings, and artificial intelligence computer systems that allowed digital neural transfer of information from the aircraft's systems to the pilot and back.

ZSU-23—A highly mobile Soviet anti-aircraft artillery weapon system on a fast-tracked vehicle, composed of four radar-guided twenty-three-millimeter cannons. Range of one mile, capable of firing eight hundred total rounds per minute against all kinds of low-flying aircraft.

# DAY OF THE CHEETAH

# Prologue

## The Connecticut Academy, USSR
*Saturday, 2 May 1985, 0748 EET*

"KEN JAMES" STAMPED his feet on the half-frozen dirt, rubbed his hands together quickly, then wrapped them around the shaft of a big Spaulding softball bat.

"C'mon, dammit," he yelled to the tall, lanky kid on the pitcher's mound.

"Wait," yelled the pitcher, "Tony Scorcelli." James made a few test swings, hitching up his jacket around his armpits. Scorcelli pounded the softball in his glove, then carefully, as if trying to toss a ring over a Coke bottle, threw the ball underhanded toward home plate.

The ball sailed clear over Ken's head.

"What do you call *that*?" James stepped away from the plate, leaned on the bat, shaking his head at Scorcelli.

The catcher, "Tom Bell," trotted back to retrieve the ball. When he picked it up from under a clump of quack grass along the backstop he glanced over at the bench, noting the displeasure of the school's headmaster, "Mr. Roberts," who was making notes on a clipboard. The catcher knew that meant trouble.

All the Academy's students were serious about these once-a-week softball games. Here, even before *perestroika*, they learned competition was necessary, even desirable. Winning was all, losing was failure. Every opportunity to prove one's superior leadership, physical and intellectual skills was monitored and evaluated.

"All right," James said as the catcher, Bell, tossed the ball back to Scorcelli. "This time open your damn eyes when you pitch."

Scorcelli's second pitch wasn't much better than the first, a high Gateway Arch that dropped almost straight down on top of home plate, but James bit on it, swung the bat with all his strength and missed.

"Hey, hot shot, you're supposed to *hit* the ball . . ."

James swung even harder at the next pitch, clipped it foul up and over the chain-link backstop.

"One more foul and you are out," the first baseman "Kelly Rogers" sang out. "Intramural rules—"

"Shove your intramural rules up your ass, Rogers," James yelled at him. The first baseman looked confused and said nothing. Roberts made another notation on his clipboard as Scorcelli got ready for the next pitch.

It was low. James wound up, gritted his teeth . . . then stopped his swing, clutched the other end of his bat with one hand. He held the bat horizontally, tracked the ball as it came in and tapped it. It hit the hard ground in front of home plate, bounced once, then rolled out between home plate and the pitcher's mound and died. James took off for first base. Bell stood up from his crouch, stared at the ball, then at James, back to the ball, then at Scorcelli—who was looking on in confusion. James had reached first base and was headed for second before someone finally yelled to throw the ball.

Bell and Scorcelli ran to the ball, nearly collided as they reached for it at the same time. Scorcelli picked it up, turned and threw toward the second baseman. But it was a lob, not overhand, and instead of an easy out at second, the softball hit the ragged mud-choked grass several feet in front of the second baseman, did not bounce and skipped off into shallow right field as Ken James headed for third. The right fielder charged the rolling ball, scooped it on the run, hesitated a second over whether he could make the throw all the way, then threw to "Johnston" at third base. Johnston corralled it with a careful two-handed catch. A perfect throw. James wasn't even halfway to third.

Johnston stepped triumphantly on third base, tossed the ball "around the horn" to second base, held up two fingers. James, though, was still running. Johnston tapped James' shoulder as he ran. "Makin' it look good for Mr. Roberts, aren't—?"

"You *idiot*," Bell was yelling to Johnston. *"You're supposed to tag him out."*

The second baseman understood and threw the ball to Bell at home plate.

By now James was getting winded. The throw was right on target, and Bell caught the ball with James still fifteen feet from home plate. Bell extended his glove, crouched down, anticipating a slide into home. James liked to do that even if it wasn't necessary—he once did it after hitting a home run.

But James wasn't sliding. As Bell made the tag, James plowed into him running at full bore, arms held up in front of him, elbows extended. The ball, Bell's mitt, his hat and most of his consciousness went flying.

Scorcelli threw his glove down on the mound, ran over to James, grabbed him by the neck, and pinned him up against the chain-link backstop. "Are you crazy?" The others, including a dazed Tom Bell, began to cluster around them. Scorcelli spun James around, wrestled him to the dirt. *"Vi balshoy sveynenah . . ."*

The others who had surrounded Scorcelli and James tensed—even Scorcelli seemed to forget that he had his hands around James' neck.

*"Enough."* Mr. Roberts walked through the quickly parting crowd and stood over the two on the ground. Scorcelli got to his feet and stood straight, almost at attention, hands at his sides, chin up. James, his chest heaving, also stood up quickly.

Roberts was a short, squat man with dark brows obscuring darker, cavernous eyes. His rumbling voice commanded instant attention.

"James deliberately ran into Bell to make him drop the ball," Scorcelli began.

"It's in the rules, pea-brain—"

"He ran right into him," Scorcelli went on. "He did not even *try* to slow down or get out of the way! James is a cheater—"

"No one calls me a cheater—"

*"Enough,"* Roberts ordered.

But James ignored the order. "I fight my own battles. If you knew the rules, Scorcelli, you'd know I have the right to home plate as much as the catcher. If he stands in front of it, I can run him down. And if he drops the ball, even after making the tag, the runner is safe and the run scores.''

"What about when you tapped the ball like that?'' Scorcelli fired back. "Were you trying to get hit by the ball? You are supposed to swing the bat, not—''

"It's called a *bunt*, you fool.'' That revelation brought a number of blank stares.

Eyes turned toward Mr. Roberts, who stared at Ken James, then announced the period was over and ordered them to report to their next class.

The students Ken James and Anthony Scorcelli were standing before their headmaster's desk. Jeffrey Baines Roberts was behind his desk. His secretary had put two file folders on his desk. She ignored Scorcelli; favored James with the hint of a smile before leaving.

"Mr. Scorcelli,'' said the headmaster, "tell me about your brother Roger.''

Scorcelli stared at a point somewhere above Roberts' head. "I have four siblings, sir, two brothers and one sister. Their names—''

"I did not ask about your other siblings, Mr. Scorcelli. I asked about your brother Roger.''

"Yes, sir . . . Kevin and Roger . . . '' He seemed to be talking to himself, then said aloud, "Roger is two years older than me, a freshman at Cornell University. He—''

"Where was your mother born?''

"My . . . mother . . . yes, sir, she was born in Syracuse, New York. She has two sisters and—''

"I did not ask you about her sisters.'' Roberts ran an exasperated hand down his forehead. "Are you not familiar with the rules of baseball, Mr. Scorcelli?''

"I was not aware that Mr. James was allowed to assault his friends and fellow players—''

"The proper term is a *battery*, Mr. Scorcelli. *Assault* is the threat of physical harm. Is it a battery if Mr. James' actions are a legal part of the game?''

"It may not be a battery, sir, but I believe Mr. James took great pleasure in the opportunity to knock over Mr. Bell—''

"Bullshit,'' James said.

"I also think, sir, that If Mr. James could legally find a way to hit me over the head with one of those bats from that stupid game, he would do it with the same enthusiasm and—''

"Right, asshole . . .''

"That's enough,'' Roberts said, his voice calm. Actually he had to strain to keep from smiling. Scorcelli would be right at home in a large corporation's boardroom or in a court of law; James would be at home in an active situation. A dangerous one with courage and physical stamina. And an ability to adjust. James was not a team player. He either led or he would choose to operate on his own. He could also be ruthless . . .

"I will not have athletics in this institution become a private battleground between students,'' Roberts said. "Mr. Scorcelli?''

Scorcelli hesitated, turned to face James and stuck out a hand.

"Apology accepted, Mr. Scorcelli,'' James said with his winning smile—a smile that infuriated Scorcelli.

"I assume you have no intention of changing your playing habits,'' Roberts said. "You will continue to take advantage of each opportunity to denigrate your compatriots, even in a baseball game?''

Ken James looked puzzled. Scorcelli may have believed he was wrestling with a moral dilemma. Roberts knew better, but was surprised when James replied: "Sir, I will take advantage of every rule and every legal opportunity to win.''

"No matter the consequences?''

"No matter, sir.''

Roberts expected and desired nothing less. "You are dismissed, Mr. Scorcelli. Mr. James will remain . . . so, Mr. Scorcelli?''

"Yes, sir?''

*"Vi balshoy sveynenah.''*

Scorcelli did not look blank, as required. Only flustered.

"Get out,'' Roberts said, and Scorcelli hustled away, closing the door behind him so gently he might have been closing a door made of fine china.

Ken James waited impassively. Roberts motioned him to a seat. Roberts watched him unbutton the top button of his sports coat and seat himself. "You even swear like one of them, Mr. James.''

No reply.

"Do you think you are ready for graduation?"

"I do."

"Mr. James, whose side are you on? Sometimes it appears only your own."

"Isn't that the American way? Knowledge is power, in baseball or business. I want all the knowledge I can accumulate. I've worked hard to accumulate it, even the things others think inconsequential. It would be a waste not to use it—"

"Do not pretend you know everything about America or how to live in it. You have lived a sheltered life here in the Academy. The world is just waiting to swallow overconfident young people like you." James made no reply but sat easily in the hard-backed upright wood chair. Roberts paused for a moment, then asked, "Tell me about your father, Kenneth."

"Not *again*, sir. All right, my father was a drunk, sir, a drunk and a scum who murdered my younger brother but was found incompetent to stand trial and was committed to a mental institution. They said he was suffering from delayed shock syndrome from his three tours as a Green Beret company commander in Vietnam. When he was released several years later he abandoned his family and went off to who knows where. Prison or another mental institution. His name was Kenneth also, but I refuse to use 'Junior' in my surname and I've even thought of changing my whole name."

Roberts looked surprised, which amused James. "Don't worry, sir. I won't. It's not as glamorous a story as Scorcelli's rich jet-setting parents, or Bell's midwestern aunties. But it's *my* story. I've learned, sir, to downplay it, push it out of my consciousness. I allow it to surface as a reminder of what I *could* become if I don't work and study very hard."

"I am not particularly interested in your opinion of your father," Roberts said, "and you would be well advised to keep such opinions to yourself."

James' response was to smile back at him with that maddening half-grin. James, it seemed, had no intention of taking such advice.

A problem. The Connecticut Academy, in operation for only thirty years, had acquired a reputation for excellence in its graduates. Only the best left the Academy, and they left only for the best colleges and universities. The rest were sent back to wherever they came from, without any ties or records of their time at the Academy. The Academy had a reputation to uphold. How would this Kenneth Francis James fit in?

His grades were never in question—he had scored in the upper one percent of his Scholastic Aptitude Tests and had passed advanced placement exams in mathematics and biology, allowing him to take nine credits of college-level courses even before stepping onto a college campus. He had even taken several Law School Admissions Tests for practice and had scored high on all of them. He had requested only the best— Columbia, Harvard, Georgetown, Oxford. It was his intention to study under such as Kissinger, Kirkpatrick, Brezezinski— and pursue a career in the Foreign Service or in politics.

Mostly autonomy was what James craved, autonomy and control, but his extremism could destroy him and hurt the Academy. In the Foreign Service, in government, one had to be a team player. Which left out Kenneth James.

But the Academy tried not to discard its students who did not fit. Especially the highly intelligent ones. The problem now was to find James a niche for his particular talents and personality and at the same time channel usefully his considerable energy and intelligence.

Roberts began to stack the folders on his desk and buzzed his secretary. "You are dismissed, Mr. James."

The sudden announcement took James by surprise, but he tried not to show it. He stood and headed for the door.

*"Das svedanya, tovarishchniy Maraklov,"* Roberts called out, glancing up at the retreating figure, waiting to catch his reaction.

There was none. James turned, hand casually on the doorknob. "I beg your pardon, sir?"

Roberts remained stone-faced but inwardly was pleased. Good, Mr. James, he said to himself. No sign of recognition— and more importantly, no sign of trying to hide any recognition. You have learned your lessons well. I think you may be ready for graduation . . .

"Dismissed, Mr. James."


"My name is Janet."

Ken James moved closer to the woman and stared into her bright green eyes. Janet Larson was thirty years old, five feet tall, with long, bouncy brown hair. She was wearing stone-

washed jeans and a red flannel shirt, the sleeves rolled up and
the top three buttons unbuttoned against the warming late spring
weather. Sitting in her apartment, Ken let his eyes travel from
her shining eyes to her white throat and down her open neck-
line to the deepening crest between her breasts. When his eyes
moved back to her face he found her looking directly at him.

"Eye contact," he said, moving closer. "When strangers
meet, eye contact is frequently broken. We've been taught here
to look everyone in the eye, that eye contact is important. Actually a woman's direct look makes many men uneasy."

She nodded, then slowly stepped even closer until her breasts
pushed against his cotton Rugby shirt. He let the Academy's
administrative secretary linger there for a moment, then reached
out, grasped her shoulders and pushed her away a few inches.

"Remember the social bubble, too," he said with a smile.
"Americans need their space. Encroachment on a person's
bubble, even by a beautiful woman, turns even the most desirable woman into an intruder."

"Do you find me desirable, Kenneth?"

He pretended to be exasperated. "Try it again," he
prompted.

She nodded, looked up, smiled and said, "Hi, my name is
Janet."

"Pretty good. But try contracting 'name' and 'is.' Americans love contractions. They slur everything together. 'Hi, my
name's Janet.' "

She nodded, took a deep breath. "Hi, my name's Janet,"
and punctuated it by invading his bubble again.

"Perfect," he said, and let his eyes deliberately roam her
body once again. She raised her lips, and their little lesson was
abruptly postponed.

She was very well trained. She started slowly, agonizingly
so. Undressing was part of the foreplay. She was controlling
him, moving slowly when she felt him hurry, speeding up when
she felt him grow impatient. She knew when and where to
touch him, what to say or do to build their sexual energy in
perfect synchronization.

Soon it became too much to control and they released their
pent-up energy. She climaxed first, the way she had been
taught, giving him one last volt to heighten his own climax.
She used her muscles to draw every drop from him, then re-

leased him moments later—she had been taught that most
American men would not remain inside a woman after sex,
sometimes refusing even to lie beside them. But this student,
however well trained, was not *that* American . . . He stayed
inside her for several minutes, then let her lie on top of him so
he could nuzzle her neck and breasts and feel her warmth all
around him. She gently rolled beside him, propped up her head
so she could look into his eyes as he traced his fingers around
her body.

She too had once been a student at the Connecticut Academy, but her training was in a far different field than his. She
had readily accepted her courtesan training and had been selected for "graduation," but instead opted to stay at the Academy as an administrator. Seducing the young students was her
chief source of excitement now, her satisfaction coming less
from the erotic than from pleasure in displaying her exceptional
skills.

She especially enjoyed displaying her skills with this young
student—control name "Ken James," born Andrei Ivanschichin Maraklov of Leningrad, the son of a Party bureaucrat and
a hospital administrator, the top student at the top-secret Connecticut Academy in the mountainside city of Novorossijsk on
the Black Sea, where young Soviet men and women were
trained to be KGB deep-cover agents.

The Connecticut Academy was a most unusual high school,
and it attracted the USSR's most unusual men and women.
Most of the students were trained at a very early age for the
intelligence field, learning foreign languages and customs of
dozens of nations. Both male and female students, like "Janet
Larson," were trained as courtesans and used for sexual espionage activities. Others were trained in demolition or assas-
sination or other forms of terrorism. And still others, like
"Kenneth James," born Maraklov, were part of a whole new
area of espionage.

Selected individuals in various countries were targeted by
the KGB because of their socio-economic status and opportunity for growth and importance. These individuals—sons and
daughters of politicians, businessmen, corporate presidents—
would be carefully studied at an early age, once identified as
being groomed for a particular position or put into the pipeline
for a given career or special responsibility. Their habits, social

life and personality were examined. Were they responsible, stable individuals, or did they squander time and money on, say, drugs and partying? If they were especially promising individuals, apparently destined for greatness, phase two of the project was invoked.

A young Russian closely matching the target's general physical and mental attributes would be trained in the same fields as the subject individual. Along with being taught the target's native language, the student would also learn everything possible to help *blend* himself into the social fabric as well as the personality of the target. After years of study and training, the student would be a virtual clone of the target.

Next, at an opportune time, the clone would be inserted to replace the target. He would assume all of the target's activities, history, future. Of course it was not possible precisely to duplicate the subject's every mood or segment of his personality, so the clones were trained to fit in, to adapt, to take control of their situations. If they did not perfectly match, they were to change the environment around themselves. The clone would, it was hoped, create the *new* norm and thereby achieve a more viable match-up.

After a suitable waiting period to allow the new mole to acclimate himself with his new surroundings, he would be directed by Moscow headquarters to begin collecting information, to maneuver closer to the seat of power in government or industry, to influence events in favor of the Soviet Union or its allies. In an emergency the mole could be used to assist other agents, collect or borrow funds, even carry out search-and-destroy missions or assassinations. Unlike informers, traitors, bribery victims or embassy employees, these "native citizens" were always to be immune to suspicion. They could pass the most exhaustive background investigation—fingerprints, if necessary, even surgically matched.

Perhaps only a handful of these super-moles could be turned loose in a year. The training was exhaustive and exhausting; many Soviet students, even though they learned English well and knew a good deal of "American," could not sufficiently adapt themselves to the very strange American culture and be a reliable espionage agent as well. And even with the apparently perfect student, there was no way of knowing what would happen to the intended target. Targets were selected for their accessibility as well as their potential value, but over the years there was no way to guarantee a useful match. Goals changed, opportunities came and went, minds changed, paths crossed. An individual who was perceived as the next President of the United States could turn out to be a corrupt congressman; a candidate-target discarded from consideration could turn out to be a future Director of the Central Intelligence Agency.

The target Ken James—the *American* Ken James—would never have been considered only a few short years earlier: He was the son of a psychotic Vietnam veteran; he grew up in a fragmented childhood punctuated by a devastating family disaster; the family was split apart. The boy himself was a loner, unpopular and remote, anti-social.

But things changed. The loner turned out to be a boy genius. The father disappeared from sight and was presumed dead. The mother married a wealthy multinational corporate president, and both the stepfather and mother were candidates for political office by election or appointment. The obscure boy was suddenly a prime candidate for "cloning." Still a loner, virtually ignored by his jet-setting parents, he was nonetheless being educated and groomed for a public life in government-service. A perfect target.

And they found a boy in the Soviet Union equal to the challenge of a match-up . . . and ultimate substitution. Andrei Ivanschichin Maraklov had a unique combination of writer's imagination and a savant's intelligence—the stuff to qualify him as Ken James' intellectual and emotional twin . . .

Janet Larson smiled as she noted the faraway expression in his eyes and propped herself up again on one elbow so she could watch him. "Where are you now, Kenneth?"

He smiled at the question. It was a game they played when they were together. As an administrative assistant to the headmaster, Janet Larson knew all about Ken James—why he was there, what was expected of him after "graduation." But some students, the special ones like Maraklov/James, gave the nuts and bolts of their alter egos a considerable amount of spice and feeling. It was forbidden for the students to talk of their "lives" with any other student, but not so with her, and especially not so with her and student Kenneth James . . .

"I'm on my way to Hawaii," he said. "One last fling before college. My mom and stepdad are in Europe on business. They

gave me a Hawaiian vacation as a graduation present. I graduated last week, remember?''

"How were your grades?''

"Straight A's, but it was an easy semester. I planned it that
way. I could have graduated and gone on to college after my
junior year—doubled up on a few classes in the summer—but
I was told by my stepdad that a guy shouldn't miss out on his
senior year in high school, that it has too many memories.
That's a crock. Anyway, I cruised through the year.''

"And what about your senior-year memories? Were they
worth delaying college?''

"I guess so,'' he said as he ran his hand up and down her
back and she saw that smile slowly spread across his face. It
was as if he was actually reliving those experiences . . .

"I was quite an athlete the whole year,'' he went on. "Soccer in the fall, basketball, baseball in the spring—I already had
all my credits for graduation and I had two gym periods every
day so I could devote full time to all of them. It was fantastic.''

Janet had trouble following—"gym'' and "soccer'' were
foreign words to her. Not, of course, baseball. The way he told
his story was eerie, as if he was relating some sort of mystical
out-of-body experience.

"That was all you did? Sports?''

"No, I had lots of dates. I went out every Friday and Saturday night. My mom and Frank—that's my stepdad—were
home only one week out of five, so I had the run of the place.
Except for the maid, of course.''

"Tell me about your dates, Kenneth.''

Again, that smile. "I saw Cathy Sawyer the most. We've
been going out almost all year. Nothing special . . . a movie,
dinner once in a while. I helped her with her homework, she
can't seem to pick up calculus no matter how hard I try to
explain it to her.''

Listening to him, watching him, it was like hearing someone
not just talk about but actually *live* another life in front of you.
They had done a complete job, it seemed, on Andrei Maraklov.
Now he *was* Kenneth James. "Were you ever passionate with
her, Kenneth?''

Suddenly his eyes grew dark. "Ken?''

"She doesn't want me that way.'' His voice had been deep,

harsh. She touched his shoulder—his body seemed to have turned to ice.

". . . She doesn't want me," he repeated in a dead-sounding voice. "No one does. My dad's an alcoholic schizoid. People think some genetic germ is going to rub off from me onto them if I get too close. Everyone thinks I'll whack out on them just like my dad whacked out on his family."

*Whack* out? More mumbo-jumbo. "Ken . . . "

"All they want is my brains and my money." His body was now as hard, as tense as his voice, his eyes were hot. " 'Help me with my homework, Ken' . . . 'Help us with the fund-raiser, James' . . . 'Come out for the team, Ken' . . . Ask, ask, ask. But when *I* want something, they all run away."

"It's only because you are better than they are, Kenneth—"

"Who cares about *that*?" It was like a cry. She gasped at the anger in his face. "When am I going to get what *I* want? When am I ever going to feel accepted by them . . . ?" He took hold of her right hand and squeezed hard. "Huh? *When?*"

He tossed her hand aside and rolled up out of bed. She gathered a sheet around her and slid out on the other side.

". . . I was glad when they asked me to be valedictorian because then I could turn them down. What's the difference? My mom was going to be in New Zealand or some other place, something too important to cancel even for her only surviving son's high school graduation—and my dad's dead or in a gutter somewhere . . . Nobody that I cared about was going to hear my speech, so I arranged to have my Regents diploma mailed to me. When I told my mom, instead of being angry, she sent me first-class plane tickets to Oahu and five thousand bucks. I got the hell out of that school as fast as I could."

Janet sat on the edge of the bed, carefully watching this Ken James as he told his story. There was something frightening in him. It was so weird listening to him tell that story, not his and yet entirely his, and the way he slid into the first-person *present* tense . . . All of the students at the Connecticut Academy studied their alter egos, but in her memory Andrei was the only one in the Academy who actually seemed to live his alter ego, experiencing everything he did, every hurt, every triumph, every sadness. And Maraklov's eyes, they were scary but held Janet—born Katrina Litkovka, the daughter of a Red Army colonel—so that she didn't want him to stop.

"What about college?" she asked.

"I've been accepted at a dozen schools," he replied in perfect mid-Atlantic American English. "I haven't made up my mind. I was even considering skipping a semester, getting away from it all. I've even thought about enlisting in the Marine Corps. I told that to my stepdad once. He said it might look good on a résumé if I want to run for a congressional seat someday. I've never forgotten that."

Janet still had a bit of trouble keeping up with his fluent English—years earlier she had been schooled in English as much as he but had lost much of her skill out of disuse. Still, she understood enough to be amazed—the clarity, the realism, the precise detail of his story . . . The Academy rarely if ever managed to teach their students to his degree of authenticity.

He stood, his back toward her. She eyed his tall, youthful, athletic frame—broad shoulders, thin waist, tight buttocks.

It seemed Andrei Maraklov had so totally immersed himself in the life of Kenneth Francis James that he had assumed his *emotional* identity as well as his documented public one. How else could Andrei reel off intimate, secretive aspects of his—James'—life so *naturally*? Of one thing she had no doubt: this man could easily beat the best interrogators, polygraphs, hypnosis or even drugs.

Andrei Maraklov *is* Kenneth James . . .

"But now I'm on my way to Hawaii," James/Maraklov continued. "I'm going to take it easy, maybe raise some hell, maybe do some painting, I don't know . . ."

He turned toward the bed once again, but she was too caught up in his eerie transformation to think about having sex with him again. Actually, he frightened her . . . he was a stranger. Uncharacteristically, she clutched the sheet tight to her breasts.

"Cathy Sawyer gets wet every time she sees me," he said, a slight smile on his lips. "I know it. But when we're alone she won't touch me." He moved toward her, and she flinched.

The smile disappeared, his eyes narrowed. "All right, damn you, you're like everyone else."

She had pulled the sheet off the bed and wrapped it around herself. He seemed to be frozen in place, his powerful chest rising and falling. As she tried to step around him, he quickly reached out and grabbed her arm.

"Kenneth—"

"No, I'm not leaving and neither are you. Not yet." He grasped her forearms with two powerful hands. The sheet fell away from her breasts. He pulled her forearms up and toward him, drawing her toward him so that she was barely touching the floor. "I'm going to show you what I did to that bitch Cathy Sawyer the night before I left. She never showed up for graduation, did I tell you that? They thought we ran off together, but we didn't. Poor Cathy . . . I wonder what happened to her . . ."

He is going to kill me, Janet thought. He's crazy, he's going to . . .

Abruptly the terrifying grin was replaced by a broad, pleasant smile. His body relaxed and he let her drop back onto her feet, then planted a playful kiss on her nose.

"Gotcha."

"What?" Her voice high, edged with fear. "What do you think you are doing?" She said it in Russian.

"Uh oh, remember, lover, English only is spoken at this academy . . ."

"I thought . . . I thought you . . ."

". . . were crazy," he said. His smile was making her even angrier. "I know what you're thinking. Every time we're together you want to hear my little stories about the American. So I tell you what I think he's like, what he's going through, what kind of life he lives."

"You scared me to *death*. Why?"

"Because you wanted it. I was only doing what you—"

"You are crazy," she said, grabbed up her clothes and put on her blouse and pants. "Get out of here."

"Janet, wait . . ."

"I don't want to see you again." She yanked open the front door to her bedroom. "Now get dressed and get out."

The smile stayed, but he obediently put on his jeans and sweatshirt, gathering his underwear and shoes in his arms. But just before he left her apartment he turned to her.

"You'll miss me," he said. "The sex you can get from any of the others. But you *need* the excitement of living with a real American. It's your high. It's the worst transgression for a female KGB operative. You love it."

"Andrei Ivanschichin Maraklov—"

"My name is Kenneth James."

"You will not be allowed to leave the Academy. You will never see America except in your own mind. That I promise—"

His smile disappeared, but she couldn't stop.

"I will make recommendations to Mr. Roberts that you never be allowed to graduate. You could compromise the whole operation."

It pleased her to see the panic in his face that had now replaced his smug expression. "What are you going to tell them, Janet? That while we've been screwing each other I somehow scared you and you think I'm crazy? You've no credibility. A thirty-year-old ex-whore having sex with a seventeen-year-old high school student. You'll make a very reliable witness." He stepped toward her, his expression softening. "You'll drag yourself down as well as me. Don't do it. I promise I won't scare you again. Janet . . ."

She pushed him away. "I don't need credibility. I can destroy you without anyone ever knowing it was me. A notation here and there, a rumor, a changed grade or a negative entry on your progress charts. You will be on your way to a border post before you know it. Now once more, get out."

"Don't do it," he was still saying as the door slammed in his face. "You'll be sorry if you do . . ."

His morning regimen had been the same for the past five years. Wakeup at five A.M., calisthenics and a morning three-mile jog, breakfast by six-thirty. The Academy even taught students to enjoy the typical American breakfast dishes while at the same time giving them healthier, more substantial foods.

Classes began at eight. Usually there was a bit of time before the morning class—today's was on the stock market and American economics—so James spent his time reviewing the latest intelligence on his "target"—the real Ken James.

How could anyone with so much going for him act the way James had? Maraklov asked himself. The report said James was going to ace every course he was enrolled in in his final semester of high school, including several advance-placement college-level courses. At the same time a police blotter report noted that James had been caught with a bag of marijuana. He was not charged with a crime, only reprimanded—his stepfather carried a good deal of influence in the small town where he lived. But James had risked his whole career on a one-ounce bag of dried grass. Stupid.

No pictures were included in the latest intelligence, but previous photographs showed a tall, handsome youth shopping in fancy stores, driving expensive cars, going to parties, every weekend. He had seemed like a normal well-adjusted teenager. Maraklov knew, of course, about James' unfortunate past, but that was ancient history. Surely that ugly episode was long forgotten? Maraklov sat back now and thought about what it was like to be Ken James . . .

I have everything I ever wanted. Brains, money, things. What am I missing? What else do I want? Why did I need to smoke marijuana and get in trouble with the cops? I have a good family, minus a brother—my natural father killed him in a drunken rage. I don't have a father, a *real* father—he's either dead or in a mental institution. I haven't seen my mom in months—the only grown-ups around are the housekeeper, the gardener once a week, and the occasional relatives of my step-father who show up and say it's okay for them to borrow the Jag or bring their mistresses in for a nooner. "Nooner" . . . Janet would have trouble with *that* Americanism . . .

The big house is lonely at night. My "friends" stop by once in a while, but they study pretty hard, and I'm not exactly popular . . . There are alarms all over the place—I have to be careful to shut them off even when I just want to get some fresh air or take a dip in the pool. Cathy Sawyer doesn't come by much anymore. I wonder where she is—?

A call on the room's intercom interrupted: "Mr. James, report to the headmaster's office immediately."

As he headed toward Roberts' office he thought of Janet Larson. *Damn her.* She had really done it, had blown the whistle on him. She would pay for this, he told himself as he straightened his tie. She would pay . . .

But Janet Larson was just as surprised, and just as fearful to see him, as she walked into Roberts' outer office. They exchanged no words, only anxious glances as he knocked on the headmaster's door. He was ushered in by Roberts himself and left standing in the middle of the office.

"The question about whether or not you will ever graduate has been made for us, it seems," Roberts began. He motioned to a message form. "A report from our agents in place in

Washington. It seems your Mr. Kenneth Francis James has decided on a college.''

Maraklov smiled. Washington, D.C. That must mean Georgetown. Ken James has decided on—

''He surprised everyone,'' Roberts went on. ''We did not even know he had applied for the Air Force Academy.''

Maraklov was stunned. ''The *Air Force Academy*?''

''He received a senatorial sponsorship last winter, obviously from his stepfather's connections,'' Roberts went on. ''We were fortunate—we learned he had cut his scheduled vacation in Hawaii short by two months, and one of our operatives did some checking to find out why. He is supposed to begin summer orientation training in six weeks.''

Maraklov's mind was beginning to catch up. ''My father,'' he mumbled, then looked at Roberts. ''I mean his father is . . . was . . . a highly decorated veteran of the Vietnam war. Even without political connections he could have received sponsorship as the son of a combat veteran. There could be a sympathy factor too. I should have known. The possibility of a military academy placement was always there . . . ''

''Whatever, this changes our plans for your graduation, Kenneth James.'' He was testing as he said it.

''Sir?''

''Your counterpart-target is about to enter the Air Force Academy. We cannot risk putting an agent into the Air Force Academy. He has a pilot-training appointment. He will be in the United States Air Force for four years—''

''Eight years, sir,'' Maraklov corrected him, eyes bright with anticipation. ''Pilot candidates must serve eight years after UPT graduation . . . ''

''You have learned well, but that is not the point, Mr. James. We have never placed a deep agent in the American air force's cadre. He would have little chance of surviving the security screening. It is very intense, especially for a pilot candidate. They check every move from present day to birth, check his parents, his relatives, his neighbors—''

''And Kenneth James will pass with flying colors,'' Maraklov said excitedly.

''But the applicant for a security clearance initiates the process with a detailed report on his background, relatives, addresses,'' Roberts said nervously. ''You would have to supply every detail of James' life from *memory*—you could not risk being caught with a dossier on yourself. And the process is repeated every five years while in the service. Could you do that?''

''Of course, sir.''

Roberts hesitated, but only for a moment. If any other student had made that confident a reply he would have dismissed it as bravado. But not Maraklov. The boy knew his counterpart so well . . . it was almost frightening. Beyond any of the other student-target linkages.

''You will need plastic surgery,'' Roberts said. ''And if the scars and bruising from surgery do not heal in time, you will be discovered.''

''I assume James will be in Hawaii until July,'' Maraklov said. ''The summer orientation course starts in mid-July, as I recall. That gives us five weeks before we need to intercept James. Five weeks is time enough for my scars to heal. And the surgery would not need to be extensive, sir. My . . . his parents won't be visiting very often. And plebes are not allowed visitors until Thanksgiving. By then his appearance will have changed enough to explain any minor differences—'' his voice dropped, sounding depressed—''if my parents notice at all.''

Roberts scarcely noticed James' changing moods, his juxtaposing of himself and the real Kenneth James, the angry distant look. But he was too busy marveling at Maraklov's extensive knowledge of even the most esoteric bits of information.

''This will have to be approved by Moscow,'' Roberts said, sounding as excited as Maraklov had earlier. ''But we have a chance to *do* it . . . And if we do, it will be the espionage coup of the century—''

''Yes, sir,'' James agreed, though he was not thinking about espionage coups, or success or failure.

He was thinking, I will be . . . complete. Yes, that was the word. For the first time in my life, I will have a chance to become a complete person. Thanks to Ken James . . .

*Wednesday, 1 July 1985, 2103 EET*

It was late that evening. As usual Katrina Litkovka, known as Janet Larson, was finishing a stack of paperwork, clearing her desk and preparing the Academy administrator's morning business. She heard the outer office door open. Before she could look up from her desk, Maraklov was in her office and had slammed the door behind him.

Katrina knew it was Maraklov, but it still took a moment for the shock to wear off—after all, it had only been a few weeks since Andrei Maraklov had had his new face. This new one was thinner, with a higher forehead and a stronger, squarer jaw. The quality of the plastic surgery was excellent—the scars were nearly invisible and the bruising had all but subsided. This Ken James could be considered very handsome—except right now what she felt was a stab of fear. Maraklov, if recognizable, was also much more a stranger now, unpredictable as any other intruder.

She forced down the anxiety she felt and managed an authoritative edge in her voice . . . "You are not to be here after hours, Mr. James."

Maraklov did not say a word but quickly scanned Litkovka's desk. His attention settled on a memo paper still in her typewriter. Before she could react he had yanked the paper out of the platen and read it, his face darkening with every word. "So," he said in a low voice, "you *are* going to try to block my mission to the United States."

"It is a report from the Academy psychologist," she said. "It has nothing to do with me—"

"He's another one you sleep with."

"You should know about *that*." Litkovka stood up and snatched the paper out of his fingers. "*He*, not I, says he is uncertain about your emotional stability. He thinks you may not be prepared to enter the Air Force Academy. It is my duty to make sure that Mr. Roberts knows about the doctor's opinion—"

"Don't do this to me," Maraklov said. "I'm the *perfect* candidate for this operation. I *am* prepared. I've prepared for years. I know exactly what I'm doing—"

"Spoken like a schizophrenic bordering on psychotic," she said with a smile. "If you 'graduate' and compromise us, all our careers are in jeopardy. I must not allow that to happen—''

Maraklov slapped his hands on the desktop, then visibly fought to relax, put on a hint of a smile, and reached inside his jacket. Her eyes widened with fear, but what he pulled out was a small half-liter bottle of amber liquid.

"This is for you, Janet," Maraklov said. "I know it's your favorite." He set the bottle down and she read the label.

"Scotch whiskey?" she said in a surprised voice. "Where did you get Scotch whiskey?"

"Never mind, Janet. It's yours. Please take it."

"But that is contraband, Andrei—"

*"My name is Ken James . . ."*

He really did seem beyond the edge, although that identification with his subject-target was what he had been trained to achieve. Still, wasn't his extreme, so much so he might lose control and endanger his mission? Her personal anger over his treatment of her helped the rationalization, if that's what it was.

"Having that in your possession is a serious offense. I suggest you get out of my office and get rid of it immediately or I will be obliged to call the headmaster—"

"No, don't do that. Please—" his tone was abruptly subdued—"I'm going . . ."

He picked up the bottle, stuck it back into his coat pocket and left without another word.

True, Litkovka had used her well-honed talents to get the school psychologist to write a perhaps more damaging psychological report on Maraklov than otherwise. But it was only a matter of degree, she assured herself. Without question, Maraklov would do anything to go to the United States—his motives were personal as well as patriotic. Why this was so she didn't know. She did know that Andrei Maraklov could be a dangerous man. Well, he had accepted the situation, finally. At least it seemed so . . .

She stayed until ten o'clock that evening—curfew for all students was ten P.M. and bed-check was shortly thereafter, so she would be safe from Maraklov just in case he tried to do something crazy when she left the office. She gathered up the papers on Maraklov and locked them in her briefcase—if Maraklov got his hands on a bottle of Scotch whiskey, he could

easily get his hands on this report if she left it in the office—
and headed for her car in the parking lot.

She found herself checking around outside her car, checking
the back seat and trunk until a passing security patrol saw her.
She had to smile. "You are acting very strange, Katrina. Go
home and get some rest and put Maraklov out of your mind."

Minutes later she was outside the front gate of the Academy
heading down the two-lane chickenseed road toward the main
highway. After turning onto the wide, two-lane asphalt highway, she switched her headlights to high-beam and roared east-
bound to her apartment complex a few kilometers from the
Academy. The road was curvy in places but it was wide and
fast and she kept the speed up to a hundred kilometers an hour.

She was rounding a gentle right-hand curve when suddenly
a figure appeared in the glare of her headlights, right in front
of her car. Litkovka jerked the wheel to the left and tromped
on the brakes. Her Zil automobile skidded in a half-circle across
the road and into the ditch on the other side. Litkovka was
wearing a seatbelt but no shoulder harness, and her head hit
hard against the steering wheel, then against the closed driver's
side window as the car sank several inches into the muddy
ditch.

She was still semiconscious, dazed by the impact, when the
passenger-side door opened. She raised her head and squinted
against the sudden glare of the interior light and saw a man
dressed in a heavy coat and gloves. The interior light went out.

"Help me, please. *Pamaghetye* . . ."

Her head was yanked backward by her hair. Before she could
take a breath a strong liquid was poured down her throat. She
coughed, tried to spit it out. The liquid burned her throat, lungs,
nose. Then a powerful gloved hand covered her mouth and
nose, trapping the liquid inside her throat. She had no strength
to resist. Only to squirm for only a moment or so, then was
still.

The shadowy figure checked the body for any sign of life,
then dumped out the contents of Litkovka's briefcase on the
car floor. Using a small penlight, he checked each paper until
he found the one he was searching for. He stuffed it into his
pocket, dropped the bottle of whiskey on the seat beside Litkovka and hurried off.

## Honolulu, Hawaii
*Monday, 6 July 1985, 2017 PDT*

Ken James was adjusting the collar on his Hawaiian flowered shirt when he heard the knock on the door.

"Housekeeping," a young woman's voice announced. "May I turn your bed down, sir?"

The hotel had some delicious-looking maids working there, Ken had recalled, young Polynesians working their way through college. This one sounded more promising than the matrons that had been coming by lately. He was on his way out but thought he might at least have a look. Who knew, once she was off duty she might make his last night in Oahu very special.

"Come in," he said over his shoulder as he admired himself in the mirror. He heard the door swing open—

A hand clamped tight over his mouth and nose. When he reached up and tried to pry his hands away from his face he felt a sharp sting on his left shoulder. He swung hard as he could, heard a muffled grunt, and then his head was snapped down and sideways. A hand was around his throat and face. The more he struggled to free himself, the weaker he became—his muscles now refusing to work. The hands left his face, but he had no more resistance. Feeling incredibly weak, he stumbled forward against the bureau, tried to balance himself and fought the urge to collapse. Slowly he turned around . . .

. . . Or *did* he turn? When he was able to focus his eyes, he found himself looking at . . . himself?

And at the same time, Andrei Maraklov stared at the object, the target of all his training for so many months—the *real* Kenneth Francis James.

Close as the resemblance was, as Maraklov studied James he noted that James' hair was thinner than his—James would be bald in five years or less while he would have his full head of hair. He was an inch taller than James and somewhat more muscular. No doubt James' dissipation, his drinking and drug taking accounted for the subtle differences that even the KGB could fail to keep up with. Still, the overall impression was of near look-alikes.

Meanwhile, Ken James studied the face that was peering at him. It *could* have been a twin but that was impossible. Some sort of hallucination. God, he'd better lighten up on the booze and grass. "Are you for real?" James asked, blinking through the growing haze that seemed to be fogging his senses.

"Yes, real . . ."

James' eyes widened, and he reached out to the apparition. Hallucination? No . . . a dream come true . . . "Matthew . . . Matthew?" James was reaching to touch the face. "Matthew—"

"No," Maraklov said. "Our brother is dead, remember? Our father killed him."

James blinked in surprise. So did the two KGB enforcers that had come with Maraklov into James' hotel room. Maraklov's voice had a pleasant, intimate tone. And the reference to "our" father momentarily startled them, though they had been briefed on this unusual young agent.

James stared at Maraklov. "Then . . . who are you?"

"I am you, Kenneth. I am Kenneth James. I've come to help you."

Through his rapidly dulling senses James clutched tighter to Maraklov to keep from falling. Maraklov held him steady.

"Give him here, *tovarisch*," one of the strong-arms muttered. "We don't have all night—"

"Shut up," Maraklov said. "And no Russian. These hotel walls are paper thin."

"Sorry," the other said. He had wheeled a large white canvas laundry cart into the room. "Drop him in here and—"

"I said be quiet. I'll turn him over when I'm ready."

James had been taking in the exchange among the three Russians. When Maraklov turned back toward him he asked what was going on, what were they going to do with him . . .

Maraklov opened his mouth to invent an easy lie for the half-dead alter ego standing before him but could not. This American, whom he had only known for a few minutes, was also someone it seemed he had known all his life . . . and the closest any human being had been to him since he left his home for the Connecticut Academy eight years earlier. He forced his voice to sound firm, reassuring. "Don't worry, everything's going to be okay. You don't have to worry about dad, or mom, or Matthew, or about Cathy or about school . . . I'm going to take care of everything, Ken. Everything will be fine. I'm strong and smart, I'll take care of our problems. Don't worry. You just go with these guys and forget about everything.''

James seemed to nod, even smile a bit. Andrei eased him over and handed him to the first man.

''Hey . . . hey . . . Who *are* you?''

Andrei smiled benevolently, brotherly. ''I am you, Ken. I told you that. I'm you and I can take care of everything. You just go on now . . .''

James was slipping away fast but still had residual instinct to resist. He turned to Maraklov. ''Ken . . .''

Maraklov was nearly mesmerized by the sound of that name, hearing for the first time an American—*the* American—call him by the name the KGB had assigned him three years ago.

''Yes . . . what?''

''You love father, don't you?''

The two enforcers were puzzled by this exchange, but Maraklov ignored them. They no longer existed. It was just the two . . . brothers. They wouldn't understand.

What could he say to ease things for this man . . . ? Kenneth James, Sr., was, he had learned, a stressed-out war veteran who had taken out his frustrations and failures in civilian life on his family. He had killed Matthew, the younger son, on one of his drunken sprees. How could a son forgive the man? But apparently Ken James, Jr., could. Or wanted to.

''Sure, Ken,'' Maraklov said quietly. ''Sure I do. He was our father, a war hero, he wasn't . . . responsible.''

But Maraklov's words seemed to make things worse. Something in James' face, misery and terror in his eyes . . . ''He wasn't responsible—'' Maraklov repeated, and James' body actually began to tremble and he shook his head. ''No . . . I did it . . . I—''

Maraklov stared at James, finally understanding what the American was saying.

''I didn't mean to do it.'' James was crying now. Maraklov motioned to one of the men with him to lay the boy down on the bed. ''I didn't hate him, I didn't really hate him. But damn it, Matthew was making father spend all his time with him. Not like it used to be when we were together so much. I felt all alone and it was Matthew's fault . . .''

Left alone . . . Maraklov knew something about that . . . ''You shot Matthew . . . ?''

"An accident, I was just going to scare him. I got father's gun and went and told Matthew to stop it and . . . the gun went off . . . "

"Go on, Ken."

"Father saw me and he saw Matthew and he told me not to worry, just like you now" . . . his eyelids were beginning to close . . . "he called the police and an ambulance and they took him away. I saw him just once when he got out of the hospital. He made me promise never to tell, it would be our secret . . . I hated mother for marrying Frank, I hate her, and Frank, hate myself too. But don't hate father. You understand . . . ?"

Maraklov tried to put it together, to readjust. Ken had killed his brother. To protect his son, his father had taken the blame for the shooting. There was no drunken rampage like Ken's mother had said. His father had endured years in a mental institution to save his son. No wonder he went crazy.

And now another thought forced itself on him. He bent down to James. "Kenneth?"

The American opened his eyes.

"Cathy. Cathy Sawyer. Where is she?"

"Gone."

Footsteps could be heard outside the hotel door. One of the KGB agents grabbed Maraklov's shoulder. "Stop this, let's get out of here."

Maraklov shrugged off the hand and bent closer to James.

"Answer me. Where? Where is she?"

"She never loved me, said she never wanted to see me again. Even laughed at me when I said I loved her . . ." He stopped, reached up as though to touch Maraklov's face, the face so like his own, just a fraction of an inch from the freshly healed plastic-surgery scars. "Thank you . . ." The hand dropped, the haunted eyes closed for the last time.

"Took longer than it should have," mumbled one of the agents, then nudged Maraklov out of the way and began to strip off James' jewelry and clothes.

"He killed his brother . . . and his girlfriend," Maraklov said half-aloud, trying to absorb it, and understood the *personal* impact of it. He rubbed his eyes, his temples.

"Get undressed, Maraklov . . . "

"James," Maraklov said as if by rote. "The name is Ken James."

"Whatever your damned name is, sir, get undressed and put these clothes on." In less than a minute they had tossed James' clothes to him and were busy putting his clothes on the corpse.

Maraklov looked at James' clothes, shook his head. "I can't wear these—" Maraklov gasped.

"We don't have time for—"

"I said, I can't." Not yet, anyway. Not until he had exorcised, or taken as his own the images that assaulted him . . . Matthew, from the only photograph acquired by the KGB weeks before his death—happy and laughing . . . Kenneth hefting the big Colt .45 caliber pistol—he could almost *feel* the weight of it, with a grip almost too big for his fingers to wrap around, a hammer almost but not quite too tight to cock, could feel the recoil, feel the weapon hot and alive, hear the blast drowning out his younger brother Matthew's cry of pain . . . then his father's face, the sorrow, the compassion in it—and he could see himself begging for forgiveness, for understanding. And his father had given it all to him. He had sacrificed his life for him.

Maraklov struggled for control. Only a few weeks ago it had been, he thought, a game he played with Janet Larson, something that always seemed to excite her. Make up stories about Kenneth James. The juicier, the better. She wanted to know if James had a lot of women, if he masturbated, if he liked older women. Maraklov always had a new story for her. Including the one about his target Ken James killing his girlfriend Cathy Sawyer. He thought he had just made it up, embroidered what the KGB reports told him. But now . . . he had thought he had an overwhelming reason to kill Janet Larson, and he had been right. Only it was not just the logical one—to do away with a threat to his mission in America. Somehow he had been duplicating what Ken James had done to Cathy Sawyer. Andrei Maraklov had become more complete with his target than he could have imagined. Cathy Sawyer had died twice—once in America, and once at the Academy in the Soviet Union . . .

He tried to clear his head, looked for the two agents who had come with him.

They were gone. So was the body of Kenneth James. He went to the door, opened it, looked outside. Nothing.

And then he heard: "What a *great* hotel." A female voice.
"Free peep shows." He turned and saw three college-age
women clustered around the elevator. Only then did he realize
he was standing in the hallway wearing only a pair of briefs.

"*Prastiti* . . . uh, sorry . . ."

"Don't be, sugar," one of them said, straining for a better
look as Maraklov ducked back into his room. "It looks to me
like you got nothin' to be sorry for."

He must get hold of himself. After all the training, the conditioning, the first word he uttered as Kenneth Francis James
to the first Americans he saw was a *Russian* word. He could
only hope they hadn't noticed. Probably not, but it was a warning to him . . .

He collapsed onto the bed. On the bedspread were some
pieces of gold jewelry, a large, heavy Rolex watch, a wallet,
some bills in a silver money clip, the hotel key and assorted
papers and receipts. The two agents had taken James' clothing,
but an open suitcase sitting on a clothes valet in a corner had
plenty more.

A drink. He needed one. The room's tiny refrigerator was
empty except for an icetray with half a dozen cubes. He thought
about calling for room service but didn't want anyone inside
the room until he had triple-checked it for any evidence of a
struggle. The drink wouldn't wait.

He selected a pair of slacks and a red polyester pullover shirt
from the suitcase, slipped on a pair of Nikes—they fit perfectly—slipped on the Rolex and gold chains, pocketed the
room key, money and wallet, brushed his hair. He studied himself in the mirror. The shirt was a bit tight across his chest,
and his thighs strained some against the pants legs. He could
detect the faintest evidence of plastic surgery scars. Never
mind. He had to get out of this room where Ken James had
died . . . and been reborn?

He made his way downstairs to the hotel's Polynesian bar
and seated himself in an area where he could watch all the
exits and windows, just as he had been taught at the Connecticut Academy.

"Good evening, Mr. James."

Maraklov willed himself not to show what he felt. A waitress in a tight sarong slit up each side nearly to her waist had

come up behind him and put down a cocktail napkin. "Hi, there, Mr. James. Your usual?"

Maraklov nodded.

"I need to see your I.D. again. Sorry."

Identification! Slowly he withdrew the wallet, opened it and held it up for the waitress.

"Not that one, silly." She reached in behind the driver's license in the front and pulled out an identical-looking laminated card. "Thank *you*, Mr. James. Back in a flash."

After she left Maraklov took a close look at the hidden card. The birthdate had been cleverly changed. A fake I.D. Apparently the hotel staff knew the routine—even better than the "new" Ken James. A few moments later the waitress returned, placing a huge frosted champagne glass on the napkin.

Maraklov looked at her. "This is my usual?" Immediately he regretted the words. A giveaway . . .

"Not tonight, lover," the waitress said. She nodded over toward the bar. "Champagne cocktails, compliments of those ladies over there." He turned and saw the three women that had seen him in the hallway at the elevator. They raised their glasses toward him, smiling.

"Well, Romeo," the waitress said. "What are you waiting for?"

Slowly, carefully, Maraklov rose to his feet. To his surprise, he found his legs and knees quite strong. Without thinking, he reached into his wallet, extracted the first bill he touched and handed it to the waitress as he picked up his cocktail. It was a twenty dollar bill.

"Thank *you*, Mr. James," she said. "A real gentleman, as always." She lowered her voice, moved toward him. "If those waihilis don't do it all for you, Mr. James, why, you just leave a message for me at the front desk. Mariana knows what you want."

Still feeling shaky inside, he made his way toward the bar, smiling. Andrei Ivanschichin Maraklov was about to experience his first night as an American named Kenneth James. Now *he* was the real Ken James. The only one.

## McConnell Air Force Base, Kansas
*August 1994*

"Required SATCOM reports are as follows," Air Force Captain Ken James said. He motioned to a hand-lettered, expertly rendered chart beside him but kept his eyes on his "audience" and did not refer to it. "As soon as possible after launch we transmit a sortie airborne report. If we launched on an execution message we transmit a strike-message confirmation report." He pointed to a large map on another easel. That depicted the strike routing of his B-1B Excalibur bomber as it proceeded on its nuclear-attack mission.

"After each air refueling we transmit an offload report, advising SAC of our aircraft status and capability to fulfill the mission. On receipt of a valid execution message, if we weren't launched with one, we would acknowledge that message as well as any messages that terminated our sortie. After each weapons release, if possible we transmit a strike report that gives SAC our best estimate of our success in destroying each assigned target. The message also updates SAC on our progress and advises them of any difficulties in proceeding with the mission. Of course, staying on time, on course and alert has priority over all SATCOM or HF message traffic. All strike messages can wait until we climb out of the low-level portion of the route and are on the way to our post-strike base. These messages can also be delivered to other SAC personnel heading stateside, to U.S. foreign offices, or to overseas military bases capable of secure transmissions to SAC headquarters."

He pointed further along the route. "Other messages will include launch reports from the post-strike and each recovery base: NUDET—nuclear detonation—position reports, GLASS EYE combat damage reports, severe weather reports, continental-defense-zone entry reports and sortie recovery and regeneration reports."

James lowered his pointer and stepped away from the charts. "SIOP communications are extremely important, and the SAC aircraft involved with the execution of our Single Integrated Operations Plan are a front-line asset in keeping the Strategic Air Command, the Joint Chiefs of Staff and the National Command Authority advised of the progress worldwide of any conflict. We feel we have the world's most up-to-date and survivable communications networks, but of course it's no good unless each aircrewman uses it effectively." He looked around the empty briefing room. "That concludes my annual Mission Certification briefing, Colonel Adams. Any questions, sir?"

"Not bad, not bad—for a pilot," came a voice from the back of the room. Kenneth frowned at the man who came in now and began to pack up the briefing charts and diagrams.

"Kiss my ass, Murphy," Ken said. "It was a perfect briefing—even for a navigator."

Captain Brian Murphy, James' offensive-systems officer on his B-1 crew, had to admit it. "Yeah, it was, Ken. No doubt about it. But why are you spending so much time on that stuff? On an Emergency War Order certification, briefing is done by the radar nav or the defensive-systems operator. Not by the pilots."

"I heard Adams likes to hit his mission-ready crews with little surprises," Ken said. "His favorite is mixing up the usual briefing routines to make sure each guy on the crew is familiar with the other guy's responsibilities. He likes to hit navs with pilot questions, too—how well do *you* know your abort-decision matrices?"

Murphy shrugged. "I'll bone up on that stuff before the briefing tomorrow. These briefings are bull anyway . . . Coming to the Club with us for lunch?"

"In a while, it's only eleven-thirty. I'll meet you there at noon."

"Man, you are so dedicated."

"Knock it off."

"No, really, I mean it," James' crew navigator said. "You're always studying. You know your stuff backwards and forwards, and you know everyone else's too. If it's not EWO communications procedures it's security or avionics or computers or target study. You got your hands in everything."

"That's my job, Murph."

"Well, at least you're getting some reward for it. Making commander of a B-1 Excalibur in less than two years was moontalk until you came along. They're saying you might make flight commander in a few weeks. You're really burning up the program."

James slapped his pencil down on the table, smiled. "You're

buttering me up, man. Okay, okay, I'll buy lunch. Just let me finish.''

"Hey, hotshot, can't you take a compliment? I know atta-boys are rare around here, but I think you can still recognize one.''

James raised his hands in surrender. "Okay, okay. Thanks, Murph, but I'm not doing anything special here. I do this stuff because it's my job and because it really interests me, and because my ass will be grass if I don't learn this communications stuff by tomorrow morning.''

"Message received. I'm outta here.'' Murphy stood and headed for the door, then stopped. "You're an Academy grad, aren't you?''

"Right.''

"Top of your class, from what I heard.''

James looked at Murphy. "Get to the point, Murph.''

"I thought so, I just want to know why you chose B-1s. You could have had your pick of any hot jet in the inventory, but you picked B-1s.''

"I liked them. I always did. They're big and sexy—just like your wife . . .''

"Asshole.''

". . . and I still have a stick and afterburners and Mach-one speed like a fighter. I hated it when Carter canceled them. I think they should build another hundred of them. At least. An-swer your question?''

Murphy nodded. "But you seem a little, I don't know, out of place.''

"Out of place?'' His stomach tightened as he looked closely at his radar nav.

"Yeah. Like B-1s are just a jumping-off place for you. I mean, you're not advertising it or anything, but somehow, old buddy, I get the feeling you're on your way somewhere. Care to tell?''

Ken James forced himself to smile. This big Irishman was hitting too close. "Just between you and me and the fence-post?''

"Sure, man.''

"I did get an assignment, I think. When I filled out my last dream sheet I was sort of . . . well, daydreaming. Appropriate, huh? Anyway, I put down that I was interested in the High Technology Advanced Weapons Center—''

"HAWC! You got an assignment to Dreamland? I don't believe it! Do they actually *give* assignments there?''

"I didn't think they did, either. Like I said, it was a long shot. And I don't have any assignment yet. But I did get a letter back from the deputy commander, a Brigadier General Ormack. He sounded interested. It was sort of a don't-call-me-I'll-call-you letter, but at least I got an answer back.''

"I don't believe it," Murphy said. "Dreamland. You realize that all of the world's hottest jets and weapons in the past thirty years went through there? Those guys fly planes and test weapons out there that are years ahead of anything that exists in the real world. And *you're* going to be assigned there—''

"I said I don't have an assignment, Murph. So keep this under your hat, okay? Besides, how do you know so much about Dreamland?''

"I don't know much of anything, except that anybody who even accidentally overflies Dreamland gets sent to our version of the old Gulag Archipelago. Every now and then you hear about an ex–Los Angeles Center air-traffic controller telling stories about Mach-six fighters or planes that fly vertically to fifty thousand feet over Dreamland. It's got to be the assignment of a lifetime.''

"Well, like I said, keep all this under your hat," James said. "Now take off. I want to polish my briefing before we do our dry runs this afternoon.''

After Murphy left, James got up from his seat, went to the door, locked it, put a chair in front of it. He returned to the small pile of red-covered books and manuals on thc dcsk in the front of the conference room and selected one marked: "COMBAT CREW EMERGENCY WAR ORDER COMMUNICATIONS PROCEDURES—TOP SECRET/NOFORN/SIOP/WIVNS.'' It was the master document used by all the American strategic combat forces all over the world—aircraft, submarines, intercontinental missile sites, and command posts—outlining every one of their communication sources and methods, procedures, frequencies, timing and locations of the nation's domestic and overseas communications facilities. The hieroglyphics after the title warned that the document was top secret, not releasable to foreign nationals, part of the Single Integrated Operations

Plan—the master plan on how the United States and its allies would conduct "the next world war." This particular volume was dated 1 October 1994, some two months from now, because it belonged to the new SIOP revision scheduled to take place at that time. The procedures in that manual would be used by all strategic forces for the next twelve months afterward.

It made it convenient for him and the KGB, Ken thought, to have to do these once-a-year briefings for the wing commander. The annual Mission Certification briefings were required by law. The wing commander of each SAC base with nuclear missions had to certify to the Commander-in-Chief of SAC, and he in turn to the President of the United States, that each crewman knew precisely what his duties were in case the SIOP was "implemented"—a euphemism for the so-called unthinkable, the declaration of World War Three. Normally the certification briefings were given once, when a crewman became mission-ready. But the SIOP was revised each year, reflecting new rules, new tactics, and so every year each crewman had to dig out the changed books, study them, then brief the wing commander on the revised mission. The top-secret books were trotted out for the certification, studied for a week, then locked away, usually never to be seen again except for basewide exercises or inspections. The opportunities were rare to have such free access to these manuals, and Ken had to work fast.

He opened the manual to section four, "ELF, LF, HF and SATCOM SIOP Frequencies and Broadcast Schedules," and propped the pages open with a couple of books. This section detailed all of the frequencies used by aircraft and submarines to broadcast and receive coded messages from SAC and the Joint Chiefs of Staff, along with what time of the day these broadcasts would be made. Anyone knowing these frequencies and times could jam or disrupt them, specific broadcasts could be intercepted and decoded. The crew charts had stickers that had only one frequency, but this book had all the frequencies for the nuclear strike force of the United States.

James unzipped a leg pocket of his flight suit and took out what looked like a thick-barreled marking pen. Moving his chair so his body would cast no shadows across the pages, he twisted and pulled the cap, held the device a couple of feet over the pages, and pressed the pocket clip to activate the shutter.

Murphy was close, James thought as he worked. He would have liked to get assigned to F-15s or F-16s, or the new F-117 Stealth fighter unit, but he went where Moscow told him to go, and that was where he could learn as much as possible about the new B-1's nuclear-strike mission. Dreamland was the most secret base in the country. B-1 Excalibur bombers were fine, but he would give anything to get his hands on the United States newest fighters.

Two minutes later Kenneth James had finished photographing the entire chapter and its accompanying appendices with the tiny microdisk camera. He wrapped the device in a handkerchief to help protect it, then zipped it safely away in his leg pocket, out of sight so no one would be tempted to ask to borrow his "pen."

Satisfied, he packed up his charts and books and turned them back to the vault custodian. He would put the camera in his car outside the alert facility to prevent discovery during one of the commander's frequent no-notice locker searches on the alert pad, then deliver it to the prearranged drop point for his KGB contact from St. Louis after he got off seven-day alert.

## Dreamland, Nevada
*Monday, 3 December 1994, 0730 PDT (1020 EDT)*

Ken James was strapped securely into a stiff, uncomfortable steel chair, wrists, ankles and chest bound by heavy leather straps. His head was immobilized by a strong steel beam. The room where he lay on the rack was dimly lit, buzzing with the sound of power transformers and smelling of the ozone created by electronic relays and microcircuits. Two men in Air Force blue fatigues rechecked his bonds, making sure they were extra tight; one of them adjusted a tiny spotlight directly onto James' right eyeball, smiling as James tried to squint against the glare. The sergeant knew there was nothing James could do to him.

James had been sweating in the steel chair for nearly an hour, the two technicians hovering over him, before another man entered the room. Tall and lanky, he looked considerably older than his mid-thirties, thanks to a bald head and a few stray shocks of gray hair that seemed to be haphazardly stuck onto his skull. He spoke briefly with the techs, then walked over to the rack and inspected the fitting and bonds. He stuck his face close to James, smiled and said, "Now, Captain James, I'll ask you once more—where were you on the afternoon of August eleventh?"

In fact, Ken James was photographing top-secret documents in a vault at McConnell Air Force Base in Kansas. He rolled his eyes in exasperation. "Very funny, Dr. Carmichael. Now can we get on with this?"

"Couldn't help it, Ken," Alan Carmichael, the white-coated researcher, said. "Seeing you trussed up gives this place the look of some futuristic interrogation chamber."

Which was precisely what Maraklov was thinking himself. He was wearing a heavy suit made of thick metallic fabric. The suit had several thick cables and conduits sewed into it that ran all through his arms, legs, feet, hands and neck. A raised metal spine ran along his backbone from head to tail, so thick that a channel had been cut into the chair to accommodate it. There was a bit of cool circulating air flowing through tubules in the suit, but it did little to relieve the oppressive heat and stuffiness.

"Have you been practicing your deep breathing exercises?" Carmichael asked.

"Don't have a choice. I either breathe deep in this getup or I suffocate. Are you ever going to tell me exactly what I'm supposed to be doing?"

"Try to relax and I'll tell." Carmichael adjusted the volume of a small speaker next to a nearby oscilloscope-like device; the speaker began to chirp in a seemingly random pattern. Carmichael motioned to one of twenty-five lines on the oscilloscope. "Your twenty-five cps beta readouts are still firing. Relax, Ken. Don't try to force it or it won't come."

"*What* won't come?" Carmichael said nothing. Ken began to take deeper breaths, trying to ignore the sweat trickling down his back and the cramp in his right calf. After a few moments, the chirping subsided. Progress?

"Very good," Carmichael said. "Beta is down . . . your Hertz waves are increasing. Good. Occipital alpha is increasing. Good. Keep it up." He turned and with the help of one of the techs lifted a huge device off a carrying cart that he had brought in with him.

"What the hell is that?" James asked as the huge object was lifted overhead. It was hexagonal, and two wide visors in the front and cables leading to various parts of the suit and to controls and boxes nearby.

"Your new flight helmet," Carmichael said. "The final component of the suit you're wearing. The project is progressing so well, we've decided to proceed with a full-scale test."

"Test of what . . . ?"

"Wait." Carmichael slid the heavy helmet over Ken's head. "Watch the ears, damn it."

"Watch your beta—you're pinging again." The helmet was set into place and fastened to a heavy clavicle locking ring on the metallic suit. The braces holding Ken's head in place took some of the helmet's weight, but his shoulders were aching after only a few moments.

A microphone clicked on, and through a set of headphones in the helmet came: "How do you hear me, Ken?"

"I think you broke my left ear off."

"You'll live. Try to relax and I'll explain." Carmichael's voice dropped into the familiar deep, even monotone that he had used weeks earlier during several days of screening: in fact, Carmichael was hypnotizing him, not with a shiny watch on a chain, but with his voice only. James' susceptibility to hypnotic suggestion had made him an especially good candidate for this secret project.

"As you know, we've been working here at Dreamland with several projects. We call them all together 'supercockpit'—designing an aircraft workspace that allows the pilot to perform better in a high-speed, high-density combat environment. You and several other pilots were working with Cheetah, the F-15 advanced technology fighter demonstrator; that's the state of the art, and her systems will be incorporated in the Air Force's new fighter in the next few years. Cheetah makes extensive use of multi-function computer screens, voice-recognition and artificial intelligence, as well as high-maneuverability technology . . . Well, we've been working on the *next* generation of fighters after Cheetah, things like forward-swept wing technology, hyper-start engines, super-conducting radar. But the most fascinating aspect of the new generation of fighters will be ANTARES—that's an acronym for Advanced Neural Transfer and Response.''

"Neural transfer? Sounds like Buck Rogers thought-control stuff." Comic books were SOP at Connecticut Academy.

A slight pause, then Carmichael said: "It is."

Inwardly Maraklov was tingling with excitement—Carmichael's electroencephalograph must be pinging off the dials, he thought. They were actually working on *thought-controlled aircraft* . . . ?

"Relax, relax," Carmichael said. "It might sound like science fiction but we demonstrated the rudimentary ANTARES technology as early as the late nineteen eighties."

"But is it possible . . . ?"

"Well, we don't know that yet. I'm hoping, I'm betting, we'll find out pretty soon . . ."

"But how can you control by thought?"

"The *idea* is simple, the mechanism is complex." He waited a few moments while the subject hurriedly fought to control his racing heartbeat.

"That's better," he said in his most soothing, uninflected voice. "Here we go. Remember back to your physiology. The human nervous system is composed of nerve cells, neurons. The neurons carry information back and forth from receptor nerves in the peripheral nervous system—nerves in the body in general—to the central nervous system, brain and spinal cord. The information carried through the nervous system is a series of chemical and electrical discharges between neurons. If one neuron is stimulated enough so that its ionic balance is changed, it releases a chemical into the synapse, the gap between neurons, and that chemical stimulates another neuron."

"Like electricity flowing through a wire?"

"Well, some discharges are purely electrical, like when neurons physically touch, but mostly the connection is chemical. Anyway, this electrochemical and ionic activity can be detected and read by electroencephalographs, which you've become very familiar with the past weeks." He would have nodded if he could. "EEGs in the past could only *measure* electrical activity—they couldn't analyze, decode that activity. It was like the Plains Indians putting their ears up to a telegraph pole, which they used to call the spirit trees, by the way. They could hear the telegraph clicks and tell that *something* was happening, but they couldn't decipher the clicks or tell which direction the clicks were coming from, and of course, they didn't know how it was being done, just as we are ignorant about so many things in the nervous system. Sure, lots of clicks usually meant the army was coming, but that was about all. Ditto for us twentieth-century wizards.''

Carmichael paused to adjust his oscilloscope. ''Well, a few years ago we built an EEG that *could* read the spirit tree. You could lift a finger or hand and this EEG could tell a researcher that you lifted a finger. And the opposite was true, too—when you generated a thought command to lift your hand, that impulse could be detected and read—in effect, we could read your mind.

''Of course, the military got their mitts on the system right away. The new-style EEG, nicknamed Spirit Tree—hey, I'm famous—was the ultimate lie detector. But there was much more potential in Spirit Tree than use as a glorified polygraph. We already knew the general path of nerves and which areas of the brain corresponded to certain thoughts or activities—that all came about during Nazi Germany's infamous lab experiments on human guinea pigs, when they would surgically remove parts of a prisoner's brain and see what the victim could no longer do. The new idea was, if we could now read the information flowing through the system, was there a way we could interject outside or foreign stimuli into the nervous system? Instead of receptors in, say, the fingers generating the initial sensory impulse, could we send information from a computer into the system and read how the brain reacted to it? And could the opposite be true—could we think about, say, moving a finger, and have a computer read that nervous instruction and execute the command *electronically*?''

The more James heard, the more excited he became, though now it was an intellectual response and his signs stayed relaxed. A computer issuing instructions to a human via his own nervous system . . . a computer reading the human nervous system . . . For a while he thought his time might better be spent making drawings or photographs of the F-15 Advanced Tactical Fighter named Cheetah. But now . . . well, the Academy hadn't imagined anything like *this* when they sent him to America. Of course nobody could have . . .

''Got all that?'' Carmichael asked.

"I think so . . . You're going to try to read my mind with this . . . whatever it is . . ."

"In a sense, yes."

"But how strong are those electrochemical discharges across the synapse? Don't you have to clip some electrodes onto my skull?"

"In the past that's how EEGs were done. Every human body has a basic electrical potential, an electrical aura, so to speak, and that potential is affected by the central nervous system. Simple electrodes could read the tiny impulses generated by the brain and nervous system. But those electrodes couldn't measure anything except the *change* in electrical potential . . ."

"Like the telegraph clicks . . ."

"Exactly. But now we have two new technologies that have improved our ability to read those electrical impulses—very high-speed integrated circuits and NRTS, near-room-temperature superconductors.

"Your helmet and that large device on your spine are huge superconducting antennae. They're so powerful they not only can measure your nervous activity, they can read it, analyze it and map its direction as the impulses move around your peripheral nervous system. And as they do, the computer issues instructions to the other large device you're wearing—that metallic flight suit. Actually, the suit is an integrated circuit that records the route each and every nervous impulse takes and studies it. After repetitions of the route the artificial-intelligence computer actually learns the route and proper timing and intervals between a certain set of impulses from certain areas of the central nervous system."

This project did sound remarkable, but it also appeared to involve a long period of passive training. Maraklov preferred action. Could he sustain the process . . . ? "You're going to map out every muscle twitch, every movement, every breath I take . . . ?"

"To the contrary," Carmichael said. "We'd be overloaded if we tried to record every muscle twitch, just as your question implies—so the idea is, we *don't want* you to twitch any muscles. We don't want mere muscular activity to show up. We don't need it—once we map out your peripheral nervous activity, we'll know what impulses are necessary to move things like muscles.

"So we need you totally relaxed, limp, deeper than relaxed—we need you as detached as you can be from your physical body. We practiced biofeedback techniques before to get you to what we call, for lack of a better term, alpha state—it simply means the propagation of alpha brain waves and the suppression of beta waves, the latter activity indicating conscious brain activity. But alpha state has many levels—nine known ones, to be exact. You've reached perhaps the second or third level, where you can totally relax both smooth and ridged muscle and even exert control over certain autonomous functions such as heart rate, respiration and blood pressure. That's fine—but we need more."

Carmichael's voice became even deeper, even more steady. There was no hint of tension, no emotional cues, no inflection. Somehow he had even managed to cut out most of the background noise in the laboratory—or was that part of the hypnotic state the subject knew he was slipping into?

"There's a level of activity called theta-alpha," the voice continued, so melodic and penetrating that it seemed to bypass his eardrums and enter directly into his brain . . . "Theta-alpha. It's a stage where the central nervous system in effect cuts out the peripheral nervous system. In higher life forms it's a defense mechanism, a way to protect the central nervous system from sensory overload.

"Without any peripheral functions to control, the brain expands its powers. Areas of the brain that normally go unused are suddenly put into service to control autonomous functions. The average person uses only thirty percent of his available brain capacity, but under theta-alpha the other seventy percent is suddenly put on line. That new seventy percent has the memory and computational power of all the computers in this building, packed into a ten-pound package that needs no power, no cooling air, no bench or field maintenance. And, like a computer built by humans, it's programmable and erasable, with its own built-in operating system."

James was finding it progressively harder to concentrate. When he tried to speak he couldn't make his jaw work. It felt as if he was asleep, but in that weird half-in, half-out state of sleep where you could hear and feel everything around you but were still deeply resting. His body felt very warm, but not sweaty or cocooned any more. The oxygen being fed into the

face mask was cool and soothing as it streamed into his lungs.
It was as if his body were somewhere else, as if he was detached . . .

Suddenly, he felt his whole body burst into flame. Every
pore, every cell, every molecule of his body spit red-hot lava.
He jerked out of his semi-sleep state and screamed.

"Easy, Ken, easy," Carmichael said. Pure oxygen flooded
his face mask. The visors on his helmet opened, and Carmichael and a medical technician peered inside to check his bulg-
ing eyes.

"What . . . what was *that*?"

"It *worked*," Carmichael said. He nodded to the med tech,
and they both disappeared out of view. Ken tried to move his
head but found it still securely fastened in place.

"Get me out of here—"

"No, Ken, relax," Carmichael was saying. The room noise
seemed louder than ever. Ken rolled his eyes, trying to blot
out the hammering in his head. "Everything's fine. Relax, relax . . . "

"I felt like . . . like I was—"

"Shocked. Electrocuted," Carmichael finished for him.
"You did it, Ken."

"Did what, dammit?"

"You entered theta-alpha. The final stage of alpha state.
You were so relaxed, relaxed in such a deep neurological sense,
that your mind opened up to its maximum capacity."

"So what was that shock—*electrocution*, you said . . . ?"

"ANTARES. The system detects when you enter theta-alpha
and begins the process of integration. The shock you felt was
the activation of the ANTARES system—it was the first time,
Ken, the very first time, so far as we know, that a computer
and the human mind have been linked, even if it was only for
a split second. You've made some history, my friend. December third, in the year nineteen hundred and ninety-four, at
seven-thirty-eight A.M., a human mind and a computer were
linked—not merely in contact, but *linked*—for the first time."

"Forget history, Carmichael. I asked you what that shock
was."

"Yes, well to facilitate the tracing of your neural impulses,
we created a slight electrical field of our own through your
suit. We charged the suit with a tiny electrical—"

"Tiny? You call that *tiny*? I felt like I was frying!"

"Milliamperes, I assure you," Carmichael replied jovially. "About the same as a nine-volt toy battery. It does no permanent damage that we can detect—"

"That's real reassuring, Doc."

"You're experiencing the same irritation that anyone feels when violently awakened from REM sleep," Carmichael said. "Try to relax. We'd like to try for another interface."

"So you can shock me like some chimpanzee?" There was a limit.

"Ken, we're on the threshold." Carmichael had turned on the microphone again and had closed the visors. "We've proven that our system works, that our equipment can respond to a specific and up to now unexplored neurological state. If we can *complete* the interface we may actually be able to establish communications between a machine and the human mind. I don't mean to sound overly melodramatic, but this is at least comparable as a scientific breakthrough to the discovery of the semiconductor. It is important that we try again. But this time you must try to ignore the electrical charge when it happens."

"And how am I supposed to do that?"

"There's no training manual for this . . . you must maintain theta-alpha through the interface process. I'm really not sure how to tell you to do that. Think of something else, try to shut out the pain. After a while the system will help you, but you must be able to endure the first wave of it until the *system* can learn how to help."

"What about drugs?"

"Drugs would interfere with the neurological impulses in your system. Besides, this program is based on creating an aircraft that responds to thought commands. We can't very well go around drugging all our pilots before sending them into combat."

The full realization of what was happening finally hit him. "You really intend to put this system on an aircraft. You say you can control an aircraft just by thinking?"

"Exactly. We already use sophisticated computers to fly our jets. But with ANTARES, we've developed the most powerful computer of all—the human brain. It's a thousand times more powerful, a hundred times faster, and a million times more reliable than any computer ever conceived or conceivable.

"You've flown Colonel McLanahan's F-15 ATF—imagine putting all this on a plane like Cheetah. Or a plane more sophisticated than Cheetah—you've seen the plans for the new fighter they're developing, the X-34. Imagine the speed and power of your mind going into the X-34. It would be all but invincible, more powerful than a squadron of F-15s. It would rewrite most everything we know about fighter combat."

Carmichael paused. "And *you* would be the first pilot."

Maraklov was stunned. This was miles beyond anything he'd hoped or bargained for. Carmichael was serious. They actually were going to move ahead with plans to put all this on an *airplane*.

"But how can all this gear go into an aircraft?"

"Ken, this is a laboratory. We do everything on huge scales because we have the room to spread out. But in the real world we'd miniaturize all this. With new microchips and superconducting technology, most of the computers in this lab can be miniaturized to the size of a steamer trunk. In three years that trunk-sized computer could be the size of a toaster. By the turn of the century it could be down to the size of a walnut."

He relaxed and smiled for the first time since entering what he had once thought of as Carmichael's chamber of horrors. It *sounded* far-fetched, but they could really be on the verge of a massive technological breakthrough. If they were, then Ken James, alias Andrei Maraklov, a newly promoted major of infantry in the KGB, was to be the principal, the key actor in a remarkable scientific discovery.

"All right," he said. "Fire it up again."

Carmichael signaled to his technicians.

"But make sure you spell the name right in the history books. It's—"

"I know," Carmichael said. "J-A-M-E-S."

No, he said to himself, beginning his deep breathing exercises, starting from his toes and consciously ordering every muscle to relax. Spell it M-A-R-A-K-L-O-V.

## The Kremlin, Moscow, USSR
*Thursday, 6 December 1994, 1451 EET (0551 EST)*

"In summary, then, General Secretary," General Boris Cherkov, Chief of Staff of the military forces of the Soviet Union concluded, "we still command a substantial lead in both conventional and nuclear forces in Europe and Asia, and we should be able to maintain that superiority through the rest of this century. I am ready to take questions."

No one in the Kollegiya raised any; few ever did during these briefings. The men and women who made up the leadership of the Soviet military, intelligence and state bureaucracy sat mute, nodding to Cherkov as if congratulating him on his presentation—the same one he had given during the past three years, and very similar to the one that the General Secretary had heard since assuming the office. Now he turned to Vladimir Kalinin, chief of the *Komitet Gosudarstvennoy Bezopasnosti*, the KGB. "Do you have a comment?"

"Just this. How is it possible that we are so superior? With respect, sir, I question the conclusions made here this afternoon. Since the late eighties and in this year of 1994 as well, the Americans have begun a steady increase in levels of conventional forces all over the world, including western Europe. We know they have a space-based strategic defense system in place that is more sophisticated than our ground-based one. Intermediate-range nuclear forces have been eliminated, our strategic nuclear forces have just been cut in half, and biological weapons have been eliminated. We have been forced to draw down the size of all our forces to help relieve our budget problems and promote *perestroika*. How can we be maintaining such a large advantage over the United States and the NATO forces—?"

"Because of our continuing five-to-one numerical advantage and our increasing technological achievements," Chief-of-Staff Cherkov broke in. "For the first time we have an aircraft carrier force that rivals the Americans'—"

"We have *three* carriers. The Americans have seventeen. Even the British have more than we do."

"We have an unrivaled worldwide cargo-transport capability. In each and every area we—"

"If we commandeer every civilian-passenger jet in Aeroflot,'' KGB chief Kalinin interrupted, ''not counting civil transports, the Americans still have more airlift capacity. We can juggle numbers, but the fact is that we have lost the advantage. The Americans have fielded two new types of fighters in Europe in the past ten years; we have fielded one. The Americans have launched two new aircraft carriers in the past ten years and equipped each one with new F-31 fighters. We still have one carrier of equivalent size in sea-trials, with fifteen-year-old fighters on board. In every area except armor and total manpower we have either lost our advantage or suffer a real lessening of whatever advantage we retain.''

''Times have changed,'' Minister of Defense Andrei Tovorin said. ''Our security is no longer based exclusively on military strength. We have treaties and agreements with many nations. We have mutual verifiable cuts in strategic and tactical nuclear weapons, beginning with the INF treaty . . .''

''But we do not agree to roll over and accept domination by the West,'' Kalinin said. ''Sir, you will be on American television in one hour, smiling at their cameras, saying how delighted you are at the progress that has been made since you signed the INF Treaty seven years ago. But, sir, the peace and security of our nation still depends on the strong arms and backs of our people, rather than on pieces of paper. Those treaties will be the first things to be set on fire in a major conflict—''

''Are you saying that this nation is in danger because we have agreed to reduce the number of nuclear weapons pointed at us?'' the General Secretary asked. ''Are you saying that we are in greater danger of destruction as a nation now than ten years ago?''

''I believe we were more secure ten years ago, yes,'' Kalinin said. ''Then I knew that we had the military capability and the national resolve to defend ourselves against any attack. Now, I am not so sure. For the first time in my career I wonder whether we could resist an invasion of western Europe or hold off a NATO invasion of western Russia. I question the security of our cities and military bases. And yet I see American stores and American hotels being built in Moscow. Where is all this taking us?''

''Into the future,'' General Cherkov said. ''The truth is we are a richer, more secure nation than ever. We also are a member of the world community, no longer the ugly Russian bear.''

Kalinin said nothing. The General Secretary, probably the most popular Soviet leader in history, was a formidable enough opponent in the government. But along with Cherkov, the military veteran and hero of Afghanistan and Africa, the opposition was all but overwhelming.

''This meeting is adjourned,'' the General Secretary said, and accepted the handshakes and good luck wishes from the Kollegiya members. Kalinin stayed behind after the rest of the members, except Cherkov, had left.

''I apologize for spoiling the mood of the meeting, sir, but I feel I have a duty to express my opinion—''

''You are correct,'' the General Secretary said. ''I encourage such discussions; you know that.''

''Yes, sir.'' The General Secretary was getting ready to leave for the new Kremlin press office for his interview. ''Sir . . . I need your authorization for additional manpower on an ongoing project. I need ten more men for five years overseas.''

The General Secretary straightened papers in his briefcase. ''Overseas?''

''The United States. Deep cover operation on an American military-research base.''

The General Secretary paused, glanced at Cherkov, then shook his head. ''It sounds like a major escalation. *Ten* people on one base?''

Kalinin tried to control his irritation. The General Secretary, it seemed, had already decided in the negative but wanted to pump his KGB chief for information before saying no. ''In one city, actually,'' Kalinin pushed on. ''Perhaps two or three on the base itself, one or two on a separate research center nearby.''

''This perhaps refers to Dreamland?'' General Cherkov asked. ''More activity there?''

''It is Dreamland,'' Kalinin admitted. The old man was well-informed. The crafty Chief-of-Staff's small but highly efficient cadre of internal investigators were still very much hard at work spying on the KGB for the General Secretary. ''We have received information on a new American project that I believe should be of great interest to us.''

''Obviously,'' the General Secretary deadpanned. ''Ten new

operatives in one area at one time is a lot. Is there a danger of discovery?''

"There is always that chance, sir. But this project is so important I feel the additional manpower is absolutely vital.''

"Wasn't your young pilot assigned to Dreamland?'' Cherkov asked. "The deep-cover agent that you managed to help transfer from their Strategic Air Command?''

"Major Andrei Maraklov, yes, and he is the one who has reported on a new American project that I must track very closely.''

"And this project?''

Kalinin hesitated—he didn't expect to be grilled like this. As reported to him so far, the new project was so unusual that he didn't fully understand it; it was going to be very difficult explaining it to the General Secretary. This was another change from practices of ten years ago—back then, the government was so large and, more to the point, so bureaucratically compartmentalized that sending ten or even fifty new agents to the United States was relatively easy. Now all personnel movement, even covert or so-called diplomatic transfers, were approved in advance.

"I'm talking about a project begun by the same research center we obtained the short takeoff and landing data from,'' Kalinin said. "Maraklov has been assigned to a project studying . . . thought-controlled fighter aircraft—''

"*Thought*-controlled aircraft?'' The General Secretary quickly looked down at the small stack of papers on his desk—apparently stifling his skepticism.

"Maraklov reports they've had *significant* success with this project,'' Kalinin said, stiffening. "I feel it is very important . . .''

The General Secretary shook his head. "I am sorry, but ten men for such a project is too much. I can authorize two in the Los Angeles consulate, and this must be coordinated with the foreign minister.''

"But, sir, I was going to use two men as handlers for Maraklov. The handlers are very important. Maraklov's movements are carefully monitored and more than one contact is essential. If I only have two new men and use them as handlers I will not have any for inside duties at the research center. I—''

"I have another meeting, Kalinin," the General Secretary said, snapping shut his briefcase. "I am scheduled to be in Los Angeles in one month. It will not look well if a large-scale deep-cover ring is discovered. I can't risk that. Two men only, Kalinin. If more information on this project comes in, I may reconsider. Now I must go."

As the General Secretary moved around his desk to leave, Kalinin quickly stepped toward him, not blocking his way but obviously wanting to hold his attention a moment longer. "Sir, I assure you, this is *most* urgent."

The General Secretary looked directly at his KGB chief. He was shorter than Kalinin by several centimeters and at least twenty years older; Kalinin had a full head of dark brown hair, the General Secretary was bald except for graying temples. The older man was solidly built and only recently giving way to fat; Kalinin was lean, as athletic as a career bureaucrat from Leningrad could manage.

Yet as they stood face-to-face, the General Secretary exuded a power that was considerably more than physical. He had a presence, an aura, an intensity that had all but mesmerized heads of government around the world. His eyes were especially effective in seizing and transfixing.

"Vladimir, the KGB has been well supported by this government. I have given you my support. I did so even when the Politburo believed I had made a wrong decision in appointing you to head the KGB. I believed the KGB needed a strong young leader for the future, and I chose you. I know that you look to something greater than merely the head of the world's largest intelligence organization—perhaps minister of defense or even General Secretary. Your ambitions are your own affair. But do not accuse me, Vladimir. I do what is in the best interest of our country and this government, *including* the KGB."

Kalinin saw the understated power in those blue eyes. After eight years in power, he was still considered by many to be the most influential man on the world scene. With *glasnost* now an important part of Soviet life, the General Secretary was much more visible in the eyes of the world. Kalinin realized confrontations at this time were pointless and even dangerous.

But the man was getting older. Older and more cautious. Nearly every decision involved weighing how it would look in the eyes of the world. Kalinin didn't much care about the eyes of the world—he cared about Russia, her security, based on her strength. The Soviet Union was not just another member of the world community—she was, or should be, its leader.

The General Secretary studied the younger man's eyes for a moment before moving toward the door. Cherkov, once the General Secretary's mentor and now his submissive guard-dog, followed him out.

The General Secretary might be, as some said, a visionary, Kalinin thought, but right now he was being dangerously short-sighted. Forget him this time, Kalinin told himself. This was a KGB project—it would remain a KGB project.

And if there was any way for this strange new American technology to advance his own position in the government, then let it happen.

# =1=

## Air Force High Technology Advanced Weapons Center (HAWC)

*Wednesday, 10 June 1996, 0430 PDT (0730 EDT)*

AIR FORCE LIEUTENANT Colonel Patrick S. McLanahan watched Captain Kenneth Francis James preparing to mount his "steed." James' tall, powerfully built frame was covered—a better term might have been "encased"—in a stiff flight suit made of nylon and metallic thread. James had to carry around a small portable air conditioning unit to stay comfortable, and the suit was so stiff that James had to be hoisted into his steed on a hydraulic lift. A small army of "squires"—military and civilian scientists and technicians, led by Doctor Alan Carmichael, the chief project engineer and Patrick's civilian counterpart—followed James on his lift up toward his incredible steed.

Both McLanahan's and James' aircraft were in a large open-ended hangar, used more to shield the two fighters from the ultra-magnified eyes of Soviet reconnaissance satellites than to protect against the weather. It was only four-thirty in the morning, but the temperature was already starting to climb; it was going to be a scorcher in the high Nevada desert test-site north of Las Vegas known as Dreamland.

But Patrick wasn't thinking about the heat. His eyes were on the sleek lines of the jet fighter before him.

DreamStar . . .

As McLanahan stood gazing at the fighter the senior noncommissioned officer of the DreamStar project, Air Force Master Sergeant Ray Butler, moved alongside him.

"I know how you feel, sir," Butler said in his deep, gravelly voice, running a hand across his shaved head. "I get a shiver every time I see her."

She was a child of the first X-29 advanced technology demonstrator aircraft built in the early and mid-1980s. Long, low, sleek and deadly, DreamStar was the only fighter aircraft anywhere with forward-swept wings, which spread gracefully from nearly abeam the cockpit back all the way to the tail. The forward-swept wings allowed air to stick to the aircraft's control surfaces better, making it possible for the aircraft to make faster and wilder maneuvers than ever thought possible. She was so agile and so fast that it took three independent high-speed computers to control her.

"Chief," Patrick said as they began a walkaround inspection of the fighter, "there's no question she's one sexy piece of hardware. Very sexy."

Butler nodded. "Couldn't put it better myself."

The cockpit seemed suspended in mid-air on the long, pointed forward fuselage high above the polished concrete floor of the satellite-bluff hangar. Beside the cockpit on each side of the fuselage were two auxiliary fins, canards, integral parts of the DreamStar's advanced flight controls. When horizontal, the canards provided extra lift and allowed the fighter to fly at previously unbelievable flight attitudes; when moved nearly to the vertical, the canards let the fighter move in any direction without changing its flight path. DreamStar could climb or descend without moving its nose up or down, turn without banking, dart sideways in, literally, the blink of an eye.

The one large engine inlet for the single afterburning jet engine was beneath the fuselage, mounted so that a smooth flow of air could still be assured even at radical flight attitudes and fast changes in direction. DreamStar had two sets of rudders, one pair on top and one on the bottom, which extended and retracted into the fuselage as needed; the lower stabilizers were to assure directional control at very high angles-of-attack (when the nose would be pointed high above the flight path of the aircraft) and low speed when the upper stabilizers would be ineffective.

Even at rest she seemed energetic, ready to leap effortlessly into the sky at any moment. "She looks like a great big cat ready to pounce," Patrick said half-aloud.

They continued their walkaround aft. DreamStar's engine exhaust was not the typical round nozzle on other fighters. She used an oblong vectored-thrust nozzle that could divert the engine exhaust in many different directions. Louvers on the top and bottoms of the nozzle could change the direction of thrust instantaneously, giving DreamStar even greater maneuverability. The vectored thrust from the engine could also act as added boost to shorten takeoff rolls, or as a thrust-reverser during dogfights or on landing to bleed off energy.

She was one hell of a bird, all right, and Patrick McLanahan figured he had the best job in the world—turning her into the world's newest and deadliest combat-ready weapon. Patrick "Mac" McLanahan, an ex-Strategic Air Command B-52 radar navigator-bombardier—especially remembered for his role on the Flight of the Old Dog that knocked out a Soviet laser installation—was the project officer in charge of development of the DreamStar advanced technology fighter. Once perfected, the XF-34A DreamStar fighter would be the nation's new air-superiority fighter.

Walking around the engine exhaust they noticed a crew chief running over to activate an external-power cart. "Looks like they're ready for power," Butler said. "I'd better go see how they're doing. Have a good flight, Colonel."

Patrick returned his salute and headed toward the plane he would be flying that morning. If the two aircraft were humans, the second jet fighter, Cheetah, would be DreamStar's older, less intelligent cousin. A by-product of the revolutionary SMTD, Short Takeoff and Landing and Maneuverability Demonstrator projects of the last decade, Cheetah was a line F-15E two-set jet fighter-bomber, heavily modified and enhanced after years of research and development in the fields of high performance flight and advanced avionics. It had come to Dreamland, this top-secret aircraft and weapons research center northwest of Las Vegas, seven years earlier. It had been at Dreamland for less than a day before then Lieutenant General Bradley Elliott, the director of HAWC, had had her taken apart for the first time. The changes to the airframe had been so extensive that it had been given a code-name Cheetah instead of keeping its original nickname, Eagle.

Hard to believe, McLanahan thought, that such a machine like Cheetah could be outdated in so short a time.

The remarkable enhancements built into DreamStar had been

tested years earlier on Cheetah, so Cheetah shared DreamStar's huge movable forward canards, vectored-thrust engines and computer-commanded flight controls. But even Cheetah was starting to show its twenty years of age. Modifications to every component of the fifty-seven-thousand-pound aircraft meant lots of riveted access panels scarred across its fuselage, performance-robbing patches that layers of paint could barely hide. With an eleven-hundred-pound remote-control camera mounted just behind her aft cockpit, her once impressive top speed of Mach two was now a forgotten statistic—she'd have a tough time, Patrick thought, of reaching Mach one without afterburners. DreamStar could easily cruise at one point five Mach without 'burners.

Where all of the high-tech components had made DreamStar the fighter of the future, those same enhancements had taken a severe performance penalty on Cheetah. But there was still one man who could make Cheetah dance in the sky like a brand-new bird. Patrick found that extraordinary young pilot asleep under Cheetah's nose, using the nosewheel as a headrest.

"J.C."

"Yo," came a sleepy reply.

Patrick went up the crew-boarding ladder, retrieved a set of ear noise protectors from the cockpit. "On your feet. Time to go aviating."

For J. C. Powell that bit of Air Force jargon was raw meat to a starving wolf—he was up, on his feet and skipping up the crew entry ladder like a kid.

"Say the word, Colonel."

"I'm stopping by to see how our boy is doing in DreamStar," McLanahan said, putting on the ear protectors to block out the noise of the external power cart. "Should be fifteen minutes to engine start. Get Cheetah ready to fly."

"You got it, boss."

In another life, Captain Roland Q. Powell, the only son of a very wealthy Virginia family, all five feet five and one hundred twenty pounds of him, must have been a barnstormer; before that he might have ridden barrels over Niagara Falls. "Plain reckless" would have been the wrong term to describe his flying, but "reckless abandon" was close. He was totally at home in airplanes, always pushing his machine to the limit but staying in control at all times. He never flew slow if he could fly fast, never made a turn at thirty degrees' bank when he could do sixty or ninety, never flew up high when he could fly down in the trees. He earned the nickname "J.C." from his Undergraduate Pilot Training instructors who would mutter "Jesus Christ" (usually followed by "help me" or "save me") when they found out they had been scheduled to fly with Roland Powell.

He became an FAIP, first assignment instructor pilot, out of Undergraduate Pilot Training, but the Air Force didn't want an entire Air Force filled with J. C. Powells, so he was assigned to Edwards Air Force Base. Flight test was the perfect place to stick Roland Powell. He knew all there was to know about aerodynamics but would still agree to do anything the engineers asked of him, no matter how dangerous or impossible it seemed. As a result Powell got the hot planes. Every jet builder wanted to see what magic J. C. Powell could conjure up with his airframe. He was soon enticed to Dreamland by General Elliott with the promise of flying the hottest fighter of them all—Cheetah. Powell's expertise both as a pilot and as an engineer helped speed up the development of DreamStar, but he chose to stay with Cheetah. From then on, he had been her only pilot.

But J. C. Powell had had his time in the spotlight. Now, it was Kenneth Francis James' turn.

When he got to DreamStar again, Patrick climbed up the ladder on the hydraulic lift and watched as James was lowered into the cockpit. His special flight suit was preformed into a sitting position, making James look like a plastic doll. Once James was lowered into place, Patrick moved toward him as close as possible without interfering with the small army of experts attending to the pilot's seat configuration.

"Feeling okay, Ken?"

James nodded. "Snug, but okay."

Patrick watched as James was set into his specially molded ejection seat, strapped into place, and had his oxygen, environmental and electronic leads connected. The image of a medieval knight being readied for combat flashed in Patrick's head, topped off when they placed James' helmet on his head and clipped it into a clavicle ring on his shoulders. The helmet was essentially a holder for a variety of superconducting sensors and terminals that covered the inner surface. Once the helmet was locked into place, the flight suit became one gigantic electronic circuit, one big superconducting transistor. It became the data-transmission circuit between James and the amazing aircraft he was strapped into.

"Self-test in progress," Carmichael said. The computer, a diagnostic self-test device as well as an electroencephalograph to monitor the human side of the system, checked each of the thousands of sensors, circuits and transmitters within the suit and their connections through the interface to DreamStar. But Carmichael chose not to let the computer do *his* work, even though he was the one who had designed the interface; the scientist manually ran through the complex maze of readouts, checking for any sign of malfunction or abnormal readings.

He found none; neither did the computer. A few minutes later, Carmichael turned to Patrick, nodded. "He's ready."

Patrick walked around the lift's narrow catwalk and knelt down in front of James. He could barely see a movement of James' eyes through the helmet's thick electro-optical lenses.

"Ready to do some flying, buddy?"

They looked at each other. There was no movement at all from James. Patrick waited, watched. James appeared to be trying to decide on something. He didn't seem fearful or apprehensive or at all nervous. He was just . . . what?

Patrick glanced at Carmichael. "Alan? How's he doing?"

"His beta is pinging off the scale," Carmichael said, rechecking the electroencephalograph readouts. "No alpha or theta activity at all."

Patrick turned again to James, bent down close to him. "We can reschedule this, buddy. Don't push it. It's not worth the grief."

"No. I'll be okay. I'm just . . . trying to get ready . . ."

"Then relax, let it come to you, don't chase it. If it doesn't happen, it doesn't happen."

"Hell of a way to fight a war," James said—the tension in his voice was obvious. "I can see a fighter pilot telling his squadron commander, 'I know the enemy is rolling across the base but I can't fly today—my damn theta isn't responding . . .' I've got to prove that I can go in and out of theta-alpha in a moment's notice."

"Making the system operational is still a few years off, Ken," Patrick told him. "Don't worry about all that. Relax, don't force yourself or the system. Let's just go up and have some fun. Finish up and buy me a beer at the Club afterward. That's all."

Patrick raised a hand in front of the test pilot, and James slapped a metallic-lined glove into it. "Punch a hole in the sky, buddy. That's an order, too." He gave James one last thumbs-up and stepped off the lift.

By the time Patrick had stepped back onto the tarmac Dr. Carmichael was shaking his head in disbelief.

"He's already under alpha-C parameters. I think he's getting to the point where he can do it anytime. If we had him hooked up outside the plane, he could probably go into theta-sine A before we strap him in."

"He gets nervous every now and then," Patrick added, "especially before a big test like this one. Back me up on monitoring him, Alan."

An external power cart was running on Cheetah by the time Patrick returned, climbed into the aft cockpit and strapped in. Aircraft power was already on, and his crew chief and test-range officers had already done a fast preflight of the telemetry and data collection instruments packed into the cockpit. Because Cheetah was the only jet around that could even try to keep up with the DreamStar, it was now used to fly photo-chase on training and test flights. The special high-speed camera Cheetah carried tracked DreamStar as it went through its paces. Patrick could monitor all of DreamStar's important electronic indications and if necessary take control of the plane by remote control.

With all of DreamStar's power off, however, there was only one readout to monitor—the EEG of Ken James himself. Like Carmichael, Patrick was amazed as he watched the electronic traces of James' different brainwave patterns. He clicked open his interphone.

"He's almost into theta-sine alpha already."

"Does that mean I can go to sleep too?" J. C. Powell said.

"How fast could *you* go into theta-alpha?" Patrick said, watching the readouts change. "I know you've flown the DreamStar simulator. Could you do any better?"

"Patrick, I'm a pilot, not a robot." J.C.'s voice had lost its sardonic tone. "Seems to me ANTARES turns pilots into near-robots. But to answer your question: sure, I could go into theta-sine-alpha quickly. Couple of minutes. *Staying* in theta-alpha was another trick. I could never quite get the hang of it. But I didn't lose DreamStar, I gained Cheetah. I figure I got the better deal.''

Which was a long speech for J. C. Powell; it underscored his dislike for ANTARES. ANTARES might be the great addition to DreamStar's already amazing array of avionics, it might be the future of air combat—but J. C. Powell didn't see it in his future.

"It doesn't turn anyone into a robot," Patrick said. "You still have full control. I don't see what your problem is about AN-TARES."

"Full control? Of what? A computer tells him what to do, and he does it."

"It's still the pilot calling the shots, J.C."

"Sure, he can pick up his own options out of a list the computer presents to him, or he can override everything and go his own way. I know that. But if a smart computer offers up a list of a hundred options, well, most guys will pick something out of that list." Powell spread his hands out across his lap. "Say you're at a fancy restaurant." He motioned an imaginary waiter to his table. "You've been to this restaurant before because they have the best steak in town, but Pierre hands you the menu. What do you do?" Powell opened his imaginary menu and pre-tended to read it. "You look at the menu. Why? Because it's there. So maybe you order the steak because that's what you always order, *but you still look at the menu.*

"See, even with ANTARES it takes time to scan the menu. A real pilot will use that time to use his head and instincts to execute a *real* maneuver. In ANTARES there's no thought, anal-ysis, decision making . . . it's been done for you. And I call that programming."

"But if it results in a better system?"

"ANTARES hasn't been proved to be better than a human pilot . . ."

"We still *use* a human pilot, J.C."

"More or less, I guess," Powell said sarcastically, returning switches to their proper positions. "But in a significant way we don't—I say ANTARES can be beat."

"Well," Patrick said, rubbing his eyes wearily, trying to mas-sage away the headache that usually happened when arguing with J. C. Powell, "it's a moot point, at least for now. Like I said, we're not concerned with how well DreamStar fights, deploying her is still a ways off. We're here to test the aircraft and test the concept.''

J.C., slumping so far down in his seat Patrick couldn't see him, said, ''But all those generals and congressmen don't care about testing the concept. They all want to know the same thing—can she win dogfights?''

''And you're saying she can't.''

''I'm saying that she *can* be beat. A pilot with the right combo of skill and balls can beat ANTARES. And if ANTARES is forced out of the combat loop, the pilot in DreamStar has to be able to take charge and fight on his own. DreamStar's not really set up for pilot-directed dogfighting. For me that's her weakness . . . And look what we're doing to our combat pilots''— J.C. motioned toward DreamStar—''Ken James is one of the best pilots in the Air Force. He's been a star ever since he graduated from the Zoo. So what have we done with him? We've trussed him up in a steel flight suit, a twenty-pound helmet and more damn electrodes than Frankenstein's monster. We're using his brain but not his *mind*. There's a big difference, I figure. Are all our best military pilots going to be used as protoplasmic circuit boards for ANTARES?''

For a guy that was only thirty years old, Powell could be a real stick-in-the-mud sometimes. Patrick scanned the EEG readouts. ''Everything looks normal. It should be awhile before he radios in that he's ready. I'll let you know when he's coming around so we can crank engines.''

''Roger that. I'm gonna do another flight-control check.''

''Didn't you just do a computer self-test?''

''Having a computer check a computer to see if a computer is working is just looking for trouble. One of these days all those computers will get together and drive us into the ground. I wanna catch them before they do it. I'm doing the check manually. Let me know when you're ready to go.''

''Rog.'' Patrick was tired of arguing. Besides, J.C. had a point. He turned again to the EEG monitors.

Theta-sine-alpha indicated that James was relaxed, but it was a much deeper level of relaxation, more neurological, much more than ordinary muscle relaxation. The ability to get to theta-sine-alpha had taken months of training. They called it biofeedback when psychologists would hook a patient up to a mini-EEG or polygraph that would beep whenever a beta wave would be detected, indicating stress or irregular muscular or nervous activity. The idea was to relax the body or control nerve activity until the beeping stopped. James had to go far beyond such muscle relaxation—he had to relax his mind, open it, create a window into the subconscious.

For Kenneth Francis James, the window to his mind did not open like a door or a window—it opened like a hot, rusty knife ripping through pink flesh. But that was the nature of the Advanced Neural Transfer and Response System that linked the brain with a digital computer. James had gone far beyond Carmichael's lectures. This was the real thing, the link-up between the computer on the plane and his suit.

The first mind-numbing phase of transition was activation of the system itself, which occurred automatically once ANTARES detected that James had entered theta-sine-alpha. In order to pick up the tiny changes in electrical activity in James' body, the metallic ANTARES flight suit itself had to be electrified. Even though the charge was very small it was applied to almost every part of the body, from the skull to the feet; it was like touching one's tongue to the terminals of a nine-volt battery and feeling the tiny current jolt the taste buds, except that James felt that sweet, tingling sensation in every part of his body. And through it all, he had to maintain theta-alpha . . .

Enduring activation of the ANTARES system was only the first step; the now familiar slight physical pain was easy to block out. The next assault, however, was on the mind itself.

Once ANTARES was open it would transmit a complex series of preprogrammed questions to various conscious and subconscious areas of James' mind. The questions, programmed months earlier by countless hours in a simulator-recording unit, would match the existing brainwave patterns of each level encountered. After scanning, recognizing and matching the patterns, ANTARES would then overpower that particular neural function, force the original pattern to a compatible subconscious level and allow the ANTARES computer to control that level. It was like submitting a series of passwords to several levels of guards, except each time ANTARES would reach a level it would hammer, not knock, on the door, demanding entry. Once admitted, it would first befriend, then overpower, the resident inside. The takeovers accomplished by ANTARES were sometimes painful, sometimes soothing. At times images would force their way out of James' subconscious, long-stored memories of childhood that Maraklov had long forgotten.

His conscious mind was now like a big living room that had just had all its furniture moved to different parts of the house. ANTARES had taken over control of most conscious activity, keeping only a few essential activities in the conscious foreground while relegating the rest to higher parts of the brain. Now ANTARES was ready to start remodeling.

With the doors and windows to James' subconscious mind wide open, his mind was ready to receive and process vast amounts of information. Normally that information would come from the five senses, and even with ANTARES some still did, but now altogether new sources of information were open. ANTARES could collect and transmit digital data signals to James' conscious mind, and James could receive that information as if it came from his own five senses. But James no longer had five senses—he had hundreds, thousands of them. The radar altimeter was a sense. The radar was a sense. So was the laser rangefinder. Dozens of thermometers, aneroids, gallium-arsenide memory chips, limit switches, logic circuits, photocells, voltmeters, chronometers—the list was endless and ever-changing.

But it was an enormous shock to the system to find that the list of senses had grown from five to five thousand, and here ANTARES was no help at all; when the "room" was full it simply began cramming in more input sources. For James the new impulses weren't coherent or understandable. They were random flashes of light or crashes of sound, battering his conscious mind, all fighting for order and recognition. Put another way, as he once had, it felt like a crushing wall of water, a wave of unbearable heat, and the swirling center of a thunderstorm all mixed up at once. And ANTARES was relentless. The instant an image or an impulse was set aside, a hundred more took its place. The computer only knew that so much had to be learned. It had no conception of rest, or defeat, or of insanity.

Suddenly, then, the flood of input was gone. The tornado of data subsided, leaving only a room full of seemingly random bits of information lying scattered about. The furniture was overturned—but it was all there, all intact. Now, like a benevolent relative or kindly neighbor, ANTARES began sorting through the jungle of information, creating boxes to organize the information, placing boxes into boxes, organizing the mountains of data into neat, cohesive packages.

The random series of images began to coalesce. Undecipherable snaps of sound became long, staccato clicks; the clicks turned to a low whine; the whine turned into waves of sounds rising and falling; the waves became words, the words became sentences. Flashes of lights became numbers. And then the numbers disappeared, replaced by numbers that James wanted to "see."

The energy surges generated by ANTARES were still coursing through James' body, but now they were acting like amphetamines, energizing and revitalizing his body. He was aware of DreamStar all around him, aware of its power waiting for release.

James' eyes snapped open, like those of a man awaking from a nightmare. Swiveling his heavy helmet on its smooth Teflon bearings, he looked across at Cheetah's open canopy. Powell was busy in the forward cockpit; McLanahan was watching his instruments. But he must have read something in the instruments in Cheetah's aft cockpit, because just then McLanahan looked over toward him. He could see the DreamStar project director with his oxygen visor in place, apparently talking on the radios. Patrick was looking directly at him now—was he talking to him . . . ?

. . . And suddenly the energy was unbearable. It was as if DreamStar was a wild animal straining on a leash, hot with the scent of prey, demanding to be released.

James looked down at the left MFD, the multi-function display, on the forward instrument panel. He imagined the index finger of his left hand touching the icon labeled "VHF-1." Immediately the icon illuminated. Now, hovering right there in front of his eyes, was a series of numerals representing the preprogrammed VHF radio channels—the image, transmitted from DreamStar's computers through ANTARES to his optic nervous system, was as clear and as real as every other visual image. He selected the proper ship-to-ship channel on the computer-generated icon and activated the radio. The whole process, from deciding to activate the radio to speaking the words, took less than a second.

"Storm Two ready for engine start," James reported. Although the ANTARES interface did not take away his ability to speak or hear, all traces of inflection or emotion usually were filtered out. So the voice that Patrick heard on the radio was eerie, alien.

"Welcome back, Captain," Patrick said. "I saw you come out of theta-alpha. Ready to do some flying?"

"Ready and waiting, Colonel."

"Stand by." Patrick switched to a secondary radio. "Storm Control, this is Storm One."

In the underground command post of the High Technology Advanced Weapons Center a four-star Air Force general seated at a large cherry desk replaced a phone on its cradle, then looked down with disgust at his right leg. He reached down, took his right calf in both hands, straightened his leg, then raised himself out of his leather seat using the stiff right leg as a crutch. Once fully standing he unlocked the graphite and Teflon bearings in the prosthetic right knee joint, allowing it to move much like a regular leg.

An aide held the office door open for General Bradley Elliott as the director of HAWC stepped out and down the short hallway to the command post. He used a keycard to open the outer door to the entrapment area. A bank of floodlights snapped on, filling the entrapment area with bright light, and the outer door automatically locked behind him.

Two security guards armed with Uzi submachine guns came through the doors on either side of the area. They slowed when they recognized who it was but didn't alter their moves. While one guard quickly pat-searched Elliott and ran a small metal scanner over his body, the other stood with his Uzi at port arms, finger on the trigger. The metal detector beeped when passed over Elliott's right leg. Elliott tolerated it.

The guards watched as Elliott signed in on a security roster and double-checked the new signature against other signature samples and the signature on Elliott's restricted-area badge pinned to his shirt. Satisfied, the guards slipped away as quickly as they had appeared.

A tall black security officer wearing a nine-millimeter Beretta automatic pistol on his waist walked quickly to the general officer as he emerged from the entrapment area. "Sorry, sir," Major Hal Briggs said, handing Elliott a cup of coffee. "New guy on the security console. Buzzed the sky cops when the metal detector in the entrapment area went crazy. He's been briefed again on your . . . special circumstances.''

"He did right. You should have commended him. The response guards too.''

"Yes, sir,'' was all Briggs had time to mutter as Elliott pushed on past him and entered the communications center. One of the controllers handed him a telephone.

"Storm Control Alpha, go ahead.''

"Alpha, this is Storm One. Flight of two in the green and ready to taxi.''

"Stand by,'' Elliott said. As he lowered the phone Briggs handed him a computer printout.

"Latest from Lassen Mountain Space Tracking Center,'' Briggs said. "Three Russian satellites will be in the area during the test-window: Cosmos 713 infrared surveillance satellite still on station over North America in geostationary orbit, but it's the other two we're concerned with. Cosmos 1145 and 1289 are the kickers. Cosmos 1145 is a low-altitude, high-resolution film-return photo-intelligence satellite. Cosmos 1289 is a radar-imaging film-return bird. We believe they're mainly ground-mapping satellites with limited ability to photograph aircraft in flight, but obviously they can be damaging. Both will be over the exercise area during the test throughout the day. Do you want to reschedule, sir?''

"No,'' Elliott said. "I don't want to give the Russians the pleasure of thinking they can disrupt my schedule with a couple of old Brownies. Just make sure DreamStar and Cheetah stay in the bluff while they're overhead.''

He took a sip of coffee, scowled at it, then set the cup down with an exasperated *thump*. "Besides, it seems like they have all the information they need on DreamStar anyway. I could have dropped my teeth when I saw the DIA photo of the Ramenskoye Flight Test Facility in Moscow with the exact same short-takeoff-and-landing runway-test devices as ours here at Dreamland. *The exact same ones.* In precisely the same position right down to the inch.''

"We've known the Russians have been working on high-performance STOL fighter-aircraft for years, sir . . .''

"Right. Exactly as long as we've been working on them here at Dreamland. We launch Cheetah, they launch an STOL fighter. We develop a supercockpit for DreamStar, and four months later we intercept plans for nearly the same design being smuggled into East Germany. The Joint Chiefs will close down Dreamland if we don't stop the leaks around here.''

''I'm rechecking the backgrounds of every person remotely connected with the project,'' Briggs said. ''DIA is rechecking the civilian contractors. But that adds up to over five thousand people and more than a hundred and fifty thousand man-years' worth of personal histories to examine. And we do this every year for key personnel. We're just overloaded—''

''I know, I know,'' Elliott said, picking up the phone again. ''But we're running out of time. For every success we have on the flight line we have one defeat with intelligence leaks. We can't afford it.'' He keyed the switch on the telephone handset. ''Storm Flight, this is Alpha. Clear for engine start. Call for clearance when ready for taxi.''

''Roger,'' McLanahan replied.

Elliott turned to Briggs. ''Join me in the tower when you've gotten the overflight update on those two Russian satellites. Before I have you work your tail off to find our security leaks, the least you can do is watch a little of our success.''

''Wouldn't miss it for all the stolen STOL plans in Ramenskoye,'' Briggs said, and immediately regretted it as Elliott gave him a look and limped out of the command post.

''Storm Two starting engines,'' James reported to Powell. The pilot of the F-15 Cheetah barely had time to acknowledge when the whine of the engine turbines pierced the early morning stillness.

Engine start was triggered by a thought impulse that selected the ''engine start'' routine from the ''home'' menu transmitted to James by ANTARES. Computers instantly energized the engine-start circuits and determined their status; since no external air or power was available, an ''alert'' status would be performed.

Less than a second later the ignition-circuits were activated and a blast of supercompressed nitrogen gas shot into the sixteenth-stage compressor of DreamStar's engine. Unlike a conventional jet engine, it was not necessary for one compressor stage at a time to spin up to full speed—all compressor stages of its engine were activated at once, allowing much faster starts. Less than twenty seconds later the engine was at idle power and full generator power was on-line. Once the engine-start choice had been activated, the computer knew what had to be done next—James just allowed the results of each preprogrammed check to scroll past his eyes as the on-board computers completed them.

"Storm Two engine start complete, beginning pre-takeoff checks."

"Amazing," Powell murmured in Cheetah. He had begun his engine-start checklist at the same time James had, but he had barely had his left engine up to idle-power by the time DreamStar's start-sequence was completed.

Immediately after James made his report to McLanahan and Powell, he commanded the start of an exhaustive computer check of all of DreamStar's systems. With the engine powering two main and one standby hydraulic pump, energy was available to DreamStar's flight controls. Outside, the check made DreamStar's wing surfaces crawl and undulate like the fins of a manta ray. From outside the cockpit the flight-control check was almost surreal . . . each wing bent and unbent in impossible angles, stretching and flexing more like a sheet of gelatin rather than hard fibersteel. The process from hydraulic system power-up to full flight-control certification had taken fifteen seconds.

Next was an electrical system check. Total time for a complete check of two generators, two alternators, one emergency generator, and two separate battery backup systems: three seconds. James stayed immobile during the checking process, allowing his senses to be overtaken by the rush of information.

The aircraft itself was like a living thing. Personnel were not allowed near the aircraft during the preflight because damaging radar, electromagnetic and laser emitters were being activated all around the aircraft at breakneck speed. The throttle advanced and retarded by itself. The mission-adaptive wings continued their unusual undulations, arching and bending so wildly it seemed they would bend clean in half or twist right off the fuselage.

Through it all James was constantly informed about each system's exact status and operation. He could no longer feel his feet or hands, but he knew which circuit in the superconducting radar was energized, and through that system he knew down to the millimeter how far Cheetah was parked from him. He knew the position of DreamStar's canards, the pressure of the fluid in the primary hydraulic system and the RPMs of the ninth-stage engine's turbine, just as one might know which way his toes were pointing without seeing them or the way one picks up a pencil and begins to write without consciously thinking about the action. ANTARES had cut James off from monitoring his own body, had relegated that function to a deeper portion of his brain and had shifted his conscious mental capacity to the task of operating a supersonic fighter plane.

Suddenly, DreamStar ceased its wild preflight movements, and the engine throttle returned to idle . . .

"Storm One, Two is in the green, ready for taxi," James reported.

"My radar's not even timed out," Patrick said to J. C. Powell. "How are you coming on your preflight?"

"Few more minutes."

"How can he accomplish an entire systems preflight in just a few minutes?"

"How long does it take you to wake up from a nap?" J.C. told him as he put the finishing touches on the preflight he had begun long before. "How long does it take you to ask yourself how you feel? That's what ANTARES is like. If something was wrong with DreamStar, Ken would feel it just like he'd feel a sprained ankle or a crink in his neck."

Where Ken had banks of computers to check his avionics, J.C. manually had to "fail" a system to check a backup system, or manually deflect Cheetah's control stick and have the wing flex checked by a crew chief to verify the full range of motion of the fighter's elastic wings. But after a few minutes of setting switches and checking off items in a checklist strapped to his right thigh, he was ready to go.

Patrick keyed his microphone: "Storm Control, this is Storm One flight. Two birds in the green. Ready to taxi."

General Elliott was now on top of Dreamland's portable control tower, a device fifty feet high that was set up and taken down for each mission to confuse attempts by spy satellites to pinpoint Dreamland's many disguised dry-lakebed runways. Major Hal Briggs had just come up the narrow winding stairs and handed Elliott another computer printout when Patrick made his call.

"Those Cosmos peeping Toms start their first pass over the range in fifteen minutes," Briggs said. "They've got our test time scoped out almost to the minute. Those satellites will be overhead every fifteen minutes for the next two hours—exactly as long as this scheduled mission."

"Another damned security leak. And I scheduled this mission only two days, ago."

"But those spy birds weren't up there two days ago," Briggs said. "I checked. You mean—?"

"I mean the Soviets took only two days—maybe less—to launch two brand-new satellites just for this test flight," Elliott said. "Well, at least they won't catch our planes on the ground." He picked up his microphone. "Storm Flight, this is Alpha. Taxi to hold point and await takeoff clearance. Winds calm, altimeter . . ." Elliott checked the meteorological data readouts on an overhead console ". . . three-zero-zero-five. Taxi clearance void time is one-zero minutes. Over."

"Storm Flight copies ten minutes. On the move." Moments later both fighters emerged from the satellite bluff and fell in behind a jeep with a large sign that read "FOLLOW ME." The caravan moved quickly across an expanse of hard-baked sand to another smaller satellite-bluff hangar that had been towed out to the end of one of the disguised runways that crisscrossed Groom Lake in the center of the Dreamland test range. Now Cheetah and DreamStar pulled alongside each other and set their parking brakes while technicians and specialists did a fast last-chance inspection of each.

"Pre-takeoff and line-up checks," Patrick said over interphone.

"Roger," J.C. replied. "In progress."

"Storm Two ready for release," James suddenly radioed in.

"Amazing," Patrick said to J.C. "He's already done with a pre-takeoff checklist twice as complicated as ours." He keyed the UHF radio switch. "Standby, Storm Two."

"Roger."

"MAW switch set to V-sub-X, max performance takeoff." J.C. read off the most critical switch positions for the mission-adaptive-wing mode, and Patrick saw that the leading and trailing edges of the wings had curved into a long, deep high-lift airfoil.

"Canard control and engine nozzle control switches set to

'AUTO ALPHA,' '' J.C. continued. "This will be a constant-alpha takeoff." J. C. Powell always briefed his back-seater on the takeoff, abort, and emergency procedures, even though he and Patrick had flown together for almost two years and Patrick knew the procedures as well as J.C. "Power to military thrust, brakes off and power to max afterburner. We'll expect negative-Y push after five seconds, with a pitch to takeoff attitude. After that we monitor angle-of-attack throughout the climb and make sure we don't exceed twenty-eight alpha in the climb-out. I'm looking to break my previous record of a seventeen-hundred-foot takeoff roll on this one . . . In case we don't get the push-down I'll cancel auto-alpha and switch to normal takeoff procedures— accelerate to one-sixty, rotate, maintain eight alpha or less, accelerate to two-eight-zero knots indicated and come out of afterburner. Same procedures if we lose vectored thrust after takeoff . . . All *right*." Powell slapped his gloved hands together, finished off the last few items of the checklist: "Circuit breakers checked. Caution panel clear. Canopy closed and locked. Seat belts and shoulder harnesses?"

"On and on," Patrick intoned.

"Checked up front. Lights set. Helmets, visors, oxygen mask, oxygen panel.''

"On, down, on, set to normal."

"Same here. Parking brakes released." J.C. touched a switch on his control stick. "Takeoff configuration check."

*"Takeoff configuration check in progress,"* responded a computer-synthesized voice. It was the final step in Cheetah's electronics array. A computer, which had monitored every step of the pre-takeoff checklists being performed, would make one last check of all systems on board and report any discrepancies.

*"Takeoff configuration check complete. Status okay."*

"I already knew that, you moron," J.C. murmured to the voice. He never relied on the computerized system although he consulted it. It was, as he would frequently remind everyone within earshot, another computer out to get him. "We're ready to go, Colonel," he said.

Patrick keyed the radio switch. "Storm Control, this is Storm flight of two. Ready for departure."

Hal Briggs, on the narrow catwalk of the portable tower, spoke four words into a walkie-talkie. "Sand storm, one-seven."

His cryptic message activated a hundred security officers spread out within some four-hundred square miles of the takeoff area. They were the last line of defense against unauthorized intrusion or eavesdropping on the test that was about to begin. Each man checked and rechecked his assigned sector with an array of electronic sensors—sound, radar, heat, motion, electromagnetic—and once secure, reported an ''all secure'' by sending a coded electronic tone. Only when all of the tones were received would a ''go'' signal be sent to Briggs.

Five seconds later he received that coded tone. ''Good sweep, General,'' he reported to Elliott. The general took one last look at the satellite overflight schedule, picked up the mike:

''Storm flight of two, clear for unrestricted takeoff. Winds calm. Takeoff clearance void time, five minutes. Have a good one.''

Patrick hit a switch, and the faint hum of the big gyrostabilized video camera mounted on Cheetah's spine could be heard. ''Camera's slaved on DreamStar, J.C.,'' he said. ''Don't lose him.''

''A cold day in hell before any machine can outrun me.''

They saw DreamStar taxi a few feet forward just ahead of Cheetah, until the tip of DreamStar's forward-swept right wingtip was just cutting into J.C.'s view of Ken James.

''Comin' up,'' J.C. said. He brought the throttles forward, keeping his toes on the brakes. Cheetah began to quiver, then shake with a sound like the distant rumble of an earthquake.

''Turn 'em loose, baby,'' J.C. murmured. He scanned his engine-instrument readouts on the main display, running down the graphic displays of engine RPM, fuel flow, nozzle and louver position, turbine inlet temperature and exhaust gas temperature. Each bar graph lined up in the normal range, everything right smack in the green—both engines in full military power, one hundred and nine percent of rated thrust, sixty thousand pounds of power. His grip on the stick and throttles unconsciously tightened. ''Turn 'em loose . . .''

James also performed a last-second engine instrument check. But he had no bar·graphs to check out with his eyes. ANTARES reported information not only through the visual nervous system in the form of words, numbers and symbols that he could ''see,'' but, to avoid overload of the visual senses, also as sensations that he could detect with his other senses. He could feel the power of the engine as clear and as real as air inflating his lungs or strength rippling down his arms. He knew in an instant that the engine was at full military thrust. At a thought-command, a computer that metered fuel flow performed a retrim of the engine to compensate for pressure altitude and outside temperature, which yielded a few hundred pounds extra thrust. The engine-fuel trim would be accomplished every six seconds thereafter as DreamStar began its test flight, accomplished as easily and as subconsciously as a person might ride a bike or drive a car along a much-traveled highway.

James briefly activated the search radar, which transmitted its signals as visual images—no obstructions or targets within thirty miles. A fast scan of VHF or UHF frequencies—no emergency calls, air traffic control challenges, no abort call from the tower. One quick check of hydraulic systems—all running normally. Electrical—one generator on the engine running a bit hot. On a mental suggestion, a digital flight-data recorder logged the time, conditions and readouts on the left generator for the crew chiefs to analyze after the flight.

The check of the secondary systems, including the flight-data recorder entry, had taken less time than it took J. C. Powell to tighten his grip on his throttle quadrant.

James now ordered the brakes to be released . . .

J.C. saw DreamStar shoot forward. "Here we go," he said.

Patrick took a firm grip on the steel "handlebars" surrounding the instrument panel in the aft cockpit. Without a stick, throttle, or pedals, Patrick could do nothing during takeoff but watch the engine instruments and hang on. He glanced at the large yellow-and-black-painted handgrip between his legs underneath the center of the instrument panel—the ejection handle—and mentally measured the distance to it . . .

DreamStar shot forward like a dragster popping off the starting line. James commanded the engine to max afterburner, increasing thrust to well over eighty thousand pounds. At almost the same instant he also commanded activation of the auto-alpha flight mode. Louvers on the top of the engine nozzle swung open, diverting one-third of the engine thrust diagonally upward, compressing the rear main landing gear struts to their lowest position and allowing the nose-gear strut to extend fully. DreamStar was now pointing ten degrees upward, in full unstick, takeoff attitude.

The trailing edges of the two canards deflected downward. The engine, coupled with the foreplanes, was now shoving DreamStar's nose skyward—its computers controlling the canards kept the one-hundred-thousand-pound fighter from flipping backward out of control. As speed increased and the canards began to fly the nose, the louvers diverting the engine thrust upward gradually swung downward, allowing the thrust to accelerate the fighter and lift the tail off the runway. At one hundred knots airspeed DreamStar's nose gear lifted off the runway. The pitch attitude increased to thirty degrees, held just below the stall by the computer-controlled foreplanes. At one hundred and fifty knots DreamStar lifted off the runway, and because the wings, foreplanes and engine were commanded for maximum lift, she rose like an elevator.

In just over one thousand feet, the same distance a small general-aviation plane used at takeoff, the fifty-ton jet fighter had left the ground. Once airborne, thrust again was automatically diverted to optimize climb performance. DreamStar was now a rocket, being propelled skyward at well over twenty thousand feet per minute. By the time it reached the end of the two-mile-long camouflaged runway, it was over eight thousand feet above the ground.

J. C. Powell's promise to keep up with DreamStar was kept for about five seconds.

He and McLanahan saw James give the signal to release brakes. "Two good engines," McLanahan called out from the aft cockpit as J.C. eased both engines into max afterburner.

"Roger. Two good cookers."

They saw DreamStar dash forward, then saw its forward fuselage jut into the sky and its canard's trailing edges snap downward . . .

Then DreamStar disappeared.

J.C. cursed. "Hang on." But try as he did, Powell could not match DreamStar's spectacular liftoff or climb rate. While DreamStar's pitch, power, and thrust controls were automatic, Cheetah's were mostly hand-controlled, relying on reaction time rather than electronics to trim the aircraft. When DreamStar dis-

appeared from view, J.C.'s first reaction was to pull back on the
stick to try to follow. But Cheetah had not reached unstick speed,
and Cheetah's computerized canard pushed the nose down to the
runway to gain speed.

*"Command override,"* the computerized voice suddenly interjected as Cheetah's nose fell and the nosewheel struts compressed. *"Stall warning."*

"Damn, too much," J.C. murmured, and let the nose fall a
few feet and watched the airspeed rise. "So much for a short
takeoff record." He let the airspeed rebuild to one hundred
eighty knots, then eased back on the stick. Cheetah glided gently
off the runway. This time, with plenty of "smash," Cheetah's
canards responded by pulling the nose higher into the air to take
advantage of the extra speed.

J.C. touched the computer interactive control on his stick.
"Gear up."

Three red "LANDING GEAR UNSAFE" lights illuminated, and
Patrick could feel the rumble as the two main wheels and the
nosewheel lifted through the slipstream. *"Landing gear unsafe,"* the computerized voice said. Five seconds later: *"Landing gear up and locked."*

"Gear's up," Patrick said. "Two hundred knots. Passing six
thousand feet."

J.C. began pulling the engines one by one out of afterburner
to conserve fuel. "Left engine to MIL power . . . right engine
to MIL . . . Okay, where is he?"

"Four o'clock high, coming down—"

DreamStar had appeared out of nowhere; it was in a full-
power descent, nose aimed straight at Cheetah's canopy.

J.C. jammed both throttles back into max afterburner and
began a hard roll to the right.

"Too late, he's gonna hit . . ."

Cheetah lunged forward but DreamStar kept on coming. Patrick could now see DreamStar's canards, deployed diagonally
underneath the fighter's belly in their high-maneuverability position. He could even see DreamStar's thirty millimeter Vulcan
cannon muzzle screaming in closer and closer . . .

But DreamStar did not hit. The closer it came, the more the
fighter began to flatten its flight path. It resembled a giant eagle
swooping in on its prey. The cannon muzzle never strayed off
Cheetah's canopy, even as DreamStar reached its prey's alti-

tude—it began to fly *sideways*, keeping the gun dead on target, paralleling Cheetah's right turn. As Cheetah began to accelerate, DreamStar snapped out of its sideways flight path and maneuvered into a right rear quartering missile-attack aspect.

"He hosed us," Patrick said. "He's at our six. He made a gun pass on us on our climbout. He's in infrared missile-launch position. Roll out and get him back into fingertip formation."

J.C. rolled wings level, paused, then rocked his wings twice. A few seconds later DreamStar was tucked in on Cheetah's right wing, so close that they could have had overlapping wingtips. "Only got a glimpse of him," J.C. said, "but he looked like he was haulin' ass. Tell him to stay with the ROE."

It was a J. C. Powell trademark to push the rules of engagement to the limits; now he was complaining about someone else pushing the ROE. "He's in fingertip," Patrick reported to Powell. "I'm sending him to the tactical frequency." Patrick extended both hands in front of him, fists clenched, one on top of the other, the signal to switch to the agreed-on scrambled tactical frequency; hand signals, used as much as possible, prevented eavesdropping. James nodded that he understood.

On the new scrambled VHF frequency, J.C. called, "Storm flight, check in."

"Two," a monotone voice immediately replied.

"Nice moves, Ken," Patrick said. "But remember the ROE. No maneuvering and no closure rate greater than two hundred knots within one mile of your target. I'd say you came close on both."

"Yes, sir." The metallic-sounding voice was James' altered by the computer. It sounded almost sarcastic. Or was Patrick imagining that?

"Okay, forget it," Patrick said, imaging Powell's face. J.C. didn't like being upstaged. He wouldn't be sore because he had been upstaged by a younger pilot but that he had been hosed by a machine called ANTARES. "Ken, ready to start some dogfighting?"

"Affirmative."

"Roger. Lead will come left, heading three-one-zero to stay inside our airspace. On roll-out, Ken, you are the fox. We'll give you fifteen seconds, then we're coming after you. Block is ten to fifty thousand feet, keep it under the Mach, please, or the camera telemetry won't keep up with you. And stay within the

ROE, gents. We're all on the same team . . . Lead, come left heading three-one-zero. Head's up.''

"Two's in.''

J.C. started a hard left turn to Patrick's assigned heading. The roll was a bit more abrupt than it should have been but it didn't seem to faze James—he stayed right in there, perhaps a few feet farther out, but still in tight fingertip formation. The instant J.C. rolled out of his turn, DreamStar merely dropped straight down out of sight.

"There he goes," Patrick said. "Straight down, I can't see him.''

"Fifteen seconds," Powell complained dryly. "He could be in the next state in fifteen seconds.''

"That's why he only gets five seconds. Go get 'em.''

Powell rolled inverted, then pulled hard on the stick. Cheetah did a tight inverted turn, losing five thousand feet. Patrick was straining against the G-forces shoving him deep into his seat, trying to look up through the canopy to where he thought DreamStar would be.

"Tally ho," J.C. sang out. "Coming up on our twelve o'clock. Right where I thought he'd be." Patrick fought a wave of vertigo as he searched for DreamStar on radar. Normally the back-seater on an F-15E fighter-bomber would use his radar and process the attack for the pilot, but Patrick was only along as a camera operator and observer—J.C. would have to find and process his own targets. But J.C. already had very unconventional help, and he quickly began working on his kill.

He hit the voice-command button. "Attack radar transmit, target report." Patrick watched as the attack radar went automatically from "STANDBY" to "TRANSMIT" and began a wide-area scan.

"*Radar transmit,*" the computer responded. Almost immediately, the computer reported, "*Radar contact, range fifteen miles.*"

"Heads up display.''

J.C.'s windscreen was filled with symbols and numbers, seemingly floating in space. Unlike regular HUDs, heads-up displays—pieces of plate glass that reflected up from the instrument console to the pilot—Cheetah's consisted of large banks of high-resolution laser projectors that created three-dimensional images that hung in space. Unlike a reflected HUD system, which relied on the pilot orienting himself directly behind the glass, Cheetah's laser-projected images were visible no matter how the pilot moved in his seat, and even bright sunlight or glare on the windshield could not wash the images away. The laser images showed an icon of DreamStar with a diamond symbol around it, indicating that Cheetah's attack radar was locked onto it. Columns of numbers surrounding the icon showed DreamStar's heading, airspeed, range and closure rate.

"Target designate . . ." Powell said. Instantly micro-wattage laser projectors in his helmet scanned his eyeballs, and a holographic circle and crosshairs was projected up onto the windscreen corresponding to exactly where he was looking. He centered the crosshairs on the icon, ". . . now."

*"Target radar lock,"* the computer reported.

"Laser slave to radar," J.C. ordered.

*"Target laser lock."* A four-pointed star superimposed itself on DreamStar's icon. Unlike Cheetah's attack radar, the laser rangefinder was undetectable by any of DreamStar's radar-detecting threat-warning receivers. Cheetah could carry a dozen laser-guided ATM-12 Cougar hypervelocity missiles, which were high-speed, nonexplosive, relatively inexpensive guided missiles. Fired from very short to very long ranges—it had no warhead and therefore no minimum-range requirements—the Cougar missile could be used to attack both air and ground targets, destroying its target by sheer force of impact.

DreamStar was still cruising along on the same heading. He hadn't been detected—yet. As James drove in closer he would eventually pick up Cheetah's radar emissions. J.C. had to control his excitement and steady his voice to issue more commands to the computer.

"Radar standby."

*"Radar standby."* The laser rangefinder would now process the entire kill without danger of detection.

J.C. took a deep breath. "Arm laser missile."

*"Arm laser missile, warning, practice missile armed."* The weapons multi-function display showed Cheetah's ten weapons stations, the belly-mounted Cougar missile rack illuminated with the number 12 on it, signifying the number of hypervelocity missiles remaining.

"Launch laser missile."

*"Launch . . . Warning! Collision warning. Collision warning."*

J.C. barely had time to react. DreamStar had just frozen in mid-air, still on its original heading, and let Cheetah drive right at him, chopping the distance between the two advanced fighters from ten miles to practically zero in the blink of an eye. Powell, with no choice, rolled hard behind DreamStar and dived past him. The computer had processed the launch command, but Powell doubted very much if he'd ever be credited with a "kill" with a closure rate and maneuver like that.

"God . . ." McLanahan breathed. He remembered how they had used the same maneuver in the B-52s in the past. Especially one particular B-52, his Old Dog Zero One, on that mission over Russia that seemed like a million years ago. "Now I know what it feels like to get sucked in . . ."

"He *knew* we'd try that dive on him," Powell said. "He was waiting for us. The minute he detected our attack radar was off he knew we were committed. He just put DreamStar on max alpha hover and chopped his power." But J.C. didn't linger on James' maneuver. He knew DreamStar could accelerate back to combat speed and pull in right behind him just as fast as he had slowed down. So J.C. selected full afterburner and yanked the nose skyward, throwing Cheetah into a near-vertical climb.

"You mean ANTARES outguessed you?" Patrick taunted as he clung to his handlebars in the steep climb.

J.C. didn't take the bait. "That was my fault. I performed like any pilot would if he sees a bogey below him. Well, enough of that. No more predictability."

Fighting in the horizontal, DreamStar, it seemed, was unbeatable—but DreamStar had only one engine and was less powerful when fighting in the vertical. In spite of Cheetah's weight penalties she was still a powerhouse when it came to dogfighting in two dimensions.

"Laser to standby. Radar to transmit," Powell spoke into the voice-recognition computer. It acknowledged his commands and gave presentations of his emitter and weapons status on the displays in the cockpit.

Cheetah was nearing the top of the altitude block when J.C. suddenly rolled her into a wild backward loop. "I'm betting he didn't have time to break out of that hover and follow us up here. I'm betting he's still right where we left him . . ."

J.C. had let the nose just barely fall through the horizon when the holographic diamond again appeared on the windscreen. "Tally ho." He didn't wait for the computer to acknowledge the radar lock-on but centered the electronic crosshairs on the icon. "Target, now. Arm missile. Launch missile."

The computer acknowledged. *"Radar missile launch."*

"Fox two, fox two for Storm One," Powell called over the interplane frequency. "Storm One descending through forty thousand. Head's up, partner."

"Fox four for Storm Two," came the reply. "Seven o'clock, one-half mile . . ." And then the voice added, "*Partner*. Heads-up."

Still inverted, Powell looked to his left, and right off his tail, also inverted, following as if it was Cheetah's shadow, was DreamStar!

"But I've got a lock-on . . ."

"On a cloud of chaff," Patrick said. "When you made your zoom, he must've popped a dozen bundles of chaff and climbed up with you and stayed on your tail. You just shot a Sparrow missile into a bunch of tinsel."

J.C. rolled wings-level and lowered his oxygen visor with an exasperated snap. "The guy's right *on* today."

Patrick checked the fuel readouts, did a quick check of his equipment and warning lights. "Looks like forty minutes to go, J.C."

Powell gave Patrick a thumbs-up. "Storm flight station check, lead's in the green with forty minutes to joker"—"joker" being the code for the minimum fuel reserves necessary on a normal training flight, about fifteen thousand pounds.

"Two has twenty minutes, all systems nominal."

J.C. said: "He's sucking gas. He's got a bigger jet, more capacity, only one engine, but half the fuel."

"And two kills," Patrick shot back. "We're not concerned about saving fuel here, J.C. I know you'd give every drop of JP-4 we've got left to get one good shot at him."

"Then turn me loose, let's get to it."

"I want you to be the fox this time, J.C.," Patrick said. "I want him on the pursuit."

"Fine, but open 'em up this time. Let's see what the boy wonder over there can *really* do."

J.C. had a point. They had really not pushed DreamStar to

the edge of the envelope. And if there was anybody who could really force DreamStar to perform, it was J. C. Powell.

"All right, J.C., you got it. But don't break the bubble . . ." Patrick lined it out. "This time lead will be the fox. We're coming up on the southeast corner of the area. Lead will come left heading three-zero-zero toward the center. Two, give us fifteen full seconds—then start your pursuit. Stay heads-up. Lead's coming left . . ."

J. C. Powell turned hard left. Patrick had time to grab hold of his handlebars before being squashed into his seat by the turn. J.C. stayed on the northwesterly heading for five seconds, then rolled inverted and pulled the nose earthward, pushing the throttles to full power, aiming the nose directly for Lookout Peak twenty thousand feet below.

Patrick watched as the altimeter readout clicked down faster than he'd ever seen it before. "I swear, Powell, you have got to have some kind of death wish"—Patrick's attention was drawn to a blinking red warning light near the radar altimeter, which read the distance between the ground and the belly of the jet. "Watch it!"

Powell checked his threat receivers—no signals from anywhere. He began to level off, pointing Cheetah toward a wide cleft in the jagged peaks below. "Colonel, if I stay at high altitude with DreamStar he'll hose me again. Let's see how he does in the rocks." He hit the voice-recognition computer switch—"attack radar standby," and threw his jet into a screeching right turn, arcing around the rugged peaks. "Fifteen seconds—he should be in his turn toward the northwest by now." Powell selected a flat valley in the desert, staying as close to the rocks as possible. Patrick stared out the top of the canopy expecting the tops of Cheetah's twin tails to scrape along the face of those rocks any second.

J.C. rolled out of his steep turn, passing only a few hundred yards from a lone craggy butte. "You're going to wait down here for him to come after you?"

"Not exactly, sir." He steered Cheetah into the narrow valley he had selected, set the autopilot, then began searching the skies far overhead. "Wondering why I selected thirty-nine thousand feet back there?"

"It's a higher altitude . . . better fuel economy—"

"Contrails."

Patrick followed J.C.'s pointing finger out the top of the canopy. Far above, they saw a thin white line against the dark blue sky, heading northwest. "You think I never listen to the morning weather briefings?"

"You're always asleep."

"I always manage to catch the contrail forecasts. The center of the vapor level was thirty-nine thousand feet. That's where we left him and that's where he is."

Patrick took a firm grip on the handlebars. J.C. had aimed Cheetah for the center of the southern ridge of the Shoshone Mountains, in the center of Dreamland's southern restricted area, and now was moving the throttles up to full afterburner. Ten seconds later they were at Mach one and building . . .

*Attack radar on . . . spherical scan . . . radar off . . .*

James checked in seconds over a half-million cubic miles of airspace for Cheetah. His superconductor technology allowed the power of a standard fighter's nose radar to be transmitted into an antenna the size and thickness of a playing card so that the antennae could be spread out all around DreamStar's skin instead of located only in the nose cone. A thousand of such micro-miniature radar arrays made a complete spherical sweep of the sky within two hundred miles of the aircraft. But except for commercial and civilian aircraft outside Dreamland's restricted airspace, the radar scan came up negative. Cheetah had disappeared!

ANTARES immediately suggested a data link with Dreamland's powerful ground-based surveillance radar, but James squelched that idea. Although DreamStar could integrate data from a variety of outside sources, he'd been ordered not to use them—and McLanahan could detect the link with his equipment on Cheetah. Never mind, he wouldn't need outside help to find Cheetah.

A pause as ANTARES weighed alternatives to an outside data-link, then suggested a ground-map scan.

Nothing. The Shoshone Mountain range was bright and prominent directly below, surrounded by dry lakebeds and nonreflecting sand. DreamStar's high-resolution radar picked out power lines, roads and tiny buildings scattered all across the desert floor. Nothing moving faster than sixty miles an hour anywhere within range.

James shut down the scan. Cheetah was obviously hiding in the Shoshone Mountains somewhere, probably ridge hopping among the rocks, staying in the radar clutter as much as possible. But this was supposed to be an air-to-air attack. Powell was screwing up big-time.

James mentally ordered another spherical radar sweep of the skies. McLanahan would probably direct Powell to climb out of the low-level regime, and then he'd—

ANTARES broke in with its warning: *"Radar contact, directly below and climbing."*

ANTARES suggested a roll and a ten-G push-over to an emergency descent. But just as James ordered the maneuver he heard on the interplane channel, "Fox four, Zero-One, three-niner thousand. Underneath you, Ken." Powell had already started shooting . . .

What was happening? Why didn't he see Cheetah coming? The questions brought spikes of pain that shot through his head and reverberated through his body. For the first time that James could remember, DreamStar had no options. The pain intensified as he continued polling the database, hunting for answers—

Abruptly the confusion that had lasted only a few seconds ended as DreamStar's sensors continued to track Cheetah. Suddenly the pain in James' head disappeared and he found himself presented with a series of maneuvers.

DreamStar inverted and began a tight descending vertical roll. If Cheetah was in a high-speed climb underneath him, J.C. would be out of airspeed at the top of the climb and would have to go inverted and begin a descent to regain lost airspeed. Now DreamStar had the power advantage. All it had to do was complete the roll and Cheetah should be dead ahead and directly in his gun sights.

But as James hit the bottom of the roll the G-forces reached their peak. Air tubules in the legs of James' flight suit inflated, which helped force blood back into the upper part of his body, but it wasn't fast enough. James' vision went to a gray-out as blood was forced out of his brain, then darkened completely as he lost consciousness.

ANTARES detected the elevated blood pressure and the interruption of theta-alpha. The computer immediately lowered the back of James' ejection seat so that his head was below heart level to improve blood flow back to the brain. Oxygen shot into

82          DALE BROWN

his face mask as he fought to regain theta-alpha. With his face mask flooded with oxygen, his breathing was slowed, making him feel light-headed.

It took a few seconds more for James to take control of AN-TARES again. He countermanded the computer's suggestion to raise the seat upright—he would need several more hard turns before he could get within firing range of his adversary and he'd be in less danger of blacking out if the seat-back stayed down. He began a hard seven-G turn back toward Cheetah, but by then he had lost his advantage. Cheetah was in a dive at nearly Mach one.

DreamStar pulled in six miles behind Cheetah and James tried for a radar lock, but Cheetah executed a vertical scissors and darted away—even though Cheetah did not have DreamStar's sophisticated high-maneuverabilities her large foreplanes and temporary speed advantage allowed her to execute such a move. DreamStar easily performed the same inverted vertical scissors to pursue. Cheetah had moved out to nine miles by then, and James ordered the throttle into min-afterburner in the descent to catch up. With the throttles up in the steep descent, the lighter, aerodynamically cleaner DreamStar fighter quickly regained the speed advantage.

*Closure rate five hundred knots,* ANTARES reported. James "heard" the stream of computer-generated reports as if he was listening to the sound of his own breathing. *Range seven miles. Action: High-maneuverability configuration, maintain speed advantage, ANTARES infrared pursuit, deactivate attack radar, laser lock, attack, close to gun range, attack, constant AOA wing mode, maintain gun range, attack.* The messages began to repeat, informing him of altitude, closure rate, weapons status, external heating, stress factors, power demands, air-conditioning faults. James accepted ANTARES' engagement suggestions— the computer had already decided how the battle would be fought several minutes in the future—why not let it go?

Using its infrared tracker and laser rangefinder, ANTARES had predicted the moves Cheetah could make in its present flight attitude and airspeed and had devised an attack for those maneuvers. There were also reversals Cheetah could make, and ANTARES had computed how to defeat them. The final moves of this aerial chess game were now being played. Cheetah was making a hard left turn, but DreamStar had the cutoff angle and the power advantage. DreamStar did not need to snap over in a hard bank to make the kill—her high-maneuverability canards and strake flaps pulled the laser rangefinder onto target and held it there. Cheetah tried another hard turn, this time to the right, but the XF-34's guns were locked on solid now—Cheetah was just burning up airspeed in each high-G turn. DreamStar was flying "uncoordinated," sideways and downward at the same time—

Suddenly James heard McLanahan over the interplane channel: *"Storm Flight, knock it off, knock it off! Storm Two, pull up!"*

*Ground-map radar,* James immediately ordered. The phased-array radars snapped on . . . revealing a sheer rock cliff no more than a thousand feet away and straight ahead. Cheetah had flown directly at two tall buttes, diving and banking away just before reaching them. ANTARES faithfully computed the deadly news—DreamStar would impact in exactly eight-tenths of a second.

Which was like eight minutes to the ANTARES computer. James canceled high-maneuverability mode and threw Dream-Star into a hard left bank. DreamStar's large canards and computer-controlled rudders kept her nose from pushing in the opposite direction in a hard turn, and she slipped between the twin towering buttes. ANTARES reported the data from the ground-mapping radars: DreamStar had missed the right butte by eight feet.

James cleared the left butte and rolled to the right, only to find Cheetah directly in his gunsights less than two miles away. He quickly lined up on him, switched to his twenty-millimeter cannon to activate the gun camera and called, "Fox four, Storm Two, your six-o'clock."

*"I said knock it off!"* McLanahan ordered. "Storm Flight, route formation, station check. Weapons on standby. Move."

James raised his ejection seat back out of the reclined anti-G setting and activated the radars that would help keep DreamStar in formation with Cheetah. "Two has twelve minutes to joker, all systems nominal."

"Lead's in the green, nine minutes," Powell reported.

"Storm Flight, right turn heading zero-four-three, direct beacon red five at ten thousand feet." Powell executed the turn, and DreamStar stayed with him in route formation.

"What the hell happened, Ken?" McLanahan said as they rolled out on the new heading. "You passed out of theta-alpha for a few seconds but you pressed the attack anyway. We watched you side-slip behind us right into that butte. You almost got yourself killed and destroyed—"

"I had contact with the ground at all times," James lied. "I was conscious during the entire attack, except at the bottom of my loop when ANTARES took over. I had clearance between the obstructions." Another lie—James would not soon forget the rivulets of ice and the lichens he saw growing on the sides of the rock . . . he was that close to it. If Patrick hadn't yelled out . . . "I had the last shot after passing between the buttes," he insisted, "and I processed the shot before you called—"

"Save it for the debriefing," Patrick said, "and the data tapes. Storm Flight, fingertip formation. Prepare for penetration and approach."

DreamStar and Cheetah were now to demonstrate their landing abilities. Powell redeemed himself for his poor takeoff. Keeping Cheetah in perfect balance, he guided the fighter to a pinpoint landing and stop within five hundred feet—he could have landed Cheetah on an aircraft carrier without the use of a tail hook or arresting cables. But DreamStar's landing was even better—it was as if the one hundred-thousand-pound fighter was a bee alighting on a flower. The combination of the large canards, mission-adaptive wings in their long-chord, high-lift configuration and thrust-vectored nozzles, all controlled by the fastest "computer" extant—the human brain—and James had DreamStar stopped within four hundred feet of touchdown, a hundred feet better than Cheetah.

Hal Briggs replaced the phone in its cradle and turned to General Elliott, who was watching the landing through binoculars from on top of the portable control tower. "Those Russian birds are still several minutes from their flyby," he said. "Good thing our guys landed early—"

"The hell it is. They even knew when the test was supposed to terminate. If they had landed on time the satellite would've been right there taking pictures and there'd be nothing we could do about it." He ran his fingers through silver hair that, Briggs noted, seemed to grow thinner every year. He turned toward Briggs. "I want you to pull out all the stops, Major." The tower controllers as well as Briggs caught Elliott's ominous tone. "Do whatever you have to do to find the leak on this installation. You have an unlimited budget, unlimited resources, and very little damn time. Search anywhere and everywhere. Go off-base with federal authorities to investigate—I'll back up whatever you do. I want answers, Briggs. Fast."

Briggs knew that at least off-base activities needed huge amounts of cooperation, hard to come by, from state and federal law enforcement. He needed some clarification, but now wasn't the time to ask for it.

Elliott thumbed the microphone on the command frequency. "Storm Flight, taxi without delay to parking. Over."

"Lead."

"Two."

Ken James had been disconnected from his fighter and hoisted out of DreamStar's cockpit. He was wheeled to an air-conditioned transfer van that drove McLanahan, Powell and him to the project headquarters, where the special flight suit was removed from James's sweat-soaked body. The two test pilots went to the locker room nearby, said not a word to each other. They were dressing when Patrick McLanahan walked up to them. "Both of you are off flying status as of right now."

James exploded. "What?" There was panic mixed in with outrage, but it belonged to Maraklov the agent, not to Ken James the pilot. Lately Maraklov had felt his alter ego taking over—this pronouncement jolted him back, some . . .

"There's a difference between evaluating the aircraft and pushing the limits to the danger level. You two cross it every time you fly together. I'm grounding you both until I figure out what to do about it."

"Then give me another chase pilot," James said quickly. "Canceling all flying isn't the answer, Colonel."

"You're assuming that Powell is the problem," and he started to walk away.

"There are a dozen guys who can fly Cheetah," James said behind him. McLanahan turned. "There's only one who can fly DreamStar. Me." James realized how this sounded and tried to soft pedal . . . "The project doesn't have to suffer, sir. I think we can continue . . ."

"Listen, hotshot, I've got six guys training to fly DreamStar.

I'd rather put this project on hold for eight months until they're ready than risk that machine and this project. You read me?''

"Yes, sir. Sorry . . ." Six guys, eight months . . . More of a shock . . . time was running out . . .

"Meet me in my office at two o'clock, both of you. The data tapes should be ready to review by then. General Elliott might be interested in what they show.''

Patrick McLanahan was waiting for an elevator up to his office when he felt a tap on his shoulder. He turned irritably. "Yeah?''

"Charming," Wendy Tork said. "Next time I'll do that with a pole.''

He managed a grin and kissed her.

"Long day, Colonel?''

"You could say so.''

"You had an early morning go, didn't you?''

The elevator arrived, and Wendy cut off the exchange, knowing that Patrick would not talk about his project in an unsecure elevator. She waited until they returned to Patrick's office and he closed the door. An electronic grid in the walls and floor, she knew, would activate when that door closed, which would offset wiretapping or any other electronic eavesdropping.

He dropped into his chair. "I've got two pilots butting heads.''

"I like them both, but I can see both of them being very competitive.''

"At least James comes right out and says it. He's an excellent pilot, and he's the only one right now who can fly DreamStar. J.C. sits there putting on an innocent and contrite act, but he's as big a show-off as James.'' He rubbed his eyes. "I can't afford to lose either one of them, but . . .''

"What will happen if you transfer either one of them?''

"I can get someone to fly Cheetah—hell, I've got enough hours, *I* could probably fly the thing. If I ground James, the project gets set back six months, maybe more. I told him I have people training on DreamStar. Who can be sure when or if they'll be ready? I exaggerated some to take him down a bit. Brad Elliott will hit the roof. The security leaks—or what seem like security leaks—are already turning him sour.''

"Are you saying you'll have to transfer or reassign J.C. if they don't get along?''

"I suppose. But Ken knows he's the only guy who can fly

DreamStar. That would be like giving him a veto in almost every other matter that comes up during this project from here on. I ended up grounding both of them, until I have a chance to talk to the general.''

Wendy smiled. ''Eight years ago you were just a captain, responsible only for a radar scope in the belly of a B-52 bomber. Your big worry was your next emergency procedures test. Now, you're a lieutenant colonel in charge of a hundred men and women and two of the hottest jets there are . . . We'll put it all on hold for a few hours. I'm here to take you to lunch. You probably don't have time to take the helicopter to Nellis, do you? General Elliott has *got* to have some decent restaurants built out in this desert.''

McLanahan grabbed his flight cap. ''We've got time to take the Dolphin into Nellis if we hurry. I'm not expected back until—'' The desk phone rang. He looked at it, then at Wendy.

''Let's go.''

She smiled, shook her head. ''You'd hate me in the morning.''

He picked it up. ''McLanahan . . . Hi, Sergeant Clinton . . . The data tapes are ready now? . . . Yeah, we had some maneuvers that may have overstressed the canards . . . how bad? All right, I'll be right down.'' He dropped the phone back on its cradle. ''I knew it. My two hotshots may have bent DreamStar some. I've got to take a look and prepare a report before this afternoon's meeting.'' He circled his desk, gave Wendy a hug and a kiss. ''Rain check?''

''Anytime.'' Especially on flying days, she reminded herself, dates were always crap shoots. She watched as Patrick hurried off.

''Wendy?''

She turned and found Captain Kenneth James standing behind her. His bright blue eyes sparkled, as usual. He was a head taller than Patrick, less broad-shouldered but still athletically built. They looked at each other for a moment. Be honest, Wendy Tork, she told herself, Ken James is a charmer. Plus he has a magnetism, a sort of masculine grace, and he's not arrogant or cocky or condescending. He also had this way of making a woman feel special, as if he had been waiting all his life just to say hello to her.

She had met him eighteen months earlier when he first joined the High Tech Advanced Weapons Center at Dreamland. He

wasn't like many of the other jet jockeys in and around Nellis
Air Force Base. Getting an assignment to HAWC was the top
achievement for any young officer, and most new test pilots
seemed not to be able to let you forget it. Not Ken James. He
took the time not only to get to know senior officers but non-
commissioned officers as well. He seemed just as interested in
the engineering and technical parts of the job as the flying. He
quickly established himself as the best pilot at HAWC . . . a
scholar of flying and aerospace, not just a participant. Quite a
package. And no wonder they had become good friends.

"If you're looking for the old man . . ." he paused at the
intentional slip, smiling winningly . . . "I mean, the colonel,
he just left."

"I know."

Maraklov understood, as everybody did, the special relationship between Wendy Tork and the colonel. Which, of course,
was the chief reason for making her his friend. And it was not
exactly hard duty. Tall, good figure, brunette with hints of gray,
still foxy for a woman going on forty. But be careful, he reminded himself. And helped himself do that by remembering
the research on her. A considerable dossier: Wendy Tork, Ph.D.,
electrical engineering. Chief of DOPY5, the cryptic office symbol of HAWC's Director of Penetration Aids, Project Y5—the
Megafortress Plus, the super-bomber and strategic escort battleship. This woman had developed many of the twenty-first-century
electronic jammers used on American military aircraft, including new jammers that could electronically defeat infrared- and
laser-guided missiles. She had built a jammer the size of a toaster
that could disrupt much of the known electromagnetic spectrum
for thirty miles in every direction. Considered a sort of outsider
in HAWC because of her former independent contractor status,
she tended, except for the colonel, to keep to herself. Scuttlebutt
said that started after the mysterious Old Dog mission that she
and most of the brass at HAWC were involved with eight years
before. It seemed to have affected her more than the others.

In any case, possibilities here, he had decided, for a special
source of information. "How about lunch?" he said easily.

"Do you have time? Don't you have a meeting this afternoon?"

"I think they'd rather not have me at this particular meeting,"
he said, pretending embarrassment. "I'm sort of in the dog-

house. But it's my lucky day. I don't have to be back until late, and I have a pretty lady to share lunch with. If she'll give me a break.''

For a moment she hesitated, then decided why not . . . they were, after all, friends.

If there was room on one of the shuttle helicopters that flew hourly to and from Dreamland, it was open for anyone at HAWC to hop a ride for the twenty-minute flight back to the "mainland," as people from Dreamland called Nellis Air Force Base. But Maraklov had a different plan. When he climbed aboard the Dolphin transport helicopter he went forward and spoke briefly with the crew. Then as the helicopter touched down on the broiling tarmac at Nellis, Ken touched Wendy's arm as she began to unbuckle her seat belt.

"We're not there yet," was all he said.

The helicopter lifted off once again and sped northwest. Ten minutes later it touched down on another military-looking airfield. As they left the chopper Wendy noticed the helicopter landing pad had been painted with a stylized Indian thunderbird symbol.

"What's this?"

"One of the best-kept secrets in the Air Force," he told her. "Indian Springs Air Force Auxiliary Field. This is where the Air Force Aerial Demonstration Team, the Thunderbirds, work and practice even though the unit is based out at Nellis. You know, the Thunderbirds do a lot of demonstrations for the brass and foreign dignitaries here—not to mention that the Thunderbird pilots get the best of everything, being on the road so much— so Indian Springs is an oasis for them out in the middle of nowhere. The base is open to all military personnel, but that's not widely advertised. I knew the Thunderbirds were gone so I asked the Dolphin pilot to get us permission to land."

They walked past immaculately groomed desert landscaped yards and freshly painted buildings to a Spanish-style stucco building with red tile veranda and cane-ceiling fans. They were seated at a table on the veranda.

"I've been coming to this *area* for eight years," Wendy said, "and I've been at HAWC for three years, and I never knew about this, or only vaguely if at all. Patrick and I are both so busy . . ."

He nodded. "The Dolphin pilot enacts a toll for side trips—I think he's got a Chris Craft on Lake Mead that needs refinishing. Guess who'll get asked to help."

"Well, it's delightful and I'm glad we came."

"You'll have to tell Patrick about it, if he doesn't know."

"Believe me, I will. I know how important his project is to him, to all of you, but I do wish he'd slow down just a little. Actually I don't know if he'd take advantage of a place like this even if he knew about it."

"Sure he would . . . but he is a busy man."

Over lunch he said, "Most people here thought you two would be married by now. You've known each other for seven years? Eight?"

"Eight," Wendy said. "Ever since the Old Dog flight . . . God, has it been that long?"

"That must have been some mission," Ken said. "I've heard about it, of course, but mostly scuttlebutt. I'd like to get the whole story from you someday."

She only nodded, smiling briefly.

"Well, the colonel joined HAWC a short time after that project . . . ended. What about you? You didn't join HAWC until recently, a little before I came here."

"I still had a civilian position in my own laboratory. Much as I wanted to, I couldn't just leave or get reassigned to Dreamland. I started to work more closely with General Brad Elliott and his group, but my home base was still in Palmdale. I visited every chance I could, but Patrick and I were still apart. When they announced the reactivation of the Old Dog project I saw my chance and got assigned to HAWC permanently. What I didn't expect was that Patrick was going to shoot up like he did under General Elliott. Don't misunderstand. I knew Patrick was good, very good, but when I first met him he was, believe it or not, thinking about leaving the Air Force and working his family's business in Sacramento. It's hard to get promoted by just being the best navigator around. And that's all I thought he wanted to be. I was wrong. In two years he went from being just another non-technical test-flight crewmember to a project director. He got promoted so fast you'd think there was a time warp. One year after becoming director of his first program he was made chief of a full-blown flight-test development program with state-of-the-art hardware. In another five or six years he'll

have his first star and probably be chief of HAWC soon after."
Through most of this she'd been looking down into her napkin.
Now she looked up abruptly. "God, if I sound like I'm complaining, I'm not. Or I don't mean to. Just for the record, I
happen to love McLanahan even more than I respect him . . .
Okay, enough of me, what about you? There's an army of ladies
in Vegas waiting to snag someone like you. When are *you* going
to take the fall?"

He laughed. "The right woman is hard to find, even in the
sun belt."

"But you're having a good time looking, right?"

"I confess . . . I'm not suffering." It had gone well, very
well, he thought.

The waiter reappeared with the check and a message.

"Helicopter's on its way," he said. "We should head back."

As they waited on the helicopter landing pad a few minutes
later, Wendy took a deep breath of warm yucca-scented desert
air and looked out at the mountains surrounding the tiny base.
"I enjoyed it, Ken. The lunch and the talk. I haven't gone on
like this for a long time. Thanks."

"We'll do it again some time."

"I don't want you to spend too many weekends refinishing
some chopper pilot's boat."

"Believe me," he said, watching her, "it's worth it."

Yes, she could be another source of information . . . on the
new ECM gear, for example.

# =2=

**East Las Vegas, Nevada**

*Wednesday, 10 June 1996, 2007 PDT (2307 EDT)*

MARAKLOV DIDN'T RETURN to his condominium in the east Las Vegas subdivision of Frenchman Mountain until late that night. The early start and the intense flying had taken their toll, and the lectures he had received from McLanahan and Elliott during the long debriefing didn't help.

He locked his car in the carport, took his briefcase, and trudged upstairs to his second-story entranceway. He wasn't able to get on the Dolphin helicopter back to Nellis and had to bump along in the electric shuttle bus from Dreamland to Nellis. Then twenty hot, steamy minutes on the freeway just to go four exits in bumper-to-bumper traffic. Maybe a cold shower, a cold beer, a casino run.

He punched his code in the lock's keypad. The door was already unlocked. He pushed it open a crack. No lights on. The lights were programmed to come on in the evening when the door was opened. Someone had overridden the programming. Someone was inside his apartment . . .

All he had for a weapon was his briefcase. Maybe he should have gotten out of there and called the cops, but the less he had to do with them, the better. He reached through the door and flicked on the lights. He strained against the faint street noises behind him but heard no sounds from inside. He flung the door open, letting it bang on the doorstep. Still no sounds.

He slowly crossed the threshold, looked down the hallway into the living room. Stereo, TV, VCR all in place. Of course, a burglar was the last thing he was worried about—he'd almost welcome that. There were others more dangerous.

He moved to the fireplace, picked up a poker and made a fast search of the apartment. Nothing. No sign of forcible entry, nothing missing. One more place to check.

He stood up on a stool and removed six books from the top shelf of the built-in bookshelves in the living room. On the back wall of the bookshelf he pressed on a board and a section sprang open about a half inch, revealing a panel hiding the steel door to a small wall safe. He had installed the safe himself shortly after moving into the apartment—one of the precautions he had taken years earlier, along with carefully arranging things in his drawers to help detect intruders, when he got his assignment to Las Vegas.

Instead of opening the hidden panel fully, he reached behind the panel with one finger and disconnected a wire leading from the door inside to the combination safe behind the panel. The wire was connected to an incendiary device inside the safe; if the door had been opened more than a finger's width the device inside the safe would incinerate the contents. The safe obviously had not been—

A faint, lingering odor. Cigarettes, or an old stale cigar. He did not smoke. He turned . . .

"Sloppy of you, Captain James." The voice came from behind him. He braced along the wall. A quick leap, a hard push and—

He heard the metallic *click*, and another voice: "Come down from there, Maraklov, before you hurt yourself, or worse."

Slowly he replaced the trip wire on the safe's hidden panel, closed it and stepped off the stool. Turning, he saw two men, one standing directly behind him holding a weapon, the other man seated on his sofa. He noted the weapon—not a pistol but a taser, a gun that shot small electrified darts. The darts, connected to the taser gun by a thin wire, were charged with twenty thousand volts at low amperage with the press of a trigger, causing instant paralysis. The dart only buried itself a fraction of an inch into the skin, but with a strong electric current from the taser short-circuiting the victim's nervous system, he was powerless to pull or shake it free. A potent weapon—quiet, effective but non-lethal. That last encouraged Maraklov. They wanted him, but they didn't want him dead.

He turned to the man on the couch. Henry Kramer was fiftyish, short, bulky but not fat, thin dark hair and beady eyes. He was dressed in a dark ill-fitting suit with a thin dark tie, looking too much a caricature of what he was—a conniving Soviet KGB agent, far more serious and dangerous than he looked.

"What are you doing here, Kramer?" Maraklov tried to control his anger as he also looked at the younger man with the taser. "Put that away. Look, you people are crazy to come here—"

Moffitt, the younger agent, lowered the taser but did not put it down. "We were worried about you, Captain James. And you should have locked your door before searching your apartment. We not only were able to get behind you, but found out where your safe is. You seem to be getting complacent . . ."

Maraklov forced himself to answer. He locked the front door, closed the blinds and began replacing books on the shelf. "Now what are you really doing here?"

"Captain," Kramer said, "people are displeased. The information stream you have been supplying has become a trickle."

"I told you why in my last report. Perhaps you've not had time to read it. They're cracking down on security at HAWC like never before. Major Briggs has been given the widest leeway to stop security leaks, and they've been promised full cooperation from the federal judges in Las Vegas. That means not only searches of military property at Dreamland and Nellis but legal searches of private non-military residences too. They could even get, probably have gotten, authority for wiretapping, no-knock searches and arrests at any time. I thought it was Briggs in here already."

"We have connections at the federal courthouse," Kramer said. "If there has been cooperation between the military and the federal courts I'm sure an anonymous tip to the Las Vegas papers will stir things up. A report about widespread military authority to search private residences? They go crazy over such things here. Especially the press. Our *perestroika* caught some of it." Kramer studied Maraklov. "Are you saying tightened security is your reason for not supplying one photograph of the XF-34A fighter plane or its components in over three weeks?"

"They haven't let me be alone with the plane or its technical data since then. I was able to be alone with a set of the aircraft's technical layouts a week ago but discovered an unusual change in the schematics that I didn't understand . . . a dogtooth modification to the wings—''

"A what?"

"A special wing design that creates two differently performing wing structures on one surface. On a mission-adaptive wing like DreamStar's, the dogtooth might increase its capabilities twenty percent."

"A significant development indeed," Moffitt said. "Why didn't you report this? If they left you alone with the specifications why did you not photograph them?"

James turned to him. "Because I think it's a fake. Or it could be. A plant. A trick. They may want me to see the dogtooth wing—and then they want to see if the dogtooth shows up on a satellite photograph of a Russian fighter at Ramenskoye or in a supposedly secure telephone message to Moscow. The dogtooth looks like a notch in the wings and is visible on satellite photography. It's not just me. I'm sure they showed something different to each of the key players—a tail modification drawing to Powell, a nozzle mod to Butler . . . Major Briggs probably cooked up dozens of these tests for security leaks. Mine was the dogtooth . . ."

"You are sure these are fakes?"

Maraklov had to pause, even though he knew the hesitation, no matter how slight, would make Kramer and Moffitt suspicious. Then: "No, I'm not sure. The dogtooth design has been incorporated in numerous advanced fighters—it would be possible for our designers to use a dogtooth wing without stealing the idea from the Americans. But I'm sticking to my hunch: I think the dogtooth wing is a fake. And *that's* why I didn't report it."

"But if it is not," Moffitt said, "our own designers will be that much farther behind in our designs. Don't you think you should have at least reported this finding? It would have alerted our agents that Dreamland has stepped up counter-espionage and security effects. Don't you think that is worth a report?"

"You people don't seem to get it. If I report this stuff as soon as it happens it makes it that much easier for Briggs and his men to hunt down the source of the leaks. I won't jeopardize my cover or anyone else's over something like this. I must be able to choose my own time, place and method of reporting activity and transferring information."

"It seems you are becoming a bit squeamish, Captain James," Moffitt said.

"You work with Harold Briggs and half the military security police breathing down your neck all day . . ."

"That's enough. Both of you."

Moffitt pressed. "I think Captain Kenneth James is becoming comfortable in his surroundings," Moffitt said. "He makes a lot of money, he has a nice apartment, attractive American women. Could it be he does not want to risk losing his rich life for the Soviet people?" Moffitt suddenly switched to Russian. "Remember, Captain? *Your* people? The ones you swore to protect? The ones who gave you this mission—"

"Speak *English*, dammit," Maraklov ordered. Anger and confusion were in his voice. Moffitt looked at him with some surprise.

"Is it possible," Moffitt said in Russian, "you don't understand what I'm saying? Or is this just a part of your little game, Comrade Maraklov—?"

*"Don't use that name."* Maraklov lowered his voice, but the anger was in his face. "My name is Kenneth James. I'm from Rhode Island. I'm an officer in the United States Air Force—"

"You are Andrei Maraklov," Moffitt pressed in Russian. "You are a Russian KGB deep-cover agent assigned to the top-secret Dreamland research laboratory in the United States. You—"

"I said speak English . . . neighbors, they could hear you—"

"Can *you* hear *me?* What are you . . . an American or a Russian—?"

*"I don't understand a goddamned word you're saying."* He turned to Kramer. "You'd better get him out of here, Kramer, before he ruins the whole deal."

"You can drop the act," Moffitt said, this time in English. "This is not a test in your Connecticut Academy—"

"That is enough," Kramer told Moffitt, on his feet now. "Stop trying to bait him—he is trained to deny any knowledge of his past." He turned to James. "But our North American Command is concerned, *Kenneth.* You give them less each contact. We were ordered to investigate. An immediate face-to-face meeting was necessary—"

"Well, you've had it. I'll get the information, but tell them I'm the only one who can control how and when I do it. It's possible the level of security intervention is so high they'll be forced to terminate the extensive searches soon. Otherwise no one will be able to get any work done. But we've got to take it easy. We can score a major espionage coup if we stay patient."

He did not add that it was no act, his not understanding their Russian. He really had lost it . . . He hadn't quite realized it himself until now . . .

"We cannot afford to be patient," Kramer said. "Our charge is to use every means to acquire this technology and build the DreamStar fighter plane. Our development of the aircraft must be parallel with the Americans'. A great deal has been invested to put you in place. For two years they've been patient. Now progress has stopped. Something must be done—"

"If you're going to pressure me like this, I might as well stop everything before I'm caught. You might as well bring me in—" He shocked himself, saying it. It was the last thing he wanted.

Kramer looked at him. "An interesting suggestion."

"What? The Command *is* considering bringing me in? That's ridiculous—"

"Why?"

"It's what they call biting off your nose to spite your face. I am in place here, Kramer. Fully in place. It would take another generation to develop another agent placed so high in the top-secret American military research organization . . ."

Kramer took a deep breath. "The lack of information was the last deciding factor, but the idea had started long ago—"

"What idea? What the hell is going on?"

"Our project to build our own version of the DreamStar aircraft was virtually doomed from the start. We knew about the F-15 fighter known as the Cheetah, of course—the Americans took it to the Paris Air Show. We built our own version shortly afterward, and with improvements it has become almost as formidable as the American version. But when we discovered what the Americans had planned for the *next* generation of fighter aircraft . . . no one believed that thought-controlled aircraft would become reality in his lifetime. Now suddenly the Americans had one in the air. Naturally we did everything in our power to learn about the technology, including authorizing the plan to put you in the Dreamland research area—"

"I don't see the problem, Kramer. Everything's going as planned."

"Not exactly."

Moffitt broke in. "Those big thinkers in Moscow can't understand the data. They've got it piled up to their ears but can't
really decipher it. They have linguists, but the Americans use
words that have no Russian equivalents. They say there are electronic parts made of atomic elements . . . I think that's it . . .
that even some of our best scientists have never heard of.

"So it takes time. In a couple of years everything they don't
understand will be commonplace. Right now they have superconducting circuitry that weighs two hundred pounds—in two
years or less they'll be putting superconductors in wrist-
watches—"

"Our people will not wait two years to build a thought-
controlled aircraft," Kramer said. "In two years the Americans
can replace their European-based fighter force with these
DreamStar aircraft. With an aircraft like DreamStar opposing
our forces, our conventional-force superiority will be offset. We
got them to reduce theirs and still leave us with an advantage.
A plane like this DreamStar can undo all our advantages."

"But DreamStar is still in its early research phase. It won't
be ready for production for two years. They *might* have a first
operational unit by the year two thousand but even that's an
optimistic estimate." He looked at Kramer. "Whoever's feeding
you or the Command this stuff is dangerous, Kramer. They're
trying to push the Kremlin into making a false move, one that
could be embarrassing to the government and deadly for us."

"What would you know about it?" Moffitt broke in. "You
don't even speak Russian any more. You've lost touch with your
country. What would you know about what goes on in the Kremlin?"

Maraklov sidestepped the accusation to firmer ground. "I
know that someone has overestimated the progress on the
DreamStar project. You listen, Moffitt—this project is as much
mine as it is yours. It's *my* life if I get caught. I can be executed
or spend the rest of my life in prison. If you get caught you pull
out your diplomatic credentials and get yourself kicked out of
the country. Big deal—"

"I said enough," Kramer interjected. "Orders have already
been received from Moscow. They are what prompted and jus-
tified this meeting with you. The Ramenskoye Research Center
in Moscow reported that your data, although revealing, is still
not sufficient for them to reconstruct the XF-34 DreamStar air-

craft. It is much more than copying the design and the components—it seems they do not have the basic knowledge of the technology involved with the craft. They estimate several years before we will have the technology to duplicate the design with sufficient quality to match the present-day aircraft." He paused, then: "The KGB has been ordered to obtain the XF-34 DreamStar aircraft from the American High Technology Advanced Weapons Center. Captain James, you are to steal DreamStar and bring it to Moscow."

"*Steal* DreamStar? Impossible! Crazy!"

"Nevertheless, we have been ordered—"

"I refuse. You would jeopardize all this work, all this time, in an attempt to get a fighter out of the most heavily defended military reservation in the United States?"

Moffitt finally let out what he had been thinking . . . "He has been turned, just as I thought—"

No hesitation, James rushed Moffitt, feinted with a right roundhouse to Moffitt's head, stepped closer and put him on the floor with a practiced kick in the groin.

He could hear Kramer trying quietly as he could to order him to stop. He wasn't listening. As Moffitt crumpled unconscious on the carpet, Maraklov grabbed the poker and held the point on Moffitt's throat . . . "The first thing I'll do if they ever turn me," he said, pressing the sharp iron shaft into Moffitt's Adam's apple, "is hunt you down and kill you. Don't give me an excuse to do it before then."

"*Enough,*" Kramer said, and grabbed away the poker.

Breathing heavily more from the adrenaline pumping than from any exertion, Maraklov told Kramer, "He knows too much. Any man with as little common sense who can name agents in the western United States is a major security risk—"

Kramer looked at Moffitt, back to Maraklov. "We are not unaware of the problem . . . diplomatic visas are being delayed. I need him, for now." He noted Moffitt was beginning to come around. "Now sit down, we need to talk about this."

James went to the kitchen, brought two cans of beer. As he opened his can he said, "The idea is impossible, Henry. I can't conceive of a plane leaving Dreamland without authorization and make it away from American pursuit. Never."

"Dreamland is like a safe, correct?" Kramer said, looking as Moffitt rolled up to his hands and knees, groaning and shaking his head. "The defenses there are to keep people *out*, not to keep anything *in*."

"Wrong. The defenses around HAWC can do both." James stood and went into his bedroom, coming back moments later with a Las Vegas visual navigation chart. He unfolded it and set it on the coffee table.

"Here. R-4808 North. Groom Lake. Emigrant Valley Road, military only. Where the road meets the south edge of Groom Lake is where the four aircraft hangars, offices, labs and weapons storage areas are. Garrisoned right there with the hangars are a detachment of twenty combat-ready security police with dogs, around the clock. They have armored vehicles, automatic weapons, guided missiles—they could hold off a regiment. Keeping one plane from leaving the security area would be a simple exercise. The buildings are surrounded by a twelve-foot concrete reinforced cyclone fence. You have to get past all that just to get into position for takeoff on Groom Lake . . . But let's say I make it and I managed to take off. Now I've got to get out of Dreamland.

"Dreamland has this country's only fixed surface-to-air missile sites. They're on Bald Mountain, on the Shoshone Mountain range, Skull Mountain, Timber Mountain and Papoose Peak. First-generation Rapier missile batteries, complete coverage from surface to thirty-thousand feet within R-4808N. Single mobile sites are located on Tonopah Test Range to the northwest and China Lake to the southwest."

Kramer took a sip of beer, grimaced at the taste, then pointed to the chart. "So, you do not go that way."

"There is *no* way to go. There are a dozen Navy and Air Force fighter bases within a thousand miles of Dreamland, and I guarantee you, every one of them will launch aircraft in pursuit. If each base launches only two aircraft, that still means there will be twenty-four advance fighter planes looking for me. Where do I run, Kramer?"

The agent studied the chart. "Mexico is only three hundred miles away . . ."

"True. But the Mexican government would allow American fighters in hot pursuit across their borders. And that's *if* DreamStar could get across the border. There are four fighter-interceptor squadrons between here and Mexico, and both the

Americans and the Mexicans conduct all-altitude surveillance of the airspace near the border. It's impossible, Kramer.''

"You've had your nose in that plane too long. Relations are strained almost to the breaking point between the United States and Mexico," Kramer said. "The U.S. pressing Mexico on re-payment of debts has turned them cold. And the pro-U.S. gov-ernment is being accused of selling out the country to Uncle Sam. The Soviet Union is the beneficiary. We have a carefully developed cordial relationship with the rest of Central America too. We can ensure that any American pursuit of DreamStar across the border will not be allowed, that Mexican military forces will interdict American aircraft penetrating their airspace. They're very proud, you know . . . Anyway, that should allow you time to evade pursuit. After that we can arrange an emer-gency refueling somewhere inside Mexico.''

"Even if all you say about their feelings toward the U.S. is true, the Mexican government would never agree to *that*.''

"There are thousands of square miles of the interior that could serve as a temporary base," Kramer said. "From what you have described, your DreamStar aircraft could land and take off any-where—on a dirt road, a grass strip, a plateau—''

"I'm not going to try to land DreamStar on some grass strip . . .''

Kramer looked closely at him. Maraklov sounded like he was talking about a personal possession. He filed it away and decided not to use it for the moment . . . "We have Mexican transport companies on private contract—they of course do not know that their contract is with the KGB—that can fly our teams in to service your aircraft without arousing the authorities—''

"And then what? I can cruise a little over a thousand nautical miles on full tanks—no air combat, no external stores, no low-altitude flight. I'd have to cross the Gulf of Mexico undetected to be able to make it into . . . Cuba. That's impossible. We both know the U.S. can track every aircraft over the Gulf unless it's down at low altitude. I'd be jumped after I went a hundred miles. If I tried to make the flight at low altitude I'd flame out before I made dry land.''

"Then forget Cuba, go somewhere else . . . Nicaragua, for instance.''

"Nicaragua? Great. And how do I get *out* of Nicaragua? The

U.S. Navy would seal off that whole region tight. I'd fly right
into a trap—"

"You are being very uncooperative—"

"I'm being realistic. I'm not going to consider this deal without a detailed plan. You expect me seriously to consider this
half-baked idea? I'm supposed to put my life on the line for some
bureaucrat's wet dream—?"

"The North American Command has issued its orders—"

"And I'm countermanding them. I'm the commander of the
Dreamland mission. That gave me the authority to decide how
my operation proceeds. Unless I receive specific orders I am not
going to consider any such operation." He stood, facing Kramer
and now Moffitt, who had struggled to a seat. "I'll keep you
updated on any developments—about DreamStar, security and
the rest. Meantime, don't contact me in my apartment again."

"You'd better reconsider," Kramer said. "An order from
Moscow cannot be ignored. You know that."

"I'll *consider* it, but only when the situation justifies the tre-
mendous loss of a trained agent in place. As of now, it doesn't.
All that's indicated is that the operation proceed with extreme
caution, which is what I intend to do." He motioned toward the
door. "Now get out. And you'd better not return directly to your
consulate in Los Angeles. There's a good chance that you'll be
followed." He paused, then said: "Go visit your buddies in
Mexico."

Moffitt left first to check the parking area and driveway for
tails. Kramer paused inside the front door.

"I will report what you have said. I warn you, do not separate
yourself from the Command any further."

Maraklov said nothing as Kramer looked out the door, got an
all-clear flash from Moffitt's cigarette lighter, went out.

After the agents had departed, James locked and bolted the
door—and suddenly felt as if he was suffocating . . .

His mind's eye could see unmarked cars roaring up the driveway toward his stairway, plainclothes FBI, CIA and DIA agents,
led by Major Hal Briggs, coming up the stairs, kicking in his
door, hauling him away in handcuffs, thrown into the back of a
van with Kramer and Moffitt, who must have been arrested already . . . The federal authorities would interrogate them, sep-
arately, of course. He could trust Kramer to keep silent, insisting
that he and Moffitt be returned to their consulate, but he was

positive Moffitt would spill his guts just for an opportunity to get back at him. He would be identified as a Soviet agent and taken into custody, charged with espionage. His career was ruined. He'd never fly DreamStar again, never experience the indescribable experience of becoming one with that amazing machine . . .

Should he just sit here waiting, or escape right now? Activate his safe's incendiary device himself so as to not risk Briggs or one of his men discovering the trip-wire and disarming the device? He'd take the money he'd hidden, go to Mexico, maybe further south, maybe to the wild interior of Brazil, out of reach of both American and Soviet intelligence units. He'd contact Moscow in hiding until he could be sure he was safe—from his own people as well as the Americans . . . He removed two of the books on the top shelf in front of the hidden wall safe. In case someone tried to break in he could reach in between the books, pop open the hidden panel and activate the incendiary device. He then shut off the lights, poured himself a glass of Scotch whiskey and sat down in the darkened living room.

Half a glass of Scotch later, sleep finally overtook him, but he was not getting any rest. For the first time since those first few months of his new life in America, Andrei Maraklov as Ken James remembered what real fear, real terror was.

Now that she was a senior civilian contractor on a small military installation, Wendy Tork's hours were much more regular than in the early years when she had spent days in her laboratory, working on some irritating software bug. She remembered slaving over a computer terminal, staring at a screen full of lines of computer code. In the early eighties debugging software and artificial intelligence-based computerized programmers were practically non-existent—human programmers, sometimes armies of them, had to disassemble a compiled routine, then read thousands of lines of code to try to find an error. One never knew if the error was on the screen or a hundred lines away or in a completely different sub-routine. Once the error was supposedly found, the code was reassembled into its compact faster form and run. It was a wonder anything as sophisticated as the B-52 I Old Dog's electronic countermeasures equipment, Wendy's first major military project, ever worked in the laboratory—not to mention in combat. Now she had computers that designed

other computers' programs, and computers that checked and de-
bugged *those* computers' work, and a master computer that supervised all of them. Her job was mostly telling her computers
what their jobs were and receiving reports from them on their
progress. What had taken dozens of scientists and engineers years
to accomplish now took one person a few days. Because of all
that she could keep regular hours, enjoy a four-day work-week—
most of the industrialized nations of the world had switched to
a four-day work-week by 1994—and spend more time at home.

But if most of the world had gone to the four-day work-week,
the military, especially military aviators, had not. It seemed to
go double for Lieutenant Colonel Patrick McLanahan. Since
Wendy joined HAWC and moved in with him, her nights had
often been long and lonely. Patrick had become an important
administrator and commander at Dreamland research center, and
it was not long before Patrick would call if he *was* going to be
home more or less on time.

Tonight was one of those. He'd be home around seven, an
early quitting time. Wendy doubted it and was right. She was
wide awake when he finally did arrive home. He walked quietly
as he could to the bedroom, tried to fumble his way, undressed
without the lights.

"Hi."

He threw his flight suit into the laundry hamper. "Sorry if I
woke you."

"Tough day?"

"You could say so." He went into the bathroom briefly, then
got into bed beside her. At first as he moved she pulled back
with a shiver. His *whole* body was like ice—he'd taken one of
his two-minute Navy shower sponge baths.

"You are *freezing*."

"Sorry." She allowed him to curl up beside her, his warm
breath on the back of her neck, punctuated by a kiss, then another. A moment or two later he asked, "How was your day
today?"

"The morning was busy—I finally finished the software up-
grades for the Megafortress. Pretty quiet this afternoon, I came
home early."

"Sorry about standing you up for lunch."

"That's okay. It looked like you were pretty busy. Anything
serious with the plane?"

"No. Some over-G warnings showed up on the computer readouts, but we couldn't find any damage. We worked right through lunch. I could have used some of the Nellis O-Club's roast beef after that flight this morning."

Wendy hesitated. "I didn't have lunch at the Officer's Club."

"You ate at the cafeteria at HAWC?"

"No . . . I had lunch at Indian Springs."

She could feel his body tense. "Indian Springs? What's at Indian Springs?"

"The Thunderbirds Club."

"You went to Indian Springs Auxiliary Field? How did you get *there*?"

"The Dolphin dropped us off."

"Us?"

"Ken James and me."

"Ken James took you to Indian Springs Field for lunch? Why?"

"Why not? I've never been there before. Ken made it sound like he goes there all the time."

"I didn't know the Dolphin ever stopped out there . . . Honey, I don't think it would be a good idea to go to Indian Springs again."

"Why?"

"Well, it's a restricted-use field. It's supposed to be for official business—"

"Sure. Whatever you say, Patrick, but Ken seems to go there a lot."

"Indian Springs is the fighter pilot's hangout. But Ken also has a habit of stretching the rules. I don't think there's any problem, but let me check it out . . ."

"Okay." She hoped it ended there. She was already sorry she'd brought it up at all.

"Damn it, if James can even find a rule, he'll stretch it every last inch he can."

"He says you grounded him and J. C. Powell today."

"He said that? Damn it, that stuff is supposed to be classified. He and J.C. came close to killing each other this morning. I should bust them both but I can't. J.C. is maybe the best pilot in the unit and one of the few that can keep up with DreamStar in our flights. And James is the only one that can fly Dream-Star with any effectiveness. I can't even officially reprimand them

until the project is declassified. I don't know if it's possible to
train another pilot for DreamStar, and I can't afford to put this
project any more behind schedule. So, I gave them a slap on the
wrist . . . they're only grounded until the next scheduled sortie.
Next week . . . So to celebrate, James takes you to lunch at a
restricted base and I have Elliott giving me the hairy eyeball all
afternoon . . .''

"I'm sorry. It's just that—"

"And I'm sorry to sound like a pompous, jealous . . . except
when you're concerned . . .''

And then she was in his arms, and there was no more time—
or need—for talk.


# Dreamland
*Thursday, 11 June 1996, 0712 PTD (1012 EDT)*

"You realize, Patrick," Dr. Alan Carmichael said, "that nothing at all may happen."

McLanahan and Carmichael were in a special steel-lined
chamber early the next morning. More a huge underground vault,
the chamber contained the original laboratory version of the AN-
TARES thought-controlled flight-and-avionics system. Concerned more with performance in the early years of the project
than size, the chamber housing the ANTARES system was massive—the size of a basketball court. The complex was controlled
by its own super-fast CRAY computer that, even though encom-
passing state-of-the-art very high-speed integrated circuits,
artificial-intelligence electronics capable of performing billions
of computations a second, was larger than a refrigerator and had
to be cooled with liquid nitrogen at two hundred seventy-five
degrees below zero.

In the center of the three-story chamber, dwarfed by massive
banks of electronics gear and environmental system ducts, was
an F-15 single-seat fighter simulator. It had none of the advanced
multi-function displays and laser-projection devices of Cheetah—it still used ordinary electric artificial horizons and pneu-
matically driven altimeters and turn-and-slip indicators, and most
of those were barely functioning. The ejection seat was an old
Mark Five "Iron Maiden"–type seat from the early 1980s, stiff,
straight-backed, and uncomfortable, its special anti-G padding

and shoulder harnesses having been cannibalized for spare parts long ago.

Patrick was not secured in that ejection seat, but neither was he free to move. He was wearing an early non-cushion version of Ken James' metallic-thread flight suit. It was far more bulky than the actual operational model, with thick fiber-optic bundles interwoven all around the suit, circuit boxes attached to every conceivable inconvenient point on Patrick's body, and, unlike James' suit, this experimental model had no integrated cooling systems built into it. Icy blasts of cold air were directed on Patrick to help keep him cool, and when the skin's resistance was completely unbalanced by sweat and vascular dilation on account of the extreme temperatures inside the suit, the session would be ended.

"I've been trying out this system for a few months now," Patrick said. "My brainwaves or whatever they are . . ."

"Theta signal threshold complex."

"Yeah, right. Anyway, they should start working, shouldn't they?"

Carmichael shook his head. "If it was that easy, we'd have a squadron of ANTARES pilots now. We don't *fully* understand how ANTARES works, how the neural interface is achieved. We can get it to work but we're not sure, for example, why it works with James and nominally for you and J.C. and not for anyone else. We're getting closer to the answer but it'll still take some time."

"What is it with James?" Patrick asked. "I can't mentally control an itch on the back of my neck. He can control a two million dollar fighter at Mach one."

Carmichael ran a hand up his forehead and across the top of his bald head—even though it was the style of the mid-1990s for some men to have a shaved head, Carmichael came by his naturally, involuntarily. "The sheer strength of his mind is enormous. The ANTARES interface is another addition to his mental gymnasium, so to speak. He's strengthened by it every time he uses it. We're learning a lot from him."

"But he's not any smarter than anyone else at HAWC."

"I'm not talking about intelligence . . . stop squirming." Carmichael motioned to one of his assistants, who ran a cool towel over Patrick's sweaty face. "He's quite intelligent—an I.Q. of well over one-fifty. But what counts more is that his mind is fluid, adaptable, agile. Are you at all familiar with taekwondo, Patrick?''

''Taekwondo? You mean martial arts?''

Carmichael nodded as he scanned an instrument panel beside the simulator. ''A special form of the martial arts that combines karate, kung fu and judo—James happens to be a black belt in taekwondo, by the way . . . did you know that? Almost made our Olympic taekwondo team. It's not an offensive, attack-style of fighting. In taekwondo the attacker is *allowed* to engage—as a matter of fact, there are few moves in taekwondo that can be performed unless in response to an attack.''

''Get to the point, Alan.''

''The point is, James' mind works much the same way as the taekwondo style of combat. He allows the flood of information created by ANTARES to invade him. He opens up his mind to it—exactly the opposite of the normal reaction to such an invasion. Most of us build barriers against such an onslaught—James allows it to move in, even expand. But he doesn't surrender to the information that bombards him. Once ANTARES unlocks the inner recesses of the mind, the ones we have no conscious access to, he's somehow able to reassert his conscious will. At first it's little more than gentle mental nudges, but then he's able to control ANTARES, steer the mass of information his way. It's the mental equivalent of a single tree changing the course of a raging river.''

''You're talking in riddles.''

''For a good reason.'' Carmichael's features turned stony. ''I've already said there's a lot we don't understand about ANTARES. We're tinkering with this technology before it's fully understood, but neither of us has the authority to stop it. I just hope I can learn enough before some disaster happens.''

He studied McLanahan. ''That was meant as a disclaimer, Patrick. You've been strapping this stuff on a few times a month now, probably with faith in me and all this high-tech government equipment. We use it because it works. Period. We don't know why it works, and so we won't know what happened if something goes wrong.'' He picked up a very large, bulky helmet with all sorts of cables and wire bundles leading to the banks of computers below. It was a much larger version of the ANTARES flight helmet, obviously not designed for flight—its wearer would be completely immobilized by its sheer size and bulk. "Still want to subject yourself to this, Colonel?"

Patrick shrugged. "Here's where I'm supposed to say 'I regret I had only one brain to give to my country . . .' "

"You're the project director, it's not your job . . ."

" 'It's not my job.' That's the most over-used and annoying phrase in the Air Force." Patrick stopped, looking at the menacing ANTARES helmet as if it was some medieval torture device, then nodded. "I need to know how it works. I need to understand what it does to the pilots that I'll order to wear this thing. Let's do it."

Carmichael and an assistant proceeded to lower the heavy helmet onto Patrick's shoulders and fasten it in place.

The helmet was very tight and heavy. Once attached to the clavicle ring on his flight suit the device pressed down on his breastbone and shoulders like a heavy yoke. The superconducting antennae pressed unmercifully on several spots on his head and neck, corresponding to the seven areas of the brain that were constantly being scanned and measured by the ANTARES. There was a smoked glass visor in the helmet, but Patrick could barely see anything outside. The thick rubber oxygen mask that enclosed his mouth and chin was hot and almost suffocating.

After a few seconds, Patrick could hear the faint click as the tiny headphone in his helmet was activated. "Patrick? All set in there?"

"Check the oxygen flow. I'm not getting any air."

"You've got a good blinker and all switches are set," Carmichael replied. Just then Patrick's oxygen mask received a steady flow of cold, dry air. "I gave you a shot of oxygen. I can't give you too much or you could hyperventilate. Try to relax. Start anytime you're ready."

Patrick sat back in the hard ejection seat and began the relaxation routine taught to him by Carmichael over a year earlier when he'd first begun experimenting with an ANTARES trainer. He began the familiar process, letting the spurts of pure oxygen in his mask slow his breathing and force the tension from his body. In his case it was his toes and calves that seemed to be perpetually clenched, like a swimmer on the starting block, as if he was always trying to grip onto something. It was refreshing to feel how good his feet felt after forcing them to relax.

Slowly, he worked his way up his body, ordering each muscle group to relax. One by one he managed to relax his body parts, letting the stiffness of the metallic flight suit support him in the ejection seat. He knew he'd have to reexamine his leg muscles now and then, but after dozens of these sessions his relaxation technique was getting much better.

"Very good," he heard Carmichael say, "much better. Minimal beta activity. Very steady alpha complex."

"It seemed to go easier this time," Patrick said. "How long did it take?"

"You did pretty well, only one hundred and thirty minutes this time."

*"Over two hours . . . ?"*

"Easy, easy, maintain your alpha level . . ."

Patrick fought to regain his body-relaxation state, despite his sudden confusion and disorientation. "I thought I was getting better, it seemed like just a few minutes."

"A good sign. You enter a state of altered consciousness, much like hypnosis but more so. Losing track of time is a good sign—if you had said it took two hours it would mean your mind is still focused on external events like time—"

And then he felt it, a tiny jolt of electricity shooting through his body. It was like diving into an ice-cold pool of water—the jolt didn't start or stop anywhere in particular but it shocked his entire body all at once. It was not totally uncomfortable, just unexpected—more attention-getting than painful, like a mild static electricity shock. His body jerked at the first jolt, and he fought to relax his body again. Surprisingly, he found it much easier to relax this time.

"Just relax, Patrick." Carmichael sounded as if he was calling from the bottom of a deep well. "You're coming along fine. Relax, Patrick . . ."

Another jolt of electricity, harder and deeper this time, creating a shower of sparks before his eyes. There was real pain this time, completely different from the first. Patrick remembered the three deadman's switches rigged to the seat—one on each hand and one on the back of his helmet, where all he had to do was release his grip on the handles or move his head in any direction and the power to the simulator box would immediately cut off. The electricity was still there, still intense . . . all he had to do was hold on long enough to command his hands to move . . .

"Remember taekwondo, Patrick," he heard a voice from nowhere say. ''Allow the fight to come to you. Accept it. Be prepared to channel it.''

Another surge of energy, powerful enough to make Patrick gasp aloud in his mask. There was a brief shot of oxygen, but now it felt blasting hot, like opening an oven door . . .

''Don't fight the energy. Relax . . .''

''The pain . . . I can't stand it . . .''

''Relax . . . regain theta-alpha.''

Another intense wave of electricity, and he involuntarily grunted against the pain. The shimmering wall of stars washed over him—but they were different this time. The lights remained, and amidst ever-growing jabs of pain throughout his body the stars began to coalesce into images. Faint, blurred, unreadable—but they were not just random stars. Something was forming . . .

Here was finally something to latch onto, to grasp and hold firm, for no other reason than to preserve his sanity and keep from screaming out in terror and pain. When the pain increased in severity, Patrick let it hit him head-on, enduring it long enough just so he could reexamine the sparks of pain floating in his mind's eye and form another concrete mental image.

He was experiencing what James already knew and had gone through . . . His whole body was on fire. The pain was continuous, but so were the sheets of light—and they were definitely taking shape. Flashes of numbers, some logical, others unintelligible, zipped back and forth in his subconscious mind. The images were beginning to organize themselves—there was now a sort of horizontal split-screen effect, with darkness above the new horizon and floating, speeding numbers and polyhedrons below. He could hear short snaps of sound, like a stereo receiver or short-wave radio gone haywire.

The sounds were the key. Patrick now began to concentrate against the pain, channeling it along with the confusion, trying to slow the jumble of numbers and letters and shapes into one positive, concrete form. With each push in the desired direction, ANTARES would give him a burst of pain for his trouble. But the pain didn't matter any more. There was an objective now, a goal to reach, if a childishly simple one . . . three letters—A, B, C—and one device—the simulator's intercom.

The letters were becoming as large as the lower half of the split screen, but they were finally becoming solid, aligning themselves beneath the blackness. Soon they remained steady, and even began to slide away from the center toward the—

"Patrick?"

The voice was like a distant, relaxing whisper, like a church bell off in the distance, like the friendly toot of a boat horn on the Sacramento River back home. "Powell?"

"Welcome back, boss. Have a nice trip?"

"Not sure. I've got a lot of pain. Dr. Carmichael?"

"Right here."

"How long did it take this time?"

"You tell me."

Patrick tried to remember back through the interfacing period, through the waves of rolling pain, through the fleeing mental images. "I felt out of control, it must've taken another hour."

"Try nine seconds," J. C. Powell said.

"Nine *seconds*?"

"Nine seconds on the dot from the moment you went into theta-alpha," Carmichael said happily. "Even faster than Ken's ever done it, although he doesn't take two hours to get to theta-alpha."

Patrick tried to turn his head, but found it impossible—it was as if two red-hot hands held his head cemented into place. "How can anyone function with all this pain? I feel like I'm being microwaved, I can't move a muscle."

"All I can say is that Ken James is different. He's also been using the ANTARES system for a long time. Don't focus on the pain, and don't worry about being able to move around. Relax and try to enjoy the ride."

A moment later, Carmichael clicked the intercom back on. "We've repositioned the simulator at thirty-five thousand feet and five hundred knots. Take the aircraft when you're ready, Colonel."

Patrick concentrated as hard as he could on the image of the instrument panel. He had managed to slide the image of the intercom channel off to the left, but the rest of the panel was blank. Like a television screen with nothing but snow across it.

Okay. Aircraft attitude was important. Maintain control. Keep the airplane flying.

Instantly an oval drew itself on the upper half of the cockpit image. It was sitting horizontal across the windscreen, a deep white line bisecting it, forming a horizon. In the exact center of the oval was a wide T, representing the aircraft.

"Release me," McLanahan said.

The T jumped up and to the right just as Carmichael said, "You're moving."

Patrick concentrated on keeping the T in the center of the oval. Slowly the T moved back in the center.

"Good start at least, now where the hell am I going?"

The oval disappeared, replaced by the image of a long ribbonlike street on the upper portion of the screen. The street was straight for a distance, but Patrick could see a few gentle twists and turns in the distance. At the bottom of the screen was a tiny picture of a jet fighter plane—it appeared to be resting right on the road.

"Hey, I've got the flight-plan depiction."

"Good," Carmichael said. "That's a major flight image. Follow it as long as you can. How's the headache?"

"It went to splitting migraine long ago, Doc, but as long as I keep my mind off the pain it'll be okay."

Keeping the simulator flying upright was more difficult without the artificial horizon, but no amount of mental effort would bring it back, so Patrick used the visual cues on the road itself— the recommended altitude was to surface on the road itself, which also represented the proper pitch and bank to follow; as long as he kept the little fighter model on the road he would be following the computer's recommended flight path. The road's curbs represented the allowable lateral flight corridor to follow, and tiny signposts represented planned turn-points and recommended altitude-changeover points.

As long as the "road" was straight and flat, the ride went well. But after a few moments the road began to make small left and right turns, and the going got much tougher. The tiny fighter icon penetrated through the road several times, porpoising up and down through the recommended altitude block, and Patrick had to apply harder and faster corrections to keep the plane steady.

"Stabilize, Patrick," he heard from J. C. Powell.

"I'm trying." The fighter icon slid through the right wall of the road, skidded sideways, then entered an uncontrolled spin.

"Let the computer recover the plane," Powell said. "Don't try to fight it."

Patrick forced himself to go along. He concentrated on the surface of the computer-generated road without thinking about the aircraft control. Suddenly he knew that ANTARES had placed both mission-adaptive wings in high-lift modes and deployed both dorsal and ventral sets of rudders to maximize directional control. The fighter icon dove through the right side of the flight path depiction, but by rapid lift, power and drag changes under precise computerized control, the fighter was soon out of its uncontrolled spin and stabilized in a steep dive. A few moments later the fighter slowly leveled out and returned to its desired flight path once again.

"Good recovery," Carmichael said. "ANTARES will always try to save the aircraft whenever possible, but you still have to tell her where you want to go, even in an uncontrolled situation."

After a few minutes of straight-and-level flight to get his confidence back, Patrick accomplished a few turns, with bank angles and altitude changes mixed in. "I think I've got the hang of it again," Patrick said.

"Still have those headaches?"

"Now that you mention it, yes, but they seem to become less noticeable when I'm concentrating on something else."

"Good. How about some formation flying? We can put up another fighter and let you fly off his wing for a while."

"No, bring up a hostile."

"Getting cocky now, aren't we, sir?" Powell cut in. "Five minutes ago you couldn't make a ten-degree turn without going out of control. Now you want to do some dogfighting."

"That's what the damned simulators are for, J.C. Bring up a high-performance model, too."

"You got it."

There was no change in the simulation after several long moments. He was going to ask if they had put up a hostile when he remembered—none of his fighter's offensive or defensive systems had been activated—

But that realization was enough. Immediately a computer synthesized voice announced, *"Attack radar activated . . . electronic countermeasures activated . . . tail warning systems activated."*

And there it was, a laser-projected image of a fighter in the upper right corner of the screen. Patrick immediately commanded the simulator's laser-tracking system to lock onto the hostile aircraft, and deactivated the attack-radar as soon as the laser had illuminated the target. But it wasn't fast enough. Flight data on the hostile aircraft showed that it had altered course and was on a head-on intercept course. The hostile had detected Patrick's brief radar emission and had turned to start the fight.

As the two aircraft merged into a nose-to-nose flight path, Patrick was suddenly flooded with information. His laser-projection screen was filled with electronic depictions of dozens of options, only a few of which included a full head-on pass. There were so many options that he lost count. His headache had come back full-force now. Beads of sweat obscured his vision, blood pounded in his ears. He was conscious, his mind still sharp, but the pain, intermingled with hundreds of bits of data predicting the outcome of dozens of maneuvers by both aircraft soon overwhelmed him.

The ANTARES simulator suddenly went inverted and pulled a heart-stopping eight-G descent. The simulator had activated the all-aspect radar as it descended, and Patrick could easily "see" his pursuer descend with him. But that was what ANTARES had been expecting. The simulator continued its inverted loop, using its high-lift canards to pull the nose up through the horizon. The throttle went to max afterburner as he went through the vertical—and Patrick had no doubt that he would have been squashed like a grape if he had been in a real jet aircraft.

As the nose dove through the horizon once again he found that the pursuer had become the pursued. Whatever kind of aircraft they had put up against him, it couldn't keep up with ANTARES. Patrick found himself directly behind his adversary, and ANTARES had already armed four laser-guided missiles and was waiting for orders to fire. Patrick issued those orders a split second later. Meanwhile, ANTARES had switched to the internal twenty-millimeter multibarrel cannon and was waiting for orders to fire as the simulator closed in on the hostile, but there was no need to open fire—all laser-guided hypervelocity missiles had hit their target.

"Ground position freeze," Dr. Carmichael ordered. Patrick heard footsteps on the catwalk around the simulator's cockpit as the cockpit indicators and the deluge of information in his head abruptly ceased. "Patrick, this is Alan Carmichael. Can you hear me?"

He found himself frozen in his seat, unable to move a muscle and barely able to move his lips . . . "Yes."

"We're going to disconnect ANTARES. Hold on."

Even though the simulator had stopped, the pain inside Patrick's head was steadily increasing. He could feel the fighter doing some lazy rolls and spins but didn't have the strength to issue the orders to maintain straight and level flight.

"I . . . I'm losing it . . ."

"Let it go, Patrick," Carmichael said. "You're off the simulation. Relax. Don't worry about the controls."

It was like telling a man hanging from a cliff to cut his lifeline. Slowly, using every last ounce of strength he had, Patrick fought the urge to counteract the spinning aircraft. But the more he let go, the more he was drawn to what was happening. As the aircraft's altitude began to decrease, he received the aircraft altitude, "heard" ANTARES' reports on terrain, engine performance, structural loads. The closer the fighter got to earth, the faster the reports came. When the fighter shot through five thousand feet above the ground, ANTARES recommended it take over. Patrick did not respond. At three thousand feet above ground, ANTARES issued the order to eject. Again, Patrick ignored it.

He just sat, transfixed, as he listened to ANTARES' neural "screams." The computer was literally begging its human occupant to do something, anything, to save it. The more the computer blasted McLanahan with pleas to issue an order to recover the aircraft, the more the pain increased and the more Patrick was unable to do anything. Carmichael was reaching to disconnect the superconducting helmet from Patrick's clavicle ring when the simulator slammed into the ground at nearly two thousand miles per hour.

When the helmet was finally lifted from McLanahan's shoulders and Carmichael saw his face, even he was shocked. McLanahan's face was a mask of pain, as in a man tortured to the very brink of tolerable agony.

"Patrick, snap out of it, it's over!" Carmichael was yelling at him. Technicians had jumped up on the catwalk beside Carmichael, and others were unfastening the shoulder harness and loosening the heavy connectors and relays on the metallic flight suit. Carmichael looped an oxygen mask over Patrick's face. "It's over. Wake up, dammit."

No response. Technicians were still trying to remove the heavy metallic gloves from Patrick's hands and undo the suit's fasteners, so Carmichael bent lower over Patrick and put his ear to his mouth.

"He's stopped breathing, cut the suit off—" An assistant hesitated, looking first at Patrick, then Carmichael. "I said cut it off. *Now*." Carmichael put his face up to Patrick's. "Patrick, wake *up*, dammit!" He grabbed a pair of steel cutters from one of the technicians as the medical team removed the oxygen mask and inserted a breathing tube down Patrick's throat, then grabbed a wire-laced seam of the suit and made a twelve-inch cut across Patrick's chest with the ultrasonic cutting tool, exposing the thin cotton undergarments soaked with sweat. "Get a heart monitor over here!" He ripped open the underwear to expose McLanahan's chest. He studied Patrick's face as the airway was opened and the respirator started. The eyes were fluttering and his facial muscles were contorting as if he was locked in some nightmare.

Then J. C. Powell stepped up on the catwalk opposite Carmichael. As the electrocardiogram leads were taped to McLanahan's chest, Powell took Patrick's head in his hands and bent down to his left ear:

"Wake up, boss," he said in a firm, quiet voice. "Show's over, Colonel. Wake up."

Carmichael studied the EKG readouts. "No pulse. Straight line. Charge the defibrillator units. Powell, get out of the way."

J.C. ignored him. "Patrick, this is J.C. I know you can hear me—"

"He can't hear a damn thing," Carmichael said. "Now stand clear—"

"He can hear me, he knows what's happening. He can feel everything. He just needs a direction—"

"What the hell are you talking about?"

J.C. did not answer. Instead, he placed both of Patrick's hands on his shoulders, moved as close as he could and said, "Patrick, you *can* hear me. Listen to me. ANTARES isn't in charge now. *You* are in control. *Wake up*."

"He's been unconscious too long, Powell," Carmichael said.

A medical technician handed him two electrode paddles from the heart defibrillator. "He'll die if we don't revive him."

"And you'll kill him if you shock him with that." Powell grabbed Patrick by his flight suit and hauled him up as far out of the ejection seat as he could. "Patrick!" he yelled. "Dammit, I said *wake up*!"

Suddenly McLanahan's eyes popped open. He grabbed J.C.'s shoulder in a crushing grip that made Powell wince. He gagged on the resuscitator tube in his throat and pulled it out, his chest heaving. Powell eased him back into his seat.

"Sinus rhythm," one of the paramedics reported. "Blood pressure high but strong. Heart rate, respiration okay."

"Are you all right?"

"I . . . I think so."

Carmichael started to put the oxygen mask on his face again but Patrick pulled it away, choosing instead to take occasional deep breaths from it.

"It was so weird," McLanahan said, trying hard to control his breathing. He seemed to be reviewing, reliving, the scene in his mind. "I was watching the intercept and the kill like a spectator. ANTARES was doing it all. It was like I wasn't there. But I felt the pain building and building, and ANTARES getting stronger and stronger, along with the pain. But then I couldn't do anything. I knew I still had to fly the aircraft on ground-position freeze but I couldn't give any commands. I felt like . . . like a million hornets were buzzing all around me. I knew those hornets carried information, important data I need to know, and I knew something was wrong. But with the pain, I couldn't do a thing . . . Suddenly everything was dark and empty. I didn't have a body, just a brain. I was searching for a way out of a room but didn't know how I was going to make it even if I found an exit. That's when I heard J.C.'s voice. The more I heard, the more . . . alive I felt. I followed his voice . . . I . . ." His voice began to fade, and he appeared to be drifting off to sleep.

"Get him out of here," Carmichael ordered.

He woke up later to find Wendy Tork asleep in a chair beside his bed, a magazine across her lap. "Wendy?"

She came upright. "Patrick? You're awake! How do you feel?"

"Tired. Thirsty." She poured him a glass of water from a plastic pitcher, then rang for the nurse. "I feel like I've just paddled a kayak across the Pacific." He found he had the strength to sit up and take the cup in his hands. "What time is it?"

"Nine P.M."

"I've been asleep for twelve hours?"

"Patrick, it's nine P.M. on *Saturday.* You've been asleep for forty-eight hours."

The water glass began to tremble in his hands, and he quickly set it on the bedside table. "Was I in a coma?"

"No—well, technically, yes," Wendy said, moving close to him and taking his hands in hers. "They called it extreme exhaustion and depletion. You lost seven pounds while you were in that simulator. You could have hurt yourself even without the strain that . . . that thing put on you. Are you sure you're okay?"

He sat up and took a few sips of water. Nothing was said until he asked, "How long have you been here?"

"I never left. I . . . I wanted to talk some more about the other night. I know how it is for you—"

"Works both ways, kid." He let out a tired sigh and his head dropped back to the pillow. He managed a short laugh. "I think I know why Doctor Jekyll drank his own potions. You want something to be so successful that you'll try anything, even making yourself into your own guinea pig. I never should have strapped myself into that simulator. I wasn't ready for it."

"It must have been terrible."

"It was . . . different," he said uneasily. "I have to give guys like James and Powell all the credit in the world for flying the real thing, never mind the simulator. It's an awesome contraption if you can keep yourself from going crazy."

"Talk about going crazy," a voice said behind them. They turned to see General Elliott and Hal Briggs enter the hospital room. Hal went over to Patrick and clasped hands with him. "You had the whole place going crazy, brother."

McLanahan thought that Elliott looked drawn, tired, as if he hadn't slept in days. His blue blouse was sweat-stained and rumpled, and he seemed to favor his artificial leg more than usual. "How do you feel, Patrick?"

"Fine, sir." A damn lie.

"Takin' a nap for a day and a half, you should be fine," Hal put in.

"We can do that SPO conference tomorrow after I get out of here," Patrick said to Elliott.

"I think we've all had enough for the weekend, Colonel," Elliott said. "I've scheduled a meeting with the senior project officers and the engineering staff for Monday morning. You're on sick leave until then. Clear?"

But something else hung in the air—Elliott was showing more than just concern for him. Elliott turned to Wendy. "Can I have him for a few minutes?"

"Visiting hours are over." She went to Patrick and kissed him. "I'll come by at nine to bail you out." Wendy nodded to Elliott and left. Briggs took a big glass of Patrick's ice water and moved unobtrusively in front of the door, casually but effectively blocking it.

"You gave us a scare, Patrick," Elliott said. Patrick sat up and watched as Elliott began to pace the small room. This, Patrick thought, was not an ordinary get-well visit. "I hope you'll forgive me for suggesting that you train in the ANTARES simulator for this project—"

"On the contrary, General, I *wanted* to do it. It was a part of the project. I think we should continue—"

"You're not expendable. I can't go on using my senior officers for experiments—"

"I'm a flyer first," McLanahan said quickly. "You needed someone with operational experience to see how well a non-ANTARES-trained person could adapt to the system. I was a logical choice."

"We've got flyers lined up around the block for a chance to do that. I can't risk you again. From here on out, no more ANTARES simulator for you."

Patrick was just too tired to argue. "Who then?" he said. He turned to Briggs. "Hal, you've got the latest clearance-list of applicants. Bring the list by my office and I'll—"

"I had a talk with Dr. Carmichael early this morning," the director of HAWC said. His tone was low, somber, like he was delivering a eulogy. "At this stage of the game we could put a hundred men through that system and we wouldn't be any closer to understanding how it really affects the human mind. There are just too many unknowns. And we just don't have the resources to study each and every one of them—"

"All it takes is time and training. I've been working with ANTARES for just a few months—"

"And it nearly killed you," Briggs cut in.

"I flew it in combat after only four months of work," McLanahan said. "I'm not a pilot but I flew the hottest jet in the world with only four months' training."

"It's not the same and you know it, Patrick . . ."

"I've made progress. I've taken the worst that machine can dish out. I can control it now. Besides, I'm an old fart. I'm forty years old. A guy half my age could master that machine a lot easier. Don't judge the whole program because of what happened to me—"

"Unfortunately we must," Elliott said. "We aren't getting the information we need from only one successful pilot in the program. We were hoping the progress you and Powell had made could clear the way for a more extensive ANTARES training program, but now it appears that we can't adequately quantify the experiences of any participant. What happens to you, or rather *why* it happens, is an unknown. We can't have training based on hit-or-miss procedures—we'll end up killing half the trainees."

McLanahan shook his head. "So you're really considering canceling the DreamStar project because of my incident the other day?"

"There are other considerations, which you're aware of. We do spend half a billion dollars a year for a plane that many congressmen may not ever see fly in their lifetimes. They hesitate continuing the funding, especially if there's some pork-barrel projects in their home districts that could get them a political leg up in *this* lifetime . . . And of course there's the security question." Elliott glanced at Briggs, who remained stone-faced. "Our security problems have tended to overshadow our advances. The way of least resistance for these Pentagon officials is simple—terminate the project, continue lower funding levels for research into the ANTARES interface but discontinue all flight operations and plans for development and deployment."

"But DreamStar's up and flying—that's a fact. We've only tried the ANTARES interface with a handful of pilots. We can't give up now."

Elliott nodded. "That's the argument I used, Patrick. We'll have our answer on Monday. Meanwhile, get some rest."

Hal Briggs stayed behind. "J.C. was by to see you, said he'd catch you tomorrow some time. Haven't seen much of James since the test flight."

Patrick shrugged. "He likes to get away from Vegas on the weekends."

A somewhat strained silence, then Briggs smiled and said, "You look like two miles of bad road, Colonel, but it's good to see you up and around."

"I've seen you look better too, buddy," McLanahan said. "The general getting on your case?"

"It's beyond Elliott," Hal said uneasily. "It's even beyond major command level now. Air Force and, I guess, the Joint Chiefs want to keep Dreamland open but close down flight operations for DreamStar—they're more concerned with the setbacks in the operations area. The White House thinks Dreamland is a classified information siphon that flows directly to the Soviets, and they want to close down the whole outfit."

"Which wouldn't look so hot for Dreamland's chief of security."

Briggs tightened. "Look, I hate lettin' the old man down—he took a chance on me ten years ago, and he really stuck his neck out when he made a brand-new major the chief of security at the Air Force's most top-secret research center. I'd hate to repay the guy with a forced retirement because I screwed up."

"I don't think you're screwing up, Hal. We've obviously dealing with very deep, very professional agents at the highest and most top-secret levels of the program. It might be a command-wide infiltration, or even a headquarters compromise, in which case we might never find the ones responsible—"

"It has to be here in Dreamland or Nellis," Hal said angrily, punching a palm with his fist. "The quality of the stolen material, and the speed with which our stuff shows up over there, tells me it comes directly from here, not through headquarters of systems command. I have got to plug this leak before the whole dam bursts wide open."

"Well, keep trying . . . but I do have to say I don't think your idea to plant phony changes in DreamStar's design will help."

Hal looked uneasy. "You figured that out?"

"It wasn't too difficult to notice those changes were out of place, Hal. If they're smart enough to recognize the changes they'll be smart enough to see that they don't make too much sense. With all the other security crackdowns you've implemented, it does smell like a setup."

"If you don't mind, I'll keep it in," Hal said evenly. "Maybe our spy isn't as all-fired smart as you think he is."

"Maybe."

There was a rather strained pause, then Hal asked, "How's Wendy?"

"Fine."

Hal nodded. "She looked great, really great." Again a pause.

"Something on your mind, Hal?"

He took a deep breath. "Hope you don't mind me asking, but . . . how are you two getting along?"

"Jesus Christ, Hal . . ."

"Dammit, Patrick, you know why I'm asking, and you know I wouldn't ask unless it was important."

"So we're peeking into bedrooms to find a spy now, is that it?"

"Easy, pal. You knew all about Elliott's orders to expand the search for these security leaks. I briefed the senior staff and outlined exactly what guidelines I'd follow and what steps my staff would take. Wendy and Ken—"

"What the hell do you mean, *Wendy and Ken* . . . ?"

"Do you know she was seen at Indian Springs Auxiliary Field the other day?"

"Yes, I *know*."

"With Ken James?"

"So what? This is getting far out—"

"You're getting defensive," Briggs shot back. "What's the story?"

"The *story* is they went to lunch."

"At Indian Springs?"

"It's James' little hideaway. It was the day of the last air combat dry-fire test. I was held up by the flight data lab, so James took her to lunch. Apparently he regularly cons the Dolphin pilot into taking him. Any more questions?"

Briggs nodded—that was the same story he'd gotten from the Dolphin pilot. "Patrick, please don't make this any tougher for me—"

"Tougher for *you*?" McLanahan propped himself up in bed, was about to get up but paled and decided against it. "What the hell are you saying? Is Wendy or Ken under *suspicion*?"

"Everyone at HAWC is under suspicion, even the Ops personnel—*especially* the Ops personnel. But when DreamStar's only pilot starts hanging around with a chief scientist from a completely different section of HAWC—who also happens to be the very close friend of the DreamStar project director—a bell has to go off—"

"She *lives* with me, Hal. Come *on* . . ."

"Do I really have to spell this out? What if you guys were having a major league argument? What if she left or you told her to? What if . . . dammit, Patrick, you *know* what the hell I'm talking about."

"I do, and it stinks."

"The leaks started when she got to Dreamland—"

"Which is also when the DreamStar project went operational," McLanahan interrupted.

"It's also the time Ken James arrived."

"Along with a dozen other people," Patrick shot back. "You're spinning your wheels, Hal. Wendy's undergone government security background checks since she was a senior in college. Ken James is an Academy grad. He's undergone far more thorough background investigations than just about anyone at HAWC, including me."

"He's also had a pretty rough family life . . ."

"Which *doesn't* make him a spy. I know all about his past, his father, his mother's suspicious death in Monaco while he was in the Zoo. But the guy's been polygraphed, examined, questioned, investigated and scrutinized on a regular basis by a dozen different agencies since entering the Academy. If he's got a questionable past it would have surfaced by now."

"Well, I've still got to check every scrap of info that's not there, Patrick. You'll end up hurting security, not helping," Hal said, not wanting to press it further at the moment. "Gotta go. I'll see you on Monday."

When the door to his hospital room closed, Patrick felt more alone, more isolated than ever before. Mercifully, his body's total exhaustion forced him to drop into a deep sleep.

• • •

*Ken James was in DreamStar's cockpit. He had no flight suit, no helmet. The canopy was closed and all power was off. He was trying to decide how to activate his fighter without ANTARES operating when a brilliant beam of light hit the cockpit from somewhere on the ramp . . . Hal Briggs was holding a huge spotlight on him. Patrick McLanahan was carrying a bullhorn. Wendy Tork stood beside McLanahan crying. She was motioning to him to come out of DreamStar . . . He lifted the canopy. It weighed only eighty pounds but it would hardly budge. He had to stand on the ejection seat to get better leverage. But as he struggled to lift the heavy Plexiglas windscreen, McLanahan rushed forward, carrying a huge fifty-caliber machine gun. Then Briggs hit him in the face with the brilliant beam from the spotlight and McLanahan raised the machine gun. "Hold it right there . . ."*

James' eyes snapped open. He was confused, disoriented. Then he heard the sounds of footsteps, coming closer, only a few feet away . . .

He scrambled for the tiny transmitter on the nightstand beside his bed—he had rigged the wall safe with a remote-control trigger to incinerate its contents from anywhere in the apartment. With his other hand he felt for the Beretta automatic pistol hidden under his pillow . . .

*". . . Don't go away, because you're listening to the solid gold voice of the solid gold strip, FM one-oh-two . . ."*

Ken pulled his finger away from the button just in time. It was his clock radio, set for the station with the two early-morning DJs with their taped sound effects. The bedroom lights, also preprogrammed to come on when the alarm clock went off, were glaring in his face. Swallowing hard, his ears ringing from tension, he carefully held the hammer of the Beretta with one hand while pulling the trigger, letting the hammer slowly uncock.

It had been another nightmare night, another confused awakening. For the past two nights he had lain in bed, dressed in shorts, shirt, and sneakers, with one finger on the remote-control detonator and one hand on the Beretta pistol beside him. Sleep had been almost impossible. Every noise, every creak, every voice outside shook him awake in an instant, and he would lie there, listening for the sounds of police feet pounding up his stairs or the sight of flashing red-and-blue lights outside his window. Each time he had decided to escape, to get out of town and head off to Mexico before they came and arrested him for

espionage, but he would always talk himself out of it, out of
deserting DreamStar. He would manage to drift off to sleep, only
to be awakened an hour later by another sound. He had managed
only a few restless hours of sleep all weekend.

Now he half-walked, half-stumbled to the bathroom. The tension was taking its toll, all right. He had dark circles under his
eyes, his face was pale, his lips cracked and dry despite the
beads of sweat rolling down his face. He turned the shower on
full cold and stepped into it, forcing himself to stand in the icy
water a full minute before feeding in warm water. He stood
there, hoping that it would wash his nightmares away. It did not.

Still, once into his morning routine, his mind began to analyze
the situation more rationally. He had holed himself up in his
apartment all weekend, afraid to leave but afraid he would be
arrested by military intelligence. The fact that no one had come
to him or called was reassuring. Perhaps no one had noticed
Kramer and Moffitt, the two Russian agents based out of Los
Angeles, at his apartment after all. Maybe Briggs wasn't conducting round-the-clock surveillance of his apartment . . .

His mood was bolstered later that morning as he drove through
Nellis toward the waiting area for the shuttle bus to the HAWC
research area. None of Briggs' men made a move for him. There
seemed no added security other than the forces that had been
added weeks earlier when the initial crackdown had been
started—if anything, the added security forces seemed more dispersed and less obvious. He felt relief as he stepped aboard the
bus that would take him to Dreamland. Surely Briggs wouldn't
let him go to Dreamland again if he had discovered his meeting
with Kramer and Moffitt.

Despite the outer calm of the place, however, there were a lot
of worried faces and hushed conversation in the hallways and
offices of the HAWC research center when James arrived. He
poured himself a mug of coffee and began to go through his
mailbox in the test squadron's mission-planning room. Among
the half-week's worth of mail were several notices telling about
a Center-wide briefing for all personnel at eight A.M. The topic
was not specified.

It was almost eight-thirty, so he put the meeting out of his
mind. He took a sip of coffee and was discarding most of the
small pile of mail in his box when J. C. Powell appeared in the
doorway.

"Ken, where you been?"

"I just got in. What's up?"

"You missed the meeting."

"I just heard about it. What was it?"

"I've been trying to reach you all weekend. Your phone's been off the hook or something."

"They're installing videophone in my apartment complex," he lied. "The phones have been screwed up ever since."

"Patrick's in his office. We better go see him."

"Now? What's the big deal?" He took another sip of coffee. It was pretty unusual to see Powell so wound up. "The Rooskies declare war or something?"

"Worse," J.C. said. "They've canceled the DreamStar Project."

James promptly poured a mouthful of coffee down into his lungs and nearly fell out of his chair. *"What . . . ?"*

"You heard me. Let's go."

They hurried down the hallway to McLanahan's office and burst in on the project director as he was signing a stack of letters.

"Glad you could be with us today, Ken," Patrick said, finishing his paperwork and dismissing the squadron clerk. He studied James for a moment. "You look like hell, Captain. Hanging out in the casinos all night again?"

Powell dropped into a chair to watch the spectacle. James blurted out, "What's this about the DreamStar project being canceled?"

"If you'd check your mailbox or put your phone on the hook you'd hear about these minor news flashes—"

"What the hell are you joking around about?" James' hands were on the colonel's desk. "Who canceled the project? *Why?*"

"The project was officially canceled by the Air Force this morning," McLanahan said wearily. He picked up a red-colored folder containing a single message-letter. "There are too many gaps in the scientists' knowledge of ANTARES to justify funding . . . at least in the opinion of the top brass. The flying phase of the project is being canceled until the gaps get filled in . . ."

James stared at McLanahan. "What do you mean, gaps? *I* can make it work. I don't get it . . ."

"The bottom line is that there's still only one person who can fly DreamStar—and that's you. J.C. can't fly it, at least not past anything more complicated than takeoff and landing. I've been trying to learn how to use it and I flunked. Carmichael and his lab can't really say why it works with *you* and so far not with anyone else. After my last flight in the ANTARES simulator, I—''

"*You* were flying in the simulator?" He sounded as if the colonel had committed a major trespass on *his* territory, his baby. "You tried to fly ANTARES? Why? I'm DreamStar's pilot, you're the project director, you—''

"I've been training in ANTARES for several months. I thought I had it down, but—''

"That wasn't a very smart idea, Colonel," James said. His voice was not sympathetic. "ANTARES can be very unpredictable . . .''

"Yeah, it damn near killed him," Powell put in.

"So you submitted a report saying that ANTARES was dangerous, and headquarters canceled the project?"

"That's *not* the way it went down, Ken. The project was slated to lose its flight-phase funding at the end of this fiscal year. The cancellation was going to happen anyway. My . . . accident only moved up the timetable a few months.''

James turned away, tried to control himself, but his mind was working overtime in its reaction to this information. He had just told Kramer and Moffitt that everything was going as planned, that he was even going to countermand the KGB's order to steal DreamStar . . . Now the project was going to be canceled. The KGB would never believe that he didn't know about the cancellation. His creditability would be totally destroyed—they would think he was double-crossing them for sure.

"Sorry, Ken," McLanahan was saying, "but it seems like they only needed an excuse to shut it down . . .''

"What will happen to us?"

"We're reforming the Cheetah ATF program. J.C. will be the senior pilot. I imagine they'll ask you to stay on in the ANTARES project. They'll want to continue their research in the laboratory . . .''

"I won't fly any more?"

"Only enough for flight-time currency. You'll get your required twenty hours a calendar quarter in the T-45A trainer, plus a lot of time in the ANTARES simulator. You'll . . .''

"You mean I'll be reduced to a guinea pig?"

"I don't think you have any choice, Ken," Powell said. "Being the only guy who can fly DreamStar can be a curse as well as a blessing. Carmichael and his people need you to continue their research. They can't figure out how to teach others to learn the ANTARES interface unless they figure out how *you* accomplished it."

Things were going to hell very, very quickly, James thought. "How soon before we stop flight operations? Will there at least be time for one more flight?" And added quickly, "I hate to see it go out this way . . ."

McLanahan rubbed his eyes and leaned back in his chair. "I had to fight like crazy to get Air Force to agree to let us complete the weapons-mating test. They wouldn't buy off on any more flight tests, though. Absolutely no way."

"But they are going to finish the mating test?"

"They've been working all weekend on it," Powell said. "They should have it finished by tonight or tomorrow morning and then start offloading the Scorpion missiles right after that. I wanted to get some pictures of DreamStar with Scorpion missiles on it—it may be the only time we'll see that for years."

The weapons-mating test—James had his answer . . . "What a waste, Colonel," he said, trying hard to act more subdued while formulating his plan . . . "An incredible waste. All this time, all this effort . . ."

McLanahan started shuffling papers, a wordless signal to both pilots that the meeting was over, he had nothing more to say.

"One thing's for sure," Powell said to James as they headed for the door. "You'll go down in the books as the first pilot of a thought-controlled aircraft."

James only murmured something and nodded. His mind was a long way away—on plans for the last flight of DreamStar.

Unlike most times, it was still light outside when McLanahan returned home that evening. Still more unusual was finding that he had actually beat Wendy home—but then he heard a faint sound from the bedroom. He opened the door and found her sitting cross-legged on the bed, her arms pulling her knees to her chest. She had the shades drawn and the room was in darkness—she must have overridden the automatic lights.

"Wendy? What's wrong? How long have you been here?"

"Not long . . . how do you feel?"

"I feel fine . . . anything wrong?"

"No."

No tears in her voice, no sadness, but it was hardly like her to coop herself up like this. "Why are you sitting here in the dark?"

"Thinking."

"About what?"

She remained curled up, staring toward the windows.

He put the light switch back on AUTO and the lights snapped on. He sat down beside her. "All right, Wendy. What's going on?" Still no answer. "Something at work? Something with the Old Dog project?"

". . . I had my flight physical this morning."

The smile disappeared from his face. "All right, enough damn mystery. Out with it." And then he saw the pamphlet in the wicker wastebasket beside the bed. Even upside down and crumpled he could read the title: "Facts About Your . . ."

"Pregnancy? You're *pregnant*?"

She looked apologetic. "Patrick, this is all wrong . . . I'm sorry—"

"Sorry? What are you *sorry* about?"

"This . . . that . . . oh, damn . . ."

"Wendy, you're babbling. Tell me what in the world you're so sorry about."

"I don't want you to think that I . . . I did this on purpose, trapping you or something—"

"Of course I don't think that." He slid over and put his arms around her. "Don't be silly, I'm trying to absorb it, but I'm delighted—"

She seemed to stiffen. She backed away and looked at him, hard and long. "Do you mean it? Because if you're just saying it—"

"Of course I do. Hey, I love you . . ."

She collapsed in his arms. "I was so worried . . . afraid you'd think I was trying the last dodge—"

He shut her up by kissing her. "Like I said, I happen to love you, I want you *and* I want our son . . . daughter . . ." And he began to kiss her again.

She pulled herself free. "I want you to make sure, Patrick. This is so important—"

"Then it's settled. Let's go."

"Go? Go where?"

"Downtown."

"Downtown? Why do you want to—?" And then she understood.

"We're living in Las Vegas, a lot of people get married here every year, some even at nine o'clock on a Monday evening—"

"What about . . . ?"

"Family? My mother's gone, and my brothers and sisters will be thrilled—relieved I finally got my act together and married you after all these years. What about *your* parents? You need to decide, Wendy. It's up to you . . ."

Her answer was to reach out to him and draw him to her . . . all the answer he needed.

At eleven o'clock, Maraklov left the Silver Dollar casino on Las Vegas' Fremont Street and made his way to the taxi stand down the block near a twenty-four-hour wedding chapel. He searched up and down the long line of taxis, then carefully checked around him. Satisfied, he ambled down the line of taxis until he was beside one that had its roof light off, signifying that it was already hired.

Maraklov got into the front seat of the cab.

"Well, well, General Big-Shot," Moffitt greeted him. *"Dobriy vyechyer* . . . looks like you have some sort of a problem—"

"Stuff it, Moffitt." He turned toward Kramer, sitting in the back seat of the cab with a copy of the Wall Street *Journal.* "They're deactivating the DreamStar project. In two days." Kramer appeared not to have heard him. "Did you hear what I said?"

"I do not think he believes you, *tovarisch*," Moffitt said.

"Speak English, asshole. Better yet, keep your trap shut. Kramer, listen to me. We've got to get DreamStar out of Nevada."

He did not look up from his paper.

Maraklov grabbed the newspaper away from Kramer and crumpled it up. "What the hell's wrong with you, Kramer?"

"With me? Nothing is wrong, Captain—except I have just conveyed your previous message to Moscow, how you have countermanded their order. Now, you tell me that you were wrong and that the KGB's original plan must be implemented. Am I now supposed to happily embrace your idea?''

"Hey, I just found out about this today. The damned project director was screwing around in the simulator and got himself hurt. He filed his report—''

"And the Joint Chiefs canceled the project," Kramer interrupted, "overriding the Air Force's recommendation for lower levels of activity.''

"You *know* about this?''

"We heard about the Pentagon's recommendation over the weekend," Kramer said. "Our superiors contacted us immediately, wanting us to explain the disparity between your contentions and the announcement. I could offer none.''

"Why the hell didn't you tell me?''

"We needed time to evaluate the situation," Kramer said. "Besides, your phone was not working.'' He had had it off the hook all weekend, afraid of contact with anyone that might have seen Kramer and Moffitt at his apartment. "But it did not matter. We knew you would contact us tonight.''

"Well, this new development changes things, makes your original plan not only necessary but, if I can pull it off, one that will give us a significant advantage. They stop, we go on . . . I think it can be done. I'll need refueling support, somewhere in Mexico. I won't know exactly where or when, so you'll have to be flexible. Arrange for a transport plane carrying fuel and supplies. You said you had some private company in Mexico, nothing connected with the KGB or anything governmental . . .''

"It can be done.''

"If I get a refueling I can fly either to Cuba or Nicaragua. I think Nicaragua would be safer, further from the U.S., less organized. After landing in Nicaragua we can make preparations to fly it to Russia with an escort.''

"So now you believe you can get this aircraft out of Nevada successfully," Kramer said. "You were sure that you could *not* do this before.''

"They're talking about mothballing my fighter. I'm not going to let them do that. No way. I'll crash the thing before they take it away from me.'' He immediately wished he could take back those last words.

Kramer was silent for a few moments, then: "The Command is concerned about you, about your motivation. They believe that you do not seem to care who has control of the fighter as long as *you* have it. This worries them—''

"They don't have to worry about a damn thing. Just make sure they have a tanker in Mexico when I get there, and make sure they have a secure, protected place to keep it in Cuba or Nicaragua or any other damn place I make it to. I'll get the fighter to Russia in one piece. You can bet on that . . .''

# =3=

## High Technology Advanced Weapons Center (Dreamland), Nevada

*Wednesday, 17 June 1996, 0400 PDT (0700 EDT)*

"GOOD MORNING, LADIES and gentlemen," Brigadier General John Ormack, the deputy commander of the High Technology Advanced Weapons Center, began. "This is the operational test flight briefing for Mission Three Sierra, first full-crew operational combat test flight of the B-52 M-model Megafortress Plus bomber.

"Our landmark mission today consists of an AIM-120 air-to-air missile test engagement, AGM-132C Tacit Rainbow III anti-radiation cruise missile test launch, and AGM-98 air-to-ground laser-guided missile weapon release."

To an outsider it hardly seemed like something to cheer about. To those assembled in the briefing room, it was something to applaud. That was especially true for those seated at the place of honor in the front row—General Bradley Elliott, Patrick McLanahan, Wendy Tork, and Angelina Pereira, surviving members of the original Old Dog's B-52 flight crew. Ormack himself had been the copilot aboard the first flight of the original Megafortress and the project director for the newly redesigned Megafortress Plus. He seemed to have grown younger since their amazing mission eight years earlier—many members of his Megafortress Plus project half his age had difficulty keeping up with him.

"The purpose of this mission is twofold," Ormack went on. "First, it's the final operational check flight for this B-52 after extensive repairs, and second, it's an operational evaluation of the Megafortress Plus weapon system, pending development authorization. The Megafortress Plus system seeks to provide long-range strategic defense suppression and attack using heavily armed B-52 bombers. These B-52s would carry air-to-air missiles, anti-radar weapons, cruise missiles, shorter-range standoff missiles, gravity bombs, and a wide array of electronic jammers and countermeasures to destroy or disrupt all kinds of enemy defenses, thereby allowing other strategic or tactical attack aircraft to transit the forward edge of the battle area and complete their missions.

"HAWC has four B-52s undergoing modification to Megafortress, including one"—Ormack motioned to a tall officer in the rear of the conference room—"commanded by Major Kelvin Carter, that will act as backup aircraft for this test." Carter's copilot, a young female captain named Cheshire, gave Ormack a look. "You included, Captain Cheshire," Ormack added quickly.

"Can it, Cheshire," Carter whispered to his copilot.

"Then don't you be hogging all the glory," she whispered back, trying to keep a straight face.

"Roll call for Mission Three Sierra: aircraft commander will be myself," Ormack went on. "Colonel Jeffrey Khan will be copilot, and in the instructor pilot's seat upstairs will be Mr. George Wendelstat from the House Armed Service Committee, acting as safety observer. Welcome, Mr. Wendelstat." Several in the room wondered how they'd manage to shoehorn Wendelstat in through the entrance hatch.

"Rounding out Dog Zero One's flight crew is radar navigator Major Edward Frost, navigator Major Linda Evanston, electronic warfare officer Dr. Wendy Tork, and fire control officer Dr. Angelina Pereira. Good luck to us all."

McLanahan had to choke down his feelings. It seemed so strange for him to be left out of the crew roster for the Megafortress' first combat-exercise flight. But it was no longer his project. He had safely flown the Old Dog from Nome back to Dreamland eight years ago, and had not stepped inside her since. It was like being reunited with an old friend who didn't recognize him any more.

The huge flat-screen liquid-crystal monitor behind Ormack changed to a digital time face. "Time hack, coming up on twelve-oh-four Zulu in fifteen seconds . . . five, four, three, two, one, hack. One-two-zero-four Zulu."

This day had been years in the making—two years of redesigning and computer testing by the engineers after the plane had returned to Dreamland; three years of rebuilding by a battalion of workers, and three years of experimentation and testing by the engineers and test flight crews. Now, the first newly redesigned B-52 bomber called the Megafortress Plus was ready to break its cherry.

A weather map came up on the screen and Lieutenant Colonel Jacobsen, HAWC's staff meterologist, stepped to the podium. "Good morning, General Elliott, General Ormack, ladies and gentlemen. You picked a wonderful day for this flight." A regional surface weather map came on the screen. "Strong high pressure dominates the region. This high pressure dome has reduced visibilities in the restricted areas in the past few days, but some overnight breezes have pushed most of the gook out of the way. You can expect clear skies, perhaps some scattered thin stratus at twelve thousand feet.

"For the air-to-air portion of your flight: no significant weather in R-4808 Pahute Mesa launch area. Possibly a few puffy clouds on the east side of mountain ranges but otherwise no restrictions to visibility. Winds forecast at twenty knots from the north at fifteen thousand feet. For the air-to-ground portion of your flight, excellent weather conditions will persist. Visibility may be as low as twenty miles on the surface, with winds light and variable. Bombing range area will be 'severe clear,' possibly some hazy conditions, temperature seventy-eight degrees. Good luck and good hunting."

Ormack took over as the screen changed again. "Status of the chase aircraft are as shown. Everyone's in the green as of this hour. Please report maintenance delays to job control on present channel eight. Colonel Towland is the operations controller in the command post and he will reassign backup aircraft as necessary."

The screen changed to a detailed high-resolution map of the restricted areas around Dreamland. The map was put into motion by computer, drawing the flight path of the Megafortress as Ormack spoke: "Route of flight is as follows: we will launch via coded message and follow the Groom Victor One departure to Angel intersection. Once at Angel, we will orbit as necessary at thirty thousand feet until one-five hundred Zulu time, then proceed downrange toward the intercept area.

"Once in the intercept area two AQM-175 tactical dome aircraft launched from China Lake Naval Weapons Center will be directed by airborne controllers to engage the B-52. The Megafortress will carry two AIM-120 Scorpion missiles in wing pylon canisters and will engage the drone aircraft at will. The engagement will continue for one hour or until the drones are destroyed. Flight crew personnel and airborne controllers will follow standard rules of engagement for safe separation of aircraft. All flight crew personnel will take directions from the airborne controllers. If not destroyed, the drones will be recovered by parachute, and the Megafortress will proceed to the missile drop zone."

The screen changed again. "The Tacit Rainbow anti-radiation loiter missile drop test will be at twelve thousand feet, in roughly the same area as the intercept zone. A simulated Soviet SA-14 surface-to-air missile site will engage the B-52 . . . Dr. Tork?"

Wendy Tork came to the podium. She was wearing a bright orange flight suit and black leather zip-up flight boots—even the baggy flight suit looked dynamite on her.

"Good morning, ladies and gentlemen," Wendy began, her energy contagious even at the early hour. "We will be testing the new array of strategic and tactical pulse-Doppler electronic countermeasure jammers aboard the Megafortress Plus, as well as the Tacit Rainbow mod three anti-radar loiter missile. The purpose of this flight is to evaluate the Megafortress' capability to penetrate sophisticated Soviet coastal defenses using its own assets, and at the same time create penetration corridors for other aircraft using the Tacit Rainbow anti-radiation missile. These will lay the groundwork for fleet modernization of existing B-52 aircraft as well as develop new capabilities for follow-on aircraft such as the B-1 Excalibur and B-2 Panther Stealth bomber."

A high-resolution photo of the anti-radar missile flashed on the screen. "First developed ten years ago, Tacit Rainbow is a small winged aircraft with a one-thousand-pound-thrust turbojet engine, a ring laser gyro inertial navigation unit and coupled autopilot, a broad-band programmable seeker head with multi-pulse and digital radiation capability, and a one-hundred-pound high-explosive warhead. The missile is released within fifty miles of a known or suspected enemy surface-to-air missile site. The missile orbits the area using its inertial autopilot until it detects emissions from the nearby enemy radar. The missile then leaves its orbit and homes in on the radar and destroys it. The missile can orbit for as long as four hours and has a small enough radar cross-section to avoid detection by hostile anti-air units. A B-52 bomber can carry as many as twenty-four of these missiles, although we see these Tacit Rainbow missiles carried with a mixed load of offensive missiles and gravity weapons aboard Navy and Air Force strike aircraft . . ."

Patrick realized how much he envied these men and women. And listening to these briefings and organization of the Mega-fortress Plus project tended to underscore his own apparent failure with the DreamStar project, now on hold mostly because he failed to keep tighter control on his test pilots and to recognize the need for more complete and useful test standards and security.

He was in charge of nothing right now except cleanup. Sure, he had been given the Cheetah program, but that was already a thriving project nearing operational deployment. He was just another caretaker, marking time.

His eyes automatically sought out Wendy's, and he found her looking in his direction. They exchanged faint smiles. She had been watching him off and on the whole time. Better snap out of it, you stupid mick, he told himself. She'll have enough on her mind without worrying about you.

The briefing ended and the flight crew moved toward the exits and the bus ready to take them to the flight line. McLanahan went to each crewmember and wished him or her a good flight.

"You should be going with us, Patrick," Angelina Pereira said, giving him a very unmilitary hug. "This is your plane. You belong on her. You and General Elliott too."

She was wearing the same orange flight suit as Wendy, and she too looked dynamite in it despite being fifteen years older than Wendy. Her hair was more gray then he remembered, but her eyes still sparkled. Angie would always be a handful for any man—she had married and divorced twice since the Old Dog's first mission. He could still see her in the denim jacket she had worn when she climbed aboard the Old Dog eight years earlier, and he could remember her gratitude when the Russian caretaker at Anadyr Airbase in Siberia gave her a full-length sealskin coat in exchange for her denim jacket, even though at the time the jacket was covered with General Elliott's blood. That coat today had to be worth at least five thousand. She would not have parted with it for five million.

He could also remember her dropping into marksman's crouch as she fired on that same Russian airbase caretaker after he discovered who they were and ran off to warn the militia. One minute she was eternally grateful to the guy; the next she was trying to blow him away. She was one tough lady, all right.

"Not this time, Angelina," Patrick said with a halfhearted smile. "But I'll have the fire trucks and the champagne ready to hose you guys off when you land."

"It's your project as well as ours."

"Not any more. Besides, you guys did all the work . . ."

"No, you did. Back over Russia." Like him, she had been thinking back to the Old Dog's first mission. "Even though you won't fly with us your name's still on the Old Dog, on the crew nameplate. It'll be there as it's flying."

"But I'm not the radar nav any more—"

"No, you're not, you're the seventh man, Patrick. Sorry to sound corny, but you're the soul of the Old Dog."

She squeezed his hand, picked up her helmet bag, and walked off. He saw Wendy then, watching him once again from the back of the conference room. He went over to her.

"How do you feel, Mrs. McLanahan?"

"Wonderful. Happy. Nervous. Excited. I've got butterflies the size of B-52s in my stomach . . . Are you going to be okay?"

"Sure."

"Wish you were going with us. You deserve it more than anyone else." She could tell he was unconvinced. She smiled at him. "When should we break the news?"

"At the post-flight reception tonight."

"Can't wait." She gave him a kiss and hurried off to join her crew.

He called out behind her. "Good luck. See you on the ground."

Wendy flashed him an exaggerated thumbs-up. "Piece of cake," she called out as she rushed off to catch the crew bus.

As the crew of the new Megafortress Plus headed off to begin their mission, Staff Sergeant Rey Jacinto was nearing the end of his tour of duty on the graveyard shift, on patrol guarding Han-

gar Number Five at the flight line at Dreamland. It was the
absolute pits.

He had done everything wrong. After four years as an Air
Force security guard he knew how to prepare himself for a
change in shifts—plenty of exercise, the right amount of rest,
not too much food, no caffeine or alcohol twelve hours before
the shift. But this time everything had gone to hell. His wife had
car trouble Monday afternoon and so he was up all morning
towing it to his brother-in-law's place. It had been hot, dusty
work and he couldn't resist a couple of beers at two o'clock in
the afternoon—that only violated the eight-hour rule by two
hours. No big deal.

His body began asking him for sleep at three o'clock, but the
car needed a new water pump and his brother-in-law insisted
they could do it before he had to leave. Then, to top it all off,
he sat down at six o'clock for homemade pizza. Knowing that
he hadn't had any sleep in twelve hours and he wasn't going to
get any in the next twelve, he downed nearly a whole pot of
coffee after polishing off four huge, thick slices of pizza.

Rey felt pretty good as he reported for duty at seven-thirty for
the shift-briefing, inspection, weapons checkout and post
changeover, but when he parked his armored assault vehicle in
front of Hangar Number Five, things began catching up with
him. The combination of caffeine and lack of rest made his muscles jittery. The night air was cold, so he turned up the heat in
his V-100 Commando armored car, which only increased his
drowsiness. He had brought his study materials for his bachelor-
degree class, but the thought of even trying to listen to an hour's
worth of audio textbooks on micro-economics was too much.

By four A.M., four hours from changeover, Sergeant Jacinto
was struggling to stay awake. Everything was quiet on the radios—no exercises, alerts, weapon movements, nothing. With
the B-52 down the way in Hangar Three being readied for a
flight, a security exercise would be too disruptive and would not
be called. The engineers who had been working on the XF-34A
DreamStar in Hangar Five had long since departed, and the
munitions-maintenance troops weren't scheduled to arrive until
after his shift-change. Even nature was conspiring to screw him
up. Thin clouds blocked most of the bright moonlight, so the
ramp and most of the area were completely dark, and there were
no birds or animals making their usual noises on the dry lakebed

aircraft ramp. It was a dark, quiet morning. If he didn't go completely crazy he was going to die from the strain of trying to stay awake.

Rey had just completed his hourly walkaround inspection of Hangar Five, checking all the doors and exits. He was so bored that he even began to pick up scraps of paper and pieces of junk on the ramp. He returned to his truck and keyed the radio.

"Red Man, this is Five Foxtrot." Red Man was HAWC's Security Control Center.

"Go ahead, Five."

"Requesting ten mike for relief."

There was a pause, then: "Five, that's your fourth potty break tonight."

"It's Rey's time of the month," someone else on the security net chimed in.

"Cut the chatter," the security controller ordered. "Five Foxtrot, unable at this time. Stand by. Break. Rover Nine, this is Red Man. Over."

"Rover Nine, go." Rover Nine was one of only two M113 armored combat vehicle-equipped crews that cruised around the huge compound, doing errands and relieving the post guards as necessary; they had numbers higher than two to hide the fact that there were only two of these heavily armed roving patrols on the flight line.

"Five Foxtrot requests relief for ten mike ASAP."

"Stand by," came the reply in an exasperated voice. A few moments later: "Red Man, we're at the shack getting coffee— Five Foxtrot's been drinking the stuff like it's going out of style." Rey Jacinto cringed as his code name was broadcast on the net— boy, was he going to get it when this shift was over. Good thing none of the other guards could leave their posts to get on his case. "We'll be another ten here, then we need to check in with the main gate. Ask Five Foxtrot if this is a number two or if he can use the piddle pack. Over."

Rey was fed up with all this—they weren't letting him off easy tonight. He was just bored and sleepy. He keyed his microphone: "Break. Red Man, this is Five Foxtrot. Cancel request for relief. Request the comedians in Rover Nine bring some water when they're done stuffing their faces at the flight line kitchen. Over."

"Roger, Five Foxtrot. Rover Nine, you copy?"

"Affirmative. Advise Five Foxtrot to stop massaging his little one-eyed helmeted reptile and stand by. Rover Nine out."

There were a few more comments on the net—no one liked to give the hot-dogs on Rover Nine the last word—but soon silence once again descended over the area.

By now Rey was struggling to keep his eyelids open. The worst part of any guard's tour, no matter how well one prepared, was the hour or two just before sunrise. It was a barrier, a psychological one—the body demanded sleep at this hour no matter how much rest it had earlier. Rey Jacinto's head was bobbing up and down off his chest. He had already stripped off his fatigue jacket, flak jacket and webbing so as much cold air could hit his skin as possible. It wasn't helping.

He was thankful to see the lights of a big blue Stepvan supply truck check in at the outer perimeter. The blue "bread truck" van, towing a missile trailer, headed right for him. He was feeling a little ornery by now, and this was his chance to get his blood pumping again. Quickly he pulled on his combat gear and webbing as the truck pulled up.

When the truck stopped in front of Jacinto's armored car, he got out, carrying his M-16 rifle at port arms, and ran in front and off to the driver's side of the van. He held up the rifle, filled his lungs with cold desert air and yelled, "Driver! Stop your engine, leave your headlights on and everyone out of the van. Now!"

The driver and one other man, both in Air Force green fatigues, jumped out of the van and stood before Jacinto in the glare of the van's headlights. The younger man, a two-striper, was shaking. The driver, a burly technical sergeant, was surprised but kept his composure as he raised his hands. "What's going on?"

"Step away from the truck," Jacinto ordered. Both men did. "What's going—?"

"Quiet! Don't move!" Jacinto still held his rifle at port arms—his voice was enough to convince the two men. Jacinto rested the automatic rifle on his hip with one hand and pulled his walkie-talkie from his web belt.

"Red Man, this is Five Foxtrot. Two males intercepted at Five, driving a blue Stepvan with missile trailer. Executing full nighttime challenge. Over."

"Copy, Five Foxtrot," the security controller replied. There was a hint of humor in the controller's voice—he knew Jacinto was going to have a little fun with his visitors. "Do you require assistance?"

"Negative. Out."

The driver of the truck said, "Sergeant, would you mind—?"

"Silence. Turn around. Both of you."

"I've got authorization—"

"I said *turn*." They did. "Where's your I.D. cards?"

"Back pocket."

"One hand, two fingers. Remove your I.D." They removed wallets from back pockets. "Over your head. Remove your I.D. cards." They did. "Drop them slowly, carefully, at your feet, then take three steps forward." When they moved away Jacinto said, "Now kneel. Hands on top of your heads."

"Give us a break, Sarge—"

"*Kneel.*"

As they did, Jacinto walked over to the I.D. cards, picked them up, and examined them. They were bent, dirty, grease-encrusted and barely readable—typical maintenance troop's I.D. cards. Jacinto stepped around the two kneeling men and shined a flashlight in their faces. The faces matched the photos.

"I need job slips now. Where are they?"

"Upper left pocket."

"Get them out." The two technicians pulled crumpled slips of paper from their pockets and put them on the ramp. Jacinto picked them up and checked them under the flashlight's beam. He couldn't check the job numbers—he'd left his clipboard with the job numbers from the squadron in his truck—but he checked the MMS squadron supervisor's stamped signoff block on the reverse side. The stamp and signature were the most frequently omitted part of the job ticket, and both were required before any work could begin on any of the birds on the line. But these guys were on the ball—both had the required stamp with the familiar signature of the MMS NCOIC.

"Okay, Sergeant Howard, Airman Crowe," Jacinto said, looping the M-16 back onto his right shoulder. "Everything checks okay."

"You're damned right it does," Howard said, hauling himself to his feet. Jacinto held out the job tickets and I.D. cards to them. Howard took his I.D. card and job ticket back with a snap of his wrist; Crowe took his with relief.

"Why can't you bozos do your little games during the day?" Howard said. He motioned to Crowe, who seemed to be cemented in place. "Move it, Airman. We're behind schedule as it is."

"Wasn't expecting you till nine," Jacinto said.

"I wasn't expecting to *be* here until nine," Howard said angrily. "So naturally I get a call in the middle of the night telling me they want the plane in premaintenance right now. I know better than to answer the damned phone after nine P.M."

Jacinto nodded. "I hear that." He put his own wife and kids on strict instructions not to answer the phone after nine P.M.

He walked back to his V-100 just as a large green M113 Armadillo combat vehicle pulled up beside his. The back door swung open and two armed soldiers jumped out and took defensive positions behind the ACV. Jacinto could see the roof turret swing in his direction, the huge twenty-millimeter Browning cannon and its coaxial 7.62-millimeter machine gun in the turret trained on the Stepvan behind him.

"Five Foxtrot, code two, report," a voice blared through the Armadillo's loudspeaker.

"Five Foxtrot, code victor ten victor, all secure," Jacinto yelled back. The security crews had been given a code sequence and number for the shift. When challenged, the guard would respond with the proper code to advise the response crew that he was not under duress. If he had responded with anything else the snipers at the back of the truck and the gunner on top of the armored vehicle with his cannon and machine gun would kill anybody in sight.

But Jacinto answered correctly. The guards behind the Armadillo raised their rifles and slung them on their shoulders. Jacinto walked over to the truck.

"Pissing off the munitions maintenance troops again, eh, Rey?"

"I gotta do something to stay awake, Sarge. These guys have no sense of humor."

"Yeah. You gotta hit the head or what?"

"Just let me refill my canteen and I'll be okay."

Jacinto went to the back of the Armadillo and hacked around with the two assault troops as he filled his canteen from the large water can and hooked it back onto his web belt. He gave the shift-supervisor NCO a snappy salute as the ACV drove away.

His blood flowing once again, Jacinto did a quick walkaround inspection of the hangar as the munitions maintenance troops punched in the number of the code lock on the hangar door opening mechanism. As the senior NCO went inside, the younger man hopped back into the Stepvan and pulled it around so that the rear was facing in toward the plane. Jacinto moved toward the front of the hangar so he could watch the rear of the truck and the driver. The young driver, obviously nervous around the flight line, finally got into position after a series of jerks and starts, maneuvering the missile trailer in beside the plane as close to the hangar wall as he could. Jacinto decided to help him out, and guided the driver in until the truck was ten feet from the nose of the plane and the trailer was just under the left wing-tip.

"Thanks," the young airman said in a high-pitched voice. He hopped out and trotted back to help his supervisor.

"Better chock the truck," Jacinto called inside the hangar. The airman froze. Sergeant Howard looked at Jacinto, then at Crowe, and finally at the Stepvan.

"Do as the man said," Howard yelled to Crowe. "You know all vehicles are supposed to be chocked out here." Crowe ran to the truck, pulled out a set of yellow wooden chocks and placed them under the rear wheels.

"And stop running around in the hangar," Howard yelled once more. "You know better. Or should."

Jacinto suppressed a smile. He remembered back to his first solo guard duties while he watched the two technicians set to work. He was a million times more nervous than this guy . . .

His interest was quickly drawn to the amazing aircraft they were servicing. He had never been any closer than this to the plane, even though he had been guarding it for a year now, but he was still amazed by the sleek, catlike aircraft. It looked even more deadly now with its two huge air-to-air missiles hanging on the belly on either side of the large intake. Jacinto had read every scrap of unclassified information on DreamStar and had repeatedly asked for permission to look inside the cockpit but was always denied.

Sergeant Howard had wheeled a maintenance platform around to the left side of the cockpit and locked it into place, then scrambled up the steps and opened the canopy. Meanwhile Crowe had started up an auxiliary power cart in the back of the hangar and was hauling air and power cables over to the receptacles near the left main landing gear. A few moments later Howard had flipped the right switches in the cockpit—the battery and external power switches, Jacinto recalled from his reading—and cockpit and position lights popped in all around DreamStar.

Howard stepped off the maintenance platform and walked over to the back of the truck. Noticing Jacinto watching him from the front of the hangar, he waved him over. Jacinto, and soon Airman Crowe, moved over beside Howard.

Over the noise of the power cart Sergeant Howard said, "Want to take look inside?"

Jacinto blinked in surprise. "Is it okay?"

"Don't see why not. Ejection seat's been deactivated, half the black boxes in the cockpit have been pulled out and the weapons are all pinned and safe. No better time."

Jacinto nodded enthusiastically. He pulled the clip out of his M-16, placed the clip in a pouch on his belt, checked the safety on the rifle and leaned the weapon on the Stepvan bumper. "All right, I been waiting to do this for—"

A hand reached across his face, covering his nose and mouth and twisting his head sideways. Jacinto tried to roll away from the arms holding his head, but Howard had run up to him and grasped his chin, holding his neck fast. A split-second later Jacinto felt a sharp, deep sting on his exposed neck.

Three seconds later he was dead.

"*Shto slochelosch?* What the hell is the matter with you, Crowe?" the man named "Howard" cursed at his young partner. "Crowe" was staring at the body, watching Jacinto's death twitch as the poison slowly destroyed the central nervous system. "You almost let him get loose."

Crowe did not reply. Howard slapped the young man hard on the shoulder. "We must hurry, idiot. Time is running out."

Pushed toward the still-quivering corpse, Crowe began unbuckling Jacinto's combat harness and webbing, jerking his hands away as the last of the dead guard's tremors left his body. Meanwhile Howard swung open the back of the Stepvan, removed several pins from the sides of the equipment racks along the inside walls of the van, then hauled the racks away from the wall.

Out from his hiding place inside the racks, wearing the AN-TARES flight suit, was Captain Kenneth Francis James.

*"Nechyega syerchyanznaga, tovarisch.* It is all clear, Comrade Captain. We are ready."

James raised the muzzle of the machine pistol and put the safety on. "Speak English, you idiot. And help me out of here."

Slowly, carefully, Maraklov was helped to his feet. Moving as if his joints were locked in place, he slowly walked to the edge of the Stepvan. Howard then lowered him to the hangar floor, where he made his way to the maintenance platform still set up beside DreamStar.

By this time Airman Crowe—real name, long unused and almost forgotten, was Andrei Lovyyev—had put on all of Jacinto's combat gear and was just replacing the ammo clip in the M-16 rifle. "Blouse your pants in your boots, Crowe," James told him as he crawled up the ladder. "And keep out of sight. You're at least thirty pounds smaller than Jacinto, someone is bound to notice."

"Yes, sir."

"Remember, your call sign is Five Foxtrot. The duress code number is twelve and the duress prefix and suffix is victor."

"I remember, sir."

He turned to Howard. "You both have been briefed on the pickup location?"

"Yes, Captain. Good luck to you, sir."

James balanced himself on the cockpit sill of DreamStar and swung his legs inside the cockpit. Then with Howard's help, he connected the maze of wire bundles from his flight suit to DreamStar's computers, set the heavy ANTARES superconductor helmet on his head and fastened it into place. By this time he was breathing hard, he could feel drops of sweat crawling down his arms and neck. Howard's hands trembled slightly with excitement as he fastened the thick shoulder straps around the metal-encased pilot and pulled them tight. "Tighter," James said in a voice muffled by the helmet. Howard braced himself and hauled on the straps as hard as he could.

"Thank you, Sergeant Howard," James said. "You pulled this off very well."

*"Nyeh zah shto."* Maraklov had been James too long. He could barely understand a word, but the KGB agent's soft tone of voice gave him the idea. The man was obviously pleased by

the compliment. He rechecked James' connections and climbed
off the maintenance platform.

Meanwhile Crowe had climbed inside the armored vehicle
outside the hangar, scanning the flight line—Howard could see
his head jerk at every crackle of the radio. It had, he now realized, been foolish to bring such a youngster on a mission like
this—it was Lovyyev's first full-scale job since sneaking across
the border from Mexico via El Paso and setting up residence
under cover in Las Vegas three years earlier. To put him in the
lion's den like this was taking a big risk.

But it was too late for second guessing. Howard disconnected
the missile trailer from the Stepvan truck and moved it out of
the way inside the hangar, closed the van's rear doors and moved
it out of the hangar and clear of DreamStar's taxi path. Next he
took several large orange-colored traffic cones marked ''DANGER
HIGH EXPLOSIVE'' out of the van and arranged them in a wide
arc around the hangar doors. This was a normal procedure—the
cones were a warning to anyone else on the flight line that work
on live weapons was going on inside. But these cones were different. Each was a miniature mortar-launcher, operated by remote control. When activated, each would fire a high-explosive
magnesium flash bomb a hundred yards away. The concussions
and blinding white light produced by the mortar rounds would
slow and presumably stop any quick-reaction forces from moving in until DreamStar was clear of the hangar.

After carefully aiming the disguised mortars at response roads
and likely targets around the hangar—being careful not to crater
DreamStar's taxi route or exit—Howard stepped inside the hangar once again and rechecked that all safing pins and streamers
were removed from the aircraft and weapons. He then walked
to the truck, retrieved a M-16 rifle with a M-203 forty-millimeter
grenade-launcher under the barrel, a metal box full of grenades
and a bag of five thirty-round clips, and went back into the
hangar to wait.

His legs were aching, sweat was pouring into the metallic flight
suit. Conditioned air from the external power cart was trickling
into the suit but was hardly enough to change the temperature.

Through the canopy he could see Crowe nervously fidgeting
inside the armored car, looking as if he was going to shoot
himself in the face with his M-16 any second. He could also

watch Howard's careful preparations for the massive assault they knew had to come. Despite their plans, the moment they tried to start engines the full force of Dreamland's security forces would be on top of them. Nearly fifty armed soldiers and two heavily armed tracked combat vehicles surrounding the flight line would be let loose to blow DreamStar to hell.

Amid it all James had to convince himself to relax, to empty his mind of all thoughts, to clear a path for the sleeping AN-TARES computer to worm its way into his subconscious. Self-hypnosis, consciously forcing each muscle group to relax, was the simplest and usually the most effective way of achieving theta-wave state, but that seemed impossible. Muscles ached from the long climb up the platform, and the lactic acid that collected in his muscle tissue from heavy exertion would act like halon gas on a fire, blocking any conscious efforts to relax those muscles.

His mind kept straying to the thoughts of Major Briggs' security forces—he had inspected those forces many times, acting only partially interested in them at the time when in fact he was taking careful notes on the exact numbers, equipment and deployment. He had examined the weaknesses of the force and planned possible escape routes out of Dreamland for himself should that ever have been necessary. He had devised several escape plans, depending on what, if anything, he was taking with him—one route was to be used if he was alone and on foot, another if he was driving a car, another if driving a truck, another if he was carrying a "black box" or another unit. But never had he expected to take DreamStar with him. Components, drawings, computers, electronic media, yes—never the whole plane.

Only one mind-set seemed to make sense—that morning in the cockpit he told himself he wasn't going to make it but it was worth it to die trying. If he did beat the odds and lift off, he had to buck even greater odds to fly the eight hundred miles from Dreamland to the deserted airstrip in central Mexico for the refueling planned by his KGB contacts in Los Angeles and Mexico City. Then he'd have both the American and Mexican air forces to beat on his way to Nicaragua, plus American forces based on El Salvador and Honduras—none of them very large or effective forces, but a deadly threat to a battered and weaponless DreamStar.

But he had no choice. If he couldn't have DreamStar, better to die in her cockpit trying to deliver her to the Soviet Union than let the Americans mothball her while they continued to perfect their research into the ANTARES interface. Were there other areas he could infiltrate, other research programs whose information could be vital to the security of the Soviet Union? Was there any other program that, if he lived, he could collect information on as valuable or as rare as his DreamStar? His? Yes, damn it, *his* . . .

The answer to all was no. Strangely, coming to that grim conclusion put him at ease, allowing him slowly to relax his knotted muscles and control his adrenaline-fired pulse and breathing.

"Do you want to live forever, Andrei Ivanschichin Maraklov?" James said into his face mask. And with that he felt his body go totally relaxed, almost limp, held upright only by the tight body harness that secured him to DreamStar's ejection seat. It was the first time in some ten years that he had spoken his given name. The words surprised him—it was such a totally *Russian* name. And right now he liked it, was proud of it. "Kenneth Francis James" sounded weak. He would not use it again.

He did not realize, though, that it had taken *two hours* for him to speak his Russian name to himself. Without warning the ANTARES interface had taken hold. He was once again one with DreamStar . . .

Patrick McLanahan could only stare. General Brad Elliott and Hal Briggs couldn't speak. Applause broke out from somewhere behind them as they stared at a reincarnation.

The doors to Hangar Three of the HAWC research flight line were opened, and a yellow "mule" tow-tractor slowly chugged out of the massive structure. The mule pulled a hulking dark beast from its lair, an aircraft so large that it seemed to blot out the faint glow of the rising sun on the horizon. It seemed to take forever to move the giant machine from the hangar, but soon there it was, sitting on the concrete ramp like a winged black dragon.

" 'Whenever science makes a discovery, the devil grabs it,' " Angelina Pereira quoted. McLanahan and Briggs turned toward her. "Alan Valentine," she added.

"Whoever . . . but that's one mean-lookin' mother," Briggs said.

Ormack began his walkaround inspection of the Megafortress Plus, General Elliott and other members of the crew following. Actually Ormack and the engineers had already completed an extensive walkaround hours earlier before the crew briefing, and all items of the before-engine-start checklist had already been performed by ground crewmen and technicians. But no matter who performed the inspection, or when, Ormack could not resist the urge to do one last visual inspection before climbing aboard— as much a ritual as a race car driver's kicking the tires of his car or a marksman's rubbing the front sight of his rifle.

Elliott pointed at the Old Dog. "I still can't believe what I'm seeing," he said to Ormack, once its copilot. What he was pointing at was the most radical change in the Old Dog's appearance—her huge wings. Instead of drooping in a huge downward curve from the fuselage to the wingtips, the wings stood straight out, tall and proud instead of arched and aged-looking.

"The newest in composite materials went into her," Ormack said. "We replaced the main wing spar, the spine, the tailplane spars and other skeletal components with fibersteel beams, the largest and thickest composite structures ever cast. I remember being called out to the hangar in Alaska when they put the wings back on—it looked like a damn optical illusion, those twenty-ton wings sticking straight out like that. They sagged when we filled them up with fifty tons of fuel, though—sagged a grand total of two inches. We used to be able to look into the outboard engines just by standing on tiptoes—now, they're all so high off the ground we need a ladder to look into them. The takeoff distance has decreased by thirty percent. It used to take forever for the Buff to lift off because those huge drooping wings would 'take off' first, leaving the fuselage still rolling on the ground. No more, Brad. When this beast hits takeoff speed, it's airborne. Period."

Ormack continued the walkaround inspection, pointing out various new changes in the huge bomber. "Only two AIM-120 Scorpion missiles on this flight, but Carter's Dog Zero Two can take up to ten on each wing now, instead of only the six we had on our first mission—that's twenty air-to-air missiles total, the same as on five F-15 fighters. And computer-controlled fuel management helps us avoid the fuel problems we had on our last flight when damage forced us out of the automatic mode. No more wing spoilers that dragged in the slipstream for aircraft control and wasted so much energy. Now we use engine-bleed air-thrusters on the wings for roll control. It allows us much faster turn control, eliminates adverse yaw.''

He pointed at the Old Dog's wingtip, which had a long, pointed oblong device trailing aft from the wingtip. ''No more twin tip-tanks on this baby. With fibersteel construction we were able to build large single jettisonable fuel tanks with greater capacity that are lighter, stronger and more aerodynamic than the twin tanks. We've also taken off the wingtip wheels—even fully fueled there's no danger of these wingtips ever striking ground. Another weight saving.''

Hal Briggs turned to Ormack. ''General, someone might think you're a lieutenant on his cherry ride.'' As he spoke Briggs glanced over Ormack's shoulder down the flight line and, by force of habit, checked the guard posts.

''I have to admit, I get clutched every time I see this beast,'' Ormack said. ''I've seen her blown up, crashed, broken, shot up, cut up, disassembled, and now I've seen her better than before. A regular phoenix, this bird.''

They walked around to the bomb bay and peered inside at the mix of glide-missiles and laser-guided smart bombs. ''If this flight is a success,'' General Elliott said, ''this could be the beginning of a new day for the B-52 bomber. Even with all one hundred B-1 Excalibur bombers operational and the first B-2 Panther Stealth bomber squadron finally operational, the anti-air, standoff and border penetration capabilities of the Megafortress Plus may mean the refitting and reactivation of *all* the G-model B-52s that were retired last year. A few squadrons of B-52 Megafortress Plus bombers could fly along with the strike bombers, clear a path for them and then return to be used in reserve or for other long-range strike missions. It's a new concept—armed flying battleship escorts for strategic bombers.''

Hal Briggs listened but his attention was continually drawn to the guard posts down the flight line. Everything appeared normal, but something *somewhere* was out of place . . .

At first Briggs dismissed the feelings. All six high-security hangars had the proper guards stationed around them—six V-100 Commando assault cars positioned properly. Straining, he could make out all six guards at their posts, a few standing to watch the crowd around the B-52, a few sitting in their V-100s. A roving patrol in an M113 Armadillo assault vehicle was moving up and down the center of the ramp, cruising slowly, a couple of SPs hanging out of the gun turret on the roof to watch the Megafortress roll out. They had taken the twenty-millimeter machine gun off its mount so two guys could squeeze up through the roof to get a better look—he'd have to get on their case for that. But overall, it appeared normal. So what was it . . . ?

"Hal?" McLanahan had stepped beside the security police commander and was scanning the flight line with him. "Problem?"

Hal noticed that Ormack, Elliott, Khan and Wendelstat had moved off toward the tail; he and McLanahan were alone beside the Old Dog's bomb bay. "No . . . nothing. I'm gonna chew some butt—those guys rubber-neckin' in the Armadillo over there." He looked at the colonel. "Where you going?"

"Take a ride out to the range, I think. Get a good seat near the ground target before the fireworks start. I was going to ask if . . ."

But Briggs wasn't listening; he was staring down the flight line toward Hangar Five, Sergeant Rey Jacinto's post. He was still sitting in his V-100, doors closed. He wasn't asleep—Jacinto was too good for that, and besides, Briggs could see him moving around inside . . .

"Hal? What about it? Can I get a ride out to the range?"

. . . but Jacinto was a high-tech aircraft freak. He knew all there was to know, all he was allowed to know, about the B-52 Megafortress Plus and the XF-34A DreamStar. He would, though, gladly give his right nut to get a look at either bird up close. Jacinto had guarded Hangar Three before, but he had never been inside . . .

"He's never seen the Old Dog before," Briggs mumbled.

"What?"

"One of my troops. Jacinto . . ."

"Rey? Yeah, nice guy. You keep on bouncing back his requests to take a peek at DreamStar. You ought to let him before they mothball her. Is he on duty this morning?"

"Hangar Five."

McLanahan squinted through the semi-darkness toward DreamStar's hangar. "I don't see him."

"He's in the Commando."

McLanahan grunted his surprise. "Looking out those tiny gunport windows? Get those guys in the Rover to relieve him on his post and have him come take a look at the Megafortress. I know he's been itching to get a look at her too."

"Yeah, right." Briggs walked off toward his sedan. Patrick was about to repeat his request for a ride out to the bombing range but changed his mind—Briggs, he decided, must have a million things on his mind.

As he walked to his car Hal Briggs decided McLanahan was right. Jacinto had wanted to get a look at the Megafortress Plus and DreamStar for years. Now, with the huge bomber not three hundred yards away, Jacinto was sitting locked up in his V-100, watching through tiny gunports when he could be outside watching it. Why? Besides, Jacinto was a well-known roamer. He couldn't stand being cooped up in a Commando for more than a few minutes.

It was then that Briggs noticed the blue Stepvan half-hidden from view beside Hangar Five. He also noticed that the doors to Hangar Five were open and that a missile-carrying trailer was parked inside. And he saw the orange safety cones arranged outside the hangar—MMS, or Munitions Maintenance Squadron, was already downloading weapons from DreamStar. They were four hours early . . .

Briggs pulled his walkie-talkie from his belt and set the channel for security control. "Red Man, this is Hotel."

"Go ahead, Hotel."

Ormack had finished his walkaround, and he, Carter and Elliott were shaking hands. Visitors began filing into buses to take them off the flight line. The crew of the Megafortress was climbing up the belly hatch into the massive bomber.

· Briggs keyed the mike button: "Status check of Foxtrot posts."

"Last status check one-five minutes ago reports all secure. Last Rover check zero-one minutes ago reports all secure."

"Copy. Break. Rover Nine, this is Hotel. Report to Five Foxtrot for relief. He wants to get a look at the monster up close. Five Foxtrot, you copy?"

Lovyyev, alias Airman Crowe, nearly pulled the trigger of his M-16 in panic when he heard his call sign over the security net. He was about to pick up the microphone and say something when he heard, "Break. Hotel, this is Rover Nine. Job Control has requested us to assist in clearing the flight line. We are moving into position. Please advise. Over."

Lovyyev's throat was stone dry. He didn't dare try to speak. Nothing would come out. Should he walk out of the car? Wave? Should he do anything . . . ?

Briggs stared at the armored car in front of Hangar Five. Jacinto sure was acting strange. Normally he would have jumped at the opportunity to check out any aircraft, from an old Piper Cub to the hypersonic spaceplane. He was being oddly reticent this morning. Well, tough. He was too late.

"Rover Nine, continue to clear the flight line. Five Foxtrot, sorry, maybe some other time."

Lovyyev still kept away from the mike button. He turned and saw KGB veteran Gekky Orlov, alias Sergeant Howard, standing inside the hangar, his M-16 out of sight, watching him. He knew Orlov had a tiny earpiece radio set to that security-net frequency. He was looking hard at him, trying to get him to calm down. Orlov could tell without seeing him that Lovyyev was ready to collapse. *Don't key that microphone*, be silent . . .

No reply. Strange.

A crew chief was hauling a huge Halon fire bottle over to the left inboard engine pylon and several of his assistants were positioning themselves around the B-52 to act as safety observers for this engine start. Briggs suddenly found himself in the middle. He got inside his sedan, closed the windows against the sound of external power carts being started, switched on the engine, and headed for the security checkpoint to watch the taxi and takeoff.

But as the first dull roar of the number four engine began to invade the early morning air, Briggs stopped the car just short of the checkpoint. He was perhaps four hundred yards from Hangar Five. Still no sign of Jacinto. Hal picked up his car microphone. "Five Foxtrot, this is Hotel. How copy?" No reply. "Five Foxtrot, this is Hotel. Come in. Over."

There may have been a reply but Briggs couldn't hear it over the steady scream of the eight turbofan engines on the massive B-52 bomber. The crew was running through their pre-takeoff equipment checks. The three-thousand-watt taxi lights on the front landing gear trucks flashed insistently at him, indicating that the B-52's attack radar was on. Briggs was parked right in front of the bomber. He started his car and moved away from the B-52's front quarter.

The pre-takeoff checks were running quietly. As Hal Briggs continued to try to raise Five Foxtrot, the crew chief ran in front of the Megafortress Plus with two lighted wands, and using hand signals ordered his assistants to pull the B-52's wheel chocks.

Hal considered cruising over to the guard post but it was too late. The crew chief swirled his wands in the air, a signal to Ormack and Khan in the cockpit that they were clear to run up their engines for taxi. The engines began a deafening roar and the huge bomber lumbered forward. It stopped briefly to test its brakes, then taxied out quickly onto the ramp and moved toward the open exit-gate. Rover Nine and Rover Seven, the two M113 combat vehicles, fell in on either side of the B-52, their gun turrets now manned and armed with automatic cannons.

Briggs let out a loud sigh of relief when the B-52 taxied clear of Hangar Five—if there had been a commando or terrorist there he would have struck then, as the Megafortress taxied right in front. He almost expected to see a bazooka or TOW anti-tank missile round hit the Old Dog's jet-black surface, but there was no movement. Hal keyed his car's mike:

"All units, be advised aircraft exiting main parking ramp heading for taxiway delta. Begin pre-launch sweep check and report to Red Man when complete. Red Man, report status to Hotel when complete."

"Red Man, wilco."

Hal put his car in gear and fell in well behind the B-52 as it headed down the taxiway toward the sand-colored four-mile-long runway. The security units surrounding Dreamland were reporting in to Red Man Security Control as briefed. Individual tactical units would report to their sector commands, who would report to their team leaders, who would report to Red Man. Everything was going smoothly.

The last to report in were the units not involved with the B-52's operations—base security, individual building security and standing flight-line checkpoints. It took several minutes, by which time all units had reported in as ordered . . . all except Five Foxtrot.

That did it. Definitely something wasn't right here. Hal Briggs stopped his car dead in its tracks and picked up the mike: "Five Foxtrot, this is Hotel. Check in immediately. Over."

He couldn't wait any longer—Lovyyev could hear the irritation in the voice of whoever this Hotel character was. Orlov had disappeared into the hangar. For an instant he thought that Orlov was running, escaping before the security patrols closed in, but he knew better. Orlov was one of the best KGB operatives in North America. He would never run out on a mission unless it was completely hopeless, and he certainly wouldn't run out on another operative.

He had to answer, but he needed to sound convincing. What was the nationality of the security guard they killed? Spanish? Mexican? Why didn't the United States use one damned race in the military like most of the rest of the world? In the Soviet Union they used *Russian* soldiers. Other nationalities swept floors or collected garbage.

Taking a deep breath, he composed his reply in his mind, as taught to him in an all-day cram course by Orlov, and keyed the mike: "Five Foxtrot, all secure. Over."

A chill ran down his spine. Hal had a tough time hearing the faint response, but even if it had been a whisper it wouldn't have made any difference.

That was not Rey Jacinto on the mike.

The Old Dog had now reached the end of the runway. It paused for a few moments as it aligned with the runway centerline. For an instant Hal thought that now would be the perfect time to strike—here, away from the ramp, isolated and vulnerable—but as he began to issue orders to cover the bomber from attack, the engines slowly accelerated to full thrust and the huge plane rolled down the runway.

Hal Briggs stared transfixed at the huge dark creature blasting down the runway. He could see huge puffs of dust and sand erupting from the edge of the semi-camouflaged runway, those could be mortar rounds impacting near the plane—which conjured up the memory of the last time he had seen the Old Dog take off eight years ago, not five hundred yards from this very spot, when there *were* mortar rounds exploding all around them. The same sense of fear gripped him . . .

But this time it turned out to be huge dust clouds kicked up by the wingtip vortices generated by the Old Dog. A few moments later the bomber was airborne, the gear was up, the SST nose retracted into flight position and the Old Dog was racing skyward once again. It climbed nose-up, more like a light fighter plane than a half-million-pound strategic bomber.

In minutes the B-52 was out of sight. No alerts, no warnings. Members of the M113 Rover crews had gotten out of their ACVs to watch the takeoff. Hal checked Five Foxtrot once again. He could see clearly inside the hangar, but there was no sign of any munitions maintenance men in there, and the missiles were still on DreamStar's handpoints beside the air intake. A power cart was hooked up to DreamStar, with hoses and cables snaking around to the fighter's service panel, and now that the Old Dog had departed, Hal could hear the roar of the external power cart's jet engine. It was as if the MMS crew had simply left the plane alone and on power to watch the Old Dog's takeoff. That was a major breach of security, not to mention good sense. You never left a plane unattended with power and air on. Jacinto knew that—where was *he* during all this? And whose was that voice on the mike? Or was he imagining . . . ?

The upper hatch on the armored car was open, and Briggs noticed that a fifty-caliber machine gun was now mounted on the armor-shielded gun bracket on the car's roof. Still no sign of Jacinto. Maybe he had watched the takeoff, after all. But why mount his machine gun now? Or had he done it during taxi?

Briggs picked up his microphone. "Five Foxtrot, report status and location of the work crew at your location. Over."

No reply.

"Red Man, this is Hotel, radio check."

"Hotel, this is Red Man. Five by."

It wasn't his radio. Was there a radio "blind spot" out here? Was Jacinto's radio malfunctioning? If it was, he should have gotten a replacement long ago—*if* it was Rey Jacinto in there.

"Roger. Break. Rover Nine, meet me at Five Foxtrot on the double. Over."

"Rover Nine on the move." Briggs could see the two alert crewmen run back inside the ACV. The low-slung, eleven-ton mini-tank made a tight turn and headed back toward the parking ramp on its twin-steel tracks.

Briggs put his car in gear and headed toward Dream Star's

hangar. Somebody was screwing up by the numbers here, it was past time to find out who and what.

Lovyyev was silently screaming at himself. Only a few hours in place, he speaks three words on the radio and is discovered.

Be calm, he told himself. Things were happening out there on the flight line—perhaps there was still time to bluff his way out of this. This Hotel person may get too busy to check on him.

But one glance out the bulletproof windscreen told him that his luck was running out. A staff car was heading his way. It was still three hundred yards off, perhaps more, but it was coming fast.

Lovyyev jumped out of his seat and crawled up into the armored open turret on the roof. He yelled back into the hangar, *"Orlov. Skaryehyeh! Etah srochnah!* Hurry. They're coming!"

"Shut up, Crowe!" Orlov was hiding against the inner front wall of the hangar, his M-16/M-203 in his arms and the remote-control detonator around his neck. "Get down!"

But it was too late. In a panic, Lovyyev swiveled the machine gun turret around, released the safety, aimed it at the approaching staff car, pulled and held the trigger.

Hal Briggs was thinking about what he was going to say to Rey Jacinto about his strange behavior when he saw what looked like exhaust smoke rising from the Commando armored car. Just as he was wondering why Jacinto was starting up, he saw a line of explosions and shattering concrete race across the tarmac directly at his car. He slammed on the brakes and dived for the floorboards under the front seat just as his windshield exploded in a shower of glass. Instantly he felt a wall of fire envelop him, and realized that the engine compartment was on fire.

His synthetic fatigue shirt began to melt on his back. He clawed for the door handle, found it, shoved the door open and crawled out of the burning car. He landed only a foot from the flaming remains of the car's hood, which had been blasted apart by the explosion, and half-crawled, half-stumbled away from the car. Thick black smoke was everywhere. He inhaled a lungful of the gas, gagged, fell to the concrete. Pieces of red-hot metal were all around him. But at least the smoke hid him from the gunner in the V-100. He stayed on his hands and knees and began to crawl to where he thought the security checkpoint was . . . He guessed right. A few moments later two guards rushed out and hauled him to his feet. He let the guards carry him to the guard shack but resisted when they tried to lay him down on the floor. He picked up the radio, switched the channel selector to one, the base-wide emergency channel, and clicked it on:

"Attention all HAWC security units, this is Hotel on channel one. Execute code echo-seven. Repeat, code echo-seven. Intruder alert, Hangar Five. Repeat, intruder alert, Hangar Five. This is not an exercise. Shots fired in front of Hangar Five by intruders from a V-100 armored vehicle. Number of intruders unknown."

Briggs paused, rubbing a pain in his right temple. Massaging it, he found a gash in his head and his hair burned off. "All Foxtrot guard units, secure your posts and stand by to repel. Break. Rover Seven, converge on Hangar Five, secure the V-100 parked there, block the front on the hangar by any means possible. Break. Red Man, notify Colonel Towland and General Elliott in Mission Control of situation, use channel nine, and have them order the flight crew on the airborne B-52 to remain clear of the area and notify the crew of the standby B-52 to prepare to evacuate. Deploy all available personnel in full combat gear to security checkpoint alpha and launch helicopter air security units one and two. Break. Rover Nine, pick me up in front of security checkpoint alpha. I will take control from Rover Nine. All units, execute . . ."

Orlov knew it was no use berating Lovyyev—he might have even saved them by keeping that sedan away from the hangar until Maraklov, or James, or whatever his name was now, could get ready. They had been out there for hours. Was Maraklov ever going to be ready?

The security forces were moving faster than Orlov ever thought possible. Seconds after Lovyyev opened fire, he was receiving return fire from Hangar Four, although Lovyyev was in no danger except from a lucky shot. M-16 rounds were pinging off the armor surrounding the turret, forcing Lovyyev to shoot from a more protected position inside the cab. But it was working. He was holding down any deadly return fire, keeping the first wave of defenders back. It wouldn't last long, but he was buying Maraklov time . . .

As was always the case, the first device to be activated under the Advanced Neural Transfer and Response System was on the radios. Usually they were quiet. This time, there was so much chatter on the area air-traffic control frequency that at first James thought he had dialed in two overlapping Las Vegas AM talk stations. The words were almost unintelligible, which at first confused him. Then he realized that the voices were talking about *them*—half the military security forces in Nevada were being called on to attack Hangar Five . . . they had already been discovered by Dreamland's security forces. If he'd spent two more minutes completing the ANTARES interface they'd all be dead.

A millisecond's mental inquiry told him all he needed to know: Sergeant Howard, if he was still alive, had done his job well. External air and power were on and available. DreamStar's body tanks were full—he had much more fuel than he had hoped for. Apparently they had drained the wing fuel tanks but left the body tanks and their thirty thousand gallons of jet fuel intact.

Both AIM-120 Scorpion missiles were loaded and even responded to a fast connectivity and continuity check—which meant they could be launched or jettisoned at any time. Whether they were armed or capable of defending him was a question that would have to wait. The twenty-millimeter Vulcan cannon was empty—a fully loaded cannon would have been too much to hope for.

Howard had removed the inlet covers, safety pins and landing gear downlocks, and had closed all the maintenance covers except for the external power cover. The man was really efficient. He'd have to thank him someday, if they made it . . . ANTARES' automatic flight-data recorder recorded the thought for later retrieval.

DreamStar had the ability to go from complete power off to full military takeoff thrust in moments. Fighters in the twenty-first century would routinely have it—now only DreamStar did. James again placed his life in the hands of a computer—only a machine could control the enormous amount of power that he was about to unleash. It was the ultimate in combat speed and efficiency—but it could just as easily turn the one hundred-thousand-pound fighter into a huge bomb.

Power, fuel, air—all engine start systems activated with a single thought. Lights and transmitters off—no use in making it easier for Briggs and the Air Force to find him. A compressed air tank, filled from the external power cart, collected twenty thousand cubic feet of air at five thousand pounds PSI pressure, then emptied it onto the sixteenth-stage compressor in DreamStar's turbofan engine in less than a second. At the same time fuel was injected into the combustion chamber and the high-voltage ignitors activated. The blast of compressed air spun the engine turbines at three thousand RPMs, mixing air and fuel in the proportions to create a huge explosive ignition equal to the force of a ton of TNT.

In ten seconds DreamStar was ready for flight. With full power available, his only concern now was to get off the ground as fast as possible.

Orlov, as Sergeant Howard, had been briefed on DreamStar's fast-reaction-start capability, but he never quite believed it. One moment the fighter was silent, cold, without power—the next, the engine was at full power with a hugh shaft of fire burning out the engine exhaust, expelling dangerous unburned gases. It reminded him of watching a tiger being fed at the Moscow Zoo—one moment the tigers were sleeping soundly, but at the first scent of blood they were unstoppable dynamos of motion and energy.

The external power cables and air hoses dropped off the service port by remote control, and before he could rush to the side of the cockpit to see if Maraklov needed anything, DreamStar was moving forward—ready to fly.

Orlov didn't hesitate. He reached up to the remote-control trigger device, pressed the button, then threw the device away in the hangar and sprinted for the V-100 armored car.

He reached the car just as columns of fire lit up the gloomy early morning sky. Orlov hadn't counted on how bright those magnesium mortar shells were—he had, though, tightly closed his eyes just as he heard the loud puffs when the mortar rounds were launched. Lovyyev, inside the V-100, had neglected to shield his eyes, and Orlov found him rubbing and blinking furiously.

"Move, get out of the way!" Orlov ordered. Lovyyev followed Orlov's grasp and tumbled into the clear area under the gun turret as Orlov scrambled into the stiff driver's seat, put the V-100 into gear and hit the gas pedal.

"Can you operate the machine gun?" Orlov called to Lovyyev and checked his assistant as he hauled himself into the gun-turret brace. Lovyyev was still trying to blink away the flashblindness, his face red and puffed, but Lovyyev, longer on courage than brains, was the kind who would say he was okay if both arms were blown away. All Orlov could do was drive. Either Lovyyev was up to the task of holding off the response forces, or they would die.

"Just don't shoot *behind* you," Orlov told him. "Maraklov and his fighter are right behind us. Shoot at anything else that moves. Don't waste a single shot. Our only hope is—"

Orlov's voice was drowned out by a rhythmic hammering sound on the hull of the armored car. He thought it was from Lovyyev's gun until he realized that the sound came from outside. He was about to warn Lovyyev to take cover when the young KGB agent's body, minus his handsome blond head, slumped into the bottom of the gun turret. Orlov stomped hard on the gas pedal. Never leave a pretty corpse for the enemy.

Dreamland's security forces had reacted much faster than Orlov had anticipated. Now the last obstacle lay ahead—the long movable steel gate that enclosed the fence surrounding the research hangars. Orlov had to work fast. Once fully closed, huge steel pilings would be lowered into place and the gate would be unmovable.

Driving with one hand on the wheel, gas pedal to the floor, Orlov reached up and swung the fifty-caliber machine gun back facing forward, then fumbled with the remote trigger mechanism, finally clipping it into place on the rifle's trigger. He was less than a hundred yards from the gate. Firing in short bursts, he swung the wheel back and forth, pointing the gun's fire at anything that moved near the gate.

To his surprise, the gate was already fully closed. Time had almost run out. Two soldiers were low-crawling along the gate, trying to reach the locking mechanism.

Orlov swung the V-100 toward them, trying to rake the fence with fire to pin them down, but the Americans refused to stop. Orlov caged the fifty-caliber forward and headed for the lock mechanism, spraying the area with bullets. But that lasted for only a few seconds—the shell-feeder on the machine gun jammed.

It was too late. One guard was dead but the other threw the handle on the locking mechanism and dropped the steel post into place.

One chance left. Keeping the throttle full open Orlov aimed the Commando right at the gate opening. If the lock could be broken and the gate dislodged from the piling he could use the V-100 to push the gate far enough open for the XF-34A to get through.

Under a hailstorm of bullets from all sides, Orlov's V-100 plowed into the gate's locking mechanism at well over sixty miles an hour—the four-ton armored car had built up enough force to demolish a house. But it was still not enough to snap the five-inch steel post securing the gate. Instead, the force of the impact snapped the motor mounts off the armored car, and the heavy armored plating in the car's nose acted like a giant piston, driving the engine and transmission into Gekky Orlov's body. The bones in his body were pulverized like dry twigs under a steam roller. The V-100 exploded, starting a fire in the electric and hydraulic lock systems and killing the second security guard. But the gate held fast.

And DreamStar was trapped.

A quick mental command, and DreamStar's attack-radar flashed on, then off, at precisely two hundred and twenty yards from where Kenneth Francis James, Andrei Ivanschichin Maraklov, had stopped his fighter short of the burning gate ahead. Six hundred and sixty feet, then over a twelve-foot-high obstacle. Another mental command: DreamStar's computers sampled the external air temperature, inertial winds, pressure altitude, relative humidity, aircraft gross weight, engine-trim-and-performance variables, then computed takeoff data at max performance best angle of climb over the obstacle.

Not good enough. DreamStar reported that it needed at least one thousand feet to clear the obstacle.

James' reaction was instantaneous. He brought DreamStar's turbofan engine to full power, moved the vectored thrust-nozzles to full reverse and released the brakes. DreamStar began to move backward toward the taxiway throat leading to the ramp in front of the hangars—back toward the melee he had just escaped from. At the same time he activated DreamStar's radar system, which scanned in every direction around the fighter.

DreamStar had moved only a hundred feet farther from the gate when he "saw" the first M113 armored vehicle approach. It was moving fast, nearly forty miles an hour, past the burning

piles of debris scattered around in front of the now-abandoned
Hangar Five less than a hundred yards away. He hit the brakes
just as the superconducting radar detected the M113's twenty-
millimeter cannon open fire.

"Hal, what's your situation?" General Elliott called over the
security net.

Hal Briggs grabbed a handhold on the M113's door for support
as he keyed his microphone: "We're approaching the plane from
the left. It's now about three hundred feet in front of us, facing
down the throat toward the gate. I'd swear the thing backed up
or somethin' . . . Over."

Elliott, now in a staff car with McLanahan at the wheel, was
racing down taxiway delta toward the hangar area, careening
over ditches and weaving through gates to get back to the ramp.
McLanahan looked at Elliott. "Did he say DreamStar was *back-
ing up*?" Elliott had no answer. "Hal," Patrick said, "what's
DreamStar's range to the gate?"

"Hard to tell until we get closer, but I'd say less than three
hundred yards."

Elliott looked at Patrick. "Is it enough . . . ?"

McLanahan didn't dare take his eyes off the road, floored the
gas pedal and gripped the wheel tighter. "Cool morning, half a
fuel load, a little headwind . . . it's enough."

"God *damn*. Who the hell's flying it?" Even then, Elliott
could not believe that James, one of only three men alive who
could possibly fly DreamStar, was in the cockpit. "How the hell
did he get in there?" Elliott pressed the mike switch hard enough
to turn his finger white. "Shoot out the tires, Hal. If the plane
moves, shoot to kill. If DreamStar moves ahead, *destroy* it."

Eight hundred twelve point seven feet. *Now.*

Keeping the brakes on hard, James commanded the throttles
to full power, let them stabilize for a few seconds, then pushed
them to max afterburner. He allowed another half-second for the
computer to perform a single full-power engine-trim adjustment,
then opened the dorsal engine louvers. DreamStar's aft end
pitched down and the nose shot up at a steep angle. He set the
flex wings and canards for high lift and max performance climb-
out . . . then released the brakes.

DreamStar had not rolled more than a hundred feet forward

when he realized he was not going to make it. He knew it even
before the performance computer, receiving data from radar on
range to the obstacle, reported a collision warning and recommended an immediate takeoff abort. Maraklov overrode the recommendation with the thought: this is how I'll die? Not after a
dogfight trying to steal and save DreamStar. Dying in a fireball
crashing into the security gate, trying something that I knew had
no chance from the beginning . . .

Five hundred feet to go. All wheels still firmly on the ground,
airspeed hardly registering. Maraklov could feel the absence of
lift on his wings, the absence of the familiar twist that the composite flex wings underwent during the takeoff acceleration.
Countering the wingtip twist was a simple computer-controlled
correction, as simple as swallowing, as simple as—

He cut short his gloomy predictions. The wingtip twist . . .
DreamStar automatically neutralized the twist in the wingtips
because the twisted wing created vortices under the wing and
fuselage, which created turbulence, which increased drag and
lengthened takeoff roll distances. But the turbulence under the
fuselage created something else—ground effect. And the power
of ground effect would be to cushion the plane a few feet off the
ground, just below flying speed but still airborne. If that was
true . . .

Four hundred feet left . . .

Maraklov overrode the order to counteract the wingtip twist.
In response, the tips of DreamStar's wings curved even more,
creating two hundred percent more lift as well as two virtual
tornados of wind that swirled counterclockwise from the wingtips down and under the wings and across the fuselage. He felt
the vortices slam into the fuselage and fought for control.
DreamStar felt sluggish, unresponsive, out of pilot control.

Ninety knots. Three hundred feet remaining . . .

A loud creak from the left wingtip, and a "CONFIGURATION"
warning flashed in Maraklov's conscious mind. He ignored it.
The wingtips were now being buffeted by winds nearing hurricane force, while the rest of the wing was wallowing in relatively
calm winds nowhere close to takeoff speed. Maraklov stiffened
the wings by twisting the inner surfaces, allowing the power
being generated in the wingtips to flow to the lazy parts of the
wing. The aircraft rumbled in protest. He was receiving "CON-
FIGURATION" and "COLLISION" warnings, and had to struggle

not only to ignore the warnings but to prevent ANTARES from taking command and aborting the takeoff. DreamStar's artificial brain was programmed for self-preservation at all costs, not self-destruction.

One hundred knots, two hundred feet remaining . . . DreamStar's nose gear popped off the runway, held aloft by the large canards and by the force of the upwardly directed thrust from the dorsal louvers. DreamStar was in takeoff attitude but she was still far, far from lift-off speed.

One hundred fifty feet . . . one chance left—he commanded the landing gear up.

One hundred feet, one hundred ten knots. An ANTARES-generated warning from the flight-configuration computer flashed in Maraklov's mind, warning him that the landing gear safety switch still showed pressure on the gear struts—DreamStar was still on the ground. Instantly he overrode the warning, commanded gear up, then closed his eyes and waited for DreamStar's tail to hit the runway.

Seventy-five feet, one hundred fifteen knots—liftoff speed for this takeoff configuration. The tail did not hit the runway.

Zero feet left . . . With the tall, bulky landing gear retracted, DreamStar accelerated to one hundred thirty knots, and was able to use the extra airspeed to lift its nose even higher, clawing for every last bit of altitude. A shower of sparks erupted from the top of the steel gate as DreamStar scraped past the reinforced barbed wire, tearing apart the two ventral rudders that had automatically deployed in DreamStar's slow-flight mode—Maraklov did not think to retract those low-speed rudders in time. DreamStar shuddered as the rudders ripped off her belly, but she did not stall or hit the ground.

DreamStar was airborne.

McLanahan and Elliott had just reached the hangar area as DreamStar lifted over the gate, the aircraft flying so slowly and at such a steep climb that it seemed almost suspended in midair, an apparition at the end of a shaft of fire. It also appeared to be falling slightly, but this was mostly an illusion; DreamStar's nose dipped slightly to build up valuable airspeed, and it began to accelerate at it crossed the deserted runways and climbed slowly into the dawn.

McLanahan slammed on the brakes in time to avoid an M113

combat vehicle that continued to fire heavy caliber rounds into
the sky until DreamStar was completely out of sight. A few
moments later Hal Briggs climbed out of the ACV, head tightly
bandaged and carrying an M-16A2 rifle, and moved over to
McLanahan's sedan. After Elliott opened a door for him, he
nearly collapsed in the backseat.

"Sorry," Briggs gasped, painfully hauling himself upright.
"Couldn't . . . couldn't stop him." Before Elliott could speak,
Briggs had pulled out a walkie-talkie. "Red Man, this is Hotel. Notify the four-seventy-fourth tactical fighter wing at Nellis. XF-
34A fighter aircraft stolen from this location. Aircraft is armed
with air-to-air missiles and must be considered hostile. Orders
from Alpha are to search and destroy."

"Copy, Hotel."

"Break. All Dreamland security units, this is Hotel. XF-34A
aircraft is airborne, last seen heading southwest out of Dreamland at slow speed. The aircraft has been hijacked by unknown
persons. It is equipped with air-to-air missiles only. Air defense
units have authorization to engage and destroy at will; report
detection or engagement to Red Man, Nellis and Las Vegas Air
Traffic Control Center ASAP. Repeat: all units, engage and destroy at will. Hotel out." He dropped the walkie-talkie into his
lap as if it weighed a hundred pounds.

"Take us over to Hangar Five, Patrick," Elliott said. He
turned to Briggs, gently lifting up the bandages to check his
wound. "Cancel that. Take us to the infirmary."

"I'm all right," Briggs said, gingerly touching the top of his
hairless head and checking his hastily applied bandages. "The
guys on the ACV fixed me up."

At least for the moment, Elliott didn't want Briggs in the
hospital any more than Briggs wanted to be there. As Mc-
Lanahan headed for the hangars he asked, "What the hell happened, Hal?"

Briggs wiped stinging sweat from his wounds and burns. "It
all happened so fast, General. The Foxtrot guard posts didn't
look right. I had them report in. Whoever was in Five Foxtrot's
Commando, it wasn't Jacinto. I headed over to check it out when
I got hit by the fifty cal. I barely made it to Rover Nine when
flash grenades start popping. Before I knew it DreamStar was
out in the throat. I've never seen anything like that takeoff, who-

ever did it. It was like he levitated right over the gate. I didn't think he'd make it . . .''

They drove up the entrance of Hangar Five. Rover Seven, the second M113 armored combat vehicle, was positioned in front, with guards covering both the front and back. Rover Seven was also aiming a huge spotlight inside the hangar.

"Seven, this is Hotel. Is the hangar secure?"

"Affirmative."

"Roger. Sergeant Macynski, follow me in. The rest cover us."

Briggs got out of the sedan, flipped off the safety lever on his M-16 and ran over to the M113. He met up with Macynski, outlined a brief tactical plan to the NCO, then approached the hangar door at a dead run. They scanned the interior of the hangar, quickly sweeping their rifle muzzles around the hangar while sighting through them, ready to fire at any sound or movement. Nothing. Briggs ordered the M113 in closer to secure the hangar, then headed back to the sedan.

In the backseat he said into the walkie-talkie, "Red Man, this is Hotel. I want an investigation unit in Hangar Five and one on the Commando ACV on the ramp gate on the double. Break. Rover Nine, secure the V-100 that crashed into the gate. Recover any bodies from the wreckage for the investigation unit. I want an I.D. on the occupants ASAP."

"Roger, Hotel," the security controller replied. "Hotel, be advised, Lance One and Lance Two F-16Fs airborne from Nellis at five past the hour. Two F-14 units from China Lake also report airborne. CATTLECAR is their controller. You can meet them on channel one-one."

"Roger, Red Man. Get all Dreamland air defense units on channel eleven and help coordinate an intercept with CATTLE-CAR. The last thing we need is for our guys to take shots at those F-14s or -16s."

"Switching all units to eleven, sir," the security controller said. "Simultaneous voice and data." Briggs switched his walkie-talkie over as well.

"CATTLECAR, this is Hotel on channel one-one. Over."

"Hotel, this is CATTLECAR," the radar controller replied. "HAWC anti-air units are reporting in now, sir. All assets should be on-line in sixty seconds."

"Any airborne radar platforms up?"

"Not yet, sir. Nellis' 767 AWACS is not an alert bird. I've requested the tac fighter unit to recall the crew, but that may take some time."

"We'll lose him without an AWACS up there to dig him out of the terrain," McLanahan said. "Ground radar won't pick him up if he stays low."

"Hotel, this is CATTLECAR. Radar contact on your hostile. I'm directing all HAWC anti-air artillery units to engage. Any further instructions?"

Briggs stopped and looked at Elliott. The general inwardly flinched but did not hesitate. "If they've got him, destroy him."

Briggs nodded and raised his walkie-talkie. "CATTLECAR, message confirmed through Alpha. Engage at will and shoot to kill. Out."

Maraklov was no more than two hundred feet above ground when ANTARES began to report the emitters all around him. As Maraklov scanned outside the cockpit, visual images were supplanted by ANTARES-generated images of catalogued terrain features around which multicolored arcs or bands undulated, disappeared and reappeared in kaleidoscopic waves. The colored bands were beams of radar energy—search radars, tracking radars, and data-links—all searching for him.

Most of the waves of color were above him, like curtains of fire stretching across a ceiling, but a few seemed to slice right through DreamStar. Maraklov had to avoid those bands. The green bands were search radars, not deadly in themselves, but they would give away his position to the searchers. The other bands of energy were yellow—tracking radars that would pinpoint his location and would begin to feed targeting information to surface-to-air or air-to-air missiles. If the yellow bands turned red, it meant that a missile had been launched. If he was inside the red band, he was within the missile's lethal envelope and would probably die within seconds unless the missile could be outmaneuvered—DreamStar carried no jammers, no decoys. Maraklov had to outrun, outmaneuver or kill his attackers, or it was over for him.

He was finally free of the dry bed of the Groom Lake area, heading south and almost into Papoose Canyon northwest of Emigrant Valley, when a single finger of green light snapped out between a narrow gap between two rocky buttes and hit

DreamStar broadside. One of the search radars had found him. The band immediately turned to yellow, but one of the buttes blocked the energy and the band turned green once again as the beam continued its three hundred and sixty degree sweep. But they now knew where he was—and were closing in on him. Maraklov dodged further away from the butte, hoping to stay in the butte's radar shadow as long as possible.

It wasn't working. The terrain was forcing him to climb, but the beam of green energy above him wasn't rising with him. He had no time to react. The green beam of energy, completing a full revolution every six seconds, hit him once again as DreamStar crested a rocky ridge line. This time, it turned yellow and stayed on him. DreamStar's threat-warning receiver immediately reported the contact, and after a few seconds analysis concluded that a British-made Rapier surface-to-air-missile was locked on.

The computer suggested a heading, altitude and airspeed to escape the Rapier missile's lethal radius, and Maraklov ordered the evasive maneuver just as the band of energy went from yellow to red—the Rapier had gone from search to missile-uplink in seconds. The missile was in the air. There was no time and no room to move. DreamStar was bracketed by hills and mountains.

Sensing Maraklov's confusion, ANTARES canceled the first suggested maneuver, immediately deployed the canards into their high-lift configuration and ordered a hard, tight Immelmann—a fast inverted half-loop—directly into the short rocky butte they had just passed. ANTARES also activated the superconducting radar, which showed the butte only three-quarters of a mile directly ahead. They would impact in less than four seconds . . .

A flash of light erupted off the right wing, and suddenly DreamStar banked hard right, pulling nine G's in the tight turn. The Rapier missile had missed by only a few short feet. Maraklov tried to search the sky for another missile, but the hard nine-G turn had blurred and tunneled his vision. Another explosion off to his right—there had, indeed, been a second Rapier missile launched at him, but that one had exploded on the butte not three hundred yards behind him.

As his ejection-seat back began to recline automatically, which would help blood to flow back into his brain while ANTARES completed evasive maneuvers, Maraklov watched as the colored bands surrounding him switched back to green. The older Rapier missile systems surrounding Dreamland carried only two missiles on each launch platform, and the system had switched back to search mode while the Rapier crew reloaded.

Maraklov watched, fascinated, as ANTARES automatically increased power to full thrust, and began to use short bursts of its multi-directional radar to scan the terrain around DreamStar and fly as close to earth as possible. His ejection seat slowly returned to its upright position as the G-forces subsided, and he actually could relax . . . he would be long gone from the range of that Rapier site by the time it was reloaded—

A warning beep sounded in the upper-center part of his cockpit, and with it a blue-triangle icon appeared, with a long green triangle protruding from the front end. Answering his mental query, ANTARES reported what it was: an F-16 Falcon fighter, sweeping the skies below with its new AEG-91 look-down radar. Although pushing age twenty-five, the F-16 had undergone so many modifications that it could hardly be considered the same aircraft as twenty-five years earlier. Not originally designed for look-down, shoot-down, low-altitude engagements, it now sported a multi-purpose "cranked arrow" effect, with huge delta wings, and was capable of attacking air or ground targets at any altitude. Its new capability was in evidence as its green triangle swept down from the sky and in moments DreamStar had once again been discovered.

Maraklov commanded an immediate hard bank and searched for terrain to hide in. He knew the F-16s rarely worked alone; only one would activate its radar, while one or two others would take vectors from the leader and close in on their prey, activating their attack radars at the last possible moment . . .

Another mental command . . . and Maraklov's heart sank. At its present low altitude, DreamStar was gulping fuel. He could not afford to get into a situation where he'd have to waste time and fuel dodging missiles from the F-16s, let alone any sort of protracted aerial battle with them. Reinforcements were surely on their way—very likely F-15s from the Air Force Reserve base at Davis-Monthan in Tucson. Maraklov's options were running out. There was only one real choice left to him.

Run like hell.

At a single request, Maraklov discovered the single best altitude to use to clear all terrain within five hundred miles—six thousand five hundred feet. He ordered the computer to maintain that altitude and set best-speed power settings for the engines. As fuel was burned off and gross weight decreased, the computer would pick the best speed versus drag settings of engine power, trim, and wing configuration to achieve the fastest possible speed. He could afford no more power changes, climbs, descents, terrain avoidance or defense maneuvers. His only option was to stay at zero Q—where the sum of all aerodynamic forces on his aircraft remained zero, the highest possible cruise efficiency—and run for the border.

A fast mental inquiry and the GPS satellite-navigation system checked DreamStar's position, computed a likely flight path around known population centers and defense areas, measured the distance between present position and the tiny dry lake, Laguna de Santiaguillo, where Kramer and Moffitt in north central Mexico were supposed to be waiting with a fuel truck. Laguna de Santiaguillo was an abandoned training facility (KGB assets utilizing locals equally receptive to rubles and dollars) in the foothills of the Sierra Madre Occidental mountains, well within range of two Mexican fighter bases at Mazatlan and Monterrey. A lousy location, Maraklov thought, but the only one possible on such short notice.

The computer had his answer after a relatively long two-second pause: three hundred miles to the Gulf of California, another seven hundred fifty miles along the west ridge of the Sierra Madre Occidental mountains, then across the Remedias River valley to Laguna de Santiaguillo. He was traveling at one point one Mach, about nine hundred miles per hour, and was consuming twenty thousand pounds of fuel an hour. He had exactly twenty-two thousand pounds of fuel remaining. Which meant, at his current setting, he would flame out right over Laguna de Santiaguillo. He would have more fuel available if he used an idle-power descent and a long glide for landing, but he'd have less if he had to dodge any more missiles or if he had to use afterburner.

Another mental command and he checked the two AIM-120C Scorpion missiles, then tried a test arming. Both were fitted with instrumented warheads, but otherwise would launch and track like fully operational weapons. He could use them if he got himself cornered. He would, though, have to shoot very carefully—without explosive warheads there would be no proximity detonation; each shot had to be a direct hit.

But up here, the possibility of anyone touching him seemed unlikely. There were still search radars all around him, resembling huge green cones rising out of the terrain, but there were large gaps between the radar cones and he was picking his way through them, using slight heading changes to put a mountain or ridge line between himself and the radar cones. Smaller yellow blobs, giant mushrooms, appeared now and then—the lethal envelope of surface-to-air missiles stationed below—but he was avoiding them as well. Now he was almost out of the Dreamland complex, accelerating past one thousand miles per hour.

Speed and stealth meant survival more than fancy flying or superior weaponry. The first time he had decided to steal DreamStar he'd imagined himself taking on the air might of the whole southeastern United States, flying rings around the best fighters and the best pilots in the world, winning out over a billion dollars' worth of hardware. Well, it wasn't going to happen that way. He was going to sneak out, hiding behind every shadow, measuring every quart of fuel.

Whatever it took . . .

For the first time he really allowed his body to relax. He had stolen DreamStar right out from under the noses of the people who wanted to give up on his baby. And now he even dared to think that he might actually make it all the way.

He was allowed that heady thought for precisely forty seconds. From out of nowhere, a green triangle of energy appeared in front of him. There was no time to evade. The green triangle enveloped him, and instantly turned to yellow . . .

This thing was truly amazing, Major Edward Frost, the radar navigator aboard the B-52 Megafortress Plus, marveled. A goddamned B-52 bomber with more gadgets and modes and functions and bells and whistles than L.A. Air Traffic Control.

Frost was studying a fourteen-inch by ten-inch rectangular video display terminal set on one-hundred-mile range. A circle cursor, automatically laid on a radar return that matched the preprogrammed parameters set by Frost, was tracking a high-altitude, high-speed target dead ahead. You told the system what you wanted to find and it did the searching. It was a hell of a lot different from only a few years ago when radar navs on B-52 bombers concentrated on terrain and cultural returns—mountains, buildings, towns. This B-52 was different.

Major Frost hit the mike button near his right foot. "Pilot, radar. Radar contact aircraft, one o'clock, eighty-five miles." He punched a function key on his keyboard. "Altitude six thousand five hundred, airspeed . . . hey, he's moving out. Airspeed one thousand one hundred knots."

He hit another function key, and the display changed to a maze of arcs, lines, grids. The computer had presented a series of options for approaching the target.

Frost shook his head. Here I am, sitting in a B-52 bomber planning to *attack* a high-speed fighter!

"Turn right heading zero-five two to IR intercept in six-two nautical miles. Automatic intercept is available." Then to Angelina Pereira: "I'm aligned for guidance-mode transfer at any time—"

"Belay that," General John Ormack said over interphone. "Weapons stay on safe—that's *our* damned plane out there, Frost."

"Sorry, got carried away."

"Auto-intercept coming on, crew." Ormack connected the digital autopilot to the intercept computer and monitored the Old Dog's turn, pushing the throttles up to ninety five percent power to keep the angle of attack low. The autopilot made several small corrections farther to the right as the distance between the two aircraft rapidly decreased.

"Exactly what are we trying to accomplish here, General?" George Wendelstat, the safety observer asked. Wendelstat was firmly strapped into the instructor-pilot's seat, wearing a backpack-style parachute on his beefy shoulders. His face was cherry red and he was sweating in spite of the B-52's cool interior temperature. "Do you mean to *attack* that aircraft?"

"What I mean to do is everything I possibly can to turn that aircraft back," Ormack said. "If I can't get him to turn around I mean to delay him long enough for help to arrive."

"But this is suicide," Wendelstat protested. "A B-52 against this DreamStar? That's a fighter plane, isn't it?"

"It's also a stolen aircraft from my research center," Ormack said. "I'm not going to let this guy go without trying to do something—"

"Including getting us all killed?"

"I know the limits of this crew and aircraft," Ormack said. "We have the capability to engage DreamStar and hopefully detain him long enough for help to arrive. I won't go beyond the limits of my responsibility or common sense—"

"You already *have*. He can launch a missile against us at any second—"

"Seventy miles and closing fast, General."

"Wendelstat, sit back and shut up," Colonel Jeff Khan, the copilot, broke in. "The general knows what he's doing."

Ormack reached up to the overhead communications console and switched his command radio to channel eleven. "CATTLE-CAR, this is Dog Zero Two. We have the hostile at our twelve o'clock, seventy miles. Closing on an intercept course. Requesting instructions from HAWC Alpha as soon as possible."

"Break. Zero Two, this is HAWC Alpha. You can't do anything up there, John. We're vectoring in the F-16s now. Get out of the area as fast as you can. Over."

"I've got a lock-on and I'm turning for an I.D. intercept, Alpha," Ormack answered back. "I can turn it into a radar pass at any time. Just say the word."

"Sixty miles."

"He's got two Scorpion missiles, John," Elliott said. "Repeat—he's armed with two live Scorpions. You won't have a chance. Disengage and leave the area—"

"*I've* got two Scorpions too, General. Plus I've got jammers that can counter the Scorpion's active radar. He doesn't."

"He can fly circles around your Scorpions—"

Ormack interrupted again. "I can engage him, maybe force him to turn back, maybe knock the sonofabitch down. Or I can let him fly our plane to Central America or wherever the hell he's going. Which is it going to be?"

No immediate reply. Ormack nodded—he'd gotten his answer. "Radar, change to Scorpion-attack profile. Crew, prepare to engage hostile air target."

Frost had his finger on the function key and hit it even before Ormack finished giving the order. Immediately the Old Dog heeled over into forty degrees of bank, then abruptly rolled out. It was now aiming for a spot several miles along DreamStar's flight path, projecting out to intersect the fighter's path at the AIM-120C's optimum flight range. Ormack pushed his throttles up to full power, then reached over to his left-side panel and flipped a gang-barred four-way switch. "Guns, you have Scorpion missile launch consent."

"Confirmed," Angelina Pereira replied. "Left pylon on automatic launch, missile counting down . . . twenty seconds to launch."

On the UHF radio Ormack said, "CATTLECAR, this is Dog Zero Two. Clear airspace for red fox engagement. Be advised, red buzzer activity on all frequencies. Dog Zero Two out." On interphone Ormack said, "Defense, clear for electronic countermeasures. Crew, prepare for air combat engagement."

"Fifteen seconds . . ."

Suddenly a metallic, computer-modified voice cut in on the frequency: "Dog Zero Two, disengage. I'm warning you."

Khan looked puzzled. "Who the hell was . . . ?"

"ANTARES. The master computer on DreamStar." Ormack flipped to the channel. "This is Dog Zero Two. Who's this?"

"This is Colonel Andrei Ivanschichin Maraklov, General Ormack." Maraklov thought before continuing: should he give his American name? But he was never going to return to America—the KGB or the CIA would see to that—and they would find out anyway. "You know me as Captain Kenneth Francis James, *sir*."

Ormack swore through his oxygen mask. "God*damn*—Ken James stole DreamStar." He switched his command radio to channel eleven. "Alpha, monitor GUARD channel. Urgent." He then quickly switched his radio to the universal emergency frequency, GUARD.

"James—Ken—Mara . . . whatever the hell it is . . . *land that plane immediately*. I have orders to attack." On interphone he told Angelina Pereira to get ready to cancel the auto attack.

"Yes, sir . . . ten seconds."

"Turn off your attack radar immediately, General Ormack," the computerized voice of Maraklov on the emergency channel said, "or I will have no choice but to defend myself."

"Damn it, James, you're about ten seconds from getting your ass blown out of the sky. Decrease speed and lower your landing gear or I'll engage."

No reply.

"Five seconds . . . four . . . three . . ."

"Any change in his airspeed or heading?"

"Negative," from Frost. "Still goin' full blast . . ."

"Launch commit," Angelina said.

There was a muffled screech of rocket exhaust from the left wing, as the first Scorpion missile raced out of its streamlined canister. It ran on course toward its quarry. Unlike previous air-to-air missiles, the C-version of the Scorpion did not glide or cruise to its target; even though it was still considered a medium-range missile it stayed powered throughout its flight.

"Uplink tracking . . . missile now tracking . . . dead on course . . ."

The bands of yellow, signifying the B-52's tracking radar illuminating his aircraft, suddenly changed to red. Maraklov caught a chill. This was *real*, Ormack wasn't bluffing. This Dog Zero Two had live missiles on board, and he was under attack. *By a B-52 bomber* . . .

He activated his attack radar. The radar image of the B-52, still over fifty miles away, seemed the size of a flying mountain. His radar wasn't picking it up but he knew the missile was only seconds from impact. His reactions were executed at the speed of thought . . .

He turned right toward the B-52, exposing only the minimum radar cross-section of his aircraft possible. He then began a series of high-speed reversals using the canards in their high-maneuverability mode, not rolling into each turn but side-stepping, darting back and forth, keeping only DreamStar's front cross-section aimed toward the B-52. The B-52 would be carrying AIM-120C, same as DreamStar. The AIM-120 was a fabulous weapon, with big fins to steer it toward its target. But its developers ten years earlier had never envisaged an aircraft that could move *sideways* like DreamStar.

Maraklov continued to shoot back and forth for another two seconds, completing two full horizontal S-slides, making each dodge wider than the other, using his high-maneuverability canards to keep DreamStar's nose pointed at where he thought the missile would be. It was a gamble. With each turn, he hoped, the Scorpion missile would have to make bigger and bigger turns to maintain lock-on. As DreamStar's side-steps got bigger, the missile's turn rates had to increase even faster to keep up—not fast enough, he hoped, for the missile to track its target at close range.

He was at the top of a right ninety-degree bank and about to execute another hard left break when he heard and felt a sharp *bang* to his left. He had been very lucky this time. Forced farther and farther out of phase, the missile was opposite his canopy when its proximity warhead detected it was within lethal range. Maraklov waited for the concussion and flak to hit, but nothing happened and all systems reported with a good status check when queried by an instantaneous mental command. Then Maraklov realized the Megafortress must have been on a test flight and so would not have live warheads in its missiles. Which diminished but hardly eliminated their threat.

He had never paid much attention to the Megafortress Plus project, thinking of it as just another one of Elliott's eccentric boondoggles. Another underestimation . . .

A quick flash of his all-aspect-attack radar showed the B-52 maneuvering hard right, moving back into attack position, its huge wings pulling it easily around and behind him. The enormous plane had to be pulling at least four or five G's, Maraklov thought. It was enough force to rip the wings off any conventional bomber and many fighters as well. Ormack obviously meant business, and he had the hardware to back him up. This was no place for a fight, even with a supposedly decrepit B-52.

ANTARES, however, always favoring the offensive, was begging for a fight and had recommended a high yo-yo maneuver—a hard vertical pull, zoom over the top, then an inverted dive to lock-on—to pull behind and above the B-52 to get into missile-firing position. Maraklov queried about fuel: now he was two thousand pounds *below* the fuel curve instead of two thousand pounds above it. He had no time to waste with a missile pass. Every time ANTARES activated its attack radar, even in small, frequency-agile bursts, the B-52 would jam it. ANTARES was being forced to use older and older data to process an attack. Besides, if the B-52 could jam DreamStar's phased-array radar, it could easily jam the AIM-120's conventional pulse-Doppler active radar. It was definitely time to bug out. Maraklov canceled the right high-G yo-yo and pulled into a sharp left turn, using radar to clear terrain until he could get established on course again.

ANTARES tried to tell him, but Maraklov wasn't listening—tried to tell him that a *left* turn was precisely the wrong thing to do.

He barely had time to roll wings-level when the missile-launch warning hammered into his consciousness. This time it wasn't a head-to-head engagement—the B-52 was in missile-launch position, behind and slightly to the left, the cutoff angle established, the missile already aiming ahead of its target's flight path. Radar, infrared, laser—whatever he had, DreamStar was wide open. The Scorpion missile was even close enough to be picked up on radar . . .

But ANTARES, literally, did not comprehend the meaning of surrender—it would compute escape and attack options until it ran out of power to energize its circuitry. And Maraklov, feeling he had no hope of survival, had surrendered control of DreamStar to ANTARES.

The computer took over. Using its high-lift wings and full canard deflection, DreamStar executed a sharp ninety-degree pitch-up at max afterburner. The Scorpion missile overshot but turned precisely with DreamStar, arcing nearly up to twenty-thousand feet before following the guidance signals from the Old Dog and pitching over hard for the kill. The missile was now aimed straight down, passing Mach four, locked on, closing in again on DreamStar's tail.

With its canards again in high-lift configuration, DreamStar continued its inverted roll, screaming below, then back up through the horizon. It was now clawing for altitude, skimming across the high desert floor by only a few feet. The Scorpion missile tracked every move, following DreamStar's high-G loop. The missile broke Mach five as it closed in on its target . . .

Which suddenly stopped in mid-air, then climbed five hundred feet straight up. The missile could make a fourteen-G turn far greater than any fighter yet designed, but not even this high-tech missile could discontinue a Mach-five diving loop and then turned a ninety-degree corner. The Scorpion missile tracked perfectly, but at such close range, and moving at almost a mile per second, its turn radius was several hundred feet greater than its altitude above ground. The missile exploded into the Amargosa Desert, just a few yards from a truck stop northwest of Jackass Airport off highway 95.

The threat gone, the maneuver accomplished, ANTARES switched to offense in less time than it took for the last of the Old Dog's missiles to disintegrate into the hard desert floor. With its attack-radar activated, it quickly searched for the enemy. At such close range even the Stealth fibersteel skin and radar energy-absorbing honeycomb arrays couldn't diminish the huge radar cross-section of the Megafortress Plus. Lock-on, data transfer, active seeker lock-on, missile stabilization test, unlock, motor firing, launch.

The thing was done before Maraklov really knew it—missile flight time was barely four seconds . . .

*"Missile launch,"* Wendy called over interphone. *"Break right."*

Ormack yanked the control stick hard right, all the way to the stops. Roll-control jets pushed the right wing down and pulled the left wing up, and nose and tail thrusters counteracted the adverse left yaw, which increased the roll rate even more. At fifty degrees of bank the B-52's right wingtip was no more than two hundred feet above ground. Ormack pulled back on the stick, letting the Old Dog's twin-tails pull the nose around even faster.

At the same time, Wendy released five rocket-powered decoys from the left ejector racks under the tail. The rockets spewed a huge globe of radar-reflecting tinsel a hundred yards from the B-52, followed by the blinding hot glare of phosphorous flares. Simultaneously Wendy activated her electronic jammers, present to the frequency of both DreamStar's track-while-scan phased-array radars and the Scorpion missile's seeker-radar, and pumped over a hundred thousand watts of energy across that frequency band.

The B-52's decoys flew past the missile's active radar seeker undetected—it had a solid lock on the B-52 itself. The seeker radar was blinded by the intense jamming, but in a millisecond it switched to the most accurate and reliable of its four backup modes: track on jam. The missile homed in on the center lobe of the jamming energy from the B-52, following the energy beam the way a hungry bat follows the echo of its hunting screech, straight to its prey. The missile flew under the B-52's tail, past the ECM emitter and under the fuselage to the right wing, impacting on the number-three engine pod.

The right wing, made of composite materials far stronger than any metal, held fast, but the number five and six engines disintegrated in a cloud of flying metal and a huge fireball. The fireball lifted the right wing fifty feet into the air, then dropped it, stalling it out. The left four engines pulled the Old Dog around in a clockwise spin. None of its huge wings was generating lift now; the plane was being held aloft only by its forward momentum, like a chewed-up Frisbee tossed awkwardly into the air.

Engine-compressor blades from the number-five engine acted like huge, powerful swords, chopping through the crew compartment. Jeffrey Khan and Linda Evanston, sitting on the right side of the plane, were pierced by hundreds of shards of white-hot metal. Wendy Tork, thrown sideways in the blast, was hit by several pieces of metal.

Ormack pulled the control stick to the left and stomped hard on the left rudder pedal. Fibersteel screamed in protest. The flat spin slowed almost to a stop, but so did the Megafortress' airspeed. Ormack knew he had pulled the plane out of its spin, but the sudden negative G's told him that the Old Dog was never going to fly. Wendelstat was screaming, clawing at his lap belt, face distorted. Blood was coming from places all over his body, his helmeted head tattered from the impact of flying metal.

Ormack reached over to the center console, finding that the centrifugal forces were gone—it felt as if he was riding a gentle elevator down to the first floor. Lowering his head caused the cockpit to tilt violently, but he fought off the sudden vertigo and flipped the EJECT WARNING switch to EJECT.

Downward ejection for the two navigators in a B-52 bomber was a crap shoot in the best of circumstances, and Major Edward Frost knew it. Driven by years of experience, it took him only a few seconds to get his hands on the ejection ring, get his back straight, chin down, knees and legs braced, elbows tucked in. He pulled his ejection handle the instant he saw the red EJECT warning light illuminate. But even then it was too late. The zero-point-two-second drogue-parachute ripped Frost's ejection seat free, automatically pulling the zero-second ripcord, but his main parachute barely had time to deploy fully from its backpack before Frost hit the earth.

Angelina Pereira had pushed Wendy back upright in her seat when she saw the bright red EJECT light. Still holding Wendy in her seat with her left hand, she carefully rotated Wendy's right ejection lever up and pulled the trigger. The fingers of her left hand broke as Wendy's armrest smashed into them, but she didn't notice the pain as she watched the seat blast skyward. Then she slammed herself back into her own seat, raised her arming levers, and pulled both triggers.

Her seat malfunctioned. Nothing happened. She reseated her triggers and activated the backup ballistic acutators, but by then it was too late . . .

Ormack heard the loud pops and surges of air as ejection seats left the plane—at least someone might make it out alive, he thought. Wendelstat had finally collapsed. There was nothing to do for him—no time to haul him downstairs for manual bailout. But Khan had a chance. He yanked up on Khan's left ejection lever and hit the trigger, watching as his long-time copilot and friend blew clear of the crippled bomber. Ormack now rotated his own arming levers and pulled the ejection triggers . . .

Khan had promptly been grabbed by the Old Dog's exhaust and blown several hundred yards back, away from the impact area, but Ormack had spent precious time rescuing Khan. He was a hundred feet above ground, his chute filling with wind and inflating rapidly, when the Old Dog slammed into the Amargosa Desert valley floor. Directly over the aircraft, face down, in position to watch the end of the B-52 Megafortress Plus, Ormack was engulfed by the two-mile wide fireball that blossomed over the desert, consumed by the flames of his beloved aircraft.

His last thought was that *somebody* had to get that son of a bitch James . . .

# =4=

## Over the B-52 crash site, Amargosa, Nevada
*Wednesday, 17 June 1996, 0712 PDT (1012 EDT)*

IT RESEMBLED THE aftermath of a fire bombing. Even from five hundred feet in the air, everything within sight was black—the rocky hills surrounding the crash site had been blackened by fires and debris. Huge craters in the earth contained burning sections of the mighty B-52 Megafortress Plus, the heat of the fireball hot enough to melt even the B-52's thick carbon and fiberglass skeletal pieces. A mile away the center-wing junction-box and forward fuselage, the piece that joined the wings to the fuselage and the largest section of the B-52 still intact, was burning, so hot and so smoky that firefighters could not get within two hundred yards of it. Debris was scattered in a ten-square-mile area of devastation, and thick black smoke obscured half the sky.

The helicopter crossed perpendicular to the axis of impact, paralleling route 95 near the evacuated town of Amargosa. A large building, a restaurant-and-truck-stop complex, was burning fiercely—one fire truck was spraying surrounding fuel pumps with water to prevent any massive explosions. Several hundred feet from the edge of the area a knot of police cars and an ambulance had pulled off the highway and encircled several dark objects lying in the charred sand.

"That's it," McLanahan shouted, not bothering to use the helicopter's interphone. "Set it down there."

The chopper pilot nodded, spoke briefly on the radio, then turned to Brad Elliott. "Sir, I can't touch down—I've got wheels instead of skids. I'd sink up to the fuselage in that mess—"

"Then hover and drop me off," McLanahan shouted.

"The medevac helicopter is only a few seconds from—"

"I don't give a damn, take me down there. *Now.*" Elliott nodded to the pilot, and the chopper pilot reluctantly circled the area once, then set the helicopter in a gentle hover, wheels up, only a few inches from the ground. McLanahan leaped out the side door and ran through the burning debris and gasoline-fired desert to the patrol cars.

It was obvious that Wendy Tork McLanahan had been under her parachute only a few seconds before hitting ground; the ejection seat was just a few yards away. Wendy was lying on her side, seemingly buried in the dirt and blackened sand, her half-burned parachute trailing behind her. Her flight suit, gloves, face and hair were black from the heat and falling debris—from the air she had looked like another burnt piece of the dead B-52 bomber. Her helmet and one boot were nowhere to be seen— they were usually lost during ejection unless secured uncomfortably tight during the mission. Her left leg was twisted underneath her body, her left shoulder, half buried in the dirt, appeared to be broken or at least separated.

Two Nevada State Troopers were maneuvering a spine board into place when McLanahan ran over to them. He dropped to his knees in front of her.

"You from the base?" one of the troopers asked McLanahan. Their voices were muffled by surgical masks.

"Yes . . ."

"What the hell hit out here? A nuke?"

"An aircraft."

They had dug a trench behind Wendy's back and were moving the board along her back. Patrick carefully swept bits and pieces of metal off Wendy's face. A few stuck fast, and pain shot through his own body, as if he was feeling the pain for her, with her.

"Get with it," one of the troopers yelled, "grab those straps and pass them over." They routed several thick straps under Wendy's body, and Patrick carefully passed them back through the brackets on the side of the board. They tightened the straps until Wendy's back was tight against the board. Several wider straps were secured over her forehead and chin, a cervical collar placed around her neck, her head immobilized on the board as well. The troopers began working to free and immobilize her legs as the medevac helicopter touched down a few yards away.

"Let the paramedics in there, pal," the troopers told Patrick, pulling him up and away from Wendy. Three paramedics rushed over. In moments they had oxygen, a respirator and electronic vital-sign monitors in operation. They finished securing thick plastic splints on her legs, placed her on a gurney and carried her to the helicopter. Patrick ran over with the gurney but was pushed away.

"No room. We've got more injured to pick up from the truck stop." The doors closed, the helicopter jumped skyward and was quickly out of sight.

Patrick's leg felt ready to buckle . . . one survivor out of a crew of seven. He'd seen the entire crew alive and well not an hour earlier. Wendy . . . his last thought of her was the thumbs-up she'd given him before heading out to the crew bus. Piece of cake, she had said.

Another aircraft appeared out of the smoke-obscured sky, not another helicopter. Resembling a remodeled C-130 transport, the CV-22 Osprey tilt-rotor transport swooped down out of the sky barely a hundred feet above the ground. Suddenly, with a roar of turboprop engines, the engine pods on the wing-tips began to tilt upward until the blades were horizontal. The aircraft then began a soft helicopter-like vertical descent, landing only yards from Patrick.

The rear cargo doors on the Osprey popped out, disgorging a dozen heavily armed security troops in full combat gear and backpacks, along with an M113 armored combat vehicle. The M113 rolled off toward route 95, and the guards began to station themselves a hundred yards apart along the perimeter of the Megafortress' impact area.

"Patrick . . ." He turned at the sound of his name. Hal Briggs was standing over him, Uzi submachine gun in hand. He was wearing a Kevlar helmet with a one-piece communications head-set in place. Now he dropped down beside Patrick and moved his face closer to his so they could talk over the roar of the Osprey's rotor-props. "You okay?"

"Wendy . . ."

"I heard, I'm glad she made it out," Briggs shouted. "They're taking her downtown to the burn unit . . . she'll be okay, they think."

"Unbelievable . . . it was James," Patrick muttered. "Stole DreamStar, shot down Old Dog . . ."

"We gotta get you out of here. I'm securing the crash site. The general is assembling an investigation unit. He wants you to help him set it up."

"Investigation unit? What about DreamStar? James is getting away with DreamStar—"

"He's heading south, right into the F-15 interceptor unit out of Tucson. They've got a squadron ready to shoot his ass down. Now let's get going."

He helped McLanahan to his feet and led him to the open cargo ramp at the rear of the Osprey. He was strapped in beside Briggs at the flight-engineer's station.

"Headquarters building," Briggs radioed to the pilot. "Helipad one should be big enough for the Osprey—"

"No," Patrick said. "I want to go to the hangar ramp. Right now."

"General Elliott is waiting—"

"I'm not going to supervise a bunch of guys crawling around in the mud, putting little flags on chunks of metal and body parts. We know what happened to the Megafortress—James shot her down, he killed six people, he damn near killed my wife . . . I want to go to the hangar ramp right now. That's an order."

Briggs shook off his immediate surprise at Patrick calling Wendy his wife. He pushed his boom microphone away from his lips and bent closer to Patrick. "You know me better than that. I take orders from Elliott, and sometimes not from him. It's how I do my job. Tell me what you want and convince me it's better than what the man with the four stars wants."

"Hal, believe me, DreamStar will blow right past the F-15s out of Davis-Monthan."

"Eight jockeys in Eagle Squadron won't buy that."

"Listen, I've flown against DreamStar for a year. If DreamStar has any more weapons on board, a whole air wing of F-15s won't be able to bring him down. Even if he doesn't, James has the skill and the hardware to evade them. Those pilots have never seen DreamStar in action. If the F-15s can't bring him down before he enters Mexican airspace, he'll lose them."

"So what are you going to—?" Briggs cut himself off. It wasn't hard to figure out what McLanahan wanted to do—"you're gonna take Cheetah . . . ?"

"It's the only fighter that can take on DreamStar head-to-head. And J. C. Powell is the only pilot that can do it. I want Powell and Sergeant Butler to meet me at Hangar Four with a fuel truck. If he can, I want Butler to get MMS out there with missiles or at least some twenty-millimeter cannon shells."

"And then what? Chase him down? He's got a huge lead on you, you won't stand a chance—"

"He's only got two hours' worth of fuel on board, maybe less," Patrick said. "He's got to land it somewhere."

"How the hell are you supposed to know where?"

"Those air defense units will be tracking him. They'll be able to pinpoint his location, even three or four hundred miles into Mexico. If he tries to land we'll know about it. And unless he's removed or deactivated them, Cheetah has telemetry and tracking equipment on board that can direct us toward him. But we need to act *now*, Hal. If we wait he could get clean away. The Mexicans aren't going to be much help. They don't exactly love us anymore."

Briggs paused. McLanahan was obviously beside himself over the crash, and about Wendy—did he say his *wife*?—but what he was saying did make sense. If Dreamland's security forces couldn't stop DreamStar, there seemed little chance that a squadron of Air Force reservists from Arizona could do it.

Hal looked at Patrick. "You said your wife?"

"We were married two days ago. We were going to tell everybody tonight." They were both silent for a moment, then Patrick asked: "How about it, Hal?"

Briggs thought about it a few moments longer, then nodded. "Hey, you're a colonel, Colonel." He reached over to the flight-engineer's console, flicked a switch on the communications panel, dialed in channel eight—the discrete channel for the flight-line maintenance section. "I was told to deliver you a message from the general and assist you in complying with those orders. *You* can do anything you want. Talk on the radio, tell Butler to do something. Look here, this radio was even on Butler's frequency, you can plug in and talk to him any time you want."

Briggs swiveled his microphone back and hit the interphone button. "Pilot, looks like I might have miscalculated. This Osprey is too big to land on the Headquarters helipad."

"No, Major," the pilot radioed back. "It's plenty big enough. I can—"

"I don't think we can chance it. Some pretty strong gusts kicking up out there."

"It's clear and calm, Major Briggs."

"Better not chance it. Drop us off at the hangar ramp."

The pilot shrugged, keyed his radio button to request different landing instructions.

McLanahan clicked on the radio. "Delta, this is Charlie on channel eight. How copy?"

A few moments later Sergeant Ray Butler replied: "This is Delta mobile, sir. Go ahead."

McLanahan glanced at the navigation readout on the flight engineer's console. "I'm fifteen minutes from touchdown on the hangar ramp, Ray. Meet me at Hangar Four. Repeat, Hangar Four in fifteen mike. Urgent. Over."

"Fifteen mike at Hangar Four. Copy that," Butler replied. "Does this have to do with our recent fireworks here, sir?"

"It does, Delta. You may want to see that the ramp is clear in front of Hangar Four. Over."

"I understand, Charlie. I'll be ready. Delta out."

Twelve minutes later the Osprey set down in the center of the hangar ramp and carefully taxied over to Hangar Four. McLanahan disembarked the cargo ramp and found an army of maintenance trucks surrounding the hangar. Cheetah had already been rolled out of the hangar and a fuel line had been hooked up to its single-point refueling receptacle on the left-side service panel.

Sergeant Butler trotted up to a surprised McLanahan with a sheaf of papers on a clipboard and a pen. "You must've forgotten to sign all these requests for maintenance support, sir," he said with a straight face. "You made this request *last week*—don't know how we missed getting all this signed off." McLanahan nodded—obviously Butler wanted the same thing he did, but he was still going to make sure his paperwork was straight. "You wanted gas, long-range fuel tanks, five hundred rounds uploaded with the M61B2 cannon, two AIM-9R infrared short-range missiles and four AIM-120 medium-range active radar missiles. I got everything? Oh, you also wanted that video camera taken off, didn't you? Good. Sign here."

McLanahan signed all the blocks. "Thank you, sir," Butler said. "Sorry about the paperwork shuffle, sir. My mistake. Won't happen again . . . I trust you'll take care of any problems General Elliott might have with my . . . procedures.''

"Nothing wrong with your procedures, Sergeant."

Butler allowed a smile. "Have a good flight, and good hunting. We should be ready to go in twenty minutes, maybe less. Captain Powell is over there. I'm very sorry about the Megafortress, sir. Well, gotta go." Butler handed Patrick his flight helmet, saluted and trotted back to the maintenance supervisor's truck.

J. C. Powell met McLanahan halfway to Cheetah. He slapped his hands together. "We're going hunting?"

"If I don't my get ass court-martialed first, yes."

"I heard Ken James stole the plane? I don't believe it. I always suspected the guy was a little whacked out but not *this* . . .''

"He's more than a little whacked out. He's jumped head-first into the shallow end, or something a lot worse."

"Such as?"

"Something Briggs said a few days ago . . . that his security problems started when James arrived at Dreamland about a year and a half ago. Briggs even suspected Wendy, who happened to get here at the same time."

"You mean, you think Ken James was some kind of damn spy?"

"It would answer a lot of questions, wouldn't it?"

"The guy's an Academy grad, passed every security screening check I have—probably more. I'm only a ninety-day wonder and I had to jump through some pretty small hoops—"

"I didn't say I had it all figured out. Maybe he was turned or recruited after he got here, or he's being blackmailed. Maybe I'm all wrong. But one thing's for sure—if the F-15s out of Davis-Monthan don't get him, we will. I just hope I get a chance to ask him why the hell he did it"—Patrick glanced at the AIM-120 missiles being raised into position on Cheetah's wings—"before we put one up his tailpipe."

## Over southwest Arizona
*Twenty minutes later*

There were eight other pilots who wanted to put one up Ken
James' tailpipe, but he wasn't going to give them the opportunity.

Ken James—that name now discarded by DreamStar's pilot,
Andrei Maraklov—could see waves of radars all around him, but
they were all search radars. He was deep within the Colorado
River valley just south of Parker Dam, following the rugged
mountain ridges as closely as he could to avoid detection. Two
longer-range F-16L cranked-arrow fighters were behind him,
their radars probing deep within the valley, but they never got a
solid lock-on and they were staying up high to try to scan as
much ground as possible. With their present tactics they were
never going to get a shot at him.

But they were no longer the main threats—they were the push-
ers, the drivers, there only to keep DreamStar headed south toward the real danger. Maraklov had caught bits and pieces of
scrambled radio conversations between the F-16s and another
aircraft. It was not hard to guess which: a Boeing 707 or 767
AWACS radar plane, stationed, Maraklov reasoned, between
Gila Bend and Yuma over Sentinel Plain. From there the older
707 AWACS could scan over one hundred twenty thousand cubic miles of airspace, from San Diego to El Paso, and most of
the way down the Gulf of California into Mexico. The radar
aboard the improved 767 was even better. No doubt the AWACS
would be accompanied by at least two F-15 fighters out of Davis-
Monthan AFB in Tucson for protective escort, plus at least two
more F-15s to hunt down DreamStar.

The fuel situation was critical. Less than an hour's worth of
fuel, less than an hour from the hastily arranged landing site in
Mexico. Staying at low altitude was badly sucking up fuel, but
he had no choice—the AWACS could have picked him up as far
north as Las Vegas if he was any higher.

Of course the maneuvering he did during the B-52 attack
pushed him under the fuel curve. Especially that last maneuver,
going from Mach one to one hundred knots one hundred feet off
the ground, thereby putting DreamStar in a virtual hover. That
took care of any reserve he'd had hopes of building up . . .

Well, the B-52 Megafortress was dead. They certainly nicknamed it right. It almost escaped, almost dodged away in time, almost managed to decoy the AIM-120 away. The Scorpion missile had to switch to home-on-jam guidance to finish the attack. Ironically the massive jamming power of the B-52 was probably what did it in—it must have been easy for the Scorpion missile to follow jamming power like that.

Who was on that plane? Ormack—good officer, better pilot, Elliott's natural successor for the command of Dreamland. Khan—a desk jockey. Had no business in the cockpit. Maraklov didn't know Frost. He had dated Evanston once but that was no more than an experiment that neither wanted to continue. Besides, navs had no information of any value to anybody.

Angelina Pereira was almost old enough to be his mother, but she liked to use men and she liked men to use her. No age limits. She was never a target for any information or recruitment, although the KGB's standard profiles fitted her. She probably would have laughed at him, just before shooting him in the balls. She was an unexpected job bonus, nothing else.

He would miss Wendy Tork most of all. Or rather miss never having had a chance to try to fulfill his fantasies about her . . . take her away from McLanahan . . . Too bad he hadn't tried to latch onto her sooner. If nothing else she had some highly useful information on electronic countermeasures research . . .

He made a slight altitude and course correction to avoid overflying a group of white-water rafters less than a hundred feet below. As he banked away to avoid them he could see several put hands over ears against the noise, but a few bikini-clad ladies waved. He had made that trip down the Colorado River several times, spending a weekend shooting the rapids, getting dumped into the swirling waters, laughing at a roaring campfire with a beer in one hand and a pretty young lieutenant from Nellis in the other.

Did they have rapids in Russia? Were the women pretty? Maraklov had forgotten more than remembered.

Things had, people said, changed over the years. *Glasnost* . . . the place was more open. But he doubted it would be to him.

Andrei Maraklov might truly be the deepest deep-cover agent ever produced by the KGB, but that didn't mean he could go back to the USSR and enjoy the gratitude of his country. Would he ever be promoted to a leadership position in the KGB or the

Mikoyan-Gureyvich Aircraft Design Bureau, the agency that designed and built the greatest fighter aircraft? No. He had been in the U.S. for nine years. Before that he had spent three years in a school that spoke more English and acted more American than parts of San Francisco and Chicago or L.A. They'd have to *reteach* him Russian, for God's sake. If they ever trusted him after his return he'd probably be given some know-nothing job or a pension and watched for the rest of his life. He might be allowed to emigrate, but he'd be safer from the CIA or the Defense Intelligence Agency in Russia. Which didn't say much. If they didn't trust him they'd pick his mind clean of every scrap of information he had, then discard him. Either way, would his life be better in his homeland? What he really felt attached to, more than anything or anyone, was this plane that he had become part of, that was part of him . . .

Up ahead, it seemed like the entire sky had turned green. Search radar—a big one. There was definitely an AWACS radar plane up there. He was in the radar shadow right now, but in only a few miles the Colorado River valley would flatten out into the Sonora Desert basin, and then he'd be trapped. The last hundred fifty miles to the border was going to turn into a gauntlet—an unknown number of F-15 fighters in front of him, waiting for him to emerge from the valley. He was also going toward Yuma Marine Corps Air Station just ahead on the border, a base for two squadrons of F/A-18 fighter bombers, and F-16 fighters from Luke AFB in Phoenix could join in. So he could be facing six squadrons of fighters from four military bases on this last hundred-mile leg.

Then, he saw it: the AWACS radar plane. DreamStar's threat receiver pinpointed the aircraft about a hundred fifty miles away, orbiting over the center of the Papago Indian Reservation west of Tucson at twenty-five thousand feet. And if DreamStar could see the AWACS plane, he could see DreamStar. At a quick mental inquiry, Maraklov had the threat-warning computer analyze the radar transmissions from the plane and learned it was the older E-3B Sentry AWACS, almost twenty-five years old but still a formidable radar platform; it was probably a drug-interdiction aircraft based out of Davis-Monthan AFB.

Suddenly, like some eerie Martian fog, green sky descended and engulfed him, and then the sky turned yellow. The AWACS had found him, started to track him. Maraklov tried to dodge

closer to the river-valley edges to hide in any available radar
shadow. No use. Once he was spotted and identified—an aircraft
at two hundred feet above ground traveling at six hundred miles
an hour could hardly be mistaken for a civilian plane—the
AWACS would change position farther west to maintain a solid
track on him in the valley . . .

"Unidentified aircraft ten miles north of Blythe, altitude
twelve hundred feet MSL, airspeed five hundred forty knots.
This is the United States Air Force air intercept controller on
GUARD." The radio message was being broadcast "in the blind"
on GUARD, the international emergency frequency, to prove to
him that he had indeed been spotted. "You are ordered to climb
to ten thousand feet MSL, reduce speed and lower your landing
gear immediately." Military aircraft being intercepted were ordered to lower their landing gear because as a safety device the
weapon systems on most fighters were automatically deactivated
when the landing gear was down. "Contact me on two-three-
three point zero immediately, repeat, contact me on frequency
two-three-three point zero."

DreamStar's weapon system did not deactivate unless Maraklov deactivated it, gear up or down, but it was a moot point—
DreamStar had only one AIM-120 missile left and very little
fuel, not enough for any sort of engagement. The F-15 fighters
would not have much chance of catching him on their own, but
with the AWACS up and locked-on they could be vectored in
with high precision and even process a missile launch, all without one watt of energy being transmitted from their own radars.
So DreamStar would have to use its attack radar to find the
F-15s, and that would give away DreamStar's position to them.

Maraklov set one of his radios to the discrete frequency but
did not reply—that would be suicidal. But he did hear:
"DreamStar, this is Colonel Harrell, Eagle Squadron commander. We're following vectors toward you. We'll be all over
you in a few seconds. Climb out of there, slow down and drop
your gear or we'll consider you a hostile and blow your shit
away. Answer up. Over."

A one-second burst of energy on the attack radar told Maraklov the story—six fighters, three pairs, all at different altitudes,
arranged along the Colorado River and spaced about twenty miles
apart. The closest was about thirty miles ahead, only two hundred feet above ground. The AWACS had moved northward a

few miles to get a better look down the valley and to get away from the radar shadows from the Kofa Mountains.

"We've got lock-on, James," Harrell said. "I got you at my twelve o'clock, twenty-eight miles. My wingmen know where you are. The Marines have set up a little surprise for you. Hiding down here in the mud ain't going to help. Give it up before you get yourself smoked."

That bit about Yuma Marine Corps Air Station was not exactly true, but it came close. The Marines could easily set up a surface-to-air missile blockade of the Colorado River mouth from Yuma Marine Corps Air Station. Harrell wouldn't reveal that, though. But the odds were starting to pile up here, and they were all against him.

There was no way to even the odds, but Maraklov decided he wasn't going to just surrender. Giving up DreamStar was unthinkable. It would make everything he'd done pointless. But if the F-15s didn't get him, his lack of fuel reserves would. Well, he wasn't going to make it easy for the F-15s to bring him down. It was time to put his DreamStar through its paces.

Maraklov pushed DreamStar to full power, trimmed for max speed and put her right down on the deck—fifty feet above the river bed.

"That was stupid, James," Harrell called over the radio. "Very damn stupid. We've got you all the way. You can't get away . . ."

Maybe, maybe not. But he wasn't about to drive right into their laps so they could take easy shots at him. If they wanted him they'd have to work for a shot. He had been cruising at about two to three hundred feet above ground, popping up occasionally to pass over bridges and power lines strung across the Colorado River. Now, two hundred feet would seem like two thousand compared to his present altitude. Using his computer-enhanced responses and DreamStar's powerful radar in terrain-avoidance mode, Maraklov kept DreamStar less than fifty feet above ground. He did not try to pop up over tall transmission lines— he went under them. He could clearly see rafters and campers lined up on the banks, plugging their ears against the sonic boom that rolled over them as he roared past at Mach one—if he could have seen behind him, he would have seen a huge plume of white exploding off the Colorado River as DreamStar's sonic

wake crashed against the water. Birds pinged and slammed into
the canopy and fuselage, but Maraklov kept going, too close
now to be brought down by a damned duck.

Near the town of Picacho the steep mountain ranges on either
side of the Colorado disappeared. He was only forty miles to the
border. He broke away from the river and headed directly south
for Yuma.

Suddenly ANTARES screamed *"missile tracking"* in his
brain. The threat receivers had detected that an AIM-120 Scorpion missile had activated its radar and was tracking him—more
likely, the F-15 had fired two missiles, since he probably was
carrying two more and had at least three other wingmen with
missiles. They had a lot of firepower on their side; they could
afford to be generous.

Maraklov commanded a hard seven-G climb, almost straight
up. He gained altitude to about a thousand feet, then flipped
over and pulled hard in a nine-G descent straight down. Fifty
feet above ground he yanked his fighter upright and pulled hard
to the left behind a hill. The missiles followed his turns but
overshot on the climbout, and when they turned to follow he had
disappeared. The missile's computer brain allowed the radar
seeker to attempt to reacquire a target for three seconds, then
tried to lock-on to any jamming signals in the area. None was
present. The missile then began following steering signals from
the E-3 AWACS radar plane and turned back toward DreamStar,
but by then it was too late. The Scorpion missiles, designed for
medium-range engagements at higher altitudes, ran out of fuel
and self-destructed seconds later.

Maraklov rolled hard right and found himself back in the Colorado River valley near Laguna Airfield. He commanded
DreamStar back down on the deck just in time to fly under a
transmission line. At that moment, the scanner on the aft fuselage detected a growing heat source and issued a MISSILE ATTACK
warning. An F-15 had dived down from its patrol altitude right
on top of DreamStar and had quickly closed in to IR missile
range.

In the literal blink of an eye Maraklov commanded DreamStar
from max speed mode to max alpha—the slowest speed
DreamStar could sustain. Within seconds DreamStar's wings
went from nearly flat to steeply curled; the two-dimensional louvers shuttled forward to redirect thrust down instead of aft; and

DreamStar's canards snapped upward, holding the nose high while the plane decelerated. In ten seconds DreamStar went from Mach one to two hundred knots—only DreamStar's composite structure, lighter than steel but a hundred times stronger, could withstand the strain.

The two F-15 fighters had closed to three miles behind DreamStar when suddenly their quarry seemed to freeze in mid-air. At only a hundred feet off the ground there was no room to maneuver, especially with two fighters together in close formation. The lead F-15 broke hard right to avoid DreamStar, then managed to pull up hard enough to escape crashing into the low hills north of Yuma. His wingman was not so lucky—not able to keep up with the five-G pull, the second F-15 fighter pancaked into the desert floor and exploded before the pilot could eject.

Twenty miles to go. Gradually, Maraklov applied power and began to transition back to max-speed, being careful not to use gas-guzzling afterburner. He was over Yuma now, skimming just above tall buildings and radio antennae. The F-15s were still behind him but they weren't attacking until DreamStar passed clear of the city. He screamed over Yuma Marine Corps Air Station with his airspeed nearly back at Mach one and saw F/A-18 fighters at the end of the runway, probably being held because of the F-15 fighters in pursuit. There was something else at the southeast end of the main runway but he didn't have time to make it out before—

AAA LOCK-ON, blared in Maraklov's mind. ANTARES reacted first, banking hard right and pulling away as warning messages flashed in his mind and streaks of black raced past his canopy. It was an M173 Bulldog anti-aircraft artillery vehicle, a small tank with two 40-millimeter radar-guided guns that fired pre-fragmented tungsten-alloy shells out to a range of over four miles. There were only a few Bulldog regiments in the United States; Maraklov was unlucky enough to run into one. Without jammers, the only defense against the Bulldog was to fly as far and as fast away from it as possible—its twin cannons could pump out two hundred rounds per minute per barrel. Maraklov now had no choice but to kick in full afterburner.

ANTARES reported damage to several mini-actuators in the wings. One Bulldog was not an effective weapon against high-speed ground-hugging fighters, but even so it had been a narrow escape. The Bulldog was quickly deactivated as the F-15s came

into range. Maraklov pulled his throttle out of afterburner as fast
as he could, but the damage had already been done. DreamStar
had no fuel reserves left. Every mile in any direction other than
toward the landing point meant one more mile Maraklov would
end up short of it.

Maraklov rolled DreamStar left and headed directly for Laguna de Santiaguillo, staying at one hundred feet above ground,
flying directly over a small town. He activated the attack radar
and completed a three-second sweep of the sky . . . the F-15
fighters had turned around, and at another mental inquiry he
found out why—DreamStar was in Mexico, two miles south of
the border, over the town of San Luis. He had made it.

## Aboard the lead F-15 over southwest Arizona

"What the hell do you mean, *turn back*?" Colonel Jack Harrell,
the Eagle Squadron commander from Davis-Monthan AFB, said
over the scrambled radio channel. He lowered his oxygen visor
with an exasperated snap. His four remaining squadron members
were arranged in extended fingertip formation around him, two
on his left and two others about a half-mile farther off to his left.
"Tinsel, verify that last transmission. Over."

"Eagle flight, this is Tinsel," the senior controller aboard the
E-3B AWACS replied, "your orders are verified. Permission to
cross into Mazatlan Fighter Intercept Region sector one with live
weapons on board has not been received. You must comply with
International Aeronautics Organization chapter one-thirteen until
permission to cross has been received."

Harrell was livid. He had watched one of his best fighter pilots
auger into the desert not two minutes earlier, and here he was
sitting by while their target was escaping—and there was nothing
between them but a lousy line on a map. Harrell made a decision—that line was not going to stop him.

"Copy, Tinsel," Harrell said. "Understand permission re-
ceived to cross into Mazatlan FIR sector one. Blue Flight and
Red Two and Three, report back to Goalie for refueling. Red
Flight is turning right in pursuit. Eagle leader out."

"Blue Flight copies," the leader of the second group of two
F-15s replied before the controller aboard Tinsel could interject.
As Harrell banked right, those two F-15s maintained their head-

ing northeast toward Goalie, their waiting KC-10 aerial-refueling tanker. But the two F-15s accompanying Harrell stayed in fingertip formation of their leader.

"Eagle Leader, this is Tinsel," the angry voice of the senior controller aboard the AWACS finally said over the command radio. "I repeat, you are *not* authorized to cross the ADIZ. Turn left heading zero-three-zero and climb to—"

Harrell shut off the radio. Out of the corner of his eye he saw the F-15 on his left wingtip raise and lower his airbrake to get Harrell's attention. The pilot extended two fingers ahead of him, visible to both Harrell and the third F-15. Harrell nodded that he understood the signal and switched his second radio to the scrambled Squadron-only frequency.

"I thought I ordered you characters to hook up with the tanker," Harrell radioed.

"If you've got radio or navigation problems, sir," the pilot of the second F-15, Lieutenant Colonel Downs, replied, "we wouldn't leave you. If you're going after that stolen fighter, we're sure as hell not leaving your wing."

"We *are* going after that guy, aren't we?" the third pilot, Major Chan, asked. "I'd hate to think we're gonna lose our wings for nothing."

"Tinsel sounds pretty pissed," Downs said. "Sure you want to do this, sir?"

"We're doing it, aren't we?" Harrell checked his heads-up display, which had been slaved to provide AWACS-generated steering signals to the stolen fighter. He was pleased to find the data-link still active. "I've still got a steer on the XF-34. Lead's coming right ten degrees, descending to two thousand feet. Two, take the mid-patrol at six thousand; three, take the high CAP at twelve. Let's waste this guy."

"Two."

"Three."

The two wingmen began slow climbs to their assigned altitudes. Harrell began a descent, following DreamStar's flight path. Moments later he received a soft beep in his headset telling him that one of his Scorpion missiles had followed the AWACS' data-link instructions and had locked onto its target. Harrell made sure his wingmen were clear, then radioed "Fox two" once on the Squadron-only frequency, and pressed the launch trigger . . .

## Over northwest Mexico

The green "sky" surrounding DreamStar was still present, meaning that the AWACS was still tracking him, but Maraklov allowed himself a moment to relax. They had turned back. He had overestimated these reservist weekend-warrior fighter-jocks. They had a reputation for tenacity, for an itchy trigger finger, for not following the rules. These guys had more to lose.

Maraklov commanded a thousand-foot climb to pad his safe terrain-clearance altitude and began to retrim his engine from best-speed to best-endurance mode. There was still a chance he could make it. In best-endurance mode the fuel computer and autopilot would work together to step-climb the aircraft to take advantage of better flying conditions and greater endurance at higher altitudes, without wasting fuel in the—

He was startled by a sudden MISSILE LAUNCH indication from the tail sensor. Momentarily stunned into indecision, he called on ANTARES to execute an evasive maneuver.

Instead of diving for the ground ANTARES pitched DreamStar up in a hard climb, lit the afterburner, leveled out, then activated the attack radar. Instantly the radar image of Harrell's F-15 appeared, dead ahead at five miles. ANTARES' radar locked on and launched the last remaining AIM-120 missile at the lone pursuer. At only five miles and slightly above the F-15, the Scorpion missile did not miss. DreamStar then flew directly toward the flaming remains of Harrell's F-15, dodging away right at the last moment. The moves were executed so quickly that Harrell's Scorpion missile, which had dutifully followed DreamStar in its wild Immelmann maneuver, now locked onto Harrell's flaming F-15 fighter and added its own destructive fury to the already doomed plane.

"Sweet mother of God . . ."

Downs banked left away from the blossoming fireball that erupted just below and in front of him. There were only a few seconds between when he left Harrell's wing and when that fireball appeared. One moment his squadron commander was lined up for a perfect missile shot, at the closest possible range without getting into an inner-range warhead arming inhabit, the target straight and level in front of him; the next moment, the target had leapt into the sky, evaded the missile, turned and launched a missile of his own. Immediately after, Harrell was part of a cloud of metal and exploding fuel.

"Eagle Three, this is Two. Lead's been hit. He's going down—no 'chute, no 'chute . . ."

"I see him, Two, I see him . . . Jesus Christ . . ."

Downs took a firm grip on his stick and throttles. "I've got the lead. Take the mid CAP and follow me in. This bastard's not getting—"

"Eagle flight, this is TINSEL on malibu"—malibu, FM frequency 660, was the Squadron's discrete scrambled channel. Great, Downs thought, they found our so-called secret channel. "Eagle flight of two, we copy that Eagle Lead is down. Search and rescue has been notified. You are to return across the ADIZ immediately or you will be considered a hostile intruder. Acknowledge and comply. Over."

"TINSEL, this is Eagle Two. That son of a bitch just shot down Colonel Harrell. Are you ordering us to *let him go*? Over."

"We don't have any damned choice, Downs." It was a new voice on the radio—obviously the AWACS mission commander cutting in over the senior controller. "We can't start a major international incident by ignoring the rules. You'll get another shot at him when we get permission to cross. Now get your asses back over the border before you have to fight off the damned Mexican Air Force—and *then* you and I get to tangle. That's an order from Air Division. Over."


DreamStar was only a dozen feet above a rocky dry-river bed snaking through the Pinacate Mountains. Occasional radar sweeps showed the skies above him were clear, but that last attack was so sudden and so close that Maraklov kept DreamStar in the dirt to avoid any more sneak attacks. He stayed in the rugged mountains and dry desert valleys until he reached the fringes of the AWACS coverage zone, then slowly step-climbed out of the rocky terrain, being careful to stay under detectable radar emissions in the area. After a few minutes, as he cruised down the Magdalena River valley at five hundred feet, he was finally out of range of all American surveillance radars. The military radar nets from Hermosillo seventy miles south of his position were searching for him as well, but they were high-altitude-only surveillance radars and not capable of finding low-altitude aircraft. As he approached the northern foothills of the

Sierra Madre Occidental mountains he was finally able to climb above ten thousand feet for the first time and reestablish best-endurance power.

Not time to celebrate, though. Maraklov was starting to search for places to crash-land DreamStar, taking seriously the fuel-endurance figures he was receiving. He was three hundred miles from Laguna de Santiaguillo with five thousand pounds of fuel. His best endurance speed was only fifty-five percent of full power—idle power, barely enough to maintain altitude and control. He was slightly over eleven thousand feet, which put him right at the minimum safe altitude for the region—he could see Cerrro Chorreras, one of the highest peaks of the Sierra Madre, looming off to his right and looking like an impenetrable wall, a fist ready to reach out and pull him out of the sky.

He didn't have the fuel to climb any higher; in fact, the best routine would command a descent soon to prevent DreamStar from stalling at such slow airspeeds. The high terrain would then force him further eastward toward the Mexican fighter base at Torreon only two hundred miles away. After successfully evading four squadrons of high-tech American fighters, Maraklov thought ruefully, he might end up dropping himself right into the very appreciative laps of the Mexican government.

ANTARES needed to search its own database for landing sites within range. Not easy. DreamStar was well within the Sierra Madre mountains now. Below were hundreds of grass-and-dirt strips—every plantation owner, every mining town, every timber mill, every drug dealer had his own airstrip. Most were simply cleared sections of land or dirt roads. Many were on high plateaus far from any usable roads or towns—if Kramer and Moffitt, his two KGB contacts from Los Angeles, were bringing a fuel truck it would take days for them to arrive.

After a few moments Maraklov was presented with a chart of north-central Mexico with landing-site choices depicted. He quickly discarded the unimproved runways of San Pablo Balleza and Rancho Las Aojuntas. Likewise the paved airport of Parral—the computerized chart showed the airport had a rotating beacon and even runway lights, which meant it probably was used by the militia or local police. Too active to maintain any secrecy.

The last choice seemed the best, a paved sixty-four-hundred-foot-long runway named Ojito. Detail of the runway showed it to be like the valley road nearby, which meant it probably *was* the road, just widened and strengthened some to serve as a runway. Several of such quasi-runways dotted central Mexico, where air access was occasionally desired but there wasn't enough room to build an airport. Ojito was a hundred miles northwest of the original landing site, and in these rugged foothills that meant at least a four-hour wait.

Once that decision had been made, Maraklov commanded radio two to a special UHF frequency. "Kramer, this is Maraklov. Come in. Over."

The radio crackled, and the pilot filtered out the noise, careful not to decrease the radio's effective range. No response. He was over two hundred miles from Laguna de Santiaguillo. Maybe they wouldn't be able to hear him in the mountains . . .

"Maraklov, this is Kramer. We read you. Welcome, you made it."

For the first time, Maraklov allowed himself to feel the exhilaration he'd not thought possible. "Kramer, listen. Change of plans. New runway is at grid coordinates kilo-victor-five-one-five, lima-alpha one-three-seven. Situation critical. Over."

"We understand. We have been monitoring your progress. We are airborne and will meet you at your designated landing point. You are almost home. Kramer out."

The official blue sedan screeched to a halt not four feet in front of Cheetah's nose gear. General Elliott jumped up from behind the wheel, threw the door open and stood behind it, drawing a thumb across his throat. He looked mad enough to hold down Cheetah even if they used full afterburner. At the same time Hal Briggs got out of the passenger's side, wearing a set of ear protectors, and holding aloft his Uzi submachine gun in an obvious warning. Patrick could see him shrug and shake his head. He had no doubt that Briggs would use that SMG on Cheetah's tires.

"Shut 'em down, J.C.," Patrick said.

J.C. muttered to himself as he touched the voice-interface switch on the stick. "Engine shutdown, power on."

*"Engine shutdown. Brakes set. External power on. Clear to scavenge,"* the computer replied.

"Clear to scavenge," J.C. said. One by one the engines revved up to eighty percent power for ten seconds, then shut themselves down. Patrick did not shut down any of his equipment but left it on standby to have it ready when—or, looking at Elliott's angry face, *if*—they received takeoff clearance. Soon the only noise left was the sound of the external power cart. Briggs holstered his Uzi as Elliott walked over to the crew ladder being put up on Cheetah's left side, pushed Sergeant Ray Butler out of the way and painfully hauled himself up the ladder.

"Where the *hell* do you think you're going? Have you gone crazy?"

"You know where I'm going," McLanahan said quietly.

"You ordered this?"

"Yes."

Elliott stared at Patrick, then at the external power cart and the screaming its turbine engine was making. "Shut that damned thing off."

"Leave it on, Sergeant," Patrick told Butler.

Elliott jabbed a finger first at Powell, then at McLanahan. "You, I *knew* you were crazy, but Patrick, you've gone round the bend. James steals a jet so you guys want to steal one too? All even up—?"

"Don't give me that, General. Don't tell me you don't understand what I'm trying to do."

"DreamStar is long gone, Patrick," Elliott said. "It's up to Air Defense to force it down or shoot it down. There's nothing we can do—"

"Like hell, Brad. We're *gonna* bring down that sonofabitch."

The change that came over McLanahan was startling but somehow familiar. This was the McLanahan, "Mac" not Patrick, that he remembered from Bomb Comp and from the Old Dog mission eight years earlier—cocky, headstrong, defiant. All part of what had attracted him to the young navigator from the very beginning. The guy was also a pro. He knew it and everyone else knew it—he didn't sugarcoat with politics or bravado or fake expertise. Some of that in his role as a project commander had been kept under wraps, but the crash of the Old Dog and seeing Wendy Tork—or rather as Hal had told him just moments ago, Wendy Tork McLanahan—lying half-dead in the ruins of the Megafortress, had transformed him back to what he'd always been . . .

"At max endurance the whole way he only had enough fuel on board to go as far as Mexico City," McLanahan was saying. "With that max alpha takeoff he made, plus all that combat maneuvering, his range has to be much less. I say he's gotta be on the ground somewhere . . .''

"So what can you do about it?" Elliott asked. "If he's on the ground—"

"Why steal DreamStar, knowing that he can fly for only a few hundred miles before he has to abandon it? Unless he's getting help, unless he planned to fly DreamStar somewhere where it can be refueled. And the nearest place obviously is Mexico, where he was chased.''

"You don't know that. What if he's just flipped out? What if he just wanted to steal DreamStar for a damned joy ride? He's gotten to be so close to that plane, he thinks he owns it.''

"He shoots down the Megafortress for a *joy ride*?''

"ANTARES could have attacked the B-52," Powell broke in. "It's possible for ANTARES to press an attack right after an evasive maneuver—as *part* of an evasive maneuver. It *could* have happened without James ever knowing about it—''

"Look, all this argument isn't getting us any closer to DreamStar,'' McLanahan snapped. "Old Dog got shot down— it happened. James has got DreamStar, that's a fact. And Cheetah is the jet that has any chance of bringing him down. We've seen what's happened to the others. The instruments on Cheetah can locate DreamStar, on the ground or in the air. If he's on the ground I can direct our forces in on him. The Mexicans can yell but I don't think they'd really try to stop us. If he's airborne we can engage him. Either way we need to get our asses in the air. Right now.''

Elliott hesitated. McLanahan might be upset but he was also thinking pretty damn clearly. The question was: what would the Joint Chiefs believe? Would they agree to let Cheetah, with McLanahan on board, try to chase down DreamStar? Obviously they had several squadrons of fighters out after him already, and Cheetah was almost as unique and as classified as DreamStar— too valuable to risk in a major fur-ball dogfight. Would they decide that everyone at Dreamland was nuts and close down the place?

"I need authorization first," Elliott said. "I have to call Washington—''

"There isn't time for that. Every minute we delay DreamStar slips further away from us.''

"You can authorize Cheetah to launch at any time, sir,'' Pow-

ell suggested. "Let us get airborne and headed south. When you
get authorization we'll continue the pursuit. If we stay on the
ground until you get the word we'll never catch him."

"This is an unauthorized mission. I don't own these air-
frames—the Joint Chiefs and the Pentagon own them. They're
experimental aircraft, *not* operational interceptors. It's illegal as
hell for me to authorize you to take off and hunt down DreamStar
or any other aircraft. Can't you understand that?"

"Sure, and now let me try to make you understand, General.
I'm just not going to let any of that stop me from bringing down
DreamStar. James is a thief, a killer and either a spy or a traitor.
I have the plane to bring him down. As far as I'm concerned all
the rest is bureaucratic horseshit that can wait until after
DreamStar has been destroyed or recaptured. Now, you can give
me authorization to launch, and you can get permission for us
to pursue DreamStar after we take off. You can play political
games if you want. But we're leaving, sir, with or without your
blessing."

Which brought matters to Hal Briggs. Would he support his
commanding officer or his best friend?

"Don't even think about it, Patrick," he said. "I can't let
you go against the general's orders. Not now . . ." But then he
turned to Elliott: "Sir, I'm a member of this organization, and
I agree with Colonel McLanahan. Let him take off and chase
down that sonofabitch. It's the best plan we have."

"If I get authorization . . ."

Briggs took a deep breath. "Sir, you've never requested authorization for half the plans you cook up. Building that Old
Dog ten years ago was unauthorized—you took a B-52 air-frame,
ripped off the parts and put the thing together in secret. That
whole B-1 bomber mission to Kavaznya was unauthorized.
Launching the Old Dog was unauthorized. Continuing the mission was technically unauthorized, and so was penetrating Soviet
airspace and attacking that laser installation. You did it, sir,
because it had to be done and you had the people and the equipment to do it."

"This is different—"

"Why? Because it's the colonel doin' the rule-breaking and
not you? Let me make a wild guess here, sir—Colonel Mc-
Lanahan here is sort of a carbon copy of Bradley J. Elliott about
twenty years ago. He's ready to go out there and kick some butt,

just like you did more than once in your career. I read your bio, General . . .'' He rushed on, afraid if he stopped he'd lose his nerve. ''They stick a hot-shot ex-test squadron commander out in some abandoned Air Force test base in Nowheresville, Nevada. They tossed you out, right? You pissed someone off and they stuck you in a hole in the wall in Nevada to get you out of the way—''

''Hal, I'm trying to be patient but this isn't getting us anywhere—''

''But you wouldn't roll over and play dead, would you? You turned Nowheresville into Dreamland. The Pentagon started tossing iffy projects your way. What the hell, sir, if the projects failed you'd get the blame. You proved them wrong. You made the projects work—and not always by following the book and getting authorization—and you got the credit. Pretty soon every new piece of military hardware went through Dreamland . . . Okay, now you're the man, General, and you're lookin' at the new Bradley James Elliott—Patrick S. McLanahan. He's pullin' the same shit you did twenty years ago.''

Elliott knew that was right. He had been drawn to Mac McLanahan from the start, not just because the guy was the best navigator in the Air Force, but because they seemed so much alike. He also knew he got a kick out of watching the transformation of Mac McLanahan—it was almost as if he was watching a videotape of what had happened with him. It had taken a disaster for Patrick to come alive, to rise above the bureaucratic morass. Now the real McLanahan had resurfaced, the one that once treated a bomb run in Russia like nothing much more than a late-night training flight in Idaho.

Elliott turned to McLanahan. ''Mac, smoke that bastard. Whatever it takes, do it.''

Elliott barely had time to lower himself off the crew ladder before Cheetah's left engine began to spin up to idle power. When Briggs reached up to pull the ladder off, McLanahan grabbed it.

''That was quite a speech, Hal,'' he said over the rising whine of the engines.

''I got a confession, buddy. I never read the old man's bio. But I guess I hit pretty close to home. You hang around the guy long enough, you learn a little about what goes on behind the brass. Now get outta here and bring us back some rattlesnake hide.''

## Over Ojito Airfield, central Mexico
*Ten minutes later*

DreamStar's database on Ojito was accurate, except it failed to account for at least a year's worth of unchecked vegetation. Maraklov had set up a computerized instrument landing system in Ojito, which used the database's field location, elevation and information on surrounding terrain to draw a glidescope and localizer beam into the runway.

But Maraklov had to yank DreamStar away from tall strands of dense trees off the approach end of the runway, and when he reached the airport's coordinates themselves he could barely see the runway through the weeds and junk scattered around. He had no choice but to ignore the low fuel warnings and go missed-approach on the field; then he adjusted his ILS for the obstructions and tried again. To use every available inch of pavement he had to drop DreamStar over a stand of trees at almost a full stall, applying power at the last moment to avoid crashing.

After touchdown he discovered that Ojito was nowhere near seven thousand feet long—another dense stand of trees and several buildings rushed up to meet him from less than *two* thousand feet away. Apparently a small corral and farm had been built on the little-used runway to make it easier to load livestock onto trucks, and the surrounding forest had been allowed to grow over the rest of the airstrip.

Maraklov threw the vectored-thrust nozzles and louvers into full reverse power, then hit the brakes. The left brake locked, its anti-skid system failed; it overheated and was quickly deactivated by computer just before it fused to the wheel. DreamStar skidded hard right, and only the lightning-fast application of thrust in the right directions kept the fighter on the narrow weed-covered runway. The left wing crashed into several small, rickety wooden buildings, sending chickens and pigs scattering in all directions. One of the small buildings burst into flames, ignited by the heat from DreamStar's exhaust.

Maraklov gunned the engine. DreamStar leapt forward away from the burning building seconds before the fire reached the left wingtip. Scattering buildings in his jet exhaust, Maraklov taxied back down the runway to the opposite end, turned and aligned himself with the runway centerline, his engine idling. If troops or police came, he would have enough fuel to take off and get two or three hundred feet before flame-out—enough to nose over and crash DreamStar.

He activated the radio on Kramer's frequency. "Kramer, what's your position?" he thought, and ANTARES transmitted the query.

*"Vstryetyemsah zahv dvah menootah, tovarisch,"* Moffitt, Kramer's assistant, replied. Maraklov wished there was a Russian-translation computer in DreamStar—once again he didn't understand enough of what Moffitt said.

This was going to be a major problem, Maraklov thought to himself. They weren't in Russia yet, but even in Mexico they were a hell of a lot closer to Moffitt's turf than Maraklov was. He would have to deal with Moffitt and all the other Moffitts that he'd meet up with—the ones that didn't trust him, the ones who'd think he might have turned, the ones who envied his life in the United States. He'd have to try to begin the transformation back to being a Russian right now.

*"Yah . . . yah nye pahnyemahyo,"* Maraklov thought haltingly. Like many before him, he thought, Russian is *hard*. But ANTARES did not transmit the Russian phrase, so Maraklov had to answer, "Say again."

"Oh, excuse me, Captain James"—Moffitt was his usual charming self—"I forgot you do not speak Russian any more. Our ETA is two minutes."

Maraklov had no time to think about Moffitt. Several villagers had begun to appear at the opposite end of the airstrip. Some went to work putting out the fires to their outbuildings; others pointed at DreamStar. Maraklov couldn't tell if any were carrying weapons but the safe assumption would be that they were armed and shouldn't be allowed to approach, even though they looked like backwoods villagers . . .

Now a large dark-green truck rumbled up the road leading to the tiny airstrip, about a dozen men piled in and slowly started down the runway toward DreamStar. So much for timid villagers.

Maraklov locked the right and the emergency brakes, set the engine louvers on full reverse, and advanced the throttle. A huge

cloud of dust rolled up from the airstrip and almost covered the
advancing truck. The truck stopped, then several villagers
jumped out and ran over to the sides of the runway. This time
Maraklov could see rifles and shotguns. The truck then began
advancing slowly toward him, the villagers with rifles advancing
on both sides.

Maraklov created another dust cloud to warn them away. It
wasn't working. He moved the louvers back to takeoff position.
The truck was closer than a thousand feet now—he wouldn't
make it if he attempted a takeoff over the truck even if his wings
weren't damaged. There was no way in hell he'd risk losing
control of DreamStar to these characters. If these guys came any
closer . . . well, he'd survived fighters, surface-to-air missiles,
anti-aircraft artillery, the best of America's defense arsenals.
Damned if he and his plane were going to give up to a bunch of
peasants in Mexico armed with shotguns.

The villagers were about a hundred yards away when a thunderous roar echoed through the mountainous valley, drowning
out the sound of DreamStar's engines. Suddenly the airfield
erupted in clouds of dust and the crackle of machine-gun fire.
The tree-line on either side of the strip was strafed with heavy-
caliber machine-gun fire, whipping the trees and branches as if
they were in the grip of a hurricane. Not surprisingly the armed
villagers bolted from the airstrip, and soon the source of the
uproar hove into view in the center of the airstrip.

Maraklov was impressed. It was a huge Boeing CH-47 Chinook transport helicopter, an old American twin-rotor job that
had to be at least forty years old. This veteran chopper, belching
smoke that could be seen for miles, was ready for action—with
a door-gunner on each side of the helicopter firing a gyro-
stabilized twenty-millimeter gun, it was more a gunship than a
trash-hauler. Its huge eight-bladed rotors, each some one hundred feet in diameter, barely made it through the trees and brush.
The KGB had at least pulled out all stops to make sure DreamStar
got out of the U.S. intact—no sooner had the monster landed
than twelve heavily armed men rushed out of the rear-cargo
ramp. Two hit the area where the burning buildings smoldered,
the fires extinguished by the downwash of the chopper's huge
rotors; the rest split up on either side of the chopper and began
to secure the perimeter of the airstrip. And then from the cargo

hold of the chopper came Kramer and Moffitt riding aboard a small black-and-green fuel truck.

As Maraklov opened the canopy, a crew from the chopper brought a ladder up to the side for Kramer. Maraklov ordered the maintenance access panels to open automatically, and a crew began to attach fuel lines to the single-point refueling adapter. Other crewmen began stripping loose chunks of fibersteel off DreamStar's tail section, while some scurried over DreamStar's wings inspecting the damage from the Bulldog AAA gun. Amid it all two photographers were taking nonstop pictures of DreamStar.

Kramer, now on the top of the ladder beside the cockpit ledge, plugged a headset into a jack offered by a maintenance technician. "Can you hear me, Maraklov?"

"Yes, I can hear you," the ANTARES-synthesized voice replied. He did not move, nor did he attempt to remove his helmet or raise his visors.

"Welcome, Andrei. What you have accomplished is incredible."

"Thank you," the computer-synthesized voice replied.

"Can you move? You must be tired. Can you get up?"

"I won't disturb the ANTARES interface until we are safely in Nicaragua. The refueling can be accomplished with the engine running. I should launch without any delay."

"I understand. We have begun refueling. We also have missiles and ammunition for your guns."

"What kind of missiles?"

"The best we have," Moffitt broke in on the interphone. He had climbed up the other side of DreamStar and was leaning inside the cockpit, watching with fascination as the multifunction screens flickered and changed at breathtaking speed while Maraklov monitored the refueling. "We have two hundred rounds of twenty-millimeter ammunition plus two AA-11 close-range dogfighting missiles and two AA-14 medium-range missiles. They—"

"Neither is enough," came Maraklov's ANTARES synthesizer voice. Moffitt tried to reach inside the cockpit to touch a button on one of the MFDs, and Maraklov immediately powered the monitor down until Moffitt withdrew his hand. "Without proper interface the missile needs to be able to lock onto a target without carrier-aircraft guidance. Neither the AA-11 or the AA-14 can do that.''

Moffitt's comment was predictable. ''Your American friends always build the best of everything, don't they?''

''Be quiet,'' Kramer told Moffitt, and then asked Maraklov, ''Can't you use the missiles as a decoy? Perhaps they could scare off—''

''They'll only add additional drag, and they could cause damage. I have no intention of letting anyone that close to me. I'll take the ammunition for the cannon—that's standard size.'' Maraklov ordered the cannon-bay door opened, and the twenty-millimeter cannon lowered itself out of its nose bay, where crewmen, along with the photographers, began to examine it in preparation for loading. ''Another important item: remove the left access panel just forward of the canard. There's a black box marked 'data transmitter.' That unit must be disconnected as soon as possible.''

''What is it?''

''An automatic telemetry-data transmitter,'' Maraklov told him. ''It sends engine and flight data to any airborne receivers within a hundred miles, including the F-15F. They can decode the information and use it to track me. It can't be deactivated by ANTARES. Do it immediately.''

Kramer gave the order to the senior crew chief, then: ''What is your plan for escaping to Nicaragua?''

So he was going to Nicaragua, as he'd guessed. Okay, so be it . . . ''I'll stay in the mountains as much as possible and avoid military bases.'' The main multi-function display screen flashed on, then scrolled through computer-generated charts of the route of flight as Maraklov continued: ''I'll fly west of Durango and east of Culiacan to avoid those bases, through the interior to avoid Aguas Calientes and Guadalajara, then into the Sierra Madre del Sur between San Mateo and Acapulco. I don't anticipate problems avoiding Tuxtla Gutierrez and Villahermosa military airfields, and crossing the border I should be unopposed through Guatemala. The problems may come crossing through Honduras,'' the computer-altered voice of ANTARES said—the metallic voice did not reveal any hint of Maraklov's real apprehension or fear. ''I may encounter large American forces from Llorango Airfield in El Salvador, and La Cieba and Tegucigalpa airfields in Honduras, but I believe resistance will not be major. There are only about two hundred miles to the Guatemalan border, through El Salvador and Honduras and into Augusto Cesar Sandino airfield—I can transit the entire distance in less than twenty minutes if necessary. I assume Sandino will be the final destination?''

"Ah . . . that reminds me," Kramer said. "The Nicaraguan government was adamant about not allowing DreamStar into Managua—those people actually believe the U.S. will send the *New Jersey* and shell the city if DreamStar shows up anywhere near it. However, we have been provided an alternate base of operations that you will find more than adequate—Sebaco Airfield, north of Managua.''

Maraklov immediately activated DreamStar's on-board database, and in an instant the computer had found the field and displayed a chart and airfield-information on Sebaco. "It's a mining town with a dirt runway?''

"Your information is dated," Kramer said, "although to tell the truth, we have made our own modifications only recently. Sebaco is now a functional airfield and military post, staffed by our people. The runway has been lengthened and paved and is protected by anti-aircraft missiles and artillery. The KGB Central American Command is based there, along with a small squadron of Mikoyan-Gureyvich-29 fighters. It will be home away from home for you—your first taste of homeland in some time.''

"Yes," Maraklov replied curtly.

Maraklov, sitting immobile in DreamStar's ejection seat, felt the life-giving flow of jet fuel into DreamStar, felt the energy and vitality as the precious liquid flowed into the fighter's tanks—and yet, watching the efficient Soviet plainclothes agents hunting down the villagers, he also felt cornered, trapped, alone. The Soviet KGB forces out there—his *countrymen*—were in a way as strange to him as men from Mars. He even felt a bit of the typical American response when seeing pictures or videotapes of Russian soldiers or airmen: curiosity, puzzlement, even a little fear. They were the enemy—no, they were his countrymen, his fellow Russians. So why did he feel this way?

He looked back toward the nose of his fighter and noted the tall, beefy frame of Kramer's assistant and chief neck-crusher, Moffitt. No matter what he'd accomplished, guys like Moffitt would always suspect him, figuring that as valuable an asset as he was to the Soviets he could be an even more valuable one for the Americans. Had he been turned? Was he a double agent? What if the returning hero turned out to be an embarrassment? At least he hadn't forgotten how they thought, never mind *glasnost*.

At a mental command, Maraklov activated DreamStar's attack radar and concentrated the energy on the right-forward nose-sector antenna-arrays. But after a few moments he turned the radar off. He would have enjoyed barbecuing Moffitt with microwaves—or at least scaring him.

He would have to deal with Moffitt, and the other Moffitts in Russia, very soon. Even being a hero could be dangerous. But he was getting ahead of himself. He was no hero. Not yet. So far he was nothing more, or less, than an uncommon traitor to the U.S.A.

"Tinsel, this is Storm One. Refueling completed with Goalie Three-Zero, squawking normal."

"Storm One, roger. Strangle mode two and four for IFF check."

"Roger, Storm One." J. C. Powell issued commands to deactivate the two military-only data channels that would help Tinsel, the E-3B AWACS radar plane, locate and identify Cheetah. One by one, Tinsel ordered J.C. to turn each transmitter on until all were activated.

McLanahan lowered his oxygen visor. The waiting was the worst part . . . waiting for special clearance for takeoff, clearance to use the KC-10 refueling tanker, clearance to join up with Tinsel and the rest of the interceptor pursuers, and now they had to wait for permission to cross into Mexican airspace. He was itching to get *on* with the chase. DreamStar had such a long head start . . . He continued to check his equipment and thought about Ken James. It was nearly unbelievable. Apparently a Soviet agent had gotten an assignment into the most highly classified research facility in the United States and had gotten to be chief test pilot—hell, the *only* test pilot—of the hottest tactical jet fighter in the world. And had now managed to steal that fighter out from under the noses of a large security force and escape with it out of the United States right past *four* interceptor squadrons.

*And* the son of a bitch had shot down the Old Dog, killed all

but three on board—they had found Major Edward Frost, the
radar navigator, badly broken up but somehow alive a mile from
the impact area; his parachute never had time to open before he
hit the ground, they said. Colonel Jeffrey Khan, the copilot,
ended up at the edge of the scorched earth in critical condition
but alive. And Wendy . . . she was alive, clinging to life. The
investigators said there was no way she could have gotten out by
herself—Angelina Pereira must have sacrificed herself to save
Wendy.

One man had caused more damage, more destruction and
more death than McLanahan could have ever imagined, not to
mention the military secrets he must already have turned over to
the Soviet Union. And if this . . . this Maraklov had replaced
the real Kenneth James *before* his assignment to Dreamland, he
would have done even more damage. The real Ken James was a
B-1 commander for three years. The phony one could have turned
over enough data on the B-1, its mission, its routes of flight, its
weapons and other top-secret information to destroy the strategic
bombardment mission of the Strategic Air Command for years.
And now, James—it was still hard to think of him as anyone else
but Ken James—had DreamStar . . .

"Storm Zero One, data-link checks completed," the controller aboard the AWACS reported. "Clearance not yet received to
proceed through the Monterrey FIR sector one. You can join
Eagle Zero Two flight of four over Luke Range Complex Seven,
or orbit within three-zero miles of REEBO intersection at flight
level two-five zero until clearance is received. Over."

"When do you expect clearance through the sector, Tinsel?"
J.C. asked.

"No idea, Storm. Our request had to be forwarded through
Air Force to the Pentagon. Pentagon will probably pass it on to
State. We lost it from there."

Patrick checked his charts. REEBO was just east of Yuma,
very close to the border; Luke Complex Seven was farther
north, closer to the tanker's orbit point. "Take the orbit at
REEBO, J.C.," Patrick told Powell.

"Tinsel, we'll take the orbit point at REEBO at two-five-oh."

"Roger, Storm One, cleared to orbit as required at REEBO.
Climb and maintain flight level two-five-zero. Orbit within three-
zero miles, stay five miles north of the southern domestic ADZ

until given a Mexican controller freq and squawk and cleared to proceed.''

"Storm One copies clearance.'' J.C. switched his outside radios to standby and said on interphone to McLanahan: "Now let me guess—this air machine ain't gonna do no orbiting.''

"You got that right. Take two-five-zero, maintain five-zero-zero knots. When we reach REEBO start a climb to three-niner-zero and switch to max speed power settings.''

"We'll be sucking fuel like crazy,'' J.C. reminded Mc-Lanahan. "It'll be real tight if we don't have tanker support on the way back.''

"We need to catch this Maraklov and get a shot at him. What counts is nailing that bastard. Right now I don't really much care if I make it back.''

General Brad Elliott sat alone in the small battle-staff operations center of HAWC's command post. A wall-size gas-plasma screen was on the far wall, depicting the southern Nevada Red Flag bombing and aerial-gunnery ranges in which the Old Dog was located. The airspace was empty except for the cluster of aircraft, mostly security helicopters and shuttles for the investigation team, around the Megafortress' impact area.

Hal Briggs entered the conference room. He was carrying his automatic pistol in a shoulder holster and wearing a communications transceiver with a wireless earpiece to allow him to stay in contact with his command center wherever he went.

He studied General Elliott for a moment before disturbing him. More than ever, the sixty-year-old commander of Dreamland looked exhausted, physically and emotionally. Working out here in the Nevada wastelands was demanding for even the healthiest, but for Elliott it was especially tough. Briggs had seen the strain on him during day-to-day activities—increased isolation, moodiness. But this disaster looked as if it might push him right to the edge. He needed some close observation from here on, Briggs decided. Very close.

Briggs dropped a piece of paper on the desk in front of Elliott. "Preliminary report from the investigation team, crew-member disposition analysis.'' Elliott said nothing. Briggs paused a moment, then decided to read on: "Two members of the crew never tried to get out; Wendelstat in the I.P. seat and Major Evanston, the nav. Right side of the crew compartment was badly chewed up; Evanston may have already been dead.'' Elliott winced as if struck in the face. Evanston was part of the "great experiment" of the early 1990s, the project exploring the possibility of military women assigned to combat duties. A graduate of the Air Force Academy, she was easily the best qualified for the program, and she was accepted and soon became the first woman crewmember in a B-52 bomber squadron. Because of her engineering background, she had been temporarily assigned to HAWC to participate in the Megafortress Plus project—obviously headed for promotion. What a terrible waste.

Hal hurried on through the report to spare Elliott as much as possible: "I guess Wendelstat in the I.P.'s seat didn't have a chance for manual bailout unless he was at high altitude." Elliott nodded numbly. "Gunner's seat was fired but apparently malfunctioned. Remains still strapped in place—I guess Dr. Pereira never tried manual bailout. Didn't have a chance . . . Remains found in the debris believed to be of General Ormack; he ejected but landed in the fireball.''

"My God . . ."

"Khan might be okay, some bad cuts and lacerations, a broken arm but that's it. Wendy Tork is in critical condition. She's on her way to the burn unit at Brooks Medical Center in San Antonio. Her progress is not favorable. Ed Frost . . . died, sir. They said he never got a 'chute . . .''

Elliott rubbed his eyes. "I want Tork's progress monitored hourly. I want to make sure she's getting the best treatment possible.''

"I'll see to it, sir.''

"What about the families?''

"Being assembled at the base chapel at Nellis, as you ordered," Briggs said. "Dr. Pereira listed no next of kin. All the rest are on their way.''

Elliott shook his head, stunned. "This is the worst since the fall of Saigon." He stared at the chart on the screen. "What the hell can I tell the families?''

"Tell them what you just told me, sir.''

"But they'll never understand, and why should they?''

"They understood the sort of job those crewmembers did, even if they weren't told specifics. What they need is every bit of support you can give them. They'll want to know their husbands or friends or sons or daughters didn't die for nothing.''

Elliott turned to Briggs. "How the hell did you get so smart?"

"Watchin' you, General. I—" Briggs stopped and listened intently on his communications earpiece. "Message coming in from the Joint Chiefs. AWACS and the Mexican government are reporting another unauthorized airspace intrusion by Powell and McLanahan in Storm Zero One. JCS want you to stand by for a secure video conference at five past the hour."

"Here's where it hits the fan, Hal," Elliott said. "The Pentagon probably thinks I've flipped out, they'll relieve me from command—"

"There was nothing you could have done—"

"There was *everything* I could have done. Like I could have screened our test pilots better, I could have secured the flight line better, I could have forbidden Ormack to engage DreamStar. It'll probably turn out I never should have let Cheetah go after DreamStar."

"They can't hang you for something you had no control over."

Elliott sat quietly for a few moments, then: "As long as I've got control, I'm going to use it." He picked up the direct line to the command post controller. "It's something I should have done from the beginning."

"You're going to recall McLanahan and Powell?"

"I've made too many mistakes. I've got a responsibility here, and I'm taking charge right now."

J. C. Powell had taken Cheetah down from forty thousand feet to one thousand feet and just below the speed of sound as they approached the area where DreamStar's data-signal indicated its position.

"Showing thirty miles to intercept," McLanahan said, reading the telemetry data being received from DreamStar's automatic encoders. "Still showing him on the ground but with engines running."

"Can you get a fix on his position?"

"Already got it," McLanahan said. "I don't show any Mexican airfields on my charts, but there're probably a lot of them around here. He . . . goddamn, just lost the data-signal."

"Which means he's got help," J.C. said. "Someone must have deactivated the data-transmitter for him." J.C. took a firm grip on his stick and throttles, experimentally shaking the stick to help himself concentrate—he was amazed at the extra amount of agility Cheetah demonstrated without the heavy camera on the spine. "Twenty miles. Stand by. Throttles coming to eighty percent." Slowly Powell brought the throttles out of military power and to the lower power setting.

"Give me a good clearing turn in each direction so I can get a look," Patrick said. "I'll call the target, then we'll come back around and try for a strafing run."

"Guns coming on," said J.C. He hit the voice-recognition computer button: "Arm cannon."

*"Warning, cannon armed, six hundred rounds remaining,"* the computer replied.

"Set attack mode strafe," J.C. ordered.

*"Strafe mode enabled."* A laser-drawn crosshair reticle appeared on J.C.'s windscreen, and weapon- and altitude-warning readouts appeared near the reticle. Adjusted for airspeed, winds and drift by the computer and attack radar, the reticle would position itself where the bullets from Cheetah's cannon would impact, no matter how Cheetah moved through the air. In strafe mode J.C. could select a ground target and the computer would direct the pilot which way to fly to keep the reticle centered on the target. It would also warn of terrain or other obstacles and warn when the ammunition count was getting low.

"Cannon's on-line," J.C. told McLanahan.

"Ten miles out." McLanahan now began to transition to visual, looking out the canopy as he could, scanning the rocks and scrub-forested hills ahead for an airfield. The inertial navigator and flight director could fly Cheetah to within sixty feet of a waypoint, but if the airstrip's coordinates in the database were not perfect they could miss the field. And in this dense, hilly terrain it was very possible to fly as close as a few hundred yards of the airstrip and not see it.

"Five miles." J.C. made S-turns around the flight path, banking sharply up without turning so Patrick and he could get a clear look all around the aircraft for the airfield, including under the belly. There were lots of clearings, even several that looked like airstrips, but in the few moments they had at each, they saw no aircraft.

"DreamStar could be hidden," J.C. said. "They've had time—"

"We'll find it."

"We'll be able to loiter only a few minutes before we have to start back—"

"Just *look* for the damned—*there it is, eleven o'clock low* . . ."

Cheetah was in a steep left bank when Patrick called the airstrip. Powell saw it immediately. It was a narrow clearing on top of a small plateau, but it was wide enough through the trees so that the edges of the tarmac could be seen. It was also difficult to miss the huge black-and-green helicopter sitting in the middle of the clearing.

"A chopper. They brought in a chopper," McLanahan called out. "If we can hit that Chinook, keep it from taking off—"

"Hang on." J.C. pulled hard, using Cheetah's large canards to pull the nose hard-left over to the helicopter in the clearing.

"Target lock." The aiming reticle began to rotate. As the helicopter moved into the center of the reticle Powell said "—now!" to complete the command.

*"Target locked,"* the computer answered. A small square appeared in the center of the reticle indicating that the firing computer was now aimed and locked onto the helicopter, and a large cross, resembling the glideslope-azimuth flight director of an instrument landing system, interposed itself on the screen. *"Fifteen seconds to firing range, six hundred rounds remaining . . . caution, search radar, twelve o'clock."*

"DreamStar," Powell said. "His search radar." As he finished saying it the search symbol on the widescreen changed to a batwing symbol.

*"Warning, radar weapon track, twelve o'clock,"* the computer announced.

"He's got us," McLanahan said. "But we got him first . . ."

"Disconnect." The computer-synthesized voice of Maraklov boomed in Kramer's headset. "Clear the area. We've been spotted. Aircraft to the east!"

Kramer, still standing on top of the crew ladder during the refueling and rearming procedure, turned and searched the horizon behind him. He saw it immediately, bearing down on them. A single F-15 fighter, dark gray, larger than DreamStar. Even from this distance he could see the missiles hanging on the wings.

*"Skaryehyeh,"* Kramer shouted to the ground crewmen. "Disconnect the fuel lines, move that fuel truck aside, launch the helicopter, *move.*" He jumped off the ladder, pulled it free

and threw it into the bushes beside the airstrip. The canopy closed with a bang. A crewman had disconnected the fuel line from the single-point refueling receptacle before the truck's pump was shut off, and a geyser of jet fuel erupted near DreamStar's front landing gear.

Cheetah. As Maraklov issued the mental command to begin the start-sequence and prepare DreamStar for flight he knew it had to be Cheetah. He didn't need to analyze the radar emissions or flight parameters. He could even guess who was on board: Powell and McLanahan. Only those two would be crazy enough to go on a search-and-destroy mission alone—but that matched Powell's cowboy attitude and McLanahan's emotional approach. They should have brought a dozen F-15 Strike Eagles or FB-111 bombers along for ground attack and carpet-bomb the area, plus another dozen fighters for backup. They were probably acting against orders—hell, they might be in as much trouble right now as he was. But he still had a chance to escape if he could get off the ground in time.

Maraklov closed the service panel and began to retract the cannon back into its bay at the same time that he activated the cannon and checked the system. The Soviet-make ammunition fed through the chamber—then suddenly jammed. It might have been the same caliber ammunition but the feed mechanisms were barely compatible. Immediately the cannon performed an auto-clear, which reversed the belt feed, ejected the cartridges where the jam had occurred and re-fed the belt, and this time the one-inch-diameter cartridges fed properly.

One last check as the engines quickly revved to full power. Two hundred rounds of ammunition had been loaded. They also had managed to onload full fuel in the body tanks and three-quarter fuel in the wings, about forty thousand pounds of it. It was enough for the seven-hundred-mile flight to Nicaragua at normal cruise speeds but not enough if he had to mix it up with Cheetah. This was not the time or place to make a stand—the order of the day was Run Like Hell Fight Only If Cornered . . .

The huge blades of the supply helicopter began to turn just as several loud sharp cracks reverberated off the canopy. Dust and concrete flew near the aft-empennage of the chopper, and smoke began to billow out of the aft rotor. But the main rotor continued to spool up. The fuel truck originally high-tailing it for the cargo ramp was waved aside and ordered into the tree line out of the way.

Maraklov set DreamStar's wings to their maximum high-lift, then had the computers check the takeoff performance. Barely enough. The computer said two thousand three hundred feet to clear the seventy-foot trees; there were only about fifteen hundred available. Maraklov activated the UHF radio on the discrete KGB frequency: "Kramer, this is DreamStar. Order your men to clear those buildings off the end of the airstrip. I need more runway for takeoff."

There was no reply, but soon several soldiers ran out of the chopper's cargo bay toward the end of the airstrip and a few moments later the fuel truck followed. They used the fuel truck to push the burned-out buildings into the tree line. Several of the Soviet soldiers fell, and others began firing into the trees—apparently there were still Mexican villagers in the forest surrounding the airstrip. The KGB soldiers would take care of them . . .

*"Five hundred fifty rounds remaining,"* the computer announced. Cheetah swooped over the trees, so close Patrick thought they had flown *between* a few of them. *"Low altitude warning . . ."*

Thanks for nothing, J.C. thought. I only had the shot for a few seconds.

"Looks like that Chinook has some heavy guns on the side," McLanahan said. "Better hit 'em from a different angle."

J.C. banked sharply left, started a hard left turn, steering to put himself at a ninety-degree angle to his first strafing run to hit the helicopter from the tail. "Did you see DreamStar?"

"Behind the helicopter about a hundred yards," McLanahan said. "He's right at the north end of the airstrip, almost under the trees."

"Had a fifty-fifty chance and blew it," J.C. said angrily. "I won't be able to hit him from this direction but if I can get another good shot at that helicopter while it's on the ground it at least should block the runway enough to keep DreamStar from lifting off."

Powell shallowed out his bank angle to allow himself more time to extend his distance from the airstrip. But by the time he had rolled out on the flight director they saw a dark, massive apparition slowly rise out of the trees, trailing thick clouds of smoke.

"It's the damn helicopter—"

J.C. hit the voice-command button, forced his voice to be steady: "Set attack mode infrared missile. Arm one missile." The Sidewinder missile's aiming reticle appeared on the windscreen centered on the slow-moving helicopter, and almost immediately the missile signaled that its infrared seeker-head had locked onto the helicopter's huge jet engines. Before the computer could acknowledge his commands Powell had punched the missile-launch button on his control stick.

*"Infrared missile launch."* Less than three miles away, the Sidewinder could hardly miss . . . the entire rotor and top half of the huge helicopter disappeared in a cloud of smoke and fire as the hulking machine rolled hard to the left and dropped into the trees. Powell and McLanahan were so close to the helicopter on impact that they could see the men inside . . .

But the helicopter crashed clear of the tiny airstrip. The runway was open.

"Damn it. Set attack mode strafe. Arm cannon." McLanahan grabbed hold of the handlebars as J.C. rolled Cheetah hard up and right, struggling to get back into firing position. They rolled into a wings-level steep descent on the attack flight director, which was still locked in strafing mode onto the spot where DreamStar had been parked. It took a few precious seconds for Powell to readjust his eyes. When he did he saw DreamStar rolling down the runway. He tried to push Cheetah's nose down and get off a few quick bursts, but his rate of descent was too steep and the flight director was ordering him to climb before he got too low. The few rounds he did get off impacted on the spot DreamStar had vacated just seconds earlier.

"I missed, he's getting away."

The instant the hulking transport helicopter lifted off, Maraklov forgot about the fuel truck, the buildings on the runway, everything except the takeoff. He saw the Sidewinder plow into the chopper, saw the machine explode and crash into the forest. But his attention was on the takeoff—until he saw Cheetah bearing straight down at him, the F-15 fighter so large it cast a shadow on Maraklov's cockpit. How could he miss?

The feeling of imminent death was so strong that the AN-

TARES interface almost shut down out of sheer panic. But Maraklov's last commands were executed, and DreamStar's turbofan engine was at full afterburning thrust and the brakes were off. He expected the rounds from Cheetah's M61B2 gun to tear through his canopy any second—then, almost as quickly, he realized that Cheetah had overshot. His guns were firing but his nose was coming up too fast and so the shells were hitting behind him. He also caught a glimpse of KGB soldiers firing into the sky, futilely trying to shoot down Cheetah with AK-47 rifles.

Maraklov considered using the same takeoff trick he had used back at Dreamland, but the wings would not respond to the wingtip back-twisting that had worked so well before. The pile of broken and burning buildings at the end of the runway rushed forward. Smoke from the destroyed cargo helicopter obscured his vision, so that he could not watch the wall of green heading straight at him . . .

. . . DreamStar's landing gear left the runway less than a hundred feet from the hastily cleared end of the runway, and the wheels were just tucking themselves into their wells when DreamStar cleared the trees. Airborne once again, Maraklov made a hard turn to the southeast, stayed in full afterburner, pushed DreamStar's nose down to build airspeed and hugged the rugged mountain ridges as close as possible. ANTARES had computed several attack scenarios, but Maraklov overrode all of them. For now escape was his best defense.

McLanahan was holding onto the canopy sill, straining against the crushing G-forces to look between Cheetah's twin vertical stabilizers.

"I see him," he called out. "He made it off, he's staying low . . ."

Powell continued his hard turn, executing a one-hundred-eighty-degree turn and thrusting his nose toward the rugged mountain foothills. Once they were rolled in McLanahan checked his radar screen. "Radar contact, J.C., twelve o'clock low—I've got radar lock. *Get him!*"

Powell hit the voice-recognition computer-button. "Set attack mode radar missile. Arm one radar missile."

*"Radar missile armed."*

"Launch radar missile . . . now."

Once again the radar-threat warning blared in Maraklov's head but this time he was ready for it. It said that Cheetah was above and behind him approximately six miles—a poor position to launch an attack at low altitude. The threat-warning receiver also did not indicate that the Scorpion missile's own seeker-head was tracking—which meant that the missile was getting its guidance information only from Cheetah's radar. A significant disadvantage in the milliseconds game they were now playing.

Maraklov began a hard four-G inverted climb directly back toward Cheetah, presenting his smallest radar cross-section to the oncoming Scorpion missile, which corrected for the sudden climb but could not complete the turn in time to avoid plowing into the Sierra Madre mountains. ANTARES immediately brought its cannon on-line and activated its attack radar to track Cheetah in as it sped toward it.

J.C. watched in frustration as DreamStar dodged away from the AIM-120 missile, but he was ready for the move. "Set attack-mode air cannon. Arm cannon."

"*Cannon armed . . . Warning, radar weapon tracking, twelve o'clock.*"

Powell touched the voice-command button. "All trackbreakers on and transmit."

"*Trackbreakers on and transmitting,*" the computer acknowledged as Cheetah's powerful internal jammers activated—the jammers would keep DreamStar's cannon from maintaining a lock-on. "I can't believe how fast he can get his guns on-line. But he's gotta be out of smash . . . Hang on."

McLanahan needed no encouragement. J.C. pulled up into a tight climb, rolled inverted only five hundred feet above ground and again tried to line up on DreamStar.

DreamStar had easily locked onto Cheetah with the attack radar, and Maraklov could now track it through its sudden climb. But when DreamStar tried to follow Cheetah around to keep the guns on him, ANTARES warned that he was approaching stall-speed. DreamStar, which had not yet reached optimal flying speed so early after takeoff, had used all its energy in its tight evasive turn and its pitch-up to track Cheetah and had no power left to continue to track him with the nose high in the air. DreamStar's canards pushed the nose down, and with that the guns were pulled off Cheetah.

• • •

Powell pushed Cheetah's nose earthward and on the downside
of the loop found himself lined up on DreamStar. He pushed on
the right rudder to slew Cheetah's nose to the right . . . no time
to get a radar lock . . . just squeeze the trigger, hoping for a
lucky hit.

"Altitude," Patrick shouted. "Pull *up*."

J.C. went to max afterburner and hauled back on the stick
with both hands. He was so fixed on the image of DreamStar
dead in his sights that he ignored the rocks and trees rushing up
at him. Then he had to roll hard left to fly behind DreamStar to
avoid hitting *him*. After that hard turn Powell found himself perilously close to stall speed and had no choice but to roll wings-
level at max afterburner and wait until he had regained speed.

"Dammit," McLanahan shouted, "you had him, J.C. You
could have nailed him—"

"This isn't no Cessna 152 we're fooling with, Patrick. He can
turn and attack faster than we can. He could have launched a
missile by now but he was only tracking us with guns—he never
got off a missile-track signal. Maybe that means he doesn't have
any missiles."

"Well, we're below half-fuel right now. We need to tag him
and head back or we'll be walking to Nevada."

J.C. started a right turn back toward DreamStar. "Safe radar
missiles," he spoke into the voice-command computer. "Set
attack mode infrared missile."

*"Infrared missile selected, warning, one missile remaining."*

"I got a visual on him," Powell said. He touched the voice-
command button. "Attack radar standby. Infrared scanner operate."

*"Attack radar standby. Infrared scanner on."* Immediately
the heat-seeking scanner locked onto DreamStar.

"He's just running," Powell said. "He's not jinking and jiv-
ing anymore." To the voice-command computer he ordered,
"Slave infrared missile to infrared scanner."

The Sidewinder missile's seeker-head followed the azimuth
directions of Cheetah's scanner, but the missile did not indicate
a lock-on. "We need to get in closer . . ."

"No," McLanahan said. "His tail IR scanner has a greater
range than our Sidewinder. Launch the Sidewinder in boresight
mode—it should lock onto him after launch."

"It's worth a try." It was easier than before for Powell to align himself with DreamStar's tailpipe—Maraklov was indeed driving straight and level, accelerating as fast as possible. When he was aligned with DreamStar's rectangular exhaust Powell commanded: "Infrared missile boresight."

*"Infrared missile boresight, caution, no target lock."* The missile would normally not launch unless it was tracking a target, but in boresight mode the missile could be launched straight ahead and the infrared seeker could attempt to lock onto a target while in flight; it also was a tricky technique used against slow-moving targets to hit them outside the missile's optimal range. It was not reliable because of the missile-seeker's narrow field of view, but against hot targets that weren't maneuvering it was at least a valid attack.

Powell hit the command button. "Launch."

*"Warning, radar target lock, seven o'clock."*

McLanahan strained again to search behind Cheetah's twin tails. "Two . . . no, four fighters, two flights of two, right behind us. I can't see what they are but they're coming on fast—"

"I gotta break it off, Patrick—"

"No, stay on him, nail him—"

But even then it was too late. DreamStar had picked up the same radar indications as Cheetah, and the advanced fighter had made a hard break to the right and an even harder one up and down to shake off the radar-lock by the advancing strangers. A boresight missile-launch was impossible.

"Infrared missiles to safe. Set attack-mode radar missiles," Powell ordered.

"Two jets going high, two coming in," McLanahan said. "I can't tell for sure but they look like . . . they're F-20s, Mexican F-20s . . ."

*"Warning, radar target lock, six o'clock . . ."*

J.C. yanked the stick hard right to stay with DreamStar, but it had regained its lost speed and was pulling away, staying at boulder level.

"They're still with us," McLanahan said. "Can you get a shot off anyway?"

"I think so . . . here we go . . ."

*"Warning, radar missile lock."* A missile was in flight, heading for them . . .

J.C. hit the voice-command button on his stick. "Chaff right."

The computer ejected two bundles of radar-decoying chaff from the right ejector rack as J.C. yanked Cheetah into a hard left bank, pulling on the stick until the computer issued a stall-warning message.

"No missile," McLanahan called out, straining his head up out of the cockpit against the G-forces pushing him into his seat. "Didn't see a missile . . ."

"They faked us out," J.C. said, "they wanted to get our attention—"

"Damn it, get back on DreamStar."

Powell began a hard right turn back toward DreamStar, but as he rolled out of the turn they heard: "American F-15 fighter, this is Mexican Air Force. You are directed to follow me at once."

"Goddamn, there he is, left wing." The F-20 Tigershark, the single-engine, high-tech version of the American F-5F Tiger fighter, was in loose route formation off Cheetah's left wingtip.

"Number two is behind us," McLanahan said. "Stay on DreamStar." He switched to the VHF GUARD international emergency frequency. "Mexican Air Force, this is the F-15 Storm One. We are on an authorized search mission for Storm Two, which is at our one o'clock position. We have permission from your government to pursue and destroy this aircraft. Over." So he lied a little.

"We have been advised that no foreign aircraft has permission to enter Mexican airspace. We will destroy both if you do not follow us immediately."

"The XF-34 Storm Two is an experimental aircraft. It's also lethal as hell. We will pursue and destroy it. Stay clear."

"No. Follow me or you will be shot down." The F-20 on Cheetah's left wing dropped back a few yards and began a climbing left turn.

*"Warning, radar target lock, six o'clock."* The F-20 following behind them had activated its tracking radar again. At this distance he could hardly miss . . .

"I'm open to suggestions, Colonel," J.C. deadpanned.

"DreamStar's moved out to ten miles," McLanahan said, checking his radar. "Those other two Mexicans are chasing him but it's no contest, he's pulling away—"

"I've got to follow," J.C. said, gently easing into a left bank. "That guy behind me will hose us if I don't."

"Damn it, we had him . . . he was so close . . . can you get away from these guys?"

"Sure. This guy ahead of us is so sloppy I can fill him full of holes right now, and I think I can get away from the guy on our tail. But then what? We're into our fuel reserves as it is. After we lose these guys we'll need afterburner the whole way back just to get within missile range of DreamStar, and then the best we got is a tail-chase until we run out of gas."

"So do it . . ."

"If that's what you really want . . ."

"What the hell does that mean . . . ?"

"That I think you better think pretty damn hard about it. If you try to chase down DreamStar from here we won't make it home. You'll risk Cheetah for a fifty-fifty chance of downing DreamStar. You've already violated Mexican air space and will take heat for that, but if you don't bring back Cheetah you're guaranteeing yourself a Big Chicken Dinner—"

"Cheetah was my responsibility. If I let James get away . . . we all go down the tubes. As long as there's a chance I'm not going to let this guy go."

"You've done everything you could. Like they say, there's a time to chase and a time to get the hell out of Dodge. I suggest we boogie."

McLanahan hesitated. J.C. rolled out behind the lead F-20 and reduced power slightly. The leader reduced his power to move beside Cheetah.

J.C. tried the last gambit he could think of to get Patrick back to reality . . . "I don't love chasing DreamStar over Mexico with two chilibeans on my tail and sucking fumes but I can live with it. But you . . . you have something worth more than DreamStar back in a hospital in Vegas. Let's get back and go after him another day."

It worked. Watching the Mexican F-20 off their left wing, with one speedbrake raised to slow himself down, McLanahan realized J.C. was right. He'd taken an incredible chance and violated a few dozen rules by coming this far. He and J.C. had almost got James . . . they'd done everything they could . . . "There's *going* to be a next time," he muttered. "Bet on it."

J.C. added: "The Russians don't have DreamStar yet—*a* Russian has it and he's still ten thousand miles from home."

"So we've still got these Mexican guys." He strained to search behind Cheetah. "Number two's back there right between the tails."

"No offense to the Mexican Air Force," J.C. said, "but I'll bet these bozos never intercepted anything but a soccer ball. The lead's got his power way back waiting for us, and his wingman's right in our jet-wash. They're both out of position. Hang on."

J.C. jerked the throttles to idle and popped Cheetah's big speedbreak. The lead F-20 noticed the sudden power reduction and, not realizing how slow he was already going, pulled back his power even more. On the verge of a stall, he had no choice but to scissor left and fall away to regain his lost airspeed. Meanwhile, the number two F-20, not watching Cheetah and distracted by his leader's sudden departure, never tried to slow down. He yanked his stick hard-right just in time to avoid slamming into Cheetah's tail, and had to spin away. At that moment J.C. retracted the speedbrake, went into full power and began to accelerate and climb away from the Mexican interceptors.

McLanahan was staring out the back of the large bubble canopy. "They're still below us . . . not climbing yet . . ."

*"Warning, radar search, six o'clock,"* from the computer.

"They dropped from radar track to search," J.C. said. "Are they getting closer?"

"I can't see them, they've dropped back."

"American F-15, this is Mexican Air Force. Follow us to base immediately. Acknowledge."

J.C. shut off the VHF GUARD channel.

"I don't think we can make it," McLanahan said a few minutes later, using the computer to check their fuel status. "We'll have to divert to a Mexican airport after all."

"We'll start a climb and then use an idle descent into a diversion base," J.C. said, gently pulling back on the stick and starting a shallow climb. "Oh, well," he sighed, "I haven't been in a Mexican jail since high school. It'll be like old times."

"Sorry I got you into this, J.C. I'm going to waste that son-ofabitch if I have to walk back to Nicaragua or Colombia or Bolivia or wherever he's headed—"

Suddenly the number one radio, still set to the refueling tanker's operating frequency, crackled to life: "Storm One, this is Cardinal Three-Seven. Over."

"I got it," McLanahan said. On the radio he replied: "Cardinal Three-Seven, this is Storm One. Over."

"Storm One, this is Cardinal. We're Sun Devil KC-135 out of Phoenix-Sky Harbor Airport, one hundred and sixty-first Air Refueling Group, Arizona Air National Guard. Set beacon code seventy-four, we've got thirty-one. We're at flight level two-niner zero, orbiting fifty miles south of Tucson near Nogales. What's your situation? Over."

"Air-to-air TACAN beacon? I haven't used that since I was a butter-bar." J.C. checked the distance readout. "He's still out of range, not picking him up yet."

"Cardinal, Storm One is approximately one hundred miles southwest of Chihuahua. Fuel situation critical. We were about to divert to Chihuahua for emergency refueling. Over."

"Copy that, Storm. I guess your boss wants you back real bad. We've been ordered to . . . how should I put it? . . . have a catastrophic navigation failure and come and get you. As I speak, our autopilot is mysteriously taking us south across the border." A pause, then: "Air-to-air TACAN shows two hundred miles, Storm. Can you make it?"

"It'll be close," McLanahan said.

"We may have visitors," J.C. added. "We left a couple sorehead Mexican F-20s in our dust."

"They should have gotten word by now that you're on an authorized sortie," the crewman replied. "Your boss tells us that they finally authorized your overflight. But that's not going to help you much. I hope you got what you came for, boys—I doubt there are going to be any high fives waiting for you."

"No," McLanahan said, "we didn't get what we came for. Not this time . . ."

# =5=

## Sebaco Military Airbase, Nicaragua
*Thursday, 18 June 1996, 0645 CDT (0745 EDT)*

ANDREI MARAKLOV AWOKE with a start but didn't try to get up—his muscles quivered with the slightest hint of exertion. He was incredibly thirsty. Beads of sweat rolled down from his eyebrows, and the dirt and salt stung his eyes.

He opened his eyes. He was lying face down on a firm mattress, his face buried in stiff white sheets. His arms were by his side. Judging by feel, he was only wearing a pair of briefs.

Suddenly he felt a cool sponge touch the back of his neck, and a young female voice said in a soft voice, *"Dobrahye otrah, tovarisch Polkovnik."*

He had prepared himself for this, ever since deciding to take DreamStar out of the United States. In hesitant, poorly phrased Russian, he replied, *"Vi gahvahretye pah angleyski?"*

"Of course, Colonel. My mistake." The sponge ran over his shoulders, across his back. He tried to look at the woman but couldn't even manage that much energy. Now in a near-perfect midwestern American accent the woman said, "Good morning, Colonel."

"Who are you?"

"My name is Musi Zaykov. I am your aide and secretary."

"Are you KGB?"

"Yes, sir. I am a *starshiy leyt* . . . I'm sorry—a lieutenant, Central American Command. I have been here in Nicaragua for almost a year."

Nicaragua. Maraklov closed his eyes. He had almost forgotten. That explained the heat and the humidity. The events of his flight across Central America came back and invaded his thoughts. That explained his debilitation—he had flown DreamStar several hours longer than he had ever done before. He routinely lost four or five pounds on every one-hour sortie in the past, and this last flight, with ANTARES in combat conditions, had taken three hours. No wonder . . .

"I have been asked to notify the base commander when you awoke, sir," she said, rinsing the sponge off in a pan on a stand by the bed, "but I'll wait and let you go back to sleep if you want."

"Thanks." He made an effort and rolled onto his back, opening his eyes wide as he did so to help him regain his equilibrium. Musi Zaykov was sitting on the bed to his right. She looked about thirty, blonde hair, blue eyes, with a bright disarming smile. She wore a khaki bush shirt with the collar open several buttons from the top against the heat.

"Musi . . . Musi . . . very pretty name."

"Thank you, sir."

"How long have I been asleep?"

"About fifteen hours, Colonel." He watched her eyes scan his body. "I'm sorry we could not provide you with better sleeping arrangements, sir. It was decided to leave you here in the hangar where the security units have been assembled. I'm sure air conditioning will be set up as soon as possible."

Maraklov nodded. "Pass the water." Zaykov quickly passed the pitcher of ice water over to him. He watched her over the rim of the plastic glass.

"They say you were close to death when they took you out of your aircraft," she said, her eyes occasionally straying down to his abdomen and legs. "Dehydration and chemical depletion."

"Ten pounds is unusual," Maraklov said, "but dehydration and chemical imbalance isn't. I have a megadose on vitamins and minerals every time I fly my plane." She was fidgeting a bit on the edge of the bed, her breathing getting deeper.

She was beautiful, but was he imagining this as a come-on? If it was real, why?

"Leave me alone," he said suddenly. "I want to get dressed."

"I have been asked to stay with you—"

"I said get out."

"I am a qualified nurse, sir, as well as an intelligence analyst and operative." She leaned closer to him, inviting him to touch her body. "In your condition I do not think it wise to leave you alone."

And he suddenly realized the real situation he was in. He was lucky the Central Command had only sent a "friendly" operative, an agent instructed to get close to him, become his confidante, including his sexual partner if necessary. Right out of Academy syllabus . . .

"You obviously didn't place too well at Connecticut Academy," Maraklov deadpanned.

Zaykov looked startled, but only for an instant. "I'm sorry, sir . . . ?"

"You're also bothering me, and I don't want the KGB watching me on the john, even an agent with big tits."

She didn't blink. "Yes, Colonel, it's true I am a KGB soldier, but right now I am here to help you in any way I can during your recovery phase. You have been through a remarkable ordeal and you have an even more difficult one ahead of you. I think it important that you not go through this alone. All I ask is that you please let me help."

So sincere, but she was using the exact hand gestures and body movements "Janet Larson" had practiced back at the Academy—her body, her mannerisms, even her accent were virtual duplicates of Janet Larson, who had tried to get him thrown out of the Academy and take away his chance to come to America . . .

*"I don't need any help—"*

"But—"

"That's an order, *Lieutenant*. Now get your butt out of here." Zaykov missed that bit of slang but got the idea, rolled off the bed and left.

The word was going to spread quickly that he was awake, so Maraklov went over to the tiny closet-sized bathroom, found toilet articles and towels and showered and shaved as fast as he could without making the room spin. He had finished and was on his seventh glass of water when the door of the small apartment opened and a man in the black battle-dress uniform of the KGB Border Guards moved aside, allowing an older officer in a dark green-and-brown camouflage flight suit to enter. The officer was tall and wiry—the flight suit, Maraklov decided, wasn't just for show; this guy looked like a fighter pilot. He looked at Maraklov for a moment, then came to attention and made a slight bow.

"It is a pleasure to see you, Colonel Maraklov. I am General Major Aviatsii Pavel Tret'yak, commanding officer of Sebaco Military Airfield." He walked over to Maraklov and extended a hand. "Welcome home."

Maraklov shook his hand. "Thank you, General. But I think I've quite a way to go before I get home."

"We consider this is a slice of Russia in the middle of Central America," Tret'yak said with a smile. "You will be home soon. Until then, this base and all its personnel are at your disposal, and I will see to it that you are treated in recognition of your feat." Tret'yak was bobbing around like a young flying cadet, showing his excitement at meeting Maraklov. "Tell me about your flight, and all about this magnificent aircraft. I took the liberty of inspecting it this morning. It seems a fantastic machine, no doubt the fighter of tomorrow . . . We must talk about your flight over breakfast."

"Thank you, sir. I could go for some coffee and breakfast before we begin DreamStar's preparations for the flight back—"

"Oh, we will see to that, Colonel. It is already being done."

Maraklov stared at Tret'yak. "What? You—?"

"Under orders from Moscow, we have already begun the process of dismantling the aircraft. In a few days it will be—"

"Dismantling DreamStar? What the hell do you mean?"

Tret'yak looked puzzled. "How else do you intend to get it out of Nicaragua? Do you intend to *fly* it back to Russia? It is sixteen thousand kilometers from here to Moscow, with North America on one side, the U.S. Navy in the center and all western Europe on the other side. I should think you would have found it dangerous enough flying a thousand kilometers across Central America."

"But I don't know how to take it apart," Maraklov said. "I didn't bring the tech manuals with me and besides, I don't want to risk—"

"That is not our concern," Tret'yak said. "We are pilots, not mechanics. When we are in the cockpit, we are in charge. But when we are on the ground the grease-monkeys and pencil-pushers are in charge."

"That isn't some rag-wing biplane out there, General. You can't just take a few screws out of her and fold it up. DreamStar may be the world's greatest jet fighter but it's as delicate as an inertial guidance computer. If it's taken apart, it will never fly again. Believe me . . .''

Tret'yak was obviously bored with the argument and anxious to hear about Maraklov's escape from the U.S. He shrugged. ''There are tropical-weight flight suits in the closet. Get dressed. We'll talk.''

''Sir, call off the dismantling until I can speak with Moscow. I don't think—''

''It is already being done, Colonel. Now—''

''I said call it off, General.''

Tret'yak turned and looked with astonishment at Maraklov. He was, after all, a general. But then he softened, seeming to understand. ''I know how you feel, Andrei,'' he said, sounding like an older brother or father. ''But these orders came directly from Kalinin himself. I must comply with them. It is an amazing war machine, I realize. You are afraid it will never fly again and I understand that—our scientists and engineers can get a little overzealous at times. They have little appreciation for what we do. But you did realize, Colonel, that they were going to get the XF-34, did you not? I cannot think of one instance where an aircraft stolen or delivered to another country in such circumstances was not used for study and research. It certainly never flies again. True, the MiG-25 that traitor Belyenko stole from Petropavlovsk and flew to Japan twenty years ago was flown a few times, but just for—''

''They can't destroy DreamStar. It's no damn lab rat. You of all people should appreciate that. DreamStar needs to be studied, true, but studied in *one piece*. We can train Russian pilots to fly her and develop an entire squadron of pilots who can fly her.'' Maraklov paused, wondering how much of this he believed, how much was his attachment to DreamStar, his communion with it. ''How would you, sir, like to be the first MiG-39 Zavtra squadron commander?''

Tret'yak broke out into a grin—he'd be dead meat in a poker game, Maraklov thought. ''Zavtra? Has it been given a name?''

''Not officially, sir. But the 39 series is the next to be developed in both the Mikoyan-Gureyvich and Sukhoi design bureaus, and you suggested the name, sir. You said it was the fighter of tomorrow—*zavtra* means 'tomorrow' in English. So . . . the first fighter of tomorrow.''

"Zavtra," Tret'yak said, nodding. "I like it."

Thank God, Maraklov thought, for Tret'yak's huge ego and the bits of elementary Russian that were coming back to him. "We can paint it on the XF-34 right away, sir—with your name as commander, of course."

"This will have to be cleared through the engineer corps working on the XF-34—"

"MiG-39, sir."

"Yes, the MiG-39. I will speak to people in Moscow. After breakfast." He left with a pleased smile, and Maraklov hurriedly dressed and followed.

His apartment was in the back of a small administrative section next to the main hangar. He passed two guard posts, one outside his door and the other at the end of the corridor leading to the hangar. The last guard at the end of the corridor moved toward Maraklov and pinned a restricted area badge on his flight suit.

*"Pazhallosta, vi mnyeh mozhitye pahkahzaht tvoye sahmahlyot, tovarisch?"* the guard asked him as he pinned the badge on his suit.

Maraklov recognized that it was a question and made out the word for plane, but the guard's stern voice also made it sound like a request to stay away from DreamStar. Maraklov ignored it, turned and walked away.

The guard looked at him. Another stuck-up pilot, he thought. All he did was ask him if he could take a closer look at his fighter. The hotshot didn't even answer him. Maybe he really *was* more American than Russian now, like some were saying . . .

Maraklov had to strain to hold back his anger when he saw DreamStar. They had, indeed, wasted no time. Every access panel and maintenance door had been opened. External power was on the aircraft—and judging by the size and high-pitched whining sound of the power cart it was probably supplying the wrong frequency. DreamStar's electrical system would kick off external power if there was any danger of damage, but if those engineers forced the circuit closed it could do irreparable damage. Then they would *have* to ship it out of Nicaragua.

Tret'yak was returning from the administrative offices wearing a big smile. "Damn you, Colonel," he said with mock irritation, "you have *got* to learn Russian again so I can stop with this damned English . . . I have a call in to Moscow outlining

your concerns about dismantling the MiG-39. I expect an answer
in an hour. Meanwhile I have no choice but to continue with my
orders, the dismantling must proceed.''

Maraklov heard it like a stab in the heart, but there appeared
nothing he could do—for now. ''I understand. However, sir, in
the future I would like to be present while any work at all is
being done on Zavtra.''

''Granted. I understand how you feel. Having these cavemen
tear into a pilot's airplane is like watching your mistress out with
another man—you want to tear the man's eyes out but there's
nothing you can do about it.''

Maraklov had to suppress a smile. Tret'yak was straight out
of central casting, a real anachronism. But at least for now he
was dazzled enough by Andrei Maraklov, his aircraft and his
feat in flying to Nicaragua that he was being cooperative. But
that wouldn't last long if Moscow insisted on ripping DreamStar
apart.

If orders came to go on dismantling DreamStar, Maraklov
thought, as Tret'yak led him away to the chow hall, he would
have to think of something else. Something drastic. He didn't
rescue DreamStar from mothballs in the U.S. to have it become
heaps of fibersteel and electronics scattered around laboratories
all across eastern Europe. DreamStar didn't deserve to die. At
least not without a fight . . .

## Washington, D.C.

''All our ground security units and anti-air missile units were at
full readiness and responded properly,'' General Brad Elliott was
saying. ''The XF-34A was able to elude all of our area defenses,
which *is* what the aircraft was designed to do, and it evaded or
defended itself against all other airborne interceptor units . . .

''The responsibility for the loss of the XF-34 is mine. It was
my responsibility to make sure that personnel assigned to HAWC
had the proper background investigations and security checks; it
was my responsibility to secure our aircraft against attack, sabotage or theft. And it was my responsibility to do everything in
my power to repel any attacks or hostile actions against personnel and resources in my center . . .''

The President sat at his desk in the Oval Office, listening to

Elliott's *mea culpa*. With him was the Attorney General, Richard Benson, his brother-in-law and, it was said, closest adviser; Paul Cesare, the President's Chief of Staff; Army General William Kane, the Chairman of the Joint Chiefs of Staff; General Martin Board, Air Force Chief of Staff; William Stuart, Secretary of Defense; Deborah O'Day, the National Security Adviser; and Speaker of the House and ranking congressional Democrat Christopher Van Keller, another close adviser and personal friend of President Lloyd Taylor.

"Your ground forces—you said you had two armed combat vehicles on the ramp at the time," Attorney General Benson said, "and you still couldn't stop that aircraft?"

"That's correct."

"What are these vehicles armed with?"

"Twelve-point-three-millimeter—half-inch—heavy machine guns. They also carry two armed security troops. They're armed with standard M-16 rifles. Some have M-203 infantry grenade launchers as well."

"And with all that they were ineffective?"

"Yes." It was the $n$-th time he had heard the word "ineffective" during this half-hour briefing, along with "incompetent" and "irresponsible." . . . "But the infiltrators set up remote-controlled mortars with concussion grenade rounds," Elliott added. "They were relatively light ordnance, but at close range and against soldiers on foot they were very effective. It gave James enough time to taxi away and take off."

"Kenneth James?" Defense Secretary Stuart said. "You mean Colonel Andrei Ivanschichin Maraklov." Stuart fixed an angry stare at Elliott. "Well, at least this happened out in Dreamland, we have a chance of keeping it out of the press. I've had my staff scan James' records and they're squeaky-clean as far back as we can go. But that's the bad news. We didn't start keeping close personal records on him until he applied for admission to the Air Force Academy. It's hard to believe, but I think this Maraklov was inserted *then*, as a cadet. He apparently worked his way through the system and found himself in Dreamland—"

"And as the test pilot for our most high-tech aircraft," Benson added. "A goddamned Russian spy flying our best fighter for *two years* . . ."

"And you take responsibility for this James, or Maraklov, being in your organization, General Elliott?" the President said.

"Yes, sir." Elliott had rehearsed a series of explanations in his mind—the fact that Maraklov had eluded ten years of Department of Defense security investigations before coming to Dreamland being the chief argument—but instead he said, "If I had uncovered Maraklov's infiltration earlier, the XF-34 wouldn't be in Soviet hands now."

"I agree," the President said. "Although the problem obviously began well before Maraklov entered your organization, Dreamland is the most sensitive research installation we have. You have security measures and procedures available to you that are not available to other commanders. But even with all these measures, you failed to present this. And that resulted in the deaths of eleven military and civilian personnel, the loss of two fighter aircraft and one B-52 bomber, millions of dollars of damage *and* the theft of a hugely valuable experimental fighter."

Taylor paused, made a note in his desk book. "But my predecessor here held you in very high regard, General. He made a point of recommending that I allow Dreamland to remain in operation and under your command, even after your injury following that . . . mission to Russia. I took his advice because I knew he meant it and not because he needed a favor. I kept Dreamland open despite your enormous budget. And I kept you in charge despite numerous calls for your mandatory retirement. You've been doing some remarkable work and up to now have a fine record, even though much of it can't be publicized . . . Well, Dreamland and the Advanced Weapons Center is to stop operations immediately until a full investigation can be conducted. General Elliott, you will see to it that your unit is properly closed and secured so that any evidence is kept intact. When the investigation is convened you will provide any and all assistance asked for. When the investigation is finished . . . I'm sorry to say I will accept your request for retirement."

Elliott said nothing.

"The Mexican government was demanding I hand over your head on a platter for sending that F-15 into their airspace without permission. You can thank the Speaker here for defusing that one."

"Deborah O'Day did the legwork," Speaker Van Keller said.

Elliott turned to look at the fiftyish, very attractive National

Security Adviser. Deborah O'Day . . . she'd had a career that Elliott had always found amazing for a woman, even in the eighties and nineties—a former professor at the Center for Strategic Studies in Washington, former Ambassador to the United Nations during the previous administration, and the first woman to hold the position as special assistant to the President on national security matters. It had been rumored that her appointment had been made only because of political expediency—Taylor was still a chauvinist of the fifties and figured he needed a woman on his White House staff for show—but O'Day had surprised him with her talent, insight and take-charge attitude. She nodded slightly to Elliott, who was surprised to see a friendly reaction in that place.

"I thought the Mexican government was dragging their heels in allowing us permission to pursue the XF-34 into their airspace," O'Day said. "I reminded the commander of Mexican air defense forces of the times their pilots have crossed into our airspace and even landed in our airports, supposedly by mistake."

Chief of Staff Cesare broke in: "But it made the President look bad, not only in their eyes but in the eyes of the world. One hotshot Reserve fighter pilot was bad enough, and he got himself killed. Then we send another plane, and *he* almost gets killed. The whole incident makes the Air Force look like Keystone Kops in flight suits, *and* it made the White House look like we weren't in control."

"Not to mention that relations are bad enough between us and Mexico," Secretary of Defense Stuart said, "without us shooting missiles all over their territory."

General Kane, Chairman of the Joint Chiefs, turned to General Board. "I expect to see the discharge papers on those crewmen that violated Mexican airspace."

Board nodded unhappily.

"That would be unwise, sir," Elliott said to the President. What the hell, he might as well speak up . . . "The first two F-15 pilots were following orders by going along with their formation leader. They're trained not to leave their leader's wing under any circumstances, and especially if they're involved in a hostile situation. They turned back as soon as they lost their leader, as ordered. The crew of Cheetah, were following *my* orders. After DreamStar downed the F-15s, I knew that the advanced-technology F-15 from Dreamland was the only fighter capable of going head-to-head with the XF-34, so I ordered Cheetah armed, to pursue DreamStar at best speed.''

"General Elliott," Secretary Stuart said, "do you think you have your own private air force out there? You don't order an attack on an enemy airfield, the President of the United States does that. You don't authorize military forces to cross a foreign border, the *President* does.''

"There wasn't time to get permission, Mr. Secretary. If we wanted DreamStar back, Cheetah was our best hope. There wasn't time to debate the question—''

" 'Wasn't time'? That's bullshit, General. You don't ignore the military chain of command because you think you don't have the time. What was next—bomb Mexico for letting that plane get away? Nuke Mexico City?''

Deborah O'Day spoke up. "I'm familiar with General Elliott's record and I think he acted at least understandably. If his crewmen could have stopped DreamStar they and he would have been called heroes. He took a risk, it almost paid off . . . The question is, what do we do about DreamStar now?''

"Do we even know precisely *where* this DreamStar is right now?'' the President asked.

"We tracked it almost its entire flight,'' General Board said, "via the Reserve 707 AWACS at first, then by an advanced 767 AWACS launched from Oklahoma and patrolling off-shore over the Gulf. The XF-34 successfully evaded attack by Mexican and Honduran fighter patrols, with a little help from Nicaraguan interceptors, and it landed in Nicaragua.''

Board nodded to an assistant who put a mounted chart of Central America up on an easel in the center of the Oval Office. "The fighter was last seen on radar somewhere north of Managua. We believe it's being kept at a small, isolated valley airbase fifty miles north of Managua called Sebaco. The base is run by the Soviet military—more specifically, by the KGB.''

He turned to the President. "Sir, I've ordered satellite reconnaissance of the area. Photo observation by aircraft would be a good idea too, perhaps by the old SR-71 Blackbird still operated by the CIA, but Managua is heavily defended by anti-aircraft artillery and missiles and is a riskier operation. A soft probe is also recommended.''

"A 'soft probe.' You mean agents?''

"CIA has assets in Managua that can possibly get close enough to verify that the XF-34 is at Sebaco," Board said.

"And if they do? Let's say they have it at Sebaco, or in Managua. We're sure as hell not going to go in with the Eighty-second Airborne or the Atlantic Second Fleet and start a war to retrieve a jet fighter . . ."

"Excuse me, sir," Elliott said, "but it's not just another jet fighter."

"Hold it. Hold on one minute, General," the President said. "I was waiting for you to say that. Let me tell you right now, General, and all of you in this room—that XF-34 is just another jet fighter in the large scheme of things. It's not some magical war machine, no matter how advanced it is. It's very important, damn right, but the United States won't start a shooting war with the Soviets or anybody else over this aircraft. Sure, the sonofa-bitches infiltrated our base, stole that plane, killed our people. We'll lodge protests, we'll demand the plane back, we'll coerce and threaten as much as possible. I'm betting they'll deny having it. They can stall forever by denying everything we say. Even if we have pictures, they can say the photos were faked. And if we *do* produce irrefutable evidence, they'll have a propaganda field day . . . 'Soviet agent infiltrates top-secret American military base, steals top-secret experimental aircraft.' The condemnation of them will be more than drowned out by the laughing aimed at *us.*"

Elliott hoped he never needed to look at *that* much of the so-called big picture. God . . . "We can't let them get away with it," he persisted.

"They *have* gotten away with it, General Elliott," the President said. "For all we know they could be taking it apart right now and shipping it off to Moscow. What would you have us do? Intercept every ship, every aircraft, every submarine that leaves Nicaragua, board it and search for a component to a fighter plane? Face it, Elliott—you lost it. *We* lost it."

The President glared at Elliott's taut face, shook his head. "I'll ask Dennis Danahall at State to lodge a stiff protest with the Soviets. We do have that tape of that agent—what's his name? Maraklov . . . ? admitting he was a KGB agent."

"The KGB will say he was just a nut-case American soldier," General Kane said, "claiming to be a Russian spy. We've had our share . . ."

"I'm still going to order Dennis to protest this incident in the strongest language. I'll ask for the return of the aircraft and compensation to the families of the crew on that B-52 and the fighters that were shot down during the chase. I want some options we can use in case, when they give us the runaround. We can threaten to cancel our participation in that joint trip to Mars in 1998 . . . I was never in favor of that cockeyed idea anyway. And we can—"

"We've already made a substantial commitment to the Mars project, Lloyd," Richard Benson said.

"Well, State has got to think of *something* to back up our protest. Kick out some of their embassy staff, raid one of their consulates . . ."

"Sir, those are all positive steps . . ." Elliott began, steaming. "But—"

"Glad you think so, General." The President motioned to his chief of staff, Cesare, who quickly rose and moved across to open the inner door to the Oval Office; to the generals in the room, opening a door was a cue to stop talking, part of their fear of being overheard outside. To the others it was word that the meeting was over. Both messages were lost on Elliott.

"Mr. President, none of these actions will help us get DreamStar back. We could use some very low-level activities that can send a clear message that we mean business. I have some suggestions—"

"You have your orders, General. Good morning." Cesare, a large, ex-football player, stepped casually in front of Elliott, physically shutting off the conversation.

Elliott turned and left the Oval Office. He was heading for the main hallway to the rear portico when he spotted Deborah O'Day ahead and called out to her.

She turned and waited as he walked up to her. She was a bit younger than Elliott, with long dark hair flecked with gray, bright blue eyes, and an athletic figure. Interesting about her eyes, Elliott thought—there were men and women he had worked with for years but still had no idea what color their eyes were. Now he met this woman for the first time and noticed her eyes right away.

"Mrs. O'Day . . ."

"Miss O'Day, General," she said, taking his hand and returning a firm grip. "But that's the Oval Office name. In the halls it's Debbie."

Elliott smiled. He hadn't done this kind of byplay maneuvering in years. "And I'm Brad."

They walked along the corridor until they came to an open doorway with a female Marine Corps officer behind a computer terminal and a male secretary leafing through some files inside the office. The secretaries' desks flanked a pair of closed oaken doors.

The Marine moved quickly to her feet when O'Day entered the office, but her eyes were on Elliott. "Good morning," she said. "Intelligence digest is on your terminal, ma'am. Coffee's fresh. Good morning, General Elliott."

"Thank you, Major. General Bradley Elliott, Major Marcia Preston, my operations officer. General Elliott is the director of—"

"The High-Technology Advanced Weapons Center. I've heard a lot about you, sir."

"Nice to meet you, Major."

The male secretary stood, ignored Elliott and handed O'Day a folder full of papers. "For your signature. I need them ASAP."

"General Elliott, Matt Conkle, my secretary." Preston hit the remote door unlock switch, and Elliott followed O'Day into her office and immediately heard the door lock behind him.

"Your secretary isn't exactly a friendly type," Elliott said.

"He hates the idea of being a secretary to a woman, even if she's the National Security Adviser. He's fine in his job, though. Marcia Preston is a rising star. Was the Marine Corps' first female F/A-18 fighter pilot. She was good. Very good. But she got so much heat from being a female pilot that she was bounced out for allegedly trying to seduce her squadron commander. Some things never change. I discovered her filing memos in San Diego, still wearing her flight suit, and brought her to Washington. She'd rather be in the cockpit—she flies my helicopter and jet— and deserves whatever she wants. She just might be giving you a call some time."

"I'm probably not going to be around—and maybe Dreamland won't be there."

"Don't be so pessimistic," O'Day said, pouring a cup of coffee for herself and Elliott and seating herself behind her desk.

Elliott eased himself into a leather-covered armchair and rebent his right leg under the chair.

O'Day noticed. "That's from your mysterious mission into the Soviet Union eight years ago?" Elliott nodded. "You know, I can't find any real information on that mission in our records. It's like it never happened."

"It's better that way. It also took the lives of some fine men."

"That was the B-52 that the Russian spy shot down, wasn't it?"

"Yes. We called it the Old Dog. We had rebuilt and upgraded it after the mission over Russia. It was the prototype of a new escort aircraft for strategic bombers. It was on its first operational flight . . . Did you know that two crewmen from my Old Dog mission died in that crash yesterday?"

"My God." She sat silent for a long moment.

"The nav on that flight was one of the Great Experiment female combat flyers, in the same group as Marcia Preston—the first female B-52 navigator. There was one other female on that B-52," Elliott continued. "A civilian. She was also on my Old Dog crew back in 1988. She's in critical condition at Brooks Medical Center in San Antonio. Her husband was on my Old Dog crew too. He was one of the F-15 crew that went into Mexican airspace and tried to get the XF-34—as a matter of fact he's the DreamStar project director, Lieutenant Colonel McLanahan."

"Jesus. Was McLanahan one of the men killed in the dog-fights with DreamStar?"

"No. He was chased away by the Mexican Air Force, missed his chance to try to even the score . . . I wanted to thank you for sticking up for me in there, and for your help with the Mexican government. I think you see how important this is to me. Maybe this sounds too dramatic, but those men and women are my *life*. I have to watch out for them—now more than ever."

"Well, now that I know that McLanahan was one of the men in those F-15s, I'm glad I stuck up for him and you. I don't think General Kane will push for any official action against McLanahan or anyone else involved."

"I appreciate it just the same . . . Look, I'm not trying to start a palace revolt here, but I just can't stand the idea of sitting by while DreamStar is chopped up into pieces and shipped off to Moscow. The President wasn't interested in my idea, but maybe you would be . . ."

"I'm interested," O'Day said. Elliott couldn't be sure she meant it or was just defusing him, but he had little choice right now, he realized. "It's true, Brad, the President isn't interested . . . But what's your idea?"

Elliott spread his hands. "Simple. Make the Nicaraguans, and the Russians, *think* we're going to strike at Managua . . . Look, *I'm not* suggesting that we send the Second Fleet over to shell Managua, but we could send it out into the Gulf, on one of the Pentagon's famous 'previously scheduled' exercises. We could land the Eighty-second Airborne next door in Honduras. That could shake them up enough at least to start dealing with us—"

"And what if? The bad old 'what if' . . . it doesn't work?"

"Then we have no choice. Mount a surgical strike. Photo intelligence would be invaluable. If we can pinpoint where DreamStar is being kept we can plan a discreet attack—"

"To destroy it?"

Elliott nodded. "Afraid so. We sure as hell couldn't *fly* it out of Nicaragua—"

"Why not?"

Elliott stopped, looked at her. He had no ready answer to that one. "Well, first of all, it would be nearly impossible to get near it anywhere on that KGB base. Second, we've no one qualified to fly it. James—Maraklov—was the only pilot . . ."

"The *only* one?"

Elliott's mind was racing now—Deborah O'Day seemed to be opening up possibilities he hadn't imagined. "We've had several men fly DreamStar's simulator, but only one man has actually flown DreamStar before. And no one has been able to control it as well as James."

"Well, you could use him then, couldn't you? If all he'd have to do is take off and land . . . ?"

"True, if we could provide him enough air cover during his escape . . . steal DreamStar back . . . There are a lot of 'ifs' here. If DreamStar is still flyable, if we can pinpoint DreamStar's location, if we can get J. C. Powell on that base . . ."

"J. C. Powell?"

"My chief test pilot. He checked out in DreamStar in the early phase but was replaced by James. He just might do it. He

can't dogfight in DreamStar like James, but he could get
DreamStar off the ground and land it again.''

"So if we knew exactly where DreamStar was, and if it wasn't
already taken apart,'' O'Day said, "we'd need a plan to get this
Powell on Sebaco and into DreamStar's cockpit. Then we'd have
to arrange air cover for him after takeoff since he wouldn't be
able to defend himself . . .''

"Right . . . put Powell in under some sort of diversionary
cover,'' Elliott said. "Hit Sebaco with a small air strike or guer-
rilla force and insert Powell. Get him into DreamStar's cockpit.
Use the guerrillas to blow a path for him out to the airstrip. With
a carrier from the Second Fleet sitting in the Gulf of Mexico we
could provide enough air cover to fight off the Nicaraguan air
force. A short flight to Texas and we'd be home free.''

"Sounds like a plan, General. Now you have just one problem . . .''

"I know. The President. It's what he *doesn't* want to do.
That's where I need your help. You have access to the man. Can
you talk to him? Try to convince him?''

She sank back in her chair. "I'm not sure how much help I can
be. The truth is, I'm not a member of the President's inner
sanctum. His brother-in-law Benson and Speaker Van Keller have
his ear, not me. I'm a political appointee, damn near a figurehead. Except I also happen to be qualified. He lucked out. I was
put here before the primaries to make the public think that Lloyd
Taylor supports women in government. I was good for a jump
in the polls, or so they say, but I'm not sure what else there is.''

"You've got to try,'' Elliott said. "Bring it up in staff meetings. Talk to the other Cabinet members. Schedule a meeting
with Van Keller or Danahall. They have got to realize that we
just can't let the Russians get away with espionage and murder.
We can yell and threaten all we want, but it doesn't work. It
didn't eight years ago with Kavaznya, and it won't work now,
even with *glasnost* and *perestroika* and all the other peaceful
coexistence stuff the Soviets have been feeding us. If the President doesn't want to authorize it he can make it a blind operation—let me loose and I'll do it and he can deny knowing or
authorizing everything.''

"You can't do that with this President,'' O'Day said. "That
might have worked with Iran-Contra, but this Democrat has a
very good memory for such screwups, especially by a Republi-

can President. No . . .'' O'Day stared at the ceiling. "Taylor is as hard-nosed as they come, and he rarely changes his mind . . . This plan . . . this operation to get DreamStar. Do you really think you can put it together?''

"I can get my staff on it—"

"No. I mean right now. Yes or no—can this J. C. Powell get in and get DreamStar?''

Elliott hesitated only a moment. *"If* I get the support from the White House I can get Powell into DreamStar's cockpit. And I believe he can get DreamStar out.''

"Okay. I'm on the case. I've a plan to shake things up around here. After that I don't know what will happen. It could blow up in our faces. But I'll bet it'll cause the White House at least to rethink its position on letting the Soviets get away with the XF-34.''

"What are you—?''

"No questions. Just be ready with a dog-and-pony show for the boss within twenty-four hours, and you better knock his socks off or it'll be too late for your XF-34. I can't promise anything except some noise, but like Yogi said, it ain't over till it's over. That might even be true for President Lloyd Emerson Taylor the Third.''

Elliott straightened his right leg, locked it and eased himself to his feet. He extended his hand, O'Day came around her desk and took it. "I bet the woman and the plan are much alike.''

"Don't be so sure—about either one, General,'' she said. "I'm expecting a few sparks around here. I'm just hoping they don't hit any vital parts.''

"Actually,'' Elliott said as he turned for the door, "I'm hoping they come too close for comfort.''

After he left, O'Day returned to her chair and felt a very rare grin on her face. *Forget* that, she told herself sternly. He may have this domineering presence that seems to fill the room when he enters, but does he really have all his facts together when it comes to this DreamStar business? Sure he wants the XF-34 back—that's understandable. But is he acting like a man with little to lose, who'll risk a major international incident to get his own way?

Having asked herself the tough questions, the answers came easy. Elliott wanted DreamStar back because a goddamn mole stole it, because his people got killed. He was willing to fight to get it back, even if his own government disowned him or worse.

She dialed a number on a private phone that could not be picked up or used by her outer office. "Marty, this is your racquetball partner . . . yes, I know it's been awhile since we've played. It's been busy . . . give me a break. I was appointed by your President, remember? Listen, can we meet for a game? Today, if we can get a court . . . better make it early. You may have a late evening . . . you heard me. Can you make it? Good. See you at seven, then . . . no, we can't count this one. That's right . . . you'll find out why. See you."

## Brooks Medical Facility, San Antonio

"Edema in her right lung, possibly from inhaling fire or burning debris. We didn't catch it right away . . ." the doctor was saying as McLanahan and Powell entered the intensive care unit.

Wendy Tork's parents were on either side of her. Her hands were heavily bandaged. She had been on a respirator ever since she was found in the crash area, but now there was a different one in place, one to keep her lungs clear of fluid and help her keep breathing. Most of her facial bandages had been removed, exposing ugly burn marks and cuts. Intravenous tubes were feeding glucose and whole blood into her arms. One small vase of flowers rested on a nightstand—ICU would tolerate no more—but Wendy had not yet been conscious to see them or her parents.

Betty and Joseph Tork glanced at Patrick and J.C. as they came into the room, quickly turned their eyes back to their daughter.

"Doctor?" McLanahan couldn't get out the obvious question.

"She's a strong woman, Colonel, but her injuries are massive . . ." He paused, moved closer to Patrick and lowered his voice. "Did you know she was pregnant?" Wendy's parents heard the words anyway. "Oh, my God," Betty Tork said, turned away from Wendy's bedside and gave in to the tears she'd been fighting back.

McLanahan could only nod and clench his fists.

"She suffered severe abdominal injuries . . ."

Powell stepped firmly between McLanahan and the doctor. "I

think that's enough, doctor. I think we ought to leave," and he took the doctor's arm and led him out of the room.

Patrick, Wendy's parents and an ICU nurse stood in silence for a long time watching Wendy, listening to the beeps of the body function monitor and the hissing of the respirator. Several times Patrick could see muscles in Wendy's face or shoulders twitch, and for a brief instant thought that she might be about to wake up.

Betty Tork noticed her daughter's movements too. "I wish they'd give her something . . . something to help her relax. It's so awful seeing her suffer. My daughter is in pain, *Colonel*. Can't anybody around here *do* something for her? What kind of hospital is this, anyway?"

Should he tell her it happened to be the best burn-and-trauma facility in the country? That as long as Wendy kept fighting for her life there was at least hope . . . ? He said nothing.

"How did this happen, Patrick?" Joe Tork asked. "She was flying the B-52, I know, but how did the crash happen?"

"I'm sorry, Joe, I can't—"

"Don't give me that crap, McLanahan." He stood up suddenly, filling the room with his size, but Patrick was immediately drawn to the lines of dried tears in the corners of his eyes. "For the past ten years, *Colonel*, that's all I've been hearing from her, from you, from everyone at that damn place. When she moved to Vegas it was as if she'd moved to Mars. Now she'd lying in a hospital in Texas probably dying from these horrible injuries and you're still playing hush-hush games with me? Goddamn, I want some answers—"

"For God's sake, Joe, that's my wife lying there—"

"She's your wife? Where's your ring? Where's *her* ring? You got a marriage certificate? We weren't invited to any wedding . . ."

"Joe, please . . ."

"The last we heard, you two weren't hitting it off all that well. You know what I think? I think you didn't marry my daughter. I think you're saying you're married so we can't sue the damned Air Force for the accident. The spouse of a military member can't sue the government, right?"

Betty Tork was staring at her husband.

"This is a rip-off. I was in the Marine Corps for six years, I know about this crap." Joe Tork moved closer and wrapped his big hands around the lapel of McLanahan's flight suit. "Answer me, you lying sack of mick shit. *Answer* me . . ."

Patrick held Joe's wrists gently as he could. The big ex-Marine could have taken his frustrations out on Patrick, and for a moment it looked like he might actually swing on him. But at the very moment Patrick thought he might do it, Tork's big shoulders began to shake. His narrow, angry eyes closed, and his grip began to loosen.

"Damn it, goddamn it all to hell . . . Wendy . . . she's been so all-fired independent ever since she was a kid. I'd get letters from Betty when I was in Vietnam telling me how smart and grown up she was. When I got back she wasn't a kid any more. I never saw her that way . . . Now she's lying there helpless as a baby and I still can't do anything for her . . ."

Patrick, feeling the same sense of anger and helplessness, could say nothing. It was Betty who broke the silence. "Patrick, when were you married?"

"What? Oh, the day before yesterday." He looked up. "Did they bring in Wendy's things?"

"In the closet."

He went to the closet and retrieved a cardboard box, took something from the box and returned to Wendy's bedside. "We're not allowed to wear rings on the flight line," he said. "Too dangerous, they say. So we started keeping each other's ring until we saw each other again." He opened his hand and revealed a tiny purple velvet bag, loosened a thin gold drawstring, dropped a hammered gold band into his palm, then slipped the ring on his left ring-finger. He then got an identical bag from a flight-suit pocket and took out another hammered-gold band, this one with a gold engagement ring fused to it. He slipped it on Wendy's finger.

The three were silent for a while. The ICU nurse came by, checked and recorded the monitor readings and left. Finally, Joe said, "Patrick, I have to know what happened out there? Can't you tell us anything?"

"Joe, you know I can't."

"But I'm a vet. I wouldn't tell anyone . . ."

"I know, but I still can't."

Tork ran his hands through what little hair was left on his head. "All right. But tell me this, just this one thing, because

I'm Wendy's father. Just promise me you're going to nail whoever's responsible for doing this to my daughter.''

Patrick's eyes were fixed on Wendy's scars and burns, he saw her muscles convulse, heard the sucking sounds as machines drew fluid from her lungs to keep her from drowning.

"Yes, Joe," he said in a low voice. "That I can promise you . . .''

## The Kremlin, Moscow, Union of Soviet Socialist Republics
*Thursday, 18 June 1996, 2103 EET (1303 EDT)*

Vladimir Kalinin walked briskly into the General Secretary's office to find several members of the Kollegiya already assembled there, all nervously pacing the floor or circling the conference table. They began to take seats immediately—obviously they had all been waiting for KGB chief Kalinin's arrival. Boris Mischelevka, the Foreign Minister, sat at the head of the conference table and presided over the meeting.

"The General Secretary is en route from West Germany," Mischelevka began. "He has directed me to begin this meeting and assemble the entire Kollegiya at ten A.M. tomorrow morning when he arrives. He will expect a briefing on our meeting first thing in the morning.

"This deals, of course, with the incident that took place yesterday morning in the United States. A fighter aircraft was stolen from a top-secret research center and flown through Central America to Nicaragua after a stop in Mexico. Apart from that information we have no details." Mischelevka turned immediately to Kalinin and asked if he could explain what had happened.

"I believe this should wait for the General Secretary," Kalinin said. "I see no reason for three separate meetings."

"The reason is simply that the General Secretary wants it," Mischelevka told him. "Obviously he intends that we be able to explain to the various governments involved *what* is going on."

Kalinin said nothing at first. The Americans called it "damage control"—everyone get their story straight and coordinated before going outside the government. With foreign journalists flooding Moscow and a press center set up in the Kremlin itself,

"damage control" was more and more important nowadays . . .
"All I can tell you is that the incident involved a Soviet helicopter and a Soviet airbase in Nicaragua. That is all I can discuss
here until I brief the General Secretary."

"We need more than that, Kalinin," Mischelevka said. "I
have received a dozen demands for explanations from several
countries, including, naturally, the United States. It is important
that we respond—"

"You will respond when the General Secretary decides you
will respond. I will not release any information until the classi-
fication of that information is determined—"

"But we must brief—"

"Brief *no one*. Is that clear enough?"

"What's wrong with you?" Mischelevka asked. "What's going on? Is this a special KGB operation in Central America?
What . . . ?"

"You will please not discuss your opinions of the incident
either," Kalinin snapped. "Say nothing. *Glasnost* does not apply here." With that, Kalinin got up and walked out.

They're like sheep, Kalinin thought as he quickly exited the
dark halls of the Kremlin. They have been lulled into compla-
cency by the garbage that has been fed to them over the years,
that openness was good, that secret information is free to all
for the asking. They were going to be this government's down-
fall . . .

And when it had fallen, with a little help from patriots like
himself, he was going to be the leader of a return to the old,
traditional ways, to the future world eminence of the Soviet
Union.


# Arlington, Virginia
*Thursday, 18 June 1996, 1905 EDT*

The Barrel Factory Racquet Club used to be just that—an old
factory and warehouse that, in pre-Prohibition days, made casks
and barrels for beer and wine. It was one of the worst eyesores
in the Washington, D.C., area for decades until Arlington's ren-
aissance in the late 1980s and early nineties, when it was remodeled into a first-class tennis, racquetball and health club. But

the area kept its old slum reputation, so the Barrel Factory was having a tough time attracting members.

But for National Security Adviser Deborah O'Day, the place was perfect for many reasons. The dues were modest, it was easy to get a racquetball court—especially during the week after seven P.M.—and the usual D.C. crowd avoided the place. She could take off the White House senior-staff facade and act like a normal human being, and as such was rarely recognized—all of which made the place ideal for an occasional surreptitious meeting.

She tossed a couple of the soft blue rubber balls out into the court and chased them, jogging up and down the court to loosen her ankles. She was pleased with how flexible and fit her body was, even at fifty-one. Exercise was never important to her until just before learning that she was being considered for the NSC position. No one much cared what you looked like as U.N. ambassador, but as part of the White House staff her image had to merge much better with that of the President, and that image was relatively young, lean and mean.

She crash-dieted during her last few weeks in New York, begging off all the bon voyage parties that she could. During the confirmation hearings, she had no time for any meals anyway, so dieting was very easy then. The same was true for her first few months in Washington. Now that the dust had settled a bit, she found that her once-a-week trips to the gym were invaluable and at times virtual life-savers. She enjoyed the challenges, relished the appreciative glances of the men in the club (some less than half her age), and felt good when she looked around the room during the White House staff meetings and knew that she could probably whip half the men in that room on the tennis or squash courts.

These late-night trips also had other valuable uses—such as tonight.

She had finished stretching out and had begun hitting the ball around when she heard a tap behind her. A tall, dark-haired, pear-shaped man in an old gray sweatsuit, elbow and knee pads, brand-new Reebok tennis shoes, wearing eye protectors and carrying an old aluminum-framed racquet, was tapping on the back Plexiglas wall of her court.

Just as he began tapping again, from seemingly out of nowhere Marine Corps Major Marcia Preston moved behind him.

She was dressed in a red jogging suit, a towel wrapped around
her neck and carrying an open gym bag—which, Deborah O'Day
knew, contained a Browning PM-40B automatic machine pistol
with a twenty-round clip and laser sight. The pear-shaped fellow
seemed to sense someone behind him and turned to face Marcia.
If he made the wrong move, Marcia could disable him in a few
seconds or kill him in less time. They exchanged glances, and
Marcia Preston never got closer than a few feet from him, but
there was no doubt that the man knew he had been efficiently
intercepted.

But at a slight hand motion from O'Day, Marcia moved on
past as if she hadn't noticed he was there. O'Day could see the
man nervously swallow, then open the half-size door to the
court and step inside. Major Preston went over to the drinking
fountain nearby, wandered around looking in the other courts,
then disappeared back into her previous unobtrusive hiding
place.

"Marcia is her usual charming self, I see," the man deadpanned, watching the major's retreating figure. He was already
sweating, and they hadn't played one point yet. He turned and
checked out Deborah O'Day in the same way he had just ap-
praised Marcia Preston. "You're looking pretty foxy yourself,
kid."

"Cool it, Marty, let's play. You warmed up?"

"For this ridiculous sport, no," Marty Donatelli said. "For
some information, yes."

"We can chat while we play. At least pretend to be trying,"
she said, gently hitting a ball off the front wall toward Donatelli.
"Besides, it'll do you some good. You could stand to lose a few
inches off that middle."

He took a huge roundhouse swipe at the ball, caroming it off
three walls, but he placed it right back in the center of the court.
O'Day chased it down easily and sent it back right to Donatelli.
"The front page goes to bed in two hours, lover. Can we make
this quick?"

"I don't care about the front page, and I'm sure as hell not
your lover." O'Day hit the ball back perfectly in the left corner;
it bounded off the left wall, the front wall, then promptly hit the
floor and died. "Okay. You serve. We'll talk."

As Donatelli moved to the center serve line, O'Day began:

"Wasn't it terrible about the B-52 crash in Nevada the other day?"

Donatelli bounced the ball experimentally a few times, bounced it once more, then hit it with all his might against the front wall. She was waiting for it and returned it up the right alley into the corner. Donatelli did not have time to move from where he had served the ball. "My serve," she said, and smiled a pretty smile.

"Yeah, I heard of it," Donatelli said. "So? I don't do aircraft accidents."

"There's some scuttlebutt around," she said, and stepped to the service line, "something about it not being an accident."

The reporter was getting impatient. "It was out in the Red Flag range, right? There's hundreds of planes out there shooting missiles. The Air Force loses a plane almost every day out there."

O'Day bounced the ball, took one glance back at Donatelli, then swung the racquet as she said, "If I only had the time I'd look into that. Some strange stories coming out of southern Nevada. There was even this weird report about a KGB agent stealing a fighter."

The blue rubber ball rebounded hard off the front wall, came straight back and hit Donatelli in the right leg. He scarcely noticed it. "Did you say, a Russian KGB agent?"

"That's just scuttlebutt. One serving zero. Still my serve."

"Hold on. Who says a Russian agent?"

"It's an unconfirmed rumor," O'Day said, getting ready for the serve. "Some stuff about a stolen fighter, some fighters shot down, about the stolen fighter heading for some pro-Soviet Central American country."

She served the ball. Donatelli knocked it into a corner.

"Two serving . . ."

"All this happened yesterday?"

"Yep. So they say."

"How can I verify this?"

O'Day walked over to pick up the ball. "Hey, I'm not a reporter. You don't tell me how to do my job and I don't tell you how to do yours. But like I said, if I had the time I'd call, say, a General Elliott through the Nellis AFB operator—he's in charge of some of the ranges down there. I might also contact the Mexican government, especially the Monterrey Air Defense Zone headquarters about those rumors about unauthorized airspace violations and dogfights over their—''

"Jesus Christ . . ." Donatelli worked to unravel the racquet's wrist strap that had wound itself tightly around his right arm. "I've got less than two hours to make these calls . . . Mexico— that'll take forever . . .''

"Remember the routine, Marty—unnamed government sources, maybe unnamed military sources. There's enough of a shake-up over there that a leak is bound to develop.''

"You mean someone else might get this story . . . ?''

"I doubt it, but you never know. I heard General Elliott got his butt chewed pretty good by the President and the senior staff today. He might be in a talkative mood.''

Donatelli whipped off his eye protectors, reprising what O'Day had just told him. "Elliott . . . Nellis . . . Mexico . . . what was that . . . ?''

"Just replay your tape recorder and listen," Deborah said.

"My tape recorder?" Donatelli looked surprised. "Our deal was no tapes. You think I'd welsh on that deal?''

O'Day tossed the blue ball at Donatelli's chest. "In a heartbeat, Marty. Just protect your sources like your life depended on it, and we'll both be okay.''

Donatelli lifted up his sweatshirt to reveal nothing but a very hairy, very sweaty chest. "I don't have a recorder. See? I've shown you mine—now you show me yours.''

"Kiss my ass.''

"With pleasure.'' They stood looking at each other.

"You're a fox, no doubt about that. Ms. National Security Adviser. But tell me—why are you doing this? Were you authorized by the White House to leak this? If so, why are they doing it?''

She began to bat the ball around the court. "I've got reasons. That's enough.''

"Care to state them for the record?''

"No. This is *off* the record, Donatelli. The President is too busy to concern himself about this incident. But the time line is very tight. There are people in the military that believe some immediate action is important.''

"And the President disagrees?''

"He believes in open negotiations, compromise.''

"So the President isn't prepared to respond with military force. I take it there is someone—"

"This isn't a damned interview, Marty. I've gone too far with you as it is. I think you've got everything you need." She chased the ball toward the back wall, then casually opened the door. Marcia Preston immediately appeared, her racquet in one hand and her gym bag in the other. She took a towel out of the gym bag, tossed it to her boss, then went to the Plexiglas-covered lockers in the left wall of the court, opened one, and stood there watching Donatelli. The threat of the machine pistol in her bag was beyond Donatelli, but the look on her face was not.

"Marcia, you're beautiful," Marty said with a contrived leer. "We have to get together some time." Marcia gave him nothing.

"Better put your paper to bed, Marty," O'Day said, holding the door open for him. Donatelli nodded and moved toward the door. Just before he exited he turned to her: "Any chance of us putting something else to bed?"

"I think we use each other enough as it is, Marty. Goodbye."

"Sounds to me like you may need a friend in the fourth estate soon, Ms. O'Day," he said.

"Marty, watch your middle and your blood pressure. 'Bye."

After he left, she closed the door and began to bat the ball around again. As she did Preston reached into her gym bag and flicked the OFF switch on a micro-tape recorder with a high-power directional microphone installed in the bag.

"Did you get everything?" O'Day asked as she returned a tricky corner bounce.

"Yes, but what good is it if anything about this conversation gets out? You lose your career, it will enhance his."

"If it gets out that Marty Donatelli can't protect his sources, his sources will dry up and he knows it. And there goes his Pulitzer Prize career. That tape proves that I gave him stuff only off the record and not for attribution. If he violates that, he's dead in this town."

"You're still taking some awfully big risks."

"I believe it's necessary, Marcia. The Taylor administration only reacts to situations. He wants to put his DreamStar incident on the back burner, take the easy way until it's too late . . . he and his New York buddies need a push to get them going. I just hope to hell it's in time.''

## The Kremlin, Moscow, USSR
*Friday, 19 June 1996, 0600 EET (Thursday, 2200 EDT)*

"I assure you," Kalinin said to the General Secretary, "events occurred so quickly in this operation that there was no time to inform you."

Kalinin had already spent the better part of an hour in the General Secretary's office, telling the weary leader about the DreamStar operation. Now the General Secretary was clenching and unclenching his hands, shaking his head as he reviewed what Kalinin had told him.

"There were only two days between when we learned of the cancellation of the DreamStar project and when our man took the fighter," Kalinin continued. "It was as much Colonel Maraklov's initiative as it was a directive from my office—"

"Be silent, Kalinin. Just be *quiet*. I do not want to hear your excuses for irresponsible behavior. I need to think about how this will be explained and handled."

"I am, of course, entirely to blame for these events, sir," Kalinin said—perhaps a complete admission of guilt, he thought, could smooth things over—"but now that it has been dealt, we should play this hand to its conclusion. We must see to it that the fighter is brought here as quickly as possible."

"I see. Have you gone completely crazy? Do you think the U.S. will not perhaps object to having the KGB steal one of their top-secret fighters?"

"Sir, I am not thinking of the Americans," Kalinin said. "I am thinking of Russia. We had the opportunity to take the aircraft and we did. Now we must capitalize on our achievement. The technology we gain will be—"

"Will be useless if they attack and kill a hundred of our people and destroy that base in Nicaragua to get their fighter back," the General Secretary said. "I will not risk a shooting war with the Americans over one damn plane!"

"If the Americans were going to attack, they would have done so," Kalinin said. "They know where the fighter is—

their radar planes tracked the XF-34 throughout its entire flight. So the point is, they will not attack. They will not risk war over the fighter—''

"You underestimate them," the General Secretary said. "I do not."

"Sir, this whole incident is part of a game," Kalinin said. "A game. Military secrets are stolen every day by both sides. Messages of protest are sent by both sides daily. I lose one or two operatives a month, sometimes more, to espionage or counter-espionage activities. Wars aren't started over such matters."

"We lost six men! The Americans lost a B-52 bomber, two fighters, and six of their people. This is a game?"

"But, sir, none of it affects the strategic balance," Kalinin said. "It is simple maneuvering, part of the give-and-take between our governments. I say the Americans will not take action or retrieve their fighter. We will open secret negotiations, perhaps eventually trade captured agents or information for the aircraft after we have learned what we want from it. We may even lose something important to us in the near future, but we should not, sir, panic. As I say, we will eventually return the aircraft—*after* we study it. Please remember, this fighter is the most advanced aircraft in the world, sir. It is controlled by *thought*. Everything—flight control, weapons, every system is activated at the speed of light, all by thought commands."

The General Secretary paused. Actually he had very little exposure to this side of his government. It was, indeed, he realized, a coup to obtain such an aircraft intact, a unique opportunity to study the best of American military technology . . . But Kalinin's apparent success also posed a danger. Kalinin's prestige and popularity would rise with the recognition of such an achievement, and the fact that he had done it all behind the General Secretary's back would make matters worse. Kalinin had to be carefully reined in. Right now . . .

"Very well," the General Secretary said, "I am opposed to this operation, but because of the unusual nature of the aircraft and the benefits of having such a machine to study, I will allow you to continue with your plans—after I review your project files. I will assign a member of the senior Politburo Central Committee to oversee your operation. He will contact your Colonel Maraklov in Nicaragua and speak with him, as well as with members of your staff, and report back to me. Control of this operation reverts to me. Is that clear?''

"Of course, sir.'' Kalinin's response was automatic—but he was thinking about who the General Secretary's representative could be. Cherkov? Tovorin? Some unknown? He would have to deal with him as he came along.

"Meanwhile, I want all activity on the American aircraft to stop. The aircraft will not be moved from Nicaragua until I give the order. Is that clear?''

"Yes, sir.''

It was a small setback—he would, of course, have to contend with an informant in his own office. But in effect, so far as he was concerned, his coup was intact. And the future was brighter than ever.

## Sebaco Military Airfield, Nicaragua
*Friday, 19 June 1996, 0445 CTD (1345 EET)*

Maraklov was startled out of a deep sleep by a ringing telephone. He took a few moments to collect himself—the feelings of imbalance, of disorientation, were still plaguing him—before he touched the speaker-phone switch.

"What?''

*"Vash vrizeveahyota peho tehyehlfono, tovarisch,"* a woman's voice replied—Musi Zaykov, he guessed. *"Moskva."* There was no apology for speaking Russian this time, he noted. Never mind. He had been studying a bit of Russian all day; because of that, plus listening to it spoken between the technicians and soldiers in Sebaco, he was able to understand more and more of it as time went on. His own vocabulary, however, was still very limited, and his reading comprehension was almost nil. Cyrillic characters were almost impossible to understand. Luckily, most of the machinery and matters relating to the flight line were the Russian export versions, which had instructions and labels printed in—of all languages—English.

*"Da,"* he replied. *"Sechyahs."* He had gotten very good at saying "wait a minute" in Sebaco, because everyone seemed to want him at once. Maraklov slipped on a flight suit

and a pair of boots and opened the door to his apartment. It was indeed Musi Zaykov, now without her seductive bush shirt but wearing a KGB casual uniform, pants and black riding boots.

"*Kahtoriy chyahs?* What time is it?" Maraklov asked, as he emerged from the apartment.

"Your Russian is improving, sir," Musi said as she led him out of the hangar. "*Byehz dvahtsatye pyetye pyaht.*" Maraklov was expecting Musi to answer in English, since she'd begun in English, and her Russian escaped him. No matter. It had to be some time before five A.M., because the guards he could see all looked bored and tired; guard-post changeover was at five.

They walked across the flight-line ramp, had their badges checked by a gruff, sleepy KGB Border Guard, then walked down a dark, mossy path toward a grove of mangrove trees. The trees disguised a twenty-foot-diameter satellite dish and other communications antennae, the only visible landmarks of the Soviet Air Force command post and KGB detachment headquarters nearby. They were stopped by still another guard post, then proceeded down a short flight of steps in the semi-underground facility.

Unlike the rest of the camp, this building was well ventilated and air conditioned—much like most of the buildings in Dreamland. They signed in, punched codes into an electronic door lock and entered the communications facility. On the right was the main communications console, with two Air Force non-commissioned officers manning it and a KGB officer supervising them; on the left was a radar console with one Air Force NCO in charge. The rest of the room was filled with smelly transformers, old teletypewriters and storage lockers.

"Ah. *Tovarisch Polkovnik* Maraklov. *Zdyehs.*" General Tret'yak motioned to Maraklov and Zaykov, who followed him into a small conference room. The general looked a bit nervous as he closed the door to the conference room.

"*Vsyo tovarisch Vorotnikov,* Andrei," Tret'yak said, motioning to a telephone on the desk at the front of the room. "*Sta Politischeskoye Buro. Yah khatyehl . . .*"

"Hold on . . . er, *prastiti,* sir," Maraklov said. "I don't understand you. Damn it, *yah nyee pahnyemahyo . . .*"

"All right, *Polkovnik, pryekrasna.* It is Comrade Luscev Vorotnikov, a member of the Politburo, representative to General Secretary for Central and South America," Tret'yak said in awkward English. "He wishes to speak with you." Maraklov reached for the phone. "I would like to know what you will say about the dismantling of the MiG-39," Tret'yak said.

"Don't worry, General. As pilot of the aircraft I have authority to decide what happens to it. It was my decision and my responsibility to recommand the halt." Tret'yak looked relieved but immediately disguised the expression and motioned to the telephone. Maraklov picked it up. "This is Colonel Maraklov."

*"Dobrayeh otrah, tovarisch Polkovnik,"* the voice on the other end began. The satellite connection was remarkably clear. *"Yah—"*

"Please speak English, sir."

There were some sounds of anger and confusion at the other end, then a much younger voice came on line: "Sir, this is Yegor Ryzhkov, an aide to Chairman Vorotnikov. Can you understand me, Colonel?"

"Yes."

His accent was British—quite possibly an exchange student or maybe a Connecticut Academy graduate; a favorite target for Academy-trained men and women was Great Britain. "I will translate for the chairman. He welcomes you back and congratulates you on your heroic work."

The congratulatory message when translated did not match the angry voices he heard in the background, but Maraklov ignored them.

"Chairman Vorotnikov has been advised by routine message traffic from Sebaco that you have recommended that the process of preparing the aircraft for shipment to the Soviet Union be halted. Can you explain this?"

"I stopped the workers from taking the aircraft apart because they were destroying it," Maraklov said. "I will not deliver a nonfunctional aircraft to Ramenskoye."

There was a pause at the other end; then Maraklov could hear the voice of Vorotnikov rising in irritation.

"The Chairman wishes to know what you recommend be done with the aircraft now," the interpreter said.

"I intend to add long-range fuel tanks to it," Maraklov told

him. "I estimate that two Lluyka in-flight refueling drop-tanks
can be added to the wings of the XF-34—these are tanks with a
retractable refueling probe built into them. The tanks will increase the effective range of the XF-34 aircraft and provide an
in-flight refueling capacity. In this way, the aircraft can be
delivered intact."

"*Ahstarozhna, tovarisch Polkovnik,*" one of the radio operators said. "*Telefoniya eahnyateh.*" Maraklov did not understand and turned to Zaykov.

"He said be careful," Musi said. "The line is not secure. Do
not mention the name of the aircraft."

The translation from Moscow took a long time, interspersed
as it was with comments and questions in the background. General Tret'yak, who was listening in on another phone, was becoming more nervous—Maraklov was sure he had just lost the
general as an ally. Then: "Colonel Maraklov, Comrade Vorotnikov has ordered that no further actions be taken on the aircraft
until further ordered. We shall transmit orders from the Kremlin
through the KGB Central Command."

"I understand," Maraklov said. "But understand, it will
take two or three days for technicians here to saw the aircraft
up into pieces, a half day to load it on a ship, at least a week
for that ship to arrive in a Russian port and another one to two
days for it to be transported to Ramenskoye. And when it arrives there it will be of *no* use to anyone—it will be nothing
but piles of circuit boards and plastic. If I am allowed to proceed it will take two days or less to modify the aircraft for
Lluyka tanks. Then, once fighter escort and tanker support has
been arranged, it will take only ten hours to fly from here
directly to Ramenskoye Research Center. When the aircraft
arrives it will be in flyable condition and ready for operational
inspection, with its computer memory and structural integrity
functional."

This explanation took even longer, but this time there were
fewer interruptions and outbursts from Vorotnikov and whoever was with him in his office. But a few moments later the
translator came back with "Colonel, Chairman Vorotnikov
has some reservations about your plan, but he would like time
to confer with his advisers. He orders you to continue your
plans for mounting the aerial refueling tanks on the aircraft
and preparing it for flight. He reminds you of the danger of

remaining in Central America and orders you to do everything
in your power to bring the aircraft home intact. Do you understand?''

''Yes,'' Maraklov said. General Tret'yak seemed happier.
''Tell the chairman that he can assure the Politburo that their
orders will be carried out.'' But the satellite link had gone dead
by then.

*''Ochin prekrahsna,''* Tret'yak said, slapping him on the shoulder. ''It looks like the pilots have beat the *ribniys* once again.''

Maraklov erased the relieved expression on his face as
Tret'yak led him out of the communications center. Well, he
had made Tret'yak a buddy once again—at least until the next
crisis blew in.

In Vladimir Kalinin's office at KGB Headquarters in Moscow,
Vorotnikov threw the phone back on its cradle. ''I did not understand most of what was going on,'' he said. He waved a
hand, dismissing Ryzhkov, waited until his assistant had left,
then reached for the bottle of fine Viennese cognac on the desk
and poured himself a glass. He took a sip, then drained the glass
in one loud gulp. ''But the pilot, your Colonel Maraklov, appears to be in charge.''

Kalinin nodded, moving the silver tray with the cognac de-
canter closer to Vorotnikov. ''An extraordinary man. His loyalty
is firmly to the Party and to his country.''

Vorotnikov shrugged, lifted his thick body far enough up off
the chair to pour himself another cognac. ''Excellent cognac,
Vladimir.''

''If you enjoy this, Luscev, I will see to it that you will have
a bottle.'' He buzzed his outer desk, and a young, blonde woman
in a red low-cut dress entered the office. ''Anna, would you
please see to it that Comrade Vorotnikov is given a bottle of this
cognac . . . at his convenience?''

Anna favored the old bureaucrat with a dazzling smile, folded
her hands behind her back, which served to accent her breasts,
and bowed slightly. ''It would be my pleasure.''

''Thank you very much, Vladimir,'' Vorotnikov said. ''Very
kind of you. Back to business—this Maraklov, can he be
trusted?''

''I believe so, sir.''

"Yet he countermanded your orders that the aircraft be dismantled and shipped back to Russia."

"He . . . what . . . ?"

Vorotnikov was too busy enjoying his cognac to notice Kalinin's confusion. "He wants to fly the thing all the way from Nicaragua to Russia, under the very noses of the Americans. Foolish. You should get that straightened out."

What was this Maraklov thinking? Kalinin was furious. *Fly DreamStar to Russia?* If he screwed up this mission now, everything he was trying to accomplish would be destroyed.

To Vorotnikov, Kalinin said, calmly as possible, "Yes, sir. Now, if you would like to review my files on the project . . . ?"

"Not necessary at the moment, Kalinin." Vorotnikov glanced at the door for a few moments, then hauled himself to his feet and straightened his tie. "I think I have heard enough to report to the General Secretary." He held out his hand, and Kalinin grasped it. "I believe the operation is being run in a satisfactory manner and I shall so report to the General Secretary in the morning. I must leave." Kalinin buzzed his outer office, and Anna arrived to escort the smiling Vorotnikov outside.

When the two had left, Kalinin hit the outer office buzzer again. "I want another secure voice-line set up to Sebaco immediately." Suddenly Kalinin realized how little he really knew about Andrei Maraklov. Vorotnikov, the General Secretary's fat spy, was easy to take care of—this Maraklov, who had spent eleven years in the United States, was a loose cannon. More than anyone else, Andrei Maraklov was now the greatest threat to his plan for ultimate power.

## The White House, Washington, D.C.
*That same morning*

The secret, Lloyd Taylor had discovered, of staying on top of things as President of the United States was information, information, and more information. Gather as much as possible from as many sources as possible, and as quickly as possible. Moreover, although he had a capable and trustworthy staff, the information should not be diluted or encapsulated by his staff. Interestingly, he found that if he got his information from the same sources that served most of the American people, he was able to stay on top of events that the people were most concerned about. He rarely found himself caught up in events in the Persian Gulf, for example, if most Americans were really concerned about the economy.

It was not a foolproof system, but it had served him well during his first three and a half years in office and, with luck, would serve him well in a second term.

Taylor's predecessor was a fanatic about daily exercise the way Taylor was about information, and so Taylor combined the two shortly after arriving in the White House. After rising at five-thirty every morning, the President would change into shorts and sneakers and make his way into the well-equipped exercise room in the back west corner of the White House.

There, in the middle of the room, sat a walking/jogging treadmill, a self-contained physical fitness evaluation device that measured and recorded two dozen different vital signs from pulse to weight to blood pressure as he walked. That was his predecessor's contribution. In front of the treadmill was Taylor's—a large-screen voice-command computer monitor and terminal.

"Good morning, Mr. President," Paul Cesare, the Chief of Staff, greeted him. Cesare set a glass of orange juice and a fresh towel on a table near the treadmill. "How do you feel this morning?"

"Just fine, Paul." The President stepped onto the treadmill. The pre-programmed machine beeped five times in warning, then automatically started. Taylor slipped his hand into a glovelike device on the handlebar that had sensors in it that would feed information to the body function monitors. As the President started walking, the computer terminal came to life.

"Good morning, Mr. President," the terminal said in a quiet feminine voice. On the screen was a recorded view of the Potomac and the Jefferson Memorial. The screen changed to several columns of information in large letters showing the weather, date, important holidays and the day's appointments. "The following is an encapsulation of your morning appointments:

"You have a Cabinet meeting at eight o'clock. At ten o'clock, a meeting with the Senate Foreign Relations committee. At noon, the luncheon with the International Kiwanas at the Ambassador Hotel. There are five desk flags." Desk flags were items left on his desk that would require some study or consultation. A brief description of each flashed on the screen; none seemed too important. "Would you like to review them now?"

"No."

"Would you like to review the afternoon appointments?"

"No."

"What would you like, Mr. President?"

The treadmill had sped up to about three miles per hour as it automatically sought to raise Taylor's heart rate to its optimum aerobic exercise rate. "Go back to bed," he said, stepping up the pace.

The computer thought about it for a moment, then, "Please make another choice, Mr. President."

"Thanks," he said, and Cesare grinned. "How about wire-service headlines?"

"Please select a keyword, or select 'All.' " The keywords were phrases used to narrow down the huge selection of news items.

" 'White House,' " the President requested.

A long list of news bulletins flashed on the screen, all containing the words "White House." The computer-synthesized voice continued: "Selected headlines as of five A.M. Eastern Standard Time: 'White House may announce decision on Korean trade bill today.' 'Foreign Relations Chairman Myers travels to White House to break impasse.' 'Russian KGB spy disaster stymies White House advisers.' 'First Lady will receive veteran's group in White House ceremony . . .' "

Taylor pounded a fist on the treadmill STOP button. "What the hell . . . ? Stop. Read item three."

"Headlines Stop," the computer acknowledged. "Review. Item three. Washington *Post* Wire Service, date twenty-one June, nineteen hundred and ninety-six. Washington desk, first paragraph: 'A Russian KGB deep-cover agent may have caused the crash of an experimental B-52 bomber in the southern Nevada desert on Tuesday, an unnamed military source said today. He may also have been responsible for the downing of an F-15 fighter over Mexico and the crash of a second F-15 over southern Arizona, with loss of life as high as six. Second paragraph: Despite the attacks, the White House has apparently decided to

take no action that may provoke the Soviet Union until more
evidence has been received and analyzed. Third paragraph:
Sources confirm—' ''

"*Stop,* dammit. Who the hell authorized that news release? I
didn't—''

"It sounds like it came from the Pentagon, sir . . .''

"The Pentagon? Get General Kane on the phone.''

Cesare hit the auto-dial button for the Chairman of the Joint
Chiefs of Staff. "I'll get hold of Walters, too," Cesare said.
Ted Walters was the White House Press Secretary. "He might
be able to keep that story from going out on the morning news
shows if we catch it in time.''

"The morning news . . . Goddamn, get on it, Paul. Of all the
things to leak out . . .''

"General Kane on your speakerphone, sir," Cesare said a few
moments later. The President punched the flashing button.

"Bill, there's an article on the Washington *Post* wire service
that mentions our discussion yesterday about the—''

"Open line, Mr. President," Cesare interrupted, his hand over
the mouthpiece of his phone.

"—the aircraft incident. Know anything about it?''

"No, sir. I certainly authorized no release about that at
all.''

"Better get over here, Bill.''

"On my way, sir.''

"Ted's on his way too, sir. He can make some calls from his
car.''

"When I catch the `sonofabitch who leaked this I'll kick his
butt out of Washington, out of the country . . .''

Cesare, always protective of the Boss and concerned about his
blood pressure, tried to soft-pedal the news. "It sounds a little
sketchy. Maybe an imaginative reporter heard about the B-52
crash and just kept on digging until he found—''

"There's no *way* any reporter could start from a B-52 crash
and end up with KGB deep-cover agents without help from this
office. We've got to assume Walters can't stop the media from
picking up on this and spreading it all over the country. So what
are we going to say about it?''

"The story is so far out," Cesare said, "that if we deny the
whole thing people will believe us. A Russian KGB agent shoot-

ing down a B-52 bomber over Nevada? Who's going to believe that?''

"Eyewitnesses. They could have interviewed someone from Dreamland. They could confirm the fact that the B-52 was shot down deliberately. There could be eyewitnesses to the plane being shot down over Mexico or the crash in Arizona. There—''

The phone rang beside Cesare. "Cesare here . . . Edward Drury? . . . Hold on." Cesare put the phone on hold. "It's Drury from CNN, Mr. President. He's asking for White House comment about a so-called KGB spy incident . . .''

So much for keeping it out of the press, the President thought. "All right, the comment is that the story about a KGB agent is false, and the cause of the crash in Nevada is still under investigation.''

"I'd advise against it, Mr. President," Cesare said. "How about 'unsubstantiated,' or 'rumors only'? If we say the story is false, and someone digs up some hard evidence . . .''

"All right, all right." A headache was already spreading from his sinuses. "The information about a Russian agent is an unsubstantiated rumor, and the cause of the B-52 crash under investigation by the Air Force has not yet been determined. Any speculation would be detrimental and injurious to the personnel involved and the best interests of the country. Got all that?''

"Yes, sir. I'll make sure Walters gets a copy.''

"Have Ted hold a press conference as soon as possible and get out a release. No one on the staff goes in front of the media, except Ted, until we get together on a statement, and Ted's only statement will either be what we just said there or 'No comment.' Got that?''

"Yes, sir." Cesare flipped through his notes. "Speaker Van Keller is scheduled to be on ABC this morning. He's the only one in on our meeting yesterday who could be pinned down on it.''

"Better get that statement out to him as soon as possible," the President said. "Have him call me or Ted so we can brief him.''

"This could be a problem, sir," Cesare continued, scanning his notes. "The first fifteen minutes of the meeting with the Foreign Relations Committee was supposed to be a photo opportunity.''

The President shook his head in frustration. "Great. In that case we'll keep it a photos-only session and cut it down to five minutes."

"Senator Myers and the committee members might have some questions about the incident—"

"We'll give them what we give the press—the crash is under investigation, we have no information on any KGB agents being involved."

Cesare finished writing. "One more thing, sir—the Russians. That wire story said we weren't going to do anything. Should we make a comment about that?"

"To hell with them." The President massaged his temples, then added, "They can think what they want. If we come out with any comment directed at the Russians we'd be admitting that they had something to do with the B-52 crash—"

The phone rang again. "Cesare here . . . Ted, what's up? . . . what? . . . any details? . . . all right. You're ten minutes away? All right, I'll pass it on."

"What now?"

"Ted just got off the phone with the *Post.* They're now saying that they have a tape of the conversation between the B-52 and the XF-34 aircraft during their engagement. The radio conversation was on a channel called GUARD, an international emergency frequency used by planes, ships . . . They have the whole thing—including the pilot of the XF-34 saying that he's a colonel in the KGB. He said the guy from the *Post* even said, 'XF-34.' That designation was top secret—until now."

"Dammit all to hell, less than twenty-four hours after our meeting and the whole country, whole world, knows about it. All right, all right," the President said. "Cancel the Cabinet meeting agenda, get the NSC and CIA and have everybody in the conference room no later than seven-thirty, briefed and ready to discuss this, but for Christ's sake do it *quietly*—don't make it look like we're circling any wagons. This is a routine Cabinet meeting. Make sure we get tapes of any news broadcasts about this thing."

"We should change the press statement," Cesare said. "I suggest—"

"The change is easy. The word now is 'No comment.' That's it, and it goes for Ed Drury and the networks and everybody.

We've got to get a handle on this thing before it gets completely away from us . . ."

Cesare got on the phone again and while he was waiting, the President turned to him and said, "Paul, I want General Elliott at the meeting, too. Has he left Washington?"

"I believe so, sir."

"Then we'll set up a secure teleconference and . . . no, I want him here. He had some ideas about this DreamStar thing that I want to hear. Wherever he is, have him back here soonest."

"Yes, sir." Cesare dialed the office of the military communications liaison and issued the President's orders, then turned back to President Taylor, who was standing near the treadmill, staring at the news item on the big screen.

"Any idea who leaked this, Paul?"

"Well, that news item mentions a military source." He paused, then asked: "Do you think it could be Elliott? Is that why you're bringing him back to Washington?"

"A guy that's just been stripped of his command and being forced to retire can do some very strange things, but no, not Elliott. He's by-the-book. I want him back in Washington to hear what he has to say about this DreamStar thing. It's been his baby."

"Are you considering a military response?"

"Maybe I won't have any choice. If we can't get control of this leak, we may *have* to do more than just protest to the Russians—"

The phone rang. Cesare picked it up. "Military communications, sir," Cesare said. "General Elliott had made a stopover at the Air Force Aeronautical Laboratories in Dayton. He can be here for the staff meeting."

"That's very good of him. I can't wait to talk to him."

"This was a deliberate information leak on someone's part," President Taylor said. "I want someone's butt, and I want it now."

He paused, scanning the faces of his Cabinet and senior White House staff members. "I expect whoever did this will have the courage to come to me later and explain why he or she felt it was necessary to reveal classified information like this. I will not tolerate this in my staff. I'll shit-can the lot of you, and senior staff, if I have to.''

He let his words linger on the wide cherry conference table for a few moments. No one appeared ready to confess or throw themselves on the sword. He also saw a few faces that allowed themselves to appear skeptical when he had mentioned dismissals. But he had no choice, the President thought—someone had to get fired over this. *Someone* had to take a fall if for no other reason than credibility, or deniability, as in Iranscam.

"The official word on this incident is 'No comment,'" the President said. "And I don't mean any of that 'Neither confirm nor deny' stuff. I mean *'No comment.'* You're not authorized to discuss anything dealing with Dreamland, the B-52 crash, experimental aircraft or any military or civilian personnel. Is *that* clear?" A few nodding heads. "If you have any difficulty with that order tell me now. I won't hold any questions against you, and I won't think that anyone who has a question has to be the guilty party. Speak up."

Silence.

"All right. If any problems come up, refer them to Ted Walters, Paul Cesare or myself. But I want a lid on this. And I want it on tight. We've got news about the Summer Olympics and the elections to take the media pressure off this incident, and that's what I want to happen."

The President turned to General Kane. "Update on that DreamStar aircraft, General?"

"Very little, Mr. President," the Chairman of the Joint Chiefs told him. "Increase in message traffic on the Soviet satellite-net out of Sebaco Airbase near Managua. We haven't been able to decode it yet but our analysts believe this reinforces our estimation that DreamStar is at Sebaco."

"How long would it take them to take that aircraft apart, General?"

Kane was anxious to get out of the sudden glare of attention and have the spotlight focus on the principal of this incident. He said, "I can't give you an accurate answer, Mr. President." He turned to General Bradley Elliott sitting beside him. "Brad?"

"It's hard to say, Mr. President." All eyes were on Elliott, but not because they were waiting to hear what he said—they all believed he was the one who had leaked the information on DreamStar to the press in the first place. "If they wanted to, they could have DreamStar in pieces in hours—it could already be crated up and ready to ship. But I don't think they would just hack it up. The XF-34 is the most advanced aircraft in the world. The Soviets will want it intact."

"Then why take it apart at all?" William Stuart, the Secretary of Defense asked. "Why not just fly it to Managua and load it onto a large freighter?"

"That can be done, sir," Elliott replied. "But they know that it would be easy to spot once it arrived in Managua, and very difficult to conceal. We could detect which ship it was loaded onto and intercept or destroy—"

*"Destroy a Russian freighter?"* from Attorney General Richard Benson. "In peacetime? That's crazy!"

"Mr. Benson," Elliott said, "that is one thing we should *never* reveal."

"I don't understand."

"Sir, many other military powers in the world would kill to keep an aircraft like DreamStar from falling into enemy hands. To the Russians, the Chinese, the French, the Israelis, the British, destroying a freighter with a torpedo from several miles away to keep that freighter from escaping with their country's most valuable military aircraft would be no big deal. They wouldn't hesitate—"

"That's *them*, not us."

"Mr. Benson, if we really want our fighter back we must at least *appear* ready at any time to commit such an act. We must convince the Russians that we are ready to do anything necessary to get our aircraft back. If we announce we will never shoot at a Russian freighter in peacetime, we invite them to load DreamStar on that freighter and sail it right under our noses back to Russia. If we tell them we'll blow your ass out of the water if we find out our plane is on board, and we convince them and the world that we *mean* it, well, they may just look for a different way to get it out of Nicaragua." He was also thinking about the Cuban missile crisis but didn't bring it up.

Heads nodded around the conference table; Elliott had apparently gotten through to most of them, at least enough to see the logic of what he was saying. And the President was at least attentive if perhaps not convinced.

"If they don't want to risk discovery by loading the entire aircraft onto a ship," Elliott pressed on, "and they don't just quickly chop it up into pieces, they have two other options: they can take their time dismantling it, making careful records and notations about how to put it back together, or they can fly it out of Nicaragua. It wouldn't take long to dismantle Dream-Star—a day or two, pull the engine and the black boxes, dissect and discard the rest. If they choose to fly it out, it may take them a few days, three at the most, to configure it for overwater flight with extra fuel tanks."

"What's keeping them from just flying the thing onto one of their new aircraft carriers?" Deborah O'Day asked. "From what I understand DreamStar can land on a carrier without an arresting hook and take off again without a catapult."

"All true," Elliott said, surprised that she knew so much, careful to use the same tone of voice with her as with the President and Stuart and the other members of the staff. He had to fight himself to keep from smiling at her. He was all but convinced that she was the one who had leaked information about DreamStar to the press to force the President's hand. He knew her feelings and those of the NSC. It was a risky maneuver but it could pay off—and it could also result in both of them being sent to Leavenworth or Eglin for ten years for conspiracy . . .

"Again, they'd be exposing themselves to a great degree of danger if they tried to fly DreamStar onto a carrier. It's a tricky operation under the best conditions; for James in DreamStar it would be that much more difficult, even with his advanced flight-control system. And the Soviets know they would risk attack if it was discovered that they had DreamStar on board. They would not, I feel, risk one of only six *Moscow*-class aircraft carriers for one fighter plane, even this one."

"These are all conjectures on your part, Elliott," the President said. "Sheer speculation not surprisingly biased in favor of a military response."

"Yes, sir, I agree. I am speculating on all of this, and I am leaning in favor of a swift, decisive, direct response—but only for the sake of time. If we could count on the Russians taking weeks to carefully dismantle DreamStar I would not even consider a direct military response. Certainly not at this point. If you recall back in 1976, when Viktor Belyenko flew his then-top-secret MiG-25 to Japan, one of the first reactions by the Ford administration was to guarantee that we would turn the MiG over to the Russians intact immediately after our investigation of the matter was completed—which, of course, gave us time to study the thing. We made that guarantee, sir, because the Russians had one-fifth of their navy within five hours' sailing time of the MiG's landing spot and the administration was convinced that the Russians would militarily intervene in Japan to get their MiG-25 back. I'm saying, sir, that is the *threat* we need to project to the Soviets in Nicaragua. It comes down to how badly we want DreamStar back.''

The President was silent, staring at Elliott. ''Did we give the MiG-25 back?''

''Yes, after we determined that the MiG-25 wasn't all our intelligence and their propaganda said it was. The MiG-25 was simply two huge jet engines with wings, built for speed at any cost. Our F-15 was operational by then, and the F-16 was in production. Both those aircraft could fly rings around the MiG-25. But DreamStar is different, sir. DreamStar is our only flying model of that concept of aircraft. It would be a huge loss for us and a quantum leap in technology for the Soviets. It would take two years to build another XF-34, and we'd be right back where we are now. Meanwhile, the Soviets would take several giant steps forward in their technology, and with their advantage in military budget and production could field a squadron of XF-34 aircraft before we could—''

''Excuse me, Mr. President,'' William Stuart broke in. ''General Elliott has made several broad statements that Defense doesn't find supportable. He's making DreamStar seem like the ultimate weapon, when in fact it's nothing more than an advanced technology demonstration aircraft. Congress hasn't voted to deploy the XF-34, nor will DreamStar even be ready for deployment for another five years. Agreed, it's an extraordinary machine, but it is not our *next* fighter aircraft. Far away from it.''

''So you're saying that it's not worth going after?''

''My point is simply that DreamStar in the hands of the Russians is not the terrible threat that General Elliott is making it out to be. It is a setback, true, but no more of a setback than if

DreamStar had crashed on a test flight or if the program had run out of funds and was canceled.''

"General Elliott?"

"I disagree with Secretary Stuart, sir. Seriously disagree. The technology transfer alone in the DreamStar theft is enormous. It's certainly of such great military importance to us that its return, or if it comes to it, destruction, is of the highest priority—''

"Not *my* highest priority," Stuart interrupted.

"It may be true that *we* were several years from deploying DreamStar, Mr. President," Elliott said, "but the Soviets could follow an entirely different timetable. We have the F-32 fighter in preproduction that will be our front-line fighter for the next five to ten years. The Soviets have their MiG-33 and Sukhoi-35 fighters operational or in production that will serve them for the next decade. Neither of those fighters can match our F-32—and *that* is a DOD assessment, not mine. With the XF-34 fighter in production in the Soviet Union, they will easily have the capability to counter our front-line fighters for the next ten years until we redevelop our own XF-34—and then we will only be *matching* the Soviets' capability. We will instantly be five years behind the Soviets if we don't react."

"General, you're blowing this whole thing out of proportion—''

"All right, enough," the President said. "We don't need to get into arguments about the future. The fact is, they got the damn plane. What do we do about it *now?*"

"I think we need to examine this problem from another perspective, Lloyd," Attorney General Benson said, "the political side. This thing's about to be splashed all over TV, newspapers and videotext terminals around the world. We can avoid feeding fuel to the fire by not providing any details, and it *may* indeed fizzle out over time, but the opposition is going to use this against us when their convention opens in Seattle next month. We need a strong, positive step to show the voters that we're in charge—''

"So you favor a military response?"

"Not necessarily, Lloyd," Benson said, leaning sideways toward the President and scarcely making himself heard in the conference room. As the President's brother-in-law (he'd taken plenty of heat for that), he was one of the few Cabinet members who called the President by his first name; when he did it usually meant he was separating himself from the Cabinet to make an especially strong point. "But we're playing catch-up ball here—the press has the advantage and we can't let that situation continue. You've got to make a move that shows that you're ready to handle the situation. We don't have to decide on an offensive against Nicaragua right now—I think it would be a bad move anyway. But you *do* have to make a move, and something stronger than a diplomatic protest. Five months from now when the voters ask what you did about this, you want to be able to point to something substantial, positive."

Benson decided after the meeting he would tell the President that the first step would be to get rid of Elliott. After all, he was the one who lost the damn plane . . .

The President held up his hand, indicating that he was going to reserve judgment, and turned to William Stuart. "Outline our responses, Bill."

"I think it's a problem for State or CIA, Mr. President," Stuart said. "We can't attack Nicaragua. It's just not an option for us. CIA might be able to suggest something, a covert operation maybe, but in my opinion it's out of DOD's hands. We can't put out a candle with a fire hose."

"That's it, Bill?"

Defense Secretary Stuart looked at Elliott. "If I may say so, the problem should have been handled long ago by General Elliott and his unit, and the aircraft should have been properly secured. We lost the aircraft. Now General Elliott wants to go in, as usual, with six-guns blazing. But if we confront the Soviets, they will probably agree to turn the aircraft over to us. It may take a few weeks, or months, but we will get the aircraft back from them. And if we do, well, that's the bottom line."

"So you'd just let them *have* it? They kill four of my flyers, two security guards and two interceptor pilots, and you're saying that we should let them alone until they've done what they want with it?"

"Don't put words in my mouth, General Elliott." Stuart's voice had risen. "What I'm saying is that we can't go off and start a war over *our* screwups or—rather, *your* screwups. I agree with the President. The X-34 is great but it isn't worth—"

"Isn't worth what? That aircraft is the most advanced in the world. We can't just build a thing like that and then hand it over to the Soviets to study, for God's sake. I don't care if they only have it for a few days, it is still too damn long."

"DreamStar, as I understand it, is twenty-first-century technology. The Soviets are having their problems with 1980s technology—"

"And *that* is a 1960s stereotype, sir," Elliott shot back. "We all learned, or I thought we did, what a fallacy that was. Ever hear of Kavaznya, Mr. Secretary? Sary Shagan? Since the late seventies the Russians have repeatedly proved that they can keep pace with any other western nation in technology, and that includes the United States. And don't forget Sputnik . . ."

"My recommendation stands, Mr. President," Stuart said.

"I'm surprised by Bill's position on this matter," Dennis Danahall, the Secretary of State, said during the pause that followed Stuart's remarks. Danahall was considerably younger than others on the Cabinet and, like Deborah O'Day, a recent White House appointee—widely thought of as a political asset to attract the support of younger voters. "I thought he'd opt for a stronger stand. But until I heard some better options I must agree with him, Mr. President. I think a strongly worded letter, perhaps from the Oval Office itself, combined with some face-to-face between myself and the Soviet Foreign Minister or their ambassador could expedite things."

"As I said, Secretary Danahall," Elliott interrupted, "in any other circumstance I would not favor a military response. But time really is of the essence here. We *must* act quickly."

"I agree," Deborah O'Day said. "My staff is working on an interagency report, sir, but I'm forced to go by what little General Elliott has told us about the XF-34. We can't allow the Russians to walk off with it . . . A small-scale military response just may be necessary."

The President looked briefly at O'Day, then turned away. "Any other inputs?" When he heard none he summarized: "Two suggestions to take the diplomatic route only, confront the Soviets and demand our property back. One to intervene directly. Frankly, I don't see how far a military response would get us. As I said before, the damage has already been done here. Whether or not the Soviets give our jet back or even admit they have it is a moot point—the fact is, we lost it and this government—and I believe the Congress—is not about to start a fight to get it back . . . Therefore I am directing Secretary Danahall to draft a letter for my signature, using the strongest diplomatic language possible, demanding the return of our aircraft immediately. I'll follow this up with more direct communications with the Soviet government, if necessary.''

The President now looked at Elliott. ''Our business in this matter is closed. I want to reopen the previous agenda in the time remaining. General Elliott, our business is concluded. Please wait for me in my outer office.''

''Yes, sir.'' Elliott stood, masking his disappointment with an expressionless stare. The Cabinet watched as the tall, thin veteran of two wars and a mission to Russia that was still only spoken of in whispers limped out of the conference room.

Cesare had alerted the President's receptionist that Elliott was on his way, and he was quickly and politely shown into the waiting area outside the Oval Office, given a cup of coffee and asked to wait.

Never, Elliott thought, had he felt so damn helpless. He was getting no support from the Air Force Chief of Staff, he had just been in an argument with the Secretary of Defense, and the President of the United States apparently thought he was some nut-case hawk. Even Deborah O'Day, who must have been the one who leaked the information about DreamStar and Maraklov to the press, didn't act supportive. Well, she said be ready with a presentation to knock the President's socks off, and he had clearly failed to do that. And if he couldn't support his own cause, he could hardly expect her or anyone else to do it for him.

He sat in the outer office for nearly an hour, jotting down occasional notes to himself on how to best organize HAWC for the upcoming investigation. There was a telephone in the outer office, and he considered using it to find out how Wendy Tork . . . now McLanahan . . . was doing, but decided against it. He'd do it on his way out. He had made a note to stop by San Antonio and Brooks Medical Center on his way back to Dreamland when the door to the Oval Office opened and Paul Cesare, wearing a grim face, opened the door for Elliott. ''This way, General.''

When he was shown into the Oval Office he was surprised at

the people assembled there. Deborah O'Day was standing beside the President, hands folded in front of her. Secretary of the Air Force Wilbur Curtis, the former Chairman of the Joint Chiefs of Staff, was there along with generals Kane and Board; only Curtis had a welcoming smile for his old friend. The other surprise addition was Speaker of the House Van Keller, the ranking Democrat in Congress. All but Curtis and O'Day were tight-faced as he made his way into the Oval Office.

"Great to see you, Brad, you old throttle jockey," Curtis said. "Sorry I couldn't be here earlier, they had me in Europe inspecting some old Russian missile silos."

"Good to see you too, sir."

"Can the 'sir' stuff, Brad. I'm wearing a suit now, and it's not a blue suit, either. And don't look so down in the mouth. We've just begun to fight."

The President took a seat at the big cherry desk, and the others found seats around him. Curtis sat beside Elliott, arranged so that he could watch both him and the President.

"I don't have a lot of time," the President said. He turned to his National Security Adviser. "Deborah, go ahead."

"As you know, Mr. President, the story broke a few hours ago. Along with questions aimed at this administration and myself, the media focused in on the Soviet Union. It was very well prepared—they had statements from our own FAA air traffic controllers, Mexican controllers, a few of our low-level military sources and local police authorities dealing with the F-15 crash near Yuma. They even got statements from air traffic controllers at Managua. The press has damn near re-created the whole sequence of events, and in very short order.

"But when asked directly, the Soviet Union still denies any involvement in the incident, denies that they have an American plane, denies they had a secret agent working in Dreamland, denies everything about James . . . Maraklov. But I've just received the preliminary report from Rutledge. His CIA confirms that the aircraft that flew through Honduras into Nicaraguan airspace did land at Sebaco Airbase."

"So we've traced it from Dreamland to a KGB airfield in Nicaragua," Curtis said, "and the Russians are denying it ever happened."

"It's not going to be another Belyenko incident," O'Day said. "The Russians aren't going to admit they have it."

"I agree," Speaker Van Keller said. "This is no disillusioned young pilot flying his jet out of the country. If they admit they have the XF-34, they admit to an international criminal act, an act of war, in effect . . ."

"It looks to me like we have no choice anymore, Mr. President," Curtis said. "It would be a political and military disaster to allow them to get away with this. Even if they should later admit it, we must do something *now.*"

"Never mind the politics, Wilbur, that's my business. As for the military, what were the Air Force and the DIA doing when this Soviet agent was planted, then allowed to exist so long in a place he gets to be the top pilot in our most advanced experimental aircraft? All right, I need a plan of action." He looked at Elliott. "General?"

"Yes, sir . . . we need to do two things immediately: first, verify exactly where DreamStar is at Sebaco, and second, show the Russians that we know that DreamStar is there and that we're prepared to do something strong about it. I propose a flyby of Sebaco by a single high-performance reconnaissance aircraft. No weapons except for self-protection. No ground-attack arsenal. It—"

"I want no weapons at all," the President said. "Unarmed. If the thing crashes in Nicaragua I don't want to see pictures of Nicaraguan fishermen dragging American missiles out of the water with their nets. Can you do it without weapons?"

"It'll be more difficult, but it can be done."

The President looked skeptical and irritable. This thing was more and more taking on the risks and implications of the Cuban missile crisis . . . "How? A high-altitude jet? I want *one* aircraft, remember—no escorts, no waves of aircraft—"

"One aircraft," Elliott said. "And it will be at low altitude. We want there to be no question that the Soviets know we mean business."

"Not another damned B-52?"

"The thought had crossed my mind," Elliott admitted, "but Managua is very heavily protected, and this would have to be a daylight mission. We would probably lose a B-1 or even a B-2 Stealth aircraft. No, no bomber aircraft."

"How do you expect one aircraft to do the job and still survive?" Van Keller asked. "Use an unmanned aircraft? A drone? A satellite?"

"No, a single aircraft but a very special one," Elliott said.
"Twice through Sebaco on photo runs, in and out, perhaps sixty
seconds over the base and five minutes in Nicaraguan airspace.
We'll have what we need."

Paul Cesare moved closer to the President: "Mr. President,
our meeting with the Foreign Relations Committee . . ."

"All right, Paul," the President said. "Wilbur, General Elliott, this is what I want: a single aircraft, unarmed, not more
than five minutes over Nicaragua. This will be the only chance
you'll get, so it had better be done right the first time. Wilbur,
you have command authority. Brief me tonight.

"One more thing. If you people screw this up I won't wait
until after the election to clean house."

As Curtis and Elliott left the Oval Office for the elevators down
to the White House garage, Curtis turned to Elliott and said, "I
knew the Old Man couldn't ignore you, Brad."

"Thanks for the support. I haven't seen much from the White
House lately."

"There's more than you think," Curtis said. "And I'm not
just talking about the National Security Adviser."

Elliott looked at Curtis. "What about her?"

"Don't play dumb with me. The lady is quite taken with you,
personally and professionally. Don't ask me why—anyone who'd
get involved with a pilot can't have all their marbles. I wouldn't
be surprised if she cooked up this morning's bombshell in the
press. Am I close?"

"Don't know what you're talking about, sir," Elliott replied
with a straight face.

"Okay, we'll leave it that way—it's safer for her too. Besides,
everyone around this place has a pipeline to some reporter.
There'd be more double-dealing and backstabbing in this place
than in the Kremlin if there wasn't the occasional leak. But get
*caught* at it, suddenly you're a leper."

In the garage they moved into waiting sedans. "I assume
you'll want to use the command center to run this operation,
Brad," Curtis said as they drove off. Elliott gave him a surprised
long look.

Curtis returned it. "Let me guess . . . you're not going to
use a bomber—that was *my* first guess. What's the hottest machine on your flight line right now? Cheetah. And McLanahan

and Powell go with it. How'm I doing? Don't answer that . . . You had Cheetah in mind from the start. You've got some sort of camera pod rigged up on it, self-protection devices up the ying-yang—you're going to have to take the missiles off, the President said no." Elliott allowed a smile. The Secretary had hit it right on the mark. "Cheetah's been ready to go ever since last night . . . Ever since O'Day agreed to help you. Right?"

"No comment, sir."

"I like it, General, I like it. You want to send a message— Cheetah will do it."

# =6=

## Sebaco Military Airfield, Nicaragua
*Friday, 19 June 1996, 0643 CDT (0743 EDT)*

WORK HAD BEGUN on DreamStar less than three hours after the last transmission from Moscow, and even though he had diverted the plan to dismantle his aircraft, every minute that Andrei Maraklov watched DreamStar's refit was like another twist of the knife that seemed to be stuck in his gut.

He was standing a few meters in front of DreamStar's hangar, just a few dozen meters from the flight-line ramp leading to Sebaco's runway. The hangar doors, which had remained closed to guard against sabotage or espionage, were now wide open because of the huge volume of trucks and workers scrambling in and out. The hangar was guarded by KGB border troops, two stationed every ten meters around the perimeter, along with a manned BMD armored vehicle or BTR-60PB armored personnel carrier on every cardinal point. Workers carried large picture I.D. cards slung around their necks, which allowed the point guards to check I.D.'s against wearers without the workers stopping.

The technicians and engineers assembled to do the job seemed to be even more ham-handed than General Tret'yak had described. They tore at fasteners they did not understand how to open, yanked at delicate data cables, got greasy hands all over the superconducting antennae arrays. They made notes about everything, in writing and by video camera, but mostly they cared about getting their jobs done on time, not on how well the fighter flew after leaving Sebaco.

Each twist of the worker's wrench brought home another re-

ality to Maraklov—that along with the delivery of DreamStar to
the Soviet Union came the end to his own usefulness. General
Tret'yak was correct, of course—DreamStar would be dismantled in ultra-fine detail once it was safely delivered to the Ramenskoye Test Facility near Moscow. It might be flown once or
twice, but more than likely its avionics would be activated arti-
ficially and all its subsequent "flights" would be confined to a
laboratory. If there was no DreamStar, there would be little need
for a DreamStar pilot, especially one who would seem more
American than Russian. They might create an ANTARES ground
simulator to study the thought-guidance system and train future
pilots on how to fly DreamStar, but that would not last long.
After that, he doubted very much that the Soviet military would
allow him to fly or even participate in any way, except as some
glorified figurehead . . . until his usefulness there ran out too.

The workers were struggling with a service-access panel on
DreamStar's engine compartment. The senior non-commissioned
officer, Master Sergeant Rudolph Artiemov, spotted Maraklov
standing outside the hangar, came over to him, gave him a half-
salute, pointed to the engine and said something unintelligible
to Maraklov.

"Speak slower, Sergeant," Maraklov said in halting Russian.
The technician squinted at him. *"Mahtor sestyema smazki nyee
khodyaht, tovarisch Polovnik. Vi pahnyemahyo?"*

"I don't understand what the hell you're saying," Maraklov
exploded in English. The startled sergeant stepped back away.
"You're tearing my damned aircraft apart and you want me to
tell you from here if it's okay? Is that it? Get out of my face."

"He said the engine-lubrication system access-panel is stuck,
Andrei," a voice said. He turned to see Musi Zaykov beside
him, her attractive smile momentarily piercing his gloom. Musi
said something to the technician in a stern voice and the sergeant
saluted, turned and trotted back to the workers.

"What did you tell him?"

"I told him that you said he is an incompetent fool, and that
you will kill him first and report him second if he is not more
careful."

"My thoughts exactly."

"They say they will have the aircraft ready for a test flight in
twelve hours," Musi said. Maraklov looked at her, then turned

away from the open front of the hangar and began walking down the flight line. Musi followed.

"Did I say something wrong?"

"No," Maraklov said. "I just feel . . ." Could he trust her? He was beginning to feel he could. She had become something of a confidante over the past few hours. If she was a KGB operative assigned to watch him, she was either doing a very good job, or a very poor one . . . "I feel a terrible mistake is being made here . . . they don't trust or respect my judgment. I brought them the U.S.'s most advanced fighter, and all they can seem to think of is taking it apart. Musi, that is no ordinary aircraft. It is . . . alive. It's part of *me* . . . Can you understand any of that?"

"Not really, Andrei. It is, after all, a machine—"

"No . . ." But he knew it was useless to try to explain. He changed the subject. "You tell me, Musi, what will they do with me after I return to Russia?"

"You will be honored as a hero of the Soviet Union—"

"Bullshit. Tell me what's *really* going to happen." She seemed to avoid his eyes. "Come on, Lieutenant."

"I . . . I don't know, Andrei." Her voice now seemed to lose its easy tone, to become almost stiff, as though she were reciting. "You will be welcomed, of course . . . following that, you will be asked to participate in the development of the aircraft for the Air Forces—"

"I want to know what kind of *life* I'll have in Russia. I want to know if I'll have a future."

"You ask me to predict too much, Andrei." Her tone changed again. "In my eyes you are a hero. You have done something no one thought possible. But there are . . . people who are distrustful of any foreigner—"

"I'm not a foreigner." Or was he?

"Andrei, I know what you are, but you know what I mean . . . You do not speak Russian. You must understand that there will be less trust at first." She took his hands in hers. "Could it be, Colonel Andrei Maraklov, that it is perhaps *you* who do not trust *us?*"

Maraklov was about to reply, stopped himself. She was right. The U.S. bias toward the Soviet Union had taken hold and was his now—distrust, fear, the works, in spite of the show of *glasnost* and *perestroika*.

He smiled at Musi, pulling her closer. "How did you get so smart, Lieutenant Musi Zaykov?"

"I am not so smart, Andrei. I think I understand how you feel. Living in Nicaragua for a year, feeling the resentment from the people, isolated in this little valley—it is easy to mistrust, even hate, those you do not understand or who seem not to understand you." She moved in closer to him, her lips parting. "I love it when you say my name. I wish you'd do it more often."

And then she kissed him, right there on the little service road next to the flight line. "I know you don't trust me, Andrei, not yet. But you will. Just trust your instincts and I will mine . . ."

Without another word they turned their backs to the flight line and headed back to the officers' quarters hidden in the trees beyond. They shut themselves in her quarters, and Maraklov gave himself up to the remarkable skills of this woman who exorcised all his earlier doubts and made him, for the moment, even forget about DreamStar . . .

## Over the Caribbean Sea
*0825 EDT*

"She's about as maneuverable as an elephant," J. C. Powell said irritably, "and five times as heavy."

Powell and McLanahan had just completed their second refueling from a KC-10 Extender refueling aircraft from the 161st Air Refueling Group "Sun Devils" out of Phoenix, the same unit—and, in fact, the same crew—that had refueled Cheetah just in time after their flight through Mexico. They were now at twenty thousand feet, still flying in tight formation with the tanker, so close that on radar screens from Texas to Florida to Cuba to the Cayman Islands to Jamaica they seemed like one aircraft—which was what they wanted.

J.C. had the throttles at full power to keep up with the KC-10, but after a few minutes the KC-10 pilot noticed the trouble the loaded F-15 fighter was having and backed off on its power. There was plenty of reason for Cheetah's sluggish performance. In addition to sixteen-hundred-gallon FASTPACK fuel tanks near each wing root, Cheetah carried an AN/ALC-189E reconnaissance pod mounted on the centerline stores station. The two-ton

recon pod carried four high-speed video cameras that pointed
forward, aft and to each side, along with data transmission
equipment that allowed the digitized imagery from the cameras
to be broadcast via satellite directly back to Dreamland for analysis. On each wing Cheetah also carried a 600-gallon fuel tank,
which normally gave it a cruising range of nearly three thousand
miles.

That cruising range was considerably shorter with the recon
pod mounted; it was even shorter with Cheetah's other special
stores: two QF-98B Hummer electronic drone aircraft, small single propfan-engined aircraft that carried several computer-
controlled radar jammers. The two Hummer drones, one mounted
on each wing, were preprogrammed to follow a specific flight
path after being released. They carried no weapons. Their flight
paths would take them close to known Nicaraguan and Soviet
early warning radar sites, where their jammers would disrupt the
radars long enough for Cheetah to make its run toward Sebaco.
After flying close to the coastal radar sites, the drones would fly
northeast toward recovery ships near Jamaica—if they survived
the expected Nicaraguan air defenses.

"You boys sure go around looking for trouble," the pilot of
the Phoenix-based tanker said over the scrambled VHF radio.
"Twenty-four hours ago I thought we'd all be in the stockade.
You must lead charmed lives."

"We found a few regs we haven't violated yet," J.C. said.

"You're coming up on your start-descent point," the nav on
the KC-10 said. "One minute."

"Time for one more fast sip before you leave?" the pilot
asked.

"I think we've had enough," J.C. said. "Thanks for the gas."

· "Thank your boss for getting us out of trouble with the brass,"
the pilot said. "I saw what was left of my retirement flash before
my eyes. You boys take it easy down there. Sun Devil starting
a climbing left turn. Out." The KC-10 wagged its wings once,
then began a steep left turn and a sharp climb, heading toward
its destination in San Juan.

"Nav computer set on initial point," McLanahan reported.
On J.C.'s laser-projection heads-up display a tiny "NAV" indicator flashed on the screen, indicating that the computer was
directing a turn. J.C. hit the voice-command switch on his control stick.

"Autopilot on, heading nav."

*"Autopilot on,"* the computer-generated voice replied. *"Heading nav mode. Caution, select altitude function."* The computer reminded J.C. that no autopilot function had been selected for holding altitude. Cheetah started a right turn, heading southwest.

In the aft cockpit McLanahan was completing his checklist items for drone release. "Release circuits safety switch to consent," he told Powell. J.C. flipped a switch far down on his left instrument panel.

"Release switch to CONSENT."

"Checklist complete. Stand by for drone release."

"Ready up here."

"Clear for zero-alpha maneuver," McLanahan said.

J.C. pushed forward on the stick and throttles. As the speed increased and pitch decreased, the angle of attack, the difference between the wing chord and relative wind, moved to zero—this was zero alpha; the wings were knifing through the air with minimum disturbance or deflection, giving the cleanest airflow for the two drones to separate from Cheetah and begin their flight.

"Zero alpha . . . now."

At that moment McLanahan hit the release button. Remote-controlled clips on the drone's carrying racks opened, and the drones began flying in formation with Cheetah.

"Showing two good releases, clear to maneuver," McLanahan announced.

"Here we go." Powell gently, carefully pulled back on his control stick, and the drones dropped away from sight. J.C. did not yank Cheetah away; the sudden turbulence could throw the drones out of control. He eased back on the stick, allowing the distance between mothership and drones to increase slowly.

"Showing good autopilot program-startup on both drones," McLanahan reported. A few moments later they saw both drones banking away to their right as they began their computer-controlled flights.

"Drones are clear to the right."

"Got 'em." J.C. verified. He watched the drones for a moment to make sure they were far enough away, then said, "We're goin' down." He hit the voice-command stud on his stick. "Autopilot attitude hold."

*"Attitude hold mode on,"* the computer acknowledged.

J.C. pressed the pitch-select switch on the control stick and pushed. Cheetah started a twenty-degree descent. When he released the select switch, the autopilot held the pitch angle.

*"Overspeed warning,"* the computer announced. J.C. pulled the throttles back to seventy percent to avoid overstressing the recon pod and external fuel tanks as Cheetah approached the speed of sound in the steep descent.

"Autopilot altitude select two hundred feet," J.C. commanded.

*"Autopilot altitude command two hundred feet."*

"We should be entering early-warning radar coverage in a few minutes. We need to be down below two thousand feet by then."

"No sweat," J.C. said. "We're descending fifteen thousand feet per minute. This baby feels like a real jet with those two loads gone."

Suddenly a tiny indicator blinked on a newly installed panel in Cheetah's aft cockpit. "Radar-warning indicator from one of the drones. Some radar's got them. He'll start jamming any minute."

"We've got five thousand feet to level-off at two hundred feet," J.C. said. "We should be ready."

And Cheetah did level off as planned. By the time it reached the San Andres y Providencia Atoll east of Nicaragua, they were at two-hundred feet above the Caribbean, traveling five hundred miles an hour. The Nicaraguan early-warning radar site at Islas del Maiz, fifty miles off the coast of Nicaragua, never had a chance to see the sea-skimming aircraft. Cheetah's automatic jammers activated once when the radar site was only a few miles away, but the Russian-built radar did not lock on or reacquire the aircraft. Fifteen minutes after passing the island radar site Cheetah was over the marshy lowlands of the east coast of Nicaragua.

"Where's all this Russian hardware the Nicaraguans are supposed to have?" J.C. said.

"We haven't hit the worst part yet." They were riding the military crest—the point on a hill where observation was the most difficult—of the lush, green Cordillera Chontalena mountain range in southern Nicaragua, heading northwest at five hundred fifty miles an hour. "We should be safe from Managua

SAM sites, but Sebaco is supposed to be loaded for bear—we could be within range of their SA-10 missile sites in five minutes. Once we bust their radar cordon we'll be assholes and elbows trying to get out of here—"

Just then, they saw two dark shapes streaking across the hills in front of them. The shapes trailed long fingers of flame that were visible even in daylight.

"Oh, God," J.C. broke out. "They look like MiG-29s, heading north."

"The drones are right on time," Patrick said, realizing the MiGs had gone for the diversionary drone targets. A few moments later two more jets screamed northward behind the first two, now less than ten miles from where Cheetah was hugging the green forested mountains. One of the MiGs appeared to start a right turn toward Cheetah, but he was really maneuvering away from his leader as they raced away. They were close enough to see the MiGs' external fuel tanks and feel their jet-wash as they passed.

"If they flushed their whole alert force to chase down the drones we just may be able to go in without visitors."

"When those guys find out they've been suckered by a couple of drones they'll be back in a hot minute and after *us*," J.C. said.

"Ten miles from the first SAM ring," McLanahan said, checking his chart and the GPS satellite navigation system. "Punch off those external tanks any time."

J.C. hit his voice-command button. "Station select two and seven."

"*Stations two and seven select,*" the computer verified. The right multi-function display showed a graphic depiction of Cheetah, with the icons of the two external fuel tanks highlighted. J.C. aimed Cheetah for a deep, thicketed stream. There was little danger of dropping the tanks on any villages or people below— they had seen no signs of habitation since crossing the coastline. The tanks might not be found for years—maybe never. They hoped.

"Ready jettison command."

"*Warning, jettison command issued, select 'cancel' to cancel,*" the computer intoned. The highlighted icons on the right MFD began to flash.

Powell hit the voice-command button. "Jettison . . . now."

*"Jettison two and seven."* McLanahan watched as Cheetah's two external fuel tanks disappeared from view. "Clean separation," he said.

"Safe all stations," J.C. told the computer. The display screen acknowledged the command, accomplishing a release-circuits check and reporting a "normal" and "safe" indication. "All *right*," J.C. said. "Throttles coming up. Time to do some flyin'," and he slowly began moving both throttles up until he had full power.

"Point-nine-eight Mach," McLanahan said. "Speed limit for the camera pod."

"I'll hold it here for now," J.C. said, nudging the throttles back a bit, "but we're not going over a Soviet military base below the Mach. I'm not getting our butts shot off just to protect a lousy camera."

"Five minutes out. Camera's activated . . . good data-transfer signal from the satellite. We're on-line . . ." And then the first warble from the radar-warning receiver could be heard through the interphone. "Search radar, twelve o'clock." McLanahan punched buttons on his forward console. "All automatic jammers active." He reached up and clicked in commands to the radar altimeter, which measured distance from Cheetah's belly to the ground. "Radar altimeter bug set to one hundred feet."

"Mine's set for ten," J.C. said.

"Ten feet?"

"If we're supposed to look inside buildings, a hundred's too high."

"Well . . . we don't have a terrain-following radar on this—" He was interrupted by a high-pitched warble and a blinking "10" on his threat-receiver scope.

*"Warning, radar search,"* the computer reported.

"SA-10 in search mode, twelve o'clock."

"Let's hope that pod can take a pounding," J.C. said, pushing the throttles to min afterburner. "Here we go."

*"Warning, external store overspeed,"* the computer intoned. J.C. ignored it.

"Mach one," McLanahan said almost immediately. "Three minutes to target."

*"Warning, radar tracking,"* the computer said.

"The SA-10's got us already," J.C. muttered.

"Impossible, unless—"

*"Warning, missile launch, missile launch."*

"Signal moved to one o'clock," McLanahan called out. "They moved the SAM site." He hit the chaff button on the left-side ejector. "Jink right . . ."

J.C. threw Cheetah into a hard right-turn. They saw the missile immediately, or rather they saw the smoke trail left by the SA-10 as it streaked by, missing them by scarcely a few dozen yards—one or two seconds slower reaction time and the missile would not have missed. "Goddamn, they put an SA-10 on that hilltop overlooking their base. That was too close . . ."

Powell started a hard left-turn away from the site and let the autopilot center back on the target. "Well, they took their best shot and missed," he said. "If they want to shoot now they'll be shooting toward their own base." Cheetah rolled out on the autopilot's command. "I've got the target," Powell said. "I'll find your precious damn jet for you, Patrick. Hang on . . ."

Andrei Maraklov was watching Musi Zaykov get dressed when the siren pierced the silence of her bungalow. By reaction learned after four years in the Strategic Air Command, Maraklov got to his feet and began pulling on his flight suit. "What's that?"

*"Opasno pavarota,"* Zaykov said, and hurriedly put on her boots and buttoned her uniform blouse. *"Bistra."* Maraklov never had a chance to understand what she said, but the urgency in her voice was clear. He ran out of the bungalow behind her.

Workers were running toward the flight line, some pointing toward the sky to the south. Maraklov started toward the flight line but Zaykov grabbed his arm. "No. If it is an attack you should not go there." Maraklov shrugged out of her grasp and headed for the flight line, crossed the access road and leaped over the low gate—none of the security forces stationed around the flight line moved to stop him, apparently confused by the sirens. He ran into the clear, into an unused part of the aircraft parking ramp and scanned the skies.

He did not see it until he was halfway down the runway—apparently neither did the anti-aircraft battery located at the south end of the runway. The aircraft slid silently down the west side of the runway, straight and level—it was so low that it looked as if it was going to try to land. Then Maraklov realized that he didn't hear the aircraft coming—it had made no noise as it passed. That meant . . . he instinctively cupped his hands over his ears and opened his mouth so the overpressure wouldn't rupture his eardrums . . .

. . . Just in time. The sonic boom rolled across the parking ramp, knocking unsuspecting workers and soldiers off their feet. The shock wave felt like a wall of wind shoving him in the face, squeezing his head and chest in an unseen grip. Men were yelling all around him, as much from shock and surprise as pain. When he opened his eyes he caught a glimpse of the aircraft as it banked hard right and climbed a few meters. The sight turned his blood cold.

*Cheetah* . . .

"I saw it, I *saw* it," McLanahan sang out.

"Me too, third hangar from the right, open doors. Hot damn, there it is, they couldn't have positioned it any better for us."

"You gotta get back over there before they close those hangar doors."

But J.C. was already pulling on the control stick. "Check, boss. Hang on."

McLanahan caught his handlebars just as J.C. yanked Cheetah into a hard right turn. He twisted in his seat so he could search in the direction of the turn for interceptors or obstructions. "Clear right," he called out. "I can see a circular barricade at the south end of the runway . . . looks like it might be a triple-A gun emplacement."

"I saw it," J.C. said, "but we're a good two miles out of range. I'm goin' for the hangar." J.C. completed his turn and leveled off barely a dozen feet above the east side of the runway. A Soviet helicopter and a small high-wing airplane blocked their path, but J.C. kept Cheetah coming down and flew between the two parked aircraft on the ramp. The hangar was the only thing in front of them now, with the cavernous doors looking like huge gaping jaws ready to devour them.

*Cheetah.* There was no mistaking it—the huge F-15 fighter with the big unmistakable foreplanes, the thundering twin engines, twin tails to match, broad wings. It was continuing its tight turn at an impossibly low altitude, barely above treetop level. In a few seconds it would turn perpendicular to the runway heading right for the main part of the base . . .

Maraklov looked down the flight line toward the hangars.

What he saw made him break out in a run. Men and equipment were pouring out of the hangar where DreamStar was parked—and they were leaving the hangar doors wide open.

"How bad do you want DreamStar, Colonel?"

McLanahan took his eyes off the recon pod control panel and glanced at the forward cockpit in surprise. "What?"

Cheetah was aimed directly for the center of the open doors, and they were skimming the runway and parking ramp with less than two thousand feet to go to the hangar. J.C. said, "I got Cheetah on hard autopilot, Patrick. You punch us out, and bye-bye DreamStar."

"You mean *crash* Cheetah into that hangar?"

One thousand feet to go. "Now's the chance, friend. You start evening up for Wendy, Old Dog right here, right now. It'll look like an accident during an authorized mission . . ."

Five hundred feet to go. The hangar doors towered above them. They could see men lying on the ramp, soldiers shooting in their direction, trucks and service vehicles taking off in all directions. They could see access doors open on DreamStar, tools lying on the hangar floor, even puddles of fluid. The camera pod was whirring away, broadcasting its information to HAWC headquarters.

Their immediate mission was finished. The Russians had DreamStar, no question about it—they apparently were in the process of dismantling it, in preparation for sending it back to Russia. Cheetah was a preproduction aircraft—the Air Force was in the process of building thousands of *them*. They would not be sacrificing anything important, and would be keeping one-of-a-kind DreamStar out of the hands of the Russians . . .

Maraklov yelled at the guards to close the doors but it was too late. Cheetah was on top of him before he could run twenty steps, and the quiet, deadly hiss of the shock wave approaching him made him dive for the tarmac . . .

Incredible . . . Cheetah was going to hit. DreamStar was going to be destroyed . . .

"Standing by for ejection . . ." Powell told his commander. It was now or never . . .

*"No."*

Less than one hundred feet from the hangar door J. C. Powell yanked Cheetah on its tail and threw in full afterburner. It cleared the hangar roof by only a few feet—Powell and McLanahan could feel the unearthly rumble of metal beneath their feet as the sonic wave pounded the tin roof. J.C. kept the climb in for a few more seconds, then rolled inverted, pulled the nose to the horizon, rolled upright and leveled off.

"Get us out of here, *sir,*" J.C. said.

"Right turn heading zero-one-zero," McLanahan said evenly. "Keep it on the deck. Ten minutes to the Honduras border."

They flew on in silence until McLanahan reported that they were crossing the border. There were some MiG-29 pursuers detected, but they were far behind them by the time they had reported in to Tegucigalpa Air Defense Control, and an entire flight of six Honduran F-16 fighters was scrambled to turn them away. J.C. ordered the voice-recognition computer to activate the IFF identification radios, then started a shallow climb at best-range power and turned northward toward home.

The roar of Cheetah's twin engines didn't subside in Maraklov's head for several minutes, until it was gradually replaced by the sound of sirens wailing up and down the flight line. Slowly he rose to his feet and surveyed the scene around him.

To his surprise, everything seemed relatively intact—Cheetah had not been carrying a bomb on its centerline station, as Maraklov had thought, or else some major malfunction had kept it from releasing. But from the quick glimpse he got, it looked more like a camera pod than a bomb. Cheetah, it seemed, had come to take pictures. Well, they definitely got what they wanted. They had caught everyone off guard, with DreamStar unprotected and vulnerable.

It had to be J. C. Powell flying Cheetah. Several pilots at Dreamland were checked out on Cheetah, but only Powell would be crazy enough to fly it so close to the ground and so close to the hangar. Any other pilot would have been happy with a hundred, even fifty feet above ground. Not Powell.

For a moment it appeared that whoever was flying Cheetah was going to kamikaze himself right into DreamStar's hangar. Cheetah and DreamStar gone together? Maybe not such a bad ending. But how different was his situation as it was? With DreamStar gone and out of his control, his career was surely at

an end. There was no good future for him in the Soviet Union—
he would be like a tiger, caged for the rest of his life, hunted
by the U.S. and distrusted or worse at "home." He would never
be closer to Brazil or Paraguay than he was right now.

And DreamStar was still safe—though for how long, now that
the Americans knew where it was? No choice but to play out
this hand and see how the cards fell. Somehow the photographic
attack on Sebaco gave him some hope—maybe, just maybe,
DreamStar would fly again. And with the right man at the controls.

It wasn't until they had completed their final air-refueling over
the Gulf that J.C. felt confident enough to approach the subject:

"We could have had them, boss," he said. "You could have
done it."

McLanahan had said nothing the entire flight, except the curt,
monotone checklist of responses required of him. But this time
he spoke up. "I know that."

"The ACES seat would have blown us clear of the impact.
We could have made it out."

"Maybe."

"Why didn't you punch us out?"

"I don't *know* why. Maybe I thought it wasn't my job to
waste Cheetah. Maybe I think we still have a chance to get
DreamStar back. Maybe I thought it was a dumb idea all on its
own. We are still alive, we haven't been captured by the Russians, Cheetah is in one piece and we've accomplished our mission. So if you can stand it, let's leave it at that."

## Sebaco Airbase, Nicaragua

"Where were your air-defense forces, General?" Maraklov said
to General Tret'yak as the commander of the KGB airbase came
over to the hangar.

"*Ahstarozhna, tovarisch Polkovnik.* Calm yourself, was anyone hurt, was there damage?"

"Do you know what that was, General? It was an American
fighter. It was carrying a camera pod or some kind of reconnaissance unit—but it could have just as easily been carrying a
two-thousand-pound bomb. We'd all be dead now if it was."

"I said calm yourself, Colonel. Our air-defense forces were dispatched in response to an intrusion northeast of here near the Nicaraguan radar site at Puerto Cabezas. Our interceptors destroyed two unmanned drones heading back out to sea. Obviously they were part of this attack, used to draw away our defense forces while this fighter staged its pass."

"Well, the lightbulb has finally come on," Maraklov said. Tret'yak obviously did not understand, but Maraklov's tone of voice was clear. "While your interceptors were being suckered away you left DreamStar wide open for attack. Here's another news flash for you, General—they'll be back. They no doubt transmitted those pictures to Washington, and they're being analyzed right now. You can expect a second wave of fighters in a few hours—and this time they won't just be carrying cameras. I know them. You have four MiG-29 fighters to counter a whole squadron of F-15 or F/A-18 fighter-bombers—"

"We will be ready for them, I assure you—"

"Never mind assurances, DreamStar is too vulnerable. We're in real danger of losing it. After all I've done to get it here. It will take your workers another twelve hours to finish the refit, plus who knows how many to get her ready to fly."

"We can transfer forces from Managua to Sebaco and other coastal bases to provide longer-range coverage—"

"You're talking about the damned Nicaraguan air force as if it was a real defensive force." Judging by the expression on Tret'yak's face, Maraklov could tell the Soviet general agreed with him. "They might be good for providing a way for the Americans to deplete their missiles, but if you rely on the Nicaraguans to defend Sebaco . . ."

He did not need to finish the sentence—Tret'yak had finished it for him. They had MiG-29 fighters at Sebaco because Tret'yak did not trust the Nicaraguans to protect it. It would be a tactical nightmare to bring Nicaraguan pilots to Sebaco. Few of them spoke Russian, few spoke English, and few had trained for longer than a month or two with their Russian counterparts. Maraklov was right—they were good for little more than target practice for the Americans.

"I understand, Colonel," Tret'yak said, "but if an attack comes we must deal with it with the resources we have. I will contact my headquarters and request additional defensive forces from Cuba. Perhaps some diplomatic pressure can be applied as well. Meanwhile, the refit of the aircraft will proceed. I will call in all shifts to increase our pace.''

## KGB Headquarters, Dzerzhinsky Square, Moscow
*Friday, 19 June 1996, 1858 EET (1058 EDT)*

Viktor Kalinin crumpled the dispatch in his hand. His senior aide, Kevi Molokov, stood by as the KGB chief swiveled in his chair and stared at a map of Central America that had been set up near his desk. ''The Americans have just flown an F-15 fighter bomber aircraft over the exact spot where the experimental aircraft is being stored. Tret'yak believes the Americans now have detailed, incontrovertible evidence that their aircraft is in Nicaragua. Tret'yak ends his message with an observation from Maraklov that the Americans may attack at any time.''

''Sir, I think General Tret'yak is overreacting,'' Molokov said. ''The United States will not take direct military action.''

''You seem so sure. Yet they sent an F-15 fighter right into the Nicaraguan and General Tret'yak's forces.''

''That was foreseeable, sir. I would have expected a high-altitude reconnaissance aircraft, such as their SR-71 or TR-1 aircraft, but I am sure they did that for show. If they were really serious about retrieving their aircraft, they have a carrier in Puerto Rico that could have been moved into the area by now. That carrier is still in port. They could have sent a squadron of fighter-bombers to destroy the aircraft on the ground, but they sent one aircraft, apparently only to take photographs. If they were going to mount an offensive it would have followed immediately.''

''I almost wish the damn plane *had* been bombed,'' Kalinin said. ''The XF-34 is slipping out of our grasp, Kevi. It's fortunate that the American government is denying the entire incident—no pressure on our government has been applied yet.'' Yet . . .

''We need Maraklov to fly the plane out of Nicaragua before real pressure begins,'' Molokov said. ''Once the aircraft is in our hands we can control events.''

''But I can't stand by waiting for the dam to burst,'' Kalinin said, slapping the table with the palm of his hand. ''I want a way to stop an American offensive *before* it begins. Never mind that *you* think they're not going to start one.''

"That would mean exposing the Central Committee," Molokov said. "Only they can initiate any direct dealings with the American government."

Kalinin paused, considering his aide's words. "We just may be able to bypass the Central Committee. To a degree, at least . . ."

"I am sure it is possible, sir, but can you take that chance? It would mean a major breach of procedure—"

"It's time to reach out," Kalinin said cryptically. "Be sure I have two secure communications lines open all evening."

"Yes, sir, they are open now. But who can you possibly contact that has the authority to act in so little time?"

"This government's golden boy. He is in a perfect position to influence the Americans. Whether he will cooperate with us depends—if he has any skeletons in his closet. I believe a call from KGB headquarters will be enough to get his attention. It is time to see if this star performer also has reason for a guilty conscience."

## The White House Conference Room
*Friday, 19 June 1996, 1605 EDT*

General Elliott watched as the President, Deborah O'Day, Wilbur Curtis, William Stuart and Richard Benson viewed the replay of Cheetah's sortie over Nicaragua. He had had an opportunity to see the tape as it was received via satellite from Dreamland after decoding, and it reminded Elliott of films shot from the first car on a roller-coaster. The viewers were twisting and squirming in their seats as it unfolded.

"This is the forward view," Elliott explained, "as the aircraft approached Sebaco. The F-15 is under attack from an SA-10 surface-to-air missile site. There—you can just barely see the missile as it misses." The huge missile could be seen easily, and Elliott watched the viewers cringe and even move to the left as the missile shot by, missing by only a few yards.

"The aircraft is now approaching Sebaco. As you can see, the base is not very large but its facilities are extensive. Here—you can see an anti-aircraft gun emplacement that we have identified as an older version of the standard S-60 air-defense weapon.

Our aircraft has come up on the base so fast there wasn't enough time for the Soviets to get this S-60 into position. Both the SA-10 and S-60 are fairly old systems. The Soviets throw nothing away."

The scene shifted to a side-looking image, with forests and hills going by in a blur. "This imagery has been slowed down fifty percent—we'll slow it down even more in a moment. Our aircraft is at Mach one—about seven hundred eighty miles an hour." The trees thinned out as the first few signs of the runway environment came into view, but the most spectacular sight was the buildings and other structures racing by—all towering over the F-15. Elliott slowed the imagery down by half again as he continued:

"We are now looking out the left-side camera of the F-15, at the rows of hangars and buildings just off the flight line at Sebaco. We will replay the image without magnification at first. Here—take a look at this hangar."

Even without increased magnification the sight was obvious—it was the XF-34 parked inside the hangar. "It's unmistakable—this is DreamStar. Notice the forward-swept wings, the canards with the trailing edges pointing downward, the chin intake, the slanted vertical stabilizers. This is what the crew saw on their first pass. Now I'll let the film go for the rest of the pass."

In normal speed the scene suddenly swung down out of view, revealing only sky and treetops—mostly treetops, since the fighter was still very low. The scene then shifted back to the forward camera, and Elliott could see Benson grabbing his chair's armrests as treetops skittered past the bottom half of the screen. The image then centered on the hangar again—and remained centered on it. They did not see the top of the hangar. The field of view was centered precisely on the aircraft inside. Their eyes widened as the mouth of the hangar raced forward. It seemed to engulf the entire screen. The needle nose of the XF-34 was aimed right at them. It seemed impossible that the fighter could turn away in time—

The hangar disappeared, to be replaced by a rearward shot as the F-15 sped a few feet above the hangar—they could see antennae and even birds' nests on the hangar roof. The image revolved once, and the trees rushed up again, snapping and whipping around in the fury of the fighter's wingtip vortices.

Attorney General Benson was the first to get out a word. *"That* was unbelievable. Who was that pilot?"

"One of my best test pilots. He flies photographic chase missions against the XF-34. He was the one who almost shot down DreamStar over Mexico."

"He must have a death wish," William Stuart said. "Or else he's completely nuts. How could you let him fly this mission? Wasn't he reprimanded by General Kane?"

"I needed the best pilot for this job. There was no final decision on a reprimand, and I needed him. Considering his performance today I believe he's in line for a commendation."

The President was still blinking from what he had just seen. "I'm very impressed, General Elliott. It certainly sent a message to the Soviets . . . There's no doubt that your DreamStar fighter is in Nicaragua. What do you think they're going to do with it?"

Elliott pressed a button on his remote control. The reconpod imagery rewound to a clear view inside the hangar, just before Cheetah dodged skyward. "That's clear in this picture, sir. You can see across panels on the sides open, and these objects here are fuel tanks. We believe they're modifying DreamStar with long-range fuel tanks. I believe their objective is to fly it out of Nicaragua as soon as possible, maybe to Cuba, maybe even to Russia."

The President nodded. "Well, for damn sure they obviously aren't about to give it back . . . I will call a meeting later this evening with the Russian ambassador and Secretary Danahall. Debbie, Richard, I'd like you to be there. We need to make an official protest. Let's set it for eight P.M. That'll get the ambassador's attention."

"But Mr. President," Elliott cut in, "that won't stop the Russians. By the time that meeting is over DreamStar could be on a Soviet-controlled airbase. We have *got* to keep it from leaving Nicaragua."

"And exactly how am I supposed to manage that? Load up your F-15 fighter with bombs and destroy that base? Send in the Marines? *Think,* General. I can't attack a country that's barely the size of Arkansas and five times poorer without a damn good overwhelming reason."

"This has very little to do with Nicaragua, sir. It—"

Stuart, still smarting from not being included in the plans on Cheetah's recon mission over Sebaco, said: "The world won't care if we say we're really after Russians. All they'll know is that we attacked Nicaragua. Your strong-arm tactics would get this government into deep trouble—"

"All right, enough," the President said. "It's late. General Elliott, I'll expect you at the staff meeting tomorrow morning at eight A.M. We'll go over the situation then and decide what next." As Elliott stood, tight-lipped, and headed for the door, the intercom phone on the President's communications panel beside his desk buzzed and he picked it up.

"Hold it, General," the President called out. His eyes widened with delight. "You're kidding . . . and he's *here?* Right now? You bet, Paul. Send him up." The President scanned the faces around him in the room. "Rewind your tape there, General. Sergei Vilizherchev just arrived. He wants to speak with us."

"The Russian ambassador is here?" Benson said.

"It's just got to be about DreamStar," Deborah O'Day said. "But I never expected them to react first. I was figuring on a world-class stall job if *we* tried to see him tonight. What are you going to do, Mr. President?"

"Listen to what he has to say. I assume he wants to talk about a way out of this. If he tries to deny that they have the aircraft we'll show him this tape." He picked up his intercom button again. "Paul, see if Dennis Danahall is available. If he can be here, we'll ask Vilizherchev to wait until he arrives."

"Yes, sir."

The President put the phone down. "I hate to admit it, Wilbur," he said to Secretary of the Air Force Curtis, "but it looks like sending that F-15 over Sebaco wasn't such a bad idea. We seemed to have gotten the Soviets' attention without getting anyone killed."

"The crew of the Old Dog," Elliott said quietly.

"I accept the reminder," the President said, "but this isn't the time to be settling a score, General. Right now, we want your airplane back. Period."

"Sir, I'm sorry, but I think they owe more than DreamStar," Elliott said. "A dozen good people are dead, plus the destruction of the B-52 and the fighters."

"What *I* want is an end to this whole business," the President said. "We'll still negotiate for reparations, but to tell the damned truth I'll settle for getting back what belongs to us and having the parties move back to their corners and call this one a draw."

Elliott considered pressing his argument further, but there seemed no point to it now. He had spent much of the day on the carpet with the President of the United States after an exhausting twenty-four hours the day before. He had organized a daylight recon mission through a heavily defended Soviet base with no losses, which apparently had forced the Russians to the bargaining table. He had been at it for eighteen hours. He was beat. All right, maybe it was time to let the big-shots do their thing.

The phone rang again. Vilizherchev had just arrived. Surprisingly, none of the few straggling members of the White House press corps had picked up on the early evening visit—since Friday was now considered the first day of the three-day weekend, few reporters hung around in the evening. Secretary of State Danahall was en route; they would make the ambassador wait about fifteen minutes until Danahall arrived and could be briefed on what was going on.

Danahall, partially briefed in his car on the way to the White House, arrived ten minutes later—Cesare had to give him a jacket and tie from the contingency closet—the Secretary of State, working late in his office, looked rumpled. Cesare handed him the coat as he finished with the tie.

"I was wondering where my jacket had disappeared to," Danahall deadpanned. ". . . So Vilizherchev just called the White House and requested a conference?"

"We figure it has to do with DreamStar," Richard Benson said. "General Elliott's group found the aircraft in Nicaragua. We got photos."

"Brad Elliott's group, eh?" Danahall said with a shake of his head. "*That* explains why Vilizherchev is coming out here at this time of night. What did you do, General—create a new Lake Nicaragua with some Star Wars neutrino bomb?"

There wasn't time for a reply. The President gave a nod to Cesare, who went to the formal waiting area and asked the Soviet ambassador inside.

Sergei Vilizherchev didn't fit the image of the stereotypical Russian bureaucrat. Young as career diplomats went, in his early fifties, dark haired, tall and athletic, he wore an Italian-tailored suit, spoke with a slight, well-trained British accent. Altogether as polite and correct as could be. A Soviet cookie-duster, or so it seemed. It was common knowledge that this man would be the next Soviet foreign minister, in a few years, and possibly could become General Secretary.

Vilizherchev strode up to the head of the conference table, where the President was seated. Taylor stood just as Vilizherchev approached him. The Russian ambassador made a slight bow before extending his hand.

"Good evening, Mr. President, very nice to see you again, sir."

*"Dobriy vyechyeer,* Mr. Vilizherchev," the President said in awkward Russian. If Vilizherchev was amused by the President's attempt, he was careful not to show it.

"Thank you very much, Mr. President. Your Russian is excellent. You will soon be able to dismiss all your interpreters." The ambassador shook hands all around and seemed quite at home in the White House conference room—until he saw General Elliott. Then, for the first time, Vilizherchev looked genuinely surprised.

"Good evening, Ambassador Vilizherchev," Elliott said, extending his hand. "I am—"

Vilizherchev took his hand as if he was accepting a delicate china cup. "General Bradley Elliott. It is a pleasure," he said. He shook hands with Elliott, clasping it firmly as he spoke. "It is an honor."

"Have we met before, Mr. Ambassador?"

"Your name and reputation are well known in the Soviet Union, General. I must admit, not always in a friendly fashion, but they are the short-sighted ones. I assure you, sir, many hold you in very high regard in my country. We recognize military genius and patriotism no matter what the nation or politics."

The man knew how to lay it on, Elliott thought. *"Spasiba,* Mr. Ambassador." Cesare motioned to a seat, and the ambassador sat down. Elliott remained standing.

"You asked to see us, Mr. Ambassador," the President asked.

"From the group assembled here tonight, Mr. President, I think we all know what the topic of discussion will be. I must, as I'm sure you can appreciate, strongly protest the overflight of our military base in Nicaragua by your aircraft. It was, as you know, a violation of restricted airspace and territorial boundaries, as well as a serious violation of international aviation regulations."

The President glanced at his advisers, looked at Vilizherchev with an exaggerated expression of confusion. "Ambassador, did you really come here at this hour to tell us this?"

Vilizherchev smiled, shook his head. Ever engaging, no matter the mission. "I would not be so impertinent as to waste your time like that, Mr. President." His accent was so flawless it was hard to remember that he was a Russian. "That was the official statement, Mr. President, and the official airspace-violation protest will be sent through the proper government channels for processing. But I doubt if the pilots on that mission will ever be identified. No, sir, I have come to relay my government's position concerning the incident with the very unusual aircraft."

President Taylor waited, said nothing.

"This is, of course, being recorded," the ambassador said. "And I understand that such a recording is for confidential use only, and I agree to the recording if you, sirs, guarantee that it will not become public and if my office is furnished an unedited copy of the transcript."

The President nodded. Formalities over, Vilizherchev continued:

"We have concluded our initial investigation into this matter, including interviews with the pilot, a reconstruction of the flight path taken by the pilot, and an examination of the aircraft. We conclude that a formal, high-level military investigation must be conducted to discover how the aircraft in question came to arrive at our installation in Nicaragua, why it is there, and what, if any, ulterior objectives the pilot may have had. We are asking your cooperation while our investigation is underway."

As Elliott stared in disbelief at Vilizherchev, Secretary of State Danahall reacted. "If I may . . . Ambassador, this sounds to me like your government is saying that you don't know *why* this aircraft is on your base, that you don't know the pilot and that you were all unaware of any aspect of the plan to steal that aircraft and deliver it to your country. Do I have that right?"

Vilizherchev appeared genuinely surprised. "Excuse me, Mr. Secretary, but I am to understand that you *believe* the media reports that the pilot of that aircraft is a Soviet KGB agent? You actually believe that a Soviet agent, somehow in place and undetected in your military for several years, actually managed to steal a top-secret military aircraft—and that this was a plan de-

vised by our intelligence service? We must clear the air right
now . . .''

"A good idea," Elliott said.

Vilizherchev ignored him. "The pilot of that aircraft is *not* a
Russian, sir. We have identified him as Captain Kenneth F.
James of the United States Air Force, a test pilot in your organization, General Elliott. He has never had any connection with
the KGB or our government in any fashion or capacity—*no as-
sociation with the Soviet Union in any way*, except that his late
parents traveled on occasion to the Soviet Union for purposes of
business and pleasure. I am aware that your press reported that
Captain James radioed he was a colonel in the KGB. That is
nonsense. James is not, never has been, a KGB agent or any
other kind of agent of the Soviet Union.''

The President glanced at Danahall and O'Day, and even
though he returned his clinical gaze back at Vilizherchev, the
momentary hesitancy in his eyes had been detected. This was
not a possibility that anyone had seriously considered. *Was* it a
KGB colonel in that jet? Just because he *said* he was KGB didn't
make it so, and the President, and the others, realized that they
had no *real* evidence to prove the true identity of the pilot.

"Our intelligence service has interviewed Captain James at
out installation in Nicaragua, and we have tapes of that interview
that you are welcome to review. Captain James is not exactly
cooperative, nor has he completely made clear his motivations,
but he has stated that he requests asylum in the Soviet Union.
His request has not been approved; it will become part of our
investigation—''

"You're saying he *defected?*" the President said.

"That, Mr. President, is precisely what I am saying.''

"That's *bullshit*—" Elliott exploded. The President held up a
hand to cut him off.

"General Elliott, I am telling you the truth," Vilizherchev
said. "Your Captain James acted on his own, without coercion
or support from my government—''

"What about the refueling in Mexico?" O'Day asked. "Our
pilots reported that it was a Soviet supply helicopter at that
mountain airfield that refueled our fighter.''

"The details of that aren't clear to us, Ms. O'Day. But apparently Captain James made contact with operatives in Las Ve-

gas and arranged for refueling support. But I am pledging to you that your Captain James had no support from us in planning and executing this operation. We concede only that we were cooperative, mistakenly in my government's view, once he left your country."

"You're lying," Elliott said. Heads turned in his direction, but no one, including the President, made a move this time to silence Elliott.

Vilizherchev turned to face Elliott. "I beg your pardon, sir?"

"Look, we identified the two men killed on my airfield in Nevada. One was an experienced KGB operative. The other was a young, inexperienced infantryman. We've also identified the mortar rounds used during the escape. All were Soviet in origin. James was a KGB agent, and he killed twelve people while stealing a top-secret aircraft from a U.S. military installation. In my book they call that an act of war. Of course, I'm a general, not a statesman."

It was all supposed to be a bluff. KGB Chief Kalinin had assured Vilizherchev that the identities of the two operatives were untraceable. By some standards, perhaps, but the Americans had sophisticated ways of identifying even a badly mutilated body. And Elliott now was describing the two operatives almost perfectly. Vilizherchev decided he had been caught in a neatly arranged trap. To use the American vernacular—he'd been set up.

But, again according to Kalinin, a trace of the mortars used in the attack should have revealed that they were Belgian in origin, not Soviet. They had never been consigned to anyone remotely connected with Russia *until* they were turned over to the two operatives by a dealer in the Dominican Republic days before the operation was to begin . . . Unless there'd been a terrific foul-up, Elliott was just talking to provoke him into reacting, showing his hand . . .

"I would like to see your report on those men and those weapons," Vilizherchev said.

"And we would like to see Kenneth James," Elliott said.

"It can be arranged very soon. I have been in contact with—"

"And I want the modification process discontinued on the aircraft," Elliott added.

"Modification?"

Elliott hit one button on the remote control he held in his

hand. The digital videotape cued itself to the preprogrammed point and the screen flared to life, showing the last clear image of DreamStar taken from Cheetah. The picture clearly showed access panels open, the fuel tanks in position under DreamStar's wings, and jacks supporting DreamStar in position. Vilizherchev studied the image.

"Thank you, sir, for verifying that it was an American aircraft that violated our restricted airspace," Vilizherchev said.

"Thank you for verifying that you have the aircraft and that you are in fact destroying something that is not your property," Elliott shot back.

The film was a surprise as well—Kalinin had not mentioned anything about a reconnaissance film of such detail. "The aircraft was heavily armed when it arrived at our airbase. Since it is obviously an unusual aircraft with systems and devices unknown to us, a thorough examination was necessary to verify that the aircraft posed no threat to our people. Otherwise, immediate disposal would have been called for."

"I'll be happy to supply you with personnel to ensure that the aircraft is safe," Elliott said quickly.

"That will not be necessary. Our technicians are well qualified to—"

"The bottom line is that the aircraft is not your property, it belongs to the U.S. We want it back immediately."

"I'm afraid that's impossible, General," Vilizherchev said, surprised that the President or one of his advisers wasn't stepping in. He turned away from Elliott and back to the President. "I trust you understand, sir, that a complete investigation must be conducted. The aircraft is material evidence in that investigation. We simply can't release it until the investigation has been completed."

Silence. Elliott was being left to carry the ball, for the moment. "That sounds like a dodge to me, Mr. Ambassador," Elliott said.

Vilizherchev's cool was wearing thin. "We have procedures that must be followed in serious matters such as this, just as you do. Let me assure this distinguished gathering that at the end of our investigation all property belonging to the United States will be returned—"

"Including James?" Deborah O'Day said.

"If he chooses to live in the Soviet Union, he will probably be allowed, just as you—"

"You still expect us to believe that James isn't a Russian spy?" Elliott said angrily.

"That's enough, General Elliott," the President said, decid-. ing the two had played out as much as was useful. "Mr. Ambassador, do you have any other message from your government?"

"Only this, sir. My government understands your reasons for the overflight of our base in Nicaragua, and we understand why you shot down our supply helicopter in Mexico. But I have tried to assure you that this aircraft intruded on our territory without our knowledge and that we must conduct an investigation to determine the facts. We expect no interference while this investigation is underway. We ask only for your patience. But we cannot, of course, tolerate any hostile or coercive acts. I remind you again that it was *your* aircraft and *your* pilot that intruded on our base and our ally's sovereign borders. You must at least recognize our right to determine the truth."

President Taylor moved forward in his chair, leaned on the conference table. "Now you give this message to the General Secretary, Mr. Vilizherchev. I don't like threats, however diplomatically put. I don't like being told what to do, especially by someone who has *our* property. You are in no position to make demands on us."

Elliott was encouraged by these opening remarks, but they stopped quickly as the President continued: "I do, however, understand your request for a period of time to conduct an investigation and I will allow it . . ."

Elliott rushed in. "Mr. President . . ."

". . . On one condition, Mr. Ambassador," the President went on, looking at Elliott out of the corner of his eye. "If your government guarantees me that the aircraft you hold will *not* be moved out of its present location, we will take no action against you for a period of five days. After that time we will take immediate steps to recover our property, including the use of naval, marine, and air forces. Clear, Mr. Ambassador?"

Vilizherchev paused. It was incredible—Kalinin apparently had actually got something right this time. The Americans did not want to precipitate a war over this aircraft. The other stuff was face-saving . . . "I will need to confer with my government about your proposal, sir."

"Agreed. But the five-day timetable starts now. If we do not have our aircraft back in five days, we'll go in and get it. I'll expect your government's reply in the morning. Good night, Mr. Vilizherchev." Vilizherchev stood, made a polite but impatient bow to the President, and left. Cesare showed him out.

"Mr. President," Elliott said, "you can't give them five days. We can't afford to give them five *hours.*"

"General Elliott, if I can get the Soviets to agree to keep DreamStar in the western hemisphere, *and* avoid hostilities at the same time, I consider that an accomplishment. Considering the situation I've been placed in." He rubbed his eyes irritably, then pounded the armrest of his chair. "I've considered a military action each time you've presented your arguments, Brad, *each time,* and I always come back to this: we would lose the aircraft, the Russians would score a major propaganda coup and it would be political suicide for this administration. That's even supposing that we destroyed the thing on the ground. If we lost some of our soldiers or flyers in the process, or failed to destroy the aircraft, it would look even worse for us. A military response is just a no-win situation."

"Sir, we've proved that the Soviets are planning to fly DreamStar out of Nicaragua. Just because we've heard from Vilizherchev doesn't mean that they've changed their minds. They can make a deal with us and then go right ahead with their plans. We need to *act,* Mr. President."

Elliott, the President thought, was relentless. Twenty-four hours earlier this guy was on the edge of a dishonorable discharge. Tonight he was interrupting senior Cabinet members, calling a credentialed ambassador a liar, and trying to negotiate with the President of the United States. Still, or maybe because of all that, and despite Benson's warning, he was starting to respect, maybe even *like,* this veteran Air Force officer. But the man was too ready to hit out with military force. He had no conception of the political realities involved. Generals rarely did.

"I have to disagree, General, at least for now. Brad, the truth here is that we have few realistic options. I just feel the repercussions of an offensive against the Russians would be far worse than the loss of this aircraft, no matter how advanced it is. Let's at least wait to see what their reaction to my proposal is."

"I'm not suggesting an *offensive,* sir. My concern right now is that they'll go ahead with their plans to take DreamStar out of Nicaragua—that this visit by Vilizherchev was just a smoke-screen to get us to relax and drop any plans to retake DreamStar. While we wait for a response from the Soviets, DreamStar could be on its way to Russia, and then we would have no recourse except to begin negotiations all over again. That could drag on for weeks, even months—as long as it took to export the XF-34's technology to their development bureaus . . ." Before anyone could interrupt, Elliott continued: "I have a plan, sir, to set up a very small-scale air cordon in the Caribbean—very small, unobtrusive, easily managed but effective. The plan revolves around one AWACS radar plane based out of San Juan, with fighter escort, to cover the eastern Caribbean, and one AWACS operating overwater out of Honduras to cover the northern and western Caribbean."

"Why couldn't DreamStar just blast its way *out* like it blasted its way into Nicaragua, General?" Stuart asked. "You said this XF-34 can fly rings around any other fighter in our inventory. If we put a radar plane and a few fighters right in its way, what's to stop it from shooting them down?"

"If the Soviets fit those external tanks to DreamStar, she won't be in nearly as good condition to fight," Elliott said. He sounded more optimistic than he felt—he was in the realm of pure speculation now. "DreamStar's wings weren't designed for external fuel tanks. My guess is that a small interceptor group can defeat DreamStar in this situation—at least the odds would be nearly even . . ."

"But your plan still calls for an armed response," Stuart said. "You're trying to force this government into a confrontation with the Russians. How many times does the President need to say no to you, General?"

"If DreamStar stays in Nicaragua, sir, there won't be a confrontation," Air Force Secretary Wilbur Curtis spoke up. "Our interceptor task force will be on just another Caribbean training flight. If DreamStar tries to break out, then the Russians will have violated our arrangement and demonstrated a cynical unwillingness to resolve this matter—" he turned to the President— "in which case, in my opinion, it justifies a much stronger response from us . . ."

The President leaned back in his chair, massaged his forehead and stared at the chart of Central America. Exhaustion and strain made the colors in the chart begin to dance before his eyes. "What forces do we have in the area?" he asked.

Elliott was already flipping to the page in his notes in anticipation. "Sir, the forces are essentially in place right now to cover the eastern Caribbean. We can step up interceptor activity to identify all low-flying high-speed aircraft that we detect. As for the northern and western Caribbean, that will be tougher. We should be able to arrange a fighter drag into the area in six to eight hours—"

"A what?"

"A fighter drag, a deployment. Nine fighters from Howard Air Force Base in the Canal Zone would deploy to our garrison staging base at La Cieba on the Honduras north coast. Three aircraft would go on station over the Caribbean immediately with the AWACS bird and a tanker, with the rest rotating in shifts. It may be possible to get support from the Cayman Islands for landing rights, but I'm anticipating difficulties with them allowing armed American aircraft to land there so I've planned this without the Cayman Islands."

The President was impressed that Elliott had already planned this mission in such detail. Still . . .

"This would continue until we could bring up naval support from New Orleans or the eastern Caribbean, either of which would take approximately forty-eight hours to reach the area," Elliott pressed on. "The best we've got available is the carrier *Theodore Roosevelt,* which is deployed north of Puerto Rico on a training cruise. She can be in position in about two days. CVN-73 *George Washington* is the better choice, but she's in port in New Orleans and may take several days to deploy. Aircraft would be armed with short- and medium-range air-to-air missiles as well as long-range fuel tanks. They would intercept any aircraft within range and visually identify each one. If they become overloaded with targets, priority would be given to high-speed, high-altitude aircraft. Although it's possible for DreamStar to make the flight at almost any speed and almost any altitude, the enormous distance he has to go would suggest he'd have to conserve as much fuel as possible, and that means high altitude and as little high-lift, low-speed flying as possible . . . Our pilot's orders would be . . . and this hurts . . . to destroy DreamStar and any other hostile aircraft that may be escorting her that engage our aircraft. But if possible they would try to harass or divert DreamStar toward a forced water landing.''

Elliott finally stopped his headlong briefing, then glanced at Secretary of the Air Force Curtis. Curtis nodded to Elliott and said to the President: ''Sir, I'm recommending adoption of this plan. It's low profile and at least the Air Force's part is easily implemented. We'll need to confer with Navy and the rest of the Joint Chiefs on the deployment of a carrier group, but I'm afraid this situation warrants an immediate go-ahead on the first phase.''

The President looked skeptical as he studied the chart. ''How much danger will it be to our pilots?'' he said, pointing to the map. ''It looks like they'll be overwater for a long time.''

Elliott nodded. ''Unfortunately, that's true, sir. The fighters will have to cover eighteen-thousand square miles of open ocean. Tanker support can keep them in the air for as long as necessary, we'll rotate another flight and another tanker in to take over every four hours.''

''Six-hour missions for them, refuelings every hour, plus the strain of visually identifying and possibly going into combat on each intercept they make,'' Curtis summarized. ''And all of it overwater—not exactly a fighter pilot's favorite place to be.''

''Sounds like you're trying to talk me out of it, Wilbur,'' the President said wryly. He held up a hand as the Secretary of the Air Force began to speak. ''I know, I know, you're just hitting me with the worst. Well, I think it's a lousy plan, gentlemen.''

Curtis and Elliott felt their hearts drop.

''You'd be placing those pilots in great jeopardy because *you* don't trust the Russians to keep their word in this thing. You act like Stalin or Khrushchev is still in charge there.'' He did not try to curb his temper; exhaustion, tension, concern and frustration had all built to a point he had to let loose. ''And all to stop one aircraft and one pilot from *possibly* being flown out of Nicaragua, and all because you two failed to uncover a Soviet agent in your own organizations. No. You're asking me to place more men's lives at risk because of your screwups. You're asking me to put this presidency in jeopardy to satisfy your need for revenge.''

The President swiveled his chair around and stared at the Central American chart. Secretary of Defense Stuart had trouble hiding his satisfaction—there was little doubt that he was going to enjoy being Taylor's hatchet man when the order came down to get rid of Elliott and Curtis. Cesare had motioned in a young steward with a pot of coffee, quietly telling him to keep the President's cup far out of reach in case his temper exploded again.

Elliott glanced at Deborah O'Day, who, to his surprise, seemed to be wearing a confident expression. What did she know? After that tirade, the President wasn't going to—

"General Elliott." The President was pointing at the chart. "I want another option for those pilots. Six to seven hours overwater in a single-seat fighter is too much, especially if they have to keep it up for days. What else have you got?"

Elliott stepped quickly to the chart, finding the place he wanted and putting a finger on it. "I'm afraid there are few other options, sir. In the eastern Caribbean we have landing rights only in Puerto Rico and Grenada, and possibly in Montserrat or Anguilla, but it still requires long overwater periods. It's worse in the western Caribbean. There are several other coastal airfields in Honduras, including Puerto Lempira here, thirty miles north of the Nicaraguan border, but they've been abandoned by the military and probably aren't secure. I wouldn't recommend landing fighters there—the drug traffickers control the area better than the militia. Honduras has a small island, the Santanilla, between Honduras and the Cayman Islands, but their airfield is very small. Nine U.S. fighters and their support teams would quickly overwhelm the place. La Cieba is the best option—"

"Maybe not," Deborah O'Day said. "General Elliott, you've already mentioned the Cayman Islands. Your assessment of that government's response to a request for landing rights may be a bit premature. Sir, I'd like to follow up on this. Allow General Elliott's fighters to take up their stations in the Caribbean. We can get permission from Honduras for landing rights in La Cieba. While the planes are airborne I'll get permission from the Cayman Islands and the Brits to land and service our fighters. The Navy goes in there all the time—I don't think a few fighters will bother them too much. I'll work on landing rights in Montserrat too."

"I don't like this," the President said. "We're risking dozens of lives to guard against a breach of a legitimate deal with the Soviets. But like Reagan once said, 'Trust, but cut the cards.' All right, the operation is approved, General Elliott. *Provided* that we get landing rights in the Cayman Islands and Montserrat. If we don't get authorization, your western fighters will refuel with their tanker, recover in Honduras for crew rest, then return to Panama, and the eastern fighters will stay in Puerto Rico. I'm not going to authorize extended overwater patrols. If they're allowed to recover in Georgetown on Grand Cayman, or Plymouth on Montserrat, I want no more than four-hour patrols over-water. I'll reserve judgment about follow-on naval operations until I get a briefing from the Navy. *Understood?*" Curtis and Elliott quickly said it was.

"Brief your pilots that I want no interference with normal air traffic in the area," the President said. "It's probably full of high-speed jets. I don't want your people scaring any airliners or, much worse, pulling the trigger on the wrong target. Is *that* clear?"

"Absolutely, sir," Curtis replied.

"I'll be on board the AWACS and take on-scene control of the situation," Elliott said.

"I've heard that one before. Wilbur, I want briefings every hour once this thing kicks off, beginning first thing in the morning. And be prepared to stand down your fighters if we get the right answer back from the Soviets."

"Yes, sir."

The President stood and walked out of the conference room without another word. Deborah O'Day went up to Elliott, a smile on her face.

"Thanks for the assist," Elliott said quietly.

She stepped closer. "You owe me one, Bradley Elliott. And I expect prompt repayment, in full."

Elliott studied her bright eyes, nodded.

"Plan on your fighters recovering in the Cayman Islands," she said. "The deputy governor of the Caymans happens to be an old family friend. I hope you can bring a two-seat fighter with you—he and members of his family will probably ask for a ride. He's a nut about fighters."

"I doubt this mission will turn out to be a joy-ride," Elliott said, and shut up as Wilbur Curtis joined them and they all walked down the hall from the Oval Office to O'Day's office. Major Preston served coffee as the three took seats.

"We need to get our staffs together and fine-tune this thing," Curtis said. "Briefing the Old Man is one thing—getting two squadrons of interceptors together for an extended deployment is another." He looked at Elliott. "Problem, Brad?"

"Something doesn't make sense." Elliott walked over to a large map of the southern United States and Central America. "Between naval units normally on-station and our airbase in Puerto Rico, we've got the eastern Caribbean covered pretty well right now. It's the western Caribbean where we don't have enough coverage. Yet we're assuming the Russians would fly DreamStar east toward Russia."

"Naturally," Curtis replied. "Where else?"

He pointed at the map. "Cuba. Cuba is only six hundred miles from Sebaco. Once DreamStar is in Cuba . . . hell, it might as well be in Russia. We couldn't touch it there. Cuba is no Nicaragua . . ."

"But why put those external tanks on DreamStar?" O'Day asked. "Why spend the extra time to bother?"

"I think they still intend to fly it to Russia," Elliott said. "But we caught them red-handed preparing for a long flight. They know we can close off the eastern Caribbean. For now, Cuba is a more logical destination."

"It doesn't make sense to go to Cuba, Brad," Curtis insisted. "Sure, they can protect it better, but Cuba is right on our back doorstep. We have round-the-clock surveillance on Cuba. If we could get the President to buy off on it, we could blockade that island by sea and air. DreamStar could never get out. Besides, we *saw* those extra tanks on DreamStar. Why would they waste the time putting those things on if they only intended to take it to Cuba?"

"I disagree with your assessment of Cuba's security," Elliott said. "We don't have the same military superiority we did back in the sixties—a cordon would be much more difficult. And I think the Russians realize that we aren't going to use a lot of military force to get DreamStar back. This is an election year— they figure Taylor won't hang it out over one fighter." He paused, then rapped his knuckles on the long, thin island south of Florida. "Nope, I'm convinced—they'll take DreamStar to Cuba instead of flying it east."

"What you're saying doesn't make sense, Brad," Curtis argued. "I think we should concentrate our forces on the southern and eastern Caribbean. It would be stupid to fly to Cuba—that wouldn't get them anywhere."

Elliott was silent for a few moments, then: "All right, sir. But we've got the eastern Caribbean covered pretty well. I'll take command of the western task force."

"The Old Man expects you to take the east."

"I only told him I'd be airborne in an AWACS—I didn't say which one. I'll be in real-time contact with the eastern forces at all times from the AWACS out of Honduras. I'll bet my pension they try to pull a fast one on us."

"Let me assure you, Brad," Curtis said, "you *are* betting your pension on this one."

## The Consulate of the Soviet Socialist Republics, Washington, D.C.
*Friday, 19 June 1996, 2015 EDT (Saturday, 0415 EET)*

The voice and data-scrambler system was experiencing severe distortion from solar-flare activity, but the elation in the KGB chief's voice was obvious.

"That is very good news," Kalinin said. He was sitting in the Kremlin communications center in Moscow, sipping tea and waiting impatiently for his aide, Molokov, to finish buttering a plate of *pirozhoks,* his favorite small turnover pastries, with fruit and creme fillings. "The Americans are obviously anxious to avoid an embarrassing conflict so close to their national elections."

"The Americans may have extended their waiting period, comrade Kalinin," Vilizherchev said from Washington, sipping a snifter of brandy, "but they have certainly not relented. They are expecting a message from Moscow in no more than twelve hours agreeing not to move their aircraft out of Sebaco and agreeing to turn the aircraft over to them in five days. If you do not comply they have well-supported and vocal elements of their military that are ready to invade Sebaco and take their property back. They're led by General Bradley Elliott of their air force."

"Elliott . . . a paper tiger, an anachronism," Kalinin said. "Too hawkish for the current government. I estimate he will be forced to retire soon. After all, we removed the XF-34 from *his* base."

"Elliott was at the White House tonight," Vilizherchev said. "Apparently he was the one who staged the overflight at Sebaco today. If he has fallen from grace in the eyes of Taylor's government, they are hiding it very well.''

"Don't worry about Elliott—"

"I am not worried about him," Vilizherchev said. "I am concerned about you, sir. On your behalf I agreed to take their message to my government. The Americans are expecting a reply. But I sense that you are unconcerned about any possible agreements and that you plan to take that aircraft out of Nicaragua regardless of any tentative agreements . . ."

"You will be vindicated in this, Sergei," Kalinin said. "The aircraft will be gone from Nicaragua long before the Americans expect a reply from the Kremlin. The KGB will accept the responsibility for the aircraft, and you can tell the Americans that the rotten KGB ignored your agreement and acted on their own. There's nothing they can do once we have the aircraft except protest. And they will get their aircraft back—after we finish studying it, of course. I understand it is a fabulous machine.''

"I agree, it must be a fantastic machine," Vilizherchev said, "because I believe the United States will retaliate in ways other than just protest.'' There was a pause, with both men listening to the crackles and snaps of solar-generated electrons interfering with the satellite transmission. Then: "About my report to the Foreign Minister . . .''

"Delay it for twenty-four hours.''

Vilizherchev had been expecting this. "That is impossible," he said. "I went to the White House. I spoke with the President. I left the Consulate at night without escort, without leaving an itinerary or contact log. What shall I report—I went on a drive around Washington to see the sights? What if someone in the White House mentions my visit to someone in Moscow and they find out I did not report it? What if this whole incident ends up in the newspapers—the media is behind every lamppost in this city.''

"Calm yourself," Kalinin said. "The missing report will not surface for at least twenty-four hours, perhaps more. By then this incident will be concluded and I will explain everything to the General Secretary and the Politburo.''

"I expect it," Vilizherchev said. "Unauthorized contact with the American government by a member of our government is still punishable, as you know, by life at hard labor. I have a desire to retire to warmer climates than Siberia.''

Kalinin broke the connection without replying. The signal, in any case, was deteriorating rapidly; so was Vilizhervchev's resolve. He was not a stupid man but he had not been in government long enough to represent a danger to Kalinin's power. Unless everything came completely unraveled, Vilizherchev could be trusted to keep silent—after all, having the director of the KGB as a co-conspirator was not such a bad position.

But now it was up to Maraklov to get that aircraft safely out of Nicaragua. All of their futures now rode on him.

## Sebaco, Nicaragua
*Saturday, 20 June 1996, 0-451 CDT*

Andrei Maraklov awoke to bedlam. Dozens of faults were being reported to him at once, ranging in severity from complete system short-circuits to oil leaks. But the familiar rush of power and energy that always accompanied a successful interface with ANTARES was a welcome feeling, in spite of the faults being reported.

DreamStar had undergone a major transformation. Her newest additions were two large cigar-shaped stainless-steel fuel tanks, one suspended under each wing. Two of the four weapon hardpoints on each wing were combined to hold the Lluyka tank's pylon; that, plus the size of the tanks themselves, left DreamStar with the capability to carry only two missiles instead of eight. Inside each tank pylon, the fuel tank's pressurization line was spliced to the wing tank's bleed air-pressurization system, which allowed fuel to flow from the tanks and feed the engines before wing-tank fuel was used. The hardpoint's jettison-circuitry was spliced into jettison-squibs in the pylon, which would blow the pylon off the wing.

There was no time to test the aerodynamic qualities of the fuel tank with DreamStar—no way to determine if DreamStar could even fly with the tanks installed. The tanks could fail to feed properly, feed unevenly, rupture the wing tanks, hit the aircraft on jettison, or flutter so badly that even a normal takeoff would result in a crash. There just was no time to test it. The flight would have to go as scheduled in spite of the risks.

DreamStar's anterior fins were replaced, and the aircraft put back together as best they could after being partially dismantled shortly after landing. The plan was to use DreamStar's own self-diagnostic computer routines to check the aircraft and direct the aircraft maintenance technicians to the problems.

As always, Maraklov activated the radios first. "How do you read, General?"

General Tret'yak stared at Musi Zaykov as the machinelike words came over his headphone. He keyed his microphone: *"Kto dyela?"*

"This is Maraklov, General."

"Colonel, are you all right? Your voice sounds different."

"My voice is altered by computer. I don't think I can speak in Russian. I have several faults that need inspection. The most serious is a left primary-bus short-circuit. The technicians will have to open the left number-four access panel. The bus-module is on the center electronics rack. I will deactivate the system when the panel is open."

*"Azhidan'yah,"* Tret'yak said. "Wait, Colonel, I do not understand you." There was a slight pause as Tret'yak passed the headphones to Zaykov.

"Andrei?"

"Yes, Musi."

Zaykov stared in surprise when she heard the voice. "Andrei, is that *you* . . . ?"

"No time to talk," Maraklov said. "Relay these instructions exactly to the chief of maintenance. I can't start my engine until this problem is corrected."

Zaykov copied Maraklov's instructions down on a clipboard, read them back to verify them, then gave the clipboard to the chief of aircraft maintenance. He read the instructions several times, then finally called to his assistant to get someone to begin removing the left access panel.

"They are removing the wrong panel," the computer-synthesized voice told Zaykov. Musi called to the workers to stop, then directed them to the correct panel. She had to repeat the instructions to the assistant crew chief, who told the crew chief, who issued the same orders back down the chain to the workers. They did not begin the job of removing the fasteners until told by their superior.

"Left primary bus-power is off," Maraklov said after issuing the mental command to redirect the power from the external power cart away from the left primary circuit. "That maintenance chief would be out on his ass in the States. Five minutes to open one access panel—we'll be here all morning.''

Sarcasm did not transmit well through ANTARES, but Zaykov nodded her understanding. ''They are all afraid to touch the aircraft,'' she said. ''They're afraid you will electrocute them. The chief has to order them to do the simplest task.''

''At this rate I'll be forced to make the crossing in daylight,'' Maraklov said.

''They should be finished in a few minutes.''

''But that's only the first of about a dozen major items that need to be inspected before I can launch. It's almost sunrise now. I'll have half the U.S. Navy on top of me before I can fly a hundred miles, and in daylight with two external tanks I'll be a sitting duck.''

''Our headquarters is coordinating with the Nicaraguan navy in sweeping the Caribbean for any American ships that might get in your way,'' Zaykov said. ''So far, they report no American ships closer than six hundred miles, except those in the Canal Zone and Puerto Rico. Besides, we have been informed by Moscow that the Americans have agreed not to take any action for five days. They will be totally unprepared for this.''

''Never mind all that,'' Maraklov said, ''just make those idiots out there work as fast as they can. Every minute I sit on the ground in this hell-hole is another mile closer the Americans can get. . . .''

## One Hundred Miles Southwest of the Cayman Islands
*Saturday, 20 June 1996, 0500 CDT*

''Dragon Five-One flight, this is Georgetown radar,'' the cheerful British voice announced over the command radio. ''Welcome to the Cayman Islands. Stand by for frequency assignments.''

''Now this is what I call a summer camp,'' Major John Coursey said happily, taking another sip of orange juice. Coursey was one of twelve F-16 ADF pilots from Howard Air Force Base in Panama taking part in an operation they had come to know simply as Barrier. Coursey was the leader of Dragon Blue, one of four three-ship cells in the huge fighter formation. The twelve fighters were all from the 107th Fighter Interceptor Group, New

York Air National Guard, from Niagara Falls International Airport, deployed to Panama in one-month rotations. They were all serving their annual training commitment, which for F-16 pilots was always more than the standard Air National Guard two weeks per year.

"One week in Panama is heaven," Coursey said over the scrambled interplane frequency, "but a secret mission to the Cayman Islands is a *real* hardship."

"Cut the chatter, Blue flight," came the order from the squadron commander, Lieutenant Colonel George Tinker. "Okay, listen up. Red, Yellow and Gold stay on me for recovery. Blue, Georgetown Radar will clear you to an orbit just outside their airspace, blocking altitudes from five to thirty thousand. You're required to squawk modes and codes even though you're outside their airspace, but you are cleared to strangle if you get into a situation. Get together with your tanker for refueling, then set up a high- and mid-CAP as directed by Barrier Control. Watch your fuel. No one goes below three thousand pounds over the high fix at Georgetown. Everyone got it?"

"Don't drink all the margaritas down there, boss," Coursey said.

"No screwing around, Blue Leader," Tinker radioed back. "We're expecting some brass on board Barrier Control for this one." Barrier Control was the 767 AWACS radar plane that would be controlling the fighters from its more protected orbit point closer to the Cayman Islands.

"Blue Lead copies. We'll look pretty for the brass."

"You'd better. Dragon flight minus Blue, come right and start descent. Blue flight, watch your gas, and good hunting."

"Blue flight is clear," Coursey reported as he watched the three groups of F-16 Falcon air-defense fighters execute a tight echelon turn to the right as they began their approach into Georgetown, the capital city of the Cayman Islands.

Coursey sucked in his breath. Against the crystal-blue shimmering backdrop of the Caribbean Sea, the large formation looked spectacular—especially to a desk-bound accountant from Tonawanda, New York, for whom the biggest excitement in life lately was having the Delaware Avenue monorail going into downtown Buffalo arrive on time. The Air National Guard was the country's biggest secret, he told himself—he was getting a great Caribbean vacation paid for by Uncle Sam, and all he had to do was fly one of the hottest jet fighters in the world.

"Dragon Five-Four flight, this is Georgetown radar. Squawk mode three code zero-zero-one-four, mode C on, and have your wingmen squawk standby," the juicy sounding controller from the Grand Cayman said.

"Anything you say, babe." Coursey was feeling altogether the hot pilot. He knew his wingmen would check that their mode three identification beacons were in standby—they were placed in standby so collision alerts between fighters in the formation would not continually show on radar—so he doubled-checked his IFF settings and got himself comfortable.

"Dragon Five-Four flight, you are cleared to orbit as required within one-zero-zero nautical miles of BRAC intersection as requested, in the block from five thousand to thirty-five thousand feet. Contact me on this frequency if you require assistance. Clear to switch to tactical frequencies. Georgetown radar clear."

Coursey was about to ask her for an after-hours phone number but it was time to get things organized. "Roger, Georgetown. You have a nice day, now. Dragon flight, push blue."

"Two."

"Three."

"Blue" was the assigned common scrambled UHF frequency to be used by Coursey's flight, the AWACS known as Barrier Control, and King 27, their KC-10 tanker out of Homestead AFB, Florida.

"Dragon flight, check," Coursey called out a few seconds after switching frequencies.

"Two."

"Three," his wingmen responded.

"Station check, report with fuel status." Coursey took a fast look at Dragon Five off his right wingtip. The big centerline fuel tank on the F-16s made the sleek bird awkward looking, not to mention the huge decrease in performance and range—those tanks would be the first to go if they engaged any hostiles out here. Each F-16 carried two AIM-132B European-built infrared-guided ASRAAM (Advanced Short-Range Air-to-Air Missiles for close-range "dogfighting" engagements) and two AIM-120C AMRAAM (Advanced Medium-Range Air-to-Air Missiles for longer-range attacks), along with five hundred rounds of twenty-millimeter ammunition. They were loaded and ready, but out here, flying quietly and peacefully over the sparkling blue Caribbean, trouble seemed a zillion miles away.

"Let's hear it, Dragon flight."

"Two's in the green, four and five hundred all safe, eight thousand." He had called out his overall status, his armament number and status, and his fuel remaining.

"Three's in the green, four and five hundred safe, seven-point-seven."

"Looks like everyone's thirsty here," Coursey said. The large external fuel tanks on the three fighters' bellies were all empty— they were usually empty shortly after a heavy gross-weight take-off—and the internal fuel loads were also depleted by half. They all had about an hour's worth of fuel left, plus the required forty-five minutes reserve. "Lead's got eight-point-one, four and five hundred. Break. King Two-Seven, this is Dragon Five-Four Flight of three on tac blue, over."

"Dragon flight, this is King Two-Seven, read you loud and clear," the KC-10 air-refueling tanker radioed back. "We're receiving your position beacons, codes verified. We're seventy miles north of your position on a heading of two-zero-zero, altitude twenty thousand feet. Over."

"Copy, Two-Seven," Coursey replied. "You've got three receivers at nineteen thousand feet, onload as briefed, point parallel auto rendezvous. Weapons all report safe and ready for refueling. We'll do a few orbits out here to stay in our assigned block, then turn northbound at thirty miles."

"Copy, Dragon."

Coursey began some gentle standard-rate turns in order to burn some time without going outside his assigned airspace. A few moments later he heard, "King Two-Seven at fifty miles."

"Copy. Dragon flight, take route spacing, stand by for auto rendezvous." The two members of Coursey's formation stayed in formation but increased the distance between aircraft to almost a mile. Dragon Four started a turn to the north, and Coursey watched to make sure his wingmen were staying with him.

"Thirty miles . . . twenty miles, stand by for turn . . ."

At seventeen miles, on the dot, Coursey's F-16 Falcon started a left turn and gentle climb. A few moments later one of Coursey's wingmen called, "Tally ho, ten-thirty position." Coursey stared harder toward the crystal-blue horizon and finally spotted the huge green converted DC-10 airliner in the distance.

"Lead's got a tally."

It appeared as if the F-16 formation was on a collision course with the huge tanker, but in auto-mode it always looked like that. Coursey pulled his throttle back to ninety percent and pegged his airspeed at four hundred twenty knots. By the time the computer-controlled turn was done, the tanker was looming over the lead F-16 fighter's nose like a storm cloud, and the autopilot beeped to remind the pilot that the rendezvous was completed.

"Dragon Five-Four flight, this is King Two-Seven boom operator, radio check."

"Dragon lead's loud and clear."

"Two."

"Three."

"Loud and clear up here. Dragon Five-Four cleared to the contact position; Two-Seven is ready."

"Dragon Five-Four moving up on auto."

The tanker's nozzle was aligned less than a thousand feet ahead. Coursey punched off the autopilot and moved the throttle to eighty percent, which, after his years of experience he knew would give him the three-hundred-knot refueling speed he wanted; tiny speedbrake deflections would take care of any excess speed. He opened the air-refueling receptacle on the F-16's spine and checked the status indications on his heads-up display. They showed ready for refueling.

"Dragon Five-Four stabilized pre-contact and ready," Coursey reported.

Coursey carefully guided his fighter under the KC-10's broad belly, following the rows of director lights arranged along the tanker's bottom, until he received a steady yellow light—which placed the front glare-shield right on the tanker's UHF antenna blade.

"Stabilize . . ." Behind Coursey's canopy the twenty-foot boom extended its tubular nozzle, and like some alien mating ritual the boom operator extended the nozzle into the F-16's receptacle. Coursey's HUD indicated CONTACT.

"Contact Five-Four."

"Contact Two-Seven," the boom operator replied. At that, the copilot on the KC-10 activated the refueling boost pumps and began transferring fuel. When the boom operator's flow panel showed a positive transfer rate, he reported, "Taking fuel."

"Give me five thousand and we'll cycle," Coursey said. Each fighter in the formation would take on a token load at first to confirm that their refueling systems were working; once all fighters could take fuel, they would spend more time on the boom and fill to full tanks. Five thousand pounds of fuel took only thirty seconds to transfer. Coursey disengaged from the tanker and swung out to the left to let Dragon Five-Five in on the boom.

The pilot aboard Five-Five, a young lieutenant who had just finished F-16 training and then reported directly into the Guard, had a bit more trouble completing the rendezvous. On his first attempt he moved no closer than ten feet from the extended nozzle.

"Forward ten, Dragon Five-Five," the boom operator prompted. Coursey could see the F-16 inch closer, but he always pulled off too much speed or ducked down away from the nozzle.

"Forward twelve."

Impatience got the better of him. This time he shoved in too much power and overcorrected. The F-16 slid under the KC-10 so far that the vertical stabilizer looked as if it was going to scrape against the refueler's boom pod.

"Breakaway, breakaway, breakaway," the boom operator called out. Not exactly an emergency situation but the KC-10's response was automatic—the boom shot full up into its retracted position, the engines went to full power, the tanker began a steady climb. Dragon Five yanked off his power and slid out of sight. Coursey and Dragon Six stayed on the tanker's wingtip as it pulled ahead.

"Two-Seven, this is Dragon Leader, Dragon Five-Five is well clear," Coursey radioed to the tanker, trying to keep Five in sight. "Cancel breakaway. Clear Dragon Five-Six to the contact position, and clear Dragon Five-Five to the right wing. Five-Five, take a breather and try to relax."

"Dragon Five-Five, clear to Dragon Five-Six's right wing," the boom operator said. The F-16 that had balked its hookup reappeared, sliding under Dragon Five-Six and moving into position on Six's right wingtip.

"Dragon Five-Five is on your right, Five-Six."

"Dragon Five-Six, clear to the contact position, Two-Seven is ready." Five-Six moved smoothly down into contact position, and fifteen seconds later it was taking fuel. A minute later he was back off Five-Five's right wing, and Dragon Five-Five was moving back into contact position.

"All right, Myers," Coursey told the pilot of Dragon Five-Five, "you've already embarrassed yourself in front of these tankers toads—try not to do it again. Remember, these Falcons don't like being muscled around. They respond to gentle inputs. Just like the ladies. Remember your visual cues and for God's sake, relax."

He watched as Dragon Five-Five again began his approach to contact position. Myers needed this hookup for much more than just to avoid embarrassment. If he didn't get his refueling on this pass he'd have to take the tanker, turn north and attempt another contact while heading for Georgetown. It would be highly embarrassing for one of Coursey's wingmen to come back alone because he couldn't accomplish a refueling, especially in near-ideal weather conditions. But whatever else Myers had on his mind, he apparently had finally managed to put it behind him as he made contact with the KC-10 on the first try.

"Fill 'er up, Two-Seven," Coursey said. "We'll top off in reverse order. I'll be on radio two." Coursey switched radios momentarily to his second non-scrambled UHF radio. "Barrier Control, this is Dragon Five-Four flight. How copy?"

"Dragon Five-Four flight, this is Barrier Control, loud and clear. Over."

"We will complete refueling in one-zero minutes," Coursey said. "Looks like we'll have three birds in the green. We'll be in the center of the assigned area at completion. Over."

"Copy all, Dragon flight," the controller replied. "First response will be in approximately zero-eight minutes. Upon completion of refueling, take flight level two-five-zero and heading two-zero-five for your first intercept."

"Copy all, Barrier. We'll report back when refueling is complete."

Dragon Five-Five was topped off in three minutes, after easing out of the boom's refueling envelope twice. Five-Six had an easier time of it, completing his refueling in two minutes. Coursey took a bit longer than two minutes, electing to use lower pump pressure from the tanker to avoid pressure disconnects, which would result in less than completely full tanks. The KC-10 then executed a right turn and headed north for its orbit point near Georgetown, and Dragon flight headed southwest toward their first intercept.

"Five-Five, you got the high CAP," Coursey said. "Top of the block is three-five-oh, so take three-three for now." The high CAP (Combat Air Patrol) was an overlook position from where he could react quickly to hostile situations below him.

Coursey hoped as Dragon Five-Five started his climb to thirty-three thousand feet that the advantages of the high-combat air patrol would make up for Myers' inexperience.

"Barrier, Dragon flight on blue," Coursey called on the scrambled command radio. "Two on heading two-zero-five and twenty-five thousand feet. One on the high CAP at three-three-oh."

"Roger, Dragon," the controller on board the Boeing 767 AWACS radar aircraft replied, "your bogey is at twelve moving to one o'clock, forty miles." Coursey checked his infrared spotting scope, which was slaved to the data-link from the AWACS— right on the money. The F-16's infrared seeker laid an aiming square on the target and began feeding targeting information to the missile's weapons computer.

"Dragon has IR lock, twelve o'clock."

"That's your target, Dragon," the controller confirmed.

Coursey started a left turn to take a greater angle into the target. The target wasn't maneuvering.

"Dragon, we've got modes and codes on this one," the controller said. "Verify I.D. and make sure he's a solo."

"Rog." Coursey allowed himself to relax a bit. "Modes and codes," meant the AWACS was picking up standard airlincr-beacon codes, such as air-traffic control codes and altitude read-outs, but they wanted each aircraft checked out visually anyway. Apparently whoever they were looking for could transmit standard codes. They were also expecting whoever they were looking for to be either traveling in a formation or trying to sneak through underneath another aircraft, a tactic that even in high-tech, super-electronic times could still only be detected visually.

"Twenty miles, one o'clock," the controller said.

"Five-Six, take spacing, coming right," Coursey ordered. Dragon Five-Six did a slow aileron roll to the right, which instantly increased his spacing from his leader to about a half-mile. When he was stabilized in route formation, Coursey started a turn toward his bogey.

"Twelve o'clock, ten miles."

"Tally Ho, Five-Four," Coursey called out. The aircraft was just off the right side of his F-16's nose, heading north. It was still not maneuvering, nor was it giving off any telltale radar emissions of its own.

"Five-Four, this is a message from Barrier command, don't let the target's crew see you out there," the controller of the AWACS said. "Select a course well aft of the cockpit and any cabin windows. Over."

"Copy, Dragon flight, check."

"Two."

"Three."

Coursey maneuvered around behind the aircraft and its left elevator, well out of sight of the pilot and anyone looking out the windows. He could understand Barrier's concern—airline pilots, not to mention passengers, got very nervous with armed fighters swarming nearby.

"Barrier, looks like we got a Boeing 707, cargo configuration," Coursey reported. As he closed in, he continued, "It has Varig colors on its tail. Stand by for serial number. Five-Six, take the right side and stay out of sight." Dragon Five-Six peeled off and began to converge on the 707's right side. Coursey pulled in close to the vertical stabilizer, well clear of the plane should it make a sudden turn. "I copy M as in Mike, five-seven-oh-seven-three alpha. No music, no weapons"—"music" meaning any hostile radar emissions or jamming.

"Belly's clear," the pilot on Dragon Five-Six reported.

"Dragon, this is Barrier. I.D. confirmed on your bogey. Resume patrol orbit and stand by."

"Roger, Barrier." Coursey rolled left away from the airliner, then took a second to check his position.

"Barrier, what are we supposed to be looking for?" Coursey asked.

A slight pause, then: "Stand by, Five-Four."

They were asking the brass on board if it was okay to tell the guard puke what he was doing in the middle of nowhere, chasing down airliners, for God's sake. He had a feeling the answer was going to be don't ask stupid questions, guard puke.

He got his answer sixty seconds later: "Five-Four, command says you'll know it when you see it."

"Say again, Barrier?"

Another pause; then a different voice came on the radio: "Dragon flight, your target is a single-seat fighter aircraft. It may be armed, and it may be escorted by one or more Soviet aircraft. It may be supported by a Soviet tanker. The aircraft may have U.S. Air Force markings on it. It must still be considered hostile."

"An American aircraft? We're going after an American aircraft?"

"The bad guys got it, Major," the voice said. "We want it back. Your job is to identify it, force it to follow you to Georgetown, or if necessary destroy it. Those are your orders, Major Coursey. Over and *out.*"

This was becoming less and less like a Caribbean vacation, Coursey thought.

"Five-Six, I've got the lead. Join on the right."

"Three."

"Five-Five, maintain your high CAP until the next refueling, then you'll swap with Five-Six. Set best endurance power. Seems this is going to be one long day."

Colonel Edward Marsch, commander of the 21st Airborne Warning and Command Squadron from Tinker AFB, looked at General Bradley Elliott and shrugged when they heard Coursey's reaction. "Air Force Reserve boys," he said.

"No need to apologize for him, Colonel," Elliott said. "I should be apologizing *to him*. He's the one putting his ass on the line."

"How long do you think we'll be on station?"

"If I'm wrong we'll get recalled in about six to eight hours. If I'm right, things will start happening in the next two, three hours."

"Which should I be hoping for, sir?"

No answer. Either way, Elliott thought, it had already turned into a nightmare.

*20 June 1996, 0840 CST*

"Dragon Five-Seven flight of three reporting airborne," the communications officer relayed to General Elliott. "ETA one-five minutes."

Elliott nodded, took another sip of coffee. It seemed that the Russians would actually honor the agreement drawn up with Vil-izherchev. They had come up empty on each of the twelve intercepts the three F-16 Falcon interceptors had performed. Although there had been no recall order it was only ten A.M. in Washington. Still plenty of time for an agreement to be struck. They could already be on the phone together making a deal.

"Dragon Five-Five, you take the lead," Elliott heard the interceptor-formation leader, Major Coursey, say on the command radio. "Five-Six, you're on his wing. I'll take the high CAP. Let's see if you guys have learned anything today."

"Two."

"Three."

Lieutenant Myers, the pilot of Dragon Five-Five, called out: "I've got the lead. Dragon Five-Four, clear to climb and clear the formation. Five-Six, clear to my right wing."

"Three," Douglas, aboard Dragon Five-Six, replied. Of all three pilots he had had the least to say the entire flight—his vocabulary had consisted of the word "three," his original formation assignment. Even when they changed leads, Douglas would always report in as "three" because he had started out in that position.

"Five-Four's outta here."

Elliott glanced at the master radar display. Another aircraft had just appeared on the scope at two hundred miles range. The operator had drawn an electronic line on the screen, depicting the airway A321 and the new target was dead on that line. This airway ran all the way from Rio de Janeiro to Goose Bay, passing near Colombia, Panama, Nicaragua, Cuba, Miami and New York—A321 was the most widely used airway in South and Central America. Every aircraft they had intercepted had been dead on this airway, and each had been transmitting the proper identification codes. When they were intercepted by Coursey and his wingmen they had turned out to be just what their I.D. codes said they were.

The exercise was beginning to wear on Coursey and his pilots, so they had been swapping leads on each intercept. For the first time, the least inexperienced pilot, Myers on Five-Five, was going to be in the lead for an intercept.

"What's the inside pitch on Myers, Ed?" Elliott asked the 767 AWACS commander.

"A hard-charger, from what I hear," Marsch replied, checking his duty roster for this mission. "Top in his class at Nellis. One of the first pilots to go directly from an Air National Guard commission to F-16 ADF training. He's low-time but he's good."

Elliott nodded. A good opportunity for Myers to get some training—he hoped that was all he'd get. He checked the data readouts on the newcomer. "Relatively low altitude," Elliott remarked. The new aircraft was at fifteen thousand feet and climbing. "Got an origin?"

"Negative, sir," the console operator said. "I should be getting his IFF data in a minute."

"Five-Four's on the high CAP," Coursey reported.

"Slow down your turn rate for me, Five-Five," Elliott heard on the radio—obviously Dragon Five-Six was having trouble keeping up with Five-Five. In many ways being a formation leader was more stressful than staying on a guy's wing—you had to think ahead all the time. On the wing all you had to worry about was staying on the wing. As lead you had to consider your wingmen's reactions to each of your moves and radio call— every throttle movement, hesitation, control input or decision had a ripple effect on everyone else.

"That's better, Bob," Douglas on Dragon Five-Six said.

Just then Ed Marsch handed General Elliott a messageform. "Message from SAC headquarters via JCS, sir," he said. Elliott read the note, lips tightening; then nodded and flipped the note onto the console.

"It seems the Russians have agreed to the President's terms. They've promised not to move the XF-34 out of Nicaragua. They're negotiating on terms for the removal of the aircraft— they say the aircraft is damaged and unflyable. The pilot will not be returned until the investigation is completed. We've been ordered to stand down. The fighters have been granted a two-night stay in Georgetown but are ordered back to Panama by Monday."

Marsch let out his breath, trying to restrain his relief at being ordered to get out of this duty. His E-5A AWACS radar plane was vulnerable out here, with no ready fighter protection and only a few minutes flying time from Cuba. "I'll order the fighters from Georgetown to RTB," he said. Elliott nodded. To the senior controller, Marsch ordered, "Tell Dragon Five-Four flight to recover to Georgetown ASAP. Set up a refueling for them if they need it—they must be down close to an hour's duration." The senior controller nodded.

"If they can properly secure your plane, Colonel," Elliott said, "request permission for you and your crew to spend the weekend in Georgetown. It beats flying all the way back to Oklahoma. I can find my own way back to Nellis." Back to Dreamland. Back to forced retirement. Back to disgrace . . . ?

"Excellent suggestion, sir," Marsch said excitedly. One weekend in the Caribbean beat a year in Oklahoma City. "I'll work on it *immediately.*"

"We've got an I.D. code on the newcomer, sir," the radar operator at the main console called out. "Checking his flight plan with Georgetown air traffic control now."

Marsch had gone over to the communications section, so Elliott said, "Let's have it, Sergeant."

"Flight plan from Georgetown says it's a flight of three—a Soviet Ilyushin-76 Midas tanker-transport plane and two MiG-29 Fulcrum fighters. One four-zero-nine-six code and one mode C." Standard civilian air-traffic beacon codes; the first transmitted aircraft-identification data, the second transmitted altitude.

"What's their origin?"

"Origin code is MMNP, sir," the operator replied. "Augusto Cesar Sandino International Airport, Managua, Nicaragua."

Elliott slipped on his headphones and keyed the mike switch. "S-One, this is S-Five. Have the fighters from Georgetown turned back yet?"

Marsch's head poked up from behind a communications console as he punched his mike button. "Affirmative, sir."

"Tell them to turn around and rendezvous with us," Elliott said.

"Excuse me, sir," Marsch said and exited the communications console and began to walk toward Elliott, "we've been ordered to stand down—"

"We got two fighters and a Soviet transport heading our way,"

Elliott said. "I want to run an intercept on them. And I want cover for us until they pass."

Marsch returned to the master radar-console and checked the readouts. "An Il-76 and a couple of MiGs. Have they got a flight plan?" The operator nodded. "They're squawking the proper codes, General. They're on the airway. I don't see what the problem is—"

"There's no problem, Colonel," Elliott said. "I just want an intercept on them and I want air cover for us until they leave."

"Sir, the mission is over," Marsch said, "we've been ordered to return to base. Besides, it's crazy running an intercept on Russian aircraft. If something goes wrong we could be in serious trouble—"

"I know what we've been ordered to do, Colonel. I also know what my responsibility is and I know what your responsibility is. Do what I tell you, goddamn it." Marsch nodded, eyes on Elliott. No question, Marsch thought, that the old man meant what he said. He turned back to the communications cabin.

"Have the mid-CAP run an intercept on the transport," Elliott told the senior controller. "But I want no hostile moves out there. Have the mid-CAP flank the fighters, but no radar and no tail-attack aspect. I just want them close enough for a visual on the transport."

"Yes, sir."

Marsch came back to the radar cabin and stood behind Elliott. "Dragon Five-Seven flight is on its way," the radar-console operator reported. "ETA twenty minutes."

"What's the ETA on the MiGs?"

"Fifteen."

"I want one of the fighters in the Dragon Five-Seven flight joined on us in twelve minutes," Elliott said. "How's the intercept running?" Elliott didn't expect an answer; he could hear the strained interchange of the pilots as they closed in on their first hostile bogeys.

"Dragon Five-Five on heading two-zero-five, level flight level two-zero-zero," Myers replied. The transition from flight lead to eventual Caribbean beach bum and back to flight lead was jarring.

"Roger, Dragon," the controller said. "Your target is one o'clock, one hundred and fifty miles, flight plan reports two

MiG-29 fighters and one Il-76 transport. Radar showing one primary target only—'' Only one of the possible three aircraft was positively being tracked.

"What the hell are we doing, Barrier?" Coursey said. He was still on the high combat air patrol, electing not to take over the lead from Myers. The kid needed the experience, and what better experience than intercepting some real Russians? But the sudden switch from stand-down to I.D.'ing some Russians was weird. "Say again our ROE. Over."

"Roger, Dragon. You are to visually I.D. and inspect the transport. Avoid hostile-attack aspects. Do *not* fire unless fired upon. Over."

"You guys got that?" Coursey said.

"Two." That was Myers—his voice was shakier, tenser than ever.

"Three." Even Douglas sounded nervous. These guys were wound pretty tight.

"Listen up, Dragon," Coursey said, "run it like all other intercepts. Take it nice and easy. As long as you don't hit 'em with an attack profile the MiGs should leave you alone—they're on a cruise to the Copacabana, that's all. They got as much right to be here as we do. Follow the ROE and the normal air-traffic rules and we'll be on the beach sipping cubra libras before you know it. Head's up."

"Two."

"Three." Douglas sounded better, but Myers sounded like someone had a vise-grip on his balls.

"One hundred miles," the controller said. "Rate of closure nine hundred sixty knots. Bogeys moving to one o'clock . . . radar now showing three primary targets, Dragon, repeat, three primary targets—"

The radar-warning receivers on the F-16s lit up. On the displays of the three Falcons was a diamond symbol. On the left display the computer identified the radar source as search-radar.

"Dragon's got music," Myers reported.

"Barrier copies," the controller said. "Transport target may be an airborne-radar aircraft, Dragon." The warning hung on the frequency; then the controller added: "Use caution."

Coursey had to laugh into his face mask.

What the controller did not convey to the F-16 pilots was that the MiGs might be planning, computing their attack on them using the long-range radar on the Il-76 just as they themselves would use the E-5's radar to direct an attack on the MiGs. The 767 AWACS controller should be setting up options for the F-16s in case the MiGs started to mix it up. Intelligence reported that the Soviets now used an AA-11 infrared short-range missile, code-name "Archer," and a copy of the AIM-120 launch-and-leave medium-range missile called the AA-15 "Abolish," but that neither was as good as the American counterpart. Well, if things went to shit they were going to find out first-hand about the Russian missile's capabilities.

"Eighty miles," the controller said. "Spacing increasing between fighters and transport aircraft. Altitude readouts on all three remain flight level one-eight-zero." The MiGs were getting some maneuvering room, Coursey thought, but it was unlikely they'd leave the transport unprotected.

"Sixty miles. Flight level one-eight-zero. Moving to one-thirty position. Distance between fighters and transport now one mile."

"Barrier, Dragon Five-Seven is zero-three minutes from join-up," Coursey heard a new voice report. That was Major Tom Duncan, the squadron operations officer and leader of the second flight. The brass must have called back the second flight of F-16s when the MiGs showed up. At least *someone* on the AWACS is thinking, Coursey thought.

"Forty miles," the controller said. "Spacing between fighters and transport now one mile. Altitude still one-eight-zero."

They should just cruise on by, Coursey told himself. As long as Douglas and Myers kept their guns away from them, they shouldn't feel threatened. Nothing's going on here, Coursey told himself, trying to convince himself this was a routine training flight, but he began heading toward the Soviet formation as if running his own intercept on the transport. Radar-warning indications illuminated his threat receiver—he had to assume that the Russians knew he was up here . . .

"Twenty miles, Dragon, moving to two o'clock position."

"Tally ho," Douglas called out. It was just a speck on the horizon, but the huge Ilyushin transport moved into view. From twenty miles away the huge saucer radome, viewed from above, could be clearly seen; it resembled an American C-141 Starlifter with a flying saucer hovering over it. "Definitely an AWACS configuration," Douglas reported.

"Five-Five has a tally," Myers finally said—a few more seconds and Douglas would have had to take the lead. "Coming right to intercept."

"Fighters moving out to two miles of the transport," the controller reported.

Two miles? They were still fairly close to the transport, but two miles' separation was a long way for escort aircraft. They were loosening up their escort duties considerably . . .

"Fighters moving to three miles . . . now four miles, Dragon," the controller said. "Report visual contact on the fighters."

"Five-Six has a tally."

"Five-Five." He didn't sound very positive—Coursey guessed that he hadn't yet picked up the fighters.

"The fighters are breaking off to join up on you individually," Coursey called out on the command channel. "Ignore them. Keep an eye on them, but all we want is a visual on the transport. Be careful—they might try to crowd you or hit you with a radar lock-on. Nice and easy."

Coursey was prophetic. "Dragon, MiGs are pairing up with you, one turning left, one turning right, both climbing. Five-Five, your bogey is at eleven o'clock, fifteen miles. Five-Six, your bogey is at two o'clock, fifteen miles."

"Lead, c'mon down here." That was Myers.

"I said ignore the fighters," Coursey said. "Keep your damned cool." But Coursey found it was getting harder and harder to believe himself—the Russians were up to something. What?

"Ten miles to the transport," the controller reported. "Five-Five, your bogey's at nine o'clock, eight miles. Five-Six, three o'clock, seven miles . . . Dragon flight, both MiGs moving rapidly on your outboard beams, closing rapidly to three miles . . . two miles . . ."

Myers could only stare out his canopy—the twin-tailed MiG-29, resembling a larger single-seat version of the Navy F-14 Tomcat, was in a shallow right bank and screaming right at him. He was not stopping his turn rate . . . Myers called on the radio—"He's gonna hit . . ."

"Hold your position . . ."

But Myers couldn't stand it any longer. With the Mig still a mile away, he selected max afterburner and yanked back on his control stick. Douglas was completely taken by surprise but somehow managed to stay within a half-mile of his leader.

Myers shot skyward, allowing his F-16 to gain at least five thousand feet before even thinking about recovering. Then, noticing his airspeed bleeding off, he rolled inverted to the left and pulled to arrest his ascent—but he had ignored his wingman trying to stay on his right wing. Douglas instinctively rolled left with Myers and found himself at the top of the roll directly over Myers and fast running out of airspeed. "Five-Five, roll right," Douglas called out as he remained inverted and pushed his nose below the horizon to gain airspeed.

Douglas dropped like a stone right at Myers' F-16. Myers had taken a few seconds to roll upright before he yanked his fighter right just in time to avoid Douglas. The second F-16 dropped another two thousand feet to regain its airspeed before rolling upright and accelerating to join up on Myers.

"Myers," Douglas called, "watch what the hell you're doing—"

"That crazy Russian almost rammed me—"

"No one's going to ram you," Coursey told him, "they're just *screwing* with you. You guys are looking like bozos. Now get back there and check out that transport. *Now*. And goddamn it, take it *easy*."

Myers scanned the sky—none of the aircraft was in sight. "Barrier, where are they?"

"Dragon, transport is at one o'clock, ten miles and northbound, two thousand feet above you. Fighters have rejoined left and right with the transport."

Murphy finally caught sight of them. "Roger. Tally ho. We're climbing to pursue."

"Stay behind them," Coursey said. "I want an I.D. on the transport, that's all. Don't mix it up with the MiGs."

Fine with Myers. He waited until Douglas caught up with him, then pushed his throttles back to min afterburner to pursue. He stared at the transport—it looked immense even from this distance. "Something strange with that transport, Barrier—"

Just then the two MiGs peeled off left and right from the transport and made a hard descending turn straight at the two F-16s.

*"They're diving right at us,"* Myers called out.

"Hold your position, Myers," Douglas told his leader. "Hang in there—"

Suddenly, when the diving fighters were less than three miles away, Myers' jaw sagged. Out of the left fuselage wingroot area he saw bright winking flashes of light and realized that . . . God, one of the MiGs had actually opened fire on him with its cannon.

"They're *shooting* at us."

Douglas saw the MiG's descending on them but it was soon clear that they were going to pass well in front of the F-16s. He yelled to Myers, "Hold your—" Too late. Myers saw the cannon firing and rolled hard left, quickly disappearing from view. One of the MiGs turned to pursue while the other MiG continued its dive, passing almost a mile in front of Douglas. But this time Douglas did not turn to stay on Myers' wing. Instead he accelerated and headed straight for the transport.

"Five-Six, where are you?" he heard Myers yelling. "I've got a MiG on my tail—"

"Join up on me," Douglas told him. "I'm on the transport."

"Dammit, get this MiG off me—"

"He's not on you, Five-Five," Douglas said. "He's just buzzing you. Ignore him. Join on me and let's I.D. this transport and go home."

The radar-threat receiver screeched a warning. "He's got missile lock." Myers again. "He's got *missile* lock . . ." The second MiG, which had crossed below Douglas, had apparently zoomed back up and behind Douglas and activated its missile-tracking radar. Douglas ignored it. "I'm almost at the transport, Barrier, there's something going on—"

"You've got one on your tail!" Myers shouted, forgetting about the MiG behind him. "I'll be there in a second—"

"I've got the lead, Five-Five," Douglas said. "Join on my left wing. *Ignore* the MiGs." Douglas stared at the transport. "Barrier, this is Five-Six. I can't yet make it out clearly but it looks like this transport's got three other planes under him. Repeat, it looks like three more planes flying tight formation underneath him. Over."

"Five-Six, look out, you've got one right at your six . . ."

"I said ignore him, Myers," Douglas said. "If he was going to shoot he would have done it before now."

Coursey felt his throat tighten. He keyed his microphone. "All Dragon units, hold your fire." But it was too late. On board

Dragon Five-Five all Lieutenant Myers heard from Dragon Five-Six was the word "shoot."

The F-16's throttle and control-stick grips were designed for rapid touch-and-feel attack-mode activation, eliminating the need for the pilot to take his eyes off the target to bring his weapons to bear. Myers had that procedure down cold. With the index finger of his right hand he hit the MSL step-button to select an AIM-120 radar-guided missile. Selection of the missile automatically activated the attack data-link between the 767 AWACS and the F-16. Target-designation diamonds appeared on the heads-up display and surrounded both Douglas' F-16 and the pursuing MiG-29. Myers hit another button on the top of the control stick with his right index finger, causing a blinking square to surround the target-designation diamond around the MiG—the attack computer was now locked onto the MiG and was transferring attack data to the selected missile. A moment later a steady beeping sound was heard in Myers' helmet, indicating that the AIM-120 Scorpion missile had received its initial flight-course information and was ready for launch.

One last check around. Myers keyed his mike switch. "Fox two," he called over the command radio, then hit the weapon-release button on the control stick with his right thumb. A streak of white roared off the left wing of Myers' fighter; the white finger extended itself directly to the MiG and touched it. A flash of orange billowed out of the MiG's tail, and the dark shape began arcing toward the bright blue Caribbean Sea far below. Large dark shapes fell free of the doomed MiG; seconds later a dark green parachute blossomed out of one of the shapes as the Russian pilot began his descent to the waters below.

"Splash one MiG," Myers called out. "Your tail's clear, Five-Six."

*"What the hell did you do?"* Coursey screamed. "Dragon flight, disengage, clear, and extend immediately . . ."

"Barrier, this is Five-Six," Douglas said. "I've got an I.D. on those birds under the transport. There's two more MiG-29s and another aircraft—looks like an X-29. Forward swept-wing job. Carrying two fuel tanks and two missiles. Repeat, we've got another two MiGs and an X-29 underneath the Midas transport. Over."

A few moments later Myers pulled up alongside Douglas' right wingtip and flashed a thumbs-up. "We're clear, Five-Six,"

Myers said on the command radio—the adrenaline pumping.
"We're—"

Myers' exhilaration was cut short by a thunderous pop, a flash
of excruciating heat, then darkness. The second MiG had instantly, silently, avenged its comrade's death. Myers had forgotten about the second MiG closing in behind him. The Soviet
infrared search-and-track system needed no radar or even a radar
data-link to attack a target—the MiG-29's infrared AA-11 dogfighting missile was slaved to directions provided by the large
infrared telescope mounted in front of the MiG's canopy. At
close range the AA-11 missile did not miss. Now it exploded
directly underneath the F-16's engine compartment, turning the
Falcon's turbofan engine into a one-ton dynamite stick. Myers
never had a chance to eject.

Aboard the 767 AWACS Elliott hammered the console with his
fist. "That's it, that's the XF-34. They're trying to fly it to
Cuba."

"General," Marsch called out, the warning words of Douglas
in Dragon Five-Six still echoing in his head, "what are you
talking about? We've just lost one of our planes. We're suddenly
up against three MiG-29s with only two F-16s for cover. We've
gotta get out of here."

Elliott ignored Marsch and keyed his microphone. "Comm,
this is General Elliott. Priority message to JCS. Give present
position and heading. Report sighting XF-34 in protective convoy with four MiG-29s and one Il-76 tanker-transport-AWACS
aircraft. Send and repeat and get confirmation."

"Yes, sir."

"Colonel, you had better take charge of this mission or I
will," Elliott warned the spooked Reserve AWACS commander.
"We're not running anywhere, so get that out of your head right
now."

"General, I've got my procedures to follow," Marsch said.
"Three against two is superior forces. The second F-16 flight
won't be here for ten minutes—by then we could be at the bottom of the Caribbean. My procedures say butt out—"

"And my orders are from the White House, Colonel," Elliott
said. "I am to find the XF-34, prevent it from leaving Nicaragua, force it to land in friendly territory . . . or destroy it. You'll
have one F-16 on us in one minute to protect this aircraft. Our

F-16s are better than the MiG-29—they can handle it. We're *not* facing superior forces, Colonel, and we're not retreating from this flight. Now take command of this engagement or I will."

"I don't have to take your orders when the safety of my crew and my aircraft are concerned—"

"Then it's no longer your aircraft. You're hereby relieved of command." Elliott seated himself in the commander's seat behind the main radar console Control One and the main defensive radar operator, Control Three; he had his own screen, Control Two, but he didn't know enough about the new system to use it. He would have to divide his attention between three screens to stay on top of this fight. Other radar operators, Controls Four through Eight, would scan the sky around the AWACS at long range for aircraft and ships as well as focus in on each friendly aircraft involved in the fight and warn him of enemy aircraft around him.

He hit the shipwide intercom button. "Crew, this is S-Five, General Elliott. I am taking command of this aircraft. Crew, prepare for air-to-air engagement." He unplugged his headset cord from the intercom box and plugged it into the commander's net. "Control Three, put Five-Seven on a high CAP over this aircraft. He's responsible for a fifty-mile diameter around us. Control Four, can Dragon Five-Eight and Five-Nine get a refueling before their ETA?"

A pause while the radar operator took in the news about the sudden change of command, then another few moments to get his mind back to the fight around them. "Affirmative, sir, but they'd have to wait zero-three minutes for the rendezvous."

"No good. Get Five-Eight and Nine in to relieve Six as fast as they can—he's gotta be low on fuel. Communications, contact Dragon Control in Georgetown and have them scramble a third flight ASAP."

"Roger."

Elliott glanced at Marsch, who stood behind him clenching and unclenching his fists—obviously angry, but also surprised at how well this four-star walk-on was deploying his fighters.

"I understand you have command responsibility for this mission, General Elliott," Marsch said, phrasing his words for the running tape recorders on the control deck.

Elliott did not take his eyes off the main screen. "Colonel, I want you on Control Two. I want you to watch that Russian

Ilyushin and track any aircraft that try to peel away from it. I
want you to identify the XF-34 and track every move it makes.
If it gets away I'll hang your ass." Marsch shut up and went to
do as he was told.

"Dragon Five-Six, bogey at your six o'clock, six miles, MiG-
29," Control One reported.

"Two fighters breaking off from the transport," Marsch called
out. "Looks like they're maneuvering to engage."

Elliott muttered to himself, "Now we *are* outnumbered. I
hoped those two would stay with DreamStar and the Russian
AWACS." Without ready help, Dragon Five-Four and Five-
Six, he thought grimly, we're going to have to get out of this
jam by ourselves.

Douglas aboard Dragon Five-Six yanked his control stick hard
right as he heard the warning from his AWACS. Meanwhile
Coursey had rolled inverted and had pointed his nose down toward the transport, searching for Douglas. He spotted him seconds later, the big MiG-29 dead on his tail. But instead of
following Douglas in his hard break, the MiG was in a dive.

"Five-Six, this is Five-Four, your MiG's going vertical.
Punch your tank. Catch him on the climb."

But by the time Douglas had jettisoned his fuel tank and completed his ninety-degree break to get away from infrared missile
firing range of the MiG, his pursuer had built up enough speed
in his dive to turn hard right and zoom upward. With his nose
high in the air, Douglas rolled out of his break directly in front
of the MiG.

*"Reverse,"* Coursey yelled.

Douglas heard the warning and banged the stick hard left. It
was the right decision—the MiG pilot was expecting another
right break to preserve his energy, was not expecting the left
turn. He tried a fast cannon burst as the F-16 crossed in front of
him but had no time to line up.

"Extend and get your speed up, Doug," Coursey ordered.
Douglas checked the airspeed readout on his heads-up display—
it was down nearly to three hundred knots. "He's coming around
behind you again. He yo-yoed on you. Don't dick with this
guy—he seems to know his shit." Coursey pulled his nose down
and aimed it at the MiG. "I'm on my way, Doug, but you be
smart, play in the vertical. Don't let him drop down on you."

The F-16 regained its speed quickly but the twin turbofans of the MiG-29 had three times the power of the Falcon. In an instant the MiG was back on Douglas' tail.

"Let's try to sandwich this guy," Coursey said after he finally got into position behind and above the MiG. "Break left."

Douglas pulled into a hard left turn but was forced to release back pressure on the stick or risk stalling. The break was not as quick or as clean as it would have been, and he offered an enticing target for the MiG, which instead of dropping down into a low-speed yo-yo maneuver chose to turn with Douglas.

Exactly as Coursey had hoped. With the MiG in a left turn, Coursey used his diving-speed advantage and pulled directly behind the MiG, then immediately went to an AIM-132B short-range infrared missile—and fired. The missile tracked perfectly, missing the fast-moving MiG by only a few feet, but the explosion of the missile's warhead damaged something vital. The MiG pilot nosed his fighter over, trailing a thick black cloud of smoke.

"Splash two MiGs," Coursey called over the radio. "Coming up on your right side, Doug."

"Dragon Five-Four, two bogeys at your four o'clock, ten miles . . ." The warning had barely been received when Coursey's radar-threat warning receiver bleeped.

"Five-Six, break left." Coursey could see chaff stream out of Five-Six's right ejector, and then the F-16 was gone in his hard defensive bank. Coursey broke right, pumping out chaff and flares from his left ejectors, and straining against the G-forces to scan out the top of his canopy for his attackers. He spotted one of the MiGs just in time to see its cannon flashing and tracers stream toward him—the missile had missed but the MiG had enough power to press the attack and go in with his twenty-three-millimeter gun.

The MASTER CAUTION light snapped on and the HUD displayed a WARNING message. Checking the caution panel on the right side, Coursey found a half-dozen cautions lights illuminated but nothing immediately serious—rudder, nozzle, fuel leaks. No fire lights. The shells had ripped across his tail from the top but missed the engine compartment. With the nozzle now stuck in the military position, engine performance in afterburner would probably be degraded, and with the rudder damaged, landing might be tricky or impossible—if he managed to make it to dry land with his fuel leak.

Such inflight emergencies ran through Coursey's mind, but he was able to dismiss them for now . . . his engine was running, his wings were still attached and personally he was undamaged except for his pride. The one overriding thought that stuck in his mind was that the Russians had gotten a shot off at him and had hurt his Falcon. They'd pay for that.

Coursey executed a nine-G turn to the right to pursue the MiGs that had passed behind him. They were in loose route formation, the double-leader formation that was very effective in covering each other, and they were both going after Douglas again. Douglas tried some hard horizontal moves but the MiGs matched him every time.

"Go over the top, Doug," Coursey told him. "Hard as you can. *Now.*"

Dragon Five-Six suddenly heeled, pointing itself straight up in the air in a sharp Immelmann maneuver, held it there for seconds, then rolled inverted and began a sharp descent.

"I'm right under you, Doug," Coursey said as he approached the area where Five-Six had begun his climb. "Roll out." Five-Six rolled upright a thousand feet above Coursey and sped away behind his leader. Coursey selected his M61 cannon and fired as the descending MiGs came into view.

A head-on gunpass was not exactly a high-percentage attack, but for sheer visual impact it was hard to beat—and this time Coursey got a bonus. As the second MiG banked away from him, he could see dark bits of material peel off the upper surface of the lead MiG's wings. It seemed a few of the F-16's twenty-millimeter shells might have caught the MiG's extended spoilers or speedbrakes and chopped them off . . .

This was turning into a battle of attrition, and Coursey knew at this rate he was going to lose it. These fighters had undoubtedly refueled off their Il-76 tanker before the fight began and had enough fuel for hours of dogfighting—Douglas in Dragon Five-Six had to be down to minimums for recovery at Georgetown, and Coursey was in danger of flaming out any minute. Something drastic was in order . . .

Coursey saw it immediately, far below him and to the left— the Ilyushin-76 AWACS-tanker-transport plane. For some reason the Il-76 pilot had driven right into the middle of the dogfight. Coursey selected a radar-guided Scorpion missile and activated his attack radar as he went over the top and aimed right for the forward cabin of the Russian AWACS.

His intentions were noted. Both MiGs broke off their attacks against Douglas and changed directions, climbing to line up on Dragon Five-Four. Coursey could see the Ilyushin disgorge bundles of radar-reflecting chaff and infrared decoy flares as the Falcon's APG-88 radar locked onto the aircraft less than two miles away. The radar-lock tone was intermittent from the Ilyushin's self-protection jamming, but the instant it steadied out Coursey hit the weapon-release button on the control stick, rolled and turned away from a murderous gun-pass by one of the MiG-29s. But the Scorpion was a "launch-and-leave" missile—it needed no guidance from the carrier aircraft after launch.

The missile hit the forward edge of the radome, chewing a large piece out of the circular device. The wind blast immediately lifted the broken, jagged edge and ripped the forty-foot-diameter radome off its support legs and back into the Il-76's T-tail stabilizer. The entire horizontal portion and half of the thirty-foot vertical stabilizer broke free of the aircraft and tumbled away. The Ilyushin transport skidded violently several times, heeling over so sharply that it appeared to be heading into a spin at any moment, but somehow its pilot managed to bring the one-hundred-seventy-ton aircraft under control. The transport made a wobbly turn and headed south, trailing a long line of thick black smoke from its aft section.

Coursey watched as the huge aircraft swerved southward. But as he was searching the skies for the two MiGs, a warning beeped in his helmet. He was down to less than fifteen minutes of fuel, and with a fuel-tank leak, probably much less than that.

"Barrier, Dragon Five-Four is bingo," he radioed as he started a turn to the right. "I'm heading north toward the margaritas. Don't forget to send someone to pick me up."

"Roger, Five-Four," the controller said. "Use channel Bravo for rescue. We will—"

Coursey never heard the end of the transmission. The damaged MiG had missed his shot at Coursey during the attack on the Russian AWACS, but his wingman did not miss. The AA-11 Archer missile detonated on target, igniting the fuel vapors in the nearly empty tanks and creating a massive fireball in the crystal-blue Caribbean skies.

• • •

There was one thing that was hard to teach new pilots and even harder to reinforce in older pilots, Maraklov thought—discipline. The two young MiG pilots on the Ilyushin's wing forgot it, and they got themselves splashed. The second two, more experienced pilots flanking the XF-34 underneath the Ilyushin, also forgot it and it cost them the effective use of the Ilyushin.

Maraklov considered himself very damn lucky to be alive. The impact of the missile on the Ilyushin's radar dome had forced the transport's nose down several meters; only his computer-fast reactions saved him from crashing into the Ilyushin's belly. He had dodged aside just in time to avoid the wild seesawing action of the transport as the pilot fought for control. Now he was tucked back on the Ilyushin's left wing, relaying damage reports to Sebaco Airbase via satellite transceiver and kicking himself for not finding his own way out of Nicaragua.

He activated his radar and picked up the two remaining MiG-29s and the one F-16 Falcon still in the fight. They were widely separated from each other, neither side anxious to mix it up again. He deactivated his radar, activated the tactical data-link, which gave him an image of what the E-5 AWACS was transmitting to the F-16s. The AWACS was still tracking all the Soviet aircraft but had not paired any fighters with them. The data-link was rescrambled in random periods, and without the scrambler's seed code it took a lengthy frequency-scan to reacquire it once it was lost, but when ANTARES was tied into the data-link it provided an excellent means to eavesdrop on the Americans and use their own radar plane to find *them*.

"Escort Three and Four, this is Zavtra," Maraklov transmitted on the convoy's command-frequency in ANTARES's computerized voice, using the Russian word for "tomorrow" as DreamStar's call sign. "Join on the transport immediately."

"We will engage the last American fighter," Escort Three replied. He was the one with flight control damage, anxious to settle the score. A real fool.

"I gave you an order, join on the transport!"

"But the American fighter is retreating, we can catch him—"

"He's trying to trap you," Maraklov said. Too bad ANTARES only transmitted his voice at one volume and one tone, because mentally he was screaming at the two Soviet pilots. "They have two American fighters waiting to bushwhack you.

Join on the transport's wing." It was only a guess—the data-link picked up only the lone F-16 Falcon heading north toward Georgetown—but the American AWACS must have called in for more air cover as soon as they discovered the MiGs. Those fighters would be arriving any minute. Finally the warning sunk in, and a few minutes later Maraklov detected the two Soviet MiGs in tight fingertip formation just above and aft of the transport.

"Escort Three, stay with the transport," Maraklov ordered. "Check your flight controls and fuel. Escort Four, you're useless staying in tight formation. This isn't a damn air show. Take a position low and to the left, into the sun so you can watch the formation and we can watch you." These Soviet pilots were like rookies, Maraklov thought as the fighters deployed themselves. Lucky for them, their machines mostly made up for their carelessness.

"We can make it, Colonel," one of the MiG pilots said. "We could have broken you free past the Americans—"

"Don't tell me what we could have done. You ruined our chances by breaking away from the Ilyushin to begin with."

"Our people were under attack, what was I supposed to do?"

"Those fools in Escort One and Two should not have broken formation either," Maraklov said. "Their actions only provoked the Americans to attack. We must return to Sebaco and reorganize . . ."

Maraklov studied the data-link image just before it scrambled once again. The first F-16 was retreating north, but three more high-speed fighters were approaching. The reinforcements had arrived.

If we can make it back before we are destroyed, Maraklov silently added.

"Dragon Five-Seven, this is Barrier Command, you have the lead of the attack formation," General Elliott radioed over the command frequency. He studied the data-link radar-depictions of the Soviet aircraft on his heads-up display. "The Soviet aircraft are at flight level one-five-zero, six-zero nautical miles, heading south. I want to draw out the XF-34, try to force it down. We'll reinforce your group with Dragon Six-Zero flight when they get on station. Take heading of two-zero-zero to intercept. Over."

Tom Duncan, commander of the second F-16 flight, which was to relieve Dragon Five-Four, was not about to stay on the E-5 AWACS's wing with two MiG-29s in the area. "Barrier, this is Dragon Five-Seven, I copy all. Dragon Five-Six, get on the tanker, then stay and cover Barrier. Gold Flight, I've got the lead, coming right heading two-zero-zero. Take combat positions. Set mil power."

"Two."

"Three." The three F-16 Falcons executed a precise right turn as they spread into a wide triangle formation, with the two wingmen about a mile away from the leader at staggered altitudes, then accelerated to two hundred knots overtake speed.

"Gold Flight, listen up," Duncan said to his wingmen. "We're looking at a three-on-three situation here, but they've lost their AWACS and we still have ours up. The MiGs have been in the fight, and they've burned down weapons and fuel." . . . On two of our F-16s, Duncan added to himself . . . "One of the MiGs may be damaged as well. I want fast attacks, mutual support and heads-up smarts. Watch your airspeed. The Falcon can burn off energy real easy in tight turns but you can extend, regain speed and get back in the fight faster than any bird flying. Keep your speed up and use your heads."

"Dragon flight, this is Barrier Command," Elliott called in on the command net. "Bogeys are at twelve o'clock, forty miles."

Elliott decided to drop the cold monotone of an air-combat controller—these guys were about to face an entirely different threat. "Listen up, you guys. This is General Brad Elliott, commander of the High Technology Advanced Weapons Center. Your target is the XF-34, an American experimental forward-swept wing fighter that was stolen from Dreamland a few days ago."

"Goddamn," Duncan said. "We're going after one of *ours*?"

"Be advised—that fighter is much more maneuverable than the F-16," Elliott was saying. "It fights at high angles of attack. It has a radar that can see in all directions and high-speed microprocessors that simultaneously process attack and defensive information at high speed." Elliott decided not to tell them about ANTARES or any thought-control capabilities—this was going to be tough enough. "It has an advanced data-link capability with the E-5 AWACS; we must assume that the XF-34 is receiving and using AWACS data-link information. The Russians aren't going to allow you to close on the XF-34. You may have to start the attack beyond visual range. I advise you not to engage the XF-34 singly or at close range. He can reverse, change directions and cause you to overshoot faster than you can believe. If you can force him to punch off his external tanks and delay overwater for several minutes, we can maybe force him to ditch. You guys are experienced fighter pilots so I won't tell you your business. But I tell you the XF-34 is a killer. Be careful when you go for a shot. If you lose sight of him, extend and clear—*don't* waste time looking for him because he'll probably be right on your tail. Use your speed and maneuverability and your buddies to get him. Good luck.''

''Bogeys at twelve o'clock low, twenty-five miles to nearest target, fifteen thousand feet,'' the controller said. ''Showing only two targets now. Second target at eleven o'clock low, thirteen thousand feet.''

''Gold Flight copies all, Barrier,'' Duncan replied. Both targets were displayed on his heads-up display as a data-link between the E-5 AWACS and the F-16. Duncan immediately selected an AIM-120C Scorpion missile and designated the leftmost target. The missile immediately received its steering information and relayed IN RANGE and ARM messages to Duncan's heads-up display.

''Let's get the ball rolling. Gold Flight, fox two,'' Duncan said, and squeezed off the first missile.

''They're twenty-five miles behind us,'' Maraklov warned. ''Escort Three and Four, stay with the transport and keep the F-16s away from it. If the Americans get any closer I'll engage and try to keep them busy while you get away. The Nicaraguan MiG-23s should be able to help as we get closer.''

''Shouldn't we counter the Americans now?'' the pilot of Escort Four asked. ''The transport will be sure to get away . . .''

Just then ANTARES transmitted a radar-threat warning to Maraklov's brain louder than any audio signal. He reacted instantly. ''All aircraft, chaff and jink, *now!*''

The MiG pilots reacted quickly, but the AIM-120 missile was detected only seconds from impact, when its internal active radar steered it into its target. A huge black cloud erupted from Escort Three's right wing, which seemed to push the fighter to the left, then hard over right into a spin. The pilot was able to eject and was even accorded the rare indignity of watching his aircraft spin into the Caribbean Sea.

Maraklov rolled upright after his own rapid left turn. A quick radar-scan showed the F-16s still just over twenty miles away—they had launched from long range, nearly the outer limit of the Scorpion. The sky should be filled with Scorpion missiles, but he and the other two aircraft of his convoy to Cuba had survived.

"Escort Four, stay as low as you can over the water," Maraklov radioed to the last remaining MiG-29. "Stay with the transport and protect it as best you can."

Maraklov issued a mental command and punched off his two Lluyka fuel tanks. With the added drag of the tanks gone, DreamStar suddenly seemed to wake up. The offensive and defensive options suggested by the ANTARES computer automatically jumped from a scant few to hundreds of options. Maraklov initiated a ten-G Immelmann, which got him turned around heading north toward the three F-16 attackers.

Maraklov carried five-hundred rounds of twenty-millimeter ammunition and two AA-13 Axe radar-guided air-to-air missiles. The AA-13 was inferior to the American Scorpion—it was a fast and powerful missile, capable at ranges out to forty miles, but it weighed twice as much as the Scorpion and required continuous radar illumination by the launch aircraft to home in on its target—carrying no missiles at all would almost have been better. If he was lucky the missiles might actually hit something—but their primary use would be to break up this well-organized combat patrol of F-16s.

Maraklov picked out the high F-16. He was the spotter, the one who was supposed to detect the enemy first and draw fire until his wingmen could get into position to press the attack. He was also the most dangerous, since in his high and fast position he could defend himself easily yet turn quickly and bring guns or missiles to bear if his wingmen were attacked. Maraklov quickly designated the high F-16 with his attack radar, and at a range of ten miles, launched his first AA-13 missile.

*"Missile launch,"* Duncan called out as his radar-warning receiver blared to life. "Check your trackbreakers, clear to maneuver, pick it up . . ."

"Tally on the missile," John "Cock" Corcoran, the pilot

aboard Dragon Five-Eight shouted. "On me at my twelve. Going vertical . . ."

Corcoran pumped out chaff to decoy the missile, activated his F-16's trackbreakers to jam the steering signals from DreamStar to the missile, and zoomed upward to force the missile to lose some of its energy. The AA-13 locked onto the chaff and almost flew right into the cloud, but finally reacquired its true target and veered upward toward the F-16 when the chaff cloud dissipated. By then the fast-burning solid-fuel propellant had burned out, and the missile was coasting toward its target, losing speed every second. The F-16 pumped out more chaff, rolled inverted and dived straight down. The AA-13 promptly locked onto the chaff once again, flew through the chaff cloud, and exploded.

It had taken the F-16 pilot only a few seconds to defeat the missile, but in that short span of time the distance between DreamStar and the F-16 had decreased from ten miles to two. Maraklov knew that the F-16 could maneuver fast enough to evade the Soviet missile, but that same violent maneuvering consumed every ounce of the pilot's concentration and took a massive physical toll—in extremely hard maneuvering in an F-16 pilots often blacked out for seconds at a time. Maraklov was hoping that the harder the F-16 pilot worked at defeating the missile—he would fall all the easier under a follow-on attack.

And it was working. The F-16 was in a headlong dive after coming over the top in a tight hairpin turn, pulling at least three negative G's. Unlike positive G's, which forced blood out of the head and produced tunnel vision or blackouts, negative G's drew blood toward the brain, creating redouts, which were much more serious. It took, he knew, at least six or seven positive G's to incapacitate a pilot, but only two or three negative G's. This guy had allowed himself to go right out on the edge.

"Dragon Five-Eight, bogey at your one o'clock low, two miles," the controller called.

Duncan heard the warning and scanned the sky for the attacker. He spotted both his wingman and the XF-34. The forward-swept-wing jet was making an unbelievable gun pass—instead of raising its nose to intercept Corcoran, the plane was climbing like . . . like a helicopter, flying horizontally but moving vertically. As Corcoran got closer the XF-34 raised its nose

and slowed its ascent, seemed to hang in mid-air, slowly raising
its nose at the oncoming F-16, tracking it perfectly.

"Bandit, twelve o'clock, Cock, *get out of there,*" Duncan
shouted. Too late. Corcoran barely had time to recover from the
disorientation and fuzzy vision caused by the negative G-forces
in the wild dive when he saw the XF-34 DreamStar angling up
for him dead ahead. He tried to roll away but DreamStar kept
on coming. Now in high-maneuverability mode, with its canards
angled downward, DreamStar's gun port easily tracked the F-16
through each turn and jink—the cannon muzzle never strayed
from the F-16 even during the most violent maneuvers. At one
mile Maraklov opened fire, spraying the F-16 with fifty rounds
of twenty-millimeter shells before dodging clear. The shells
ripped across the F-16 from canopy to tail, killing the pilot in a
fireball of exploding fuel.

"Five-Eight's been hit," Duncan called out. "No 'chute."
The full significance of Barrier Command's warning was obvious now. The forward-swept wing aircraft, the XF-34, appeared to hover, virtually suspended in mid-air as it cut down
Corcoran. No aircraft except a subsonic Harrier Jump-jet or a
helicopter could do that.

But now it was the prey, not the hunter. It had slowed itself
down to practically nothing, which made it, he thought, an almost laughingly easy target. Duncan selected an AIM-132 missile, lined up on the XF-34 and waited until the missile had
locked—

In the blink of an eye the XF-34 had flat-turned, faced Duncan
and began firing its cannon. Astonished, Duncan rolled hard left
and dived, trying to put as much distance between his F-16 and
those cannon shells as he could. He dived five thousand feet,
ejected one chaff and one flare bundle to decoy any missile the
Russian might have fired, then pulled hard on the stick and
zoomed skyward.

The XF-34 was waiting for him. As Duncan brought his F-
16's nose up to reacquire his target he saw that the Russian had
positioned himself to take a shot as he flew above the horizon.
Duncan hit the afterburner and snapped his Falcon into tight
aileron rolls to spoil the Russian's aim . . .

"Extend, Dunk," he heard a voice call out. It was Lee Berry
in Dragon Five-Nine. "Break right and *extend* . . ."

Duncan could hear cannon shells buzzing, pinging around him. A warning horn sounded but he didn't stop to check the malfunction. He halted his wild last-ditch roll, banked hard right, rolled upright and scanned the sky for his attacker as he waited for his airspeed to build.

The XF-34 was nowhere to be seen.

Duncan forced his attention back inside the cockpit to check his instruments and the warning panel. The OIL PRESS light was lit—he had taken a hit in the engine. No smoke in the cockpit or fire lights, so he still had time to head back to Georgetown, but in a single engine aircraft an oil pressure problem was a land-as-soon-as-possible inflight emergency. "Barrier, this is Five-Seven. I've got an oil pressure light," Duncan reported on the command channel as he headed north. "I need a vector to Georgetown."

"Copy, Five-Seven. Heading zero-three-five, vectors to Georgetown Airport, one-one-five nautical miles. Climb as required. Emergency channel Bravo. Search and rescue has been notified."

Duncan angrily clicked his mike in response. They were already preparing to fish him out of the Caribbean. Thanks a bunch.

He keyed his mike. "Gold Flight, check in." No answer. "Berry, where are you?" Still no reply.

"Barrier, where's Five-Nine?"

"No contact with him, Five-Seven," the controller replied. "No IFF, no primary target."

Oh, God, Duncan thought. That guy got Berry, too. He closed his eyes, trying to force the image of his two squadron buddies out of his mind. It was no use. Two hours ago they were together making plans for a luau on the beaches near the casinos—now he'd have to make plans for a funeral.

That last guy was good, Maraklov thought as he pulled his power back from full afterburner to military power. Very good. The F-16 pilot had maneuvered so fast that he never got a clean shot off at him, but he had apparently taken some damage because he wasn't pressing the fight. Maraklov had taken his shot, then immediately turned south at full power and headed back toward Nicaragua to join up with the stricken Il-76 transport and Escort Four.

Dream Star . . . *his* plane . . . was still safe, still with one AA-13 missile and two hundred rounds of ammunition. Fuel was the problem now—almost none left for another dogfight with any more F-16s. He'd have perhaps fifteen minutes of fuel remaining once he returned to Sebaco.

"Escort Four, this is Maraklov," he called on their assigned frequency. "Approaching your formation at fifteen thousand feet, twenty miles behind you. Area is clear." There had been three F-16s in the attack formation, but his spherical scan showed clear. The third F-16 must have returned with his leader.

The pilot in Escort Four acknowledged. The Ilyushin transport and the MiG-29 had managed to climb back to a safer altitude, but the transport looked worse every second. "Clear to approach. Flight Kepten Kameneve reports that the Ilyushin is very unstable and landing may be impossible. He is briefing the crew on ditching procedures at this time."

"Understood."

It seemed the game was up. The Americans weren't likely to send in another jet with a camera over Sebaco. Next time they'd send in bombers. One aircraft carrier loaded with F/A-18 fighter-bombers, or one B-52 like the Old Dog he destroyed in Nevada, could devastate Nicaragua's whole defense network and waste Sebaco. Should he fly his plane back to Sebaco—or to Nicaragua for that matter?

Maraklov initiated a computer database search for all available runways within DreamStar's current safe-endurance range. Possibilities—Belize, Costa Rica, offshore islands belonging to Colombia. All had isolated runways along with possible nearby sources of fuel.

The Americans, it now seemed, were out to destroy DreamStar if that was the only way to keep it from escaping, and the Russians seemed incapable of stopping them. Why shouldn't *he* take charge of defending his aircraft? Besides, maybe if *no one* knew where DreamStar was he'd have a better chance of getting it to Russia . . .

. . . or anywhere else. He tried to be practical, not sentimental. DreamStar was a commodity, wasn't it? A bargaining chip. If he was so worried about what would happen to him in the Soviet Union, maybe the Soviet Union wasn't where he should be. The Americans, Elliott and the rest, would pay a stiff price to have DreamStar back, enough for Maraklov to live like a . . . like an American—

The warnings came in rapid succession. Aware that he hadn't scanned the skies for a few minutes, Maraklov commanded a two-second spherical sweep of the skies, and instantly an aircraft was detected directly beneath them, climbing right toward them at terrific speed.

"Warning, target beneath us . . ." But at that same moment the MISSILE LAUNCH warning sounded—a radar-guided missile was in the air. "Escort Four, break away, bogey at your five o'clock low—"

Escort Four ejected chaff, rolled inverted and began a steep dive toward the ocean, but with the combat damage he had taken in the dogfight he could not maneuver fast enough. The Scorpion missile plowed directly into the center of the canopy, and the last MiG-29 fighter exploded and crashed into the sea.

DreamStar had no chaff or electronic countermeasures, but it had maneuverability that equaled the Scorpion missile. Maraklov turned DreamStar as hard as he could directly for the F-16 that had appeared out of nowhere. He found himself eyeball-to-eyeball with the Scorpion missile itself, seconds before impact.

The plan had worked, nearly to perfection, Berry had said to himself. It was obvious why the XF-34 could defeat them so easy—if he had access to the AWACS's data he could see the attack coming and plan against it. So Berry had decided to disappear from the AWACS scope—shut off the IFF and the data transceivers and drop down low enough to the ocean that his radar blip would be surrounded by clutter from the ocean. It was easy for him to approach the Russian aircraft unseen from sea level, climb directly underneath them, designate both fighters on his attack computer and launch his two AIM-120 Scorpion missiles at the Russians.

The first fighter went down with near-textbook precision, but something must have gone wrong with the second AMRAAM. It was running hot and true right on target, but the missile's plume passed by the XF-34 without even a proximity explosion. Berry flipped on his IFF and data-link transceiver.

"Barrier, this is Five-Nine, splash one MiG."

"Five-Nine, this is Barrier Control . . . Roger . . ." came

the confused voice of the surprised AWACS controller. "Do you
need a vector?"

"Berry, where the hell are you?" Duncan called out, interrupting the controller.

"Head to head with that stolen fighter," Berry said. "He's
mine." The data-link image of the last fighter seemed to hover
in front of him—his velocity had decreased to less than three
hundred knots. Berry selected an AIM-132 missile and centered
the line-of-sight infrared aiming-reticle on the target. This was
easy. The reticle eased into place, and the missile's computer
reported a lock-on—

But Berry did not notice the range rapidly decreasing until it
was much too late. DreamStar had heeled sharply downward to
avoid the Scorpion missile attack; the maneuver had been so fast
that it appeared that the fighter had stopped all forward motion.
The only warning Berry had was the rapidly growing black spot
under the reticle and the sudden SHOOT indication on the heads-
up display, but by the time his right thumb had pressed the
weapon-release button, DreamStar had cut loose with its cannon
in a Mach-one gun-pass. The twenty-millimeter shells missed
the cockpit but tore into the fuselage and engine compartment.
FIRE and EJECT lights snapped on as the cockpit filled with smoke.
Berry clawed for the ejection handle just as the first rolling waves
of fire hit the fuel tanks.

"Emergency locator-beacon coming from Five-Nine's last plotted position," the controller reported. Elliott could hear the faint
clicks of the intercom as the controller relayed position-data to
Communications, which would relay them to the tilt-rotor CV-
22 Osprey search-and-rescue aircraft out of Guantanamo Naval
Base and Puerto Rico.

"Dragon Five-Seven looks like he'll make it, sir," the controller reported. "He's approaching the initial approach-fix for
landing at Georgetown."

"Dragon Six-Zero flight of three will be on station in ten
minutes," a third controller reported. "Do you want them on a
high CAP?"

Elliott had kept silent ever since the third F-16 got hit. He
could do nothing but watch DreamStar head south with the
stricken Ilyushin transport.

"Soviet aircraft moving out of range," Marsch, the AWACS

commander, reported from his console. "Shall I reposition to maintain contact?" No reply—Elliott closed his eyes as the computer data block that read "XF-34 USSR" froze on the edge of the screen while it cruised out of range. "Sir?"

"I heard you, Colonel," Elliott said. "I heard you. We will stay on station over Five-Nine's locator beacon until the Osprey picks him up. Bring the tanker south and arrange a refueling for us if we need it. Arrange a refueling with Dragon Six-Zero flight and have them stay with us until we withdraw from the area."

"Are you going to pursue the XF-34 any further, sir?" Marsch pressed, his own anger rising. "We've got three more fighters on the way, plus three more on the ground—maybe you can waste the entire squadron this morning. Like the commercials used to say—'we do more by nine A.M. than most people do all day . . .'"

"Knock it off, Colonel," Elliott said, too tired to react to Marsch's heavy sarcasm. "If you're looking to get yourself busted . . . oh hell, we've got a pilot in the water—I want you to make sure he gets picked up ASAP. Okay?"

"May I remind the general, we've got pilots in little *pieces* in the water," Marsch said. "We got three pilots killed, sent up against known superior forces. For what? One lousy fighter already in Soviet hands?"

"You just worry about getting that pilot out of the water, Colonel."

Marsch glared at Elliott, but turned to his interphone to give the orders. Elliott slumped in his high-backed seat overlooking the master consoles. Any other thoughts except the images of five out of six F-16s damaged or destroyed and three out of six pilots dead was all but impossible. True, they had exposed the true intentions of the Soviets, but at a shocking cost. Now the decision had to be made—what were they going to *do* about it? DreamStar may have been headed back for Nicaragua, but it was certainly not going to stay there for long. It might just refuel, arrange for another escort and try again—with the U.S. air taskforce decimated by fifty percent it now had a much better chance of making it.

Elliott hit his intercom button. "Communications, this is Elliott. I want a secure satellite link direct with JCS set up soon as possible. Get Air Force on the line, Secretary Curtis direct—

he should be standing by for a report on transponder kilo seven. Set up the call with JCS on that channel if possible.''

"Yes, sir. Kilo seven is active. I should be able to conference JCS and Air Force in a few minutes.''

The mission had gone sour, but its objective, no matter how terrible the price, had been achieved—to intercept the XF-34 and prevent it from leaving Nicaragua. The question remained— would the price Elliott paid to reveal the Soviet Union's deceit be too high for the President of the United States to accept? And what would he do about it?

Orbiting at five thousand feet over the marshy northeast coast of Nicaragua, Maraklov watched as, one by one, crewmen bailed out of the stricken Ilyushin-76 AWACS transport. Because the aircraft was no longer structurally sound, ditching was not recommended; instead, they decided to crash the aircraft in the peat bogs of the Mosquito Coast after the crew bailed out. The Ilyushin had been trimmed for a shallow left-turning descent to allow time for the pilot to run back to the cargo door and jump out. Maraklov watched each crewman bail out, electronically measuring and recording the location of each man as he hit the marshy ground, then watched as the huge transport, still streaming smoke from its mangled tail and ruptured fuselage, continued its left turn, pointed itself toward the ocean and pancaked in just a half-mile offshore.

They had hoped to retrieve the aircraft relatively intact and salvage as much of the expensive electronic gear on board as possible, but their estimates of the aircraft's poor structural integrity were on-target. Even though the plane made a rather gentle belly-flop into the warm Caribbean, the weakened fuselage cracked and tore apart as if made of balsa wood. The last Maraklov saw was the huge wings of the Ilyushin flying and spinning in the air; then the sea swallowed the plane and it quickly disappeared from sight.

"Control, this is Zavtra," Maraklov reported as he electronically recorded the impact point and the point at which the fuselage disappeared from view. "Ilyushin is down and submerged. Stand by for transmission of impact coordinates for possible naval salvage. Requesting immediate clearance to land.''

"Request approved, Zavtra," the controller replied in English, then added: "Plenty of parking space available now.''

The reply, a bitter one, underscored the fast-worsening situation Maraklov faced. Sebaco was virtually defenseless. All four of the MiG-29s assigned to Sebaco had been destroyed—the only aircraft available were borrowed MiG-23 fighters from the Nicaraguan Air Force at Managua and possibly some of Nicaragua's Sukhoi-24 swing-wing fighter-bombers to counter any naval forces that might threaten Sebaco. Sebaco did not even have Russian pilots to man these twenty- to thirty-year-old aircraft—they'd have to rely on poorly trained Nicaraguan or Cuban pilots until Russian pilots could be flown in.

As Maraklov approached Sebaco he noticed the small anti-aircraft artillery guns at the end of the runway. They had piled up more sandbags and scrap-armor plates around the gun's bunker to protect the gunners, but the extra buttresses decreased the gunner's visibility and reaction time. Those too would be useless in a fight.

Tret'yak and his men, isolated for so long in this damned never-never land, had no conception of what was about to be unleashed on them.

Whatever, Maraklov was determined not to allow their short-sightedness spell the end of DreamStar.

# ≡7≡

**Brooks Medical Center, San Antonio, Texas**
*Saturday, 20 June 1996, 1730 CDT (1830 EDT)*

McLANAHAN WAS AWAKENED from a fitful sleep by a hand shaking his shoulder. "Colonel McLanahan? Colonel?"

It was Wendy's doctor. His face looked weary. Patrick's heart began to race and he leapt to his feet. A nurse was removing the plastic airway in Wendy's throat, and aides were wheeling in a gurney. "Wendy . . . ?"

The doctor immediately held up his hands. "She's all right, Colonel, at least for the time being." He paused, referring to a chart he had brought with him. "She has some extensive damage in her lung tissues . . . pneumonectomy may be necessary. I doubt we can wait any longer."

Patrick watched as the orderlies moved his wife onto the gurney and began attaching a portable respirator. "How long will it be?"

"Several hours. I suggest you go home and get some rest. We won't know until morning."

"Call if there's any news."

"I will." The doctor followed Wendy's gurney and the technicians out of the intensive care unit.

It had been an exhausting two-day vigil over Wendy's bedside, waiting to see if she would ever regain consciousness. He wandered in a near-daze out of intensive care and down the silent corridor toward the exit.

Usually victims of an airplane crash were assumed to be dead—the human body was simply not designed to survive the crushing force of a plane crash. The doctors and nurses, although hard-working and very professional, carried out their duties as if they were demonstrating to the victim's family that the Air Force was doing everything possible, while trying to steel the family into accepting the worst. It was evident in the damned attending physician. He seemed more concerned with making the family comfortable than with saving Wendy's life—

McLanahan stopped dead in the hallway. He realized that he had been walking very fast down the middle of the corridor, storming past patients and nurses, his fists tight-clenched. Get a grip, McLanahan, he told himself as he stepped aside and slowed his pace through the corridor. This is no time to go bananas.

As he passed an open doorway on his way out to the parking lot he heard the words "Air Force" from the room's television set. He stopped outside the door to listen:

". . . today would not comment on reports from a Mexican news service that U.S. Air Force jets were shot down by Russian fighters today in the Caribbean Sea south of Cuba. Pentagon officials will only confirm that American military planes were in the area on routine training missions, and that those aircraft were harassed by Soviet, Cuban and Nicaraguan military aircraft. Air Force officials say the aircraft were part of a month-long exercise called Tropical Thunder, an annual joint U.S.–Central American military exercise . . ."

McLanahan turned away to look for a telephone. "Tropical Thunder" was the name of a joint U.S.–Latin American military exercise, but it rarely involved more than a few dozen Marines and a few transports, and it was usually conducted in the United States or Panama. This had to have something to do with DreamStar.

He found a telephone, and got the base operator, who dialed the command post number at Dreamland.

"Command Post, Captain Valentine."

"Kurt, this is Colonel McLanahan—"

"Yes, sir," Valentine, the senior controller at HAWC interrupted, "General Elliott is expecting your call. Can you stand by, sir?"

"Yes, this is not a secure line."

"Understand. Stand by." He heard clicks and digital dial tones in the background; then a voice said, "Barrier, Charlie one, go ahead. Over."

The HAWC command post had hooked him into a UHF or

satellite phone patch with some ship or aircraft. McLanahan considered using his Dreamland call sign on the open frequency, but this guy wouldn't know what he was talking about. He said: "Barrier, this is Colonel McLanahan. Connect me with General Elliott."

"Stand by one, sir."

There was only a slight pause, then the booming voice of General Elliott came on. "Patrick, how's Wendy?"

"Still critical, sir. They might be operating tonight."

"You know we're all thinking of her . . . How you doing?"

"Okay . . . I was watching the news and heard this story—"

"I know which one you mean," Elliott interrupted. "We need to discuss it. If you feel up to it, make your way to the electronic security command post at Kelly. I'll leave instructions on how you can contact me directly."

"I'll get out there as soon—"

"Listen, Patrick. You don't have to do this. If you think you shouldn't leave—"

"I won't know anything more about Wendy for several hours, she's stable now . . ."

Things were obviously happening fast, he thought. There was no telling what sort of aircraft Elliott was in—it was very possible for him to be in some emergency airborne command post, much like his former Strategic Air Command position in the Airborne Command and Control Squadron, ready to take charge of a wide array of military forces. He was probably right on the scene of whatever happened in the Caribbean earlier that day.

But should he leave Wendy now? If she could, she would tell him that even now, with DreamStar in enemy hands, he was still the key in the DreamStar program. At least his place was with the people trying to get DreamStar back, not wringing his hands and letting self-pity take over . . . "I'll be there in a half hour, sir."

"I'll be waiting for your call. Barrier out."

He hurried back to the ICU nurse's station, grabbed a piece of paper and wrote a number on it. When the duty nurse came over he gave her a number to call in case of any change in Wendy's condition. "Tell the controller anything you have, this is my command post number, they'll—"

"I'm sorry, sir, we're only allowed to contact you in person. We can't leave any message in situations like—"

"Then get your supervisor over here. I'm tired of people around here telling me what I have to do or should do or can do. Do you follow me?"

The nurse reached over and took the slip of paper. "I'll take care of it, sir."

"Thank you. Remember, *any news at all.*"

## Sebaco Airfield, Nicaragua
*Saturday, 20 June 1996, 1735 CDT*

Maraklov woke up with the most crushing headache he had ever had—the pain this time so great that the slightest movement of his head or the least bit of light penetrating the room made everything spin. It was severe dehydration, as always. It was like a fierce case of cotton-mouth and hangover after an all-night drunk—the ANTARES interface soaked up vast amounts of water and essential minerals from his tissues to facilitate the computer-neuron connection, causing the sickness—except this was far far worse. This was the second time he had been taken unconscious from DreamStar's cockpit—it was getting very unnerving. He decided not to rush things, but lay in bed quietly with his eyes closed and tried to will the pain away.

A few minutes later he heard voices and footsteps. They were talking in Russian. They did not try to knock before entering, but came right in. Maraklov decided to pretend to be asleep.

"So this is the great pilot?" one voice was saying.

"After today, who can tell?" the other said. "He is the only one who returns out of six aircraft—either he is very lucky or he let the others do the fighting for him.

"Check his arm, check the drip against your wristwatch, then administer ten c.c.'s of—" Maraklov could not understand the word—"if he is not conscious . . ."

Ten c.c.'s . . . ? Maraklov experimentally flexed each arm and felt the stiff tubules and dull pain of an intravenous needle in his left arm. He quickly opened his eyes. There was a plastic bottle with clear liquid suspended over his head to his left. His left arm was taped onto a stiff plastic board, and an intravenous tube ran into a vein in the crook of his elbow. His eyes focused just in time to see a white-jacketed man injecting something into his intravenous feeding tube with a hypodermic needle.

"Hey, Karl, he's awake . . ."

With strength Maraklov thought he wasn't capable of, he drew his legs up to his chest, swung around to his left, planted his feet on the white-coated man with the hypodermic and kicked out as hard as he could. The man stumbled back and crashed against the far wall, slipping to the floor.

"Easy, easy . . ." The other man threw himself over Maraklov and tried to pin his arms and legs down. Maraklov brought the thick edge of the plastic board down on his right temple. He was still struggling but the blow had taken a lot of fight out of him. Maraklov sat up, forcing away the rush of dizziness, rolled away from the second attacker and struggled to his feet. When the entire room seemed to sway Maraklov dropped to one knee and tried to steady himself.

Two arms suddenly reached around him from behind and pinned his arms to his sides. "*O myenya*, Ivan, I have him, get—"

Maraklov bent his head forward, then snapped it backward as hard as he could. He heard bone and cartilage splinter as the man's nose took the full force of the blow. Still on one knee, Maraklov braced himself against the bed and shoved backward. The man landed hard on his back. Maraklov rolled away from him, giving him a chop to the throat. He found a chair, and held it between the second attacker and himself—using it as much for balance as for self-defense.

The second man was done. "*Stoy, stoy,*" he said, holding up his hands. Maraklov had never seen him before.

Suddenly the door to his room opened and Musi Zaykov and two KGB Border Guards appeared, all with rifles trained on the three men. Musi was the first one in. She scanned the room, then: "Colonel Maraklov, are you all right?" She saw the blood seeping from his left arm, shouldered her rifle, turned to one of the guards. "*Pazavetya vrachya. Skaryeye!* Call a doctor. Be quick!" She went over to Maraklov, took a towel from the bedstand and wrapped it around the point where the I.V. needle had come out.

"What happened, Colonel?"

"These men . . . never saw them before . . . shooting me up with something . . ."

Zaykov finished tightly wrapping Maraklov's arm, then helped him back into bed. As he collapsed onto the pillow she checked the two men. The unconscious one was being checked over by one of the Border Guards.

"Karl Rodovnin," the KGB soldier said. "He is badly hurt."

Zaykov turned toward the second man. "What are you doing in here, Boroschelvisch?"

"Administering an injection," the orderly said. "We checked his intravenous needle and were administering his mineral solution into his drip meter when the guy goes berserk."

"I've found the hypodermic, Lieutenant," one of the guards said, holding the plastic syringe. "It's still full and intact."

"Take it and that bag of solution to the infirmary," Zaykov ordered, pointing to the overturned plastic bag of clear liquid seeping onto the floor. "Have them analyze it. I want to know what's in it. Boroschelvisch, you are under arrest. Take him and Rodovnin into custody."

Zaykov turned back to Maraklov. She had not seen him in several days because he was involved in the preparations for taking the XF-34 to Cuba—and she had never expected to see him again when he left. But even in the brief time they had been apart, the changes in the man were frightening. He looked old, emaciated, pale skin stretched over cheekbones, hollow eyes, thinning hair. "Andrei . . ."

She could feel his body stiffen. He stared in shock at Zaykov. "Janet?"

Musi looked puzzled. Janet? The name was somehow familiar, and she scanned her memory trying to make the connection. Nothing. Perhaps someone Andrei knew in the United States . . . "Andrei, it's Musi Zaykov."

His tongue moved across cracked lips. Slowly, his eyes seemed to focus on her instead of some shadowy figure in the distance, and he now seemed to recognize the woman sitting beside him. "Musi . . . ?"

"Yes, you will be all right."

He seemed to relax, let himself fall limp against the pillow, his breath coming in shallow gasps. "Water." Zaykov poured a glass of lukewarm water for him and held the glass as he drank. She soaked a towel and wiped sweat off his face and chest.

"What happened?"

"I don't know. I woke up and saw those guys shooting something into the I.V. I guess I panicked."

"I should say," Zaykov said with a wry smile. "You almost killed Rodovnin. I am having the syringe and the intravenous solution analyzed, and Rodovnin and Boroschelvisch are in custody. The doctor will also tell us if he ordered an intravenous feeding for you. I wasn't notified of it."

He rolled painfully up out of bed, taking deep breaths, trying to force his equilibrium back to normal, then turned angrily to Zaykov. "I don't want any more damned I.V.'s stuck into me."

"The doctor obviously felt it was necessary, you are so dehydrated—"

"I said no more I.V.'s." He got carefully to his feet and began to test the strength of his legs. She was shocked at the appearance of his body—he looked as if he had lost well over seven kilograms since she had first seen him. Ribs and joints protruded, and his muscles, once lean and powerful, looked stringy, weak. "My body recovers just fine with rest, vitamins and water," he told her. "I've never needed intravenous fluids before."

"And I have never seen you so thin before, Andrei. Perhaps the doctor was right—"

"I'm thin because the food around here is *lousy*. Hasn't the KGB ever heard of steaks? The only protein around here is from chicken and beans. Back in Vegas you could get a twenty-ounce steak dinner for five bucks. You could eat like a pig for nothing . . ."

Maraklov paused, resting a hand on the bedstand. He half-turned to Musi. "Vegas," he said shaking his head. "It seems like a century ago." Actually it was only a few days.

"Las Vegas is not your life any more, Andrei. It never was."

"Then what is my life? When do I get to live *my* life? When I arrive in the Soviet Union? I think we both know my life will be anything but mine back in Russia . . ."

Musi had seen this before but never believed it could happen to a man as gifted and professional as Colonel Andrei Maraklov. It was more than the sickness caused by that machine he flew. It was common among turncoats, traitors, double agents, informers, even hostages held for long periods of time who began to identify with their captors. The feeling of profound loneliness, aloneness, invades even the strongest men, the feeling that no one trusted you then, that no one really wanted or cared about you then. But Andrei Maraklov's situation was very different. He had been a Soviet agent pretending to become an American—

actually *two* Americans, as a boy and as a man. Now he had to leave that part of his life and revert back to a strange new world. It was supposed to be his world, but it was now as alien—in a way more so—as America was to the young Russian teenager so long ago.

As a young graduate of the Connecticut Academy years ago, deep-cover agent reorientation and surveillance had been one of Musi Zaykov's first assignments. She had been trained in studying the men and women who had returned from deep-cover assignments, analyzing them emotionally, seeking out any lingering loyalties to their former lives or resentments toward their new ones. Although the personalities were always different, their emotional roller-coaster rides were not. She had hoped Andrei would be different, stronger, better balanced. She was wrong. Hopelessness, paranoia, anger, loneliness, guilt, even impotence—all common symptoms.

The intravenous solutions and injections would all check out, she was sure of that. They would find no trace of contamination, no evidence of conspiracy. Rodovnin and Boroschelvisch would check out as well.

Maraklov had already made complaints about the food—that was typical. He had also complained about the Soviet worker's sloppiness and inefficiency, about shortcomings in the Soviet government, about his new military commanders, about his clothing, water and surroundings. Telling stories about his former environment, making comparisons, was also to be expected. Unfortunately, so was violence.

The instructors at the Connecticut Academy suggested that the closer one could get to the repatriated man or woman, the better the transition would be. Strong emotional ties often resulted—but they could be negative or positive emotions. The "handler" was often the target of the repatriated person's rage as well as his or her love and trust. In this case it was easier to accept Maraklov's love—she hoped that she would not have to bear his hate as well.

She had thought about the Connecticut Academy several times in just the past few minutes, while in the past few years she had hardly given that place even a passing thought. What was it about that place . . . ?

"Andrei, please believe what I say," Musi said, "your country wants you back. They *need* you back. You will be the guiding force of an entire new generation of soldiers and citizens. You will be honored and respected wherever you go. And it has nothing to do with that machine out there. Military secrets are the most transient of all. It will be your strength, your courage, your determination *and* your patriotism that make you a hero to our people, not that plane out there.''

''That's bullshit,'' he said, turning away from her. ''They want me because of what I *know*, not because of what I'm supposed to be.''

''That's only partly true,'' she said. ''Of course, the knowledge you possess is important, even vital to our national defense and security. Naturally, imparting that knowledge will be your primary function when you return. But your usefulness as a man and as a Russian will not end with that.'' She moved toward him and put a hand on his shoulder. ''I can prove it to you, Andrei.''

''How?''

''Come back with me. Right now. Leave the airplane here—''

Maraklov spun around. ''Leave it? *Here?*''

''You are killing yourself every time you fly it,'' she said. ''Look at yourself. It drains you like some kind of electronic parasite. It will kill you if you continue. Leave it. I can order a transport to take us to Moscow in the morning. Take whatever you want from the aircraft—its most vital computers, diagrams, memory tapes, whatever. Or take nothing. The aircraft is in the hands of the KGB. You have done your duty—now let them do theirs. Come back with me to Russia and I guarantee you, you will be treated like the national hero you are.''

He stared at her, apparently considering her words. Her message finally seemed to be getting through to him, she thought. He was finally beginning to believe her . . .

''So that's it,'' Maraklov said. ''You don't think I can deliver. That's it, isn't it? The Politburo doesn't think I can deliver DreamStar—''

''No, Andrei, that is *not*—''

''They don't want me flying DreamStar any more,'' he continued angrily. ''They never did. I delivered it. They think they can debrief me and get rid of me. Now you want me to go back to Russia immediately. Bring him back before he snaps, is that what they said? Pick his brain before he freaks. Is that it?''

"Of course not—"

"Lady, I am the only hope of getting that bird out of here in one piece. They don't have a chance without me."

"I know that, Andrei," she said. "If they want to get the fighter out of Nicaragua you must fly it. But there is a very good possibility that they will not *want* to fly the aircraft out of Nicaragua."

"Not fly it out of Nicaragua . . . ?"

"Andrei, our government tried to make a deal with the Americans for the return of their fighter. They told the Americans they would turn the plane over to them in five days. The same day they concluded that agreement we were caught trying to fly the plane to Cuba. The Americans no longer believe us. You've said it yourself—we can't defend ourselves here. If the U.S. mounts an attack they'll destroy this base. It would seem the only way we can save ourselves is to turn the fighter over to them."

"Like hell . . ." He recalled he'd momentarily considered it himself, but only in his bitterness about what probably waited for him back "home." But he could never seriously go through with that . . . "Do you know what I've done? Do you realize what I've gone through to get that aircraft here? I was the top pilot in the United States Air Force's most top-secret research center. In ten years I could have been *running* the place. I sacrificed it to protect and deliver this aircraft and I will *never* surrender it . . ."

He went to the closet, found a fresh flight suit and began pulling it on. "I'll talk to the general—hell, I'll talk to Moscow. I doubt that the Americans will attack this base. But if they do we can move DreamStar to another location until the attack is over. Unless the U.S. declares war, they won't threaten the peace in Central America by bombing a base, even over this fighter. And they're not going to declare war." Maraklov pulled on a pair of boots and left his room.

Zaykov remained there for several minutes. The strain, she decided, was getting to him. Even more than before, the fighter was *his* personal possession, more than the U.S.'s or the USSR's, and he was determined to ignore official orders and political realities and do with the fighter as *he* thought best. The signs of paranoia were stronger as well. She'd never thought he'd agree to leave DreamStar in Nicaragua, but at the very least she thought

her words would comfort him if not altogether reassure him. It
had had the opposite effect. He clearly now believed that the
Soviet military would discard him like a spent shell casing after
his mission was completed. (She did not consider the likelihood
that he might be right . . .)

She had to try to convince him to trust his countrymen. That
was now more important than ever. With the threat of American
retaliation hanging over them, a battle-fatigued and alienated
mind of Colonel Maraklov could mean disaster for himself, the
mission and all Soviet personnel in Nicaragua.

He had to be brought back to the fold—or he had to be eliminated.

Maraklov went to the command post, where he found General
Tret'yak in his office sitting in front of a computer terminal,
staring at a half-filled screen. "I need to talk to you, General."

Tret'yak looked up, motioned to a chair. Maraklov ignored
it. "I am composing a detailed report on this morning's incident," Tret'yak said in a distracted tone. "Five aircraft lost.
Watching that Ilyushin go in—I have never felt so helpless—"

"Sir, we have to discuss the XF-34 fighter," Maraklov interrupted. "It's not secure here. I recommend it be moved as soon
as possible to a secret location and prepared for another flight to
the Soviet Union as soon as possible."

Tret'yak stared at the screen for a few moments; then, to
Maraklov's surprise, began typing again. "Colonel Maraklov,
personally, at this moment, I don't care *what* happens to our
fighter," he said without looking up from his work. "I have lost
seven men and five aircraft today—that is more men and more
equipment than I have lost in four years as a squadron commander in Afghanistan. I will certainly lose my command and
possibly my pension. The safety and security of your wondrous
aircraft is out of my hands. I have no more resources to defend
it with."

He reached over to a stack of papers, selected one and tossed
it to Maraklov without looking up from the computer screen.
"Here are your orders, transmitted by the chief of the KGB.
You are authorized to take any actions necessary to protect the
aircraft. Authorization has already been obtained to allow you
access to Sandino Airport in Managua, Aeroflot hangar number
twelve, and Puerto Cabezas Airport, main transient hangar. You

will take weapons with you. I have already ordered my men to load Lluyka tanks, ammunition and missiles on your fighter—we suddenly seem to have plenty to spare. It's *your* responsibility now.''

Maraklov picked up the message. It was true—he had been given almost unlimited authority to protect DreamStar from destruction until the chief of the KGB, Kalinin, could consult with the Soviet Kollegiya. Trucks, trains, ships, tankers, weapons, hangars, men, money—anything he felt was necessary, so long as DreamStar was safe. It was an exciting prospect, but he realized that if he failed, the Kollegiya would demand repayment—and not in money.

Maraklov almost felt sorry for the man—he had, in effect, just been relieved of command because of something he had no control over. ''I understand, sir, *spasiba*—''

''Get out, Colonel,'' Tret'yak said. ''You have everything you need.''

''I want to ask your opinion, sir,'' Maraklov said quickly, ''about where you recommend I take *Zavtra*.''

The old fighter pilot looked up from his work. ''You want my opinion?''

Maraklov saw the old glimmer in his eyes, at least something of the fire he'd noted when they'd met that day he arrived at Sebaco. Tret'yak wanted a piece of the action, no matter what. ''I'm glad you asked, because I have given it some thought.'' Tret'yak motioned to a chair, then poured a tall glass of ice water for Maraklov. ''I am very, very glad you asked.''

## Washington, D.C.
*Saturday, 20 June 1996, 1900 EDT*

President Taylor cursed, his New England accent, rarely heard after years in Washington, leaking through.

The full National Security Council had been summoned for an early-evening meeting at the White House conference room. They had just been briefed on DreamStar by General Elliott via two-way satellite videophone from the E-5 AWACS plane, in which he was still orbiting over the Cayman Islands. The President turned his face away from his advisers at the conference table, his jaw tight. ''They just went ahead and lied to me.''

"According to Ambassador Vilizherchev, the military detachment in Nicaragua acted on their own without clearing it with Moscow," Secretary of State Danahall said. "Vilizherchev insists there was no intention of deceiving us."

"I don't care what he insists. For starters, I want Vilizherchev's ticket pulled—he's *persona non grata*. And I want to make sure that the press knows he's not being 'recalled to confer with his government' or any such bull—I want them to know that I'm *kicking* him out."

"Do you want the press to know why?" Danahall asked.

"Because he lied to me, he lied to this government." He pointed a finger at Danahall. "You don't need to go into details." Danahall shook his head as the President turned back to the image of Elliott on the three-sided monitor set up in the center of the conference table. Yes, Danahall thought, the President needed to go into detail for something as serious as kicking out an ambassador, especially the ambassador from the Soviet Union.

"So we definitely know that the XF-34 was flown back to Nicaragua, back to this Sebaco airfield?" the President asked Elliott.

"Positively, sir," Elliott radioed back. "We've had continuous AWACS radar coverage of Sebaco since the XF-34 withdrew. It has definitely landed at Sebaco, and so far no aircraft have departed or arrived at Sebaco except for two MiG fighters from Managua that had tried to chase our AWACS plane away from Nicaragua. Our Falcons convinced him that it was all right for us to stay. We've been keeping watch on Sebaco via our AWACS plane, by satellite surveillance, and by sketchy reports from covert operatives in Nicaragua when possible."

"But that doesn't mean they can't move it again," William Stuart said testily. "It's still a no-win operation, Elliott. So you caught the Russians trying to move the thing. They're still not going to give it back until they're good and ready—"

"We *can* stop them from moving that aircraft out of Nicaragua," Elliott said, "if we act fast enough."

"Is it true, General," the President asked, "that we can't detect them if they move it out of Sebaco?"

"I'm afraid so, sir. We have satellite overflights every ninety minutes to scan the base, and our radar plane can track anything in the sky. Our agents in the field are keeping watch on the area surrounding Sebaco, but the Russians have stepped up security around that base and our agents can't get too close. There are gaps . . . But we don't have to know the XF-34's exact location,'' Elliott added, readjusting his headset. ''We know they have it—we don't need to know anything else—''

''You're recommending that we *bomb* Sebaco, regardless of whether we know that fighter is there or not?''

''Yes, sir, I am. It would help if the plane were returned to its hangar where it was first spotted, but there's not too much chance of that. I'd expect them to hide it in the jungle or transport it to Sandino Airport, where we'd be less inclined to attack—''

'' 'Less inclined' is right, General,'' Stuart said. ''We will *not* attack a civilian airfield.''

''Sandino is a military airfield, sir. The Nicaraguans don't operate any civilian airfields. Sandino is operated by the military but accepts civilian traffic. A surgical strike—''

''We're getting off the point, General,'' the President said. ''I'll end this right now—we will *not* attack Sandino Airport. It may in fact be a military airfield, but it is considered a civilian airfield. If the Soviets ship it to Sandino, then it's just another step out of our reach.''

''Yes, sir,'' Elliott said. ''Sebaco is our target in any case. Our objective is to send a message that we don't accept our fighter being stolen, our people killed and our so-called agreement being broken.''

For a brief moment the President thought about the upcoming election, the scrutiny he was under already, the criticism he could expect when the country learned that he had mounted an attack against Nicaragua. But Elliott's carefully phrased statement seemed the bottom line—the Soviets had been banking on this election year to get away with killing American servicemen and stealing a multi-million-dollar aircraft . . .

''Let's send that message, General Elliott,'' the President ordered, and said a silent prayer.

**Moscow, USSR**
*Sunday, 21 June 1996, 0700 EET (Saturday, 2300 EDT)*

The General Secretary, as always, began the emergency meeting of his senior advisers precisely on time. He was dressed in a business suit and tie, in spite of the early hour, and bestowed a disgusted look on any of his civilian or military advisers who arrived in rumpled suits or unpolished shoes or who did not shave. The man set high standards for himself and he expected each of those around him to measure up to the same standards. And, contrary to much of the rest of the world, Sunday was still a day of work in the Kremlin.

The General Secretary got right to business. He turned to his foreign minister, interlaced his fingers on his desk. "Comrade Tovorin, Vilizherchev has been expelled from the United States. Why?"

Tovorin looked anxiously at Kalinin, then cleared his throat. "I had intended to brief you this morning on Vilizherchev, sir. This deals with the experimental aircraft taken by Comrade Kalinin's agent in the United States. Vilizherchev was called to the White House and questioned about the fighter. He agreed to consult with you and the Kollegiya on the Americans' demands for returning the aircraft. Comrade Kalinin, however, was unaware of this. He ordered his agent in Nicaragua, Colonel Maraklov, to fly the aircraft to Cuba. When the Americans learned this they expelled Vilizherchev—"

"Why wasn't I notified of any of this, Kalinin?"

"Vilizherchev met with the President very early Saturday morning, our time," Kalinin said quickly. "The operation to fly the fighter from Nicaragua to Cuba began only a few hours after that meeting. You were in Leningrad for the day, sir—there was no time to consult you—"

"There was ample time to consult with me. Perhaps you *chose* not to consult me?"

"I didn't wish to intrude on your holiday, sir."

"Very considerate of you, Kalinin. Did you authorize any agreements with the American government yesterday morning?"

"No, sir," Kalinin lied. "Vilizherchev consulted with me because the fighter was in our hands. I advised him to wait for a reply from Moscow before proceeding further."

"The order expelling Vilizherchev says that he lied to the

American President and gave assurances to the Americans that were not honored. Did Vilizherchev do these things?''

"I don't know, sir," Kalinin said, "but I doubt it. Sergei Vilizherchev is one of the most loyal and trusted of your advisers. More likely, the Americans are angry about their fighter and expelled Sergei in protest.''

"I want Vilizherchev to report to me immediately after he arrives," the General Secretary said.

"Yes, sir." Tovorin was relieved that the questioning on that score was over, at least for the moment.

"We lost five aircraft over the Caribbean yesterday," the General Secretary said, "including a one-billion-ruble airborne-warning-and-control aircraft, of which we only have thirty. We have two pilots dead, two captured by the Americans, and four men from the Ilyushin transport seriously injured." He never ranted or raved, never seemed to get too upset or angry—but the deep, resonant voice, the fixated stare that seemed to bore a hole right into your skull, the hawklike eyebrows, the knotted fists—all told their story.

He turned on Kalinin. "Your mission to bring this American super-fighter to Russia is becoming very expensive, Kalinin."

"Our fighters were outnumbered four to six," Kalinin said, "and we shot down four of their fighters and forced the other two to retreat. The XF-34 fighter shot down one and crippled another. If the XF-34 hadn't been carrying long-range fuel tanks, sir, it could have destroyed all six American fighters—it is *that* superior, sir."

"It's no use to us, Kalinin, if we must kill off half our air force to get it . . . What's the status of the project? Can you get this fighter to Russia in one piece without starting World War Three?''

"Yes, sir. We will make another attempt to fly the aircraft intact out of Nicaragua. Colonel Maraklov, the pilot, now believes it would be safer to fly it in a circuitous route to Moscow rather than trying to fly it first to Cuba. He tried that. It was a good plan . . . Cuba is more stable than Nicaragua, but—''

"When will he make the attempt?"

"Tonight, sir." Kalinin stood and walked to a large chart of the region. "I have arranged a diversion—a large formation of aircraft flying from Nicaragua to Cuba, much the same as the first attempted convoy to Cuba. This force will directly challenge the Americans. At the same time, Maraklov and a small escort force will launch, stay clear of American radar sites in Panama and in the Lesser Antilles archipelago and out over the Atlantic Ocean; we can expect support if needed from Venezuela and Trinidad and Tobago, both of whom have been glad to accept large amounts of aid from our government in recent years, as you know. We have arranged tanker and fighter support for Maraklov over the Atlantic, well away from commercial air-traffic routes or ground-based radar sites. The force will continue north, steering well clear of known or detected naval vessels. We can expect support from Mauritania and Algeria and we can land for crew rest and replenishment in Algiers in northern Algeria or Tamanrasset in southern Algeria. After that I believe it will not be too difficult to penetrate the relatively weak NATO southern flank or the eastern Mediterranean area and recover into Tbilisi or Odessa.''

The General Secretary appeared to be only half listening. "You seem to be very confident of success, Kalinin. You were confident about the ease at which you would get this aircraft to Cuba. Yet this aircraft is still in Nicaragua.''

"I realize that this will be a difficult mission,'' Kalinin said. "Maraklov must fly his aircraft nine thousand kilometers, prepared at any moment to defend himself against the Americans' most advanced fighters, both land- and sea-based. Yet this is the fighter that can do it, sir. This XF-34 fighter has already fought its way out of the United States and survived a large coordinated assault against it. We *must* have this aircraft. Much of the balance of power between the Soviet Union and the United States depends on it.''

"I suspect you are overstating the case, Kalinin'' . . . although for *you* it is crucial, he added to himself . . . "We have already lost five aircraft and had our ambassador declared *non grata*. I can't accept much more.''

He turned away from Kalinin, considering the options . . . It would be a coup for both of them, he thought, if the fighter could be brought to Russia. *And* they would give it back, but only *after* all possible information on the machine was obtained and a suitable trade arranged.

Should the mission fail, Kalinin, his chief rival for power, would be ousted, an irritating memory, taking with him the blame for the incident. Should Kalinin succeed, his strength and authority in the government would surely increase, but enough for a takeover? He doubted it, but he would need to be very, very vigilant . . .

"What will you require?" the General Secretary asked.

"Because of the time involved, sir, very little," Kalinin said. "Authorization for another Ilyushin-76 radar plane, another Il-76 tanker aircraft, six MiG-29 aircraft with *our* pilots from Cuba, and landing rights and defense arrangements with Trinidad and Tobago, Mauritania, Algeria, Libya and Syria. These forces to be placed under my authority for the next seventy-two hours."

The General Secretary shook his head. " 'Very little,' you say, Kalinin?" He turned to the chief of staff. "Marshal Cherkov, can these be provided in so short a time?"

Marshal Boris Cherkov, one of the oldest members of the General Secretary's senior staff, pondered the question so long and without any apparent reaction that for a moment Kalinin and some of the others thought he was asleep. Then: "I trust young Comrade Kalinin has investigated the source of the Ilyushin aircraft and the fighters? From Cuba, I understand?"

"Yes, sir. There are a total of two Il-76 radar planes at Havana, four Il-76 tankers and twenty-one MiG-29 fighter aircraft."

Cherkov nodded. "It seems he has his aircraft. Obtaining landing rights from any of these nations mentioned will not be a problem. Obtaining mutual-defense operations will be virtually impossible without days of precise planning—half the government of Trinidad and Tobago is on holiday, and it sometimes takes a whole day for our embassy to contact anyone in Mauritania's government. Besides, none of these nations has any appreciable air or naval forces. I would not expect any resistance to your operation from these nations, but neither would I expect any assistance."

Kalinin nodded. He had hoped these governments would exclude American fighters from their airspace while allowing Russian fighters to land, but obviously that wasn't to be. "Never mind," he said. "Permission to cross their airspace and landing rights for our jets will be enough."

"As for the radar aircraft, tanker and fighters," Cherkov went on, "that must be your decision. The forces are available. Of course, if the Americans launch some sort of attack against Cuba in retaliation, then those aircraft would be needed for defense . . .''

Kalinin was pleased. He had thought Cherkov, a close ally of the General Secretary, was going to raise a lot more problems . . .

"However," Cherkov said, as if on cue, "I feel I must object to this operation." The bastard did not let him down, Kalinin thought grimly.

"It is extremely dangerous to provoke the Americans in their own 'backyard.' Remember the Cuban missile crisis and that fool Khrushchev. We could invite retaliation and open conflict in an area of the world where we are hardly dominant—"

"The U.S. is in no position to retaliate," Kalinin said angrily. "If I had decided to put the aircraft on an ocean-going vessel or even a transport plane, I will admit the danger of attack in those cases would be high. If we were holding the fighter in place for some sort of trade, there would be danger of attack by the Americans. But the fighter is a *moving* target. The Americans will not blindly lash out and attack unless they know precisely where the aircraft is located. Besides, they are not in good standing with most of Latin America . . .''

Cherkov's hands shook with emphasis. "Nicaragua is hardly an ideal safe haven. Your base at Sebaco is a prime target—you must feel the same way, judging by the haste with which you want to fly the fighter out of there. I expect Sebaco will come under attack. It is an isolated base, obviously not part of the Nicaraguan armed forces, and now nearly unprotected. The President can call it a 'communist-terrorist headquarters,' a rallying cry for most Americans. If I were Secretary Stuart or General Kane, I would order an attack on Sebaco immediately."

"Then it is even more urgent that the fighter be moved without delay," Kalinin said. "It's too late for talking about what *should* have been done. I have instructed Colonel Maraklov, the XF-34's pilot, to do everything in his power to see that the aircraft survives. I want to order him to fly the aircraft to the Soviet Union, and I want to provide him with all available military support. If we hesitate, we are, as you say, inviting defeat. If we act now, we can be successful . . .''

There was silence around the conference table. The General Secretary stared at Kalinin, and from across the table Kalinin forced himself to return the General Secretary's icy stare with one as determined and convincing as he could manage. He was sure that the General Secretary was trying to think days and weeks ahead, assessing possible consequences of defeat and failure for both of them. But he also realized that the General Secretary really had no choice—to back away from this operation now, when the Americans had given them such a lengthy chance to recover and regroup, would show indecision and timidity. Over time that lack of initiative could be translated into political weakness, which would mean a further loosening of his tenuous grasp on the reins of power.

"Very well," the General Secretary said, "you are authorized to requisition and command the forces you have outlined to bring this aircraft home. But understand, I am not convinced that this one fighter is worth a major confrontation with the U.S., no matter how advanced it may be. Be prepared to terminate your operation and obey the orders of the Kollegiya should you be so ordered. Am I clearly understood?"

"Yes, sir," Kalinin said automatically. The General Secretary had relented, as Kalinin expected. His caveat was pro forma, face-saving.

Vladimir Kalinin's rise to power had begun.


## Over the Caribbean Sea
*Sunday, 21 June 1996, 2100 CDT*

"Tegucigalpa Control, Sun Devil Three-Two is with you at flight level one-eight zero, position one-zero—zero nautical miles north of La Cieba. Over."

The Honduran military radar operator checked his display and quickly located the data block, then the primary radar return belonging to the American aircraft one hundred miles north of the military airbase on the north coast of Honduras. He cross-checked the information with the newcomer's flight plan. The aircraft, he knew from the flight plan, was a modified McDonnell-Douglas DC-10 belonging to the U.S. Air Force—that would explain the very large radar return even at this distance.

Satisfied, he replied in thick Latino-accented English, "Sun Devil Three-Two, this is Tegucigalpa Control, radar contact. Clear to intercept and track airway Bravo eight-eight-one until overhead Goloson Airport, then follow airway alpha seven-five-forty to Toncontin International, maintain flight level one-eight-zero. Over.''

The copilot of the KC-10 Extender tanker from the 161st Air Refueling Group, the very same group unlucky enough to get involved with all these "questionable" (for which read technically illegal) missions into Central America, checked the clearance with his computer flight plan and nodded to his pilot—it was the clearance he had been expecting. "Sun Devil Three-Two, roger. Out.''

The pilot switched over to the scrambled number-two radio. "Storm Zero Two, we're in contact with Tegucigalpa. Cleared on course.''

"Roger, Mike,'' J. C. Powell replied. "Right on time.''

The KC-10's copilot said, "You expected something else?''

McLanahan scanned outside Cheetah's bubble canopy at the huge gray-green tanker, a massive, shadowy figure in the growing twilight. The tanker aircraft was on its third mission for him and J.C. in almost as many days—they had gotten to know each other very well during their videophone flight-planning sessions. Although Tegucigalpa and all the other Central American radar operators only knew of a single aircraft on this flight plan, there were actually two—McLanahan was borrowing the tactic the Russians had used the morning before to try to get DreamStar to Cuba. The two aircraft were sticking tightly together in order to merge their radar returns.

Cheetah was right on the tanker's left wingtip. She was carrying two conformal FAST PACK fuel tanks for added range, and she was armed with four AIM-120 Scorpion missiles in semi-recessed wells along the underside of the fuselage, four AIM-132 infrared homing dogfighting missiles on wing pylons, and five hundred rounds of ammunition for the twenty-millimeter cannon. Cheetah also carried a combination infrared and laser seeker-scanner under the nose that could provide initial steering signals for the AIM-120 missiles without using any telltale emissions from the attack radar.

It was armed and ready for a preemptive strike against the KGB base at Sebaco. The mission was to retaliate against the theft of DreamStar and the Soviet reneging on the deal struck between Moscow and Washington. It was also to try to flush out

DreamStar and engage it in one last aerial battle. Better a dead
bird than in Soviet hands to copy . . .

But Cheetah was on this mission only if DreamStar or other
high-performance fighters challenged the strike aircraft. The
original plan proposed by General Elliott had Cheetah armed as
both an air-to-air and air-to-ground fighter, but surprisingly J.C.
had vetoed the idea—surprising because Powell rarely backed
away from a challenge, and because he was an excellent air-to-
mud pilot. He had argued that Cheetah would be too heavily
loaded down if it had to carry any bulky iron bombs or complicated laser-infrared target designators. He recognized the real
possibility that the Russians would use DreamStar to defend Sebaco against attack, and he wanted to be ready with all the power
and maneuverability he could get. If DreamStar was going to
launch, he wanted to be right there on top of him.

There was a surprise third party on the satellite conference
call involved with planning the strike mission, a project director
from HAWC. He had been silent most of the conversation, until
J.C. had voiced his objections. Then he had stepped in, presenting his options and his estimates for success. In short order
his proposals had been approved by General Elliott, and less
than an hour later approved by the Secretary of the Air Force.

This fight had become personal—it was as if the President and
the DOD had agreed to let the men and women of HAWC deal
with the traitor from their own ranks, because that was how they
thought of him—as Ken James, not a Soviet man named Maraklov. There were more concrete reasons, of course: The unit
was cloaked in secrecy, with fewer persons involved who could
alert the media or enemy agents; they commanded the most high-
tech weapons in the American military arsenal; and, especially
during the recent events, were able to generate a strike sortie
faster than an active-duty military unit.

The two men in Cheetah's cockpit were quiet. J.C. concentrated on maintaining close fingertip formation with the KC-10,
and McLanahan checked and rechecked his equipment and
watched the setting sun dipping behind the low Maya Mountains
near the coast of Belize off the right side of the fighter. The Islas
de la Bahia island chain was off to the left, with tiny lights
twinkling in the growing Caribbean twilight. It was a pleasant,
romantic sight—until the view of those tranquil islands was obscured by the row of AIM-132 missiles slung under Cheetah's

wings, the missile's large foreplanes slicing the Isla de Roatan neatly in half.

"How are you doing back there, sir?" Powell asked, finally breaking the strained silence. "You're quiet."

"I'm okay."

"Radio's free. Want to call back to the command post again?"

"No, not right now." Since leaving Dreamland earlier that afternoon he had made one UHF radio phone-patch back to HAWC's command post to ask about Wendy. She was, they told him, undergoing laser surgery to remove areas of scarred and damaged tissue in her lungs. The last word he had gotten was that they were searching for possible donors for a single lung transplant. Only a few hundred of these transplants had been done in the United States in the past few years, and only a handful of recipients were still alive.

"She'll be okay," J.C. said.

Patrick said nothing.

Silence again as they approached the Honduras coastline and the tiny city of La Cieba came into view. Then J.C. asked, "You figure we'll run into James up here?"

"You mean *Maraklov*."

"Still can't help thinking of him as Ken James."

"By any other name he's still a murderer. I don't think of him as a Russian or an American or even as a person. I won't have any trouble pulling the trigger on him."

According to General Elliott's plan, Cheetah was meant to go up against DreamStar, to engage with missiles from long range, close, engage at medium range with missiles, and if necessary close and engage with guns.

"Ken . . . Maraklov seems like he's still on top of his game," J.C. said. "He scared the hell out of those F-16 Air National Guard guys. Faked one with a missile shot, follows him in a horizontal climb, then hoses him while the F-16 descends on him. He busted up one other guy—"

"I don't want to talk about him."

But that wasn't altogether true—in reality, McLanahan was, in a way, fascinated by him. Not just because of the amazingly successful espionage operation that he had managed all these years, but because of what sort of *person* was out here. He was a Russian, a Soviet agent—he *must* have been worried about being captured every day, yet he not only successfully penetrated the most top-secret flight research lab in the U.S. but became the only pilot of the most advanced flying machine in the whole world. How anyone could keep calm and collected through all that without going crazy was unbelievable. Add on that he had to fly DreamStar itself—and in Maraklov's case take it into battle, with no "knock it off" calls or prearranged attack scenarios, no "wait ten seconds then come and get us" stuff. And Maraklov had proved himself in battle, handily defeating two F-16 ADF interceptors . . . "How the hell does he do it?"

"He's tuned into the ANTARES computer as if it was made especially for him," J.C. replied immediately, as if he was thinking the very same thing as McLanahan. "It's logical, though—if he's a Russian mole like they say he is, he had to forget completely about being a Russian and transform himself into an American. It's like he can ram-flush his own mind and fill it with whatever he wants. The same with ANTARES—he can empty his mind of everything and allow that machine to take over. I don't know how he snaps out of it—he must keep back a bit of his brain, enough to remind himself that he's a human being—sort of like leaving bread crumbs behind in a maze to help find your way out . . ."

"But how can a guy *fight* like that? I've flown lots of different high-performance fighters, including Cheetah's simulator, and it takes every ounce of concentration I have just to keep the thing flying straight. How can a schizy guy like that fly one?"

"Practice helps," J.C. said. "Sure, you've flown a lot of fighters—always with an instructor pilot and always in ideal day VFR conditions—but you don't have many hours. Maraklov has got hundreds of hours in DreamStar. And let's face it—the man *is* good. With or without DreamStar, he's a top fighter pilot. I'm no psychologist, so I don't know too much about his mental state, but just because you're schizy doesn't mean you can't function normally or even *above* norm. Hell, they say most of us fighter pilots are schizoids anyway . . . But ANTARES is the key, Patrick. If you had a full-time, high-speed computer telling you what to do each and every second you were at the controls, you could fly *any* jet in the inventory. The problem you and I have is that we can't interface with ANTARES. Maraklov is the opposite: he's probably at a point where he can't exist *without* ANTARES. He's not whole unless he's hooked up to that machine. When he's not hooked up he's less than himself. He's probably more dangerous when he's *not* hooked up. When he's hooked into ANTARES he's sort of at the mercy of it.''

"What do you mean?''

"Well, no matter how far we've come with high-speed integrated circuits, micro-miniature computers and neural interfaces, there's no unlimited amount of info you can take on board an aircraft. We call ANTARES artificial intelligence, and in a way it is, but the critical difference between my brain and ANTARES' computer is that ANTARES can't *learn*. And learning creates an unlimited pool of info that you rely on in combat. There's a lot of it available on DreamStar, but it has a limit, and we know what the limit is. James—Maraklov—can call on his own experience and training to improve his own pool of information, but we've seen before that he doesn't do that. He relies more and more on ANTARES to make crucial decisions for him. So his advantage can become a disadvantage for him, and that's a one-up for me. On Cheetah I've got a lot of options available. Including ones I dream up or choose. He doesn't—''

"But ANTARES has hundreds of options available,'' McLanahan said, "and it can execute them much faster than you can—''

"ANTARES executes a maneuver based on what it figures out I'm doing, true,'' J.C. said, "but he also makes moves based on the probability of what I'll do in the future, based on what I do now. ANTARES is thinking ahead and maneuvering to counter or press the attack based on what it *thinks* I'll do. But what if he's thinking the *wrong thing*?''

"The chances of it computing the wrong thing are slim,'' McLanahan said. "It computes dozens, sometimes hundreds of combinations to any situation—''

"But it can only execute *one* of them,'' J.C. said. "The one it executes is based on current activity and probability—highly accurate mathematical statistics and historical averages but still chance, educated guesses.''

"So if you do something different, it recomputes on that move, executes the maneuver, and computes another dozen situations . . .''

"You got it. And when it stops and thinks—and I don't care how fast it does it—I have some advantage. If it's thinking instead of fighting that's good for me.''

McLanahan's head was pounding. "You've got a machine

that can think and react faster than a human being. A *lot* faster. How can *you* get the advantage over that?''

"Because of the way it's programmed," J.C. said.

"DreamStar is a fighter," McLanahan said. "It's been programmed to fight. Attack. It can compute a dozen different ways to attack every second. Where's the advantage?''

"What would you do?'' J.C. asked, "if you were chasing down a bogey at your twelve o'clock and you had the overtake on him but you both had a lot of smash built up? What would you do? Would you go max AB, firewall the throttle, close on the guy and attack?''

"I could, but it wouldn't be smart.''

"Why?''

"Because if I had a lot of overtake, the bogey could reverse on me easier. Then I'd be on the defensive—''

"Exactly. DreamStar does *not* think like that. DreamStar has not been programmed to hang back, match speed and power, maintain spacing, look for an opening. DreamStar goes for the kill when the target is presented to it. It will *always* engage. If you're ever in doubt about what it will do, it will attack. You can count on it. Remember our last flight test with DreamStar?''

"Sure. James almost pancaked into those buttes.''

"He did that because even in what we would call an unsafe situation, DreamStar's computers will press the attack no matter what. If there's the slightest opening, the tiniest chance for success, DreamStar will use it in its attack equation.''

"I wasn't involved with the programming part of DreamStar's computers," McLanahan said, "but to me it doesn't make sense. Isn't defense as much a part of dogfighting as offense? Why wouldn't DreamStar's computer programmers teach it about defense?''

"Who knows? DreamStar was probably programmed by some computer weenie who never was in a cockpit. But then again, I suppose if you have the ultimate fighter, the most agile and fastest there is, it would be easy to ignore defense and concentrate on offense. But it can afford to ignore cut-and-run options because it has the speed and the agility to turn tiny mistakes into victories. Guys lose because they're amazed by how fast it is. It's not fast—you're dead because you did exactly what DreamStar figured you would do, and it was right there waiting for you. Boom. Dead meat.''

"So if you make DreamStar play defense . . ."

"DreamStar *does not play defense*, Patrick," J.C. said, pounding on the canopy sill to drive home his point. "The only defense maneuver programmed into that system is high-speed escape, and that's only if the ANTARES interface is broken or damaged. As long as it's fully functional, it never thinks defense. DreamStar is always thinking attack. *Always*. If you force it into a defensive role you know that DreamStar is thinking about how to attack in response. And when it's thinking, you have the advantage. True, it may only be for a second or two, but during that time you have an advantage, and that's when you have to take him out."

"Sounds like you got this all figured out, J.C."

"Hey, DreamStar's a fantastic machine, you can't beat it in technology or maneuverability—you have to *think* at a level where even ANTARES has a weakness. You fly unpredictable, fly in three dimensions, fly by instincts instead of by the book or by some computer. ANTARES has problems handling that . . ."

As the KC-10 began a shallow turn right toward Tegucigalpa in southern Honduras, J.C. gently yawed Cheetah around to follow. They had just crossed the north coast of Honduras directly over the Honduran Air Force base of La Cieba. Even though the Hondurans had only twenty-five aircraft, La Cieba was a large, modern, high-tech base—mostly because of the U.S. military, which used the base for "joint training missions," and subsequently "assisted" with base improvements that virtually built an American air base at La Cieba. There were often more American planes at La Cieba than other aircraft in all of Honduras.

"Storm Two, Sun Devil Three-Two is ready for your final refueling any time," the copilot aboard the KC-10 tanker reported. "Airspeed coming back. Cleared to pre-contact position."

"Roger, Sun Devil," J.C. replied. "Moving to pre-contact." J.C. pulled the throttles back to eighty percent power and watched as the KC-10 moved slowly ahead. Cheetah would get one more refueling as they transited Honduras; then Sun Devil Three-Two would land as scheduled at Tegucigalpa and refuel, and Cheetah would continue on its strike-escort route.

The refueling went without a hitch. They stayed in contact position right up until the KC-10's initial approach fix to Toncontin International Airport at Tegucigalpa, so Cheetah could fill up to full tanks right until the last possible minute—Cheetah had to complete its mission, escort the strike aircraft out of the danger area, then return to La Cieba and land. Every drop of gas was critical.

"Well, boys, you got another ten thousand pounds courtesy of the people of the great state of Arizona," the pilot of the KC-10 radioed after he had started his approach to Tegucigalpa, "Take care, I don't want to read about you in the papers."

"Likewise," J.C. replied. "We'll see you in about three hours if we need you. Over."

"We'll be waiting and ready. Sun Devil out."

The channel went dead. J.C. ordered the voice-command computer to reset the radios to the strike mission channelization, with the command radio on the strike-aircraft frequency and a scan on all UHF and VHF frequencies for ground-controlled intercept activity in Nicaragua. At the same time, Powell started a turn toward the east and a rapid descent to five-thousand feet, which would put him about a thousand feet over most of the lush tree-covered mountains of northwestern Nicaragua. They were skirting the northern Nicaragua border, staying deep within the Cordillera Entre Rios valley to avoid Nicaragua's main surveillance radar site situated on top of a fifty-seven-hundred-foot mountain near Cuyali in the center of the country.

"Shouldn't we have heard from them?" J.C. asked a few minutes later. He had fitted a night-vision visor over his eyes to help him pick out the rugged peaks and valleys surrounding them in the rapidly growing darkness.

"Few more minutes," McLanahan told him. He had the satellite transceiver unit set on the strike frequency as briefed back at Dreamland; because of the high terrain all around them, UHF or VHF communications would be impossible. "Then all hell will break loose."

It wasn't like the old days, Major Kelvin Carter told himself. It was a damned sight better.

He was sitting in what could best be described as the inside of a computer surrounded by multi-function, multi-color computer monitors, LED readouts and synthesized voices. The cockpit windscreen undulated with laser-drawn images describing search radars, terrain and performance data. The big two-horned yoke and massive center-console throttle quadrant were gone, replaced by static force side-stick controls, a special control stick that did not move but sensed the amount of pressure being delivered and commanded the appropriate input to the flight controls, and electronic mini-throttles.

He was sitting in what probably was the most advanced electronic cockpit outside DreamStar's—the cockpit on the upper deck of Dog Zero Two, the second experimental B-52 M-model Megafortress Plus.

She was a more potent weapon than her predecessor, Old Dog. Every possible system in the aircraft, from flight controls to navigation to weapons, was controlled by computer—and many of those systems could be activated or monitored by voice commands, helping to reduce workload even more. The Megafortress Plus had been virtually rebuilt from the spine up with advanced composite materials, even lighter and stronger than fibersteel.

But her most outstanding feature was her weapons fit: she had been redesigned to carry almost every missile or bomb in the Air Force inventory. In her role as a defense suppression ''super escort'' battleship, as on this mission, she carried enough weapons to equip a dozen tactical aircraft—and she could carry those weapons almost eight thousand miles without refueling.

For self-defense, the Megafortress Plus carried fifty aft-firing Stinger ''air mine'' missiles, which had a range of almost two miles and could be steered by the fire-control radar operated from the gunner's position, and six AIM-120C Scorpion air-to-air missiles, three on each wing pylon, for defense against fighter attack. She also carried a wide array of electronic jammers and decoys to confuse or shut down enemy radars. Her terrain-following capability, where she could automatically fly any desired altitude above ground ''hands off,'' was also a valuable self-protection feature.

For destroying enemy radars and weapon sites, the Old Dog Two carried four AGM-136 Tacit Rainbow anti-radar drones, two on each wing external pylon, which would home in on enemy radars from long distances. These were planned for use against the four known fixed-radar defense sites along the flight route. For unexpected threats she carried six AGM-88 HARM High-speed Anti-Radar Missiles on a rotary launcher in the aft bomb bay, designed to destroy mobile anti-aircraft guns or missile sites.

For attacking the KGB airbase itself, she carried four AGM-130 Striker glide bombs in the forward bomb bay, which could be launched from as far as twelve miles away against the aircraft hangars or other high-value targets at Sebaco. To destroy runway, taxiways and parking ramp she carried two cluster-bomb dispenser drones on the rotary launcher in the aft bomb bay, small winged vehicles that would fly around a preprogrammed or designated spot and scatter (one hundred) twenty-pound bomblets over a wide area, cratering concrete and destroying aircraft or vehicles unlucky enough to be there at the time.

Twenty-two attack weapons, plus the fifty mini-rockets in the tail—the weapons on Old Dog Two could outfit four or five modern F-15 or F-11 fighter-bombers. The aged B-52 bomber—this particular airframe first rolled off the assembly line in 1963—had been given a new lease on life, ensuring its usefulness in a major combat role beyond the year 2000.

"One minute to start countermeasures," the navigator, Captain Alicia Kellerman, reported. The call shook Carter out of his reverie. It was so easy to slip into a sort of hypnotic trance flying this beast—it was as quiet as an airliner and as comfortable as the leather recliner back in his own living room.

Carter checked the threat radar display projected onto his windscreen after first tearing his attention away from the sight of the iridescent dark green sea rushing past as they skimmed only a hundred feet above the Caribbean. A green dome not far in the distance signified their first electronic barrier, the surveillance and GCI radar at Puerto Cabezas, the large combined Soviet–Nicaraguan airbase on the Nicaraguan northeast coast. They were aiming right for the northern edge of the dome, but because of the interference from the sand dunes and marshes of Punta Gorda they were able to fly just under the radar coverage. But in less than sixty seconds they would lose the protection of even that low spit of land.

Carter hit the voice-command button on his control stick. "Set countermeasures release switches to consent," he said in a slight Louisiana bayou accent, reaccented and measured to make it easier for the voice-command computer to understand his voice. It was a humorous problem back in the early years of the project, he recalled—he refused to believe *he* was the problem when the computer continually rejected his commands during testing.

"*Pilot's countermeasures release consent,*" the computer

confirmed. Then to warn the rest of the crew about the move, the computer came on shipwide interphone and announced, *"Caution, pilot release consent."*

"Coming up on SCM point, crew," Kellerman said.

*"Caution, radar navigator release consent,"* the computer said.

"You're all a bit early," the electronic-warfare officer, Captain Robert Atkins, said.

"If it hits the fan up here," Carter said, watching the green radar sky slowly inching down on top of him, "I don't want to be fumbling with switches."

"Amen," radar navigator Captain Paul Scott chimed in.

Just then Carter heard, *"Caution, electronic warfare release consent. Warning, weapon release consent complete."* The last safety interlock belonging to Robert Atkins had been removed.

They were sixty miles from the coastline, about seventy-five miles northeast of Puerto Cabezas. This part of the mission was almost as crucial as the attack phase. For the next one hundred twenty miles until they reached the Cordillera Isabella mountains in north-central Nicaragua, they were vulnerable to attack—no mountains to hide in, only marshes and featureless lowlands—and they would be in range of the powerful search radar at Puerto Cabezas. Although the exact strength of the defenses was unknown they had been briefed to expect SA-10 air-defense missiles, MiG-29 and MiG-23 fighters to be operating in the no-man's land before them.

But at least this sortie had been planned to challenge those defenses. They were not relying on air cover, nor were they taking advantage of overflying friendly territory. This mission was designed as much for effect as well as results—the idea that a large American strike aircraft could make it across Nicaragua and strike a heavily defended target was planned to demoralize and confuse as much as it was to destroy.

The green radar dome had almost touched them. "I show contact with that search radar any second," Carter called out. "Clear all weapons for release. Station check and report by compartment when ready."

Nancy Cheshire performed the pilot's station check, choosing not to rely on the computer to check switch positions but doing the checks visually. She was the first female test pilot at HAWC and one of the first ever anywhere, and the public attention she

had attracted three years earlier at the beginning of the Megafortress Plus program had threatened to undermine her goal to
be the best pilot in the organization.

"Offense ready," Scott reported.

"Defense ready," Atkins responded.

"Station check complete, Kel, warning light coming on,"
Nancy reported as she hit the EJECT press-to-test button. The
last item on the list.

Carter looked at the small, red-haired woman for a moment,
studying her face underneath her lightweight flyer's helmet.
"How you doing over there?" he asked cross-cockpit.

She looked back at him. "I'm scared to death, Kel." But she
sounded more angry than scared. "And why don't you ask anyone else if they're scared?"

"Because you're my copilot," Carter shot back. "That's *all*.
Hell, I never know what you're thinking and you're wrong . . ."

His attention was pulled away from his copilot as he watched
the green dome descend over his aircraft like some unearthly fog.
"*Caution, search radar, ten o'clock,*" the computer reported.

"I've got a second search radar, ten o'clock, estimated range
sixty miles," Atkins reported. "Search and height-finder . . .
looks like our shoreline SA-10. Hasn't found us yet, though."

"Take it out, EW," Carter said. "Jam the search radar—I
don't want to be tracked by anyone out here over water. Kory,
send a warning message on the HAWC satellite net. Tell 'em
we're coming."

"Roger," Master Sergeant Kory Karbayjal, the crew gunner
and defense systems officer, replied, flipping down the SAT-
COM keyboard and punching commands to send the preformat-
ted message out on the satellite channel.

"Kel?"

Carter turned to Cheshire.

"Thanks for asking," she said, giving the control stick a slight
shake.

Carter nodded, lowered his oxygen visor and checked his system. "Get on oxygen." She raised her mask.

"Stand by for missile launch, crew," Atkins said. "Radar
programming complete. I need a hundred feet, pilot."

"Rog." Carter pulled back on the control stick, manually
flying the Megafortress Plus a hundred feet higher. "Set."

"Rainbow away," Atkins called out.

The Rainbow was the AGM-136 Tacit Rainbow air-to-ground missile, a subsonic winged drone aircraft with a small jet engine that could seek out and destroy enemy radars. If the enemy radar was operating, it would home in and destroy it with a one-hundred-pound high-explosive warhead; if it did not detect a radar it would orbit within ten miles of the target area until a signal was detected, then fly toward it and destroy it. So even if the enemy radar was shut off or moved, the missile could still seek out and destroy.

Carter shielded his eyes from the sudden glare of the AGM-136's engine exhaust as the missile appeared briefly past the long pointed nose of the Megafortress Plus, banked left, then disappeared into the darkness. Just then the green-radar warning "sky" projected onto the windscreen changed to yellow.

"Tracking radar," Atkins called out over the computerized warning voice. "SA-10, ten o'clock. I'm getting warning messages on UHF and VHF GUARD channels." The yellow sky seemed to undulate, then disappear and reappear at long intervals, showing the effectiveness of Atkins's jamming.

Kellerman activated her navigation radar. "Land fall in two minutes. First terrain, fifteen miles, not a factor at this altitude. First high terrain twenty-five miles, starting to paint over it." She plotted her position on a chart, cross-checked it with the GPS satellite navigation readout, then turned the radar to standby.

Carter released his back pressure on his control stick, allowing the terrain-following autopilot to bring the B-52 back to one hundred feet above the Caribbean. The radar warning had changed to solid yellow, then changed briefly to red before being blotted out.

"Did they get a missile off, EW?" Cheshire called out.

"No uplink signal," Atkins replied. "We're at the extreme outer range of the SA-10. I don't think they can . . ."

"*There, I see it*," Cheshire said. She pointed out the left windscreen. Just over the horizon was a short glowing line of fire spinning in a tight circle, growing larger and larger by the second.

Carter jerked the control stick hard left toward the missile. "Chaff, flare." Atkins hit the ejector buttons, sending bundles of radar-decoying chaff and heat-decoy flares overboard.

Carter hit the voice-command stud. "Set clearance plane fifty feet."

"*Clearance plane fifty feet, warning low altitude, clearance plane one hundred feet.*" Carter's turn was so tight that, had the computer set the lower clearance plane, the B-52's left wingtip would have dragged the water.

"It's still coming," Cheshire called out as Carter rolled out. The B-52 dipped as the lower clearance plane setting kicked in.

"I can't find the uplink, something must be guiding it but I can't find it . . ."

The glow was getting brighter—Carter would swear he heard the roar of the missile's rocket-motor as it sped closer and closer, jamming wasn't working . . . what . . . ?

"Stop jamming, EW," Carter suddenly called out. "It must be homing in on the jamming source. Go to standby. Fast."

The result was near-instantaneous. The fast-circling flight-path of the missile began to wobble, and the tail flame of the missile's engine began to elongate just as it burned out. Carter nudged his B-52 as low as he could safely go. It was too late to try to make a turn, too late even for more decoys . . .

They heard a *thud* against the fuselage, then silence. The B-52 shook as if a giant hammer had hit it.

"It missed," Cheshire shouted, "that was the supersonic shock wave, it missed . . ."

"It must have been a SA-15 SAM," Atkins said. "SA-15s . . . they just started deploying SA-15s in the Soviet Union. Now they got them in Nicaragua?"

Carter forced calm into his own dry throat. "Be ready—our intelligence briefing was obviously missing a few details."

But Atkins was still rattled. "SA-15 . . . I'm sorry, I didn't recognize it . . . they're not supposed to have SA-15s in Nicaragua . . . I could've gotten us all killed . . ."

"Snap out of it, Bob." But Carter understood what Atkins was going through. No one on this crew, including himself, had ever flown a combat mission—as a matter of fact, until Dog Zero Two was ready to fly two months ago, none of his crew members had been aboard a military aircraft for several months. After months or years with their mostly deskbound duties at Dreamland they had become more like engineers than combat crew members. Now they were being shot at by the Soviet Union's most advanced surface-to-air missile. He was sure the rest of the crew was steeling a panic—Atkins was just the first one to let loose.

"All of you, settle down and pay attention," Carter called over interphone. "They took a shot and missed. Fly this mission as briefed. But we've gotta pull together and back each other up. All of you know your stuff—now it's time to put it into action. All right. Check your stations and minimize electronic emissions. Nancy, get another power-plant check."

The radar sky had turned back to yellow. Carter maintained his new heading for a few moments, then turned back to the right and let the autopilot take control.

"Do you think we should go back on the same course?" Scott asked. "It'll be easier to find us that way."

"No use in doing that until we get over the mountains," Carter said. "The faster we get inland the better. Besides, I'll bet there's no big secret where we're heading. The entire Nicaraguan air force is probably waiting up there for us."

"Crossing the coast now," Kellerman announced. Carter checked out the cockpit window—when only fifty feet above the surface, the transition from water to land occurred very fast. He double-checked that the terrain-following system was working properly and set a two-hundred-foot clearance plane.

"Tracking radar up again," Atkins said shakily. The yellow sky was back for only a few moments when it completely blanked out again.

"They get another missile off?"

"I don't think so," Atkins said. "The Rainbow indicates impact—*we got it*."

Cheshire slapped her armrest. "All *right*."

"Celebration over, copilot," Carter said. "We've got a long long way to go."

In a matter of only a few minutes the Nicaraguan military airbase of Puerto Cabezas was in chaos. One moment it was quiet and peaceful, a warm, lazy summer evening with a hint of an evening storm brewing. The next, air raid sirens were screaming into the night, Russian missiles raised from concrete canisters like demons rising from their crypts, and the roar of jet fighters began to fill the air with the pungent odor of kerosene.

The first SA-15 missile, installed on the coastal Nicaraguan base only a month earlier in the ongoing Russian fortification of Nicaragua, screamed off its launch rails less than twenty seconds later, filling the air with burning acidic exhaust gas. The missile crews, Nicaraguan with Russian commanding officers, stood and watched the missile disappear into the night sky until a Soviet officer yelled an order to prepare the launcher for reload. Another SA-15 missile was completing its gyro-alignment—the Nicaraguan soldiers were skilled at aligning one missile at a time for launch . . .

It was this deficiency that had probably saved the crew of the Megafortress Plus. Just before the second missile was ready for launch a huge explosion lit up the small sandy hill where the SA-15 tracking and guidance radome was positioned. The golf-ball-like radome exploded like a burst balloon, scattering pieces of the antenna within for hundreds of meters.

From his vantage point in a low-covered concrete revetment near the flight line, Maraklov saw the golf-ball radome split apart and explode; now it looked like a cracked egg in a boiled egg holder. Men were running toward the flight line, but he knew the attack on the SA-15 guidance radome was a prelude to the real assault. If it was a Tacit Rainbow cruise missile the attack would not be for a few minutes because the AGM-136 had a range of almost a hundred miles; if it was an AGM-88 HARM missile the follow-on attack could be any second. Either way it was going to be an air raid—the attackers had obviously been waiting for the SA-15 to come up before blowing it up, and with the radar gone the whole north coast of Nicaragua was open to air attack.

Maraklov took a deep pull from a plastic jug of distilled water as he watched the radar control center begin to burn. Sebaco, he was sure, was next—except whoever was staging this attack wasn't going to stop at a radar site.

But DreamStar—it was safe. He was sitting in DreamStar's cockpit, still wearing his flight suit, his helmet resting on his lap in front of him. Less than one hour earlier he had landed at Puerto Cabezas after a low-altitude run from Sebaco. Because he knew that the American AWACS radar planes would be looking for a high-speed aircraft leaving Sebaco, he had made the flight under two hundred miles an hour and at the lowest altitude he could muster, flying deep within mountain valleys and jungle river beds to avoid detection. His gamble that his flight-profile would resemble anything but a jet fighter had apparently worked.

To avoid detection he had landed on the taxiway at Puerto Cabezas instead of the broad ten-thousand-foot runway, taxied

to the semi-underground concrete shelter and waited with engines running for any sign of pursuit. None. He shut down but
maintained the ANTARES interface and remained strapped in
place, configured and ready to fire up DreamStar. But still no
sign of pursuit. Exhaustion overtook him, so he shut down the
interface and directed the ground crewmen to begin refueling
his fighter. He had been off the ANTARES interface only fifteen
minutes when the attack began.

DreamStar was ready for a fight. She carried two more Lluyka
in-flight refueling tanks on the wing pylons plus two radar-guided
missiles on wing pylons and, this time, two infrared-guided missiles on hardpoints on the underside of the fuselage. The two IR
missiles were more of a hazard than a help—if DreamStar's canards were down in their high-maneuverability position, the missiles could possibly hit the canards after launch—but for the long
ferry mission, the extra weapons were considered necessary. The
twenty-millimeter cannon was also fully reloaded—DreamStar
was at its heaviest gross weight ever, well over one hundred-
thousand pounds.

But Maraklov himself wasn't as prepared for either a long
flight or a fight with American fighters. This had been the first
time he had made two flights in DreamStar within twenty-four
hours and the physical and mental strain was immense—like running the Boston Marathon, getting twelve short hours of rest,
then going out and running a few more Heartbreak Hills. His
body had not recovered from the first mission, but the necessity
was clear—DreamStar was in danger if it was left there at Sebaco. That had just been confirmed.

The whine of high-speed jet engines made Maraklov painfully
turn to scan down the runway. Four MiG-23 fighters were taxiing
to the end of the runway preparing for takeoff. The Soviet government had not been able to send any more MiG-29s or Russian
pilots to Nicaragua on such short notice, so those four MiG-23s
were manned by Nicaraguan pilots. The Mig-23s were twenty
years old, the pilots young or ill trained in night intercepts. If
whoever was attacking Nicaragua destroyed the search and
ground-controlled intercept radars as well as the surface-to-air
missile radars, the MiG pilots would be forced to hunt for the
attackers blind, using their own look-down, shoot-down pulse-
Doppler radars to scan thousands of square miles of territory for
their quarry.

Maraklov took another drink. It didn't matter, he thought—he'd be out of this backwater country in a few hours. And who knew . . . maybe one of the MiGs would get lucky. It happened . . .

A soldier came up to Maraklov's revetment, showed an I.D. card to the guard, and ran to the platform set up beside DreamStar. He was hesitant to climb up the ladder, but Maraklov saw that he had a message in his hand, motioned him up, and asked for the paper.

He got an instant headache after reading the first word. Assuming he could read Russian, the Spanish-speaking radio operators had scrawled the message out in childlike Cyrillic characters. Maraklov had enough trouble reading Russian, but reading this gobbledygook would be next to impossible. He had to get the soldier's attention away from the interior of Dream-Star's cockpit by hammering his shoulder.

"Read this for me," he said in English.

The soldier looked at him in surprise. "You speak English, mister?"

"Yes."

The soldier looked at the message for a moment, then looked at Maraklov as if he was going to hit him. "I am sorry, I cannot read this. This is Russian, no?"

"This is garbage Russian, yes. Go back to the radio operator and tell him to write the message out in English." Maraklov grabbed a pencil from the soldier's shirt pocket just before he scrambled off the platform—at least while he was getting the message translated he could work on deciphering this junk.

The MiG-23s were still idling at the end of the runway—that probably meant that the GCI radar was being jammed or had been destroyed, and the pilots were being held until a heading to the intruder's position could be established. Don't bother launching, Maraklov thought. Let the MiGs at Sebaco handle the American attackers—Sebaco was obviously the American's target—and leave the Puerto Cabezas MiGs in reserve for when the attackers try to withdraw. If they chase the attackers they could wind up getting shot down themselves or run out of fuel before engaging the stragglers . . . But a moment later the MiG-23s began their runup and minimum-interval takeoffs. So much for reserve interceptors. Maraklov guessed that none of these MiGs would return.

Maraklov had the scribbled Cyrillic characters deciphered now, but remembering the phonetic pronunciations for each character was tougher, and it took a few minutes to make the message intelligible—luckily, most of it was numbers. It was a satellite message from Moscow informing him that Soviet air forces would be in place in five hours, ready to escort him out of the Caribbean basin into the open Atlantic. The message gave last-minute backup or anti-jam frequency changes and other use-less information. If the Americans were broad-band jamming their primary communications frequencies, they were listening in as well and were probably vectoring fighters into the source of their transmissions. With such a large force of combat aircraft involved, everything relied on secrecy and radio silence, not secondary and tertiary frequencies.

The fighters were on the downwind side of the runway, the long, bright flames of their afterburners still visible. They had no tankers in Nicaragua (except the one that was lying on the bottom of the Caribbean), so if those guys in the MiG-23s didn't come out of afterburner they'd flame out before getting a shot off at the intruders.

Maraklov asked himself, "Why am I ragging on those pilots? DreamStar is safe—if the Americans had pinpointed DreamStar here in Puerto Cabezas this whole base would be a smoking hole."

Was it because he itched to get into battle? No, even if he had enough energy to take DreamStar aloft, which he didn't, he wouldn't risk it. With the MiG-29s gone Nicaragua was wide open to attack—for all he knew there was an aircraft carrier sitting off the coast with fifty F-18 fighter-bombers ready to take him on. It would be suicide to try.

He took another drink of water, emptying the bottle. The real problem here was that he just wanted a future, and every step being taken just seemed to drive him farther and farther from it. DreamStar, he felt, *was* his life. His whole being was inter-meshed with it, and the thought of its eventual dismantling or, worse, destruction was as obscene to him as the idea of a mother killing her newborn baby. But he was also a soldier, obliged to obey orders—and he had been ordered to deliver DreamStar to Russia. But could he obey those orders, knowing what they would do to his aircraft—and what they would probably do to *him* as well? He was already suspect . . . too American . . .

All the dead-end thoughts he was having were giving him a headache even worse than before. He tossed the plastic water bottle at one of the Nicaraguan military guards at the mouth of the revetment. *"Agua, por favor"*—probably the only three words of Spanish he knew. The soldier began filling the bottle from one of his canteens—no doubt more of the brackish, parasite-ridden water of this country. The thought of getting diarrhea while in the metallic flight suit made him laugh and cry, but dying of thirst and trying to withstand these migraine headaches were even worse prospects.

Soon, it would be over, he thought. He'd be on his way out of this godforsaken country and back to . . . Russia. Back to . . . what?

He was too tired to think any more about that. As the flickering lights of the fires in the SA-15 radome subsided, exhaustion overtook him, and he drifted off into a fitful sleep.

"Rainbow two showing impact," Atkins reported. The green search radar indication on Carter's laser-projection cockpit display had disappeared—the Tacit Rainbow missile had destroyed the Cuyali radar site, the last large-scale search radar system before Sebaco.

"Coming up on the initial point, crew," Alicia Kellerman announced. They were deep within the Rio Tuma river valley, which snaked out of the Cordillera Dariense mountains north of Managua and fed Managua Lake. Their initial point was, of all places, the town of Los Angeles thirty miles upriver from Sebaco.

"Bomb run briefing, crew," Paul Scott, the radar navigator, began, "we'll be approaching Sebaco from the northeast on the military crest of the river valley. There's one SA-10 site on the top of Iinotega Mountain at our one o'clock position, but according to Powell and McLanahan in Cheetah it's a mobile site."

"The system can use infrared to acquire its targets," Atkins chimed in. "Even though it needs radar for guidance they can launch on IR azimuth commands and then go to guidance uplink once the missile is in flight. We could see a snap-launch profile, where all we get on the threat-warning receivers is a MISSILE LAUNCH warning—we won't get a symbol or MISSILE WARNING." Carter was relieved to hear Atkins back on top of his game—he was pretty shook after their first encounter with the SA-15.

"Our last hazard on the run is the town of Matagalpa, where some Soviet troops could be garrisoned. Watch out for triple-A radars. SA-14 or SA-7 shoulder-fired missiles may also be a factor but if we stay low and fast we should be able to beat an SA-14.

"We'll approach Sebaco from the southeast side of the base. Powell and McLanahan saw one antiaircraft artillery battery on each end of the runway—it'll be worth lobbing a HARM or even a Striker in there if it engages us. They also saw helicopter gunships on the base. These can carry air-to-air heat-seeking missiles too. Our targets are the three hangars on the southwest side of the base and the underground headquarters building three hundred yards southeast from the hangars. The hangars are primary. We'll also drop the CBU cluster-bomb units on the runway and the taxiway-parking ramp area, with emphasis on destroying any aircraft. If the defenses are minimal we can make a circle to the north or northeast and come around for another pass. After the attack, we beat feet to the northeast, terrain-follow in the Cordillera Isabella mountains, and exit along the Honduran border. If we're drowned and each module crew gets separated, evade north or northwest toward Honduras and get a ride to Tegucigalpa. We've all been briefed on the pick-up points in Nicaragua where we can maybe get assistance from Contadora sympathizers. We're using channel Charlie on the survival radios."

They had time to prebrief the details of the mission and talk about their recommended actions in case they were shot down or somehow separated, but it was much different this time—they were actually over hostile territory, surrounded by the military forces of two nations. It had suddenly all become very real.

"J-band search radar at six o'clock," Atkins called out. "Batwing symbol—there's a fighter up there looking for us."

"I.P. inbound, crew," Kellerman said. The Megafortress made a slight left turn, hugging the side of the rugged, tree-covered mountains.

Suddenly a green mushroom-shaped dome appeared briefly on Carter's windscreen. *"Warning, search radar, twelve o'clock."* "We've got something out ahead of us," Carter called out.

"Looks like triple-A," Atkins said, studying his threat receiver. The computer confirmed it seconds later by drawing a tiny gun-icon underneath the green mushroom. "I've got a HARM aligning against it." Just then, the mushroom turned yellow.

"*Warning, threat radar tracking, twelve o'clock.*"

"Should we go around it?" Carter asked.

"No room," Cheshire said. "We'd have to climb five thousand feet to clear these mountains."

"Descend and accelerate," Atkins said. "Stand by for missile launch . . . now."

The yellow BAY DOORS OPEN light came on. "*Caution, bomb doors open . . . warning, HARM missile launch command . . . missile launch . . . bomb doors closed.*"

"Missile away." The one-thousand-pound HARM missile was a yellow streak as it roared away into the darkness. Seconds later there was a splash of fire on the horizon and the glow of flames. The yellow mushroom was gone.

"*Warning, airborne threat radar, six o'clock.*"

Karbayjal activated his fire-control radar and slaved it to the threat receiver so the beam from the tail-mounted tracking radar would look in the exact direction of the threat. The readout he got made him yell into his oxygen visor. "Fighter at six o'clock, five miles, descending rapidly." He hit the voice-command button on his armrest. "Radar lock. Airmine launch one. Launch two. Launch three."

A warning tone sounded on interphone, followed by the hard, short thuds of the Stinger airmine rockets being shot away. "*Radar lock automatic . . . warning, launch command issued . . . airmine launch . . . launch two . . . launch three.*"

But moments later the fighter was still coming—all three airmine rockets had missed. "He's still coming. Prepare for infrared missile attack," Karbayjal called out. "Two miles . . . one mile . . . —break left now."

Carter yanked the Megafortress into a hard left turn. The terrain-following computer immediately commanded a climb to allow for terrain clearance. At the same time Karbayjal punched two flares and chaff out the right side ejectors.

"One mile . . . half mile . . . he's still coming." Nothing was decoying this guy—chaff, flares, jammers, even airmine rockets . . .

The fire-control radar tracked the fighter as it flew closer and closer, but a few seconds later the reason for its daringly close

pass became obvious as Karbayjal watched the fighter's altitude
wind down lower and lower until it finally read zero.

"He *crashed*," Karbayjal called out. "He—"

Suddenly they heard on the scrambled discrete strike frequency, "Dog Two, this is Storm Two. Your tail's clear."

"Powell. McLanahan." Cheshire shouted the names. "Way
to go."

Carter let out his breath. He tasted blood and found he had
bit his lower lip almost all the way through. As he steered the
Megafortress back on course he opened the radio channel.
"Thanks, guys."

J.C. raised Cheetah's nose until he was level with the tops of
the tree-covered mountains, making several tight turns left and
right to clear behind them, searching for a second fighter.
McLanahan, his night-vision visor lowered, searched the sky
behind the F-15. "Clear visually, clear on the threat receiver,"
he said.

"That MiG pilot had balls," J.C. said. "Diving down from
twenty-thousand feet like that, it could have paid off for him."

"But where's his buddies?" McLanahan asked.

J.C. climbed another five-thousand feet, well above the
mountains, and continued his clearing turns. He used the radar
sparingly, relying more on the infrared-laser scanner to avoid
telltale electronic emissions that could give away their location.
"Nothing. One MiG working alone? Unusual."

"They're not up here," McLanahan said. "That means they've
got to be on the deck, flying down that same river valley as the
Old Dog. We either use the radar to look for them . . ."

"Or we go down into the valley ourselves and dig 'em out,"
J.C. said. "I was afraid you'd say that." Powell lowered the
nose once more, plunging Cheetah back into the jungle abyss
below.

They had to dodge far south of course, around sprinkles of ore
mines and tiny villages to avoid the spot where the antiaircraft
artillery gun had been destroyed by one of the Old Dog's HARM
missiles. Carter set five hundred feet in the clearance plane to
allow more leeway in terrain clearance as they roared through a
high valley and across a ridge-line south of the town of Matagalpa.

"We should have met up with that SA-10 site by now," Atkins said nervously. The calm that he had restored in himself after the strike against the SA-15 site had come back full force after the MiG encounter. He was reproaching himself loud enough to trigger the voice-activated interphone, and Karbayjal had to reach across the aisle beside him and touch his shoulder, trying to calm him down. The navigators were quiet. Kellerman had to be prompted to activate the ground-mapping radar to check terrain. Scott was quiet too. He had activated his laser-scanner in preparation for the strike, but the scanner was not moving in any sort of search pattern.

"Nav, brief us on this axis of attack," Carter said, trying to bring his crew back together any way he could think of. "You said we're five miles south of course—how will this affect our attack plan?"

"What?"

"Alicia, get with it," Carter said. "Brief the crew on the attack profile."

A strained pause, then: "We . . . we'll be heading more directly down the runway instead of perpendicular to it," she replied in a ragged voice. "The triple-A will be at our twelve o'clock. It might be harder to pick out from this direction."

"You hear that, Paul?"

"Y . . . yes."

"What else, Alicia?"

"The CBUs," Kellerman said. "We should launch the first pod down the runway after we defeat the triple-A site."

"I can designate the hangars on that pass," Scott put in. He could lock the gyro-stabilized laser-scanner on up to five different images, and no matter how the B-52 turned, the designated targets could be recalled and attacked at any time once they were back within range.

"And the smoke and fire should cover our turn when we line up on the target," Cheshire added.

Carter smiled behind his oxygen visor. "All *right*," he said. "We're starting to sound like a combat crew again. Now let's do it and get out of here."

General Tret'yak stood in the control tower of his small airfield, presiding over preparations for the defense of Sebaco like a modern-day Nicholas I, with his almost medieval forces, defending the battlements of Sevastopol in the Crimea against the then-high-tech forces of the upstart Napoleon III and the unstoppable if inept British. He fancied the defense of Sebaco as a symbol of Soviet power in the western hemisphere, and he was going to repel the invaders of his twenty-five-square-kilometer airfield.

His forces were at the ready, poised for battle as soon as the message from Puerto Cabezas had been received. An exact number of attackers could not be determined—Tret'yak had been bracing for an entire carrier air wing of bombers, but no reports of an American fleet within striking range of Sebaco had been reported. That meant it was a smaller, less formidable strike force on the way, perhaps only a few aircraft. Good—his forces could handle that.

To counter the American attackers, four MiG-23s were idling at the northwest end of the runway, each loaded with four AA-8 missiles on fuselage stations and two infrared-guided close-range AA-11 missiles on underwing pylons, plus a twin-barreled GSh-23 gun and a centerline fuel tank. Two more were in reserve, cannibalized for parts earlier but quickly being repaired and readied for combat.

In addition to the fighters Tret'yak had an SA-8 surface-to-air missile-battery brought up from Managua situated near the center of the runway on a small hill about a kilometer north of the field. The SA-8 was a small, fast missile, capable of destroying the American navy's F/A-18 Hornet fighter-bomber even during a supersonic bomb run. The SA-10 missile site had been moved once again, down from the hills above Sebaco into the Rio Tuma river valley, and it appeared they had positioned it perfectly— any aircraft flying toward Sebaco from Puerto Cabezas had to fly down that valley, right into the jaws of the SA-10 system. The SA-10 was a longer-range missile, capable of defeating attackers from treetop level up to eighty thousand feet. For close-in defense, they still had the two fifty-seven-millimeter guns on each end of the runway, which could create a virtual wall of lead around Sebaco for two miles.

They had other defenses, including Nicaraguan anti-air artillery units deployed in three areas around Sebaco. One of them was located in the Rio Tuma valley, again in perfect position to engage the American attackers.

Tret'yak's forces were in excellent position.

"Message from People's Militia Group seven, sir," an aide reported.

"Who?"

"The Nicaraguan militia force northeast of the base, in Matagalpa," the aide replied. "They report they are under attack. One ZSU-23 anti-aircraft artillery unit destroyed, nine casualties, ten wounded by rocket attack."

"I need details, Lieutenant," Tret'yak said. "What kind of rockets? What kind of aircraft? Speed? Direction?"

As the aide turned to the radio operator, Tret'yak checked his chart of the area, then looked to the tower controller. "Clear the flight for launch, Sergeant. Send them down the Rio Tuma valley and engage the intruders at low altitude."

The controller nodded, picked up his microphone and said in Spanish, "Sebaco flight of four, target at heading zero-nine-five, range twenty miles, cleared—"

Suddenly they saw a flash of light north of the runway, followed by a streak of fire. One of the SA-8 missiles leaped off its launch rail and roared toward the southeast, the missile so low and flying in such a flat trajectory that it looked as if it would hit one of the hangars. The first group of two MiG-23s, which had already gone into afterburner and had begun their takeoff roll, abruptly pulled their engines out of afterburner and stopped as the SA-8 missile roared across the departure end of the runway.

"Missile site two engaging low-altitude targets," the radio operator reported, "bearing one-six-zero true, range twenty kilometers."

"I can *see* that," Tret'yak shouted. "Get those fighters airborne."

"Missile-site two reports multiple targets, sir. They recommend holding the launch until they engage again—"

"No." Then to be on the safe side Tret'yak said, "Tell missile site two to hold fire to let two aircraft depart. Launch aircraft one and two. Tell three and four to hold position. Get five and six ready for takeoff."

The controller called out the new orders, and soon the first two MiG-23s were in afterburner once again and roaring down the runway.

"Afterburner blowout on fighter two," Tret'yak's aide called out. Only one glowing engine was visible in the nighttime sky.

Tret'yak sucked in his breath as he watched the fighter skim the trees to the southeast to build up enough speed for the climb-out. But soon both birds were climbing and turning northeast to find the attackers.

"Have missile site two reengage," Tret'yak ordered. "If they are still picking up targets we'll have three and four head south to—"

His words were drowned out by the roar of another SA-8 missile leaving its rails, following the first missile's flight path except on an even flatter trajectory. The smoke had barely cleared from the second missile launch when Tret'yak saw a brief flash of gunfire from the southern fifty-seven-millimeter triple-A emplacement.

"What is he shooting at . . . ?" His question was interrupted by another bright flash and explosion from the mission site, the boom rolling across the airfield and slamming into the slanted windows of the control tower—but this time no missile left the site.

Tret'yak stared in amazement at the remains of the SA-8 site on the small hill overlooking the runway—half the hill had been blown away, men and vehicles scattered around like a child's upended toy box. The sudden destruction was clearly visible in the glare of a massive fuel fire on top of the hill.

"The missile site has been hit," Tret'yak called out. "Launch the fighters, send units three and four south to engage the aircraft that is launching those missiles, get five and six airborne—"

Another volley of gunfire from the fifty-seven-millimeter unit, followed by an explosion and fireball not a half-kilometer off the end of the runway that lit up almost the entire base. The shock wave from the explosion knocked Tret'yak sideways. The area was littered with secondary explosions, and fires erupted in the forests surrounding Sebaco.

"We got one," someone in the tower yelled. "We got an American aircraft . . ."

The celebration was cut short by another volley of gunfire from the fifty-seven-millimeter gun emplacement. Tret'yak, back on his feet, stared out to watch the gun's tracers streak into the night. Suddenly the significance of what he was watching hit him full force: "Why is the anti-aircraft artillery unit firing tracers?" he yelled. "Their gun is radar-guided and it's nighttime—they don't need tracers. It will only give away their position. Order them to—''

Too late. As Tret'yak watched, the gun site was obliterated. When the glare of the explosion cleared from Tret'yak's eyes, he saw that the gun's radar-trailer, located inside a bunker of its own fifty meters away from the gun itself, had been destroyed. There was collateral damage to the gun itself but it was still intact.

''Anti-radar missiles,'' Tret'yak said angrily. ''They are launching anti-radar missiles. Order the north gun site to use infrared and electro-optical guidance. I want an ambulance over to that south gun sight to—''

''Another missile,'' someone yelled, pointing toward the southeast. In the glare of the forest fires and the burning radar trailer, Tret'yak saw it—a large, sleek, slow-moving winged-missile. It drifted lazily past the burning trees, past the fifty-seven-millimeter gun emplacement—Tret'yak could see men pointing at the missile, but the gun never slewed around and never got a shot off at the object. As if the thing was doing an approach to the runway, the missile cruised right onto the field just to the south of the taxiway, right on the northern edge of the parking ramp. As soon as the missile was over the ramp area, objects like small boxes began to eject themselves from both sides of the craft.

And then huge columns of fire began erupting from the parking ramp every ten or fifteen meters. The main taxiway was hit almost directly down the center, carving large craters in the tarmac. The bombs did the same to the north half of the parking ramp, lifting sections of concrete as if the earth itself was opening up. Bombs fell on the two fully loaded and fueled MiG-23s on the ramp, creating a destruction that spread across the parking ramp. Burning missiles from the MiGs arched across the base, and twenty-three-millimeter gun rounds pinged off the control tower, creating jagged holes in the shatterproof glass. Tret'yak, the controllers and the radiomen dove for the floor. The cluster-bomb drone continued on, dropping its load of destruction. It missed the two MiGs parked on the runway hammerhead by several meters, showering the fighters with pieces of concrete.

Tret'yak stumbled to his feet, grabbing for a microphone. ''Sebaco three and four, take off.'' He did not issue the order in Spanish, but the MiG pilots needed little prompting. The number three MiG put his plane in full afterburner and roared down the runway, pulling his nose up in a hard fast climb. The fourth MiG taxied up to the end of the runway but chose to wait until the third MiG was clear before starting its takeoff.

Finally the fourth MiG lined up with the runway, slapped in max afterburner, released brakes and sped away. The fighter just managed to get its gear up at the end of the runway when an explosion ripped off the MiG's tail section. The MiG flipped up and backward, and the pilot ejected just as the fighter continued its backward spiral and slammed into the ground about a mile off the end of the runway.

A nightmare, Tret'yak thought—except this one was real. One by one, Sebaco's defenses had been neutralized—and not one enemy fighter had yet been spotted—a blur of motion off to the south attracted his attention, and then he did see it . . . a massive dark shape hugging the ground no higher than the ten-story control tower. It flew diagonally across the south end of the runway about a half-mile from the tower. It was *huge*, one of the biggest aircraft Tret'yak had ever seen. The sound of its engines was like a freight train rumbling by at full speed.

The aircraft banked sharply left, aligning itself with the row of buildings and hangars along the parking ramp area. Tret'yak could see a few soldiers firing their rifles at the apparition, but to the KGB general it was as if they were trying to kill a whale with squirt guns. The aircraft roared down the runway with the sound of a gigantic waterfall. Illuminated as it was in the fires on the parking ramp, Tret'yak could see that the monstrosity had a long pointed nose, no visible tail-control surfaces and huge sprawling wings with missiles of different sizes hanging from them. It was not like any aircraft he had ever seen.

Just as quickly as the thing appeared it was gone, leaving in its wake clouds of dust and smoke swirling around the few remaining fires. The silence was awesome, as if the huge black craft had sucked all air and all sound away with it. Tret'yak stood in the control tower, staring through the shattered glass of the control tower at the scene below. What had been an important Soviet military base a few minutes before had been turned into chaos.

"What *was* that thing?" the senior controller asked, shaking bits of glass off his tunic. "I've never seen anything like it."

"It had to be some sort of bomber," Tret'yak said, shaking his head. "But I've never known such a large aircraft to fly so low on a bomb run. It was obviously the aircraft that launched the anti-radar missiles and set off those bombs that cratered our ramp."

"Could it have destroyed our fourth fighter?"

"It could not have—" But Tret'yak paused. A bomber carrying air-to-air missiles? Why not? That bomber that passed by seemed to be carrying several kinds of weapons under its huge wings. Instead Tret'yak replied, "Any reports from our radar sites? Any reports from Managua?"

"No, sir, not yet. We should have communications reestablished shortly."

Tret'yak turned to the communications operator. "I want a rescue crew out to find the pilot of our fourth MiG. And I want that ramp cleared as soon as possible. Our fighters will need to land in about an hour." The operator nodded and began to issue the orders. Lights snapped on, further revealing the damage caused by the strange drone. But as men and machines moved out to the ramp to put out the fires, the extent of the damage was not as total as first thought.

"We have been hit, but not put out of action," Tret'yak said. "The runway appears open, our fuel stubs and hangars are intact and only half our ramp space has been affected. This base is still operational."

"We've been fortunate, sir," the senior controller said, "that bomber looked large enough to carry a hundred bombs. It could have caused much destruction . . ."

Tret'yak was about to reply, but the words caught in his throat. He remembered seeing weapons hanging off the wings . . . the bomber did not drop any bombs over the base . . .

He suddenly turned to the communications operator. "Clear that ramp immediately, shut off the lights."

"But, sir, the firefighters—"

"That bomber is coming back. It did not withdraw—it only found more targets. Order the gun sites to—"

Too late. An explosion erupted in the northern fifty-seven-millimeter gun-emplacement bunker—Tret'yak didn't need his binoculars to know that the north gun had just been destroyed.

"Tell the south gun to open fire. Forget the radar guidance—just fire the gun to the north, bracket the area. *Quickly*."

But the radio operator froze, gaping out the windows to the north across the runway. Tret'yak grabbed the microphone and was about to push the man out of the way when he too looked up and followed the man's stare.

The dark shape roared out of the jungle surrounding Sebaco like some sort of prehistoric bird, swooping so low over the trees that it appeared to be skimming the tops, the wing vortices and engine thrust snapping branches and parting the forest. When it cleared the trees it dropped even lower, not more than twenty or thirty meters above ground. It was headed right for the control tower, aiming its pointed nose at a spot, it seemed, right between Tret'yak's eyes.

In rapid succession four dark streaks arced away from the bomber's belly. The first headed straight ahead, plowing into the center of Sebaco's two-kilometer runway. The explosion obscured the bomber for several seconds until the behemoth crashed through the column of smoke, bearing down on the control tower.

A second missile missed the control tower by a few meters, flew by and hit a building somewhere behind the tower—Tret'yak immediately thought of his headquarters building a few hundred meters directly in that weapon's path. The missiles seemed to be massive bombs with wings, more flying whales than missiles. A third and forth explosion rocked the hangars off to Tret'yak's left, blowing out the hangar doors, collapsing both buildings and scattering pieces of steel and concrete in all directions. Secondary explosions blew the roofs off another hangar, adding more fuel to the fires now burning out of control all along the flight line.

The massive aircraft then executed an impossibly tight left turn toward the southeast. The roar of the bomber's engines was so great that it threatened to collapse the control tower. As it banked away, its broad jet-black fuselage missing the tower by only a dozen meters, the remaining glass panels exploded as if grenades had been set off inside the room. Tret'yak was thrown off his feet, blinded and deafened by the hurricane-like aftermath. Tables, books, chairs and pieces of equipment flew everywhere.

Tret'yak could not move for several moments, and even

though he was awake and alert he felt as if he had been dis-
membered. Finally he shook off the piles of debris on his back
and struggled to his feet. The control tower was beginning to
fill with smoke as the fires in the nearby hangars intensified;
the underground fuel pits, containing over forty thousand deca-
liters of jet fuel, were in danger unless the fires could be
contained.

He helped his men to their feet and toward the exits as he
surveyed what he could see of his airbase. The runway had
one huge crater in the center, leaving about nine hundred meters usable on either side of the crater—not enough to recover
the MiG-23s. It would take a day to repair it; the fighters
would have to land at Sandino International, Bluefields or
Puerto Cabezas. The taxiway was destroyed and the parking
ramp was unusable. Two fifty-seven-millimeter guns and one
SA-8 missile site out of commission—the SA-10 site in the
Rio Tuma valley had apparently been destroyed as well. Not
to mention the one MiG-23 fighter destroyed right after takeoff. Tret'yak checked the area behind the tower and found the
second American glide-bomb had hit the roof of the underground headquarters building, but caused no apparent serious
damage or fire.

*One aircraft* had done all this. He had planned on taking
on the combined might of an American carrier air group, and
*one bomber* had wiped out all his defenses in less than ten
minutes.

He needed to transmit a report as soon as possible back
to Moscow. The stolen American fighter was safe, but the
Americans had just raised the price of keeping it to an all-
time high.

The flight out of Nicaragua was no cakewalk for the Megafortress and her crew, but the loss of all ground-controlled intercept
capability over Nicaragua and the loss of contact with Sebaco
seemed to take the fight out of the Nicaraguan MiG pilots. One
had been destroyed by Stinger fire from the Megafortress as it
tried to tail-chase the bomber at low altitude, and another was
damaged by a near-miss from one of Cheetah's dogfighting AIM-
132 missiles; the rest turned around and headed for Sandino
International Airport. Powell and McLanahan followed the B-52

out over the Caribbean until it was picked up by the E-5 AWACS radar plan orbiting over the Cayman Islands.

"First things first," Bradley Elliott said when secure communications with the strike formation had been established. "Patrick, Wendy's out of surgery. She's still officially in critical condition. I can't get any other information out of the hospital staff. We could airlift you from Georgetown and have you in San Antonio in four hours—"

"No . . . as long as she's being taken care of. I'm where I need to be right now."

"We've got other back-seaters for Powell—"

"*I* am Powell's back-seater. Maraklov's gotta break out sooner or later and I have to be there when he does. Oh hell, of course I'd like to go to her, but I also know I can't do her any good. Not now. And I've got more hours in Cheetah than anyone else. I'm the only one familiar enough with her systems to take her into combat. If DreamStar got away while I was in Texas it would be a disaster for us all. And if I know Wendy, she'd kill me if I sat around her bedside while . . . well, you know what I mean."

Aboard the E-5 AWACS, Elliott still considered pulling McLanahan, but not because of Wendy. His near-fixation on evening it up with Maraklov had come perilously close to personal, and soldiers on a vendetta made poor fighters. Still, he was right, he was the best-qualified crewman for Cheetah, and only Cheetah could hope to take on DreamStar in air-to-air combat. The time to have the first team on the line was right now, when the chances of DreamStar leaving Nicaragua were most likely . . .

"All right, Patrick," Elliott said. "Agreed, at least for now. Break. Kelvin, job well done to you and your crew. Radar shows your tail is clear. Climb to flight level two-six-zero. Your tanker is orbiting over Grand Cayman at two-seven-zero. Everyone okay?"

"Affirmative," Carter replied on the scrambled UHF channel. "We're beat but unhurt. We might have picked up some blast damage from the last run we did—we were a little close to the explosion when we dropped a Striker on the runway, and with our bay doors open we might have picked up some fuel leaks—but we should be able to recover in Dreamland. I'd like to have a tanker meet us over the CONUS in case we have a leaking aft body tank.''

"We'll work on that for you right away," Elliott said.

"While you're at it," Cheshire cut in, "maybe you can get us clearance to land in Georgetown for a few days.''

"I thought of that, Nancy," Elliott replied, "but we had a little trouble convincing the government to let the F-16s, the KC-10s and the AWACS in—a Buff would have been out of the question. Besides, technically the Megafortress Plus is still classified. But we can arrange a short TDY for a debriefing, I think. Break. J.C., Patrick, any problems with Cheetah?''

"We're in the green," Patrick told him. "I just wish our late friend had showed for the party.''

"It was a long shot, Patrick," Elliott said. "There's fifty-thousand square miles of nothing in Nicaragua where they could have hidden DreamStar. We've intercepted radio traffic that seems to indicate it might be in Puerto Cabezas but we're not positive.''

"It's worth a look.''

"We're not loaded for air-to-mud, Patrick," J.C. cut in. "There's nothing we can do to him except wave as we fly by. Besides, we'd fly right into the teeth of that SA-15 Atkins said was there.''

"We've done more than the White House wanted to authorize. We'll maintain our surveillance in case they try to fly DreamStar out. We're changing your flight plan, though, because of this new intelligence," Elliott continued. "We've secured landing rights at Puerto Lempira, a Honduran army base seventy miles north of Puerto Cabezas—that was the original base for this operation until we got landing rights in the Cayman Islands. We're trying to get authorization now from the White House to set up a photo-run at Puerto Cabezas like the one you did on Sebaco. We've got fuel and weapons being airlifted there to meet you. It's not Georgetown but you'll be in position in case DreamStar tries to make another run for it.''

"Sounds good," McLanahan said. "I want to be there when he tries to get away again.''

## The Kremlin, Moscow, USSR
*Monday, 22 June 1996, 0932 EET (0132 EDT)*

Outside the foreboding walls of the Kremlin the bright, clear summer morning belied the internal struggle taking place. There, two of the government's most powerful men were sitting across from each other, locked in a silent combat.

The Chief of Staff of the Soviet military, General Cherkov, had just delivered a briefing to the General Secretary and Vladimir Kalinin, Chief of the KGB. The General Secretary nodded to Cherkov, who was unsure whether or not he had just been directed to leave; he kept his seat, with no objections from the two principals with him.

"I disagree with General Cherkov's analysis of the information provided from General Tret'yak," Kalinin said. "He says that the American experimental fighter is safe in hiding at Puerto Cabezas, guarded by both KGB and Nicaraguan troops, but then he says that the aircraft is in danger. That is inconsistent. Tret'yak is understandably shaken after sustaining the Americans' preemptive attack—"

"Your rhetoric is the only thing that is inconsistent here, Kalinin," the General Secretary said. "The Americans destroyed one of our military bases, shot down two of our fighters and decimated our defenses. Yet you can sit there and say your plan is progressing well and that there is no cause for alarm?"

"We won't know the true extent of the damage for several hours," Kalinin hedged. "But what happens to Sebaco is irrelevant to our mission. The XF-34 is *safe*, it is still combat ready and can make the flight to Ramenskoye. In two hours, we will begin launching escort aircraft from Cuba, and the decoy aircraft from Managua will make their way north to—"

"Your plan has failed, Vladimir," the General Secretary said. "Admit it before any more men are killed and we lose any more aircraft or bases." He shook his head. "It is only a matter of time before they discover the fighter in this, this Puerto Cabezas place. Then they will proceed to destroy *that* airfield—" he scanned the report, tossing it away with a dramatic flourish— "with one bomber. *One bomber*. What do we do against one of their aircraft carriers or a *squadron* of these bombers?"

"The attack on Sebaco was expected," Kalinin argued. "That was the reason why we moved the fighter out of there. Tret'yak described some sort of new bomber that carried defense-suppression weapons as well as air-to-ground weapons, and it possibly carried air-to-air—" Kalinin suddenly stopped. "The *kryepahst ezometyelna*," he said half-aloud.

"The what?"

"The Megafortress project," Kalinin said. "The highly modified B-52 bomber developed in the Nevada research area, the same place where the XF-34 was built. The American Air Force general, Bradley Elliott, flew a Megafortress against our strategic-defense laser-installation at Kavaznya eight years ago; it carried the same unusual mix of weapons as the bomber that attacked Sebaco. It must have been a Megafortress they used to beat down our defenses and attack Sebaco." Kalinin slapped a hand on the conference table, muttering to himself. "*Parazetyel'na!* Vilizherchev said he met Elliott in Washington at the White House. We should have *known* Elliott would be called on to formulate an attack plan—"

"You mean you knew the man who would direct this attack?" the General Secretary interrupted, staring at the KGB chief. "You knew about this meeting—which did not appear in your report or Vilizherchev's report—and you knew that this Elliott would be involved with the planning yet you failed to anticipate the attack and failed to take actions to protect our base from attack. I am ending this craziness—"

"You can't stop it now—all the forces are in place and ready—"

"Then order them to stand down," the General Secretary said. "Kalinin, how much more do you want? The Americans want their fighter back, and as long as the aircraft is in Central America they have the resources to offset every effort we make to bring it out."

"One more attempt," Kalinin said. His voice softened, and he opened his hands, virtually pleading. "I ask for one more try. All our forces are in readiness, it can begin in two hours . . ."

"Request denied."

"If our aircraft are detected and intercepted I will order them to turn around and return to Nicaragua without a battle," Kalinin said. "But if we surround the XF-34 with fighter aircraft, even if the formation is detected I think the Americans will have no choice but to allow us to proceed.''

"*I* disagree," Cherkov put in. "I believe the Americans would attack the formation. Even if they didn't openly attack, which they did *not* do over the Caribbean on your first attempt to smuggle the XF-34 out of Nicaragua, there is too much chance for disaster. An air battle would almost certainly result. I cannot endorse such an operation—''

"You'd do anything to save your pension and your *dacha* . . .''

"Silence, Kalinin.''

"Your defense of me is not necessary, sir," Cherkov said. "Actions speak louder than words and *young* Kalinin's actions in this operation prove what sort of tactician he is.''

"It was not *my* pilot that tried to ram the American fighters," Kalinin said quickly. "It was not my ineffective pilots that could not defeat inferior American forces." Kalinin chose not to mention that the air-defense troops around Sebaco were all KGB. Cherkov did not bring it up either.

Kalinin turned to the General Secretary, trying to put on his best humble, earnest face. "Then allow me to bring the fighter out on one of our carriers, sir. A Kiev-class cruiser with escorts can be brought from Havana to Puerto Cabezas within the hour. The XF-34 can easily land on one, and the Americans would not dare attack a carrier . . .''

"But one of these Megafortress bombers could send a few of the carrier's escorts to the bottom of the Caribbean," the General Secretary said. "Vladimir, I have lost count of the number of fighters, transports, men and equipment we have lost trying to bring that fighter out of Nicaragua. Even if what you say is true—if this DreamStar fighter is worth ten of our front-line fighters—we are definitely on the minus side of the ledger. We have lost six MiG fighters along with the Ilyushin radar plane, which I understand is worth ten or twenty fighters, plus the transport helicopter and its men and crew in Mexico. If we then lost a seven-thousand-metric-ton capital ship to an American attack, we would all be deposed by the Politburo. That could still happen . . .''

He reached to the phone on his desk and buzzed his confidential secretary. "I am going to order Vilizherchev to open negotiations with the Americans for the transfer of the aircraft back to them. You will not move the aircraft from its present location. You will not remove or damage any of its components. I do want you to collect as much information about the aircraft as you can without damaging it—we had better get more out of this nightmare operation than a dozen caskets.''

"Sir, you *must* reconsider," Kalinin said. "If we stop now, if we don't attempt to get the aircraft to Russia, all those men will have been killed for nothing, all of our efforts will have been for nothing."

"All of *your* efforts, Kalinin," the General Secretary said. "*Your* operation. I must remind you that I was against this operation from the beginning. I told you it would never succeed. I will not accept responsibility for an operation that I never approved and that was conducted largely without my knowledge."

The General Secretary's senior aide came into the office, carrying notepaper and pencil. "Now see to it that the XF-34 is secured and ready for transport."

"I ask you once more," Kalinin said. The General Secretary was turned away from him. "If we succeed, and I stake my life that we will, there will be huge assets for both of us, sir. We are already committed, we must—"

"Your career is already at stake here, Kalinin," the General Secretary said. Mine too, he thought gloomily. "I will concentrate on repairing the damage caused by your ill-conceived plan. Do as I've ordered."

Outside, Molokov, Kalinin's aide, fell in behind him. "Sir . . . ?" Kalinin gave his instructions.

"Back to KGB headquarters," Molokov told the driver. To Kalinin he asked, "What is the situation, sir?"

Kalinin filled him in, needing to unload his feelings. "I have no more authority in this. I am only authorized to collect as much data as possible on the aircraft without damaging it, then prepare to *turn it over to the Americans*."

They drove through the streets of Moscow in silence until approaching KGB headquarters, then Molokov said, "Maraklov will not like this. Turning over that fighter to the Americans, after all he's done, will be like asking him to turn over one of his legs to a shark."

Kalinin suddenly turned to Molokov, an idea forming in his

head, becoming clearer every moment. "Maraklov . . . yes, perhaps he can secure the aircraft for us . . ."

"Sir?"

"Maraklov . . . I need a secure satellite channel to Puerto Cabezas. The General Secretary will brief Vilizherchev in less than an hour, and Vilizherchev will ask to confer with the President by seventeen hundred hours Moscow time—I must talk with Maraklov immediately."

"There is a transponder set up with the command post at Puerto Cabezas now, sir," Molokov said. "What will you do?"

"This operation is still on, my friend," Kalinin said. "There may still be a way . . ."

# =8=

## Puerto Lempira Airbase, Honduras
*Sunday, 21 June 1996, 0612 CDT (1512 EET)*

PATRICK McLANAHAN AND J. C. Powell might have thought they had been transported to the set of a low-budget Vietnam war movie. They were sitting on a plastic fold-up picnic table inside a musty green canvas tent, eating cold scrambled eggs and canned ham out of tin mess kits. Outside, it was warm and impossibly humid, with occasional heavy downpours that seemed to erupt with no warning and then, just as abruptly, end a few minutes later as if God had simply shut off a faucet somewhere in the heavens. Their sweaty flight suits, now going on their second day of use, stuck to their bodies like strips of papier-mâché and smelled like the saltwater swamps that surrounded the tiny Honduran airbase.

"Airbase" might have been a flattering term for Puerto Lempira. The base was actually a small airstrip clinging to a marsh near the ocean on the northeast corner of Honduras, only forty miles from the Nicaraguan border. The place had a nine-thousand-foot concrete runway, but only six thousand feet of it was usable, the encroaching swamps having retaken almost half a mile of the eastern end; workers were busy sandbagging the end of the runway, trying to drain it. There was a small concrete aircraft parking area where a prefabricated aircraft hangar had been erected for Cheetah. Outside the ramp area was a half-sand, half-rock clearing where the tents and a communication trailer had been airlifted in—except for the runway, the entire base may have occupied a total of five acres.

Almost all the personnel at Puerto Lempira were security

guards, here to guard Cheetah and the support equipment that had been moved in. Over the years Puerto Lempira had been used more by smugglers and drug runners than military forces. Four guards stood watch in Cheetah's portable hangar, two guarded the communications trailer, and another thirty were stationed around the airbase's perimeter. Everyone expected trouble.

"When do you suppose we'll get out of here?" J.C. asked, frowning at the lump of canned ham in his mess kit and pushing it away.

"No idea." McLanahan glanced at the device that had been set up on the picnic table beside him. "We should find out soon."

The device was a field communications unit linked to the system of power generators and electronics in the trailer. They had instant satellite, UHF, VHF and HF communications capability with most of the rest of the world through that tiny unit, which was about the size of a cereal box.

The rains began coming down again, lightly at first, then in virtual sheets with big fat rain droplets that threatened to shred their canvas roof. The rain rattled the metal roof of Cheetah's hangar. Cheetah had been rearmed for air combat with both long- and short-ranged missiles, but intelligence had been received that DreamStar might have been moved to Puerto Cabezas in Nicaragua less than a hundred miles away, and a crew was standing by to arm Cheetah with its photo-reconnaissance pod again—as well as an array of air-to-ground weapons.

The sound of the rain almost drowned out the gentle beeping of the satellite communications transceiver. McLanahan picked up the receiver, laying his finger on the SCRAMBLE/DESCRAMBLE button. When he heard the snaps and whine on the other end he hit the button. The static disappeared, replaced by a faint hiss.

"McLanahan."

"Patrick, this is Brad Elliott." His heart began pounding— Elliot rarely used his first name, even to his closest friends and most senior officers, unless something was wrong.

"Go ahead, sir."

"I've sent a F-15E down to pick you up. It should arrive in about an hour from now."

"Wendy . . . ?"

"They've asked you to come back."

Suddenly, in the heat and humidity, he felt very, very cold. He forced himself to ask, "What about DreamStar?"

A slight pause, then: "No word yet. We're bringing your replacement on the F-15, a guy from the tactical bomb squadron at Luke Air Force Base. He'll fly Cheetah if DreamStar tries to make a break. The F-15E will fly you directly back to Brooks AFB."

This time he did not try to rationalize staying with Cheetah in Honduras. She had spent hours in surgery and a full day in post-operative intensive care. Now even General Elliott was telling him to come back . . .

Or maybe he finally realized that it was time for him to start facing up to reality. He had flown three missions in Cheetah since she was hurt, tearing himself away—no, *running* away—from her agony, claiming that he was the only one who could do the job, the only one who could defeat James in DreamStar. In fact, a young F-15E back-seater in Cheetah could probably do a better job than a forty-year-old desk jockey. His responsibility was with his wife and her family—not hiding behind an oxygen mask and a radar scope.

"How's J.C. and your bird?" Elliott asked.

"Okay. Ready to go."

"Okay. We've scheduled Cheetah for a photo-recon run over Puerto Cabezas—we'd like to pinpoint DreamStar's location but that's unlikely. But they well might think it's another prelude to an attack, help convince them to turn DreamStar over to us *intact*."

Silence.

"Patrick, about Wendy. What can I say? I wish to God she hadn't been on that plane—"

"General, I'm sick and tired of everyone giving Wendy up for dead. And as far as I'm concerned we should stop pussyfooting around with the damned Russians. No more damn messages, no more warnings. If we think DreamStar is in Puerto Cabezas let's go in and get it. Right now. If we send Cheetah up to take pictures they'll just move DreamStar somewhere else. Bring the carrier *George Washington* in with a naval bombardment squadron, level Puerto Cabezas and let's stop jacking around."

When there was no response from the other end he thought

the connection had been broken. Then Elliott said: "Keep us advised on Wendy's condition, Patrick. Elliott out."

He dropped the phone back on its cradle. J.C. was looking at him carefully. "I'm leaving as soon as my plane gets here," McLanahan told him.


## The White House, Washington, D.C.
*Sunday, 21 June 1996, 0815 EDT*

"All I want to know from you, Vilizherchev," President Taylor said as the Russian ambassador entered the Oval Office, "is where our aircraft is and when it will be returned to us."

Sergei Vilizherchev was taken off guard but shrugged it off and continued inside the office. He was followed by Secretary of State Danahall, who had met the ambassador at the rear entrance to the White House. Secretary of Defense Stuart, Secretary of the Air Force Curtis, Secretary of the Navy John Kemp, National Security Adviser Chairperson Deborah O'Day, Speaker Van Keller and Attorney General Benson were already in the Oval Office, summoned there immediately after learning of the Russian's hurried request for a meeting. The President's advisers formed a semi-circle around Vilizherchev as the ambassador approached the President's desk. Taylor ignored Vilizherchev's offered hand; he did not stand to greet the ambassador.

The Russian smiled and made a slight bow. "Very nice to see you again, sir . . ."

"I asked you a question, Mr. Ambassador," the President said. "I want that fighter. Immediately."

"Mr. President, I am here to deliver my government's most emphatic protest of the attack on our military installation last night," Vilizherchev said, as if ignoring the President's outburst. "That attack cost the lives of three pilots, four men on the ground, and millions of dollars worth of equipment and property destroyed. The attack was inexcusable—"

Taylor interrupted: "Mr. Curtis."

Wilbur Curtis flicked on a high-resolution video monitor and began rolling a tape. "This was transmitted to us less than ten minutes ago, Mr. Ambassador," Curtis said. The monitor showed a concrete bunker, open at both ends, inside a depressed rain-soaked aircraft parking area. Soldiers surrounded the structure. A few could be seen pointing rifles in the air, obviously taking aim at the aircraft taking the photographs. Inside one open end of the hangar the unmistakable forward-swept wings of DreamStar could clearly be seen in the early-morning sunlight.

"You moved our aircraft to a different base and we found it," the President said. "If I don't get the answer I'm looking for I pick up this phone and I order the Navy to level that base like they leveled Sebaco. In fifteen minutes this whole thing will be over—I guarantee it."

"The attack will fail," Vilizherchev said quickly. "Such an offensive has been anticipated. We have strengthened the coastal defenses and are ready for such an assault—"

"The crew of this recon jet reported no defenses anywhere," Curtis said. "We have pictures of the destroyed SA-15 missile sites—want to see them, Mr. Ambassador?"

"I must also tell you, sir, that Soviet forces in the region are prepared to retaliate. If American bombers cross the border again, orders have been issued to attack Honduran airfields with Soviet supersonic bombers from Cuba. They will destroy one airfield, military or civilian, for every Nicaraguan base destroyed. The bombers are armed with supersonic cruise missiles that cannot be intercepted. If naval forces are encountered they have been ordered to attack them as well. Your new aircraft carrier *George Washington* is in the area, I believe—will you risk a three billion dollar vessel for one aircraft? Pride is a poor reason to go to war, sir."

"Likewise stupidity," the President said. "I don't need to remind you what would happen if the Soviet Union tries to start a shooting war in the Caribbean."

"We have two aircraft-carrier groups, three strategic air divisions and nine tactical air divisions ready to send into the area," Stuart said. "That's twenty capital ships and twelve hundred aircraft that can be deployed in less time than it will take you to get back to your office."

"And all I need, mister, is one Russian cruise missile," the President said. "Just one. It doesn't even have to *hit* anything. One missile or one bomber aimed at American forces and we end the Soviet presence in the Caribbean for good. I'll wipe out everything with a red star on it."

Vilizherchev stood in front of the President's desk, virtually in shock. "You . . . you are talking a major war, Mr. President," he said. "You are threatening war over this . . . this mere aircraft . . ."

"I'm threatening over your lies, your deceit. And your murdering. You stole our aircraft, murdered our soldiers, killed and destroyed and killed again all through Central America just to steal one fighter. What you've done is declare war on the United States. I'm going to start answering you by destroying Puerto Cabezas." He picked up the telephone and punched two digits on the keypad.

"This is the President. Unlock file nine-six-zero-six bravo, authenticate with line charlie-charlie and execute immediately. Send reports to the Situation Room. I'll be there in ten minutes." He hung up the phone and pointed to Vilizherchev. "Good day, sir."

"Will we not discuss this, Mr. President . . . ?"

Just then two beepers went off—Vilizherchev spun around at the sound as if it had been a gunshot. Both Kemp and Curtis retrieved their tiny credit-card-sized pagers from jacket pockets and checked the message on its tiny liquid-crystal screen.

"Execution cross-checks, Mr. President," Curtis said. "Crews are responding. I'd like to take it in the Situation Room."

"You're dismissed, John, Wilbur . . ."

"Wait, Mr. President, Secretary Curtis, Secretary Kemp, please," Vilizherchev said. "We must discuss this . . ." Curtis and Kemp turned and headed for the door.

The President turned to his Secretary of State and his aide. "Dennis, Paul, escort the ambassador out of the White House. Deborah, I need you to call your staff down to the Situation Room in ten minutes to—"

"I am authorized to release the aircraft to you, Mr. President," Vilizherchev shouted. Everyone in the room froze. The President pointed to the Secretary of the Navy.

"Get going, John. This sounds like a stall to me. Get your planes from the *George Washington* airborne. I want a prestrike briefing from the Navy when I get there. Wilbur, hang on for a minute." Kemp opened his mouth, was about to say something, then decided against it and hurried out.

"I came here to organize a transfer of the aircraft back into your control, Mr. President," Vilizherchev said, staring at the closed door of the Oval Office through which Kemp had just exited. He turned back to the President. "The General Secretary has directed that the aircraft be turned over to you immediately."

"So what about all that garbage about retaliatory strikes, bombers and cruise missiles?" Deborah O'Day asked. "Was that a bluff?"

"The same as your bluff with the attack on Puerto Cabezas . . ."

"That is no bluff, Vilizherchev," the President said. "I've got bombers from the *George Washington* lined up to attack that base, whether DreamStar is there or not. When the air attack is completed I've ordered a company of Marines to land, occupy that base and take control of the area. If they don't find that aircraft they'll move down to Bluefields and level that base. After Bluefields they'll move inland all the way to Managua."

"This is not a bluff, Mr. Ambassador," Curtis said. "Once those planes are airborne, we're committed."

"The President has approval from Congress, sir," Van Keller said. The Speaker of the House of Representatives and the congressional Majority Leader was sweating. "The plan was presented early this morning to the Senate and House committee chairmen. We stand behind the President."

"All *right*," Vilizherchev said. "The bombers, the cruise missiles, the attacks against Honduras . . . I invented them. I had to find a way to regain at least some of my bargaining position—"

"This is not the time for diplomatic face-saving, Mr. Ambassador," the President said. "In five minutes those planes launch."

"I have been ordered to negotiate a way to turn the fighter back to you," Vilizherchev said. "No conditions. The General Secretary has directed it be done immediately."

"Is the aircraft flyable?" Curtis asked.

"Yes. It is at Puerto Cabezas, as you already know. It was flown there to avoid the attack against Sebaco."

"What about the pilot? What about James?"

"A KGB agent, the project was run by the KGB. The General Secretary learned of the theft of the aircraft only after it landed in Nicaragua. The General Secretary never agreed to keep the aircraft in Nicaragua—he never knew of the plan to move it out of your country. The whole affair was run by Vladimir Kalinin of the KGB.''

''So why should the KGB turn the aircraft over to us now?'' Deborah O'Day asked. ''If they control the aircraft . . .''

''The aircraft is now in the hands of the Soviet army, not the KGB. Colonel Maraklov has been ordered to return to Sebaco to await transportation to Moscow via Managua. The army has orders to make the aircraft ready to be flown out of Nicaragua.''

Deborah O'Day looked at the President. ''Sir, it is over . . .''

''Not yet,'' the President said. ''I'll cancel the air strike, but I'm keeping the *George Washington* on station. I don't trust these people. Not any more. Wilbur, I want you in the Situation Room for a meeting. Postpone the air strikes for now.'' Curtis nodded, a faint hint of a smile on his face not detectable by anyone, and departed.

''Then I suggest sending in a security force to guard the aircraft,'' Stuart said, ''until we can figure out how we can get the aircraft out of there.''

''General Elliott is in the Cayman Islands in control of the air forces,'' O'Day said. ''He has a man that can fly DreamStar— only specially trained pilots can fly it. He can send in a security unit with the pilot and some technicians that can inspect the aircraft. He can make the decision on how to get DreamStar out.''

The President nodded to O'Day, then looked at the Russian ambassador.

Vilizherchev understood that look. ''I assure you, the General Secretary is anxious to be done with this . . . incident.''

''Bill, get down to the Situation Room, advise Mr. Kemp to hold the Second Fleet's air raid but tell them to stay on the alert.'' Stuart nodded and departed.

''Deborah, set up a satellite call in the conference room with General Elliott. We will plan this thing together so the ambassador knows what we'll want from his people and the Nicaraguans. I'll meet you all there in a minute.'' Van Keller, Danahall and Vilizherchev filed out of the Oval Office, led by Cesare, but Deborah O'Day stayed behind.

''What is it, Debbie?''

''Did I hear all this correctly a minute ago? Did I hear you say you had elements of the Second Fleet ready to invade Nicaragua?''

"You must have heard it correctly," the President said with the hint of a smile. "Kemp and Curtis heard it, too."

O'Day said, "Strike aircraft with heavy bombs on board usually have to jettison their bombs before recovering back on the carrier. But I'm confused. I didn't know anything about an invasion plan. Did you formulate a plan with John and—" She stopped, then stared at the President. "You *made that up*?"

"I thought Vilizherchev might be lying to me again," the President said, "so I raised the stakes on him. He had nothing in his hand but he wanted to challenge me. The guy has balls. Without authorization, without anything to back himself up with, the guy stood in front of me and threatened us with war if *we* didn't back off."

"So what will you do if the Russians won't turn DreamStar over to us? Will you invade Nicaragua after all?"

"Yes. He forced my hand, whether he knew it or not. Now we both have to live with that threat. Hell, I wish we did have congressional authorization for an invasion. Van Keller makes a good poker player, too. He played right along, just like you and Wilbur.

"If the Russians don't turn over DreamStar, I'm prepared to destroy Puerto Cabezas, then order the Marines to occupy it. We'll have to make a decision on whether or not to go after those other airfields and bases after that."

## Sebaco, Nicaragua
*Sunday, 21 June 1996, 1132 CDT (1032 EDT)*

"Am I under arrest?" Andrei Maraklov said, pulling himself away from the KGB Border Guards that had escorted him into Sebaco's command post.

General Tret'yak turned toward him, waving at the guards to leave him. "Arrest? No, Colonel, you are not under arrest. Why would you think such a thing?"

"Because some Russian and Nicaraguan army bozos dragged me out of DreamStar and threw me into a helicopter to take me back here," Maraklov said. "What the hell is going on? I can't allow DreamStar to be left alone and unprotected like that. And I want my flight suit back. That's a delicate piece of equipment—"

"It's no longer your concern, Colonel. You don't look so well, Colonel Maraklov. Apparently Central America does not agree with you."

Actually Maraklov did look in poor health. Most of the men under Tret'yak's command, because of bad water, stress and the spicy food had lost weight after coming to Nicaragua, but Maraklov had only been here a week and he looked emaciated. The elastic belt on his flight suit was drawn in so much that the ends overlapped halfway around his waist, and his eyes looked almost ghostly in the command center's stark overhead lighting. He also seemed to be losing hair. Could he be on drugs? No—Maraklov was guarded night and day and observed through hidden cameras while in his room. If he was doing drugs he was being very crafty indeed to escape detection.

Maraklov's anger flared. "Forget my waistline, General. What do you mean, DreamStar is no longer my concern?"

"The army has been ordered to take control of the aircraft, effective immediately."

"And what are they going to do with it?"

"I don't know or care. My job is to get this base operational again. Your fighter, or you for that matter, are no longer my concern."

"My mission was to deliver that aircraft to Ramenskoye Test Center in Moscow," Maraklov said. "I have authority to demand assistance from all Soviet or allied forces. That includes you—"

"*Nyet*. My last order concerning you was to see to it that you board an Aeroflot plane in Managua for Moscow when you are told to do so, which will be in the next two or three days. Meanwhile you are not to return to Puerto Cabezas or go anywhere near the DreamStar aircraft. You will not be placed under arrest but I trust you will do as you are told."

"This is nuts. Why is the KGB abandoning the project now? We can still get DreamStar to Russia—why are they giving up like this?"

"I don't know," Tret'yak said. "The KGB troops under my command have not been used to secure the fighter—they are using only Red Army troops. Who knows, perhaps they have made a bargain with the Americans for the return of the fighter . . ." He paused, staring at Maraklov. "Perhaps they do not trust you any longer."

"What do you mean by that?"

"I *mean*, Colonel Maraklov, where were you when Sebaco was under attack? You had four missiles and extra fuel on board your fighter, and yet you stayed in Puerto Cabezas and hid in your concrete bunker while my airbase was being blown to hell by an American B-52 bomber. You—"

"A B-52 bomber? You mean *one* B-52 bomber?"

"Yes, one B-52," Tret'yak said, "armed with air-to-air and air-to-ground weapons. Certainly your amazing fighter plane could have shot it down with ease—if you had bothered to join in the fight."

"Well how the hell was I supposed to know it was only one plane? We were expecting a major assault—I got into the bunker and shut down before they could track me. Besides, I was never informed—"

"It was never your intention to help defend the base," Tret'yak said. "One plane or a hundred—you were not going to come to our aid." He rubbed his eyes irritably, then held up a hand before Maraklov could speak. "Your special metallic flight suit has been impounded—you will have no use for it. It will be sent with you when you leave for Moscow. Lieutenant Zaykov has asked to remain your aide until you leave, and her request has been granted. You are dismissed."

"I want to contact Moscow for clarification of instructions."

Tret'yak waved toward his office. "Do what you want. KGB headquarters wanted to speak with you when you arrived from Puerto Cabezas anyway. The channel has already been set up. But until I receive orders to the contrary, Lieutenant Zaykov is to escort you to Managua first thing in the morning and to see that you are on your way to Moscow. Good-bye, Colonel Maraklov."

Maraklov hurried into Tret'yak's office and ordered the call be put through to KGB headquarters in Moscow. Things had gone to hell real fast, he thought. Tret'yak was naive if he thought Moscow would risk using DreamStar to defend his little jungle base. Hell, Sebaco, Puerto Cabezas, Bluefields, even Managua were going to be sacrificed—anything to get DreamStar off safely. Somebody changed their minds in Moscow. The B-52 must've really shaken them up. Kalinin must have screwed up. The responsibility of getting DreamStar out of Nicaragua was obviously his, and he slipped up—this was the first time anybody but KGB troops had had anything to do with Dream-Star. Obviously there had been some sort of shakeup in Moscow and someone else was in charge now . . .

So the question was—what could *he* do to get around this? How could he turn disaster to his advantage?

The satellite transmission went through after several attempts—the American bomber attack had done extensive damage to the power transformers and underground communications cables, and they had only a patchwork setup still running. Maraklov shook his head as he thought of a single B-52 bomber attacking Sebaco. It had to be another of Elliott's toys, he thought—another Megafortress Plus, or maybe the resurrection of the one he had shot down? Would he never be rid of Dreamland's ghosts?

*"Tovarisch Polkovnik, dobriy vyechyer,"* the voice on the other end of the line greeted him. *"Ehtah General-Major Kalinin. Kahk dyela . . . ?"*

"You have to speak English, sir," Maraklov said. "My Russian is still very poor. *Vi gavaretye angleyski?"*

"Of course, yes, I speak English," the man replied. "I am Director Kalinin."

Damn . . . it was the KGB director himself on the line.

"I assume you have received your orders from General Tret'yak, *vyehrna?"*

"Yes, sir."

"What is your . . . *kak gavaretye* . . . how do you say, thoughts?"

"My opinion? Of my orders, sir?"

"Yes, your opinion."

What the hell was going on? The director of the KGB was asking *him* if he agreed with his orders? He was screwed either way he answered. Well, no use dodging this . . . "I do not agree with them, sir. We must not give the aircraft to the Americans. We have already paid a very dear price for it—it is ours now . . ."

To his surprise he heard Kalinin say he *agreed* with him.

There was a long pause on the channel. What was going on? Was Kalinin going to disobey his own orders and bring DreamStar back to Russia? Were they trying to set him up, use what he said against him in a trial once he returned to the Soviet Union?

"Colonel, I will transmit message to you, in confidence, soon. It will be in English. The message for you only. Not Tret'yak. *Vi pahnyemahyo*?"

"No, I don't understand, sir."

"I will give you orders. New orders. Carry them out if you can. *Etah sroch'nah*. It is urgent. *Da svedahneya*." And the line went dead.

## Brooks Medical Center, Brooks AFB, San Antonio, Texas
*Sunday, 21 June 1996, 1305 CDT (1405 EDT)*

"O God of heavenly powers, who, by the might of thy command, drivest away from men's bodies all sickness and all infinity; be present in thy goodness with this thy servant, that her weakness may be banished and her strength recalled; that her health being thereupon restored, she may bless thy holy Name; through Jesus Christ our Lord. Amen."

Patrick and J.C., who had come back with him, then would return as needed, stood apart from the small circle of Wendy's parents and relatives around her bed in the intensive care unit as the doctor checked Wendy's eyes and skin. They had had no time to change out of their flight suits. After securing the still heavily armed Cheetah in a guarded hangar they had gone right from the aircraft parking ramp to a waiting Air Force sedan and on to the hospital. McLanahan had knelt beside his wife only briefly, then backed away when he noticed the number of relatives present and their faces. Now, with the minister and relatives crowded around her, he felt more excluded, more isolated than ever.

A minister had been there for the last twelve hours. When he first arrived the prayers were full of uplifting, optimistic words. Now the prayers had taken a sudden shift toward the irremediable.

The doctor finished his examination, took notes on the monitor readouts, changed an intravenous fluid bag, then moved away. McLanahan saw the minister touch the doctor's arm, and they spoke briefly. Did he see the doctor shake his head? He drove murderous thoughts out of his mind and got the doctor's attention.

"What's the story, doctor?"

"The right lung sounds clear. I think we stopped the edema. But she's very weak. I'm sorry, but we have to expect respiratory failure—"

*"No . . ."*

"The damage was massive. She's a strong woman, Colonel. But for every step she takes forward, her body takes two backwards. She's fought back bravely, but . . ."

McLanahan could not stand to look at the doctor any more. He sought his wife's face from the foot of her bed. They had removed the larger tubes from her throat, leaving only the nasal cannula in place to feed her oxygen. Many of the bandages had also been removed, and the burns on her face and neck looked markedly better. Wendy's mother had even brushed out her hair. "She looks better to me," McLanahan said. The doctor made no comment. "Why isn't she on a respirator? If you say her respiratory system can collapse, why can't she be on life-support . . . ?"

"We can keep her alive indefinitely, Colonel, but is that what you really want?"

"Yes."

"Think of the pain you'd be subjecting her family to—"

"I'm her family too." He ignored the faces around her bedside. "Stop trying to spare us pain and help *her*, dammit. Right *now*." The doctor nodded, put his hand on McLanahan's shoulder and turned away. The relatives and friends turned away; some filed out of the intensive care ward, not looking at him or saying anything. A few minutes later he felt a hand on his shoulder. Hal Briggs was standing beside him. "Man, I came as soon as I could . . ."

"Thanks for coming, Hal. I appreciate it. Is the general here?"

"He's still . . . away," Hal said. McLanahan knew that meant the Cayman Islands, as leader of the air cordon around Nicaragua. "There's DOD investigators all over the Center, and they have authority to go any damn place they want. I got sick of them and took off."

"I'm really glad you guys are here," he said to both Powell and Briggs. He noticed Briggs wearing his earpiece transceiver. He was also armed, his ever-present Uzi submachine pistol on his waist. Hal nodded, then motioned his eyes off toward the door, and all three men walked outside and found an isolated area in the hallway.

"How is she?"

"The doctor says she's worse. Who the hell knows? What's going on, Hal?"

"J.C. might have to return to Puerto Lempira right away," Briggs said. "They made a deal with the Russians. They're going to turn DreamStar over to us—maybe tomorrow morning. They say it's flyable, so the general wants J.C., Dr. Carmichael and Master Sergeant Butler to go out to Puerto Cabezas and inspect her. J.C. might be able to fly the thing back to Dreamland."

"That's good, real good . . . What about Ken James?"

"You mean Colonel Andrei Maraklov. The Russians say the guy really *is* a KGB agent," Briggs said. "Do you believe it? We had a damned KGB agent in Dreamland for almost two whole years. Heads are gonna roll for that—mine in particular."

At the mention of James' real Russian name, the old fury came back. "What's supposed to happen to him?"

"The White House says he's on his way back to Russia," Briggs said. "The next time we see him will probably be on the podium beside the head man at the Great October military parade."

Briggs suddenly touched the earphone. "Briggs. Go ahead." The earpiece acted as a microphone as well as a speaker, picking up sinus- and osteo-vibrations and transmitting them like a conventional radio system. Briggs listened for a few moments, then replied, "Copy all. Briggs out." He turned to McLanahan. "Word's in, Colonel. The plane's been sealed off in a concrete shelter on Puerto Cabezas airfield. Tomorrow morning at six A.M., we've been cleared to fly no more than four more people in to inspect DreamStar—that means Carmichael, Butler, J.C. and myself. If we can fly it out, they'll let us. If we can't, we'll be able to sail a barge into the docks at Puerto Cabezas and ship it out. The general wants J.C. back immediately. I've got to get his gear together back at Dreamland."

McLanahan glanced down the hallway and saw Wendy's doctor and several nurses and technicians wheeling a large machine into Wendy's ICU ward at a run. "Wait here," he said, and ran down the hallway and followed the doctor back into the ward.

When he entered the room a low, high-speed electronic beeping was coming from Wendy's body-monitor. The relatives were crowded around her bedside, blocking the doctors and technicians from reaching her. The minister was kneeling beside her . . .

*"Get away from her,"* McLanahan shouted and pushed his way through the knot of people. The doctor, after seemingly being paralyzed by the scene, rushed over to the monitor. "What the hell are you doing? Get away from her and let the doctors through . . ."

"Respiratory arrhythmia," McLanahan heard the doctor say to one of the technicians, "but I've still got a heartbeat. She's hanging in there. Put her on the respirator and take her to the CDV lab." They began to insert the tracheal tube in her throat and worked to reinflate her lungs.

McLanahan pushed the minister aside and stood beside the doctor. "Can you help her?"

"I don't know, dammit." He was watching as the technicians quickly transferred the body-function leads from the wall unit to the portable device. "Her respiratory system has shut down." He pointed to an electronic electrocardiogram readout on the portable respirator. "But that could be her saving grace. Strong as a horse. There may still be time." He turned to the people surrounding the bed as a gurney was wheeled into the room. "All right, please move aside, everyone." Wendy was transferred to the gurney, and the hospital technicians rushed out.

McLanahan saw Wendy's parents staring at him as if he was crazy. "Wendy will be all right," he told them.

"Why are you doing this, Patrick?" Betty Tork said in a low voice.

"I'm *doing* this because I want Wendy to live. You're all waiting for her to die. I'm sick of it. I'm sick of *you.*" He turned, pushed past the relatives still packing the small room and hurried out.

He was met by Powell and Briggs in the hallway. "I'm going with J.C. back to Honduras," he told them. The two officers stared at him. "We'll fly back in Cheetah. Hal, go back and get J.C.'s flight gear and Carmichael and Butler and meet us in Puerto Lempira."

J.C. said gently, "Do you think you should?"

"Wendy's back on a respirator. I think she's going to make

it. I believe she's going to pull out of it. I've got to be there
when we get DreamStar . . .''

"Man, are you sure you're all right?" Briggs asked. "Maybe
you should stop and think about this . . ."

"Listen, I've got to do it this way. The more I stay around
this place the more I feel like I'm on a death watch. I won't do
that. I got to believe she's going to make it. Now let's get going.
Until DreamStar is out of Nicaragua I won't stop. And I want
Cheetah there in case something goes wrong . . ."

"Nothing can go wrong," Briggs said. "Maraklov is on his
way to Russia. He's the only one that could fly DreamStar. They
can blow DreamStar up, destroy it or disable it, but either way
we've at least kept the Russians from getting their hands on it.
We've won, man."

"Not yet, we haven't. As long as Wendy's fighting, I'm fighting too. And I can't fight wringing my hands in this place. Let's
get the hell out of here."


## Sebaco, Nicaragua
*Sunday, 21 June 1996, 2141 CDT (2241 EDT)*

Out of some one hundred troops originally stationed at Sebaco,
fewer than twenty were still there, all pressed into service in
cleaning up and preparing the base for rebuilding. Since there
were no aircraft at Sebaco, security had been cut back to only a
couple of guards roving the base. With workers on the job from
twelve to sixteen hours a day, the base was practically deserted
by nine P.M.

It would be that much easier to get away from Sebaco. Maraklov had decided on a plan nobody would expect, he hoped—
return to Puerto Cabezas and try to steal DreamStar again.

Earlier that day he had taken a military sedan that had a full
tank of gas and hidden it, keeping the keys. It was less than two
hundred miles to Puerto Cabezas, but the first one-third was on
mountainous gravel roads, which were dangerous enough when
driven by day—he would have to make the drive in the middle
of the night. The first fifty miles would take at least two hours,
maybe more. The rest would be easier—he could make the trip
in five hours, maybe a little less. According to KGB director

Kalinin, the Americans would be at Puerto Cabezas to get DreamStar shortly after dawn. He had to be there ahead of them.

There were only two things left to do: get back his metallic flight suit and helmet from Lieutenant Musi Zaykov, who was holding the equipment in preparation for sending it back with him to Moscow, and—what would be the hardest of all—subdue, or eliminate, Musi herself. She was scheduled to drive him to Managua at six A.M. the next morning and put him on a nine A.M. Aeroflot flight to Moscow. If he could keep Musi quiet, maybe tie her up and hide her in the jungle where she'd eventually be found, they would think they had left for Sandino International Airport as scheduled. They wouldn't know until the Aeroflot's departure time of nine A.M. that they never showed up—and by then he would be airborne once more in DreamStar.

That evening he dressed in a dark flight suit and spit-shined boots—into which he slipped a large hunting knife in a leather sheath—and left his room; he had, of course, already deactivated the surveillance camera set up in his room, and he was sure it had not been reactivated since the attack. He slipped outside through a back window, retrieved the sedan and drove it over to Musi's barracks several buildings away—being an officer as well as one of the few women on the base, Musi had a cabin to herself.

He stopped the engine a few dozen yards from her cabin and coasted to a stop several yards from the back door. He considered trying to sneak into the cabin, but Zaykov would probably shoot him as an intruder. Instead he simply went to the front door and knocked.

"*Kto tam?*"

"Andrei."

A slight pause, then, in a light, excited voice, Musi replied in English, "Come in, Andrei."

She was standing in the middle of her small living room, wearing a T-shirt that outlined her breasts, a pair of tropical-weight shorts and French-made tennis shoes. She came over to him and kissed him lightly on the right cheek. "Come in, Andrei." She tugged him into the living room and around toward the sofa. "Please, sit down. How do you feel?"

"Physically, great, emotionally, lousy . . . I can't believe we're just going to give up DreamStar. After all that's happened."

"Orders are orders, I suppose," she said, curling up like some exotic cat on the loveseat beside the sofa. "There's nothing any of us can do."

"Doesn't make me feel better."

"No, but we are both soldiers," she said. "Never mind, won't you be glad to get back home? It's been so long since you have been there . . ."

Maraklov had to work at his reaction. "Sure, but it would be better if you were going with me."

"I will join you in Moscow before long," she said. "We will see each other very soon." She motioned to a small bar in the corner behind Maraklov. "Fix us some drinks? I think I have something interesting in there."

He got up, found ice and glasses, then started checking out her stock. He picked up one especially fancy bottle. "Well, look at this! Glenkinchie single malt Scotch whiskey . . . I never expected to see this in this godforsaken place."

"You can try some of that," Musi said. "It is very special. It is my favorite." As he dropped ice cubes into a couple of glasses she added, "It was Janet's favorite, too."

"Who?"

"Janet. Janet Larson. Her real name was Katrina Litkovka—the woman you murdered eleven years ago."

He froze, then, willing his muscles to move, turned around. Musi Zaykov was standing in the center of the room holding a silenced nine-millimeter automatic pistol in her right hand. Her seductive smile had vanished, leaving a stone-cold murderous glare.

"What in hell is going on, Musi?" He put the glass down on the bar but kept the Scotch bottle in his left hand, sliding it down his leg to hide it as best he could. "Put that thing down."

"You are under arrest, Colonel Maraklov," Zaykov said, "for the act of murder."

"What are you talking about? Is this some kind of sick joke?" Loosen up, he told himself. Find out what she knows and use the time to figure out something . . . He forced himself to put on a broad smile. "What's gong on, Musi? Put that thing away. Are you crazy? I'm no threat to you—"

"Stay where you are." She reached into her jacket pocket and took out a sheet of paper. "A copy of a message transmitted to

you from Moscow, directing you to go to Puerto Cabezas and
steal the DreamStar aircraft. What is this about?''

"Just what it says, Musi. I've been ordered to steal the damn
thing again and fly it to a secret base in Costa Rica." As he said
it he took the opportunity to take a half-step toward her. "They
figured I did such a good job the first time, they wanted to see
if I could do it again."

"If that was meant to be humorous, Andrei, you failed,"
Zaykov said. "*My* last orders from General Tret'yak were to see
to it that you are confined to the base until morning."

"Well, I have orders too, Musi. Given to me by Vladimir
Kalinin. I'm sure you have ways of confirming that. I don't have
much time to waste."

"I must check this with General Tret'yak. If what you say
is true, this contradicts previous orders. Orders must be verified—"

"There's no damn time to verify anything. DreamStar will be
gone in ten hours, maybe less."

"And you had to come here to get your flight suit and helmet," Zaykov said. "Then you had to do one more thing—kill
me. You could not make it appear that we had gone to Managua
as scheduled unless I was out of your way."

"I wasn't going to kill you. I could never do that. I'm much
too fond of you . . . you know that . . ." He searched her face,
found little softening in it. "You can help me, Musi. You can
get a helicopter to take me to Puerto Cabezas—"

"I can't do that. Even if these orders were fully authorized I
would not do it."

Something else was wrong. "Musi, what is it?"

She let the first letter drop to the floor, then drew another one
from her jacket. "Some research I did when you left Sebaco for
Puerto Cabezas . . . The morning after your attempt to fly to
Cuba you were delirious from dehydration. You called out a
woman's name—Janet."

"Janet? You mentioned that name moments ago. I don't know
a Janet."

"You did know a Janet, Andrei—or should I say, Kenneth
James. I knew a Janet too. Janet Larson. We were good friends
. . . back at the Connecticut Academy."

Now the words hit Maraklov like a baseball bat against his
skull. He had forgotten the name the minute he left the Soviet

Union for Hawaii all those years ago. The delirium caused by the ANTARES interface somehow had unearthed it—unfortunately, in the presence of another Connecticut Academy graduate who knew her.

"Yes, I knew Janet . . . Janet Larson. What has she got to do with my orders?"

"Perhaps nothing—perhaps everything," Zaykov said. "Janet Larson—Katrina Litkovka—was found dead in a car crash. They say she had been drinking, that her car went off the road. But Katrina was fond of having affairs with many of the students at the Academy. You were one of them." She paused, then said, "I was one of them too."

"You and Larson were *lovers*?"

"Those of us in courtesan training at the Academy were taught to . . . to please women as well as men," she said. "It was all part of the game at the Academy. But mostly we were friends, damn it, *friends* . . . She apparently had been drinking an expensive Scotch whiskey. Even though she didn't have much alcohol in her blood, drunk driving was blamed for the accident. But the whiskey was very suspicious. Under questioning, a truck driver that delivered supplies to the Academy admitted that he sold or traded bottles of contraband foreign liquor to students and employees. One of the students he sold the whiskey to was *you*."

Zaykov took a tighter grip on the weapon. "All of Katrina's lovers were suspects in the investigation. All of us were officially cleared—all but you. No investigation was started on you because you had just been inserted into the United States Air Force Academy training program. After a time interest in the case disappeared. Katrina Litkovka's murderer was never found."

"I still don't see what this has to do with anything," Maraklov said. "Are you accusing *me* of her murder? Now, after all these years, you're on a manhunt for a murder that happened over a decade ago and ten thousand miles away?"

"There is no statute of limitations on murder." She held up the paper. "I did some more checking, Mr. Kenneth James. A report done by a KGB agent that assisted you in killing the real Kenneth James in Hawaii during the substitution. He reported that the dying American admitted to two murders in his presence—the murder of his infant brother, and the murder of his high school girlfriend."

Maraklov took a step forward. The gun did not waver. "Musi, I still don't understand. What does this have to do with what's going on here? Yes, the real Kenneth James killed his brother— he admitted that. He was seconds away from death when he said he killed his girlfriend. He was delirious—"

"Perhaps. Perhaps not. My friend Katrina Litkovka used to tell me about you, about the stories you supposedly made up, about how realistic they were. She told me about how you told her about how James killed his girlfriend before he went to Hawaii. Katrina said you were close to killing *her* then. Strange, isn't it—the real Kenneth James confessed to the very crime that you described to Katrina."

That made Maraklov stop in hopeless confusion. The parallels between the real Ken James and what he *thought* was James' life were indeed startling, but he had never thought of it as *his* thoughts versus James' *real* life. At the very instant that he realized he had been left alone in that hotel room in Honolulu, he became the ultimate extreme of his training . . . he *became* Kenneth Francis James. He evaded the security checks, the encounters with James' friends and lovers, even related intimate details about James' childhood because he had ceased to be Andrei Ivanschichin Maraklov and had become Ken James. Which was more than they wanted at the Academy.

Zaykov let the report fall to the floor and took out still another piece of paper from her jacket. "I am detaining you so we can speak with General Tret'yak, but I am also reopening the investigation of Katrina Litkovka's murder.

"Motive: She told me you threatened to kill her if she exposed your behavior to Headmaster Roberts. That would have destroyed your chances to go to America, something you had spent half your life and every part of your peculiar mind training for. I recall the talk that your mission was to be canceled because you were unprepared emotionally for the role. Opportunity: The whiskey you bought two days before the accident. The security guards testified that Litkovka was not drunk before leaving the Academy. You arranged the accident, made it look like Katrina had been drinking, then killed her, Kenneth James . . ."

"I am not Kenneth James," Maraklov said. "I am Colonel Andrei Maraklov, an officer in the *Komitet Gosudarstvennoy Bezopasnosti*, a trained deep-cover agent just like yourself. And I am not a murderer . . ."

Zaykov held up the last piece of paper in her hand. It was a photograph. She tossed it across to him. Maraklov stepped forward to pick it up, she moved backward to stay out of his reach. "Look at it."

Sweat popped off his forehead as he studied the picture. It was an old photocopy of a picture of Kenneth James, the real Kenneth James, taken in Hawaii, obviously by a KGB hidden camera. It appeared to have been taken not long before he had arrived in Hawaii to make the switch—possibly it was the photo used by the plastic surgeons to give him his new face before replacing James.

Even though the photo was much enlarged and grainy, Maraklov could still make out the drawn features, the thinning hair, the sickly appearance. The guy had been tearing himself apart from the inside out for ten years over the murder of his infant brother. He had destroyed not only his own life but the life of his natural father as well. No wonder he had expressed such relief when he realized he was dying and had confessed the truth to Maraklov that evening.

"What about this, Musi? We're wasting time . . ."

She motioned to a mirror on the living room wall. "Take a look."

Maraklov dropped the photograph and moved over to the mirror. He stared at the face in the mirror. It was Kenneth Francis James—at least the face of James in the photograph. The plastic surgery Maraklov had undergone before coming to America kept most of his face looking like it was still seventeen years old, but it couldn't hide the thinning hair, the hollow cheeks, the sunken eyes, the thin neck and protruding Adam's apple . . . in his case, the strain of the ANTARES interface and the other attritions in the theft of DreamStar had chewed away at Maraklov's body, much as the murders of his brother and girlfriend had eaten away at James.

"I'm arresting you for the murder of Katrina Litkovka," Musi Zaykov said. "You come with—"

Ignoring the weapon pointed at his chest, he reared back and hurled the Scotch bottle at the mirror. The bottle hit the glass and exploded. Instinctively Zaykov turned at the sound, the gun still pointed at Maraklov, but her head turned toward the shattered mirror. It was the opening Maraklov needed. Forgetting the pistol she still held, he covered the few steps between him and Zaykov, and with the skill and precision developed from years of training, turned the pistol away from his left hand and delivered a solid roundhouse kick with his right foot. Zaykov collapsed to the floor, but Maraklov could not take control of the gun. As she doubled over and fell, she swung the gun back up and squeezed the trigger.

The gun exploded, he felt his left shoulder yanked backward, there was a loud buzzing in his ears and the blood drained from his head. His knees buckled and he dropped backward, clutching his shoulder. There was no pain—yet—only a steady rivulet of blood leaking from between his fingers, and the disorienting feeling of confusion mixed with fear. The room began to spin. He felt lightheaded, almost intoxicated.

Gasping, Musi crawled up to her hands and knees, reaching for the pistol. Maraklov caught it first. Musi dug her nails into the back of his left hand, raked the nails of her right hand across his face. He let go of the gun. She tried to grab the gun but the hot silencer-barrel burned her fingers, and before she could grab the stock he had tumbled on top of her. He rolled her over onto her back and sat on top of her, trying to pin her arms down.

"Musi, don't . . ."

Blood ran down from his shoulder over her T-shirt, covering her chest, her face and hands. He put one hand over her mouth, ignoring the pain as she bit into it. With his other hand he pulled the hunting knife out of his boot. "Musi, all I want is the flight suit . . ."

Zaykov freed her right arm, punched Maraklov in the left shoulder, then on the jaw. He toppled off her and she rolled to her right away from him, reached out and grabbed the pistol. She swung it up and fired.

The bullet just missed Maraklov's left ear. Before she could get off another shot he had knocked the pistol aside, swung around and, before he realized what he was doing, plunged the hunting knife into her abdomen. The blade pierced her diaphragm and punctured the right lung. She took one more breath, exhaled, blood coming from her open mouth in spasmodic coughs. She shuddered slightly, stared at him with a look of surprise, and then lay motionless underneath him.

He rolled off her, staring back at her lifeless eyes, then away. Janet Larson, James' girlfriend . . . all over again . . .

He shook himself back to the present . . . pulled the pistol from her fingers and crawled to the window, checking outside. Nothing. He checked the side windows, the bedroom, the back door. Nothing. The gunshots that had shocked him had not carried beyond her secluded quarters.

He went back to the living room. Forcing himself back to her, forcing himself to touch her, he grabbed her hands and dragged her to the bedroom, then into her closet. There was little blood—her heart had stopped beating almost instantly. He rested her as best he could in the closet and closed the door. She would not likely be discovered until morning.

His shoulder wound hurt badly now, but the bullet had only taken a shallow, ragged gouge out of his left shoulder muscle. Maraklov found bandages, disinfectant ointment and tape and wrapped the wound tightly as he could. The pain began to build, but he decided against any of the pain-killers he found in Zaykov's medicine cabinet—the drive would be long enough, and any drugs might later interfere with the ANTARES interface. The pain also acted like a stimulant, helping to clear his mind. Fortunately, he thought wryly, he could fly DreamStar without a fully functioning left arm.

He found the two aluminum cases in a living-room closet and made a fast check of the flight suit and superconducting helmet—both were as he had packed them the day before. He pocketed the pistol, picked up the two aluminum cases and headed for the back door. After checking outside for several minutes he brought the cases out to the car, got behind the wheel, and drove off.

He followed the access road out from the southeast runway hammerhead toward the destroyed anti-aircraft gun emplacement, then turned onto a dirt road that led toward the perimeter. No patrols were in sight. He followed the road right to the base perimeter fence and found a long-unused gate secured by a chain and a rusty lock that gave way when he rammed it open with the sedan. Ten minutes later he was on the Isabella Highway heading east toward Puerto Cabezas.

## Puerto Lempira Airbase, Honduras
*Monday, 22 June 1996, 0515 CDT (0615 EDT)*

Powell and McLanahan had just finished refueling and securing
Cheetah in its portable hangar on the Honduran coastal airbase
about eighty nautical miles north of the concrete bunkers at
Puerto Cabezas. They were also watching the construction of a
second portable aircraft shelter right beside Cheetah's hangar.
The second hangar was for DreamStar. After leaving Puerto Cabezas, Powell was to take it here to Puerto Lempira, where technicians would give it a thorough going over before Powell would
fly it first to Houston, and then on to Dreamland in Nevada.

Cheetah was still armed for combat—there had not been time
in nearly two days to disarm her. She still carried four AIM-
120C Scorpion radar-guided missiles in semi-recessed fuselage
stations, and two AIM-132 infrared-guided missiles on wing pylons—two other AIM-132 missiles had been expended on Soviet
fighters during the bombing raid on Sebaco—plus FASTPACK conformal fuel tanks and five hundred rounds of 20-millimeter ammunition.

"The Russians figured out how to put external fuel tanks on
DreamStar," Powell was saying as they watched the final parts
being assembled onto the steel-and-fiberglass structure. "We
should be able to do it. With external tanks I'm sure I can fly
her all the way back to Dreamland."

"I'm sure you can, but it's too risky. From what you said
yourself, you'll be flying DreamStar right on the edge of your
capabilities to begin with—it's been at least two years, J.C.,
since you've flown her. The Russians probably didn't bother
testing DreamStar with the external tanks—they just slapped them
on and hoped they'd work. I don't know about you, but I'd
rather make a few fuel stops along the way than trust those
tanks."

"I know. Well, I've no big desire to fly that thing all the way
from Central America to Nevada in one leg. Four hours hooked
up to ANTARES? Gives me a migraine just thinking about it."

"A bad time for a headache," McLanahan said. "We want
that plane out of there *today.*"

"Hell, why don't *you* fly it out of Nicaragua then? You at
least flew in DreamStar's simulator a couple weeks ago. You'd

probably do better than me. I could fly Cheetah on your wing and keep you company . . .''

"It's an idea. But you know what happened the last time I flew in the simulator—I crashed and burned, in more ways than one. If you think you can't do it, we'll just call Elliott on the horn and get that Navy barge in here. No, I think I'll let you have all the pleasure of flying DreamStar. I'll be in Cheetah on *your* wing.''

Powell looked at him. "I'll be happy if I can just keep it upright.''

A few minutes later they heard the steady rhythm of helicopter blades approaching. An Air Force HH-65A Dolphin helicopter swung in over the saltwater marshes, down the runway and over to the asphalt and concrete parking area. A security guard directed in the chopper with lighted wands, and it settled gently in for a landing. As the rotors began to spin down, a fuel truck and maintenance crew began making their way toward the chopper, and the passengers began to deplane. Powell and McLanahan went over to greet them.

"These helicopters have some real possibilities," Master Sergeant Ray Butler said as he exited the Dolphin. "But I'll take solid wings and big turbofans any day." He shook hands with McLanahan. "How are you, sir?''

"Okay, Ray.''

"Sorry about Dr. Tork," he mumbled.

Alan Carmichael wrapped his big arms around McLanahan before saying a word. "I called Brooks before we left La Cieba, Patrick. Wendy's hanging right in there. Still on full respiratory life support but she's a fighter. I thing she's going to pull out of it.''

"Me too. Thanks for the news, Alan.''

There were a few extra security guards along, plus several cases of supplies that were hauled out. The last man off the chopper was Major Hal Briggs. "Patrick, J.C., things are looking better," he said. "Wendy's gonna do okay, and we're gonna get our baby back." He checked his watch. "It'll take us less than an hour to get to Puerto Cabezas. We should plan to leave in about forty-five minutes, right?''

"Wrong," McLanahan said. "I want the chopper fueled and ready to go fifteen minutes max.''

"But they said we can't be there any earlier than eight A.M.''

"Push them. Ask for immediate clearance into Nicaraguan airspace and clearance onto Puerto Cabezas. If they won't let us near the plane until eight, fine—but I want to get on the base as fast as possible."

"You're the colonel, Colonel." Briggs stuck his head back in the helicopter cockpit to talk to the Dolphin's pilot and have him arrange for clearances.

McLanahan turned to Butler. "Got everything you need? I know this was short notice."

"I could've brought half my shop if Briggs had let me," Butler said. "I've got two portable logic test units, assorted toolkits and supplies, about a thousand pounds worth. The best test unit we have, though, will be Captain Powell. Once he's interfaced with ANTARES, we can diagnose and fix any problems."

"Good." McLanahan found Carmichael alone with J. C. Powell in one of the nearby tents. Powell was leaning back against a tent pole, his head bent down as if he was napping; Carmichael was just a few inches from his ear, saying something to him. As McLanahan approached, Carmichael held up his hand to keep him away. A few moments later Carmichael pulled a stethoscope from a jacket pocket and placed the electronic pickup against Powell's chest, then stood and walked over to Patrick.

"I saw it right away," Carmichael said. "He was jumpy as hell."

"J.C.? I didn't notice anything. He seemed himself."

"He's like that. He's the most laid-back guy I've ever met. The differences were subtle, but after working with him for eight months on the early ANTARES project I can tell when he's nervous. I put him in a mild hypnotic state to help him relax— actually he took my suggestion and put himself in a hypnotic state."

"Will he be able to interface with ANTARES?"

"We won't be able to tell until he tries it, but I'd say yes. He put himself right into alpha-state as if he had been doing it for years. He should be able to go into theta-alpha. Whether or not he can maintain it during the interfacing—well, we'll find out soon enough."

"Sooner than you thought," Briggs said as he came over to McLanahan and Carmichael. "We've got clearance to cross the border and into the Puerto Cabezas control zone. Final clearance onto the base will be issued through the control tower. The Dolphin will be topped off in five minutes."

"Then tell everyone to get back on board," McLanahan told Briggs. "Let's go get our fighter back."

## Puerto Cabezas Airbase, Nicaragua
*Monday, 22 June 1996, 0605 CDT (0705 EDT)*

This was the one of the hardest jobs General Tret'yak had ever performed in peacetime, rivaling the unpleasant duty of telling mothers or young wives of their son's or husband's death in some training accident. To be ordered by the Kollegiya, the senior political-military staff in Moscow, to give back the DreamStar aircraft was one thing—to have the Americans *land* here and take it from him was doubly embarrassing.

The DreamStar aircraft was right where Maraklov had left it two nights ago. The airfield at Puerto Cabezas, originally built in 1987 as a combined air force and navy base, was designed as the primary air-defense base in Nicaragua besides Managua itself. A series of semi-underground aircraft shelters had been constructed to house Nicaragua's alert fighter-interceptors. The shelters, six in all, were concrete pads with six-foot-high walls and concrete roofs. They were located one hundred meters north of the west end of Puerto Cabezas' single east-west runway, well distanced from the rest of the base.

But as the strategic importance of Nicaragua had tended to diminish over the years, fewer and fewer shelters were used until all alert air-interceptor operations were relocated to Managua. These revetments had been unoccupied for years, used only for annual Soviet-Nicaraguan exercises. Until now.

Tret'yak and two armed KGB Border Guards waited outside the revetment where DreamStar had been parked. All of the Nicaraguan troops on the base were kept away from the alert shelters—that was as much to avoid the embarrassment of the Nicaraguans finding out that they were turning over DreamStar to the Americans as it was for security. A landing pad had been prepared just inside the alert area fence on the throat or exit-taxiway from the alert area. A three-meter-high fence surrounded the entire alert area. Tret'yak's men had checked the perimeter and found the fence in disrepair but intact.

"Why must we even be here, sir?" one of the guards asked
Tret'yak. "Let the Americans get their own plane."

"We are here because I personally want to meet the men who
built this incredible machine," Tret'yak told him. He studied
the amazing shape of DreamStar for at least the tenth time since
arriving on the base. "She's a masterpiece of aeronautical design." The guard looked disgusted. Tret'yak shook his head.
"It may be hard for you to understand, but building a machine
like this is an art. And sometimes art can transcend politics."
But don't quote me, he added to himself.

A few moments later Tret'yak heard the rhythmic beating of
helicopter blades. They looked up to find an American HH-65
transport helicopter flying down the runway. It slowed to just a
few miles per hour as it approached the west end of the runway,
then barely to walking speed as it flew up the throat and over
the security fence. Tret'yak signaled to one of his men, who
pulled a flare from his belt, popped it and set it on the edge of
their prepared landing area. The HH-65 dropped its landing gear
and settled in for a landing.

The first man out of the helicopter was a tall, thin black man.
One of the Border Guards smiled. "There is your artist, sir,"
he said to Tret'yak.

"Quiet," the KGB general said. "He's carrying a weapon,
obviously a security guard." The others quickly moved off the
helicopter—one civilian, a non-commissioned officer in dark
green fatigues, and two U.S. Air Force officers in light green
flight suits. As the rotor blades slowly moved to a halt and the
turbine noise subsided, the five men walked toward Tret'yak.
The short, thickly muscled officer in the flight suit headed over
to Tret'yak while the others stopped about ten paces behind.

"My name is Lieutenant Colonel Patrick McLanahan, United
States Air Force," the man said in slow English. In hesitant but
obviously pre-rehearsed Russian, he asked, *"Vi gavaretye an-
gleskiy?"*

"Yes, I speak English," Tret'yak said. "I am General-Major
Pavel Tret'yak, senior KGB field commander in Nicaragua." He
looked over McLanahan's shoulder at the other men. "I was
told there would only be four persons coming here."

"My fault and my responsibility," McLanahan said, and
turned toward them. "Major Briggs, my security chief. Dr. Alan
Carmichael, chief engineer. Sergeant Butler, senior maintenance

non-commissioned officer. And Captain Powell, senior test pilot.''

"And your function, Colonel?''

"Officer in charge of the DreamStar project.''

"Ah. Captain Kenneth James' senior officer.'' McLanahan's only reaction was to narrow his eyes, his mouth tightening.

Tret'yak nodded toward the four men. "Well, you are here, and I would prefer to get this business over with as quickly as possible. You are cleared to enter.'' McLanahan nodded, then waved the four men behind him to follow.

Butler was the first to react when he saw the XF-34. "Oh, boy,'' he muttered, ran ahead and into the shelter. Carmichael and Powell followed. McLanahan studied the two Lluyka tanks and the missiles hung on the fighter. "I see you made a few modifications.''

"Modifying a fighter for external ferry tanks, in-flight refueling and foreign-made weapons is a major task. Our devices worked very well.''

"You didn't need extra tanks to fly to Cuba.''

"But to fly to Russia, our original and eventual destination . . .''

"This plane and its pilot shot down two American fighters—*after* you stole it.''

"Come now, Colonel, the theft, the air battles, all part of the game. We both played it.''

McLanahan shook his head. Get on with it, he told himself.

Butler finished a cursory inspection and came back to McLanahan. "Looks like they used two pylon hardpoints on each wing to stick those tanks on. Simple electronic pyrotechnical jettison squibs. Same with the missiles. We can punch 'em off here but there's no telling what damage it might cause.''

"Leave them on, then,'' McLanahan told him. "I want DreamStar out of here fast as possible.'' Butler nodded and trotted back to the helicopter to get his gear. McLanahan turned back to Tret'yak. "Where is Maraklov?''

"On his way to Moscow. He will be debriefed. Even though he was not given the opportunity to bring this aircraft back with him, he carries a great deal of information. His talks with our intelligence people should be revealing.''

"And after that?''

"After that, I cannot say. He is a difficult man, but if I were the General Secretary of the Kollegiya I would make Colonel Maraklov a Hero of the Soviet Union. We like to reward loyalty, courage and initiative," Tret'yak said.

"Thanks for the compliments, General," a voice behind them said. Tret'yak and McLanahan turned. And saw Andrei Maraklov emerging from behind the concrete walls of the revetment. Tret'yak and McLanahan saw the man, but the two KGB Border Guards accompanying Tret'yak saw the pistol he held. They lifted their rifles and swung them toward Maraklov. With two muffled puffs of the nine-millimeter automatic pistol, they were dead as fast as they had reacted.

Maraklov then turned the pistol toward Hal Briggs, who had only gotten as far as reaching for the Uzi at his hip. "Don't do it, Hal. Left hand, unbuckle your holster and toss your gun over here." Briggs hesitated, his hand still poised near the Uzi. "I'll kill you otherwise." Briggs had no choice, did as he was told. Maraklov picked up the Uzi and took its safety off.

"You had a detour on your way to Moscow," McLanahan said.

"There's been a change in plans, Colonel. It happens."

"Where is Lieutenant Zaykov?" Tret'yak said.

At that, Maraklov's attention seemed to wander, but only for a moment. "She found out about our plan."

" 'Our' plan?' " McLanahan said, turning to Tret'yak. "You never intended to turn DreamStar over to us."

"I know absolutely nothing about this," Tret'yak told him. "He obviously has killed the officer I ordered to escort him to Managua."

"What counts," Maraklov said, "is that DreamStar is mine. It always has been. I decide what to do with it." Not quite the case, he realized, but by now it felt like it was . . . "It's not going back to the United States, and it's not going to be hacked up in the Soviet Union. I'm flying it out of here to a place where it'll be safe." He stuck the automatic pistol in his pocket, cocked the Uzi, raised it and aimed at them—

Out from behind the Dolphin helicopter, Sergeant Butler appeared holding one of the computer logic test devices, a large suitcase-sized object, up before his body like some huge heavy shield. And proceeded to run full speed at Maraklov, who whirled, dropped to one knee—more out of surprise than to help his aim—and fired at Butler.

The Uzi had been set for single-shot. Maraklov squeezed off two, three rounds, swore and reached down to move the action lever. Butler had eaten up all but a few yards of the distance between them before Maraklov switched the weapon to full automatic and sprayed the charging man. But Butler had finally reached Maraklov and crashed into him before one of the bullets found Butler's unprotected legs and cut him down. Butler drove the test device into Maraklov's face, then used his body weight to haul him to the ground.

Lying on top of Maraklov, Butler tried to raise the test device over his head and drive it into Maraklov's skull. But he was too late. Maraklov put the muzzle of the Uzi into Butler's stomach and pulled the trigger. The senior NCO's gut exploded, he dropped over backward, dead before he hit the ground.

McLanahan yelled, *"Run for cover,"* and made a dash for the helicopter. The pilot immediately started the engines in the Dolphin, and Powell and Carmichael, both inside DreamStar's shelter, ran for the helicopter.

Briggs made his run at Maraklov, but to his surprise, General Tret'yak turned, blocked his path, then pushed him back toward the helicopter. As Briggs stumbled backward and fell to the concrete taxiway, Tret'yak turned on Maraklov. *"Ehtat yah svenyena mo sahm. This pig is mine."*

Tret'yak never had a chance. He'd take no more than three steps when Maraklov raised the Uzi and emptied its magazine into the KGB general.

"Hal, run for it," Patrick called out. The Dolphin's rotor blades were spinning up to takeoff RPMs. Hal got to his feet and sprinted for the open door.

Maraklov got to his knees, took aim at Briggs, squeezed the trigger. Nothing. He had emptied out the magazine on Tret'yak. He tossed the machine pistol aside and pulled out the nine-millimeter silenced pistol. Briggs had just gotten to the Dolphin's starboard side-door and jumped inside, so Maraklov swung his aim left to the two running figures and squeezed off a shot.

Alan Carmichael grabbed the right side of his chest and pitched forward. J. C. Powell skidded to a halt, knelt down and began to drag Carmichael toward the helicopter. Maraklov took aim once again, and before McLanahan or Briggs could react, fired.

Powell flew backward away from Carmichael's inert form, and lay still.

"*You bastard.*" McLanahan was screaming, rushing out of the helicopter and heading toward Maraklov. He had just cleared the Dolphin's right door when the Dolphin pilot yanked the chopper off the ground, hovering less than three feet above ground, and aimed the helicopter at Maraklov. McLanahan, knocked aside, crawled on hands and knees toward Powell and Carmichael, trying to shield his eyes from the flying gravel and sand.

Maraklov took aim on the helicopter's canopy, fired. The shot missed the pilot by inches, but it sped through the cabin and through a circuit breaker panel, showering the cockpit with sparks. The helicopter engine faltered, lost power, then regained it. Maraklov tried to get off another shot but the rotor's downwash forced him to his knees, and he had no choice but to crawl away from the blast, though he was still sideswiped by the Dolphin's fiberglass nose.

Meanwhile Briggs had jumped out and run over to Carmichael. McLanahan took Powell, and together they began to drag the wounded toward the helicopter.

The pilot halted his advance at the body of Sergeant Butler. McLanahan and Briggs dragged Carmichael and Powell through the side door, then together they picked up Butler's body and carefully as they could manage put his body in the helicopter. Blood and viscera were everywhere, on their faces, covering their uniforms. Briggs and McLanahan jumped inside the chopper, ignoring whatever they were stepping or slipping on. Patrick shouted to the pilot, "go," and the chopper lifted off.

Maraklov had crawled back to DreamStar's shelter just as the chopper rose off the concrete. Again he took aim at the canopy and fired, but at this angle the bullets were ricocheting off, not penetrating. He fired once more on the retreating helicopter, doing no more damage that he could see—but the chopper's engine was definitely faltering. He had hit something vital—no way it would make it back to Honduras. No reason to worry about McLanahan any more—he would be long gone before McLanahan could call in a counterstrike, and Powell was definitely no worry.

But Maraklov had a new worry: the Nicaraguans. If anyone from the base came out here to investigate, the game would be over. He ran back to the taxiway and dragged the bodies of the two KGB Border Guards and General Tret'yak out of sight in the aircraft shelter, then checked the ammunition in his pistol. Three shots left. Two for any curious spectators that decided to investigate—and perhaps one for himself.

He sat down in front of DreamStar's nose gear, peering up over the edge of the semirecessed parking stub, waiting for anyone to approach. After ten minutes there was still no sign of activity. Either no one had heard the shots—unlikely—or no one cared enough to interfere.

Maraklov felt a rush of excitement. He had snatched DreamStar out of the hands of the Americans once more, just as he had done back in Dreamland. This fighter was *destined* to be his. More than ever, he felt it must be.

He ran out the back of the shelter toward the perimeter fence, checking for any sign of intruders or surveillance. He went to where he had hidden the cases containing his flight suit and helmet and quickly brought them back to the shelter. He checked the perimeter once more—once he had the metallic flight suit on, it was going to be impossible for him to defend himself. The aircraft shelter had a set of steel doors that could be motored in place, but Maraklov had no choice but to keep them open—there was no one alive to open them again.

No matter. In two hours, perhaps less, he'd be airborne, heading away from this damned place, once and for all.

Maraklov dragged the aluminum cases up onto the service platform beside the cockpit, then climbed up the ladder and began opening them. Already, he was beginning the deep-breathing exercises that would relax his body, open his mind and allow the electronic neural interface to begin. In five minutes he had stripped down, put on the pair of thin cotton underwear, and began connecting the fiber-optic electrical connections between the suit and helmet and from the suit and helmet to the interface inside the cockpit. He could feel the familiar, soothing body cues beginning to wash over him as he entered the first level of alpha-state, the primary self-hypnosis level of his mental relaxation. Coincidentally, this alpha-state was helping to block out the throbbing pain in his shoulder and calm the quivering in his muscles as adrenaline began to be dissipated from his bloodstream.

He opened DreamStar's canopy and climbed inside. No longer needing the platform, he unlatched and collapsed it, then kicked it away as hard as he could. The ladder rolled across the stub, hit the revetment wall and fortunately did not roll back toward DreamStar's wings or canards.

Next he activated DreamStar's internal battery power and did a fast system self-test to make sure he had all the connections right—the self-test reported fully functional and ready to receive computer commands. The test also reported on any ground saf-ing pins, access panels, or covers out of place. The standby gauges read full tanks, full twenty-millimeter ammunition drum and connectivity with the four remaining air-to-air missiles. DreamStar was ready for engine start as soon as the ANTARES interface was completed.

Finally, standing on the ejection seat, Maraklov began to put on the flight suit. He had thought it would be impossible to do it without help, but it was turning out to be less of a problem than he'd anticipated. In twenty minutes he had put on and ad-justed the sixty-pound suit, then carefully lowered himself into the ejection seat and fastened as many body restraints as he could. The suit was not designed for free range of motion—it resisted any movements that departed from the normal cockpit flight po-sition—but he was soon strapped in tight.

After a few moments of concentration he had his breathing back to normal, then well below normal as he reentered full alpha-state hypnosis. Still no sign of interference as he closed his eyes to begin the progressively deeper levels of self-hypnosis.

Soon, DreamStar would be his once more. And he would be DreamStar's . . .

"Mayday, Mayday, Mayday, Air Force helicopter Triple-Echo Three-Four on GUARD frequency, twenty miles east of Lecus Southeast airport at two thousand feet. We are a United States Air Force military flight. Three on board plus three casualties, seven thousand pounds of fuel, heading two-niner-zero degrees magnetic toward Buena Vista airport at one hundred knots. En-gine and electrical damage and uncontrollable fuel loss. Request-ing search and rescue meet us along southern Honduran border south of Puerto Lempira. Emergency. Please respond. Over." There was no reply. The pilot repeated the call on both UHF and VHF GUARD emergency frequencies.

"Nothing from the Nicaraguan military?" McLanahan asked.

"It's like they all disappeared off the face of the earth," the pilot said. "When we crossed the border into Nicaragua, they were all over us every second. Now they don't even answer a distress call."

"They might not hear you," Briggs said, checking the overhead circuit-breaker panels. "Your radio panel looks like it might be damaged." The pilot kept trying. Briggs moved up beside McLanahan, who was scanning a chart and keeping track of their progress. "Patrick . . . J.C. . . . he's had it."

The chart dropped from his lap. His mouth turned dry as sand. His fingers trembled. "Jesus, no . . ." He shut his eyes. "J.C., J.C., dammit . . ." His only immediate relief was to allow the grief to overflow into blinding rage at Maraklov. That sonofabitch was going to pay, somehow, he was going to pay . . .

McLanahan's anger was disrupted by a hard *thump* and a low-frequency vibration that began to echo through the helicopter. The pilot tapped him on the shoulder. "Behind your seat, in the survival kit, there's a hand-held radio." He was also struggling against a sudden vibration that shook the entire helicopter. "We were briefed to use rescue channel alpha on this mission. See if you can raise anyone with that." But before Briggs could retrieve the kit the chopper took a steep dive. The pilot had to pull with all his strength on the collective to keep the helicopter airborne.

"I'm losing it fast," the pilot said. "I've gotta set it down."

McLanahan picked up the chart and relocated their position. "Try to make it across the Rio Coco river into Honduras. No way we want to go down in Nicaragua."

The pilot shook his head. "I don't know how far we can go but I'll try. You two better strap in." McLanahan stuck the chart in a flight-suit pocket. Briggs grabbed the survival kit, found a seat between the bodies on the chopper's aft deck and strapped in.

Somehow the helicopter did manage to stay intact for ten more minutes. McLanahan directed the pilot farther west toward a road leading northeast, and the pilot found it just as a yellow caution light lit up on the front instrument panel. "She's seizing up," the pilot said. "We can't autorotate with all these trees around us. We land now or crash."

Following the road as best they could, they glided in over the forests, searching for a clearing. They found a bend in the road, and the pilot headed for it. He had timed it well. The Dolphin hit the road, hard, just as the overspeed safety system in the chopper's transmission automatically uncoupled the rotor.

*"Out!"* the pilot yelled, cutting off fuel and power and activating the automatic fire-extinguishing system. "Form up off the nose. Fast." The three men dashed from the helicopter and ran a hundred yards away from the chopper, then turned and waited for an explosion or fire. Smoke billowed from the engine and power-train compartment behind the cockpit, but there was no explosion or fire. The three collapsed on the driest spot they could find beside the road, too weak from fear, tension, and worn-off adrenaline to stand any longer.

After a few silent minutes McLanahan unfolded the chart he had stuck in his flight suit and pointed to the bend in the road. "Here we are, I think, about three or four miles from this town, Auka. Puerto Lempira is about twenty-five miles by this road. Hal, see if you can raise someone on the survival radio." Briggs got out the radio, set it to emergency channel alpha and GUARD and began calling for help.

"I got Puerto Lempira," Briggs said a few moments later. "Storm Control, this is Air Force helicopter Triple-Echo Three-Four. You are weak and barely readable. We are down zero-three miles south of town of Auka. Requesting pickup for three souls and three fatalities. Over." He listened for a few moments, made a few responses and orders for priority assistance, signed off.

"Our base says they don't have another helicopter at Puerto Lempira," Briggs said. "They've called for one from La Cieba. They might be able to get one from private companies but we can expect at least an hour before pickup, maybe ninety minutes. We have to get to Auka, then find a clearing and vector the chopper in. That's the soonest they can make it."

"Too damn long," McLanahan said. "Maraklov will be off in DreamStar before then. We've got to get hold of Elliott and tell him to set up the air cordon again."

"What about fighters from Puerto Lempira?" Briggs asked. "Don't you have that F-15E there any more?"

"They withdrew it to the States when the Russians cut their deal. We had to take down the whole air cordon out of the Cayman Islands as a sign of good faith. Let's just secure the chopper and get *moving*."

As they headed back to the Dolphin, McLanahan asked Briggs

if General Elliott wasn't supposed to be on his way to Puerto Lempira by now.

"Should be."

"You think you can set up a patch with General Elliott through Puerto Lempira? He can get the air cordon put back up around Nicaragua—at least get the AWACS back up there to watch for DreamStar when it heads out."

"I can try. Reception is pretty poor from here but at least I can get the ball rolling." He began another call to Puerto Lempira as they walked. When they got to the Dolphin, McLanahan and the chopper pilot locked up the helicopter while Briggs stayed in as much clearing as he could find to maintain radio contact with the Honduran military base.

"No good," Briggs said as McLanahan and the chopper pilot joined him on the road heading toward Auka. "Can't raise the base any more. We'll have to wait until we get to Auka and find a telephone, or just get to a clearing where we've got a straight shot to Puerto Lempira."

McLanahan muttered as they set off on a fast walk. "After everything . . . J.C. . . . Maraklov is still going to get away with DreamStar? And there's nothing we can do to stop him?"

## Over the Caribbean Sea
*Monday, 22 June 1996, 0748 CDT*

"What the hell was that?" General Elliott said into his earset microphone. He was on a C-21B military Learjet en route from Georgetown in the Cayman Islands to La Cieba, where he would pick up a helicopter from there to Puerto Lempira. The relief he'd felt as he left Grand Cayman to see DreamStar safe and sound in U.S. hands was shattered once again. "Say again that last transmission."

"Message received from a Major Briggs, crewmember aboard Air Force helicopter Triple-Echo Three-Four," the communications man said. "Briggs requested immediate emergency assistance. He said his helicopter was down four miles south of Auka, approximately thirty miles south of Puerto Lempira. He reported three survivors and three fatalities."

"Oh, God," Elliot muttered. Over the radio he said, "When did the rescue chopper depart?"

"We dispatched your HH-3 from La Cieba immediately after receiving the call," the operator replied. "ETA to Auka is 0815 local."

"From *La Cieba*? That was the only chopper available?"

"Affirmative, sir."

Elliott slammed a fist against the C-21's front instrument console, then keyed his mike button. "Control, did Briggs report what happened?"

"We lost contact shortly afterward, sir," the operator reported. "He was calling in on a rescue channel, apparently using a hand-held survival radio. I think he's been trying to call us but we can't pick him up."

Elliott clicked on the C-21's interphone and turned to Marine Corps Major Marcia Preston, National Security Adviser Deborah O'Day's aide and the C-21's pilot. "Major, head toward Puerto Lempira airbase instead of La Cieba at best possible speed. We'll fly near where Briggs went down and try to find out what's going on."

"Yes, General." The C-21 jet banked left as Preston took up a rough heading to the Honduran airbase, then began calling up the base's coordinates on the inertial navigation unit and calling La Cieba air traffic control for a change in her flight plan.

Elliott left his seat and went back to sit with Curtis and O'Day. They had flown from Washington to the Cayman Islands after the deal had, they thought, been set to recover the XF-34, and Elliott had gone along with them in the C-21 for the flight to Honduras. "We've got a big problem," Elliott told them. "My security chief Briggs is on the ground in Honduras with two other survivors and three casualties from our recovery party. No other information. There's a chopper on the way, but it won't arrive for another forty-five minutes—"

"What are we going to do, Brad?" O'Day asked.

"I want to get in contact with Briggs soonest—he's on a survival radio and our people at Puerto Lempira lost contact. I've told Marcia to head over to where the pickup point will be and we'll try to contact Briggs ourself."

"What the hell do you make of it?" Curtis said.

"Not enough information to tell, but we'll act on what you guys like to call worst-case scenario . . . they tried to make the swap for DreamStar, the Russians reneged, shot up our chopper and our people. Major Briggs and whoever's with him managed to get away across the border but not all the way back to base."

"So that means the Russians still have DreamStar," O'Day said. "And if they reneged on the deal and went so far as to attack our people, they'll probably be trying to get it out of the country as fast as they can."

"And there's very damned little we can do about it," Elliott said. "We've got no assets close enough to stop them. We've still got the AWACS and some of the F-16s in the Cayman Islands, but we'd have to get a tanker from Puerto Rico or Florida down here to support us—that'll take a few hours at least. The two F-15E ground-attack fighters we brought to Honduras are on their way back to Arizona. We've got some Honduran ground-attack planes, but if the Honduran air force gets into the act we'll start a war in Central America. The President will never go for it . . ." Elliott paused for a moment, then: "Cheetah . . ."

"What?"

"*Cheetah*. My modified F-15F fighter. It's down in Puerto Lempira—Powell and McLanahan flew it back to the States and then back to Honduras. It can do both air-to-air and ground attack."

"But you said that McLanahan and Powell went on this mission into Nicaragua. That means—"

"That means that one or both of them may be dead," O'Day said. "Can't anyone else fly it?"

Elliott rubbed his throbbing right leg—the developing headache he had was starting to rival the pain in his leg. "It's like asking if anyone can race in the Indianapolis 500. Sure, anyone can drive the cars, and you *might* even survive the race without killing yourself. But only a very few can *really* race in it . . . Only a few people can fly Cheetah well enough even to have a chance of getting DreamStar," Elliott said gloomily. "Most of them, my senior test pilots, are two thousand miles away in Dreamland right now. Two may be lying dead in the jungle in Honduras—Powell and McLanahan. And another turned out to be a goddamned Russian spy—"

"General Elliott, this is Major Preston," the pilot said over the cabin intercom. "We're crossing the coast now, ETA to Puerto Lempira nine minutes. We've got clearance to fly near the Nicaraguan border, but we'll only have enough fuel to loiter about ten minutes before we need to head back to Puerto Lempira for fuel.''

"Thanks, Major. Take us down to two thousand feet and head south of Puerto Lempira, then ask Storm Control on what frequency they talked to Major Briggs. We'll scan that frequency plus GUARD and hope he comes back." Preston gave General Elliott enough time to strap himself in back in the right cockpit seat before descending quickly to five thousand feet and getting on the radio to Puerto Lempira. A few minutes later she had set up the radios on UHF and VHF GUARD and Air Force discrete emergency channel alpha. Elliott put on his earset and keyed the microphone:

"Air Force helicopter Triple-Echo Three-Four, this is Storm Commander on alpha. How do you read?"

The three crewmen of the mission to bring DreamStar out of Nicaragua reached Auka in less than an hour, but all hope of finding a telephone was quickly squelched—Auka was little more than a group of abandoned old shacks, half flooded and long overgrown by jungle. The road was still wide and paved—it was part of the main coastal highway running through Central America—but there was almost no traffic anywhere except for a few horseback riders and some youngsters herding a small knot of uncooperative goats through the streets. They had no intention of talking to a group of dirty-looking strangers, and as fast as the children appeared, they were gone.

The road through Auka branched out just on the north side of town off to the west—the fork in the road was on a small cleared-away rise with a shrine to the virgin Mary in the intersection. From that spot they could see for about five miles in any direction before the trees shrouded the horizon. "This looks like the best vantage point," McLanahan said. "Hal, go ahead and—"

"Wait," Briggs said. He held the survival radio up to his ear, then hit the TRANSMIT button. "Storm Commander, this is Hal Briggs. I read you loud and clear. Over." To McLanahan: "It's General Elliott! He's coming this way!"

"All *right*."

Briggs handed McLanahan the survival radio. "General, Colonel McLanahan."

"Patrick, damn good to hear you." Then he realized—the

third survivor must be the chopper pilot . . . "Who did you lose?"

"J.C., Carmichael and Ray Butler . . ."

Elliott slumped back in his seat. Powell dead—that was their last hope, the man who could fly Cheetah well enough to take on DreamStar in air-to-air combat. He keyed the microphone: "How did it happen? Were they killed in the crash?"

"No. They were killed by Andrei Maraklov—Ken James."

"*James?* He's supposed to be in Moscow . . ."

"He's alive and he's got DreamStar."

"But what about the deal? The transfer?"

"I had the impression that James came out of nowhere, completely unexpected. Even by the local Russian general. He killed the KGB general and two Russian soldiers and who knows who else to get DreamStar. He might be working for himself, or for someone else. General, DreamStar is flyable. We've got less than fifteen minutes to put together an attack package and take it out before he gets away."

"I see Elliott's jet," Briggs shouted, pointing skyward.

"General, we've got a visual on you. Range about three miles. Come right twenty degrees. There'll be an east–west road off your right wing. Follow the road until it ends. We're right at the intersection in the clearing."

Aboard the C-21 Marcia Preston made the correction and immediately spotted the intersection. "I've got it," she said.

Elliott turned to her. "Major, can you . . . ?"

"Tell everyone to hang on. Speed brakes coming out . . ."

The three men watched as the blue-and-white Air Force C-21 made a sudden hard-left bank. They heard the turbine whine decrease to a whisper as the C-21 turned in the opposite direction, paralleling the east–west road out of Auka. McLanahan could hear the loud, angry sound of rumbling air. "It's slowing down," he said.

"Landing gear," the Dolphin pilot shouted. "He's gonna *land*."

The C-21 made the turn to final approach only a few feet above the trees at the edge of the clearing, its nose high in the air, flying just above the stall. As soon as it cleared the last row of trees, the jet dropped almost straight down, touching down precisely and firmly in the center of the asphalt road. The speed brakes stayed up and the flaps were retracted to put as much weight as possible on the main landing-gear brakes. This jet did not have thrust reversers but the short-field approach technique was executed so well by Marcia Preston that they were not needed—with only a few hard taps on the brake, the C-21 Learjet-35 slowed and came to a stop right at the road intersection. Engines running, the left side airstair door opened and Briggs, McLanahan and the Dolphin pilot climbed on board.

Deborah O'Day gasped as she saw Briggs and McLanahan. Blood covered their bodies. Quickly they found seats in the back of the eight-passenger jet.

Elliott moved past her in the narrow center aisle, blocking her view of the three newcomers. "Deborah, sit up front, would you?" The NSA chief nodded and quickly changed places. Elliott took her seat and strapped himself in, waited until Secretary Curtis had the airstair door closed, then touched the intercom button. "Ready for takeoff, Major Preston. Best possible speed for Puerto Lempira. Call for medical assistance on arrival."

The C-21 executed a tight left turn as Preston lined up again on the road for takeoff. Sixty seconds later they were airborne.

"We don't need medical assistance, what we need is an attack against Puerto Cabezas. Right now or it may be too late." McLanahan turned and recognized the Secretary of the Air Force. "Secretary Curtis, I think Ken James—Andrei Maraklov—will try to fly DreamStar out of Puerto Cabezas as soon as possible. He killed J.C. and five other men out there. He's gotta be stopped."

"Colonel, we're trying to work out something, but we don't have any assets out here. We withdrew everything when the Soviets agreed to this turnover."

"We've got Cheetah," McLanahan said. "I want to fly Cheetah out there and get him." Curtis and Elliott said nothing, sat back in their seats. "I can fly it, I know I can. I've flown it in the simulator and I've had lots of stick time—"

"*I've* flown in the F-15F's simulator," Curtis said, "but that doesn't mean I can take it into combat, especially against a plane like the XF-34. We'd be risking you and Cheetah against impossible odds."

"Wilbur is right," Elliott said. "Even J.C. couldn't beat

DreamStar and James half the time in flight-test *exercises*. You would have *no chance*. I just can't endorse it—''

"And I won't authorize it," Curtis added.

"J.C. told me the key to beating DreamStar, he had it figured out and he taught it to me."

"It takes more than a second-hand theory to—"

"Besides, James himself has changed. You should have seen him—he looks like he's lost thirty pounds and aged twenty years. I know how it can eat at you from the inside, from the brain. It's been eating at James for almost two years. ANTARES has changed him into . . . into something else—"

Hal Briggs broke in. "The man has become a cold-blooded murderer. He gunned down those KGB soldiers, and J.C. and Dr. Carmichael, like he was shooting at paper targets.

"He's gotten compulsive—acts like DreamStar is *his*. I think that may be our chance . . . His entire *being* is centered around that machine. But one thing he isn't—he's not a cool-headed fighter pilot any more. He's changed into something else."

"But you're not a fighter pilot either, Colonel . . ." Curtis pointed out.

"No, I'm not, but what I am is the only chance we've got to keep DreamStar out of the hands of the Russians or an obsessed type like Maraklov. We don't have any choice, we've *got* to do it."

Elliott looked at Curtis. "What about it? He makes sense."

"We'd be throwing Cheetah *and* McLanahan away. We'd have another dead officer on our hands and lose *both* our advanced fighters all in one morning."

"That's bull, General Curtis, and you know it," McLanahan snapped. "There's only one thing we know for certain here—if I don't go, Ken James, Maraklov, gets away with DreamStar. Sure, if James gets away we still might get DreamStar back from the Russians, but only after they've copied all our technology and duplicated the ANTARES interface. After that, we'd be *forced* to build the F-34 fighter because we'd know that the Russians would build and deploy their own DreamStar—but we'd be building the F-34 *knowing* that it would be a trillion-dollar waste of money because the Russians would have developed defenses and countermeasures against it and its weapons . . . Worse than surrendering DreamStar is letting James get away. He's killed a dozen Americans to get his hands on Dream-

Star. He blew away three of his own people right in front of us. He's gone round the bend. I want him, General Curtis."

There was silence again in the C-21 cabin. Marcia Preston made an announcement that they were about to land in Puerto Lempira, but no one reacted. As they touched down and taxied to the parking area, Elliott said quietly, "I'll fly as your weapon-systems officer."

"Out of the question," Curtis said.

"I'll go alone," McLanahan said. "Cheetah is designed to fly air combat with one pilot—"

"I won't allow any of you to fly this mission," Curtis said as the C-21's engines were shut down. "It's suicide, a major breach of regulations—"

"I'll go," a voice said behind Curtis. They turned and saw Major Marcia Preston standing in the aisle behind Curtis and Elliott. "It'll solve your problems, General Curtis. I'm high-performance twin-turbine qualified, also a qualified military instructor pilot. If General Elliott makes me part of his unit it'll at least be a legal flight. All nice and by the book."

'Done," Elliott said. He turned to Briggs and said something to him in a low voice.

"And as senior project officer I can sign you off as qualified in the F-15F—judging by the way you handle this C-21, the F-15 should be a piece of cake," McLanahan said. "I can also make you air-weapons qualified. And as a flight instructor qualified in the F-15F I can then legally fly front seat in Cheetah. Like you say, by the book."

"McLanahan's not a pilot, he's not qualified to fly in combat—"

"I've got a hundred hours of stick time in Cheetah, including air combat maneuvers, General."

"And I've got two hundred hours flying time in the F/A-18 Hornet—air-to-air, air-to-ground, carrier ops, and even Red Flag, sir," Marcia put in. "You'll have the experience up there. But what Colonel McLanahan needs more than anything is a pair of air-combat-experienced eyes in his back seat. You've got the people you need, sir."

"It's still a suicide mission, damn it . . . I still at least need to get authorization from the White House—"

McLanahan stood and motioned to Preston. "We're wasting time. Let's go." Preston pushed open the airstair door and exited the C-21. McLanahan followed her out, along with Hal Briggs and the Dolphin helicopter pilot, and together they ran for the portable hangar in which Cheetah was tied down, yelling orders to the crew chiefs.

"McLanahan, get your butt back here," Curtis called out. "That's an—" But Brad Elliott had put a hand on his shoulder.

"The decision's been made, Wilbur."

"Like hell." Deborah O'Day joined the two men in the C-21 cabin. "I'm in charge of this operation. It's *my* butt on the line. Yours too, Brad."

"My butt's been chewed off long ago. I don't really care what the suits in Washington say. I say let them go."

"And as one of the suits, I agree with General Elliott," Deborah said. "You're outvoted."

"Don't give me this," Curtis said. "You two can stand side by side in the Oval Office and explain to the President why you authorized this mission. But I'm going to call for authorization from the top. And I don't want those planes to launch until I get it." He moved toward the airstair door, only to find Hal Briggs rearmed with an M-16B2 automatic rifle slung on his shoulder, blocking the stairs. Curtis turned back toward Elliott, fixing him with a disbelieving look. He then turned on Briggs. "You have a problem, Major?"

Briggs looked at Elliott with a silent request for an order. Elliott paused until Curtis turned back toward him again. "Brad, don't do this . . ."

Elliott met Curtis' stare. He had stepped up to the very edge of insubordination, something he had never quite done. He nodded, abruptly. "The Secretary has a call to make, Hal. Let him by."

"Just wanted to pass along to you, sir," Briggs said straight-faced. "We can't seem to make contact with La Cieba. They're saying another two hours to fix the problem with the radio, maybe longer."

"Don't hand me that crap, Major."

"Wilbur," Elliott said, "the radio works fine. I told him to rig it. But you know what we're facing. We need a decision *now*. You have to make it. Launch Cheetah."

Curtis hesitated, clenching and unclenching his fists. Outside he heard a low whine and the whine of a turbine—the sound of an external power-cart being started.

"You made a decision eight years ago that changed my life," Elliott said. "You sent another crew and another machine on what was considered a no-win mission. You could have ignored the Old Dog, brought back the B-1 bombers and let the politicians handle things. You didn't. You took over and did what had to be done, and it worked. Do it again. Launch Cheetah."

Curtis said nothing. Out the starboard windows of the C-21 he could see Preston already in Cheetah's aft-cockpit seat, strapping in and familiarizing herself with the layout. McLanahan was standing on the top of the boarding ladder, helmet and flight gloves on, hand on the edge of the front windscreen—but he had not yet entered the cockpit.

"He's gone through a lot of hell, Wilbur," Elliott said when he saw what Curtis was looking at. "He's seen more blood, more death in eight years than a dozen men will in their lifetime. He's also got a score to settle—a blood-score—but he'll stand on that ladder until you give the word. I think you've known that all along."

Curtis nodded, leaned back in the seat and closed his eyes. "Major Briggs, launch Cheetah. Now."

# =9=

## Over Nicaragua

CHEETAH'S CONTROL STICK felt alive, pulsating with power. Mounted on the right side of the cockpit instead of in the center as in most pre-1990s fighters, it was almost rigid. Tiny pressure-sensitive switches in the fixed stick detected hand movements and applied the inputs to the triple-redundant flight-control computers, which then transmitted movement instructions to the hydraulic systems that moved the canards and tail stabilators, as well as the micro-hydraulic systems that recurved Cheetah's wings.

The system was ultra-sensitive, very fast—not like the old gear, bell-crank and cable flight-control systems, or even the newer fly-by-wire electronic systems. The slightest touch on the stick would send Cheetah into an unexpected pitch-up or away. He tried to loosen his tight grip on the control stick, but it was hard to reprogram his head to the realities of electronic fiber-optic controls—and J.C. had set the system to its lowest sensitivity.

To complicate matters, a universe of information kept flashing on the windscreen, changing so quickly that McLanahan didn't have time to read it before it disappeared and another line of numbers or symbols danced across his eyes. He had experimented with turning off most of the laser-projected symbiology but found himself repeatedly calling the information back up a few moments later. Finally he decided to leave it there and just deal with it—he hoped it wouldn't distract him too much when

the shooting started. How J.C. could assimilate all this information was beyond him.

Suddenly Patrick saw a gloved hand reach across his shoulder.
"By the way, I'm Marcia Preston." He realized only then that
he had not said a word except "prepare for takeoff" to his new
back-seater. With all the things going on in Cheetah's cockpit,
he managed to reach across with his left hand and shake Marcia's extended hand.

He had just leveled Cheetah off at only five thousand feet as
once again he steered it southward toward Puerto Cabezas. At
full power he was maintaining just under Mach one as he raced
across the lush tropical forests and salt marshes of northeastern
Nicaragua. He hit the voice-command control on the stick and
in a deliberate voice said, "Autopilot, on, altitude, hold." The
computer repeated the command, which reminded McLanahan
to double check the autopilot status indicators. Cheetah's voice-
command system had been programmed by J.C., and although
it was supposed to be adaptable to any pilot, the subtle differences in pitch, accent and volume of voices sometimes confused
the computer.

"Marcia," McLanahan said after setting the autopilot, "I've
got a question—why the hell did you volunteer for this mission?"

"Because you needed me, and mostly because I wanted to
go."

"There's a chance we won't make it back."

"Not to toot my own horn, sir, but your chances of making
it back are much better now."

"Can the 'sir,' okay?"

"Okay, Patrick. Where to?"

"It's an outside chance but it's possible that DreamStar could
still be on the ground. We need to check the shelter at Puerto
Cabezas."

At seven miles per minute they reached Puerto Cabezas in a
little over ten minutes. McLanahan pulled the power back to
eighty percent. "I'll line up so I can give you a good look out
the right side," he said. "The shelter is pretty low but you
should be able to see if an aircraft is in there."

Their arrival at the Nicaraguan military base was greeted by
a cacophony of warning messages in English, Spanish and Russian, ordering them to turn away. He ignored them—and there

were no radar threat-warnings anywhere in the vicinity. They had decreased speed to less than five miles per minute to get a good look in the shelter. As they approached the base Mc-Lanahan hit the voice-command switch: "Arm, cannon, mode, strafe."

"*Warning, cannon armed, strafe mode, five hundred rounds remaining.*" An holographic aiming-reticle appeared on the windscreen in front of McLanahan. He switched off the autopilot, descended to one thousand feet and began to line up on the shelter.

"You're arming the guns?"

"If DreamStar is in there I want to shoot before he gets off the ground." He hit the command button again: "Target select." The reticle began to blink. He moved his head until the aiming reticle, slaved to follow the pilot's head movements, was directly on the mouth of the shelter, then hit the voice-command button again: ". . . Now." The reticle stopped blinking and a series of lines drew themselves on the windscreen like an instrument-landing director. Once McLanahan centered those lines, the cannon would blast the target to pieces.

"*Target designated, select target off to cancel.*"

"Watch your altitude," Marcia Preston said. "You're less than five hundred feet AGL with autopilot off."

"Thanks." McLanahan put the altitude-hold autopilot back on.

As they raced across the Nicaraguan base they could see men and vehicles darting all across the airfield, even over the runway—it was much too crowded on the flightline for normal air traffic. A number of emergency vehicles crowded the throat taxi-ramp that led to the alert parking shelters.

When they were about two miles from the alert area Marcia called out, "I can see the shelters. No aircraft in any of them." Men were running from the shelter. "They think you're going to bomb them, I think."

"I *should* put a few rounds in there."

"Waste of ammo."

"It would make me feel better, though." Instead of firing, however, McLanahan hit the voice-command button. "Target off. Cannon safe." The computer repeated and verified. He shut off the autopilot and began a shallow climb, putting in full military power once again.

"Long gone," Marcia Preston said. "Which way now?"

"Not sure." Patrick McLanahan climbed to ten thousand feet, well above the mountains of central Nicaragua far off to the west. "James' original plan was to fly DreamStar to Cuba. More secure than Nicaragua. Then on to the Soviet Union . . ." He switched frequencies to the channel set up with the communications facility at Puerto Lempira. "Storm Control, this is Storm Two. How copy?"

"Loud and clear, Storm Two," General Elliott replied immediately.

"Our target wasn't at Puerto Cabezas. Is the AWACS up?"

"Affirmative," from Elliott. "He's got complete coverage of the Caribbean north of Nicaragua. He's got one F-16 with him. No word from him yet."

"Target must be heading south, back to Sebaco or Managua." McLanahan called up Managua on the inertial navigation unit and set the autopilot on course. "We're en route back to Sebaco to check it out, then Managua."

"Roger. Keep us advised. Storm Control out."

They flew on for another few minutes, then Marcia clicked on the interphone: "Colonel, you said we're flying to Sebaco, then Managua . . . What kind of air defenses does Sebaco have? I know Managua is heavily protected. Isn't Sebaco that KGB base where they kept DreamStar?"

"Yes," he replied testily, the questions interrupting his train of thought. "Sebaco was protected by fifty-seven-millimeter guns and SA-10 missiles and a few MiG-29 fighters. We destroyed them two days ago."

"Are they back in place?"

"I don't know."

"What about Managua? What kind of defenses does it have?"

"Probably like Puerto Cabezas. SA-15 missiles, MiG-29 or MiG-27 fighters, probably tactical anti-aircraft artillery. Why?"

"Why? Well . . . do you think the Nicaraguans are just going to let us fly over their cities? Don't you think they're going to throw everything they got at us?"

"We're going anyway. I don't care what defenses they have, we've penetrated them before, and—"

"No, sir—J. C. Powell and you defeated their defenses. You were in the backseat—"

"What the hell does *that* mean?"

"It means that you can't just charge in over Managua and Sebaco without some kind of a game plan," she said. "We were lucky over Puerto Cabezas, sir—you assumed that the defenses that were destroyed by the B-52 two days ago were still destroyed, or they didn't bring in more fighters just waiting for you to fly over looking for DreamStar. What if they'd been replaced? We would have been dead ten minutes in the sky. You can't assume anything."

No response from McLanahan. "I'm not trying to chicken out. I'll fly wherever you want, and I'll help you defend this aircraft the best I can. But we've got to do this the smart way or we'll be dead without ever getting off a shot at Ken James . . ."

"You're right. I took off from Puerto Lempira with no idea where I was going after checking Puerto Cabezas. And we did receive intelligence that the runway at Sebaco had been repaired—they could have moved in a whole squadron of MiGs by now. We could be jumped at any moment, and we have no air cover, no surveillance and only six missiles to defend ourselves. Stupid. Damned stupid . . ."

"The question is—what are we going to do now? We can't just drone around in circles."

"We've got to get an idea which way we went." But how . . . He ordered the voice-command computer to set a frequency in the number two VHF radio.

"Sandino Tower, this is Storm Zero Two on one-one-eight point one. Over."

"Storm Zero Two, this is Augusto Cesar Sandino International Airport tower," a controller with a thick Spanish accent replied. "State your position, altitude, type of aircraft, departure airport and destination. Be advised, we have no flight plan for you. You may be in violation of the air traffic laws of Nicaragua. Respond immediately."

"Tower, Storm Zero Two is an American military fighter. I am in pursuit of an American aircraft piloted by a Russian criminal. I intend to overfly Sebaco and Managua in search of this aircraft. I request assistance. Over."

"Storm Zero Two, overflight of Nicaragua by American military aircraft is prohibited. You are in violation of national and international law. You are directed to land at Sandino International immediately or you will be fired on without warning. Over."

"Sandino Tower, I say again; I am in pursuit of a criminal piloting an American aircraft. He is a danger to *you* as well as to the United States. I request assistance in pursuing this aircraft. I am *not* hostile to Nicaragua. Please assist. Over."

"It's not going to work," Preston said. "They're just triangulating our position. We've got to get out of here, head back across the Honduran border—"

"Storm Zero Two, this is Sandino Tower. Please stay on this frequency for important message. Acknowledge."

He did not reply. A message flashed on his windscreen, warning him that a search radar was in the vicinity. From the rear seat Preston said, "We're getting close to Managua's search radar."

"Storm Zero Two, contact the man on frequency one-three-one point one-five VHF. Important. Sandino Tower out."

He began a left turn away from Managua and changed channels. Preston asked, "Are you going to talk on that frequency? It could be a military ground-controlled interceptor's direction-finder. They could pin-point our location as soon as you key the mike without using radar."

"Maybe. But I don't think so." He hit the mike button. "This is Storm Zero Two on one-three-one point one-five. Over."

"Storm Two, this is General-Lieutenant Viktor Tcharin, Deputy Commander of Operations for Soviet Central America Operations Base Sebaco. Whom am I addressing?"

"It's a damned Soviet general," Preston said. "What the hell does *he* want?"

Patrick keyed the mike. "General Tcharin, this is Lieutenant Colonel Patrick McLanahan, United States Air Force. State your request. Over."

"McLanahan . . . McLanahan . . ." Then, sounding as if he was reading from a script, went on: " 'Senior project officer, Midnight Sky. Code name for XF-34 DreamStar advanced tactical fighter aircraft flight technology validation project. Age forty-one, white male.' *Ochin kharasho.* Very good. Colonel McLanahan, I believe we want very nearly the same thing. You want the XF-34. We want Colonel Andrei Maraklov. Perhaps we can make an arrangement—"

"I want Maraklov *and* the XF-34, General. Do you know where Maraklov is headed?"

"We have evidence to that effect, yes," Tcharin told him.

"We believe we have tracked his course on radar. But we do not have the air assets to pursue him. You reported to the Nicaraguan tower controller that you are in command of a fighter plane. Is it your intention to attack Colonel Maraklov?"

"Yes."

"We have information that may be of use to you. In exchange for this information we want you to deliver Colonel Maraklov to us, should he survive. Is that agreeable to you, Colonel Mc-Lanahan?"

"I'm not making any deals," McLanahan told him. "I don't trust you any more than I trust Maraklov. But if you tell me where he went, and if he survives, I promise not to kill him myself. What happens to him after that is up to our governments. How about that?"

A pause, then: "I agree. Colonel Maraklov had received instructions" . . . he did not say from whom . . . "to fly the aircraft south, to an isolated landing strip somewhere in Costa Rica. He was detected flying forty nautical miles west of Blue-fields in southern Nicaragua about ten minutes ago. We have no other information. He was at twenty thousand feet, flying at five hundred nautical miles per hour."

"Copy that down for me, Marcia," McLanahan said. On the radio: "How do I know you're telling the truth? He could be flying north to Cuba, or east. He could even be on the ground in Managua or Sebaco."

"*You* contacted *us* for assistance and I have given it to you. If you do not trust us, your request makes no sense."

"Why can't you get Maraklov by yourself? Isn't he delivering the XF-34 to you?"

"It's not clear *what* orders Colonel Maraklov has chosen to follow. Our last orders, from the Kollegiya, were to turn over the XF-34 to you at Puerto Cabezas. Why he took the aircraft, I do not know. We want to question him about that matter, as well as the killing of two Soviet officers and two soldiers. My orders are to capture Colonel Maraklov for questioning, but I have no resources to do it. That is where you can help . . ."

If this Soviet general was lying, every mile he flew south could be two miles that Maraklov was increasing the distance on his way to Cuba or someplace to the east. Yet he had no other possible options.

"Marcia?"

"I don't see much of a choice. I don't trust him either, and I sure as hell don't like making deals with him, but it's the only lead we have. Our AWACS from Grand Cayman is covering the north Caribbean—so south seems like a good direction for us to be heading. Might as well try it."

McLanahan keyed the radio again as he began a right turn toward the south. "General Tcharin, if I get Maraklov alive I promise you'll have an opportunity to question him about the murders. I was a witness to three of them in Puerto Cabezas."

"Unfortunately an American is an unacceptable witness in our military court of law," Tcharin said, "but I believe we have a deal . . . Colonel McLanahan, the XF-34 is armed with twenty-millimeter shells, two radar-guided missiles and two infrared-guided missiles—not the most modern Soviet weapons but proved effective against your F-16s over the Caribbean. One more item: Maraklov is wounded. We have tested and found his blood at a site here in Sebaco as well as the blood of one of his victims. You have clearance to transit Nicaraguan airspace west and south of Bluefields. Costa Rican approach control frequency for crossing border restricted airspace MRR Three is one-one-nine point six, El Coco Control."

And the channel went dead. McLanahan told the computer to set the frequency, and he checked the computer flight-information database and double-checked the flight information files for Costa Rica—Tcharin's information seemed right on.

"Well, you wanted a plan, Marcia," he said as they approached the border. "I never expected to get it from the Russians, but we'll take it."

Pain. Intense, burning.

For at least the past year the pain that always came to Andrei Maraklov when the ANTARES interface was completed was fairly easy to suppress. The concentration and the exhilaration of flying a machine like DreamStar usually did the trick, but this time it wasn't working. Obviously the shoulder wound was the culprit. Every time he thought about his throbbing left shoulder his body would receive a jolt of pain from the ANTARES system.

So far it didn't seem to affect his flying performance or his ability to monitor his ship's functions. In spite of the hard flying that DreamStar had done during the past week she was running

perfectly. Her automatic monitors detected a higher than normal
level of metal particles in the oil, suggesting an overdue engine
overhaul or contaminated oil; other systems detected clogged
fuel-metering systems from dirty fuel, moisture in computer
components and a few loose panels. He made a mental command to have a list of these items recorded and played back to
him just before the next shut-down, to remind him to have them
checked. It was a long list, but Maraklov told himself he would
have time to check over his bird. In any case, these minor discrepancies did not seem to be affecting DreamStar's performance.

He was flying in the deep mountain valleys of the Cordillera
de Guanacaste mountains of northwestern Costa Rica, staying as
low as possible to avoid detection from radar sites at Santa Maria
International Airport to the east and Lomas Guardia International to the west. Although Costa Rica had an air force deployed at Santa Maria Airport and a few other small training
bases, it was made up of a handful of aging American-built F-5
day VFR fighters to scare away drug smugglers, plus several
single-engine piston prop planes for surveillance. The federal
military forces were very small—the nation's popular phrase
nowadays was "we have more teachers than soldiers," and fortunately for him that was true.

It was also true in Costa Rica that most provincial and mu-
nicipal security (it could not be called "law and order") came
from privately funded and equipped armies, which was legal in
this country of only three million people. If you were rich enough
you could own a good-sized town in Costa Rica, which could
eventually turn into one's own little nation—including one's own
army, and it was legal for certain citizens to make their own
stamps, set prices, deal with other countries, appoint their
own judges and mayors.

One such privately owned city-state was Venado, a thirty-
thousand-acre plantation in the heart of the Guanacaste Mountains. Two thousand people lived and worked on this plantation,
nearly half of whom were soldiers. The entire plantation, the
well-equipped army and the airport within it were all funded
and maintained by the KGB, one of dozens of secret KGB bases
scattered over the world, bases so secret, so well disguised, that
most party members outside of a few ranking officers in the KGB
knew nothing about them. This was Maraklov's destination.

Finding the airport was no problem, but making an approach to it in daytime without being seen was going to be difficult. Maraklov had already had to weave around scores of private airstrips dotting the San Juan Valley and the northern Costa Rican jungles to stay out of sight; he could not afford just to shoot directly into Venado, with some farmer or peasant watching his approach and blabbing to his boss or the police. Maraklov's plan was to hug the northeast rim of the Guanacaste Mountains, stay as deep in the valleys as possible, sweep around the valleys to the southwest and then come back up over Venado from the west. This way, he should be shrouded by mountains almost all the way to landing.

There was another summer storm brewing out over the Pacific to the west as Maraklov started his low-altitude swing to the southeast along the mountain range. His holographic display showed slivers of surveillance radar above him, but most of the energy was blocked out by the tall mountains of central Costa Rica. The area was sparsely settled, but occasional glances out the cockpit showed a few very beautiful haciendas below, where men had retaken the jungle and turned it into lush fields of coffee or fruit. Maraklov throttled back on the power as much as possible, balancing his energy to avoid making as much noise as possible but keeping up his speed to avoid letting anyone on the ground get a good look at him.

The inertial navigation computer warned Maraklov that its precision was not great enough to find Venado with less than the usual quarter-mile accuracy, and since the satellite-navigation unit was unavailable for use (it required a daily code) it recommended that the attack radar be activated in ground-mapping mode to update the computer's position. Any radar emissions were dangerous, but Maraklov had no choice—DreamStar was not the type of aircraft specifically designed for pilotage or for navigating by use of visual references.

He allowed the computer to activate the radar, which transmitted in thirty-mile range for five seconds, then went back to standby. DreamStar steered west-southwest for a few miles, until the very rim of a beautiful mountain lake could be seen, then began a right turn on top of a ridge-line toward Venado. After an instantaneous mental inquiry he knew that they were exactly four point one nautical miles from the center of the runway. One pass over the field was all it would take to make a radar survey of the field for landing data, and the computer would do the rest. The turbofan engine throttled back to seventy-five percent, the canards moved from cruise position to high-lift position, and the mission-adaptive wings began to reshape for approach speed—

"DreamStar, this is Cheetah on GUARD channel. We've found you."

The sudden radio message screamed in Maraklov's brain like a siren. Instinctively he increased power to ninety percent and reshaped the wings and moved the canards back to high-speed, high-maneuverability position, ready to evade a missile or gun attack. The attack radar also activated in air-to-air search mode for three seconds before Maraklov commanded it to stand by— at this altitude he would see very little on radar, while his own radar energy could be seen for miles by aircraft at higher altitude. He also punched off the Lluyka tanks in preparation for the fight—he hoped he could somehow fool Kalinin into getting him another pair of external fuel tanks. As for Cheetah, by denying DreamStar a long-range cruise capability once again, it had already won a considerable victory.

Maraklov found it hard to believe. *Cheetah?* Cheetah was *here?* How was that *possible?* Who was flying it?

"Got him," Marcia said. "Brief airborne search radar at one o'clock position. Hot damn. This time the Russians were telling the truth."

McLanahan hit the voice-command switch: "Arm, missiles, arm, cannon."

*"Warning, all weapons armed, select safe to safe all weapons."*

"Weapon, select, radar, missile." The computer repeated the command, and on the weapon-status display one of the four radar-guided AIM-120C Scorpion missiles on the fuselage stations was highlighted.

"Radar, mode, air, range, maximum. Radar on." The attack radar came on, showing no air targets within one hundred miles.

"Check your radar," Marcia said. "You've been transmitting for twenty seconds at full power."

"I know," McLanahan said. "I want him to know we're here."

"Sir," Preston said, "he doesn't need any of *our* help to hose us."

"The smart thing for him to do would have been to land," McLanahan said. "If I was close to my destination I'd hightail it over there and hide and not risk an air-to-air engagement. But if I look inviting enough for him, maybe he'll come up and fight."

"Don't take unnecessary chances," Marcia said. "You might flush him out, sure, but then you have to deal with him on your tail. Don't be so anxious to mix it up with him. The fight will happen."

He smiled. Her words in his helmet sounded a lot like J. C. Powell. Powell had been a skilled flight instructor, with seemingly infinite patience in spite of some of the stupid mistakes McLanahan would make—Marcia Preston seemed a lot like him.

"Radar, standby," he commanded. "Thanks, Marcia."

"Electronic jammers are on," she reported. "Keep your power up. Remember, you're the power fighter, he's the angles fighter. He might be able to move like greased lightning but you have the speed and the power . . . You've been too long on this constant heading, too," she said. "Give me a few clearing turns. Let's take a look—*bandit, three o'clock, low. Break right!*"

He slammed the stick hard right. Cheetah executed a hard right full roll, then another half-roll until he could regain control. When his eyes were adjusted after the spin, he saw DreamStar headed right at him, less than a hundred yards away, with its nose high in the air but tracking Cheetah's every move as if the two were mechanically linked. And in a way they were, now in more ways than one . . . He saw DreamStar's nose light up as he fired his cannon.

McLanahan pushed the stick full forward, sending Cheetah in a screaming dive. He released the back pressure almost immediately, but Cheetah wasn't pulling out.

"Pull *up*," he heard Preston yell. He hauled back on the stick. It did not move—it was as if Cheetah's controls were locked, which made McLanahan push or pull harder each time. He realized that was the reason for the steep dive—the rigid side-stick control had no play, which automatically made him push even harder to try to move it. He zoomed Cheetah up into a climb, gaining two thousand feet in altitude but losing two hundred knots of precious air speed. Finally he leveled off and took a deep breath, the first one he remembered taking since the attack began.

"He's right above us, still at ten thousand feed," Preston said. "Be careful dogfighting with this guy. He knew exactly which way we were going. Keep your speed up. That's your advantage."

He took a look at DreamStar's position once more. "I'm going for a shot. Hang on." He pulled back on the stick and aimed the nose at DreamStar, then waited for the radar-lock-on tone. When he heard it he moved his right thumb over to the missile-launch button and pressed.

*"Warning, min range inhibit,"* the computer announced. The AIM-120C Scorpion was too close to its target to arm its warhead, so the computer automatically overrode the launch command.

McLanahan slipped his right index finger down onto the cannon trigger, but just as he squeezed, DreamStar turned as if doing a pirouette in mid-air and dived so fast and so sharply that it virtually disappeared from sight.

"I see him," Preston said, grasping the back of her ejection seat to turn herself around so she could watch DreamStar. "Four . . . five . . . six o'clock, he's coming around on us. God, I've never seen a plane *move* so fast."

Suddenly McLanahan and Preston *felt* a banging and shuddering sound throughout Cheetah, as if a giant hand had grabbed the F-15's entire tail section, held it fast and started shaking it back and forth. The laser-projection screen reported a half-dozen faults. "Right rudder actuator out," he said. "Right radar warning receiver and ECM antennas—looks like he shot off our right rudder."

"Fox Four, at your six o'clock," they heard on the radio. It was a cold, monotonous, mechanical voice, as eerie as listening to strangers' faraway voices in a dark cave.

"What the hell is that?" Preston asked.

"It's his," he told her. "His voice is computer-synthesized."

"He's right behind us, right between our tails."

"Who is in command of Cheetah?" the eerie voice said on the GUARD channel. "McLanahan? Elliott?"

Before McLanahan could reply, Preston called out, "He's right beside us—"

Patrick snapped his head around. DreamStar was precisely on Cheetah's right wing, flying in perfect formation. At first, a completely disoriented feeling came over him—this was like it always had been, Cheetah in the lead, DreamStar on the wing. They had flown like this for months, talking over a maneuver, doing the maneuver, then forming up as they repositioned themselves, critiqued the previous maneuver's results and talked over the next one. But this wasn't Dreamland, and that wasn't Ken James.

"Marcia, there's a satellite transceiver unit on your right rear panel. Ever use one before?"

"Yes, we have a larger version in the NSC office."

"Send a clear-text message to Storm Control and to the Joint Chiefs about our location. Tell them we found DreamStar in Costa Rica." On the emergency radio frequency he said, "Maraklov, I want you to land. I've been in contact with the Russian authorities. What you're doing isn't authorized even by your government. You've got the U.S. and the USSR both wanting your head on a platter. Give it up."

"Colonel McLanahan, I will never give up DreamStar," Maraklov replied. "I am ordering you to withdraw across the border immediately. Otherwise I will destroy Cheetah piece by piece before I put the final missile into her. Comply immediately."

"Maraklov, there's no place you can run. The KGB knows where your landing base in Costa Rica is, and pretty soon we'll know it too."

As he watched, DreamStar began to slip aft. "Patrick, he's moving behind us again," Preston called out.

This was it, Patrick thought. Ken James is going to shoot me out of the sky. He had no place to run. DreamStar already had an attack planned for every climb, descent and turn imaginable . . . It was time to act . . .

*No.* J. C. Powell's words came back full force . . . DreamStar does not play defense. Act unpredictably, force her into a defensive situation and take advantage of its programming deficiency to try to turn the tables—

The computerized voice of the ANTARES computer cut in: "You have been warned, Colonel McLanahan. This is your last chance. I will open fire if you—"

He did not wait for the rest of Maraklov's warning. He yanked the throttles to idle. On the throttle-quadrant on the left side-panel, a large guarded switch read REVERSE. McLanahan flicked the guard away, selected full-reverse thrust on the two-dimension vectored-thrust nozzles and cut in full military power. The rectangular engine-exhaust nozzles reduced down to their smallest size, and steerable exhaust louvers over and underneath the engines opened, blowing the engine exhaust toward the nose. As the thrust came back to full power, Cheetah's airspeed was cut in half in a matter of seconds.

Cheetah's steel and titanium airframe shrieked, and the computerized stall and airframe overstress warning messages blasted in their helmets. McLanahan's and Preston's bodies were thrown forward against their shoulder harnesses. Struggling against the G-forces, he waited until he was abeam DreamStar again, then yanked the control stick over, and rolled right into Dream-Star . . .

Even if the ANTARES computer had not warned Maraklov of Cheetah's sudden decrease in airspeed, he had seen Cheetah's engine exhaust nozzles snap closed and the ventral louvers open, and had time to react. What he wasn't expecting was the suicide-move that McLanahan made after that. Before he knew it Cheetah had banked up on its right wing and was turning directly into DreamStar on a collision course.

Maraklov's first decision was to roll with Cheetah and out-turn him, but the radar quickly informed him that he had no room to bank away from the sudden roll—Cheetah was so close that if DreamStar went into a right bank his left wingtip would certainly strike Cheetah's right wing. Maraklov was near-transfixed by the sight of Cheetah swooping in on him. He had no place to run. Only a few yards remaining . . .

Suddenly the pain that had been with him ever since his successful interface with ANTARES returned full-force. It was so intense it nearly blinded him. His shoulder throbbed, the pain seemed to spread out across his entire body, intensifying the electrical shock generated by the metallic flight suit. The headache that had seemed to go away when he attacked Cheetah was now like a red-hot thing buried in his head. He knew he did not black out—his seat was still upright and he was not being force-fed blasts of oxygen—but he was out of control as he tried to figure a way to escape Cheetah's attack.

At some point during the maneuver ANTARES took control. The computer commanded full down deflection on the nose canards, full downward thrust from the vectored-thrust nozzle, full adverse pitch on the flap strakes in the tail. The effect was a rapid elevator zero-pitch descent at negative seven G's, almost at the structural limit of DreamStar's airframe and, more important, twice the normal safe negative-G limit of the human body. Cheetah's right wingtip missed DreamStar's bubble canopy by a few yards—if the canopy had been made of anything but ultra-strong polymer plastics it would have shattered from the hurricane-like force from Cheetah's wingtip vortices.

Maraklov, already partially incapacitated by the sudden intense sheets of pain rolling across his body, was on the verge of unconsciousness from the negative G's. He was quickly past the red-out stage, where blood was forced up into his brain. Blood vessels burst in his eyeballs and nostrils, and one eardrum exploded. The computer sensed Maraklov's semi-conscious state, immediately reclined his ejection seat and shot pure oxygen into his face mask. But the increased pressure in his face only forced blood from his nostrils back into his throat, nearly drowning him.

Once DreamStar's all-aspect radar detected that Cheetah had rolled well clear, it discontinued the hard horizontal descent, selected full afterburner and began a hard climb up to a safer altitude. But DreamStar was flying on full-computer control as Maraklov fought for consciousness. The pain had suddenly subsided, but Maraklov was still trying to recover from the effects of the negative G's as DreamStar zoomed to thirty thousand feet, then leveled off.

ANTARES performed a systems self-test and prepared to issue an all-systems-nominal report—as soon as Maraklov regained full consciousness.

The system self-test never included the pilot.

*"Colonel, what the hell are you doing?"* Preston called out. "Recover, dammit, recover."

McLanahan immediately let up on the stick pressure, allowing Cheetah's automatic roll-and-yaw damping mechanisms slow the roll rate. When he firmly saw which way his roll was going, he eased in left-stick force and rolled Cheetah wingslevel.

"Where is he, Marcia? Where did he go?"

She was still shaken from the sudden maneuver but quickly pulled herself together. "God, what a *ride*. I don't see him anywhere."

"I've gotta risk using the radar." He hit the voice-command

button while continuing to search the skies around Cheetah. "Radar, search, transmit, voice warning."

*"Attack radar transmit,"* the computer replied. *"Voice warning activated. Fifty mile range selected, no targets."*

"Get some altitude back," Preston said. "He had the upper hand when he got above you. You can use your power more effectively if you stay above him."

He began a rapid climb. "But remember, DreamStar is a new kind of fighter. It's hard to explain—it took J.C. years to figure it out and months to explain it to me. There's only one way to get him, and I just showed it works."

"By almost killing us? By pulling a kamikaze on him? If that's how we're going to play we might as well get out—"

The computerized voice cut in: *"Target, range twenty miles, bearing ten left."*

"There he is," Preston called out. "Eleven o'clock high, straight and level."

"Tally ho. I'm going for a shot." He hit the voice-command button. "Radar target designate . . ." The blinking circle-aiming cursor appeared on the windscreen, superimposed on DreamStar as the only radar target in range. "Now."

*"Radar lock."* McLanahan hit the missile-launch button and watched as one of the AIM-120 Scorpion missiles streaked out from underneath the fuselage toward its target.

"Missile's tracking by itself," Preston said, scanning her weapons indications. The Scorpion missile needed guidance from its launch aircraft only until its own on-board radar locked onto the target. Then the carrier aircraft could disengage and look for other targets. "Try a left turn, get around behind him in case he gets past the missile."

"He'll get past it—guaranteed," McLanahan said. To the computer: "Select radar missile. Arm missile."

*"Warning, radar missile armed."* He hit the launch button and a second Scorpion missile streaked out.

DreamStar abruptly heeled over to the right, making a turn so tight that the Scorpion missile's automatic proximity detonation missed by over a hundred feet—the proximity detonation circuits could not keep up with DreamStar's remarkably fast jink. McLanahan watched, transfixed, as DreamStar headed directly down at Cheetah, rapidly closing the distance even before his AIM-120 medium-range missile left the rails. Shaking himself,

McLanahan banked hard right and up, selected zone-five full afterburner, trying to get underneath DreamStar, spoil his aim and get out of the way before Maraklov could finish his sudden attack.

Maraklov had recovered from the effects of negative G's just in time to receive the new warning of radar lock-on and missile uplink—a Scorpion missile was in flight. This time there was no pain—in an instant Cheetah's location was plotted, its direction and all three of its axis velocities were recorded and assimilated and a counter-offensive move and several alternate maneuvers processed. He selected the first choice a fraction of a second later. It had been timed perfectly, and the missile rushed well past DreamStar without detonating until it had passed out of lethal range.

In the same instant ANTARES had selected an AA-11 infrared-guided missile and had just received a lock-on signal from the missile's seeker-head when a new threat was detected—a second missile in flight from Cheetah. A moment later he saw Cheetah head straight for him, chewing up the distance. Now two threats were closing on him—the second Scorpion missile and Cheetah itself, fast approaching optimal cannon range.

ANTARES commanded the AA-11 to launch. At the same time it made a tight right roll followed by a hard break, turning in a tight circle to align once again with Cheetah.

"Missile launch! Dead ahead!"

McLanahan hit the voice-command button. "Chaff. Flare." As the radar and infrared decoys ejected off into space, he jerked the control stick right, descended a few hundred feet, then lit the afterburners and pulled up. But not fast enough. DreamStar's AA-11 missile followed Cheetah's turn and descent, then detonated its ninety-pound warhead just as McLanahan began to hard six-G pull. The missile detonated ten feet to the right and slightly aft of the right engine, piercing the engine case and sending showers of metal and compressor blades in all directions.

But at the same time ANTARES detected Cheetah's second Scorpion missile still in flight—the two or three seconds it had taken to launch the jury-rigged Soviet missile gave the big, high-speed AIM-120 missile time to lock on and reach full speed. The all-aspect radar detected the missile still closing fast.

The radar range to Cheetah's second missile turned into a high-pitched squeal of warning, transmitted directly to Maraklov's already exhausted brain. ANTARES had no choice but to evade the missile—DreamStar's jammers were ineffective against Cheetah's radar or the Scorpion missile's on-board radar—they had reprogrammed the AIM-120's on-board radar to a different frequency outside DreamStar's known jammer-range in anticipation of this fight—and DreamStar could not continue the right turn to pursue Cheetah with the missile closing in.

With Maraklov allowing ANTARES now to select the fighter's maneuvers and counter-maneuvers, ANTARES reversed its direction of flight, went to full afterburner, and aimed its nose right at the missile, presenting its lowest radar cross-section. At the last possible moment DreamStar jinked upward hard . . . and the missile passed underneath.

"Engine fire on the right," Preston called out. McLanahan yanked the right throttle to idle, lifted it out of its idle detent and moved it to cut-off, then hit the voice-command switch: "Right engine fire, execute." The computer commanded the right-engine fuel valves and supply lines closed and fire retardant sprayed inside the engine compartment.

"I'm showing fuel cutoff and engine fire light out," Preston said. She turned in her seat, scanning the area for damage. "We might have a fuel leak on the aft body tank. The smoke is clearing."

"Where's DreamStar? Is he behind us?"

Preston scanned the skies, expecting to see that unreal plane diving out of nowhere with guns blazing. But it was nowhere to be seen. "I can't see him."

"I'm getting some altitude. Power coming back to mil," McLanahan said. With an engine fire and the potential of more damage in the left engine casing, the use of afterburner was unwise except in an emergency. "I've still got full flight control." The engines were close enough together on the F-15 so that single-engine handling was not a problem, and the vectored-thrust nozzles, mission-adaptive wings, and canards would compensate for the loss of rudder control and the asymmetric thrust.

"Airspeed's down below five hundred knots," Preston said, continuing to search for DreamStar. "And you're hardly climbing. We've had it, we don't have the power to even consider dogfighting with him any more.''

''I'm not giving up. Listen, something's happening here. If Maraklov was flying at one hundred percent we'd be dog meat by now. He's not engaging, I think *maybe* he's reached his limit . . .'' Wishful thinking . . . ? He began a turn back in the opposite direction and activated the air-to-air attack radar.

Immediately the computer reported, *''Radar target, range twelve miles, bearing right.''*

He hit the voice-command button: ''Select radar missile. Launch missile. Launch missile.''

The pain that racked Maraklov's body was constant now, rolling across every nerve ending like a brush fire out of control. The numbness in his left shoulder spread to his left arm and elbow— it was the first time in two years that Maraklov ever noticed anything about his appendages while flying under the neural– computer interface system. The sensory dichotomy created momentary confusion. He became aware of still more problems with his body—he was incredibly thirsty, weak as a kitten. He was aware of the taste of blood—he could even feel blood dripping down the side of his head and pooling inside his oxygen mask. Taste? Feel? These sensations were as foreign to him while under ANTARES as mental radar images had been when he first saw one.

At the same time, ANTARES was warning him about a hundred other things. Cheetah was in a left turn, heading back for him. Fuel state was critical—less than twenty minutes fuel left, without reserves. Oxygen was low. That last Scorpion missile's miss was not altogether harmless—ANTARES was now reporting minor ventral fin actuator damage and a few sectors of the ventral superconducting radar arrays malfunctioning.

It was time to destroy Cheetah, once and for all.

But DreamStar had barely completed its turn back toward Cheetah when more missiles were detected in flight. And now they were in a head-on engagement, with one, then two missiles in flight. Maraklov began a series of high-speed random maneuvers, trying to make the missiles swing farther and farther away on each turn. At the same time he moved farther and farther from Cheetah, getting a few more yards of lateral separation, waiting for the moment to begin a lead turn into the F-15 to start his gun pass.

This time, Maraklov thought, he could not miss. McLanahan had become lazy—never go head-to-head with his DreamStar.

"Scorpion missile tracking . . . stay with him, Patrick, he's getting outside you . . ."

McLanahan blinked beads of sweat out of his eyes as he nudged the control stick farther right toward Cheetah. He had a steady JOKER indication on the heads-up display—less than fifteen minutes of fuel remaining, enough to get him back to La Cieba or Puerto Lempira. If he continued to fight much longer the number of possible landing sites, in Honduras or Panama, would steadily decrease to zero until he would be forced to put down somewhere in Costa Rica.

"Patrick, watch it," Preston called out, "he's turning in on you—"

He had let his mind drift off at the worst possible moment. That momentary lapse of concentration had allowed DreamStar to get the angle on him. Maraklov was now bearing in on Cheetah from the right side. A turn in either direction would expose himself even more to a cannon attack.

He lit the left afterburner and pulled Cheetah up into a hard climb. Preston hung from the handlebars in the back seat, straining against the G-forces as she tried to keep DreamStar in sight over her right shoulder.

"*Warning, missile launch,*" the computer threat-receiver blared. Then: "*Warning, airspeed low. Stall warning. Stall warning.*"

"He's turned inside us. Missile launch. *Get out of here.*"

McLanahan hit the voice-command button: "Chaff . . . Flares," he grunted, forcing the words out from the pressure against his lungs. He saw the decoys-eject indications on the heads-up display.

"Where is he?" he called out to Preston.

"Five o'clock low, climbing with us. He's still coming . . ."

McLanahan pulled back on the stick even harder, his neck and jaw muscles quivering against the pressure. He rolled inverted, ejected more chaff and flares to decoy the missiles, then plunged Cheetah earthward. They were head-to-head once again, but this time they were fighting in the vertical, not the horizontal—Cheetah was in a full-power descent, rapidly building airspeed, and DreamStar was in a screaming climb, heading right at him . . .

ANTARES adjusted each flight control surface and every pound of two-dimensional vectored thrust to keep Cheetah centered in its crosshairs. Measuring by DreamStar's precision millimeter-wave radar and calculating by computer several times a second, Maraklov commanded DreamStar to open fire seconds before McLanahan's finger even closed on his trigger. They were still almost two miles apart when DreamStar opened fire, dead on target . . .

The cannon reported locked-on and firing—then stopped.

After several days of misuse, inexperienced handling, and lack of routine preventive maintenance, and because the Russian-made ammunition was not precisely compatible with its American counterpart, DreamStar's twenty-millimeter cannon fired five rounds, then jammed solid. The M61A5 cannon's automatic jam-clearing mechanism tried to reverse the cartridge belt-feed, spin past the portion of the belt where the jam occurred and refeed the belt through the firing chamber, but the jam could not be cleared in flight.

At the speed of thought, ANTARES transmitted several bits of data to Maraklov's exhausted mind. The cannon jam was reported in minute detail—he knew exactly where the jam was, the status of the unsuccessful attempts to clear it and the changing status of all the attack options that had been computed using the cannon. He also knew the range to Cheetah, knew Cheetah's Doppler-measured velocity, and knew that Cheetah was within lethal gun range. And he knew to the nearest one-tenth of a knot his own decreasing airspeed and the position of his wings and canards to overcome his speed deficit. He commanded his last AA-11 missile to launch, but it was a desperate snap-shot, with only one or two seconds guidance time and launched with a much higher launch angle of attack than the Russian missile was designed for.

With the realization that a defensive turn and descent away from Cheetah was the last available option, the pain returned full-force to Maraklov's already tortured nervous system. This time, the pain was unbearable . . . He never knew that ANTARES' stabilization system automatically corrected the impending stall condition. He also was not conscious enough to realize that DreamStar had taken several direct hits all across its wings and upper fuselage as ANTARES pulled its nose back to the horizon.

Warning messages began flooding in from almost every system on board the fighter, but Maraklov was too dazed by exhaustion and too overloaded with pain to assimilate them all—now the ANTARES computer was forced to take over all safety and flight control functions. The computers aboard DreamStar detected a fire in the engine compartment, momentarily shut down the engine, put out the fire and restarted the engine all in a few seconds. Engine-fuel feed was rerouted to draw fuel from leaking tanks before they ran dry. The mission-adaptive wings reshaped themselves to compensate for hydraulic actuators damaged by gunfire.

But through it all, Maraklov hovered on the brink of unconsciousness. And without him, for all ANTARES' capability, DreamStar was no longer capable of fighting.

McLanahan came out of military power and set the throttles to eighty percent. He saw the BINGO low fuel warning projected onto his windscreen—less than ten minutes of fuel remaining—but for now he ignored it. He clicked open the interphone. "He's *what*?"

"I see smoke coming out of his exhaust," Preston said. "Not heavy but I can see it. He's flying straight and level, not maneuvering. You *got* him . . ."

McLanahan looked over far to his right and spotted DreamStar. He turned toward him. Preston said, "You've got two-hundred rounds remaining and two missiles. Take the shot. We're low on fuel."

He lined up on DreamStar, selected an AIM-132 infrared missile, aligned it, hit the voice-command button: "Safe all missiles. Safe cannon."

*"Caution, all weapons safe."*

"Patrick, what are you *doing*? You got to bring this guy down. There's no other choice. He can turn on us . . ."

McLanahan's reply was to click open the emergency frequency: "DreamStar, this is Cheetah. I'm at your six, five miles. I'm joining on your right side. Do you hear me?"

"Stay away . . ." The pain in his voice was obvious, even

through the computerized distortion. ''Do not come any closer . . .''

''It's over, I'm joining on your wing. When you see me stay on my wing. We're landing. Do you *understand*?''

He maneuvered Cheetah closer to DreamStar, finally overtaking him. ''I've got the lead, coming right. You're on the wing, stay there.'' He began a shallow right turn.

''I am not giving up this aircraft . . .'' the computer-synthesized voice said. ''I am not . . . not going to surrender DreamStar . . .''

''It's over. Listen to me. DreamStar is damaged, you're hurt bad. You'll destroy DreamStar or force me to destroy you. You've got a chance to live. Take it—''

Suddenly Marcia called out, ''He's turning behind us . . . !''

But it was only a momentary deviation. A moment later DreamStar moved into perfect fingertip formation with Cheetah. ''That's it, stay in position.'' On interphone McLanahan said, ''Marcia, get on the radio to any air traffic facility you can reach. Tell them we need vectors to a hard-surface runway ASAP.''

He paused, taking his first real deep breath, then added: ''Two American military aircraft landing, both require assistance.''

# Epilogue

## Brooks AFB Hospital, San Antonio, Texas
*Thursday, 25 June 1996, 2037 PDT (2337 EDT)*

"SHE'S A REMARKABLE woman," the doctor told him. "You were right. She just refused to give up."

He bent over and kissed her. "She's a tough broad."

Wendy returned the kiss, reached up and touched his face, ran her fingers across his temples. "You've gotten a few gray hairs in the past few days, Colonel." Her smile dimmed as she saw his eyes, remembering. "I'm sorry I won't be there for J.C.'s service tomorrow. I'm going to miss him . . ."

He nodded. "I've never felt as secure, or as happy in an aircraft until I started flying with J.C. And he was a *friend*." McLanahan was silent a few moments. "But seeing you like this again, it overwhelms everything . . . How do you feel?"

"Like they say, lucky to be alive. Also tired as hell. The doctor says I'll be out of here in a couple of weeks, then a few months' convalescent leave. I think that's too much. Four, five weeks should do it." She took his hand, squeezed it tight. "I . . . I heard about what you did before you left for Honduras again. I heard everyone was ready to let me go. I—"

Patrick put a finger on her lips. "I did it because I'm selfish. What the hell would I do without you?"

He knelt down beside her bed and she wrapped her arms around him, pulled him close to her. They didn't say a word. Even one would have been superfluous.

They heard a polite cough behind them. Joe and Betty Tork were standing in the doorway. "May we come in?" Betty asked.

McLanahan moved aside. Wendy's parents gave their daughter

a hug and spoke in low whispers. Then Joe Tork stood and faced Patrick.

"Congratulations, Patrick," he said in a low voice. "Thank God Wendy is doing all right."

"Yeah, well, I have to be going." Joe put a big hand on his shoulder.

"Hey, McLanahan, I'm trying to apologize."

"Colonel, it's not so bad for an ex-Marine. Okay?"

"Okay. All even."

There was one spot in the thousand-square-mile Dreamland complex not classified top-secret or restricted access, although it was one of the most difficult places to get in to visit. Surrounded by a simple picket fence and a grove of trees, a green oasis in the middle of miles of desert and rocks, was a cemetery dedicated to the most extraordinary aircrewmen and support personnel in the world.

The cemetery, belonging to the men and women who died in the service of the top-secret weapons and aircraft laboratory in the high desert of southern Nevada, had seen a lot of use in the past few days. The services for the dead security guards and the crew of the Old Dog had already taken place here; their grave sites, only a few yards away, still bore fresh flowers. Granite walls had been erected near the plots, telling who these men and women were and how they died; the walls were concealed by black plastic covers because the incident was still classified and under investigation. Now three more burial places and another granite wall, covered with secretive black as well, had been prepared for Alan Carmichael, Raymond Butler and Roland Powell.

No matter how much he prepared, the sound of the shots from the seven rifles over the graves of his friends stung McLanahan right to the heart. The echoes of the twenty-one shots reverberated off the surrounding Groom Mountains, seemingly rolling off the hills and echoing on forever.

As taps were played by a lone bugler, McLanahan heard the roar of jet engines passing overhead. At first he had no desire to watch the planes—the realization that he would never see these three men again had hit him with full force. They were such an important part of his life that their loss made him feel weak, completely drained. Then he looked across to the grave site, and the further realization of the deaths of Ormack, Pereira and the other members of the Old Dog's crew made it especially hard. There seemed to be no future beyond this place . . . his future seemed to be lying at his feet . . .

He felt a hand on his shoulder, turned and saw Brad Elliott. Standing on one side of Elliott was Deborah O'Day, and on his other side was Hal Briggs. Elliott motioned skyward with his eyes, and McLanahan looked up and saw the astonishing formation passing overhead.

The sky seemed to be filled with planes. The lead formation was composed of some of the most high-tech machines in the world, led by a B-52 Megafortress. The formation also had "flying-wing" B-2 stealth bombers, a B-1 Excalibur bomber, one of the new stretched FB-111 bombers and a large aircraft that looked a lot like a smaller version of the B-1, with its wings pulled back to its fully swept high-speed setting. The second formation was composed of five F-15F fighter-bombers, and it was from this formation where one aircraft, J.C.'s Cheetah—he recognized it immediately, its right vertical stabilizer was still missing—peeled off from the rest to form the "missing man" formation.

Among the onlookers was a man who had had more than a little to do with this ceremony. Ken James . . . Maraklov. He had been allowed, over protests of some members of HAWC, to attend the service, handcuffed and surrounded by two security guards. Eventually he was taken away by the security agents.

Elliott and McLanahan turned back toward the three grave sites as the ceremony ended and the crowd dispersed. "I feel like everything's come to an end here, General."

"Not quite." Elliott motioned skyward again, and McLanahan followed his lead. The unusual B-1 lookalike had moved its wings up from its full aft-sweep position to a forward-swept position like the XF-29 fighter's high-maneuverability wings. The amazing hybrid plane then pulled up out of the formation, lit its twin afterburners with a rolling boom and did a spectacular climbing roll, accelerating quickly out of sight.

"The new XFB-5 Tracer," Elliott said in a low voice. "First generation, designed for strategic escort-duties like the Megafortress. We combined the technology of the F-29 and the B-1 and came up with a plane that's twice as good as the sum of its parts. It's as fast and agile as a fighter, but with almost the same payload and power as a supersonic bomber."

The officer in charge of the ceremony handed the folded American flags to Secretary of the Air Force Wilbur Curtis, who in turn handed them to the widows and families. Elliott said, "Meet me in my office tomorrow afternoon, three o'clock," and walked off with Deborah O'Day and Briggs to join Curtis and pay his respects to the families.

The next day McLanahan walked into Elliott's office in the heart of the HAWC complex. Elliott, O'Day, Preston and Briggs all had snifters of brandy, and Hal offered one to McLanahan.

"To our friends," Elliott said, raising the glass. He took a sip, then set the snifter down on his desk. "I never realized how young Powell was. His *parents* still look like college graduates."

"Powell was the one who made it happen," McLanahan said. "He gave me the key to beating DreamStar . . . no matter how advanced a system is, *human* unpredictability and flexibility can overcome it. Funny, the very thing that made DreamStar supposedly unbeatable actually led to its defeat—its single-minded command to attack meant it didn't know what retreat or caution were. J.C. had the intelligence and insight to discover that."

"Well, he gave you the key just in time," Elliott said. He turned to O'Day. "It was very . . . generous of you also to recommend that James be allowed to attend the ceremony."

"*Very,*" Briggs said.

McLanahan said nothing. His sentiments were obvious. This was his buddy.

"My lieutenant says Maraklov wants to make a deal—asylum for information," Briggs said. "I'm going to talk with him. Frankly, I'd just as soon turn his butt over to the Russian government. I'm sure *they'd* show him a good time."

"I have some bad news, people," Elliott said. "As you know, the Defense Intelligence Agency, the CIA, and the Pentagon are all conducting investigations at HAWC. I don't know what the future of the Center will be. But we do know some of the first casualties. As expected, Hal and I have been relieved of our assignments, effective at the end of the year."

"That's lousy," McLanahan said. "Neither of you deserve it—"

"There will be another casualty." He looked at McLanahan. "Sorry, Patrick. I think the housecleaning will be total."

McLanahan looked neither shocked nor even surprised. "If *any-one* didn't deserve this, it's you. Your actions during this whole business have been above and beyond."

"So were J.C.'s. So were General Ormack's. Maybe I deserve what I got—they sure as hell didn't."

"It's not the end, though," Elliott said. He turned to Deborah O'Day, who took another sip of brandy and got to her feet.

"No, it is *not* the end. The fact is, in this room right now is the heart of an entirely new outfit. We have groups that can specialize in many different types of operations, all working directly for the President, and all supervised to various degrees by Congress. This group, including Marcia Preston, will carry on with the type of work you've been doing for the past few years, except now you'll be doing it directly and accountably for the White House."

She picked up her brandy snifter. "Of course, all of this might come to a crashing halt if Lloyd Taylor doesn't get reelected. But that's not up to us." She held up her glass. "Ladies and gentlemen, all those here present interested in working more long hours for low pay and probably lower recognition, but having the absolute time of their lives, signify by saying 'aye.'"

The ayes had it. Unanimous.

"Here's to the charter members of Future Flight. And may heaven have mercy on the bad guys."

The whole second floor of Dreamland's small detention facility had been turned into a huge high-security area. Guards were posted on the stairways and in every hallway. All personnel were screened and checked any time they came in or out of the building.

Andrei Maraklov was the floor's only occupant. He had a room to himself in the center of the second floor, guarded inside and out by armed soldiers and undercover CIA operatives. All in all, twenty soldiers and agents were assigned to him round-the-clock.

Even for other agents, it was tough to get near him. From the time he came onto the grounds of the High Technology Advanced Weapons Center, Defense Intelligence Agency operative Anthony Scorcelli, Jr., was searched, had his I.D. checked and was electronically scanned for weapons as well as by teams of bomb dogs. He went through one metal detector at the entrance, one before getting into the elevator and one before getting near Maraklov's room. After the last machine he was carefully pat-searched and sniffed over by an explosives dog as his name and I.D. were checked once again.

"No gun?" the Air Force soldier asked. "Doesn't the DIA carry guns?"

"I don't chase bad guys," Scorcelli told him. "I wait until they're in custody, surrounded by blue-shirts. What do I need a gun for?"

"He checks," another guard said. The pat-search revealed a few pens—the guards even pushed the plungers on them and scribbled circles on a sheet of paper to make sure they worked—a small notebook, an appointment book with a credit-card-sized computer inside, wallet with seven dollars in it and a set of car keys from a rental car agency. "He's okay."

"What are you doing here this late?" the second guard asked, taking a sip of coffee as Scorcelli retrieved his belongings.

"First opportunity the DIA's had to interview him," Scorcelli said. The first guard consulted his log to double-check that fact—he was the first DIA representative here today. "This is the CIA's and the Air Force's ballgame. We just want to see what the guy has to say. I understand he wants to make a deal."

"Go ahead," the guard said. "Twenty minutes, max. Doctor's orders."

Scorcelli entered Maraklov's room and closed the door—and was immediately grabbed from behind by another guard. "You scared the crap out of me," Scorcelli said.

"Sorry," was all the guard said, but he didn't loosen his grip. Scorcelli then heard two beeps on a walkie-talkie the guard carried on his belt, and the guard replied with two beeps of his own. Finally the guard released him. "Go ahead, sir."

"Man, with all these searches I forgot what I was going to ask this guy," Scorcelli said. The guard smiled and walked back to his seat on the far side of the room.

"Where's our friend?"

"Taking a leak," the guard said. He got up and knocked on the door to the adjacent bathroom. "Someone to see you."

"I'll be out in a minute," Maraklov called from inside the bathroom.

"He doesn't sound like a Russian to me," Scorcelli said.

"He's a Russian, all right. He says he's been trained to act like an American. Can you believe it?''

"Sounds weird." Scorcelli unbuttoned his jacket, then pulled out the small notebook and a pen. He was about to write something when he looked up at the floor beside a sofa near the wall. "You got rats in here."

When the guard walked in front of Scorcelli to check for rats, Scorcelli jabbed the point of the pen into his neck. The guard was conscious just long enough to reach up to his neck, then instantly fell asleep. Scorcelli lowered him to the floor, dragged him out of sight, then took his sidearm from his holster. Hiding behind the bathroom door, Scorcelli took the second pen from his shirt pocket, twisted the cap and pressed the pocket-clip.

When Maraklov emerged from the bathroom, Scorcelli reached around behind him, grabbed his chin with his left hand, pulled his head over to the left to expose his neck and pressed in the point of the pen. When he depressed a plunger, a one-inch long needle shot out and injected its contents directly into Maraklov's carotid artery.

Maraklov managed to push Scorcelli away, but the poison was already starting to take effect. He sagged to his knees, trying but unable to call for help. He strained to focus his eyes on Scorcelli. "What . . . who are you?"

"Don't you remember, buddy?" Scorcelli said. "C'mon, you remember."

Maraklov shook his head.

"You're a smart guy, *Ken*. You remember. I'll give you a hint. We went to school together." Maraklov's eyes suddenly opened, and he struggled to get to his feet. Scorcelli put a hand on his shoulder, and in Maraklov's weakened condition it was easy to hold him steady.

"I'm your old buddy, Tony Scorcelli," the DIA "agent" said. "Remember? We played softball together. I'll never forget that last game we played, *Ken*, the one we played just before you went to Hawaii. You got me busted back after that little scuffle, did you know that? I wanted to go to law school in the United States. But after that fight, Roberts busted me back and I ended up in a nowhere little job in the DIA pushing papers."

Maraklov tried to rise again but was too weak. "But I got an interesting call from my handler the other day, and guess what? The KGB wants my old buddy Ken James dead. It seems he began spilling his guts to the Americans. Actually wanted to defect or something like that. Fell in love with an airplane, can you beat it? There was word that he was responsible for killing that nympho secretary back at the Academy. When I heard all this I just had to run right over from Washington, get myself clearance to enter your little condo here . . .''

Scorcelli pulled Maraklov up and sat him on the chair. "Sorry I can't stay and shoot the breeze, old buddy, as us Americans say, but you've got a date in hell and I'm on my way back to my Black Sea condo. It's beautiful there this time of year."

Just then the door opened behind Scorcelli and McLanahan and Briggs walked in. "Hey," McLanahan called out when he saw Scorcelli standing over Maraklov. "What the hell are you doing?"

Briggs drew his sidearm just as Scorcelli reached for the gun he had taken from the drugged guard. He pushed McLanahan aside, fired one shot into Scorcelli's chest and dropped him. Briggs checked over Scorcelli and the Air Force guard as more security agents ran into the room. McLanahan went over to Maraklov.

"Ammonium cyanide," Maraklov got out, barely strong enough to draw breath. "Standard KGB issue. Scorcelli's KGB. Deep cover, like me . . ."

McLanahan found the doctor's call button and pressed it. "Easy . . ."

"No, listen. Wall safe in my apartment . . . behind the bookcase. Careful . . . I wired it. Names of KGB handlers and Academy grads. Not many but it'll help . . ." Dying, he looked as if he was falling asleep.